BREAK IN
&
BANKER

Dick Francis has written over forty-one international best-sellers and is widely acclaimed as one of the world's finest thriller writers. His awards include the Crime Writers' Association's Cartier Diamond Dagger for his outstanding contribution to the crime genre, and an honorary Doctorate of Humane Letters from Tufts University of Boston. In 1996 Dick Francis was made a Mystery Writers of America Grand Master for a lifetime's achievement and in 2000 he received a CBE in the Queen's Birthday Honours list.

Also by Dick Francis in Pan Books

Dick Francis

BREAK IN
&
BANKER

PAN BOOKS

Break In first published 1985 by Michael Joseph.
First published in paperback 1987 by Pan Books in association with Michael Joseph.
Banker first published 1982 by Michael Joseph.
First published in paperback 1983 by Pan Books in association with Michael Joseph.

This omnibus first published 2006 by Pan Books
an imprint of Pan Macmillan Ltd
Pan Macmillan, 20 New Wharf Road, London N1 9RR
Basingstoke and Oxford
Associated companies throughout the world
www.panmacmillan.com

ISBN-13: 978-0-330-44667-9
ISBN-10: 0-330-44667-3

3 5 7 9 8 6 4 2

A CIP catalogue record for this book is available from
the British Library.

Printed and bound in Great Britain by
Mackays of Chatham plc, Chatham, Kent

BREAK IN

With love and thanks
to my son
MERRICK
racehorse trainer

and to

NANCY BROOKS GILBERT
bureau coordinator
for WSVN

CHAPTER ONE

Blood ties can mean trouble, chains and fatal obligation. The tie of twins, inescapably strongest. My twin, my bond.

My sister Holly, sprung into the world ten minutes after myself on Christmas morning with bells ringing over frosty fields and hope still wrapped in beckoning parcels, my sister Holly had through thirty years been cot-mate, puppy-companion, boxing target and best friend. Consecutively, on the whole.

My sister Holly came to Cheltenham races and intercepted me between weighing room and parade ring when I went out to ride in a three-mile steeplechase.

'Kit!' she said intensely, singling me out from among the group of other jockeys with whom I walked, and standing four-square and portentously in my way.

I stopped. The other jockeys walked on, parting like water round a rock. I looked at the lines of severe strain in her normally serene face and jumped in before she could say why she'd come.

'Have you any money with you?' I said.

1

'What? What for?' She wasn't concentrating on my question but on some inner scenario of obvious doom.

'Have you?' I insisted.

'Well . . . but that's not . . .'

'Go to the Tote,' I said. 'Put all you've got on my horse to win. Number eight. Go and do it.'

'But I don't . . .'

'Go and do it,' I interrupted. 'Then go to the bar and with what's left buy yourself a triple gin. Then come and meet me in the winners' enclosure.'

'No, that's not . . .'

I said emphatically, 'Don't put your disaster between me and that winning post.'

She blinked as if awakening, taking in my helmet and the colours I wore beneath my husky, looking towards the departing backs of the other jockeys and understanding what I meant.

'Right?' I said.

'Right.' She swallowed. 'All right.'

'Afterwards,' I said.

She nodded. The doom, the disaster, dragged at her eyes.

'I'll sort it out,' I promised. 'After.'

She nodded dumbly and turned away, beginning almost automatically to open her shoulder bag to look for money. Doing what her brother told her, even after all these years. Coming to her brother, still, for her worst troubles to be fixed. Even though she was four years married, those patterns of behaviour, established

2

in a parentless childhood, still seemed normal to us both.

I'd sometimes wondered what difference it would have made to her if she had been the elder by that crucial ten minutes. Would she have been motherly? Bossy, perhaps. She felt safer, she'd said, being the younger.

I walked on towards the parade ring, putting consciously out of my mind the realization that whatever the trouble this time, it was bad. She had come, for a start, one hundred and fifty miles from Newmarket to see me, and she disliked driving.

I shook my head physically throwing her out. The horse ahead, the taxing job in hand, had absolute and necessary priority. I was primarily no one's brother. I was primarily Kit Fielding, steeplechase jockey, some years champion, some years not, sharing the annual honour with another much like myself, coming out top when my bones didn't break, bowing to fate when they did.

I wore the colours of a middle-aged princess of a dispossessed European monarchy, a woman of powerful femininity whose skin was weathering towards sunset like cracked glaze on porcelain. Sable coat, as usual, swinging from narrow shoulders. Glossy dark hair piled high. Plain gold earrings. I walked towards her across the parade-ring grass; smiled, bowed, and briefly shook the offered glove.

'Cold day,' she said; her consonants faintly thick,

vowel sounds pure English, intonation as always pleasant.

I agreed.

'And will you win?' she asked.

'With luck.'

Her smile was mostly in the eyes. 'I will expect it.'

We watched her horse stalk round the ring, its liver chestnut head held low, the navy rug with gold embroidered crest covering all else from withers to tail. North Face, she'd named it, from her liking for mountains, and a suitably bleak, hard and difficult customer he'd turned out to be. Herring-gutted, ugly, bad-tempered, moody. I'd ridden him in his three-year-old hurdles, his first races, and on over hurdles at four, five and six. I'd ridden him in his novice steeplechases at seven and through his prime at eight and nine. He tolerated me when he felt like it and I knew his every mean move. At ten he was still an unpredictable rogue, and as clever a jumper as a cat. He had won thirty-eight races over the years and I'd ridden him in all but one. Twice to my fury he had purposefully dropped his shoulder and dislodged me in the parade ring. Three times we had fallen together on landing, he each time getting unhurt to his feet and departing at speed with indestructible legs, indestructible courage, indestructible will to win. I loved him and hated him and he was as usual starting favourite.

The princess and I had stood together in such a way in parade rings more often than one could count, as

4

she rarely kept fewer than twenty horses in training and I'd ridden them constantly for ten years. She and I had come to the point of almost monosyllabic but perfectly understood conversation and, as far as I could tell, mutual trust and regard. She called me 'Kit', and I called her 'Princess' (at her request) and we shared a positive and quite close friendship which nevertheless began and ended at the racecourse gates. If we met outside, as occasionally happened, she was considerably more formal.

We stood alone together in the parade ring, as so often, because Wykeham Harlow, who trained North Face, suffered from migraine. The headaches, I'd noticed, occurred most regularly on the coldest days, which might have been a truly physical phenomenon, but also they seemed to develop in severity in direct ratio to the distance between his armchair and the day's racing. Wykeham Harlow trained south of London and very seldom now made the north-westerly traverse to Cheltenham: he was growing old and wouldn't confess he was nervous about driving home in the winter dark.

The signal was given for jockeys to mount, and Dusty, the travelling head lad who nowadays deputized for Wykeham more often than not, removed North Face's rug with a flick and gave me a deft leg-up into the saddle.

The princess said, 'Good luck,' and I said cheerfully, 'Thank you.'

No one in jump racing said 'Break a leg' instead of

'Good luck', as they did in the theatre. Break a leg was all too depressingly possible.

North Face was feeling murderous: I sensed it the moment I sat on his back and put my feet in the irons. The telepathy between that horse and myself was particularly strong always, and I simply cursed him in my mind and silently told him to shut up and concentrate on winning, and we went out on to the windy track with the mental dialogue continuing unabated.

One had to trust that the urge to race would overcome his grouchiness once the actual contest started. It almost always did, but there had been days in the past when he'd refused to turn on the enthusiasm until too late. Days, like this one, when his unfocused hatred flowed most strongly.

There was no way of cajoling him with sweet words, encouraging pats, pulling his ears. None of that pleased him. A battle of wills was what he sought, and that, from me, was what he habitually got.

We circled at the starting point, seven runners in all, while the roll was called and girths were tightened. Waited, with jockeys' faces turning pale blue in the chilly November wind, for the seconds to tick away to start time, lining up in no particular order as there were no draws or stalls in jump races, watching for the starter to raise the tapes and let us go.

North Face's comment on the proceedings took the form of a lowered head and arched back, and a kick like a bronco. The other riders cursed and kept out of his way, and the starter told me to stay well to the rear.

It was the big race of the day, though heavier in prestige than prize money, an event in which the sponsors, a newspaper, were getting maximum television coverage for minimum outlay. The Sunday Towncrier Trophy occurred annually on a Saturday afternoon (naturally) for full coverage in the *Sunday Towncrier* itself the next morning, with self-congratulatory prose and dramatic pictures jostling scandals on the front page. Dramatic pictures of Fielding being bucked off before the start were definitely not going to be taken. I called the horse a bastard, a sod and a bloody pig, and in that gentlemanly fashion the race began.

He was mulish and reluctant and we got away slowly, trailing by ten lengths after the first few strides. It didn't help that the start was in plain view of the stands instead of decently hidden in some far corner. He gave another two bronco kicks to entertain the multitude, and there weren't actually many horses who could manage that while approaching the first fence at Cheltenham.

He scrambled over that fence, came almost to a halt on landing and bucked again before setting off, shying against coercion from the saddle both bodily and clearly in mind.

Two full circuits ahead. Nineteen more jumps. A gap between me and the other runners of embarrassing and lengthening proportions. I sent him furious messages:

Race, you bastard, race, or you'll end up as dogmeat, I'll personally kill you, you bastard, and if you think you'll get me off, think again, you're taking me all the way, you sod, so get on with it, start racing, you sod, you bastard, you know you like it, so get going . . .

We'd been through it before, over and over, but he'd never been worse. He ignored all take-off signals at the second fence and made a mess of it and absolutely refused to gallop properly round the next bend.

Once in the past when he'd been in this mood I'd tried simply not fighting him but letting him sort out his own feelings, and he'd brought himself to a total halt within a few strides. Persevering was the only way: waiting until the demonic fit burned itself out.

He stuck his toes in as we approached the next fence as if the downhill slope there alarmed him, which I knew it didn't; and over the next, the water jump, he landed with his head down by his feet and his back arched, a configuration almost guaranteed to send a jockey flying. I knew his tricks so well that I was ready for him and stayed in the saddle, and after that jolly little manoeuvre we were more than three hundred yards behind the other horses and seriously running out of time.

My feelings about him rose to somewhere near absolute fury. His sheer pigheadedness was again going to lose us a race we could easily have won, and as on other similar occasions I swore to myself that I'd never ride the brute again, never. Not ever. Never. I almost believed I meant it.

As if he'd been a naughty child who knew its tantrums had gone too far, he suddenly began to race. The bumpy uneven stride went smooth, the rage faded away, the marvellous surge of fighting spirit returned, as it always did in the end. But we were a furlong and a half to the rear, and to come from more than three hundred yards behind and still win meant theoretically that one could have won by the same margin if one had tried from the start. A whole mile had been wasted; two left for retrieval. Hopeless.

Never give up, they say.

Yard by flying yard over the second circuit we clawed back the gap, but we were still ten lengths behind the last tired and trailing horse in front as we turned towards the final two fences. Passed him over the first of them. No longer last, but that was hardly what mattered. Five horses in front, all still on their feet after the long contest, all intent on the final uphill battle.

All five went over the last fence in front of North Face. He must have gained twenty feet in the air. He landed and strode away with smooth athletic power as if sticky bronco jumps were the peccadillo of another horse altogether.

I could dimly hear the crowd roaring, which one usually couldn't. North Face put his ears back and galloped with a flat, intense, bloody-minded stride, accelerating towards the place he knew was his, that he'd so wilfully rejected, that he wanted in his heart.

I flattened myself forward to the line of his neck to cut the wind resistance; kept the reins tight, my body still, my weight steady over his shoulders, all the urging a matter of mind and hands, a matter of giving that fantastic racing creature his maximum chance.

The others were tiring, the incline slowing them drastically, as it did always to so many. North Face swept past a bunch of them as they wavered and there was suddenly only one in front, one whose jockey thought he was surely winning and had half dropped his hands.

One could feel sorry for him, but he was a gift from heaven. North Face caught him at a rush a bare few strides from the winning post, and I heard his agonized cry as I passed.

Too close for comfort, I thought, pulling up. Reprieved on the scaffold.

There was nothing coming from the horse's mind: just a general sort of haze that in a human one would have interpreted as smugness. Most good horses knew when they'd won: filled their lungs and raised their heads with pride. Some were definitely depressed when they lost. Guilt they never felt, nor shame nor regret nor compassion: North Face would dump me next time if he could.

The princess greeted us in the unsaddling enclosure with starry eyes and a flush on her cheeks. Stars for success, I diagnosed, and the flush from earlier embarrassment. I unbuckled the girths, slid the saddle over my arm and paused briefly before going to weigh in, my head near to hers.

'Well done,' she said.

I smiled slightly. 'I expected curses.'

'He was especially difficult.'

'And brilliant.'

'There's a trophy.'

'I'll come right out,' I said, and left her to the flocking newsmen, who liked her and treated her reverently, on the whole.

I passed the scales. The jockey I'd beaten at the last second was looking ashamed, but it was his own fault, as well he knew. The Stewards might fine him. His owners might sack him. No one else paid much attention either to his loss or to my win. The past was the past: the next race was what mattered.

I gave my helmet and saddle to the valet, changed into different colours, weighed out, put the princess's colours back on, on top of those I would carry in the next race, combed my hair and went out dutifully for the speeches. It always seemed a shame to me when the presentation photographs were taken with the jockey not wearing the winner's colours, and for owners I cared for I did whenever possible appear with the right set on top. It cost me nothing but a couple of minutes, and it was more satisfactory, I thought.

The racecourse (in the shape of the chairman of directors) thanked the *Sunday Towncrier* for its generosity and the *Sunday Towncrier* (in the shape of its proprietor, Lord Vaughnley) said it was a pleasure to support National Hunt racing and all who sailed in her.

Cameras clicked.

There was no sign anywhere of Holly.

The proprietor's lady, thin, painted and good-natured, stepped forward in smooth couturier clothes to give a foot-high gilded statue of a towncrier (medieval version) to the princess, amid congratulation and hand shaking. The princess accepted also a smaller gilt version on behalf of Wykeham Harlow, and in my turn I received the smile, the handshake, the congratulations and the attentions of the cameras, but not, to my surprise, my third set of golden towncrier cufflinks.

'We were afraid you might win them again,' Lady Vaughnley explained sweetly, 'so this year it's a figure like the others,' and she pressed warmly into my hands a little golden man calling out the news to the days before printing.

I genuinely thanked her. I had more cufflinks already than shirts with cuffs to take them.

'What a finish you gave us,' she said, smiling. 'My husband is thrilled. Like an arrow from nowhere, he said.'

'We were lucky.'

I looked automatically to her shoulder, expecting to greet also her son, who at all other Towncriers had accompanied his parents, hovering around and running

12

errands, willing, nice-natured, on the low side of average for brains.

'Your son isn't with you?' I asked.

Most of Lady Vaughnley's animation went into eclipse. She glanced swiftly and uncomfortably across to her husband, who hadn't heard my remark, and said unhappily, 'No, not today.'

'I'm sorry,' I said; not for Hugh Vaughnley's absence, but for the obvious row in the family. She nodded and turned away, blinking, and I thought fleetingly that the trouble must be new and bad, near the surface of tears.

The princess invited Lord and Lady Vaughnley to her box and they happily accepted.

'You as well, Kit,' she said.

'I'm riding in the next race.'

'Come after.'

'Yes. Thank you.'

Everyone left their trophies on the presentation table to be taken away for engraving and I returned to the changing room as the princess moved away with the Vaughnleys.

She always asked me to her box because she liked to discuss her horses and what they'd done, and she had a loving and knowledgeable interest in all of them. She liked most to race where she rented a private box, namely at Cheltenham, Ascot, Sandown and Lingfield, and she went only to other courses where she had standing invitations from box-endowed friends. She was not democratic to the point of standing on the open stands and yelling.

I came out in the right colours for the next race and found Holly fiercely at my elbow immediately.

'Have you collected your winnings?' I asked.

'I couldn't reach you,' she said disgustedly. 'All those officials, keeping everyone back, and the crowds . . .'

'Look, I'm sorry. I've got to ride again now.'

'Straight after, then.'

'Straight after.'

My mount in that race, in contrast to North Face, was unexciting, unintelligent and of only run-of-the-mill ability. Still, we tried hard, finished third, and seemed to give moderate pleasure to owners and trainer. Bread and butter for me: expenses covered for them. The basic fabric of jump racing.

I weighed in and changed rapidly into street clothes, and Holly was waiting when I came out.

'Now, Kit . . .'

'Um,' I said. 'The princess is expecting me.'

'No! Kit!' She was exasperated.

'Well . . . it's my job.'

'Don't come to the office, you mean?'

I relented. 'OK. What's the matter?'

'Have you seen this?' She pulled a page torn from a newspaper called the *Daily Flag* out of her shoulder bag. 'Has anyone said anything in the weighing room?'

'No and no,' I said, taking the paper and looking

where she was pointing with an agitated stabbing finger. 'I don't read that rag.'

'Nor do we, for God's sake. Just look at it.'

I glanced at the paragraph which was boxed by heavy red lines on a page entitled 'Intimate Details', a page well known to contain information varying from stale to scurrilous and to be intentionally geared to stirring up trouble.

'It's yesterday's,' I said, looking at the date.

'Yes, yes. Read it.'

I read the piece. It said:

Folk say the skids are under Robertson (Bobby) Allardeck (32), racehorse-trainer son of tycoon Maynard Allardeck (50). Never Daddy's favourite (they're not talking), Bobby's bought more than he can pay for, naughty boy, and guess who won't be coming to the rescue. Watch this space for more.

Robertson (Bobby) Allardeck (32) was my sister Holly's husband.

'It's libellous,' I said. 'Bobby can sue.'

'What with?' Holly demanded. 'We can't afford it. And we might not win.'

I looked at the worry in her normally unlined face.

'Is it true, then?' I said.

'No. Yes. In a way. Of course he's bought things he can't pay for. Everyone does. He's bought horses. It's

15

yearling sale time, dammit. Every trainer buys yearlings he can't pay for. It's natural, you know that.'

I nodded. Trainers bought yearlings at auction for their owners, paying compulsorily for them on the spot and relying on the owners to reimburse them fairly soon. Sometimes the owners backed out after a yearling had been bought; sometimes trainers bought an extra animal or two to bring on themselves and have ready for a later sale at a profit. Either way, at sale time, it was more common than not to borrow thousands short-term from the bank.

'How many has Bobby bought that he can't sell?' I asked.

'He'll sell them in the end, of course,' she said, staunchly.

Of course. Probably. Perhaps.

'But now?'

'Three. We've got three.'

'Total damage?'

'More than a hundred thousand.'

'The bank paid for them?'

She nodded. 'It's not that it won't be all right in the end, but where did that disgusting rag get the information from? And why put it in the paper at all? I mean, it's pointless.'

'And what's happened?' I asked.

'What's happened is that everyone we owe money to has telephoned demanding to be paid. I mean, horrible threats, really, about taking us to court. All day yesterday . . . and this morning the feed-merchant rang and said he wouldn't deliver any more feed unless we paid our bill and we've got thirty horses munching their heads off, and the owners are on the line non-stop asking if Bobby's going to go on training or not and making veiled hints about taking their horses away.'

I was sceptical. 'All this reaction from that one little paragraph?'

'Yes.' She was suddenly close to tears. 'Someone pushed the paper through the letter box of half the tradesmen in Newmarket, open at that page with that paragraph outlined in red, just like this. The blacksmith showed me. It's his paper. He came to shoe some of the horses and made us pay him first. Made a joke of it. But all the same, he meant it. Not everyone's been so nice.'

'And I suppose you can't simply just pay everyone off and confound them?'

'You know we can't. The bank manager would bounce the cheques. We have to do it gradually, like we always do. Everyone will get paid, if they wait.'

Bobby and Holly lived in fairly usual fashion at permanent full stretch of their permitted overdraft, juggling the incoming cheques from the owners with the outgoing expenses of fodder, wages, overheads and taxes. Owners sometimes paid months late, but the horses had to be fed and the lads' wages found to the minute. The cash flow tended to suffer from air locks.

'Well,' I said, 'go for another triple gin while I talk to the princess.'

CHAPTER TWO

The Princess Casilia, Mme de Brescou (to give her her full style), had as usual asked a few friends to lunch with her to watch the races, and her box contained, besides herself and the Vaughnleys, a small assortment of furs and tweeds, all with inhabitants I'd formerly met on similar occasions.

'You know everyone, don't you?' the princess said, and I nodded 'Yes', although I couldn't remember half their names.

'Tea?' she asked.

'Yes, thank you.'

The same waitress as usual smoothly gave me a full cup, smiling. No milk, no sugar, slice of lemon, as always.

The princess had had a designer decorate her boxes at the racecourses and they were all the same: pale peach hessian on the walls, coffee-coloured carpet and a glass-topped dining table surrounded by comfortable chairs. By late afternoon, my habitual visiting time, the table had been pushed to one side and bore not lunch but plates of sandwiches, creamy pastries, assorted alcohol, a box of cigars. The princess's friends tended to linger long after the last races had been run.

One of the women guests picked up a plate of small delicious-looking cakes and offered it to me.

'No, thank you,' I said mildly. 'Not this minute.'

'Not ever,' the princess told her friend. 'He can't eat those. And don't tempt him. He's hungry.'

The friend looked startled and confused. 'My dear, I never thought. And he's so tall.'

'I eat a lot,' I said. 'But just not those.'

The princess, who had some idea at least of the constant struggle I had to stay down at a body weight of ten stone, gave me a glimmering look through her eyelashes, expressing disbelief.

The friend was straightforwardly curious. 'What do you eat most of,' she asked, 'if not cake?'

'Lobster, probably,' I said.

'Good heavens.'

Her male companion gave me a critical glance from above a large moustache and long front teeth.

'Left it a bit late in the big race, didn't you, what?' he said.

'I'm afraid so, yes.'

'Couldn't think what you were doing out there, fiddling about at the back. You nearly bungled it entirely, what? The princess was most uncomfortable, I can tell you, as we all had our money on you, of course.'

The princess said, 'North Face can behave very

badly, Jack. I told you. He has such a mind of his own. Sometimes it's hard to get him to race.'

'It's the jockey's job to get him to race,' Jack said to me with a touch of belligerence. 'Don't you agree, what?'

'Yes,' I said. 'I do agree.'

Jack looked fractionally disconcerted and the princess's lips twitched.

'And then you set him alight,' said Lord Vaughnley, overhearing. 'Gave us a rousing finish. The sort of thing a sponsor prays for, my dear fellow. Memorable. Something to talk about, to refer to. North Face's finish in the Towncrier Trophy. Splendid, do you see?'

Jack saw, chose not to like it, drifted away. Lord Vaughnley's grey eyes looked with bonhomie from his large bland face and he patted me with kindly meant approval on the shoulder.

'Third time in a row,' he said. 'You've done us proud. Would you care, one Saturday night, to see the paper put to bed?'

'Yes,' I said, surprised. 'Very much.'

'We might print a picture of you watching a picture of yourself go through the presses.'

More than bonhomie, I thought, behind the grey eyes: a total newspaperman's mentality.

He was the proprietor of the *Towncrier* by inheritance, the fiftyish son of one of the old-style newspaper barons who had muscled on to the scene in the nineteen thirties and brought new screaming life to millions of breakfasts. Vaughnley Senior had bought a dying provincial weekly and turned it into a lusty voice read nationwide. He'd taken it to Fleet Street, seen the circulation explode, and in due course had launched a daily version which still prospered despite sarcastic onslaughts from newer rivals.

The old man had been a colourful buccaneering entrepreneur. The son was quieter, a manager, an advertising man at heart. The *Towncrier*, once a raucous newsheet, had over the last ten years developed Establishment leanings, a remarkable testimony of the hand-over from the elder personality to the younger.

I thought of Hugh Vaughnley, the son, next in the line: the sweet-tempered young man without strength, at present at odds, it appeared, with his parents. In his hands, if it survived at all, the *Towncrier* would soften to platitude, waffle and syrup.

The *Daily Flag*, still at the brassiest stage, and among the *Towncrier*'s most strident opposition, had been recently bought, after bitter financial intrigues, by a thrusting financier in the ascendant, a man hungry, it was said, for power and a peerage, and taking a well-tried path towards both. The *Flag* was bustling, go-getting, stamping on sacrosanct toes and boasting of new readers daily.

Since I'd met Lord Vaughnley several times at various racing presentation dinners where annual honours were dished out to the fortunate (like champion jockeys, leading trainers, owners-of-the-year, and so on) and with Holly's distress sharp in my mind, I asked him if he knew who was responsible for 'Intimate Details' in the *Flag*.

'Responsible?' he repeated with a hint of holier-than-thou distaste. 'Irresponsible, more like.'

'Irresponsible, then.'

'Why, precisely?' he asked.

'They've made an unprovoked and apparently pointless attack on my brother-in-law.'

'Hm,' Lord Vaughnley said. 'Too bad. But, my dear fellow, pointless attacks are what the public likes to read. Destructive criticism sells papers, back-patting doesn't. My father used to say that, and he was seldom wrong.'

'And to hell with justice,' I said.

'We live in an unkind world. Always have, always will. Christians to the lions, roll up, buy the best seats in the shade, gory spectacle guaranteed. People buy newspapers, my dear fellow, to see victims torn limb from limb. Be thankful it's physically bloodless, we've advanced at least that far.' He smiled as if talking to a child. 'Intimate Details, as you must know, is a composite affair, with a whole bunch of journalists digging out nuggets and also a network of informants in hospitals, mortuaries, night clubs, police stations and all sorts of less savoury places, telephoning in with the dirt and collecting their dues. We at the *Towncrier* do the same sort of thing. Every paper does. Gossip columns would be non-starters, my dear fellow, if one didn't.'

'I'd like to know where the piece about my brother-in-law came from. Who told who, if you see what I mean. And why.'

'Hm.' The grey eyes considered. 'The editor of the *Flag* is Sam Leggatt. You could ask him of course, but even if he finds out from his staff, he won't tell you. Head against brick wall, I'm afraid, my dear fellow.'

'And you approve,' I said, reading his tone. 'Closing ranks, never revealing sources, and all that.'

'If your brother-in-law has suffered real positive harm,' he nodded blandly, 'he should get his solicitor to send Sam Leggatt a letter announcing imminent prosecution for libel unless a retraction and an apology are published immediately. It sometimes works. Failing that, your brother-in-law might get a small cash settlement out of court. But do advise him, my dear fellow, against pressing for a fully fledged libel action with a jury. The *Flag* retains heavyweight lawyers and they play very rough. They would turn your brother-in-law's most innocent secrets inside out and paint them dirty. He'd wish he'd never started. Friendly advice, my dear fellow, I do assure you.'

I told him about the paragraph being outlined in red and delivered by hand to the houses of tradespeople.

Lord Vaughnley frowned. 'Tell him to look for the informant on his own doorstep,' he said. 'Gossip column items often spring from local spite. So do stories about vicars and their mistresses.' He smiled briefly.

'Good old spite. Whatever would the newspaper industry do without it!'

'Such a confession!' I said with mockery.

'We clamour for peace, honesty, harmony, common sense and equal justice for all,' he said. 'I assure you we do, my dear fellow.'

'Yes,' I said. 'I know.'

The princess touched Lord Vaughnley's arm and invited him to go out on to the balcony to see the last race. He said, however, that he should return to the *Towncrier*'s guests whom he had temporarily abandoned in a sponsors' hospitality room, and, collecting his wife, he departed.

'Now, Kit,' said the princess, 'while everyone is outside watching the race, tell me about North Face.'

We sat, as so often, in two of the chairs, and I told her without reservation what had happened between her horse and myself.

'I do wish,' she said thoughtfully, at the end, 'that I had your sense of what horses are thinking. I've tried putting my head against their heads,' she smiled almost self-consciously, 'but nothing happens. I get nothing at all. So how do you do it?'

'I don't know,' I said. 'I don't think head to head would work, anyway. It's just when I'm riding them, I seem to know. It's not in words, not at all. It's just there. It just seems to come. It happens to very many riders. Horses are telepathic creatures.'

She looked at me with her head on one side. 'But

you, Kit, you're telepathic with people as well as horses. Quite often you've answered a question I was just going to ask. Quite disconcerting. How do you do it?'

I was startled. 'I don't know how.'

'But you know you do?'

'Well . . . I used to. My twin sister Holly and I were telepathic between ourselves at one time. Almost like an extra way of talking. But we've grown out of it, these last few years.'

'Pity,' she said. 'Such an interesting gift.'

'It can't logically exist.'

'But it does.' She patted my hand. 'Thank you for today, although you and North Face between you almost stopped my heart.'

She stood up without haste, adept from some distant training at ending a conversation gracefully when she wished, and I stood also and thanked her formally for her tea. She smiled through the eyelashes, as she often did with everybody: not out of coquetry but in order, it seemed to me, to hide her private feelings.

She had a husband to whom she went home daily; Monsieur Roland de Brescou, a Frenchman of aristocratic lineage, immense wealth and advanced age. I had met him twice, a frail white-haired figure in a wheelchair with an autocratic nose and little to say. I asked after his health occasionally: the princess replied always that he was well. Impossible ever to tell from her voice or demeanour what she felt about him: love, anxiety, frustration, impatience, joy . . . nothing showed.

'We run at Devon and Exeter, don't we?' she said.

'Yes, Princess. Bernina and Icicle.'

'Good. I'll see you there on Tuesday.'

I shook her hand. I'd sometimes thought, after a win such as that day's, of planting a farewell kiss on her porcelain cheek. I liked her very much. She might consider it the most appalling liberty, though, and give me the sack, so in her own disciplined fashion I made her merely a sketch of a bow, and went away.

'You've been a hell of a long time,' Holly complained. 'That woman treats you like a lap dog. It's sickening.'

'Yeah . . . well . . . here I am.'

She had been waiting for me on her feet outside the weighing room in the cold wind, not snugly in a chair in the bar. The triple gin anyway had been a joke because she seldom drank alcohol, but that she couldn't even sit down revealed the intensity of her worry.

The last race was over, the crowds streaming towards the car parks. Jockeys and trainers, officials and valets and pressmen bade each other goodnight all around us although it was barely three-forty in the afternoon and not yet dusk. Time to go home from the office. Work was work, even if the end product was entertainment. Leisure was a growth industry, so they said.

'Will you come home with me?' Holly asked.

I had known for an hour that that was what she would want.

'Yes,' I said.

Her relief was enormous but she tried to hide it with a cough, a joke and a jerky laugh. 'Your car or mine?'

I'd thought it over. 'We'll both go to the cottage. I'll drive us in your car from there.'

'OK.' She swallowed. 'And Kit . . .'

'Save it,' I said.

She nodded. We'd had an ancient pact: never say thank you out loud. Thanks came in help returned, unstintingly and at once, when one needed it. The pact had faded into abeyance with her marriage but still, I felt, existed: and so did she, or she wouldn't have come.

Holly and I were more alike in looks than many fraternal twins, but nowhere near the identical Viola and Sebastian: Shakespeare, most rarely, got it wrong. We each had dark hair, curly. Each, lightish brown eyes. Each, flat ears, high foreheads, long necks, easily tanned skin. We had different noses and different mouths, though the same slant to the bone above the eye socket. We had never had an impression of looking into a mirror at the sight of the other, although the other's face was more familiar to us than our own.

When we were two years old our young and effervescent parents left us with our grandparents, went for a winter holiday in the Alps, and skied into an avalanche. Our father's parents, devastated, had kept us and brought us up and couldn't in many ways have been better, but Holly and I had turned inward to each other more than might have happened in a normal family. We had invented and spoken our own private language, as many such children do, and from there had progressed to a speechless communication of minds. Our telepathy had been more a matter of knowing what the other was thinking rather than of deliberately planting thoughts in the other's head. More reception than transmission, one might say: and it happened also without us realizing it, as over and over again when we'd been briefly apart we had done things like writing in the same hour to our Australian aunt, getting the same book out of the library, and buying identical objects on impulse. We had both, for instance, one day gone separately home with roller skates as a surprise birthday present for the other and hidden them in our grandmother's wardrobe. Grandmother herself by that time hadn't found it strange as we'd done similar things too often, and she'd said that right from when we could talk if she asked, 'Kit, where's Holly?' or, 'Holly, where's Kit?' we would always know, even if logically we couldn't.

The telepathy between us had not only survived the stresses and upheavals of puberty and adolescence but had actually become stronger: also we were more conscious of it, and used it purposely when we wanted, and grew in young adulthood into a new dimension of friendship. Naturally we put up a front to the world of banter, sarcasm and sibling rivalry, but underneath we were solid, never doubting our private certainty.

When I'd left our grandparents' house to buy a place

of my own with my earnings, Holly had from time to time lived there with me, working away in London most of the time but returning as of right whenever she wished, both of us taking it for granted that my cottage was now her home also.

That state of affairs had continued until she fell in love with Bobby Allardeck and married him.

Even before the wedding the telepathy had begun to fade and fairly soon afterwards it had more or less stopped. I wondered for a while if she had shut down deliberately, and then realized it had been also my own decision: she was off on a new life and it wouldn't have been a good idea to try to cling to her, or to intrude.

Four years on, the old habit had vanished to such an extent that I hadn't felt a flicker of her present distress, where once I would somehow have had it in my mind and would have telephoned to find out if she was all right.

On our way out to the car park I asked her how much she'd won on North Face.

'My God,' she said, 'you left that a bit late, didn't you?'

'Mm.'

'Anyway, I went to put my money on the Tote but the queues were so long I didn't bother and I went down on to the lawn to watch the race. Then when you were left so far behind I was glad I hadn't backed you. Then those bookies on the rails began shouting five to one North Face. Five to one! I mean, you'd started at odds-on. There was a bit of booing when you came past the stands and it made me cross. You always do your best, they didn't have to boo. So I walked over and got one of the bookies to take all my money at fives. It was a sort of gesture, I suppose. I won a hundred and twenty-five, which will pay the plumber, so thanks.'

'Did the plumber get Intimate Details?'

'Yes, he did.'

'Someone knows your life pretty thoroughly,' I said.

'Yes. But who? We were awake half the night wondering.' Her voice was miserable. 'Who could hate us that much?'

'You haven't just kicked out any grievance-laden employees?'

'No. We've a good lot of lads this year. Better than most.'

We arrived at her car and she drove me to where mine was parked.

'Is that house of yours finished yet?' she asked.

'Getting on.'

'You're bizarre.'

I smiled. Holly liked things secure, settled and planned in advance. She thought it crazy that I'd bought on impulse the roofless shell of a one-storey house from a builder who was going broke. He'd been in the local pub one night when I'd gone in for a steak: leaning on the bar and morosely drowning his sorrows in beer.

31

He'd been building the house for himself, he said, but he'd no money left. All work on it had stopped.

I'd ridden horses for him in his better-off days and had known him for several years, so the next morning I'd gone with him to see the house; and I'd liked its possibilities and bought it on the spot, and engaged him to finish it for me, paying him week by week for work done. It was going to be a great place to live and I was going to move into it, finished or not, well before Christmas, as I'd already exchanged contracts on my old cottage and would have to leave there willy nilly.

'I'll follow you to the cottage,' Holly said. 'And don't drive like you won the Towncrier.'

We proceeded in sedate convoy to the racehorse-training village of Lambourn on the Berkshire Downs, leaving my car in its own garage there and setting off together on the hundred miles plus to the Suffolk town of Newmarket, headquarters of the racing industry.

I liked the informality of little Lambourn. Holly and Bobby swam easily in the grander pond. Or had done, until a pike came along to snap them up.

I told her what Lord Vaughnley had said about demanding a retraction from the *Flag*'s editor but not suing, and she said I'd better tell Bobby. She seemed a great deal more peaceful now that I was actually on the road with her, and I thought she had more faith in my ability to fix things than I had myself. This was a lot different from beating up a boy who pinched her bottom twice at school. A little more shadowy than making a salesman take back the rotten car he'd conned her into buying.

She slept most of the way to Newmarket and I had no idea at all what I was letting myself in for.

We drove into the Allardeck stableyard at about eight o'clock and found it ablaze with lights and movement when it should have been quiet and dark. A large horsebox was parked in the centre, all doors open, loading ramp down. Beside it stood an elderly man watching a stable-lad lead a horse towards the ramp. The door of the place where the horse had been dozing the night away shone as a wide open oblong of yellow behind him.

A few steps away from the horsebox, lit as on a stage, were two men arguing with fists raised, arms gesticulating, voices clearly shouting.

One of them was my brother-in-law, Bobby. The other . . . ?

'Oh my God,' Holly said. 'That's one of our owners. Taking his horses. And he owes us a fortune.'

She scrambled out of the car almost before I'd braked to a halt, and ran towards the two men. Her arrival did nothing, as far as I could see, to cool the flourishing row, and to all intents they simply ignored her.

My calm-natured sister was absolutely no good at stalking into any situation and throwing her weight about. She thought privately that it was rather pleasant to cook and keep house and be a gentle old-fashioned woman: but then she was of a generation for whom that way was a choice, not a drudgery oppressively imposed.

I got out of the car and walked across to see what could be done. Holly ran back to meet me.

'Can you stop him?' she said urgently. 'If he takes the horses, we'll never get his money.'

I nodded.

The lad leading the horse had reached the ramp but the horse was reluctant to board. I walked over to the lad without delay, stood in his way, on the bottom of the ramp, and told him to put the horse back where he'd brought it from.

'What?' he said. He was young, small, and apparently astonished to see anyone materialize from the dark.

'Put it back in the box, switch off the light, close the door. Do it now.'

'But Mr Graves told me . . .'

'Just do it,' I said.

He looked doubtfully across to the two shouting men.

'Do you work here?' I said. 'Or did you come with the horsebox?'

'I came with the horsebox.' He looked at the elderly man standing there who had so far said and done nothing. 'What should I do, Jim?'

'Who are you?' I asked him.

'The driver,' he said flatly. 'Keep me out of it.'

'Right,' I said to the lad. 'The horse isn't leaving. Take it back.'

'Are you Kit Fielding?' he said doubtfully.

'That's right. Mrs Allardeck's brother. Get going.'

'But Mr Graves . . .'

'I'll deal with Mr Graves,' I said. 'His horse isn't leaving tonight.'

'Horses,' the boy said, correcting me. 'I loaded the other one already.'

'OK,' I said. 'They're both staying here. When you've put back the one you're loading, unload the first one again.'

The boy gave me a wavering look, then turned the horse round and began to plod it back towards its rightful quarters.

The change of direction broke up the slanging match at once. The man who wasn't Bobby broke away and shouted to the lad across the yard, 'Hey, you, what the shit do you think you're doing? Load the horse this minute.'

The lad stopped. I walked fast over to him, took hold of the horse's head-collar and led the bemused animal back into its own home. The lad made no move at all to stop me. I came out. Switched off the light. Shut and bolted the door.

Mr Graves (presumably) was advancing fast with flailing arms and an extremely belligerent expression.

'Who the shit do you think you are?' he shouted. 'That's my horse. Get it out here at once!'

I stood, however, in front of the bolted door, leaning my shoulders on it, crossing one ankle over the other, folding my arms. Mr Graves came to a screeching and disbelieving halt.

'Get away from there,' he said thunderously, stabbing the night air with a forefinger. 'That's my horse. I'm taking it, and you can't stop me.'

His pudgy face rigid with obstinacy, he stood about five feet five from balding crown to polished toecaps. He was perhaps fifty, plump, already out of breath. There was no way whatever that he was going to shift my five feet ten by force.

'Mr Graves,' I said calmly, 'you can take your horses away when you've paid your bill.'

His mouth opened speechlessly. He took a step forward and peered at my face, which I dare say was in shadow.

'That's right,' I said. 'Kit Fielding. Holly's brother.'

The open mouth snapped shut. 'And what the shit has all this to do with you? Get out of my way.'

'A cheque,' I said. 'You do have your chequebook with you?'

His gaze grew calculating. I gave him little time to slide out.

I said, 'The *Daily Flag* is always hungry for tit-bits for its Intimate Details. Owners trying to sneak their horses away at dead of night without paying their bills would be worth a splash, don't you think?'

'That's a threat!' he said furiously.

'Quite right.'

'You wouldn't do that.'

'Oh yes, I certainly would. I might even suggest that if you can't pay this one bill, maybe you can't pay others. Then all your creditors would be down like vultures in a flash.'

'But that's ... that's ...'

'That's what's happening to Bobby, yes. And if Bobby has a cash-flow problem, and I'm only saying if, then it's partly due to you yourself and others like you who don't pay when you should.'

'You can't talk to me like that,' he said furiously.

'I don't see why not.'

'I'll report you to the Jockey Club.'

'Yes, you do that.'

He was blustering, his threat a sham. I looked over his shoulder towards Bobby and Holly, who had been near enough to hear the whole exchange.

'Bobby,' I said, 'go and fetch Mr Graves's account. Make sure every single item he owes is on it, as you may not have a second chance.'

Bobby went at a half-run, followed more tentatively by Holly. The lad who had come with the horsebox retreated with the driver into the shadows. Mr Graves and I stood as if in a private tableau, waiting.

While a horse remained in a trainer's yard the trainer had a good chance of collecting his due, because the law firmly allowed him to sell the horse and deduct from the proceeds what he was owed. With the horse whisked away his prospects were a court action and a lengthy wait, and if the owner went bankrupt, nothing at all.

Graves's horses were Bobby's security, plain and simple.

Bobby eventually returned alone bringing a lengthy bill which ran to three sheets.

'Check it,' I said to Graves, as he snatched the pages from Bobby's hand.

Angrily he read the bill through from start to finish and found nothing to annoy him further until he came to the last item. He jabbed at the paper and again raised his voice.

'Interest? What the shit do you mean, interest?'

'Um,' Bobby said, 'on what I've had to borrow because you hadn't paid me.'

There was a sudden silence. Respectful, on my part. I wouldn't have thought my brother-in-law had it in him.

Graves suddenly controlled his anger, pursed his lips, narrowed his eyes, and delved into an inner pocket for his chequebook. Without any sign of fury or haste he carefully wrote a cheque, tore it out, and handed it to Bobby.

'Now,' he said to me. 'Move.'

'Is it all right?' I asked Bobby.

'Yes,' he said as if surprised. 'All of it.'

'Good,' I said, 'then go and unload Mr Graves's other horse from the horsebox.'

CHAPTER THREE

'Do what?' Bobby said, astonished.

I remarked mildly, 'A cheque is only a piece of paper until it's been through the bank.'

'That's slander!' Graves said furiously, all his earlier truculence reappearing.

'It's an observation,' I said.

Bobby shoved the cheque quickly into his trouser pocket as if fearing that Graves would try to snatch it back, not an unreasonable suspicion in view of the malevolence facing him.

'Once the cheque's been cleared,' I said to Graves, 'you can come and pick up the horses. Thursday or Friday should do. Bobby will keep them for nothing until then, but if you haven't removed them by Saturday he will begin charging training fees again.'

Bobby's mouth opened slightly and shut purposefully, and he walked without more ado towards the horsebox. Graves scuttled a few steps after him, protesting loudly, and then reversed and returned to me, shouting and practically dancing up and down.

'I'll see the Stewards hear about this!'

'Most unwise,' I said.

'I'll stop that cheque.'

'If you do,' I said calmly, 'Bobby will have you put on the forfeit list.'

This most dire of threats cut off Graves's ranting miraculously. A person placed on the Jockey Club's forfeit list for non-payment of training fees was barred in disgrace from all racecourses, along with his horses. Mr Graves, it seemed, was not quite ready for such a social blight.

'I won't forget this,' he assured me viciously. 'You'll regret you meddled with me, I'll see to that.'

Bobby had succeeded in unloading Graves's first horse and was leading it across to its stable, while the lad and the driver closed the ramp and bolted it shut.

'Off you go, then, Mr Graves,' I said. 'Come back in the daytime and telephone first.'

He gave me a bullish stare and then suddenly went into the same routine as earlier: pursed his mouth, narrowed his eyes and abruptly quietened his rage. I had guessed, the first time, watching him write his cheque without further histrionics, that he had decided he might as well write it because he would tell his bank not to cash it.

It looked very much now as if he were planning something else. The question was, what?

I watched him walk calmly over to the horsebox and wave an impatient hand at the lad and the driver, telling

41

them to get on board. Then he himself climbed clumsily up into the cab after them and slammed the door.

The engine started. The heavy vehicle throbbed, shuddered, and rolled away slowly out of the yard, Graves looking steadfastly ahead as if blinkered.

I detached myself from the stable door and walked across towards Bobby.

'Thanks,' he said.

'Be my guest.'

He looked round. 'All quiet. Let's go in. It's cold.'

'Mm.'

We walked two steps and I stopped.

'What is it?' Bobby asked, turning.

'Graves,' I said. 'He went too meekly.'

'He couldn't have done much else.'

'He could have gone shouting and kicking and uttering last-minute threats.'

'I don't know what you're worrying about. We've got his cheque and we've got his horses . . . er, thanks to you.'

His horses.

The breath in my lungs went out in a whoosh, steaming in a vanishing plume against the night sky.

'Bobby,' I said, 'have you any empty boxes?'

'Yes, there are some in the fillies' yard.' He was puzzled. 'Why?'

'We might just put Graves's horses in them, don't you think?'

'You mean . . . he might come back?' Bobby shook

his head. 'I'd hear him. I heard him before, though I admit that was lucky because we should have been out at a party, but we were too worried about things to go.'

'Could Graves have known you would be out?' I asked.

He looked startled. 'Yes, I suppose he could. The invitation is on the mantelpiece in the sitting room. He came in there last Sunday for a drink. Anyway, I'd hear a horsebox coming back. Couldn't miss it.'

'And if it parked at three in the morning on that strip of grass along from your gate, and the horses were led out in rubber boots to deaden the noise of their hooves?'

Bobby looked nonplussed. 'But he wouldn't. Not all that. Would he?'

'He was planning something. It showed.'

'All right,' Bobby said. 'We'll move them.'

On my way back to fetch the horse I'd been guarding I reflected that Bobby was uncommonly amenable to advice. He usually considered any suggestion from me to be criticism of himself and defensively found sixteen reasons for not doing what I'd mentioned: or at least not until I was well out of sight and wouldn't know. This evening things were different. Bobby had to be very worried indeed.

We walked Graves's horses round to Bobby's second yard behind the main quadrangle and installed them there in two empty boxes, which happened (all to the good, I thought) not to be side by side.

'Does Graves know his horses by sight?' I asked Bobby; which was not by any means a stupid question, as many owners didn't.

'I don't know,' he said dubiously. 'It's never come up.'

'In other words,' I said, 'he always knows them because they're where he expects to see them?'

'Yes. I should think so. But it's not certain. He might know them better than I think.'

'Well . . . in that case, how about rigging some sort of alarm?'

Bobby didn't say certainly not, it wasn't necessary, he said, 'Where?'

Incredible.

'On one of the boxes they are normally in,' I said.

'Yes. I see. Yes.' He paused. 'What sort of alarm? I haven't any electric gadgets here. If I need any special tight security before a big race I hire a man with a dog.'

I did a quick mental review of his house and its contents. Saucepan lids? Metal trays? Something to make a noise.

'The bell,' I said. 'Your old school bell.'

'In the study.' He nodded. 'I'll fetch it.'

Bobby's study contained shelves of tidily arranged mementoes of his blameless early life: cricket caps, silver cups won at school sports, team photographs, a rugger ball . . . and the hand bell which as a prefect he had rung noisily through his House to send the younger boys to bed. Bobby had been the sort of steadfast team-spirited boy that made the British public school system work: that he had emerged complacent and slightly pompous was probably owing to his many good qualities being manifest to all, including himself.

'Bring a hammer,' I said. 'And some staples if you have any. Nails, if not. And some heavy-duty string.'

'Right.'

He went away and in due course returned carrying the bell quietly by its clapper in one hand and a toolbox in the other. Between us we installed the bell as near to Bobby's house as possible and rigged it in such a way that a good tug to the string tied to its handle would send it toppling and jangling. Then we led the string through a long line of staples to the usual home of one of Graves's horses, and fastened the end of it out of sight to the top of the closed door.

'OK,' I said. 'Go into the house. I'll open this door and you see if you can hear the bell.'

He nodded and went away, and after a fair interval I opened the stable door. The bell fell with a satisfying clamour and Bobby came back saying it would wake the dead. We returned it to its precarious pre-toppling position and with rare accord walked together into the house.

There had been Fieldings and there had been Allardecks in racing further back than anyone could remember: two families with some land and some money and a bitter mutual persisting hatred.

There had been a Fielding and an Allardeck knifing each other for favour with King Charles II when he held court not in London but in Newmarket, thereby making foreign ambassadors travel wearily north-east by coach to present their credentials.

There had been an Allardeck who had wagered three hundred sovereigns on a two-horse race on Queen Anne's own racecourse on Ascot Heath and lost his money to a Fielding, who had been killed and robbed before he reached home.

There had been a Mr Allardeck in the Regency years who had challenged a Mr Fielding to a cross-country contest over fearsome jumps, the winner to take the other's horse. Mr Allardeck (who lost) accused Mr Fielding (an easy victor) of taking a cheating short cut, and the dispute went to pistols at dawn, when they each shot carefully at the other and died of their wounds.

There had been a Victorian gentleman rider named Fielding with a wild moustache and a wilder reputation, and an Allardeck who had fallen off, drunk, at the start of the Grand National. Fielding accused Allardeck of being a coward, Allardeck accused Fielding of seducing his (Allardeck's) sister. Both charges were true: and those two settled their differences by fisticuffs on Newmarket Heath, Fielding half killing the (again) drunk and frightened Allardeck.

By Edwardian times the two families were inextricably locked into inherited hostility and would accuse each other of anything handy. A particularly aggressive Fielding had bought an estate next door to the Allardecks on purpose to irritate, and bitter boundary disputes led to confrontations with shotguns and (more tamely) writs.

Bobby's great-grandfather burned down Great-grandfather Fielding's hay-barn (Great-grandfather Fielding having built it where it most spoiled the Allardeck's view) only to find his favourite hunter shot dead in its field a week later.

Bobby's grandfather and Grandfather Fielding had naturally been brought up to hate each other, the feud in their case extending later to bitter professional rivalry, as each (being a second son and not likely to inherit the family estate) had decided to set up as a licensed racehorse trainer. They each bought training stables in Newmarket and paid their lads to spy and report on the other. They cockily crowed when their horses won and seethed when the other's did, and, if coming first and second in the same race, lodged objections against each other almost as a matter of course.

Holly and I, being brought up in Grandfather Fielding's tempestuous household, were duly indoctrinated with the premise that all Allardecks were villainous madmen (or worse) who were to be cut dead at all times in Newmarket High Street.

Bobby and I, I dare say, each having been taught from birth to detest the other, might in our turn have come to fists or fire, were it not for my father dying, and Bobby's father leaving Newmarket with his family and going off into property and commodities. Not that Bobby's father, Maynard, could bear even the mention of the word Fielding: and the reason he was not speaking to Bobby (as truthfully noted in Intimate Details) was because Bobby Allardeck had dared, despite a promise of disinheritance, to defy his father's fury and walk up the aisle with Holly Fielding.

When Holly was thirteen her one absolute heroine had been Juliet in *Romeo and Juliet*. She learned almost the whole play by heart, but Juliet's part particularly, and became hopelessly romantic about the dead young lovers uniting the warring families of Montague and Capulet. Bobby Allardeck, I reckoned, was her Romeo, and she had been powerfully predisposed to fall in love with him, even if he hadn't been, as he was, tall, fair-haired and good-looking.

They had met by chance (or did she seek him out?) in London after several years of not seeing each other, and within a month were inseparable. The marriage had succeeded in its secret purpose to the extent that Bobby and I were now almost always polite to each other and that our children, if we had any, could, if they would, be friends.

Bobby and Holly had returned to Newmarket, Bobby hoping to take over as trainer in his by then ailing grandfather's yard, but the quarrelsome old man, calling his grandson a traitor to the family, had made him pay full market price for the property, and had then died, not leaving him a penny.

Bobby's current financial troubles were not simple. His house and yard (such small part of it as was free from mortgage) would as a matter of course be held by the bank as security for the extra loans they'd made him for the buying of yearlings. If the bank called in the loans, he and Holly would be left with no home, no livelihood, and an extremely bleak future.

As in many racing houses, a great deal of life went on in the kitchen, which in Holly and Bobby's case was typically furnished with a long dining table and a good number of comfortable chairs. A friendly room, with a lot of light pine, warmly lit and welcoming. When Bobby and I went in from the yard Holly was whisking eggs in a bowl and frying chopped onions and green peppers in a large pan.

'Smells good,' I said.

'I was starving.' She poured the eggs over the onions and peppers. 'We must all be.'

We ate the omelette with hot French bread and wine and talked of nothing much until we had finished.

Then Holly, making coffee, said, 'How did you get Jermyn Graves to go?'

'Jermyn? Is that his name? I told him if he stopped the cheque Bobby would put him on the forfeit list.'

'And don't think I haven't thought of it,' Bobby said.

'But of course it's a dead loss from our point of view really.'

I nodded. The Jockey Club would refrain from putting an owner on the forfeit list if he (or she) paid all training fees which had been owing for three months or more. Unfortunately, though, the forfeit list leverage applied to basic training fees only, and not to vets' or blacksmiths' fees or to the cost of transporting horses to race meetings. Bobby had had to pay out for all those things already for Graves's horses, and putting the owner on the forfeit list wouldn't get them reimbursed.

'Why is he in such a hurry to take his horses away?' I asked.

'He's just using our troubles as an excuse,' Holly said.

Bobby nodded. 'He's done something like this to at least two other trainers. All young and trying to get going, like us. He runs up big bills and then one day the trainer comes home and finds the horses gone. Then Graves pays the bare training fees to avoid the forfeit list, and the trainer's left with no horses as security and all the difficulties and expense of going to court to try to get what he's owed, and of course it's seldom worth it, and Graves gets away with it.'

'Why did you accept his horses in the first place?' I said.

'We didn't know about him, then,' Holly said gloomily. 'And we're not exactly going to turn away people who ask us to take two horses, are we?'

'No,' I said.

'Anyway,' Holly said, 'Jermyn's just another blow. The worst crisis is the feed-merchant.'

'Give him Graves's cheque,' I said.

Holly looked pleased but Bobby said dubiously, 'Our accountant doesn't like us doing that sort of thing.'

'Yeah, but your accountant hasn't got thirty hungry horses on his doorstep staring at him reproachfully.'

'Twenty-nine, really,' Holly said.

'Twenty-seven,' Bobby sighed, 'when Graves's have gone.'

'Does that include the three unsold yearlings?' I asked.

'Yes.'

I rubbed my nose. Twenty-four paying inmates were basically a perfectly viable proposition, even if in his grandfather's day there had been nearer forty. They were, moreover, just about to enter their annual rest period (as Bobby trained only on the Flat) and would no longer be incurring the higher expenses of the season.

Conversely they could not until the following March win any prize money, but then nor would they be losing any bets.

Winter, in flat-racing stables, was time for equilibrium, for holidays, for repainting, and for breaking in the yearlings, sold or not.

'Apart from the unsold yearlings, how much do you owe?' I asked.

I didn't think Bobby would tell me, but after a pause, reluctantly, he did.

I winced.

'But we can pay everything,' Holly said. 'At our own pace. We always do.'

Bobby nodded.

'And it's so unfair about the yearlings,' my sister said passionately. 'One of our owners told Bobby to go up to fifty thousand to get one particular yearling, and Bobby did, and now the owner's telephoned to say he's very sorry he can't afford it after all; he just hasn't got the money. And if we send it back to the next sale, we'll make a loss. It's always that way. People will think there's something wrong with it.'

'I'll probably be able to syndicate it,' Bobby said. 'Sell twelve equal shares. But it takes time to do that.'

'Well,' I said, 'surely the bank will give you time.'

'The bank manager's panic-stricken by that damned newspaper.'

'Did someone deliver it to him too?' I asked.

Holly said gloomily, 'Someone did.'

I told Bobby what Lord Vaughnley had said about the *Flag*'s informant being someone local with a grudge.

'Yes, but who?' Bobby said. 'We really haven't any enemies.' He gave me a sidelong look in which humour was definitely surfacing. 'Once upon a time it would have been a Fielding.'

'Too true.'

'Grandfather!' Holly said. 'It couldn't be him, could it? He's never forgiven me, but surely . . . he wouldn't?'

We thought of the obstinate old curmudgeon who still trained a yardful of horses half a mile away and bellowed at his luckless lads on the Heath every morning. He was still, at eighty-two, a wiry, vigorous, cunningly intelligent plotter whose chief regret these days was that Bobby's grandfather was no longer alive to be outsmarted.

It was true that Grandfather Fielding had been as outraged as Grandfather Allardeck by the unthinkable nuptials, but the man who brought us up had loved us in his own testy way, and I couldn't believe he would actively try to destroy his granddaughter's future. Not unless old age was warping him into malice, as it sadly could sometimes.

'I'll go and ask him,' I said.

'Tonight?' Holly looked at the clock. 'He'll be in bed. He goes so early.'

'In the morning.'

'I don't want it to be him,' Holly said.

'Nor do I.'

We sat over the coffee for a while, and at length I said, 'Make a list of all the people who you know had the *Flag* delivered to them with that paragraph marked, and I'll go and call on some of them tomorrow. All I can get to on a Sunday.'

'What for?' Bobby said. 'They won't change their

minds. I've tried. They just say they want their money at once. People believe what they read in newspapers. Even when it's all lies, they believe it.'

'Mm,' I said. 'But apart from telling them again that they'll be paid OK I'll ask them if any of them saw the paper being delivered. Ask them what time it came. Get a picture of what actually went on.'

'All right,' Holly said. 'We'll make the list.'

'And after that,' I said, 'work out who could possibly know who you deal with. Who could have written the same list. Unless, of course,' I reflected, 'dozens of other people who you don't owe money to got the paper delivered to them as well.'

'I've no idea,' Holly said. 'We never thought of that.'

'We'll find out tomorrow.'

Bobby yawned. 'Scarcely slept last night,' he said.

'Yes. Holly told me.'

There was suddenly a loud clanging from outside, a fierce and urgent alarm, enough to reawaken all the houses, if not the dead.

'God!' Bobby leapt to his feet, crashing his chair over backwards. 'He came back!'

We pelted out into the yard, all three of us, intent on catching Jermyn Graves in the act of trying to steal away his own property; and we did indeed find an extremely bewildered man holding open a stable door.

It was not, however, Jermyn Graves, but Nigel,

Bobby's ancient head lad. He had switched on the light inside the empty box and turned his weatherbeaten face to us as he heard us approach, the light carving deep canyons in his heavy vertical wrinkles.

'Sooty's gone,' he said anxiously. 'Sooty's gone, guv'nor. I fed him myself at half-six, and all the doors were shut and bolted when I went home.' There was a detectable tinge of defensiveness in his voice which Bobby also heard and laid to rest.

'I moved him,' he said easily. 'Sooty's fine.'

Sooty was not the real name of Graves's horse, but the real names of some horses tended to be hopeless mouthfuls for their attendant lads. It was hard to sound affectionate when saying (for instance) Nettleton Manor. Move over Nettleton Manor. Nettleton Manor, you old rogue, have a carrot.

'I was just taking a last look round,' Nigel said. 'Going home from the pub, like.'

Bobby nodded. Nigel, like most head lads, took the welfare of the horses as a personal pride. Beyond duty, their horses could be as dear to head lads as their own children, and seeing they were safely tucked up last thing at night was a parental urge that applied to both species.

'Did you hear a bell ring?' Holly said.

'Yes.' He wrinkled his forehead. 'Near the house.' He paused. 'What was it?'

'A new security system we're trying out,' Bobby said.

'The bell rings to tell us someone's moving about the yard.'

'Oh?' Nigel looked interested. 'Works a treat then, doesn't it?'

CHAPTER FOUR

Work a treat the bell might, but no one came in the small hours to tug it again to its sentinel duty. I slept undisturbed in jeans and sweater, ready for battle but not called, and Bobby went out and disconnected the string before the lads arrived for work in the morning.

He and Holly had written out the list of *Flag* recipients, and after coffee, when it was light, I set off in Holly's car to seek them out.

I went first, though, as it was Sunday and early, to every newsagent, both in the town and within a fair radius of the outskirts, asking if they had sold a lot of copies of the *Flag* to any one person two days ago, on Friday, or if anyone had arranged for many extra copies to be delivered on that morning.

The answer was a uniform negative. Sales of the *Flag* on Friday had been the same as Thursday, give or take. None of the shops, big or small, had ordered more copies than usual, they said, and no one had sold right out of the *Flag*. The boys had done their regular delivery rounds, nothing more.

Dead end to the first and easiest trail.

I went next to seek out the feed-merchant, who was not the one who supplied my grandfather. I had been struck at once, in fact, by the unfamiliarity of all the names of Bobby's suppliers, though when one thought about it, it was probably only to be expected. Bobby, taking over from his grandfather, would continue to use his grandfather's suppliers: and never, it seemed, had the lifelong antagonists used the same blacksmith, the same vet, the same anything. Each had always believed the other would spy on him, given the slightest opportunity. Each had been right.

No feed-merchant in Newmarket, with several thousand horses round about, would find it strange to have his doorbell rung on his theoretical day of rest. The feed-merchant who waved me into the brick office annexe to his house was young and polished; and in an expensive accent and with crispness he told me it was not good business to allow accounts to run on overdue, he had his own cash-flow to consider, and Allardeck's credit had run out.

I handed him Jermyn Graves's cheque, duly endorsed by Bobby on the back.

'Ah,' said the feed-merchant, brightening. 'Why ever didn't you say so?'

'Bobby hoped you might wait, as usual.'

'Sorry. No can do. Cash on delivery from now on.'

'That cheque is for more than your account,' I pointed out.

'So it is. Right then. Bobby shall be supplied until this runs out.'

'Thank you,' I said, and asked him if he had seen his copy of the *Flag* delivered.

'No. Why?'

I explained why. 'This was a large scale and deliberate act of spite. One tends to want to know who.'

'Ah.'

I waited. He considered.

'It must have been here fairly early Friday morning,' he said finally. 'And it was delivered here to the office, not to the house, as the papers usually are. I picked it up with the letters when I came in. Say about eight-thirty.'

'And it was open at the gossip page with the paragraph outlined in red?'

'That's right.'

'Didn't you wonder who'd sent it?'

'Not really . . .' He frowned. 'I thought someone was doing me a good turn.'

'Mm,' I said. 'Do you take the *Flag* usually?'

'No, I don't. *The Times* and the *Sporting Life*.'

I thanked him and left, and took Holly's winnings to the plumber, who greeted me with satisfaction and gave me some of the same answers as the feed-merchant. The *Flag* had been inside his house on the front door mat by seven o'clock, and he hadn't seen who brought it. Mr Allardeck owed him for some pipe-work done way back in the summer, and he would admit, he said, that he had telephoned and threatened him pretty strongly with a county court action if he didn't pay up at once.

Did the plumber take the *Flag* usually?

Yes, he did. On Friday, he got two.

'Together?' I asked. 'I mean, were they both there on the mat at seven?'

'Yes. They were.'

'Which was on top of the other?'

He shrugged, thought, and said, 'As far as I remember, the one marked in red was underneath. Funny, I thought it was, that the boy had delivered two. Then I saw the paragraph, and I reckoned one of my neighbours was tipping me off.'

I said it was all very hard on Bobby.

'Yes, well, I suppose so.' He sniffed. 'He's not the only bad payer, by a long shot.' He gave me the beginnings of a sardonic smile. 'They pay up pretty quick when their pipes burst. Come a nice heavy freeze.'

I tried three more creditors on the list. Still unpaid, they were more brusque and less helpful, but an overall pattern held good. The marked papers had been delivered before the newsboys did their rounds and no one had seen who delivered them.

I went back to the largest of the newsagents and asked the earliest time their boys set out.

'The papers reach us here by van at six. We sort them into the rounds, and the boys set off on their bicycles before six-thirty.'

'Thanks,' I said.

They nodded. 'Any time.'

Disturbed by the stealth and thoroughness of the operation I drove finally to see my grandfather in the house where I'd been brought up: a large brick-built place with gables like comic eyebrows peering down at a barbed-wire-topped boundary fence.

The yard was deserted when I drove in, all the horses in their boxes with the top doors closed against the cold. On the day after the last day of the Flat season, no one went out to gallop on the Heath. Hibernation, which my grandfather hated, was already setting in.

I found him in his stable office, typing letters with concentration, the result, I surmised, of the departure of yet another beleaguered secretary.

'Kit!' he said, glancing up momentarily. 'I didn't know you were coming. Sit down. Get a drink.' He waved a thin hand. 'I won't be long. Damned secretary walked out. No consideration, none at all.'

I sat and watched while he hammered the keys with twice the force necessary, and felt the usual slightly exasperated affection for him, and the same admiration.

He loved horses beyond all else. He loved Grandmother next best and had gone very silent for a while the winter she'd died, the house eerily quiet after the years they'd spent shouting at each other. Within a few months he had begun shouting at Holly and me instead, and later, after we'd left, at the secretaries. He didn't intend to be unkind. In an imperfect world he was a perfectionist irritated by minor incompetencies, which meant most of the time.

The typing stopped. He stood up, the same height as myself, white-haired, straight and trim in shirt, tie and excellently cut tweed jacket. Casual my grandfather was not, not in habits or manners or dress, and if he was obsessive by nature it was probably just that factor which had brought him notable success over almost sixty years.

'There's some cheese,' he said, 'for lunch. Are you staying tonight?'

'I'm, er, staying with Holly.'

His mouth compressed sharply. 'Your place is here.'

'I wish you'd make it up with her.'

'I talk to her now,' he said, 'which is more than can be said for that arrogant Maynard with his rat of a son. She comes up here some afternoons. Brings me stews and things sometimes. But I won't have him here and I won't go there, so don't ask.' He patted my arm, the ultimate indication of approval. 'You and I, we get along all right, eh? That's enough.'

He led the way to the dining room where two trays lay on the table, each covered with a cloth. He removed one cloth to reveal a carefully laid single lunch: cheeses, biscuits under clingfilm, pats of butter, dish of chutney, a banana and an apple with a silver fruit knife. The other tray was for dinner.

'New housekeeper,' he said succinctly. 'Very good.'

Long may she last, I thought. I removed the clingfilm and brought another knife and plate, and the two of us sat there politely eating very little, he from age, I from necessity.

I told him about the paragraph in the *Flag* and knew at once with relief that he'd had no hand in it.

'Nasty,' he said. 'Mind you, my old father could have done something like that, if he'd thought of it. Might have done it myself,' he chuckled, 'long ago. To Allardeck.' Allardeck, to Grandfather, was Bobby's grandfather, Maynard's father, the undear departed. Grandfather had never in my hearing called him anything but plain Allardeck.

'Not to Holly,' my grandfather said. 'Couldn't do it to Holly. Wouldn't be fair.'

'No.'

He looked at me searchingly. 'Did she think it might be me?'

'She said it couldn't be, and also that she very much didn't want it to be you.'

He nodded, satisfied and unhurt. 'Quite right. Little Holly. Can't think what possessed her, marrying that little rat.'

'He's not so bad,' I said.

'He's like Allardeck. Just the same. Smirking all over his face when his horse beat mine at Kempton two weeks ago.'

'But you didn't lodge an objection, I noticed.'

'Couldn't. No grounds. No bumping, boring or

crossing. His horse won by three lengths.' He was disgusted. 'Were you there? I didn't see you.'

'Read it in the paper.'

'Huh.' He chose the banana. I ate the apple. 'I saw you win the Towncrier yesterday on television. Rotten horse, full of hate. You could see it.'

'Mm.'

'You get people like that, too,' he observed. 'Chockful of ability and too twisted up to do anything worthwhile.'

'He did win,' I pointed out.

'Just. Thanks to you. And don't argue about that, it's something I enjoy, watching you ride. There never was an Allardeck anywhere near your class.'

'And I suppose that's what you said to Allardeck himself?'

'Yes, of course. He hated it.' Grandfather sighed. 'It's not the same since he's gone. I thought I'd be glad, but it's taken some of the point out of life. I used to enjoy his sour looks when I got the better of him. I got him barred from running his horse in the St Leger once, because my spies told me it had ringworm. Did I tell you that? He would have killed me that day if he could. But he'd stolen one of my gullible lady owners with a load of lies about me never entering her horses where they could win. They didn't win for him either, as I never let him forget.' He cut the peeled banana into neat pieces and sat looking at them. 'Maynard, now,' he said, 'Maynard hates my guts too, but he's not worth the ground Allardeck stood on. Maynard is a power-hungry egomaniac, just the same, but he's also a creeper, which his father never was, for all his faults.'

'How do you mean, a creeper?'

'A bully to the weak but a boot-licker to the strong. Maynard boot-licked his way up every ladder, stamping down on all the people he passed. He was a hateful child. Smarmy. He had the cheek to come up to me once on the Heath and tell me that when he grew up he was going to be a lord, because then I would have to bow to him, and so would everyone else.'

'Did he really?'

'He was quite small. Eight or nine. I told him he was repulsive and clipped his ear. He snitched to his father, of course, and Allardeck sent me a stiff letter of complaint. Long ago, long ago.' He ate a slice of banana without enthusiasm. 'But that longing for people to bow to him, he's still got it, I should think. Why else does he take over all those businesses?'

'To win,' I said. 'Like we win, you and I, if we can.'

'We don't trample on people doing it. We don't want to be bowed to.' He grinned. 'Except by Allardecks, of course.'

We made some coffee and while we drank I telephoned some of Grandfather's traditional suppliers, and his vet and blacksmith and plumber. All were surprised at my question, and no, none of them had received a marked copy of the *Flag*.

'The little rat's got a traitor right inside his camp,'

Grandfather said without noticeable regret. 'Who's his secretary?'

'No one. He does everything himself.'

'Huh. Allardeck had a secretary.'

'You told me about fifty times Allardeck had a secretary only because you did. You boasted in his hearing that you needed a secretary as you had so many horses to train, so he got one too.'

'He never could bear me having more than he did.'

'And if I remember right,' I said, 'you were hopping up and down when he got some practice starting stalls, until you got some too.'

'No one's perfect.' He shrugged dismissively. 'If the little rat hasn't got a secretary, who else knows his life inside out?'

'That,' I said, 'is indeed the question.'

'Maynard,' Grandfather said positively. 'That's who. Maynard lived in that house, remember, until long after he was married. He married at eighteen . . . stupid, I thought it, but Bobby was on the way. And then he was in and out for at least another fifteen years, when he was supposed to be Allardeck's assistant, but was always creeping off to London to do all those deals. Cocoa! Did you ever hear of anyone making a fortune out of cocoa? That was Maynard. Allardeck smirked about it for weeks, going on and on about how smart his son was. Well, my son was dead, as I reminded him pretty sharply one day, and he shut up after that.'

'Maynard wouldn't destroy Bobby's career,' I said.

'Why not? He hasn't spoken to him since he took up with Holly. Holly told me if Maynard wants to say anything to Bobby he gets his tame lawyer to write, and all the letters so far have been about Bobby repaying some money Maynard lent him to buy a car when he left school. Holly says Bobby was so grateful he wrote his father a letter thanking him and promising to repay him one day, and now Maynard's holding him to it.'

'I can't believe it.'

'Absolutely true.'

'What a bastard.'

'The one thing Maynard is actually not,' Grandfather said dryly, 'is a bastard. He's got Allardeck's looks stamped all over him. The same sneer. The same supercilious smirk. Lanky hair. No chin. The little rat's just like them, too.'

Bobby, the little rat, was to any but a Fielding eye a man with a perfectly normal chin and a rather pleasant smile, but I let it pass. The sins and shortcomings of the Allardecks, past and present, could never be assessed impartially in a Fielding house.

I stayed with Grandfather all afternoon and walked round the yard with him at evening stables at four-thirty, the short winter day already darkening and the lights in the boxes shining yellow.

The lads were busy, as always, removing droppings, carrying hay and water, setting the boxes straight. The long-time head lad (at whom Grandfather never shouted) walked round with us, both of them briefly discussing details of each of the fifty or so horses. Their voices were quiet, absorbed and serious, and also in a way regretful, as the year's expectations and triumphs were all over, excitement put away.

I dreaded the prospect of those excitements being put away for ever: of Grandfather ill or dying. He wouldn't retire before he had to, because his job was totally his life, but it was expected that at some point not too very far ahead I would return to live in that house and take over the licence. Grandfather expected it, the owners were prepared for it, the racing world in general thought it a foregone conclusion; and I knew that I was far from ready. I wanted four more years, or five, at the game I had a passion for. I wanted to race for as long as my body was fit and uninjured and anyone would pay me. Jump jockeys never went on riding as long as flat jockeys because crunching to the ground at thirty miles an hour upwards of thirty times a year is a young man's sport, but I'd always thought of thirty-five as approximately hanging-up-the-boots time.

By the time I was thirty-five, Grandfather would be eighty-seven, and even for him . . . I shivered in the cold air and thrust the thought away. The future would have to be faced, but it wasn't upon me yet.

To Grandfather's great disgust I left him after stables and went back to the enemy house, to find the tail end of the same evening ritual still in progress. Graves's horses were still in the fillies' yard, and Bobby was feeling safer because Nigel had told him that Graves had at least twice mistaken other horses for his own when he'd called to see them on Sunday mornings.

I watched Bobby with his horses as he ran his hand down their legs to feel for heat in strained tendons, and peered at the progress of minor skin eruptions, and slapped their rumps as a friendly gesture. He was a natural-born horseman, there was no doubt, and the animals responded to him in the indefinable way that they do to someone they feel comfortable with.

I might find him a bit indecisive sometimes, and not a razor-brain, but he was in truth a good enough fellow, and I could see how Holly could love him. He had, moreover, loved her enough himself to turn his back on his ancestors and estrange himself from his powerful father, and it had taken strength, I reckoned, to do that.

He stood up from feeling a leg and saw me watching him, and with an instinct straight from the subconscious stretched to his full height and gave me a hawk-like look of vivid antagonism.

'Fielding,' he said flatly, as if the word itself was an accusation and a curse: a declaration of continuing war.

'Allardeck,' I replied, in the same way. I grinned slightly. 'I was thinking, as a matter of fact, that I liked you.'

'Oh!' He relaxed as fast as he'd tensed, and looked confused. 'I don't know . . . for a moment . . . I felt . . .'

'I know,' I said, nodding. 'Hatred.'

'Your eyes were in shadow. You looked . . . hooded.'

It was an acceptable explanation and a sort of apology; and I thought how irrational it was that the deep conditioning raised itself so quickly to the surface, and in myself on occasions just the same, however I might try to stop it.

He finished the horses without comment and we walked back towards the house.

'I'm sorry,' he said then, with a touch of awkwardness. 'Back there . . .' He waved a hand. 'I didn't mean it.'

I asked curiously, 'Do you ever think of Holly in that way? As a Fielding? If her eyes are in shadow, does she seem a menace?'

'No, of course not. She's different.'

'How is she different?'

He glanced at my face and seemed to find it all right to explain. 'You,' he said, 'are strong. I mean, in your mind, not just muscles. No one who's talked to you much could miss it. It makes you . . . I don't know . . . somehow people notice when you're there, like in the weighing room, or somewhere. People would be able to say if you'd been at a particular race meeting or not, or at a party, even though you don't try. I suppose I'm not making sense. It's what's made you a champion jockey, I should think, and it's totally *Fielding*. Well, Holly's not like that. She's gentle and calm and she hasn't an ounce of aggressiveness or ambition, and she doesn't want to go out and beat the world on horses, so she isn't really a Fielding at heart.'

'Mm.' It was a dry noise from the throat more than a word. Bobby gave me another quick glance. 'It's all right,' I said. 'I'll plead guilty to my inheritance, and also exonerate her from it. But she does have ambition.'

'No.' He shook his head positively.

'For you,' I said. 'For you to be a lasting success. For you both to be. To prove you were right to get married.'

He paused with his hand on the knob of the door which led from the yard to the kitchen. 'You were against it, like all the others.'

'Yes, for various reasons. But not now.'

'Not on the actual day,' he said with fairness. 'You were the only one that turned up.'

'She couldn't walk up that aisle by herself, could she?' I said. 'Someone had to go with her.'

He smiled as instinctively as before he'd hated.

'A Fielding giving a Fielding to an Allardeck,' he said. 'I wondered at the time if there would be an earthquake.'

He opened the door and we went in. Holly, who bound us together, had lit the log fire in the sitting room and was trying determinedly to be cheerful.

We sat in armchairs and I told them about my morning travels, and also assured them of Grandfather's non-involvement.

'The marked copies of the *Flag* were on people's mats at least by six,' I said, 'and they came from outside,

71

not from Newmarket. I don't know what time the papers get to the shops in Cambridge, but not a great deal before five, I shouldn't think, and there couldn't have been much time for anyone to buy twenty or so papers in Cambridge and deliver them, folded and marked, to addresses all over Newmarket, twenty miles away, before the newsboys here started on their rounds.'

'London?' Holly said. 'Do you think someone brought them up direct?'

'I should think so,' I nodded. 'Of course that doesn't necessarily mean that it wasn't someone from here who arranged it, or even did it personally, so we're not much further ahead.'

'It's all so pointless,' Holly said.

'No one seems to have been looking out of their windows by six,' I went on. 'You'd think someone would be, in this town. But no one that I asked had seen anyone walking up to anyone's door with a newspaper at that time. It was black dark, of course. They said they hardly ever see the newsboys themselves, in winter.'

The telephone on the desk beside Bobby's chair rang, and Bobby stretched out a hand to pick up the receiver with a look of apprehension.

'Oh . . . hello, Seb,' he said. There was some relief in his voice, but not much.

'Friend,' Holly said to me. 'Has a horse with us.'

'You saw it, did you?' Bobby made a face. 'Someone

sent you a copy . . .' He listened, then said, 'No, of course I don't know who. It's sheer malice. No, of course it's not true. I'm here in business to stay, and don't worry, your mare is very well and I was just now feeling her tendon. It's cool and firm and doing fine. What? Father? He won't guarantee a penny, he said so. Yes, you may well say he's a ruthless swine . . . No, there's no hope of it. In fact on the contrary he's trying to squeeze out of me some money he lent me to buy a car about fourteen years ago. Yes, well . . . I suppose it's that sort of flint that's made him rich. What? No, not a fortune, it was a second-hand old banger, but my first. I suppose I'll have to pay him in the end just to get his lawyers off my back. Yes, I told you, everything's fine. Pay no attention to the *Flag*. Sure, Seb, any time. Bye.'

He put down the receiver, his air nowhere near as confident as his telephone voice.

'Another owner full of doubt. Load of rats. Half of them are thinking of leaving without waiting to see if the ship will sink. Half of them, as well, haven't paid their last month's bills.'

'Has Seb?' asked Holly.

Bobby shook his head.

'He's got a cheek, then.'

'That wretched paragraph reached him by post yesterday: just the Intimate Details column. A clipping, he said, not the whole paper. In an ordinary brown envelope, typed. From London, like the others.'

'Did all the owners get a clipping?' I asked.

'It looks like it. Most of them have been on the phone. I haven't exactly rung the rest to ask.'

We sat around for a while, and I borrowed the telephone to pick up my messages from the answering machine in the cottage, and to call in return a couple of trainers who'd offered rides during the week, and to talk to a couple of jockeys who lived in Newmarket, asking for a lift down to Plumpton in Sussex for racing the next day. Two of them were already going together, they said, and would take me.

'Will you come back here?' Holly said, when all was fixed.

I looked at the anxiety in her face and the lack of opposition in Bobby's. I wouldn't have expected him to want me even in the first place, but it seemed I was wrong.

'Stay,' he said briefly, but with invitation, not grudge.

'I haven't been much help.'

'We feel better,' Holly said, 'with you here.'

I didn't much want to stay because of practical considerations. I was due to ride in Devon on the Tuesday, and one reason I preferred to live in Lambourn, not Newmarket, was that from Lambourn one could drive to every racecourse in England and return home on the same day. Lambourn was central.

I said apologetically, 'I'll have to get a lift back to Lambourn from Plumpton, because I need my car to go

to Devon on Tuesday. When I get back to Lambourn
on Tuesday evening, we'll see how things are here.'

Holly said, 'All right,' dispiritedly, not attempting to
persuade.

I looked at her downcast face, more beautiful, as
often, in sorrow than in joy. A thought came unexpectedly into my head and I said without reflection,
'Holly, are you pregnant?'

CHAPTER FIVE

Bobby was dumbstruck.

Holly gave me a piercing look from the light brown eyes in which I read both alarm and stimulation.

'Why did you say that?' Bobby demanded.

'She's only a short while overdue. We haven't had any tests done yet,' Bobby said; and to Holly, 'You must have told him.'

'No, I haven't.' She shook her head. 'But I was thinking just then how happy I was first thing on Friday, when I woke up feeling sick. I was thinking how ironic it would be. All those months of trying, and the first time it may really have happened, we are in such trouble that the very last thing we need is a baby.'

Bobby frowned. 'You must have told him,' he repeated, and he sounded definitely upset, almost as if he were jealous.

'Well, no, I didn't,' Holly said uncertainly.

'On the way back here yesterday,' he insisted.

'Look,' I said. 'Forget I said it. What does it matter?'

Bobby looked at me with resentment and then more

forgivingly at Holly, as if some thought had struck him. 'Is this the sort of thing you meant,' he said doubtfully, 'when you told me once about you and Kit reading each other's minds when you were kids?'

She reluctantly nodded. 'We haven't done it for years, though.'

'It doesn't happen nowadays,' I agreed. 'I mean, this was just a one-off. A throw-back. I don't suppose it will happen again.'

And if it did happen again, I thought, I would be more careful what I said. Stray thoughts would be sieved.

I understood Bobby's jealousy perfectly well because I had felt it myself, extraordinarily strongly, when Holly first told me she had fallen in love. The jealousy had been quickly overlaid by a more normal dismay when she'd confessed just who it was she'd set her heart on, but I still remembered the sharpness of not wanting to share her, not wanting my status as her closest friend to be usurped by a stranger.

I'd been slightly shocked at my jealousy and done a fair amount of soul-searching, never before having questioned my feelings for my sister: and I'd made the reassuring but also rueful discovery that she could sleep with Bobby all she liked and leave me undisturbed: it was the mental intimacy I minded losing.

There had been sexual adventures of my own, of course, both before and after her marriage, but they had been short-lived affairs with no deep involvement, nothing anywhere approaching Holly's commitment to Bobby. Plenty of time, I thought, and maybe, one of these days; and platitudes like that.

Bobby made at least a show of believing that telepathy between me and Holly wouldn't happen again, although both she and I, giving each other the merest flick of a glance, guessed differently. If we chose to tune in, so to speak, the old habit would come back.

The three of us spent the evening trying not to return over and over to the central questions of who and why, and in the end went wearily to bed without any possible answers. I lay down again in jeans, jersey and socks in case Graves should return, but I reckoned that if he'd ever planned it, he had had second thoughts.

I was wrong.

The bell woke me with a clatter at three-thirty-five in the morning, and I was into my shoes, out of the house and running down the drive, in the strategy that Bobby and I had discussed the night before, almost before it stopped ringing.

Out of the open gateway, turn left; and sure enough, on a stretch of roadside grass that sometimes accommodated gypsies, stood the wherewithal for shifting horses. A car, this time, towing a two-horse trailer. A trailer with its rear ramp lowered; ready, but not yet loaded.

I ran straight up to the car and yanked open the driver's door, but there was no one inside to be taken by surprise. Just keys in the ignition; unbelievable.

I lifted up the trailer's ramp and bolted it shut, then

climbed into the car, started up, and drove a couple of hundred yards to a side road. I turned into there, parked a short way along, left the keys in the ignition as before, and sprinted back to Bobby's yard.

The scene was almost a repeat of the time before, at least as far as the lights, the shouting and obscenity went. Bobby and Jermyn Graves were standing outside the empty box where the alarm had been rigged and had all but come to blows. A thin boy of perhaps sixteen stood a short distance away, holding a large carrier bag, shifting from foot to foot and looking unhappy.

'Give me my property,' Graves yelled. 'This is stealing.'

'No, it's not,' I said in his ear. 'Stealing is an intention permanently to deprive.'

'What?' He swung round to glare at me. 'You again!'

'If you're talking law,' I said, 'it is within the law to withhold property upon which money is owed, until the debt is discharged.'

'I'll ruin you,' he said vindictively. 'I'll ruin you both.'

'Be sensible, Mr Graves,' I said. 'You're in the wrong.'

'Who the shit cares. I won't have some pipsqueak jockey and some bankrupt little trainer get the better of me, I'll tell you that.'

The attendant boy said nervously, 'Uncle . . .'

'You shut up,' Graves snapped.

The boy dropped the carrier and and fell over his feet picking it up.

'Go away, Mr Graves,' I said. 'Calm down. Think it over. Come and fetch your horses when your cheque's been cleared, and that'll be the end of it.'

'No, it won't.'

'Up to you,' I said, shrugging.

Bobby and I watched him try to extricate himself without severe loss of face, which could hardly be done. He delivered a few more threats with a good deal of bluster, and then finally, saying 'Come on, come on' irritably to his nephew, he stalked away down the drive.

'Did you immobilize his horsebox?' Bobby asked.

'It was a car and a trailer, and the key was in it. I just drove it out of sight round the nearest corner. Wonder if they'll find it.'

'I suppose we needn't have bothered,' Bobby said. 'As Graves went to the alarm box first.'

We had thought he might go to his other horse's box first, find it empty, think he had the wrong place, and perhaps remove one of the horses from either side. We thought he might have brought more men. In the event, he hadn't done either. But the precaution, all the same, might have been worth it.

We closed the empty stable and Bobby kicked against something on the ground. He bent to pick it up, and held it out for me to see: a large piece of thick felt with pieces of velcro attached. A silencer for a hoof. Fallen out of the carrier, no doubt.

'Not leather boots,' Bobby said, grimly. 'Home-made.'

He switched off the yard lights and we stood for a while near the kitchen door, waiting. We would hear the car and trailer drive off, we thought, in the quiet night. What we heard instead, however, were hesitant footsteps coming back into the yard.

Bobby turned the lights on again, and the boy stood there, blinking and highly embarrassed.

'Someone's stolen Uncle's car,' he said.

'What's your name?' I asked.

'Jasper.'

'Graves?'

He nodded and swallowed. 'Uncle wants me to ring the police and get a taxi.'

'If I were you,' I said, 'I'd go out of the gate here, turn left, take the first turn to the left along the road a bit, and use the public telephone box you'll find down there.'

'Oh,' he said. 'All right.' He looked at us almost beseechingly. 'It was only supposed to be a lark,' he said. 'It's all gone wrong.'

We gave him no particular comfort, and after a moment he turned and went away again down the drive, his footsteps slowly receding.

'What do you think?' Bobby said.

'I think we should rig the bell so that anyone coming up the drive sets it off.'

'So do I. And I'll disconnect it first thing when I get up.'

We began to run a blackened string tightly across the drive at knee level, and heard Graves's car start up in the distance.

'He's found it,' Bobby said. He smiled. 'There's no telephone box down that road, did you know?'

We finished the elementary alarm system and went yawning indoors to sleep for another couple of hours, and I reflected, as I lay down, about the way a feud could start, as with Graves, and continue through centuries, as with Allardecks and Fieldings, and could expand into political and religious persecutions on a national scale, permanently persisting as a habit of mind, a destructive hatred stuck in one groove. I would make a start in my own small corner, I thought sardonically, drifting off, and force my subconscious to love the Allardecks, of which my own sister, God help her, was one.

Persistence raised its ugliest head first thing in the morning.

I answered the telephone when it rang at eight-thirty because Bobby was out exercising his horses and Holly was again feeling sick: and it was the feed-merchant calling in his Etonian accent to say that he had received a further copy of the *Daily Flag*.

'I've just picked it up,' he said. 'It's today's paper. Monday. There's another piece outlined in red.'

'What does it say?' I asked, my heart sinking.

'I think . . . well . . . you can come and fetch it, if you like. It's longer, this time. And there's a picture of Bobby.'

'I'll be there.'

I drove straight round in Holly's car and found the feed-merchant in his office as before. Silently he handed me the paper, and with growing dismay I looked at the picture which made Bobby seem a grinning fool, and read the damage in Intimate Details.

Money troubles abound for Robertson (Bobby) Allardeck (32), still training a few racehorses in his grandfather's once-bustling stables in Newmarket. Local traders threaten court action over unpaid bills. Bobby weakly denies the owners of the remaining horses should be worried, although the feed-merchant has stopped deliveries. Where will it end?

Not with manna from heaven from Daddy.

Maynard 'Moneybags' Allardeck (50), cross with Bobby for marrying badly, won't come to the rescue.

Maynard, known to be fishing for a knighthood, gives all his spare cash to charity.

Needy Bobby's opinion? Unprintable.

Watch this space for more.

'If Bobby doesn't sue for libel,' I said, 'his father surely will.'

'Greater the truth, greater the libel,' the feed-merchant said dryly, and added, 'Tell Bobby his credit's good with me again. I've been thinking it over. He's always paid me regularly, even if always late. And I don't like being manipulated by muck like that.' He pointed to the paper. 'So tell Bobby I'll supply him as before. Tell him to tell his owners.'

I thanked him and went back to Bobby's house, and read Intimate Details again over a cup of coffee in the kitchen. Then I pensively telephoned the feed-merchant.

'Did you,' I said, 'actually tell anyone that you intended to stop making deliveries to Bobby?'

'I told Bobby.' He sounded equally thoughtful. 'No one else.'

'Positive.'

'Not even your secretary? Or your family?'

'I admit that on Friday I was very annoyed and wanted my money immediately, but no one overheard my giving Bobby a talking to about it, I'm quite certain. My secretary doesn't come in until eleven on Fridays, and as you know, my office is an annexe. I was alone when I telephoned him, I assure you.'

'Well, thanks,' I said.

'The informant must be at Bobby's end,' he insisted.

'Yes. I think you're right.'

We disconnected and I began to read the *Daily Flag*

from start to finish, which I'd never done before, seeking enlightenment perhaps on what made a newspaper suddenly attack an inoffensive man and aim to destroy him.

The *Flag*'s overall and constant tone, I found, was of self-righteous spite, its message a sneer, its aftertaste guaranteed to send a reader belligerently out looking for an excuse to take umbrage or to spread ill will.

Any story that would show someone in a poor light was in. Praise was out. The put-down had been developed to a minor art, so that a woman, however prominent or successful, did not 'say'; instead she 'trilled', or she 'shrilled', or she 'wailed'. A man 'chortled', or he 'fumed', or he 'squeaked'.

The word 'anger' appeared on every single page. All sorts of things were 'slammed', but not doors. People were reported as denying things in a way that interpreted 'deny' as 'guilty but won't own up'; and the word 'claims', in the *Flag*'s view, as, for instance, in 'He claims he saw...' was synonymous with 'He is lying when he says he saw...'

The *Flag* thought that respect was unnecessary, envy was normal, all motives were loved; and presumably it was what people wanted to read, as the circulation (said the *Flag*) was increasing daily.

On the premise that a newspaper ultimately reflected the personality of its owner, as the *Towncrier* did Lord Vaughnley's, I thought the proprietor of the *Daily Flag* to be destructive, calculating, mean-spirited and dangerous. Not a good prospect. It meant one couldn't with any hope of success appeal to the *Flag*'s better nature to let up on Bobby, because a better nature it didn't have.

Holly came downstairs looking wan but more cheerful, Bobby returned from the Heath with reviving optimism, and I found the necessity of demolishing their fragile recovery just one more reason to detest the *Flag*.

Holly began to cry quietly and Bobby strode about the kitchen wanting to smash things, and still there was the unanswerable question: Why?

'This time,' I said, 'you consult your lawyer, and to hell with the cost. Also this time we are going to pay all your worst bills at once, and we are going to get letters from all your creditors saying they have been paid, and we'll get those letters photocopied by the dozen, and we'll send a set of them out to everyone who got a copy of the *Flag*, and to the *Flag* itself, to Sam Leggatt, the editor, special delivery, and to all the owners, and to anyone else we can think of, and we'll accompany these with a letter of your own saying you don't understand why the *Flag* is attacking you but the attacks have no foundation, the stable is in good shape and you are certainly not going out of business.'

'But,' Holly said, gulping, 'the bank manager won't honour our cheques.'

'Get the worst bills,' I said to Bobby, 'and let's have a look at them. 'Specially the blacksmith, the vets and the transport people. We'll pay those and any others that are vital.'

'What with?' he said irritably.

'With my money.'

They were both suddenly still, as if shocked, and I realized with a thrust of pleasure that that plain solution simply hadn't occurred to them. They were not askers, those two.

Holly couldn't disguise her upsurge of hope, but she said doubtfully, 'Your new house, though. It must be taking you all you've saved. You haven't been paid for the cottage yet.'

'There's enough,' I assured her. 'And let's get started because I'll have to be off to Plumpton pretty soon.'

'But we can't . . .' Bobby said.

'Yes, you must. Don't argue.'

Bobby looked pole-axed but he fetched the bunch of accounts and I made out several cheques.

'Take these round yourself this morning and get watertight receipts, and in a minute we'll write the letter to go with them,' I said. 'And see if you can get them all photocopied and clipped into sets in time to catch this afternoon's post. I know it's a bit of a job, but the sooner very much the better, don't you think?'

'And one set to Graves?' Bobby asked.

'Certainly to Graves.'

'We'll start immediately,' Holly said.

'Don't forget the feed-merchant,' I said. 'He'll write

you something good. He didn't like being made use of by the *Flag*.'

'I don't like to mention it . . .' Holly began slowly.

'The bank?' I asked.

She nodded.

'Leave the bank for now. Tomorrow maybe you can go to the manager with a set of letters and see if he will reinstate you. He darned well ought to. His bank's making enough out of you in interest, especially on the yearling loans. And you do still have the yearlings as security.'

'Unfortunately,' Bobby said.

'One step at a time,' I said.

'I'll telephone my solicitor straight away,' he said, picking up the receiver and looking at his watch. 'He'll be in by now.'

'No, I shouldn't,' I said.

'But you said . . .'

'You've got an informant right inside this house.'

'What do you mean?'

'Your telephone,' I said, 'I should think.'

He looked at it with disgusted understanding and in a half-groan said, 'Oh, God.'

'It's been done before,' I said: and there had in fact been a time in Lambourn when everyone had been paranoid about being overheard and had gone to elaborate lengths to avoid talking on their home telephones. Illegal it might well be to listen uninvited, but it was carried on nevertheless, as everyone knew.

Without more ado we unscrewed all the telephones in the house, but found no limpet-like bugs inside. Horses, however, not electronics, were our speciality, and Bobby said he would go out to a public box and ring up the telephone company and ask them to come themselves to see what they could find.

It happened at one point that Bobby was on his knees by the kitchen wall screwing together the telephone junction there and Holly and I were standing side by side in the centre of the room, watching him, so that when the newcomer suddenly arrived among us unannounced it was my sister and I that he saw first.

A tall man with fair hair fading to grey, immensely well brushed. Neat, good-looking features, smoothly shaven rounded chin; trim figure inside a grey City suit of the most impeccable breeding. A man of fifty, a man of power whose very presence filled the kitchen, a man holding a folded copy of the *Daily Flag* and looking at Holly and me with open loathing.

Maynard Allardeck; Bobby's father.

Known to me, as I to him, as the enemy. Known to each other by frequent sight, by indoctrination, by professional repute. Ever known, never willingly meeting.

'Fieldings,' he said with battering hate; and to me directly, 'What do you think you're doing in this house?'

'I asked him,' Bobby said, straightening up.

His father turned abruptly in his direction, seeing

his son for the first time closely face to face for more than four years.

They stared at each other for a long moment as if frozen, as if relearning familiar features, taking physical stock. Seeing each other perhaps as partial strangers, freshly. Whatever any of us might have expected or wished for in the way of reconciliation, it turned out to be the opposite of what Maynard had in mind. He had come neither to help nor even to commiserate, but to complain.

Without any form of greeting he said, 'How dare you drag me into your sordid little troubles.' He waved his copy of the *Flag*. 'I won't have you whining to the Press about something that's entirely your own fault. If you want to marry into a bunch of crooks, take your consequences and keep me out of it.'

I imagine we all blinked, as Bobby was doing. Maynard's voice was thick with anger and his sudden onslaught out of all proportion, but it was his reasoning above all which had us stunned.

'I didn't,' Bobby said, almost rocking on his feet. 'I mean, I haven't talked to the Press. I wouldn't. They just wrote it.'

'And this part about me refusing you money? How else would they know, if you hadn't told them? Answer me that.'

Bobby swallowed. 'You've always said . . . I mean, I thought you meant it, that you wouldn't.'

'Of course I mean it.' His father glared at him. 'I

won't. That's not the point. You've no business snivelling about it in public and I won't have it. Do you hear?'

'I haven't,' Bobby protested, but without conviction.

I thought how much father and son resembled each other in looks, and how little in character. Maynard had six times the force of Bobby but none of his sense of fair play. Maynard could make money work for him, Bobby worked to be paid. Maynard could hold a grudge implacably for ever, Bobby could waver and crumble and rethink. The comparative weaknesses in Bobby, I thought, were also his strength.

'You must have been blabbing.' Maynard was uncompromisingly offensive in his tone, and I thought that if Bobby ever wanted to announce to the whole world that his father would let him sink, he would have every provocation and every right.

Bobby said with a rush, 'We think someone may have been tapping our telephone.'

'Oh, you do, do you?' Maynard said ominously, casting an angry look at the silent instrument. 'So it's on the telephone you've been bleating about me, is it?'

'No,' Bobby said, half stuttering. 'I mean, no I haven't. But one or two people said ask your father for money, and I told them I couldn't.'

'And this bit,' Maynard belted the air furiously with the newspaper, 'about me fishing for a knighthood. I won't have it. It's a damned lie.'

It struck me forcibly at that point, perhaps because

of an undisguisable edge of fear in his voice, that it was the bit about the knighthood which lay at the real heart of Maynard's rage.

It was no lie, I thought conclusively. It was true. He must indeed be trying actively to get himself a title. Grandfather had said that Maynard at nine had wanted to be a lord. Maynard at fifty was still the same person, but now with money, with influence, with no doubt a line to the right ears. Maynard might be even then in the middle of delicate but entirely unlawful negotiations.

Sir Maynard Allardeck. It certainly rolled well off the tongue. Sir Maynard. Bow down to me, you Fieldings. I am your superior, bow low.

'I didn't say anything about a knighthood,' Bobby protested with more force. 'I mean, I didn't know you wanted one. I never said anything about it. I never thought of it.'

'Why don't you sue the newspaper?' I said.

'You keep quiet,' he said to me vehemently. 'Keep your nose out.' He readdressed himself to Bobby. 'If you didn't mention a knighthood on the telephone, how did they get hold of it? Why did they write that . . . that damned lie? Answer me that.'

'I don't know,' Bobby said, sounding bewildered. 'I don't know why they wrote any of it.'

'Someone has put you up to stirring up trouble against me,' Maynard said, looking hard and mean and deadly in earnest.

We all three stared at him in amazement. How anyone could think that was beyond me.

Bobby said with more stuttering, 'Of course not. I mean, that's stupid. It's not you that's in trouble because of what they wrote, it's me. I wouldn't stir up trouble against myself. It doesn't make sense.'

'Three people telephoned me before seven this morning to tell me there was another paragraph in today's *Flag*,' Maynard said angrily. 'I bought a copy on my way here. I was instantly certain it was your poisonous brother-in-law or his pig of a grandfather who was at the back of it, it's just their filthy sort of thing.'

'No,' Holly said.

Maynard ignored her as if she hadn't spoken.

'I came in here to tell you it served you right,' he said to Bobby, 'and to insist on your forcing the Fieldings to get a full retraction printed in the paper.'

'But,' Bobby said, shaking his head as if concussed, 'it wasn't Kit. He wouldn't do that. Nor his grand-father.'

'You're soft,' Maynard said contemptuously. 'You've never understood that someone can smile into your face while they shove a knife through your ribs.'

'Because of Holly,' Bobby insisted, 'they wouldn't.'

'You're a naive fool,' his father said. 'Why shouldn't they try to break up your marriage? They never wanted it, any more than I did. They're a wily, shifty, vengeful family, the whole lot of them, and if you trust any one of them, you deserve what you get.'

Bobby gave me a quick glance in which I read only discomfort, not doubt. Neither Holly nor I offered any sort of defence because mere words wouldn't dent the opinions that Maynard had held all his life, and nor would hitting him. Moreover we had heard the same sort of invective too often from Grandfather on the subject of the Allardecks. We were more or less immune, by then, to violent reaction. It was Bobby, interestingly, who protested.

'Kit and Holly care what becomes of me,' he said. 'You don't. Kit came to help, and you didn't. So I'll judge as I find, and I don't agree with what you say.'

Maynard looked as if he could hardly believe his ears, and nor, to be honest, could I. It wasn't just that what Bobby was expressing was a heretical defection from his upbringing, but that he also had the courage to stand up to his father and say it to his face.

He looked, as a matter of fact, slightly nervous. Maynard, it was said, inspired wholesale nervousness in the boardroom of any business his eye fell on, and as of that morning I understood why. The unyielding ruthlessness in him, clearly perceptible to all three of us, was central to his success, and for us at least he made no attempt to disguise it or dress it with a façade of charm.

Bobby made a frustrated gesture with both hands, walked over to the sink and began to fill the kettle.

'Do you want any coffee?' he said to his father.

'Of course not.' He spoke as if he'd been insulted. 'I've a committee meeting at the Jockey Club.' He looked at his watch, and then at me. 'You,' he said, 'have attacked me. And you'll suffer for it.'

I said calmly but distinctly, 'If I hear you have said in the Jockey Club that a Fielding is responsible for what has appeared in the *Flag*, I will personally sue you for slander.'

Maynard glared. He said, 'You're filth by birth, you're not worth the fuss that's made of you, and I'd be glad to see you dead.'

I felt Holly beside me begin to spring forward in some passionate explosion of feeling and gripped her wrist tight to stop her. I was actually well satisfied. I had read in Maynard's eyes that he was inclined to take me seriously, but he didn't want me to know it, and I understood also, for the first time, and with unease, that the very fact of my being successful, of being champion, was to him, in his obsession, intolerable.

Along at the Jockey Club, which had its ancient headquarters in Newmarket's main street, and where he had been one of its members for four or five years, Maynard would with luck now pass off the whole *Flag* thing with a grouchy joke. There, in the organization which ruled the racing industry, he would show all courtesy and hide the snarl. There, where he served on dogsbody committees while he made his determined way up that particular ladder, aiming perhaps to be a Steward, one of the top triumvirate, before long, he would now perhaps be careful to say nothing that could get back to my ears.

There were no active professional jockeys in the Jockey Club, nor any licensed trainers, though a few retired practitioners of both sorts sprinkled the ranks. There were many racehorse owners, among whom I had real friends. The approximately 140 members, devoted to the welfare of racing, were self-perpetuating, self-elected. If Maynard had ever campaigned quietly to be chosen for membership it might have helped him to be a member of an old-established racing family, and it might have helped him to be rich, but one thing was certain: he would never have unsheathed for the civilized inspection of his peers the raw, brutal anti-Fielding prejudice he had given spleen to in the kitchen. Nothing alienated the courteous members more than ill-mannered excess.

The preserving of Maynard's public good manners was very much my concern.

He went as he'd come, private manners non-existent, walking out of the kitchen without a farewell. We listened to the firm footsteps recede and to the distant slam of a car door, and his engine starting.

'Do you realize,' Bobby said to me slowly, 'that if he's made a Steward and you're still a jockey . . . you'd be horribly vulnerable . . .?'

'Mm,' I said dryly. 'Very nasty indeed.'

CHAPTER SIX

I rode at Plumpton. A typical day of four rides; one win, one third, one nowhere, one very nearly last, with owner reactions to match.

Far more people than in the previous week seemed to have seen the pieces in Intimate Details, and I spent a good deal of the day assuring all who asked that, no, Bobby wasn't bankrupt, and yes, I was certain, and no, I couldn't say for sure what Bobby's father's intentions were in any respect.

There was the usual small scattering of racing journalists at the meeting, but no one from the *Flag*. The racing column in the *Flag* was most often the work of a sharp young man who wrote disparagingly about what was to come and critically of what was past, and who was avoided whenever possible by all jockeys. On that day, however, I would have been satisfied enough to see him, but had to make do with his equivalent on the *Towncrier*.

'You want to know about the *Flag*? Whatever for? Disgusting rag.' Large and benevolent, Bunty Ireland, the *Towncrier*'s man, spoke with the complacency of a more respectful rag behind him. 'But if you want to know if the parts about your brother-in-law are the work of our sharp-nosed colleague, then no, I'm pretty sure they're not. He was at Doncaster on Friday and he didn't know at first what was in the gossip column. Slightly put out, he was, when he found out. He said the gossip people hadn't consulted him and they should have done. He was his usual endearing sunny self.' Bunty Ireland beamed. 'Anything else?'

'Yes,' I said. 'Who runs Intimate Details?'

'Can't help you there, old son. I'll ask around, if you like. But it won't do Bobby much good, you can't just go and bop us fellows on the nose, however great the provocation.'

Never be too sure, I thought.

I cadged a lift home to Lambourn, ate some lobster and an orange, and thought about telephoning Holly.

Someone, it was certain, would be listening in on the line. Someone had probably been listening in on that line for quite a long period. Long enough to make a list of people Bobby dealt with in Newmarket, long enough to know where he banked, long enough to know how things stood between him and his father. The owner who had telephoned to say he couldn't afford to pay fifty thousand for his yearling must have been listened to, and so must Bobby's unsuccessful attempts to sell it to anyone else.

Someone must indeed have listened also to Bobby's

racing plans and to his many conversations with owners and jockeys. There was no trainer alive who wouldn't in the fullness of time have passed unflattering or downright slanderous opinions about jockeys to owners and vice versa, but nothing of that nature had been used in the paper. No 'inside' revelations of betting coups. No innuendoes about regulations broken or crimes committed, such as giving a horse an easy race, a common practice for which one could be fined or even have one's licence suspended if found out. The target hadn't in fact been Bobby's training secrets, but his financial status alone.

Why?

Too many whys.

I pressed the necessary buttons and the bell rang only once at the other end.

'Kit?' Holly said immediately.

'Yes.'

'Did you try earlier?'

'No,' I said.

'That's all right, then. We've left the receiver off for most of the day, the calls were so awful. But it just occurred to me that you might be trying to ring, so I put it back less than a minute ago . . .' Her voice faded away as she realized what she was saying. 'We've done it again,' she said.

'Yes.'

She must have heard the smile in my voice, because it was in hers also when she replied.

'Look,' she said. 'I've been thinking . . . I've got to go out, now. I'll ring you later, OK?'

'Sure,' I said.

'Bye.'

'Bye,' I said, and disconnected. I also waited, wondering where she would go. Where she'd planned. She called back within fifteen minutes and it was unexpectedly from the feed-merchant's office. The feed-merchant, it appeared, had let her in, switched on the heater, and left her in private.

'He's been terribly good,' Holly explained. 'I think he'd been feeling a bit guilty, though he's no need to really. Anyway I told him we thought our telephone might be bugged and he said he thought it highly possible, and I could come in here and use the phone whenever I liked. I said I'd like to ring you this evening . . . and anyway, here I am.'

'Great,' I said. 'How are things going?'

'We spent the whole day doing those letters and we're frankly bushed. Bobby's asleep on his feet. Everyone took your cheque without question and gave us paid-in-full letters, and we photocopied those and also the rebuttal letter we all wrote before you went to Plumpton, and by the time we'd finished putting everything in the envelopes the last post was just going, and in fact the postman actually waited at the post office while I stuck on the last ten stamps, and I saw him take the special delivery one to the editor of the *Flag*, so with luck, with luck, it will be all over.'

'Mm,' I said. 'Let's hope so.'

'Oh, and Bobby went to see the solicitor, who said he would write a strong letter of protest to the editor and demand a retraction in the paper, like Lord Vaughnley told you, but Bobby says he isn't sure that that letter will have gone today, he says the solicitor didn't seem to think it was frantically urgent.'

'Tell Bobby to get a different solicitor.'

Holly almost laughed. 'Yes. OK.'

We made plans and times for me to talk to her again the next evening after I got home from Devon, but it was at eight in the morning when my telephone rang and her voice came sharp and distressed into my ear.

'It's Holly,' she said. 'Get a copy of the *Flag*. I'll be along where I was last night. OK?'

'Yes,' I said.

She disconnected without another word, and I drove to the village for the paper.

The column would have been printed during the past night. The special delivery envelope wouldn't reach the editor until later in the present morning. I thought in hindsight it would have been better for Bobby to have driven the letter to London and specially delivered it himself, which might just possibly have halted the campaign.

The third broadside read:

Don't pity Robertson (Bobby) Allardeck (32), strapped for cash but still trying to train racehorses

101

in Newmarket. It's the small trader who suffers when fat cats run up unpaid bills.

In his luxury home yesterday Bobby refused to comment on reports he came to blows with the owner of one of the horses in the stable, preventing the owner taking his horse away by force. 'I deny everything,' Bobby fumed.

Meanwhile Daddy Maynard ('Moneybags') Allardeck (50) goes on record as prize skinflint of the month. 'My son won't get a penny in aid from me,' he intoned piously. 'He doesn't deserve it.'

Instead Moneybags lavishes ostentatious handouts on good deserving charities dear to the Government's heart. Can knighthoods be bought nowadays? Of course not!

Bobby wails that while Daddy lashes out the loot on the main chance, he (Bobby) gets threatening letters from Daddy's lawyers demanding repayment of a fourteen-year-old loan. Seems Moneybags advanced a small sum for 18-year-old Bobby to buy a banger on leaving school. With the wheels a long-ago memory on the scrapheap, Daddy wants his money back. Bobby's opinion of Daddy? 'Ruthless swine.'

Can stingy Maynard be extorting interest on top? Watch this space.

Thoughtfully I got the feed-merchant's number from directory enquiries and pressed the buttons: Holly was waiting at the other end.

'What are we going to do?' she said miserably. 'They're such pigs. All those quotes . . . they just made them up.'

'Yes,' I said. 'If you could bear to put together another batch of those letters you sent yesterday, it might do some good to send them to the editors of the other national newspapers, and to the *Sporting Life*. None of them likes the *Flag*. A spot of ridicule from its rivals might make the *Flag* shut up.'

'Might,' Holly said, unconvinced.

'Doing everything one can think of is better than doing nothing,' I said. 'You never know which pellet might kill the bird when you loose off the shot.'

'Poetic,' Holly said sardonically. 'All right. We'll try.'

'And what about the solicitor?' I asked.

'Bobby says he'll find a better one today. Not local. In a London firm. High powered.'

'Some of his owners may know who's best,' I said. 'If not, I could get him a name from one of the people I ride for.'

'Great.'

'But do you know something?' I said.

'What?'

'I'm not so sure that Maynard was very far wrong. All this aggro is aimed as much at him as at Bobby.'

'Yes,' Holly said slowly. 'When we read today's bit of dirt, that's what Bobby thought too.'

'I wouldn't mind betting,' I said, 'that a fair few copies of Intimate Details, episodes one, two and three,

will find their way to the attention of the Honours'
Secretary in Downing Street. And that this was chiefly
what was at the bottom of Maynard's anger yesterday.
If Maynard is really being considered for a knighthood,
Intimate Details could have put the lid on his chances,
at least for just now.'

'Do you think it would? Just a few words in a paper?'

'You never know. The whole Honours thing is so
sensitive. Anyway it's about now that they send out
those ultra-secret letters asking Mr Bloggs if he would
accept a medal if invited. They'll be drawing up the
New Year's Honours' List at this moment. And the
sixty-four dollar question is, if you were the Honours'
Secretary drawing up a list for the Prime Minister's
approval, would you put Maynard on it?'

'But we don't know that anything like that is happening.'

'No, we sure don't.'

'It's probably just the *Flag* being its typically vicious,
mean, destructive self.'

'Perhaps,' I said.

'You know how nasty the Press can be, if they want
to. And the *Flag* seems to want to, all the time, as a
matter of policy.'

'Mm,' I said. 'Maybe you're right.'

'But you don't think so?'

'Well . . . It would make more sense if we could see
a purpose behind these attacks, and stopping Maynard
getting a knighthood would be a purpose. But why

they'd want to stop it, and how they got to hear of it . . . hell alone knows.'

'They didn't hear about any knighthood from our telephone,' Holly said positively. 'So perhaps they're just making it up.'

'Everything else in those stories is founded on things that have happened or been said,' I pointed out. 'They've taken the truth and distorted it. Shall I write to the Honours' Secretary and ask if Maynard's on his provisional list?'

'Yes, yes, funny joke.'

'Anyway,' I said. 'How did Bobby get on with the telephone people?'

'They said they would look into it. They said telephone tapping is illegal as of 1985. They didn't send anyone here yesterday looking for bugs. They said something about checking our exchange.'

'The exchange? I didn't know people could tap into an exchange.'

'Well, apparently they can.'

'So no actual bugs?'

'We told them we couldn't find any and they said we probably didn't know where to look.'

'Well, at least they're paying attention.'

'They said a lot of people think they're being bugged when they aren't,' Holly said. 'All the same, they did say they would look.'

'Keep them up to it.'

'I'll ring you this evening when I get back from

Devon,' I said. 'If I don't get back ... I'll ring sometime.'

'Yes,' she said. 'Take care of yourself.'

'Always do,' I said automatically; and both she and I knew it was impossible. If a steeplechase jockey took too much care of himself, he didn't win races, and there were days occasionally when one couldn't drive oneself home. I was superstitious to the extent of not making binding commitments for the evenings of race days, and like most other jump jockeys accepted invitations with words like 'If I can' and 'With luck'.

I drove the two hours to the Devon and Exeter meeting with my mind more on Holly and Bobby and Maynard than on the work ahead. None of the five horses I was due to ride posed the problems of North Face, and I'd ridden all of them often enough to know their little quirks and their capabilities. All I had to do was help them turn in the best they could do on the day.

The Devon and Exeter racecourse lay on the top of Halden Moor, a majestic sweep of bare countryside with the winds blowing vigorously from the Channel to the Atlantic. The track itself, with its long circuit of almost two miles, stretched away as a green undulating ribbon between oceans of scrub and heather, its far deserted curves as private a place as one could imagine for contest of horse and man.

Unfashionable in Ascot terms, distant geographically, drawing comparatively small crowds, it was still one of my favourite courses; well run, well kept, with welcoming locals, nice people.

The princess liked to go there because friends of hers maintained one of the few private boxes, friends who had a house down by a Devon beach and who invited her to stay regularly for the meetings.

She was there, lunched, fur-coated and discreetly excited, in good time for the first race, accompanied in the parade ring by a small bunch of the friends. Three friends, to be exact. The couple she stayed with, and a young woman.

The princess made introductions. 'Kit . . . you know Mr and Mrs Inscombe . . .' We shook hands. ' . . . And my niece. Have you met my niece, Danielle?'

No, I hadn't. I shook the niece's hand.

'Danielle de Brescou,' the niece said. 'Hi. How're you doing?' And in spite of her name she was not French but audibly American.

I took in briefly the white wool short coat, the black trousers, the wide band of what looked like flowered chintz holding back a lot of dark hair. I got in return a cool look of assessment; half interest, half judgement deferred, topped by a bright smile of no depth.

'What shall we expect?' the princess asked. 'Will Bernina win?'

Wykeham, naturally, had not made the journey to Devon. Moreover he had been vague when I'd talked to him on the telephone, seeming almost unclear as to Bernina's identity, let alone her state of readiness, and it had been Dusty, when I'd handed him my saddle to put on to the mare before the race, who had told me she was 'jumping out of her skin and acting up something chronic'.

'She's fit and ready,' I said to the princess.

'And Wykeham's riding instructions?' Mr Inscombe enquired genially. 'What are those?'

Wykeham's instructions to me were zero, as they had been for several years. I said diplomatically, 'Stay handy in fourth place or thereabouts and kick for home at the second last hurdle.'

Inscombe nodded benevolent approval and I caught the ghost of a grin from the princess, who knew quite well that Wykeham's instructions, if any, would have taken the form of 'Win if you can', an uncomplicated declaration of honesty by no means universal among trainers.

Wykeham produced his horses fighting fit from a mixture of instinct, inherited wisdom, and loving them individually as athletes and children. He knew how to bring them to a peak and understood their moods and preferences, and if nowadays he found the actual races less interesting than the preparation, he was still, just, one of the greats.

I had been his retained jockey for the whole of the main part of my career and he frequently called me by the name of my predecessor. He quite often told me I would be riding horses long dead. 'Polonium in the big race at Sandown,' he would say, and, mystified, I would ask who owned the horse as I'd never heard of it. 'Polonium? Don't be stupid. Big chestnut. Likes mints. You won on him last week.' 'Oh . . . Pepperoni?' 'What? Yes, Pepperoni, of course, that's what I said. Big race at Sandown.'

He was almost as old as my grandfather, and gradually, through their eyes, I was coming to see the whole of racing as a sort of stream that rolled onwards through time, the new generations rising and the old floating slowly away. Racing had a longer history than almost any other sport and changed less, and sometimes I had a powerful feeling of repeating in my own person the experience of generations of jockeys before me and of being a transient speck in a passing pageant; vivid today, talked about, fêted, but gone tomorrow, a memory fading into a footnote, until no one alive had seen me race or cared a damn whether I'd won or lost.

Dead humbling, the whole thing.

Bernina, named after the mountain to the south of St Moritz, had by four years old produced none of the grandeur of the Alps, and to my mind was never going to. She could, however, turn in a respectable performance in moderate company, which was all she was faced with on this occasion, and I hoped very much to win on her, as much for the princess's sake as my own. I understood very well that she liked to be able to please the various hosts around the country who offered her multiple invitations, and was always slightly anxious for her horses to do well where she felt they might contribute to her overnight bread and butter. I thought that if people like the Inscombes didn't enjoy her company for its own sake they wouldn't keep on asking her to stay. The princess's inner insecurities were sometimes astonishing.

Bernina, without any of the foregoing complications of intent, took me out of the parade ring and down to the start in her best immoderate fashion which included a display of extravagant head-shaking and some sideways dancing on her toes. These preliminaries were a good sign: on her off days she went docilely to the starting gate, left it without enthusiasm and took her time about finishing. Last time out she'd had me hauled in front of the Stewards and fined for not trying hard enough to win, and I'd said they should have understood that a horse that doesn't want to race won't race; and that mares have dull days like anyone else. They listened, unimpressed. Pay the fine, they said.

The princess had insisted on reimbursing me for that little lot, where other owners might have raged. 'If she wouldn't go, she wouldn't go,' she'd said with finality. 'And she's my horse, so I'm responsible for her debts.' Owners didn't come more illogical or more generous than the princess.

I'd told her never to let her friends back Bernina on the days she went flat-footed to the start, and she'd acknowledged the advice gravely. I hoped, sitting on top of the bravura performance going on in Devon, that she, the Inscombes and the niece would all be at that moment trekking to the bookmakers or the Tote. The mare was feeling good, and, beyond that, competitive.

The event was a two-mile hurdle race, which meant eight jumps over the sort of fencing used for penning sheep: hurdles made of wood and threaded with gorse or brushwood, each section unattached to the hurdle on either side, so that if a horse hit one, it could be knocked over separately. Good jumpers flowed over hurdles easily, rising little in the air but bending up their forelegs sharply; the trick was to get them to take off from where the hurdle could be crossed in mid-stride.

Bernina, graciously accepting my guidance in that matter, went round the whole course without touching a twig. She also attacked the job of beating her opponents with such gusto that one mightn't have blamed the Stewards this time for testing her for dope, such was the contrast.

She would, if she'd had serious talent, have won by twenty lengths, especially as the chief danger had fallen in a flurry of legs about halfway round. As it was, she made enough progress, when I gave her an encouraging kick between the last two hurdles, to reach the last jump upsides of the only horse still in front, and on the run-in she produced a weak burst of speed for just long enough to pass and demoralize her tiring opponent.

Accepting my congratulatory pats on her victorious neck as totally her due, she pulled up and pranced back

111

to the winners' enclosure, and skittered about there restlessly, sweating copiously and rolling her eyes, up on a high like any other triumphant performer.

The princess, relieved and contented, kept out of the way of the powerful body as I unbuckled the girths and slid my saddle off on to my arm. She didn't say much herself as the Inscombes were doing a good deal of talking, but in any case she didn't have to. I knew what she thought and she knew I knew: we'd been through it all a couple of hundred times before.

The niece said, 'Wow,' a little thoughtfully.

I glanced briefly at her face and saw that she was surprised: I didn't know what she was surprised at, and didn't have time to find out as there was the matter of weighing in, changing, and weighing out for the next race. Icicle, the princess's other runner, didn't go until the fourth race, but I had two other horses to ride before that.

Those two, undisgraced, finished fifth and second, and were both for a local trainer who I rode for when I could: besides Wykeham I also often rode for a stable in Lambourn, and when neither of them had a runner, for anyone else who asked. After, that is, having looked up the offered horse in the form book. Constant fallers I refused, saying Wykeham wouldn't give his approval. Wykeham was a handy excuse.

Icicle, like his name, was the palest of greys; also long-backed, angular and sweet-natured. He had been fast and clever over hurdles, the younger horses' sport, but at a mature eight years and running over bigger fences, was proving more cautious than carefree, more dependable than dazzling, willing but no whirlwind.

I went out to the parade ring again in the princess's colours and found her and the friends deep in a discussion that had nothing to do with horses but which involved a good deal of looking at watches.

'The train from Exeter is very fast,' Mrs Inscombe was saying comfortingly; and the niece was giving her a bright look of stifled impatience.

'Most unfortunate,' Mr Inscombe said in a bluff voice. 'But the train, that's the thing.'

The princess said carefully as if for the tenth time, 'But my dears, the train goes too late . . .' She broke off to give me an absent-minded smile and a brief explanation.

'My niece Danielle was going to London by car with friends but the arrangement has fallen through.' She paused. 'I suppose you don't know anyone who is driving straight from here to London after this race?'

'Sorry, I don't,' I said regretfully.

I looked at the niece: at Danielle. She looked worriedly back. 'I have to be in London by six-thirty,' she said. 'In Chiswick. I expect you know where that is? Just as you reach London from the west?'

I nodded.

'Could you possibly ask,' she waved a hand towards the busy door of the weighing room, 'in there?'

'Yes, I'll ask.'

113

'I have to be at work.'

I must have showed surprise, because she added, 'I work for a news bureau. This week I'm on duty in the evenings.'

Icicle stalked methodically round the parade ring with two and a half miles of strenuous jumping ahead of him. After that, in the fifth race, I would be riding another two miles over hurdles.

After that ...

I glanced briefly at the princess, checking her expression, which was benign, and I thought of the fine she'd paid for me when she didn't have to.

I said to Danielle, 'I'll take you myself straight after the fifth race ... if, er, that would be of any use to you.'

Her gaze intensified fast on my face and the anxiety cleared like sunrise.

'Yes,' she said decisively. 'It sure would.'

Never make positive commitments on race days ...

'I'll meet you outside the weighing room, after the fifth, then,' I said. 'It's a good road. We should get to Chiswick in time.'

'Great,' she said, and the princess seemed relieved that we could now concentrate on her horse and the immediate future.

'Kind of you, Kit,' she said, nodding.

'Any time.'

'How do you think my old boy will do today?'

'He's got bags of stamina,' I said. 'He should run well.'

She smiled. She knew 'bags of stamina' was a euphemism for 'not much finishing speed'. She knew Icicle's ability as well as I did, but like all owners, she wanted good news from her jockey.

'Do your best.'

'Yes,' I said.

I mounted and took Icicle out on to the track.

To hell with superstition, I thought.

CHAPTER SEVEN

It wasn't Icicle I had trouble with.

Icicle jumped adequately but without inspiration and ran on doggedly at one pace up the straight, more by good luck than anything else hanging on to finish second.

'Dear old slowcoach,' the princess said to him proudly in the unsaddling enclosure, rubbing his nose. 'What a gentleman you are.'

It was the hurdler afterwards that came to grief: an experienced racer but unintelligent. The one horse slightly ahead and to the right of us hit the top of the second hurdle as he rose to the jump and stumbled on to his nose on landing, and my horse, as if copying, promptly did exactly the same.

As falls went, it wasn't bad. I rolled like a tumbler on touching the ground, a circus skill learned by every jump jockey, and stayed curled, waiting for all the other runners to pass. As standing up in the middle of a thundering herd was the surest way to get badly injured, staying on the ground, where horses could more easily avoid one, was almost the first lesson in survival. The bad thing about falls near the start of hurdle races, however, was that the horses were going faster than in steeplechases, and were often bunched up together, with the result that they tended not to see a fallen rider until they were on top of him, by which time there was nowhere else to put their feet.

I was fairly used to hoof-shaped bruises. In the quiet that came after the buffeting I stood slowly and stiffly up with the makings of a new collection, and found the other fallen jockey doing the same.

'You all right?' I said.

'Yeah. You?'

I nodded. My colleague expressed a few obscene opinions of his former mount and a car came along to pick us up and deliver us to the ambulance room to be checked by the doctor on duty. In the old days jockeys had got away easily with riding with broken bones, but nowadays the medical inspections had intensified to safeguard the interests not altogether of the men injured but of the people who bet on them. Appeasing the punter was priority stuff.

Bruises didn't count. Doctors never stopped one from riding for those, and in any case bruises weren't visible when very new. I proved to the local man that all the bits of me that should bend, did, and all the bits that shouldn't bend, didn't, and got passed fit to ride again from then on.

One of the two volunteer nurses went to answer a

knock on the door and came back slightly bemused to say I was wanted outside by a woman who said she was a princess.

'Right,' I said, thanking the doctor and turning to go.

'Is she?' the nurse asked dubiously.

'A princess? Yes. How often do you come to race meetings?'

'Today's my first.'

'She's been leading owner three times in the past six jumping seasons, and she's a right darling.'

The young nurse grinned. 'Makes you sick.'

I went outside to find the right darling looking first worried and then relieved at my reappearance. She was certainly not in the habit of enquiring after my health by waiting around outside ambulance room doors, and of course it wasn't my actual well-being which mattered at that point, but my being well enough to drive the niece to work.

The niece was also there and also relieved and also looking at her watch. I said I would change into street clothes and be ready shortly, and the princess kissed the niece and patted my arm, and went away saying she would see me at Newbury on the morrow.

I changed, found the niece waiting outside the weighing room, and took her to my car. She was fairly fidgeting with an impatience which slightly abated when she found the car was a Mercedes, but changed to straight anxiety when she saw me wince as I edged into the driving seat.

'Are you OK? You're not going to pass out, or anything, are you?' she said.

'I shouldn't think so.'

I started the car and extricated ourselves from the close-packed rows. A few other cars were leaving, but not enough to clog the entrance or the road outside. We would have a clear run, barring accidents.

'I guess I thought you'd be dead,' the niece said without emotion. 'How does anyone survive being trampled that way by a stampede?'

'Luck,' I said succinctly.

'My aunt was sure relieved when you stood up.'

I made an assenting noise in my throat. 'So was I.'

'Why do you do it?' she said.

'Race?'

'Uh-huh.'

'I like it.'

'Like getting trampled?'

'No,' I said. 'That doesn't happen all that often.'

We swooped down the hill from the moor and sped unhindered along roads that in the summer were busy with holiday crises. No swaying overloaded caravans being towed that day, no children being sick at the roadside, no radiators boiling and burst, with glum groups on the verges waiting for help. Devon roads in November were bare and fast and led straight to the

119

motorways which should take us to Chiswick with no problems.

'Tell me truthfully,' she said, 'why do you do it?'

I glanced at her face, seeing there a quality of interest suitable for a newsgatherer. She had also large grey eyes, a narrow nose, and a determined mouth. Good-looking in a well-groomed way, I thought.

I had been asked the same question many times by other newsgatherers, and I gave the standard answer.

'I do it because I was born to it. I was brought up in a racing stable and I can't remember not being able to ride. I can't remember not wanting to ride in races.'

She listened with her head on one side and her gaze on my face.

'I guess I never met a jockey until now,' she said reflectively. 'And we don't have much jump racing in America.'

'No,' I agreed. 'In England there are probably more jump races than Flat. Just as many, anyway.'

'So why do you do it?'

'I told you,' I said.

'Yeah.'

She turned her head away to look out at the passing fields.

I raced, I thought fancifully, as one might play a violin, making one's own sort of music from coordinated muscles and intuitive spirit. I raced because the partnership with horses filled my mind with perfections of cadence and rhythmic excitement and intensities of communion: and I couldn't exactly say aloud such pretentious rubbish.

'I feel alive,' I said, 'on a horse.'

She looked back, faintly smiling. 'My aunt says you read their thoughts.'

'Everyone close to horses does that.'

'But some more than others?'

'I don't really know.'

She nodded. 'That makes sense. My aunt says you read the thoughts of people also.'

I glanced at her briefly. 'Your aunt seems to have said a lot.'

'My aunt,' she said neutrally, 'wanted me to understand, I think, that if I went in your car I should arrive unmolested.'

'Good God.'

'She was right, I see.'

'Mm.'

Molesting Danielle de Brescou, I thought, would be my quickest route to unemployment. Not that in other circumstances and with her willing cooperation I would have found it unthinkable. Danielle de Brescou moved with understated long-legged grace and watched the world from clear eyes, and if I found the sheen and scent of her hair and skin fresh and pleasing, it did no more than change the journey from a chore to a pleasure.

Between Exeter and Bristol, while dusk dimmed the day, she told me that she had been in England for three weeks and was staying with her uncle and aunt while she found herself an apartment. She had come because she'd been posted to London by the national broadcasting company she worked for: she was the bureau coordinator, and as it was only her second week there it was essential not to be late.

'You won't be late,' I assured her.

'No ... Do you always drive at eighty miles an hour?'

'Not if I'm in a real hurry.'

'Very funny.'

She told me Roland de Brescou, the princess's husband, was her father's eldest brother. Her father had emigrated to California from France as a young man and had married an American girl, Danielle being their only child.

'I guess there was a family ruckus when Dad left home, but he never told me the details. He's been sending greetings cards lately though, nostalgic for his roots, I guess. Anyway, he told Uncle Roland I was coming to London and the princess wrote me to say come visit. I hadn't met either of them before. It's my first trip to Europe.'

'How do you like it?'

She smiled. 'How would you like being cosseted in a sort of mansion in Eaton Square with a cook and maids and a butler? And a chauffeur. All last week the chauffeur drove me to work and picked me up after. Same thing yesterday. Aunt Casilia says it's not safe here after midnight on the subway, the same as it isn't in New York. She fusses worse than my own mother. But I can't live with them for too long. They're both sweet to me. I like her a lot and we get along fine. But I need a place of my own, near the office. And I'll get a car. I guess I'll have to.'

'How long will you be in England?' I asked.

'Don't know. Three years, maybe. Maybe less. The company can shift you around.'

She said I didn't need to tell her much about myself on account of information from her aunt.

She said she knew I lived in Lambourn and came from an old racing family and had a twin sister married to a racehorse trainer in Newmarket. She said she knew I wasn't married. She left the last observation dangling like a question mark, so I answered the unasked query.

'Not married. No present girlfriend. A couple in the past.'

I could feel her smile.

'And you?' I asked.

'Same thing.'

We drove for a good while in silence on that thought, and I rather pensively wondered what the princess would say or think if I asked her niece out to dinner. The close but arms-length relationship I'd had with her for so many years would change subtly if I did, and perhaps not for the better.

Between Bristol and Chiswick, while we sped with headlights on up the M4 motorway, Danielle told me about her job, which was, she said, pretty much a matter of logistics: she sent the camera crews and interviewers to wherever the news was.

'Half the time I'm looking at train schedules and road maps to find the fastest route, and starting from when we did, and taking the road we're on right now, I expected to be late.' She glanced at the speedometer. 'I didn't dream of ninety.'

I eased the car back to eighty-eight. A car passed us effortlessly. Danielle shook her head. 'I guess it'll take a while,' she said. 'How often do you get speeding tickets?'

'I've had three in ten years.'

'Driving like this every day?'

'Pretty much.'

She sighed. 'In dear old US of A we think seventy is sinful. Have you ever been there?'

'America?' I nodded. 'Twice. I rode there once in the Maryland Hunt Cup.'

'That's an amateurs' race,' she said without emphasis, careful, it seemed, not to appear to doubt my word.

'Yes. I started as an amateur. It seemed best to find out if I was any good before I committed my future to what I do.'

'And if it hadn't worked out?'

'I had a place at college.'

'And you didn't take it?' she said incredulously.

'No. I started winning, and that was what I wanted

most. I tried for the place at college only in case I couldn't make it as a jockey. Sort of insurance.'

'What subject?'

'Veterinary science.'

It shocked her. 'You mean you passed up being a veterinarian to be a jockey?'

'That's right,' I said. 'Why not?'

'But . . . but . . .'

'Yeah,' I said. 'All athletes . . . sportsmen . . . whatever . . . find themselves on the wrong side of thirty-five with old age staring them point-blank in the face. I might have another five years yet.'

'And then?'

'Train them, I suppose. Train horses for others to ride.' I shrugged. 'It's a long way off.'

'It came pretty close this afternoon,' Danielle said.

'Not really.'

'Aunt Casilia says the Cresta Run is possibly more dangerous than the life of a jump jockey. Possibly. She wasn't sure.'

'The Cresta Run is a gold medal or the fright of a lifetime, not a career.'

'Have you been down it?'

'Of course not. It's dangerous.'

She laughed. 'Are all jockeys like you?'

'No. All different. Like princesses.'

She took a deep breath, as if of sea air. I removed my attention from the motorway for a second's inspection of her face, for whatever her aunt might think of my ability to read minds I never seemed to be able to do it with any young woman except Holly ... I was aware also that I wanted to, that without it, any loving was incomplete. I thought that if I hadn't had Holly I might have married one of the two girls I'd most liked: as it was, I hadn't reached the living-in stage with either of them.

I hadn't wanted to marry Holly, nor to sleep with her, but I'd loved her more deeply. It seemed that sex and telepathy couldn't co-exist in me, and until or unless they did, I probably would stay single.

'What are you thinking?' Danielle asked.

I smiled wryly. 'About not knowing what you were thinking.'

After a pause she said, 'I was thinking that when Aunt Casilia said you were exceptional, I can see what she meant.'

'She said what?'

'Exceptional. I asked her in what way, but she just smiled sweetly and changed the subject.'

'Er ... when was that?'

'On our way down to Devon this morning. She's been wanting me to go racing with her ever since I came over, so today I did, because she'd arranged that ride back for me, although she herself was staying with the Inscombes tonight for some frantically grand party. She hoped I would love racing like she does, I think. Do you think sometimes she's lonesome, travelling all those miles to racemeets with just her chauffeur?'

'I don't think she felt lonesome until you came.'

'Oh!'

She fell silent for a while, and eventually I said prosaically, 'We'll be in Chiswick in three minutes.'

'Will we?' She sounded almost disappointed. 'I mean, good. But I've enjoyed the journey.'

'So have I.'

My inner vision was suddenly filled very powerfully with the presence of Holly, and I had a vivid impression of her face, screwed up in deep distress.

I said abruptly to Danielle, 'Is there a public telephone anywhere near your office?'

'Yeah, I guess so.' She seemed slightly puzzled by the urgency I could hear in my voice. 'Sure . . . use the one on my desk. Did you remember something important?'

'No . . . er, I . . .' I drew back from the impossibility of rational explanation. 'I have a feeling,' I said lamely, 'that I should telephone my sister.'

'A feeling?' she asked curiously. 'You looked as if you'd forgotten a date with the President, at least.'

I shook my head. 'This is Chiswick. Where do we go from here?'

She gave me directions and we stopped in a parking space labelled 'Staff Only' outside a warehouse-like building in a side street. Six-twenty on the clock; ten minutes to spare.

'Come on in,' Danielle said. 'The least I can do is lend you a phone.'

127

I stood up stiffly out of the car, and she said with contrition, 'I guess I shouldn't have let you drive all this way.'

'It's not much further than going home.'

'You lie in your teeth. We passed the exit to Lambourn fifty miles back.'

'A bagatelle.'

She watched me lock the car door. 'Seriously, are you OK?'

'It's nothing that a hot bath won't put right.'

She nodded and turned to lead the way into the building, which proved to have glass entrance doors into a hallway furnished with armchairs, potted plants and a uniformed guard behind a reception desk. She and he signed me into a book, gave me a pass to clip to my clothes, and ushered me through a heavy door that opened to an electronic buzz.

'Sorry about the fortress syndrome,' Danielle said. 'The company is currently paranoid about bombs.'

We went down a short corridor into a wide open office inhabited by six or seven desks, mostly with people behind them showing signs of packing up to go home. There was also a sea of green carpet, a dozen or so computers, and on one long wall a row of television screens above head height, all showing different programmes and none of them emitting a sound.

Danielle and the other inhabitants exchanged a few 'Hi's, and 'How're you doing's, and no one questioned my presence. She took me across the room to her own domain, an area of two large desks set at right angles with a comfortable-looking swivelling chair serving both. The desk tops bore several box files, a computer, a typewriter, a stack of newspapers and a telephone. On the wall behind the chair there was a large chart on which things could be written in chinagraph and rubbed off: a chart with columns labelled along the top as SLUG, TEAM, LOCATION, TIME, FORMAT.

'Sit down,' Danielle said, pointing to the chair. She picked up the receiver and pressed a lighted button on the telephone. 'OK. Make your call.' She turned to look at the chart. 'Let's see what's been happening in the world since I left it.' She scanned the segments. Under SLUG someone had written 'Embassy' in large black letters. Danielle called across the room, 'Hank, what's this embassy story?' and a voice answered, 'Someone painted "Yanks Go Home" in red on the US embassy steps and there's a stink about security.'

'Good grief.'

'You'll need to do a follow-up for *Nightline*.'

'Right . . . has anyone interviewed the Ambassador?'

'We couldn't reach him earlier.'

'Guess I'll try again.'

'Sure. It's your baby, baby. All yours.'

Danielle smiled vividly down at me, and I recognized with some surprise that her job was of far higher status than I'd guessed, and that she herself came alive also when she was working.

'Make your call,' she said again.

'Yes.'

I pressed the buttons and at the first ring Holly picked up the receiver.

'Kit,' she said immediately, full of stress.

'Yes,' I said.

Holly's voice had come explosively out of the telephone, loudly enough to reach Danielle's ears.

'How did she know?' she asked. Then her eyes widened. 'She was waiting . . . you knew.'

I half nodded. 'Kit,' Holly was saying. 'Where are you? Are you all right? Your horse fell . . .'

'I'm fine. I'm in London. What's the matter?'

'Everything's worse. Everything's terrible. We're going to lose . . . lose the yard . . . everything . . . Bobby's out walking somewhere . . .'

'Holly, remember the telephone,' I said.

'What? Oh, the bugs? I simply don't care any more. The telephone people are coming to look for bugs in the morning, they've promised. But what does it matter? We're finished . . . It's over.' She sounded exhausted. 'Can you come? Bobby wants you. We need you. You hold us together.'

'What's happened?' I asked.

'It's the bank. The new manager. We went to see him today and he says we can't even have the money for the wages on Friday and they're going to make us sell up . . . he says we haven't enough security to cover all we owe them . . . and we're just slipping further into debt because we aren't making enough profit to pay the interest on the loan for those yearlings, and do you know how much he's charging us for that now? Seven per cent over base rate. Seven. That's about seventeen per cent right now. And he's adding the interest on, so now we're paying interest on the interest ... it's like a snowball ... it's monstrous ... it's bloody unfair.'

A shambles, I thought. Banks were never in the benefaction business.

'He admitted it was because of the newspaper articles,' Holly said wretchedly. 'He said it was unfortunate ... unfortunate! ... that Bobby's father wouldn't help us, not even a penny ... I've caused Bobby all this trouble ... it's because of me ...'

'Holly, stop it,' I said. 'That's nonsense. Sit tight and I'll come. I'm at Chiswick. It will take me an hour and a half.'

'The bank manager says we will have to tell the owners to take their horses away. He says we're not the only trainers who've ever had to sell up ... he says it happens, it's quite common ... he's so hard-hearted I could kill him.'

'Mm,' I said. 'Well, don't do anything yet. Have a drink. Cook me some spinach or something, I'm starving. I'll be on my way ... See you soon.'

I put down the receiver with a sigh. I didn't really want to drive on to Newmarket with stiffening bruises and an echoingly empty stomach, and I didn't really want to shoulder all the Allardeck troubles again, but a pact was a pact and that was the end of it. My twin, my bond, and all that.

'Trouble?' Danielle said, watching.

I nodded. I told her briefly about the attacks in the *Flag* and their dire financial consequences and she came swiftly to the same conclusion as myself.

'Bobby's father is crass.'

'Crass,' I said appreciatively, 'puts it in a nutshell.'

I stood up slowly from her chair and thanked her for the telephone.

'You're in no shape for all this,' she said objectively.

'Never believe it.' I leaned forward and kissed her fragrant cheek. 'Will you come racing again, with your aunt?'

She looked at me straightly. 'Probably,' she said.

'Good.'

Bobby and Holly were sitting in silence in the kitchen, staring into space, and turned their heads towards me apathetically when I went in.

I touched Bobby on the shoulder and kissed Holly and said, 'Come on, now, where's the wine? I'm dying of various ills and the first thing I need is a drink.'

My voice sounded loud in their gloom. Holly got heavily to her feet and went over to the cupboard where they kept glasses. She put her hand out towards it and then let it fall again. She turned towards me.

'I had my test results since you phoned,' she said

blankly. 'I definitely am pregnant. This should have been the happiest night of our lives.' She put her arms around my neck and began quietly to cry. I wrapped my arms round her and held her, and Bobby stayed sitting down, too defeated, it seemed, to be jealous.

'All right,' I said. 'We'll drink to the baby. Come on, loves, businesses come and go, and this one hasn't gone yet, but babies are for ever, God rot their dear little souls.'

I disentangled her arms and picked out the glasses while she silently wiped her eyes on the sleeve of her jersey.

Bobby said dully, 'You don't understand,' but I did, very well. There was no fight in him, the deflation was too great; and I'd had my own agonizing disappointments now and then. It could take a great effort of will not to sit around and mope.

I said to Holly, 'Put on some music, very loud.'

'No,' Bobby said.

'Yes, Bobby. Yes,' I said. 'Stand up and yell. Stick two fingers up at fate. Break something. Swear your guts out.'

'I'll break your neck,' he said with a flicker of savagery.

'All right, then, do it.'

He raised his head and stared at me and then rose abruptly to his feet, power crowding back into his muscles and vigour and exasperation into his face.

'All right then,' he shouted, 'I'll break your fucking Fielding neck.'

'That's better,' I said. 'And give me something to eat.'

Instead he went over to Holly and enfolded her and the two of them stood there half weeping, half laughing, entwined in privacy and back with the living. I resignedly dug in the freezer for something fast and unfattening and transferred it to the microwave oven, and I poured some red wine and drank it at a gulp.

Over the food Bobby admitted that he'd been too depressed to walk round at evening stables, so after coffee he and I both went out into the yard for a last inspection. The night was windy and cold and moonlit behind scurrying clouds. Everything looked normal and quiet, all the horses dozing behind closed doors, scarcely moving when we looked in on them, checking.

The boxes that had contained Jermyn Graves's horses were still empty, and the string which led to the bell had been detached from the door and hung limply from its last guiding staple. Bobby watched while I attached it to the door again.

'Do you think it's still necessary?' he asked dubiously.

'Yes, I do,' I said positively. 'The feed-merchant will have paid in Graves's cheque yesterday, but it won't have been cleared yet. I wouldn't trust Graves out of sight and I'd rig as many strings to the bell as we can manage.'

'He won't come back again,' Bobby said, shaking his head.

'Do you want to risk it?'

He stared at me for a while and then said, 'No.'

We ran three more strings, all as tripwires across pathways, and made sure the bell would fall if any one of them was tugged. It was perhaps not the most sophisticated of systems, but it had twice proved that it worked.

It worked for the third time at one in the morning.

CHAPTER EIGHT

My first feeling, despite what I'd said to Bobby, was of
incredulity. My second, that springing out of bed was
a bad idea, despite the long hot soaking I'd loosened
up with earlier; and I creaked and groaned and felt
sore.

As I took basic overnight things with me permanently in a bag in the car – razor, clean shirt, toothbrush
– I was sleeping (as usual in other people's houses) in
bright blue running shorts. I would have dressed, I
think, if I'd felt more supple. Instead I simply thrust
my feet into shoes and went out on to the landing, and
found Bobby there, bleary-eyed, indecisive, wearing the
top half of his pyjamas.

'Was that the bell?' he said.

'Yes. I'll take the drive again. You take the yard.'

He looked down at his half-nakedness and then at
mine.

'Wait.' He dived back into his and Holly's bedroom
and reappeared with a sweater for me and trousers for
himself, and, struggling into these garments en route,

we careered down the stairs and went out into the windy night. There was enough moonlight to see by, which was as well, as we hadn't brought torches.

At a shuffle more than a run I hurried down the drive, but the string across that route was still stretched tight. If Graves had come, he hadn't come that way.

I turned back and went to help Bobby in the yard, but he was standing there indecisively in the semi-darkness, looking around him, puzzled. 'I can't find Graves,' he said. 'Do you think the bell just blew off in the wind?'

'It's too heavy. Have you checked all the strings?'

'All except the one across the gate from the garden. But there's no one here. No one's come that way.'

'All the same . . .' I set off down the path to the gate to the garden, Bobby following: and we found the rustic wooden barrier wide open. We both knew it couldn't have blown open. It was held shut normally with a loop of chain, and the chain hung there on the gatepost, lifted off the gate by human hands.

We couldn't hear much for the wind. Bobby looked doubtfully back the way we had come and made as if to return to the yard.

I said, 'Suppose he's in the garden.'

'But what for? And how?'

'He could have come through the hedge from the road into the paddock, and over the paddock fence, and then down this path, and he'd have missed all the strings except this one.'

'But it's pointless. He can't get horses out through the garden. There are walls all round it. He wouldn't try.'

I was inclined to agree, but all the same, someone had opened the gate.

The walled garden of Bobby's house was all and only on one side, with the drive, stable yard and outhouses wrapping round the other three; and apart from the gate where we now stood, the only way into the garden was through French windows from the drawing room of the house.

Maybe Bobby was struck by the same unwelcome thought as myself. In any case he followed me instantly through the gate and off the paving-stone path inside on to the grass which would be quieter underfoot.

We went silently, fast, the short distance towards the French windows, but they appeared shut, the many square glass frames reflecting the pale light from the sky.

We were about to go over to try them to make sure they were still locked when a faint click and a rattle reached my ears above the breeze, followed by a sharp and definite 'Bugger'.

Bobby and I stood stock still. We could see no one, even with eyes fast approaching maximum night vision.

'Get down,' a voice said. 'I don't like it.'

'Shut up.'

Feeling highly visible in my long bare legs and electric blue shorts I moved across the grass in the direction of the shadows which held the voices, and as policemen will tell you, you should not do that; one should go indoors and telephone the force.

We found, Bobby and I, a man standing at the bottom of a ladder, looking upwards. He wore no mask, no hood, simply an ordinary suit – incongruous as a burglar kit.

He was not Jermyn Graves, and he was not the nephew, Jasper.

He was under forty, dark haired, and a stranger.

He didn't see us at all until we were near him, so firmly fixed upwards was his attention, and when I said loudly, 'What the hell do you think you're doing?' he jumped a foot.

Bobby made a flying rugby tackle at his knees and I took hold of the ladder and pushed it sideways. There was a yell from above and a good deal of clattering, and a second stranger tumbled down from the eaves and fell with a thud on to an uninhabited flower bed.

I pounced on that one and pushed his face down into the November mud and with one hand tried to search his pockets for a weapon, with him heaving and threshing about beneath me, and then when I found no weapon, for some sort of identification, for a diary or a letter, for anything. People who came to burgle dressed as for going to the office might not have taken all suitable precautions.

I couldn't get into his pockets – it was too dark and there was too much movement – but somehow I found myself grasping the collar of his jacket, and I pulled it backwards and downwards with both hands, temporarily fastening his arms to his sides. He plunged and kicked and managed to throw my weight off his back, but I held fiercely on to the jacket, which was entangling his arms and driving him frantic.

To get loose he slid right out of the jacket, leaving it in my hands, and before I could do anything he was up from his knees to his feet, and running.

Instead of chasing him I turned towards Bobby, who was rolling on the ground exchanging short jabbing blows and breathless grunts with the man who'd been holding the ladder. Throwing the jacket into the deep shadow against the house wall I went to Bobby's help, and between the two of us we managed to pin the intruder face down on to the grass, Bobby astride his legs and I with a foot on his neck. Bobby delivered several meaningful blows to the kidneys, designed to hurt.

'Something to tie him with,' he said.

I bent down, gripped the collar of that jacket also, and pulled it as before backwards over the burglar's shoulders, pinning his arms, and then yanking it right off, I took my foot off the neck and said to Bobby, 'That's enough.'

'What? Don't be stupid.'

The intruder rolled under him still full of fight. Bobby punched him wickedly on the ear and again in the small of his back.

I shoved a hand into an inside pocket of the jacket and drew out a wallet.

'See,' I said to Bobby, pushing it under his nose. He shook his head, ignoring it, not wanting to be deterred.

I put the wallet back into the jacket and threw that jacket too into the shadows, and for a second watched Bobby and the now shirt-sleeved intruder tearing at each other and punching again, half standing, half falling, the one trying to cling on and hit, the other to escape.

Bobby was tall and strong and angry at having his house attacked, and no doubt erupting also with the suppressed and helpless fury of the past traumatic days: in any case he was hitting his adversary with tangible hatred and very hard, and I thought with spurting sudden alarm that it was too much, he was beating the man viciously and murderously and not merely capturing a burglar.

I caught Bobby's raised wrist and pulled his bunched fist backwards, upsetting his balance, and his victim twisted out of his grasp and half fell on his knees, coughing, retching, clutching his stomach.

Bobby shouted 'You bugger' bitterly and hit me instead, and the intruder got unsteadily to his feet and staggered towards the gate.

Bobby tried to follow and when I grasped at him to stop him he jabbed his fist solidly into my ribs, calling me a bloody Fielding, a bloody sod, a fucking bastard.

'Bobby . . . Let him go.'

I got a frightful cuff on the head and another clout in the ribs along with some more obscene opinions of my character and ancestors, and he didn't calm down, he kicked my shin and shoved me off him, tearing himself away with another direct hit to my head which rattled my teeth.

I caught him again in a couple of strides and he swung at me, swearing and increasingly violent, and I said to him, 'For God's sake, Bobby . . .' and just tried to hang on to his lethal fists and parry them and survive until the fireball had spent itself.

The generations were all there in his intent face: Allardecks and Fieldings fighting with guns and swords and bare knuckles in malice and perpetuity. He had transferred the intruder-born fury on to the older enemy and all rational restraints had vanished. It was me, his blood's foe, that he was at that point trying to smash, I the focus of his anger and fear and despair.

Locked in this futile archaic struggle we traversed the lawn all the way to the gate; and it was there, when I was wedged against the heavy post and finally in serious trouble, that the killing rage went out of his hands from one second to the next, and he let them fall, the passion dying, the manic strength draining away.

He gave me a blank look, his eyes like glass reflecting the moonlight, and he said 'Bastard', but without much force, and he turned and walked away along the path to the yard.

I said 'God Almighty' aloud, and took a few deep

breaths of rueful and shaky relief, standing for a while to let my hammering heart settle before shoving off the gatepost to go and fetch the burglars' coats. Bobby's fists hadn't had the same weight as the hurdlers' hooves, but I could well have done without them. Heigh ho, I thought, in about twelve hours I would ride three tricky jumpers at Newbury.

The coats lay where I had thrown them, in the angle of the empty flower bed and the brick wall of the house. I picked them up and stood there looking at the silvery ladder which had reached high up the wall, and then at the wall itself, which stretched in that section right to the roof, smooth and unbroken.

No windows.

Why would burglars try to break into a house at a point where there were no windows?

I frowned, tipping my head back, looking upwards. Beyond the line of the roof, above it, rising like a silhouette against the night sky, there was a sturdy brick chimney, surmounted by a pair of antique pots. It was, I worked out, the chimney from the fireplace in the drawing room. The fireplace was right through the wall from where I stood.

Irresolutely I looked from the ladder to the chimney pots and shivered in the wind. Then, shrugging, I put the jackets back into the shadow, propped the ladder up against the eaves, rooted its feet firmly in the flower bed, and climbed.

The ladder was aluminium, made in telescopic sections. I hoped none of them would collapse.

I didn't much like heights. Halfway up I regretted the whole enterprise. What on earth was I doing climbing an unsteady ladder in the dark? I could fall and hurt myself and not be able to race. It was madness, the whole thing. Crazy.

I reached the roof. The top of the ladder extended beyond that, four or five more rungs going right up to the chimney. On the tiles of the roof lay an opened tool kit, a sort of cloth roll with spanners, screwdrivers, pliers and so on, all held in stitched pockets. Beside it lay a coil of what looked like dark cord, with one end leading upwards to a bracket on the chimney.

I looked more closely at the chimney and almost laughed. One takes so many things for granted, sees certain objects day by day and never consciously sees them at all. Fixed to the chimney was the bracket and mounted on the bracket were the two terminals of the telephone wires leading to Bobby's house. I had seen them a hundred times and never noticed they were fixed to the chimney.

The wire itself stretched away into darkness, going across the telephone pole out on the road; the old above-ground wiring system of all but modern housing.

Attached to the telephone bracket, at the end of the dark cord leading from the coil, there appeared to be a small square object about the size of a sugar cube, with a thin rod about the length of a finger extending downwards. I stretched out a hand precariously to touch it and found it wobbled as if only half attached.

The moon seemed to be going down just when I needed it most. I fumbled around the small cube and came to what felt like a half-undone screw. I couldn't see it, but it turned easily anti-clockwise and in a few moments slipped out into my hand.

The cube and the rod fell straight off the bracket, and I would have lost them in the night if it hadn't been for the coil of stiff cord attached to them. Some of the cord unwound before I caught it, but not a great deal, and I put the coil, the cube and the rod on to the row of tools and rolled up the canvas kit and fastened it with its buckle.

The flower bed, I thought, wouldn't hurt the tool kit, so I dropped the rolled bundle straight below, and went down the ladder as slowly as I'd gone up, careful to balance and not to fall. There was no doubt I felt more at home on horses.

Retrieving the jackets and the tool kit but leaving the ladder, I went out of the garden and walked along the path and round to the kitchen door. Holly in a dressing gown and with wide frightened eyes was standing there, shivering with cold and anxiety.

'Thank goodness,' she said when I appeared. 'Where's Bobby?'

'I don't know. Come on in. Let's make a hot drink.'

We went into the kitchen where it was always

warmest and I put the kettle on while Holly looked out of the window for her missing husband.

'He'll come soon,' I said. 'He's all right.'

'I saw two men running . . .'

'Where did they go?'

'Over the fence into the paddock. One first, then the other a bit later. The second one was . . . well . . . groaning.'

'Mm,' I said. 'Bobby hit him.'

'Did he?' She sounded proud. 'Who were they? They weren't Jermyn. Did they come for his horses?'

'Which do you want,' I asked, 'coffee, tea or chocolate?'

'Chocolate.'

I made chocolate for her and tea for myself and brought the steaming cups to the table.

'Come and sit down,' I said. 'He'll be back.'

She came reluctantly and then watched with awakening curiosity while I unbuckled and unrolled the tool kit.

'See that?' I said. 'That tiny little box with its rod and its coil of cord? I'll bet anything that that's what's been listening to your telephone.'

'But it's minute.'

'Yes. I wish I knew more. Tomorrow we'll find out just how it works.' I looked at my watch. 'Today, I suppose one should say.' I told her where I'd found the bug, and about Bobby and me disturbing the intruders.

She frowned. 'These two men . . . Were they fixing this to our telephone?'

'Taking it away, perhaps. Or changing its battery.'

She reflected. 'I did say to you this evening on the telephone that the telephone people were coming tomorrow to look for bugs.'

'So you did.'

'So perhaps if they heard that, they thought . . . those two men . . . that if they took their bug away first, there wouldn't be anything to find, and we'd never know for sure.'

'Yes,' I said. 'I think you're right.' I picked up the first of the jackets and went through the pockets methodically, laying the contents on the table.

Holly, watching in amazement, said, 'They surely didn't leave their coats?'

'They didn't have much choice.'

'But all those things . . .'

'Dead careless,' I said. 'Amateurs.'

The first jacket produced a notepad, three pens, a diary, a handkerchief, two toothpicks and the wallet I had shown to Bobby in the garden. The wallet contained a moderate amount of money, five credit cards, a photograph of a young woman, and a reminder to go to the dentist. The name on the credit cards was Owen Watts. The diary not only gave the same name but also an address (home) and telephone number (office). The pages were filled with appointments and memos, and spoke of a busy and orderly life.

'Why are you purring like a cat with cream?' Holly said.

'Take a look.'

I pushed Owen Watts's belongings over to her and emptied the pockets of the second jacket. These revealed another notepad, more pens, a comb, cigarettes, throwaway lighter, two letters and a chequebook. There was also, tucked into the outside breast pocket, a small plastic folder containing a gold-coloured card announcing that Mr Jay Erskine was member number 609 of The Press Club, London EC4A 3JB; and Mr Jay Erskine's signature and address were on the back.

Just as well to make absolutely certain, I thought.

I telephoned to Owen Watts's office number, and a man's voice answered immediately.

'*Daily Flag*,' he said.

Satisfied, I put the receiver down without speaking.

'No answer?' Holly said. 'Not surprising, at this hour.'

'The *Daily Flag* neither slumbers nor sleeps. The switchboard, anyway, was awake.'

'So those two really are . . . those pigs.'

'Well,' I said. 'They work for the *Flag*. One can't say if they actually wrote those pieces. Not tonight. We'll find out in the morning.'

'I'd like to smash their faces.'

I shook my head. 'You want to smash the face of whoever sent them.'

'Him too.' She stood up restlessly. 'Where is Bobby? What's he doing?'

'Probably making sure that everything's secure.'

'You don't think those men came back?' she said, alarmed.

'No, I don't. Bobby will come in when he's ready.'

She was worried, however, and went to the outside door and called him, but the wind snatched her voice away so that one could scarcely have heard her from across the yard.

'Go and look for him, will you?' she said anxiously. 'He's been out there so long.'

'All right.' I collected the bugging device, the tools and the pressmen's things together on the table. 'Could you find a box for these, and put them somewhere safe.'

She nodded and began to look vaguely about, and I went out into the yard on the unwelcome errand. Wherever Bobby was, I was probably the last person he wanted to have come after him. I thought that I would simply set about rigging the alarm bell again, and if he wanted to be found, he would appear.

I rigged the bell and got back some night vision, and came across him down by the gate into the garden. He had brought the ladder out so that it lay along the path, and he was simply standing by the gatepost, doing nothing.

'Holly's wondering where you've got to,' I said easily.

He didn't answer.

'Do you think you can hear the bell from here?' I

said. 'Would you climb up someone's house if you'd heard an alarm bell?'

Bobby said nothing. He watched in flat calm while I found the string and shut the gate, fastening everything as before so that the bell would fall on the far side of the house if the gate was opened.

Bobby watched but did nothing. Shrugging, I opened the gate.

One could hear the bell if one was listening for it. On a still night it would have been alarming, but in the breeze the intruders had ignored it.

'Let's go in,' I said. 'Holly's anxious.'

I turned away to walk up the path.

'Kit,' he said stiffly.

I turned back.

'Did you tell her?' he asked.

'No.'

'I'm sorry,' he said.

'Come on in. It doesn't matter.'

'Yes, it does matter.' He paused. 'I couldn't help it. That makes it worse.'

'Tell you what,' I said, 'let's go in out of this bloody cold wind. My legs are freezing. If you want to talk, we'll talk tomorrow. But it's OK. Come on in, you old bugger, it's OK.'

I put the journalists' belongings under my bed for safety before I went achingly back to sleep, but their owners seemed to make no attempt to break in to get them back. I derived a great deal of yawning pleasure from picturing their joint states of mind and body, and thought that anything that had happened to them served them very well right.

Owen Watts and Jay Erskine. Jay Erskine, Owen Watts.

They were going to be, I decided hazily, trying to find an unbruised area to lie on, the lever with which to shift the world. Careless, sneaky, callous Owen Watts, battered half unconscious by Bobby, and stupid, snooping, flint-hearted Jay Erskine, fallen off his ladder with his face pressed into the mud. Served them bloody well right.

I dreamed of being run over by a tractor and felt like it a bit when I woke up. The morning after falls like the day before's were always a bore.

It was nearly nine when I made it to the kitchen, but although the lights were on against the grey morning, there was no one else there. I heated myself some coffee and began to read Bobby's daily paper, which was the *Towncrier*, not the *Flag*.

On page seven, which was wholly devoted to the Wednesday comments and opinions of a leading and immensely influential lady columnist, the central headline read:

WHAT PRICE FATHERLY LOVE?

And underneath, in a long spread unmissable by any *Towncrier* reader, came an outline of Maynard Allardeck's upwardly thrusting career.

He had journeyed from commodity broker, she said, to multi-storey magnate, sucking in other people's enterprises and spitting out the husks.

His *modus operandi*, she explained, was to advance smilingly towards an over-extended business with offers of loans of life-saving cash. Easy terms, pay when you can, glad to help. His new partners, the journalist said, welcomed him with open arms and spoke enthusiastically of their benefactor. But oh, the disillusionment! Once the business was running smoothly, Maynard would very pleasantly ask for his money back. Consternation! Disaster! Impossible to pay him without selling up and closing. The workforce redundant. Personal tragedies abounding. Can't have that, Maynard agreed genially. He would take the business instead of the money, how was that? Everyone still had their job. Except, hard luck, the proprietor and the managing director. Maynard presently would sell his now financially stable newly acquired business at a comfortable profit to any big fish looking out for manageable minnows: and so back, one might say, to the start, with Maynard appreciably richer.

How do I know all this? the lady journalist asked; and answered herself; less than three weeks ago on the TV programme *How's Trade*, Maynard himself told us. Classic takeover procedure, he smugly called it.

Anyone could do the same. Anyone could make a fortune the same way that he had.

It now seemed, she wrote, that one particular over-extended business in dire need of easy-terms cash was the racehorse training enterprise of Maynard's own and only son, Robertson (32).

Maynard was on record in this one instance as obstinately refusing to offer help.

My advice to someone in Robertson's (known as Bobby) position, said the lady firmly, would be to not touch Daddy's money with a bargepole. To count his rocky blessings. Daddy's fond embrace could find him presently sweeping the streets. Don't forget, she said, this parent is still grasping for car money he lent his son as a kid.

Is Maynard, she asked finally, worth a knighthood for services to industry? And she answered herself again: in her own opinion, definitely not.

There was a photograph of Maynard, polished and handsome, showing a lot of teeth. The word 'shark' sprang to mind. Maynard, I thought, would be apoplectic.

Bobby's first lot of horses clattered back into the yard from their morning exercise on the Heath, and Bobby himself came into the kitchen looking intensely depressed. He fixed himself a cup of coffee and wouldn't look at me, and drank standing by the window, staring out.

'How's Holly?' I asked.

'Sick.'

'Your father's in the paper,' I said.

'I don't want to read it.' He put down his cup. 'I expect you'll be going.'

'Yes. I'm riding at Newbury.'

'I meant . . . because of last night.'

'No, not because of that.'

He came over to the table and sat down, looking not at me but at his hands. There were grazes on the knuckles of both fists, red-raw patches where he'd smashed off his own skin.

'Why didn't you fight?' he said.

'I didn't want to.'

'You could have hurt me to hell and gone. I know that now. Why didn't you? I could have killed you.'

'Over my dead body,' I said dryly.

He shook his head. I looked at his face, at the down-cast blue eyes, seeing the trouble, the self-doubt, the confusion.

'What I fight,' I said, 'is being brainwashed. Why should we still jump to that old hate? It was a Fielding you were trying to kill. Any Fielding. Not me, Kit, your brother-in-law who actually likes you, though I can't quite see why after last night. I'll fight my indoctrination, I'll fight my bloody ancestors, but I won't fight you, my sister's husband, with whom I have no quarrel.'

He sat for a while without speaking, still looking at his hands, then in a low voice he said, 'You're stronger than me.'

'No. If it makes you feel better, I don't know what I'd have done if I'd been through all you have in the past week and there had been an Allardeck handy to let it all out on.'

He raised his head, the very faintest of glimmers reappearing. 'Truce, then?' he said.

'Yeah,' I agreed; and wondered if our subconscious minds would observe it.

CHAPTER NINE

The vans swept into the yard as if conducting a race; one red, one yellow. Out of each emerged more slowly a man in dark clothes carrying, from the red van, the day's letters, and from the yellow, a clipboard. The Royal Mail and British Telecom side by side.

Bobby went to the door, accepted the letters, and brought the phone company man back with him into the kitchen.

'Bug-hunting,' the latter said heartily, as the red van roared away again outside. 'Got termites in the telephone, have you? Been hearing clicking noises on the line? No end of people hear them. False alarms, you know.'

He was large, moustached, and too full of unnecessary bonhomie. Bobby, making a great effort, offered tea or coffee, and I went upstairs to fetch the non-imaginary equipment from the chimney.

I could hear the phone man's voice long before I could see him on my way back.

'You get your M15, of course, but your average left-wing militant, they call us in regular. In Cambridge, now, false alarms all the time.'

'This is not,' Bobby said through gritted teeth, 'a false alarm.'

'We found this,' I said calmingly, putting the tool kit on the table, unrolling it, and producing for inspection the small metal cube with its rod and its coil of attached stiff cord.

'Ah now,' the telephone man's interest came to life, 'now you know what this is, don't you?'

'A bug,' I said.

'Now that,' he said, 'is your transformer stroke transmitter and your earth. Where's the rest?'

'What rest?'

He looked at us with pity. 'You got to have the tap itself. Where did you get this little lot?'

'From the chimney stack, where the phone wires reach the house.'

'Did you now.' He blew down his nose. 'Then that's where we'd better look.'

We took him outside the house rather than through the drawing room, walking down the path from the yard and through the gate. The telescopic aluminium ladder still lay on the path, but the phone man, eyeing the height of the chimney, decided against its fragile support and went back to his van for much sturdier rungs. He returned also with a busy tool-belt buckled round his rotund middle.

Planting and extending his workmanlike ladder he

lumbered up it as casually as walking. To each his own expertise.

At the top, with his stomach supported, he reached out to where the telephone wire divided to the two terminals, and with tools from his belt spent some time clamping, clipping and refastening before returning unruffled to earth.

'A neat little job,' he said appreciatively. 'Superior bit of wire-tapping. Looks like it's been in place for a couple of weeks. Grimy, but not too bad, see? Been up there just a while in the soot and rain.'

He held out a large palm on which rested a small cylinder with two short wires leading from it.

'See, this picks up the currents from your phone wire and leads them into that transformer you took down last night. See, voice frequencies run at anywhere between fifty Hertz and three kiloHertz, but you can't transmit that by radio, you have to transform it up to about three thousand megaHertz. You need an amplifier which modulates the frequency to something a microwave transmitter can transmit.' He looked at our faces. 'Not exactly electronics experts, are you?'

'No,' we said.

With complacent superiority he led the way back to the yard, carrying his heavy ladder with ease. In the kitchen he put the newly gathered cylinder alongside the previous night's spoils and continued with the lecture.

'These two wires from the cylinder plug into the transformer and this short little rod is the aerial.'

'What's all that cord?' I asked.

'Cord?' He smiled largely. 'That's not cord, it's wire. See? Fine wire inside insulation. That's an earth wire, to complete the circuit.'

We looked no doubt blank.

'If you'd have closely inspected your brickwork below your chimney these last weeks you'd have seen this so-called cord lying against it. Running through clips, even. Going down from the transmitter into the earth.'

'Yes,' Bobby said. 'We're never out there much this time of the year.'

'Neat little job,' the telephone man said again.

'Is it difficult to get?' I asked. 'This sort of equipment.'

'Dead easy,' he said pityingly. 'You can send for it from your electronic mail order catalogue any day.'

'And what then?' I asked. 'We've got the tap and the transmitter. Where would we find the receiver?'

The phone man said judiciously, 'This is a low-powered transmitter. Has to be, see, being so small. Runs on a battery, see? So you'd need a big dish-receiver to pick up the signals. Line of sight. Say a quarter-mile away? And no buildings to distort things. Then I'd reckon you'd get good results.'

'A big dish-receiver a quarter of a mile away?' I repeated. 'Everyone would see it.'

'Not inside a van, they wouldn't.' He touched the cube transmitter reflectively. 'Nice high chimney you've got there. Most often we find these babies on the poles out on the road. But the higher you put the transmitter, of course, the further you get good reception.'

'Yes,' I said, understanding that at least.

'This is an unofficial bit of snooping,' he said, happy to instruct. 'Private. You won't get no clicks from this, neither. You'd never know it was there.' He hitched up his tool-belt. 'Right then, you just sign my sheet and I'll be off. And you want to take your binoculars out there now and then and keep a watch on your chimney and your pole in the road, and if you see any more little strangers growing on your wires, you give me a ring and I'll be right back.'

Bobby signed his sheet and thanked him and saw him out to his van; and I looked at the silent bug and wondered vaguely whose telephone I could tap with it, if I learned how.

Holly came in as the yellow van departed, Holly looking pale in jeans and sloppy sweater, with hair still damp from the shower.

'Morning sickness is the pits,' she said. 'Did you make any tea?'

'Coffee in the pot.'

'Couldn't face it.' She put the kettle on. 'What happened out there last night between you and Bobby? He said you would never forgive him, but he wouldn't say what for. I don't think he slept at all. He was up walking round the house at five. So what happened?'

'There's no trouble between us,' I said. 'I promise you.'

She swallowed. 'It would just be the end if you and Bobby quarrelled.'

'We didn't.'

She was still doubtful but said no more. She put some bread in the toaster as Bobby came back, and the three of us sat round the table passing the marmalade and thinking our own thoughts, which in my case was a jumble of journalists, Bobby's bank manager, and how was I going to warm and loosen my muscles before the first race.

Bobby with apprehension began opening the day's letters, but his fears were unfounded. There was no blast from the bank and no demands for payment with menaces. Three of the envelopes contained cheques.

'I don't believe it,' he said, sounding stunned. 'The owners are paying.'

'That's fast,' I said. 'They can only have got those letters yesterday. Their consciences must be pricking overtime.'

'Seb's paid,' Bobby said. He mentally added the three totals and then pushed the cheques across to me. 'They're yours.'

I hesitated.

'Go on,' he said. 'You paid our bills on Monday. If

those cheques had come on Monday you wouldn't have had to.'

Holly nodded.

'What about the lads' wages this Friday?' I asked.

Bobby shrugged frustratedly. 'God knows.'

'What did your bank manager actually say?' I said.

'Sadistic bully,' Bobby said. 'He sat there with a smirk on his prim little face telling me I should go into voluntary liquidation immediately. Voluntary! He said if I didn't, the bank would have no choice but to start bankruptcy proceedings. No choice! Of course they have a choice. Why did they ever lend the money for the yearlings if they were going to behave like this five minutes later?'

The probable answer to that was because Bobby was Maynard's son. Maynard's millions might have seemed security enough, before the *Flag* fired its broadside.

'Isn't there any trainer in Newmarket who would buy the yearlings from you?' I said.

'Not a chance. Most of them are in the same boat. They can't sell their own.'

I pondered. 'Did the bank manager say anything about bailiffs?'

'No,' Bobby said, and Holly, if possible, went paler.

We might have a week, I thought. I didn't know much about liquidation or bankruptcy: I didn't know the speed of events. Perhaps we had no time at all. No one, however, could expect Bobby to be able to sell all his property overnight.

'I'll take the cheques,' I said, 'and I'll get them cashed. We'll pay your lads this week out of the proceeds and keep the rest for contingencies. And don't tell the bank manager, because he no doubt thinks this money belongs to the bank.'

'They lent it to us quick enough,' Holly said bitterly. 'No one twisted their arm.'

It wasn't only Maynard, I thought, who could lend with a smile and foreclose with a vengeance.

'It's hopeless,' Bobby said. 'I'll have to tell the owners to take their horses. Sack the lads.' He stopped abruptly. Holly, too, had tears in her eyes. 'It's such a mess,' Bobby said.

'Yeah . . . well . . . hold tight for a day or two,' I said.

'What's the point?'

'We might try a little fund-raising.'

'What do you mean?'

I knew only vaguely what I meant and I didn't think I would discuss it with Bobby. I said instead, 'Don't break up the stable before the dragon's breathing fire right in the yard.'

'St George might come along,' Holly said.

'What?' Bobby looked uncomprehending.

'In the story,' Holly said. 'You know. Kit and I had a pop-up book where St George came along and slew the dragon. We used to read it with a torch under the bedclothes and scare ourselves with shadows.'

'Oh.' He looked from one of us to the other, seeing

dark-haired twins with a shared and private history. He may have felt another twinge of exclusion because he smothered some reaction with a firming of the mouth, but after a while, with only a hint of sarcasm and as if stifling any hope I might have raised, he came up with an adequate reply. 'OK, St George. Get on your horse.'

I drove to Newbury and solved the stiff muscle problem by borrowing the sauna of a local flat race jockey who spent every summer sweating away his body in there and had thankfully come out for the winter. I didn't like water-shedding in saunas as a daily form of weight-control (still less diuretics), but after twenty minutes of its hot embrace on that cold morning I did feel a good deal fitter.

My first two mounts were for the Lambourn stable I normally rode for, and, given a jockey with smoothly working limbs, they both cleared the obstacles efficiently without covering themselves with either mud or glory. One could say to the hopeful owners afterwards that yes, their horses would win one day; and so they might, when the weights were favourable and the ground was right and a few of the better opponents fell. I'd ridden duds I wouldn't have taken out of the stable and had them come in first.

My final mount of the day belonged to the princess, who was waiting, alone as usual, for me to join her in the parade ring. I was aware of being faintly disappointed that Danielle wasn't with her, even though I hadn't expected it: most illogical. The princess, sable coat swinging, wore a pale yellow silk scarf at her neck with gold and citrine earrings, and although I'd seen her in them often before I thought she was looking exceptionally well and glowing. I made the small bow; shook her hand. She smiled.

'How do you think we'll do today?' she said.

'I think we'll win.'

Her eyes widened. 'You're not usually so positive.'

'Your horses are all in form. And . . .' I stopped.

'And what?'

'And . . . er . . . you were thinking, yourself, that we would win.'

She said without surprise, 'Yes, I was.' She turned to watch her horse walk by. 'What else was I thinking?'

'That . . . well . . . that you were happy.'

'Yes.' She paused. 'Do you think the Irish mare will beat us? Several people have tipped it.'

'She's got a lot of weight.'

'Lord Vaughnley thinks she'll win.'

'Lord Vaughnley?' I repeated, my interest quickening. 'Is he here?'

'Yes,' she said. 'He was lunching in a box near mine. I came down the stairs with him just now.'

I asked her if she remembered which box, but she didn't. I said I would like to talk to him, if I could find him.

'He'll be glad to,' she said, nodding. 'He's still

165

delighted about the Towncrier Trophy. He says literally hundreds of people have congratulated him on this year's race.'

'Good,' I said. 'If I ask him a favour, I might get it.'

'You could ask the world.'

'Not that much.'

The signal came for jockeys to mount, and I got up on her horse to see what we could do about the Irish mare: and what we did was to start out at a fast pace and maintain it steadily throughout, making the mare feel every extra pound she was carrying every stride of the way, and finally to beat off her determined challenge most satisfactorily by a length and a half.

'Splendid,' the princess exclaimed in the winners' enclosure, sparkling. 'Beautiful.' She patted her excited 'chaser. 'Come up to the box, Kit, when you've changed.' She saw my very faint and stifled hesitation and interpreted it. 'I saw Lord Vaughnley up there again. I asked him to my box also.'

'You're amazingly kind.'

'I'm amazingly pleased with winning races like this.'

I changed into street clothes and went up to her familiar box high above the winning post. For once she was there alone, not surrounded by guests, and she mentioned that she was on her way back from Devon, her chauffeur having driven her up that morning.

'My niece telephoned yesterday evening from her bureau to say she had arrived promptly,' the princess said. 'She was most grateful.'

I said I'd been very pleased to help. The princess offered tea, pouring it herself, and we sat on adjacent chairs, as so often, as I described the past race to her almost fence by fence.

'I could see,' she said contentedly. 'You were pushing along just ahead of the mare all the way. When she quickened, you quickened, when she took a breather down the bottom end, so did you. And then I could see you just shake up my horse when her jockey took up his whip . . . I knew we'd win. I was sure of it all the way round. It was lovely.'

Such sublime confidence could come crashing down on its nose at the last fence, but she knew that as well as I did. There had been times when it had. It made the good times better.

She said, 'Wykeham says we're giving Kinley his first try over hurdles at Towcester tomorrow. His first ever race.'

'Yes,' I nodded. 'And Dhaulagiri's taking his first start at a novice 'chase. I rode both of them schooling at Wykeham's last week, did he tell you? They both jumped super. Er . . . will you be there?'

'I wouldn't miss it.' She paused. 'My niece says she will come with me.'

I lifted my head. 'Will she?'

'She said so.'

The princess regarded me calmly and I looked straight back, but although it would have been useful I couldn't read what she was thinking.

'I enjoyed driving her,' I said.

'She said the journey went quickly.'

'Yes.'

The princess patted my arm non-committally, and Lord and Lady Vaughnley appeared in the doorway, looking in with enquiring faces and coming forward with greetings. The princess welcomed them, gave them glasses of port, which it seemed they liked particularly on cold days, and drew Lady Vaughnley away with her to admire something out on the viewing balcony, leaving Lord Vaughnley alone inside with me.

He said how truly delighted he'd been with everyone's response to last Saturday's race, and I asked if he could possibly do me a favour.

'My dear man. Fire away. Anything I can.'

I explained again about Bobby and the attacks in the *Flag*, which by now he himself knew all about.

'Good Lord, yes. Did you see the comment page in our own paper this morning? That woman of ours, Rose Quince, she has a tongue like a rattlesnake, but when she writes, she makes sense. What's the favour?'

'I wondered,' I said, 'if the *Towncrier* would have a file of clippings about Maynard Allardeck. And if you have one, would you let me see it.'

'Good Lord,' he said. 'You'll have a reason, no doubt?'

I said we had concluded that Bobby had been a casualty in a campaign mainly aimed at his father. 'And it would be handy to know who might have enough of a grudge against Maynard to kill off his chance of a knighthood.'

Lord Vaughnley smiled benignly. 'Such as anyone whose business was pulled from beneath them?'

'Such as,' I agreed. 'Yes.'

'You're suggesting that the *Flag* could be pressured into mounting a hate campaign?' He pursed his mouth, considering.

'I wouldn't have thought it would take much pressure,' I said. 'The whole paper's a hate campaign.'

'Dear, dear,' he said with mock reproof. 'Very well. I can't see how it will directly help your brother-in-law, but yes, I'll see you get access to our files.'

'That's great,' I said fervently. 'Thank you very much.'

'When would suit you?'

'As soon as possible.'

He looked at his watch. 'Six o'clock?'

I shut my mouth on a gasp. He said, 'I have to be at a dinner in the City this evening. I'll be dropping into the *Towncrier* first. Ask for me at the front desk.'

I duly asked at his front desk in Fleet Street and was directed upwards to the editorial section on the third floor, arriving, it seemed, at a point of maximum bustle as the earliest editions of the following day's papers were about to go to press.

Lord Vaughnley, incongruous in tweed jacket, dress

trousers, stiff shirt and white tie, stood at the shoulder of a coatless man seated at a central table, both of them intent on the newspaper before them. Around them, in many bays half separated from each other by shoulder-high partitions, were clumps of three or four desks, each bay inhabited by telephones, typewriters, potted plants and people in a faint but continuous state of agitation.

'What do you want?' someone said to me brusquely as I hovered, and when I said Lord Vaughnley, he merely pointed. Accordingly I walked over to the centre of the activity and said neutrally to Lord Vaughnley, 'Excuse me . . .'

He raised his eyes but not his head. 'Ah yes, my dear chap, be with you directly,' he said, and lowered the eyes again, intently scanning what I saw to be tomorrow's front page, freshly printed.

I waited with interest while he finished, looking around at a functional scene which I guessed hadn't changed much since the days of that rumbustious giant, the first Lord Vaughnley. Desks and equipment had no doubt come and gone, but from the brown floor to the yellowing cream walls the overall impression was of a working permanence, slightly old-fashioned.

The present Lord Vaughnley finished reading, stretched himself upwards and patted the shirt-sleeved shoulder of the seated man, who was, I discovered later, that big white chief, the editor.

'Strong stuff, Marty. Well done.'

The seated man nodded and went on reading. Lord Vaughnley said to me, 'Rose Quince is here. You might like to meet her.'

'Yes,' I said, 'I would.'

'Over here.' He set off towards one of the bays, the lair, it proved, of the lady of the rattlesnake tongue who could nevertheless write sense, and who had written that day's judgement on Maynard.

'Rose,' said the paper's proprietor, 'take care of Kit Fielding, won't you?' and the redoubtable Rose Quince assured him that yes, she would.

'Files,' Lord Vaughnley said. 'Whatever he wants to see, show him.'

'Right.'

To me he said, 'We have a box at Ascot. The *Town-crier* has, I mean. I understand from the princess that you'll be riding there this Friday and Saturday. No point, I suppose, my dear chap, in asking you to lunch with me on Saturday, which is the day I'll be there, but do come up for a drink when you've finished. You'll always be welcome.'

I said I'd be glad to.

'Good. Good. My wife will be delighted. You'll be in good hands with Rose, now. She was born in Fleet Street the same as I was, her father was Conn Quince who edited the old *Chronicle*; she knows more of what goes on than the Street itself. She'll give you the gen, won't you, Rose?'

Rose, who looked to me to be bristling with

reservations, agreed again that yes, she would; and Lord Vaughnley, with the nod of a man who knows he's done well, went away and left me to her serpent mercies.

She did not, it is true, have Medusa snakes growing out of her head, but whoever had named her Rose couldn't have foreseen its incongruity.

A rose she was not. A tiger-lily, more like. She was tall and very thin and fifteen to twenty years older than myself. Her artfully tousled and abundant hair was dark but streaked throughout with blonde, the aim having clearly been two contrasting colours, not overall tor-toiseshell. The expertly painted sallow face could never have been pretty but was strongly good-looking, the nose masculine, the eyes noticeably pale blue; and from several feet away one could smell her sweet and heavy scent.

A quantity of bracelets, rings and necklaces decor-ated the ultimate in fashionable outlines, comple-mented by a heavy bossed and buckled belt round the hips, and I wondered if the general overstatement was a sort of stockade to frighten off the encroachment of the next generation of writers, a battlement against time.

If it was, I knew how she felt. Every jump jockey over thirty felt threatened by the rising nineteen-year-olds who would supplant them sooner or later. Every jockey, every champion had to prove race by race that he was as good as he'd ever been, and it was tough at the top only because of those hungry to take over one's saddle. I didn't need bangles, but I pulled out grey hairs when they appeared.

Rose Quince looked me up and down critically and said, 'Big for a jockey, aren't you?' which was hardly original, as most people I met said the same.

'Big enough.'

Her voice had an edge to it more than an accent, and was as positive as her appearance.

'And your sister is married to Maynard Allardeck's son.'

'Yes, that's right.'

'The source of Daddy's disapproval.'

'Yes.'

'What's wrong with her? Was she a whore?'

'No, a Capulet.'

Rose took barely three seconds to comprehend, then she shook her head in self-disgust.

'I missed an angle,' she said.

'Just as well.'

She narrowed her eyes and looked at me with her head tilted.

'I watched the Towncrier Trophy on television last Saturday,' she said. 'It would more or less have been treason not to.' She let her gaze wander around my shoulders. 'Left it a bit late, didn't you?'

'Probably.'

She looked back to my face. 'No excuses?'

'We won.'

'Yes, dammit, after you'd given everyone cardiac

173

arrest. Did you realize that half the people in this building had their pay packets on you?'

'No, I didn't.'

'The Sports Desk told us you couldn't lose.'

'Bunty Ireland?'

'Precisely, Bunty Ireland. He thinks the sun shines out of your arse.' She shook an armful of baubles to express dismissal of Bunty's opinions. 'No jockey is that smart.'

'Mm,' I said. 'Could we talk about Maynard?'

Her dark eyebrows rose. 'On first name terms, are you?'

'Maynard Allardeck.'

'A prize shit.'

'Olympic gold.'

She smiled, showing well-disciplined teeth. 'You read nothing in the paper, buddy boy. Do you want to see the tape?'

'What tape?'

'The tape of *How's Trade*. It's still here, downstairs. If you want to see it, now's the time.'

'Yes,' I said.

'Right. Come along. I've got the unexpurgated version, the one they cut from to make the programme. Ready for the rough stuff? It's dynamite.'

CHAPTER TEN

She had acquired, it appeared, both the ten-minute edition which had been broadcast as well as the half-hour original.

'Did you see the programme on the box?' Rose said.

I shook my head.

'You'd better see that first, then.'

She had taken me to a small room which contained a semi-circle of comfortable chairs grouped in front of a television set. To each side of the set various makes of video machine sat on tables, with connecting cables snaking about in apparent disorder.

'We get brought or sent unsolicited tapes of things that have happened,' Rose explained casually. 'All sorts of tapes. Loch Ness monsters by the pailful. Mostly rubbish, but you never know. We've had a scoop or sixteen this way. The big white chief swears by it. Then we record things ourselves. Some of our reporters like to interview with video cameras, as I do sometimes. You get the flavour back fresh if you don't write the piece for a week or so.'

While she talked she connected a couple of wandering cable ends to the back of the television set and switched everything on. Her every movement was accompanied by metallic clinks and jingles, and her lily scent filled the room. She picked up a tape cassette which had been lying on the table behind one of the video machines and fed it into the slot.

'Right. Here we go.'

We sat in two of the chairs, she sprawling sideways so she could see my face, and the screen sprang immediately to life with an interesting arrangement of snow. Total silence ensued for ten seconds before the Maynard segment of *How's Trade* arrived in full sharp colour with sound attached. Then we had the benefit of Maynard looking bland and polished through a voice-over introduction, with time to admire the hand-sewn lapels and silk tie.

The interviewer asked several harmless questions, Maynard's slightly condescending answers being lavishly interrupted by views of the interviewer nodding and smiling. The interviewer himself, unknown as far as I was concerned, was perhaps in his mid-thirties, with forgettable features except for calculating eyes of a chilling detachment. A prosecutor, I thought; and disliked him.

In reply to a question about how he got rich Maynard said that 'once or twice' he had come to the rescue of an ailing but basically sound business, had set it back on its feet with injections of liquidity and had subsequently acquired it to save it from closure when it had been unable to repay him. To the benefit, he suavely insisted, of all concerned.

'Except the former owners?' the interviewer asked; but the question was put as merely fact-finding, without bite.

Maynard's voice said that generous compensation was of course paid to the owners.

'And then what?' asked the interviewer, in the same way.

Naturally, Maynard said, if a good offer came along, he would in his turn sell: he could then lend the money to rescue another needy firm. The buying, selling and merging of businesses was advisable when jobs could be saved and a sensible profit made. He had done his modest best for industry and had ensured employment for many. It had been most rewarding in human terms.

Neither Maynard nor the interviewer raised his voice above a civilized monotone, and as an entertainment it was a drag. The segment ended with the interviewer thanking Maynard for a most interesting discussion, and there was a final shot of Maynard looking noble.

The screen, as if bored silly, reverted to black and white snow.

'Allardeck the philanthropist,' Rose said, jangling the bracelets and recrossing her long legs. 'Have you met him?'

'Yes.'

'Well, now for Allardeck the rapacious bully.'

'I've met him too,' I said.

She gave me a quizzical look and watched me watch the snowstorm until we were suddenly alive again with Maynard's charm and with the introduction and the first few harmless questions. It wasn't until the interviewer started asking about takeovers that things warmed up; and in this version the interviewer's voice was sharp and critical, designed to raise a prickly defensive response.

Maynard had kept his temper for a while, reacting self-righteously rather than with irritation, and these answers had been broadcast. In the end however his courtesy disintegrated, his voice rose and a forefinger began to wag.

'I act within the law,' he told the interviewer heavily. 'Your insinuations are disgraceful. When a debtor can't pay, one is entitled to take his property. The state does it. The courts enforce it. It's the law. Let me tell you that in the horse racing business, if a man can't pay his training fees, the trainer is entitled to sell the horse to recover his money. It's the law, and what's more, it's natural justice.'

The interviewer mentioned villainous mortgage holders who foreclosed and evicted their tenants. Hadn't Maynard, he asked, lent money to a hard-pressed family business that owned a block of flats which was costing more to maintain than the rental income, and couldn't afford the repairs required by the authorities? And after the repairs were done, hadn't

Maynard demanded his money back? And when the family couldn't pay, hadn't he said he would take the flats instead, which were a loss to the family anyway? And after that, hadn't mysterious cracks developed in the fabric, so that the building was condemned and all the poor tenants had to leave? And after that, hadn't he demolished the flats and sold the freehold land to a development company for ten times his original loan for repairs?

The inquisitional nature of the interviewer was by now totally laid bare, and the questions came spitting out as accusations, to which Maynard answered variously with growing fury:

'It's none of your business.'

'It was a long time ago.'

'The building subsided because of underground trains.'

'The family was glad to be rid of a millstone liability.'

'I will not answer these questions.'

The last statement was practically a shout. The interviewer made calming motions with his hand, leaning back in his chair, appearing to relax, all of which cooling behaviour caused Maynard to simmer rather than seethe. A mean-looking scowl, however, remained in place. Nobility was nowhere to be seen.

The interviewer with subterranean cunning said pleasantly, 'You mentioned racehorses. Am I right in thinking your own father was a racehorse trainer and that you at one time were his assistant?'

Maynard said ungraciously, 'Yes.'

'Give us your opinion of investing in bloodstock.'

Maynard said profits could be made if one took expert advice.

'But in your case,' the interviewer said, 'you must be your own expert.'

Maynard shrugged. 'Perhaps.'

The interviewer said very smoothly, 'Will you tell us how you acquired your racehorse Metavane?'

Maynard said tightly, 'I took him in settlement of a bad debt.'

'In the same way as your other businesses?'

Maynard didn't answer.

'Metavane proved to be a great horse, didn't he? And you syndicated him for at least four million pounds ... which must be your biggest coup ever – bigger than the Bourne Brothers' patents. Shall we talk about those two enterprises? First, tell me how much you allow either Metavane's former owners or the Bourne Brothers out of the continuing fruits of your machinations.'

'Look here,' Maynard said furiously, 'if you had a fraction of my business sense you'd be out doing something useful instead of sitting here green with envy picking holes.'

He stood up fiercely and abruptly and walked decisively off the set, tearing off the microphone he had been wearing on his tie and flinging it on the ground. The interviewer made no attempt to stop him. Instead

he faced the camera and with carefully presented distaste said that some of the other businesses, big and
small, known to have benefited from Mr Allardeck's
rescue missions were Downs and Co. (a printing
works), Benjy's Fast Food Takeout, Healthy Life
(sports goods manufacturers), Applewood Garden
Centre, Purfleet Electronics and Bourne Brothers (light
engineers).

The Bourne Brothers' assets, he said, had proved to
include some long overlooked patents for a special
valve which had turned out to be just what industry
was beginning to need. As soon as it was his, Maynard
Allardeck had offered the valve on a royalty basis to
the highest bidder, and had been collecting handsomely
ever since. The Bourne Brothers? The interviewer
shook his head. The Bourne Brothers hadn't realized
what they'd owned until they'd irrevocably parted with
it. But did Maynard Allardeck know what he was
getting? Almost certainly yes. The interviewer smiled
maliciously and pushed the knife right in. If Allardeck
had told the Bourne Brothers what they owned, collecting dust in a file, they could have saved themselves
several times over.

The interviewer's smugly sarcastic face vanished into
another section of blizzard, and Rose Quince rose lan-
guidly to switch everything off.

'Well?' she said.

'Nasty.'

'Is that all?'

'Why didn't they show the whole tape on *How's Trade*? They obviously meant to needle Maynard. Why did they smother the results?'

'I thought you'd never ask.' Rose hitched a hip on to one of the tables and regarded me with acid amusement. 'I should think Allardeck paid them not to show it.'

'What?'

'Pure as a spring lamb, aren't you? That interviewer and his producer have before this set up a pigeon and then thoroughly shot him down, but without the brawl ever reaching the screen. One politician, I know for certain, was invited by the producer to see his hopelessly damaging tape before it was broadcast. He was totally appalled and asked if there was any way he could persuade the producer to edit it. Sure, the producer said, the oldest way in the world, through your wallet.'

'How do you know?'

'The politician told me himself. He wanted me to write about it, he was so furious, but I couldn't. He wouldn't let me use his name.'

'Maynard,' I said slowly, 'has a real genius for acquiring assets.'

'Oh, sure. And nothing illegal. Not unless he helped the trains to shake the block of flats' foundations.'

'One could never find out.'

'Not a chance.'

'How did the interviewer rake all that up?'

Rose shrugged. 'Out of files. Out of archives. Same as we all do when we're on a story.'

'He'd done a great deal of work.'

'Expecting a great deal of pay-off.'

'Mm,' I said, 'if Maynard was already angling for a knighthood, he'd have paid the earth. They could probably have got more from him than they did.'

'They'll curl up like lemon rind now that they know.' The idea pleased Rose greatly.

'How did you get this tape?' I asked curiously.

'From the producer himself, sort of. He owed me a big favour. I told him I wanted to do a shredding job on Allardeck, and asked to see the interview again, uncut if possible, and he was as nice as pie. I wouldn't tell him I knew about his own little scam, now would I?'

'I suppose,' I said slowly, 'that I couldn't have a copy?'

Rose gave me a long cool look while she considered it. Her eyelids, I noticed, were coloured purple, dark contrast to the pale blue eyes.

'What would you do with it?' she said.

'I don't know yet.'

'It's under copyright,' she said.

'Mm.'

'You shouldn't have it.'

'No.'

She bent over the video machine and pressed the eject button. The large black cassette slid quietly and smoothly into her hand. She slotted it into its case and held it out to me, gold chains tinkling.

'Take this one. This is a copy. I made it myself. The originals never left the building, they're hot as hell about that in that television company, but I'm fairly quick with these things. They left me alone in an editing room to view, with some spare tapes stacked in a corner, which was their big mistake.'

I took the box, which bore a large white label saying 'Do not touch'.

'Now listen to me, buddy boy, if you're found with this, you don't get me into trouble, right?'

'Right,' I said. 'Do you want it back?'

'I don't know why I trust you,' she said plaintively. 'A goddamn jockey. If I want it back I'll ask. You keep it somewhere safe. Don't leave it lying about, for God's sake. Though I suppose I should tell you it won't play on an ordinary video. The tape is professional tape three-quarters of an inch wide, it gives better definition. You'll need a machine that takes that size.'

'What were you going to do with it yourself?' I asked.

'Wipe it off,' she said decisively. 'I got it yesterday morning and played it several times here to make sure I didn't put the uncut version's words into Allardeck's mouth in the paper. I don't need suing. Then I wrote my piece, and I've been busy today ... but if you'd come one day later, it would all have been wiped.'

'Lucky,' I said.

'Yes. What else? Files? There's more on the tape, but Bill said files, so files you can have.'

'Bill?'

'Bill Vaughnley. We worked together when we were young. Bill started at the bottom, the old Lord made him. So did I. You don't call someone sir when you've shared cigarette butts on a night stint.'

They had been lovers, I thought. It was in her voice.

'He says I have a tongue like a viper,' she said without offence. 'I dare say he told you?'

I nodded. 'Rattlesnake.'

She smiled. 'When he's a pompous fool, I let him know it.'

She stood up, tawny and tinkling like a mobile in a breeze, and we went out of the television room, down a corridor, round a few corners, and found ourselves in an expanse like a library with shelves to the ceiling bearing not books but folders of all sorts, the whole presided over by a severe looking youth in spectacles who signed us in, looked up the indexing and directed us to the section we needed.

The file on Maynard Allardeck was, as Rose had said, less informative than the tape. There were sundry photographs of him, black and white glossy prints, chiefly taken at race meetings, where I supposed he was more accessible. There were three, several years old now, of him leading in his great horse Metavane after its win in the 2000 Guineas, the Goodwood Mile and the Champion Stakes. Details and dates were on flimsy paper strips stuck to the back of the prints.

There were two bunches of newspaper clippings, one from the *Towncrier*, one from other sources such as the *Financial Times* and the *Sporting Life*. Nothing critical had been written, it seemed, before the onslaught in the *Flag*. The paragraphs were mainly dull: Maynard, from one of the oldest racing families... Maynard, proud owner... Maynard, member of the Jockey Club... Maynard, astute businessman... Maynard, supporter of charity... Maynard the great and good. Approving adjectives like bold, compassionate, far-sighted and responsible occurred. The public persona at its prettiest.

'Enough to make you puke,' Rose said.

'Mm,' I said. 'Do you think you could ask your producer friend why he hit on Maynard as a target?'

'Maybe. Why?'

'Someone's got it in for Maynard. That TV interview might be an attack that didn't work, God bless bribery and corruption. The attack in the *Flag* has worked well. You've helped it along handsomely yourself. So who got to the *Flag*, and did they also get to the producer?'

'I take it back,' she said. 'Some jockeys are smarter than others.'

'Very few are dumb.'

'They just talk a different language?'

'Dead right.'

She returned the file to its place. 'Anything else? Any dinky little thing?'

'Yes,' I said. 'How would I get to talk to Sam Leggatt, who edits the *Flag*?'

She let out a breath, a cross between a cough and a laugh. 'Sam Leggatt? You don't.'

'Why not?'

'He walks around in a bullet-proof vest.'

'Seriously?'

'Metaphorically.'

'Do you know him?'

'Sure, I know him. Can't say I like him. He was political correspondent on the *Record* before he went to the *Flag*, and he's always thought he was God's gift to Fleet Street. He's a mocker by nature. He and the *Flag* are soulmates.'

'Could you reach him on the telephone?' I asked.

She shook her head over my naivety. 'They'll be printing the first edition by now, but he'll be checking everything again for the second. Adding stuff. Changing it round. There's no way he'd talk to Moses let alone a . . . a jumping bean.'

'You could say,' I suggested, 'that you were your editor's secretary, and it was urgent.'

She looked at me in disbelief. 'And why the hell should I?'

'Because you trade in favours.'

'Jee-sus.' She blinked the pale blue eyes.

'Any time,' I said. 'I'll pay. I took it for granted that this . . .' I held up the tape, 'was on account.'

'The telephone,' she said, 'makes it two favours.'

'All right.'

She said with amusement, 'Is this how you win your races?' She turned without waiting for an answer and led the way back roughly to where we had started from but ending in a small, bare little room furnished only with three or four chairs, a table and a telephone.

'Interview room,' Rose said. 'General purposes. Not used much. I'm not having anyone hear me make this call.'

She sat on one of the chairs looking exotically sensuous and behaving with middle-class propriety, the baroque façade for frighteners, the sensible woman beneath.

'You'll have about ten seconds, if that,' she said, stretching out the bracelets for the telephone. 'Leggatt will know straight away you're not our editor. Our editor comes from Yorkshire and still sounds like it.'

I nodded.

She got an outside line and with long red nails tapped in the *Flag*'s number, which she knew by heart; and within a minute, after out-blarneying the Irish, she handed me the receiver silently.

'Hello, Martin, what goes?' an unenthusiastic voice said.

I said slowly and clearly, 'Owen Watts left his credit cards in Bobby Allardeck's garden.'

'What? I don't see . . .' There was a sudden silence. 'Who is this?'

'Jay Erskine,' I said, 'left his Press Club card in the same place. To whom should I report these losses? To the Press Council, the police or my member of parliament?'

'Who is that?' he asked flatly.

'I'm speaking from a telephone in the *Towncrier*. Will you talk to me in your office, or shall I give the *Towncrier* a scoop?'

There was a long pause. I waited. His voice then said, 'I'll ring you back. Give me your extension.'

'No,' I said. 'Now or never.'

A much shorter pause. 'Very well. Come to the front desk. Say you're from the *Towncrier*.'

'I'll be there.'

He crashed the telephone down as soon as I'd finished speaking, and Rose was staring at me as if alarmed for my wholeness of mind.

'No one speaks to editors like that,' she said.

'Yeah . . . well, I don't work for him. And somewhere along the way I've learned not to be afraid of people. I was never afraid of horses. People were more difficult.'

She said with a touch of seriousness, 'People can harm you.'

'They sure can. But I'd get nowhere with Leggatt by being soft.'

'Where do you want to be?' she asked. 'What's this scoop you're not giving the *Towncrier*?'

189

'Nothing much. Just some dirty tricks the *Flag* indulged in to get their Allardeck story for Intimate Details.'

She shrugged. 'I doubt if we'd print that.'

'Maybe not. What's the limit journalists will go to to get a story?'

'No limit. Up Everest, into battlefields, along the gutters, anywhere a scandal leads. I've done my crusading time in rotten health farms, corrupt local governments, nutty religions. I've seen more dirt, more famine, more poverty, more tragedy than I need. I've sat through nights with parents of murdered children and I've been in a village of lifeboatmen's widows weeping for their dead. And then some damn fool man expects me to go sit on a prissy gilt chair and swoon over skirt lengths in some goddam Paris salon. I've never been a women's writer and I'm bloody well not starting now.'

She stopped, smiled twistedly, 'My feminism's showing.'

'Say you won't go,' I said. 'If it's a demotion, refuse it. You've got the clout. No one expects you to write about fashion, and I agree with you, you shouldn't.'

She gave me a long look. 'I wouldn't be fired, but he's new, he's a chauvinist, he could certainly make life difficult.'

'You,' I said, 'are one very marketable lady. Get out the famous poison fangs. A little venom might work wonders.'

She stood up, stretching tall, putting her hands on her heavily belted hips. She looked like an Amazon equipped for battle but I could still sense the indecision inside. I stood also, to the same height, and kissed her cheek.

'Very brotherly,' she said dryly. 'Is that all?'

'That's all you want, isn't it?'

'Yes,' she said, mildly surprised. 'You're goddam right.'

The *Daily Flag*, along Fleet Street from the *Towncrier*, had either been built much later or had been done over in Modern Flashy.

There was a fountain throwing out negative ions in the foyer and ceiling-wide chandeliers of thin vertical shimmering glass rods, each emitting light at its downward tip. Also a marble floor, futuristic seating and a security desk populated by four large men in intimidating uniforms.

I told one of them I'd come from the *Towncrier* to see Mr Leggatt and half expected to be thrown out bodily into the street. All that happened, however, was that after a check against a list on the desk I was directed upwards with the same lack of interest as I'd met with on friendlier territory.

Upstairs the decorative contrast continued. Walls in the *Flag* were pale orange with red flecks, the desks shining green plastic, the floor carpeted with busy orange and red zigzags, the whole a study in unrestfulness. Anger on every page, I thought, and no wonder.

Sam Leggatt's office had an opaque glass door marked 'editor' in large lower-case white letters, followed some way below by smaller but similar letters telling callers to ring bell and wait.

I rang the bell and waited, and presently with a buzz the door swung inwards a few inches. Sam Leggatt might not actually wear a bullet-proof vest but his defences against people with grievances were impressive.

I pushed the door open further and went in to another brash display of rotten taste: black plastic desk, red wallpaper flecked in a geometric pattern, and a mottled green carpet, which as a working environment would have sent me screaming to the bottle.

There were two shirt-sleeved men in there, both standing, both apparently impervious to their surroundings. One was short, stubby and sandy-haired, the other taller, stooped, bespectacled and going bald. Both about fifty, I thought. A third man, younger, sat in a corner, in a suit, watchful and quiet.

'Mr Leggatt?' I said.

The short sandy-haired one said, 'I'm Leggatt. I'll give you five minutes.' He inclined his head towards the taller man beside him. 'This is Tug Tunny, who edits Intimate Details. That is Mr Evans from our legal department. So who are you, and what do you want?'

Tug Tunny snapped his fingers. 'I know who he is,'

he said. 'Jockey. That jockey.' He searched for the name in his memory and found it. 'Fielding. Champion jockey.'

I nodded, and it seemed to me that they all relaxed. There was a trace of arrogance all the same in the way Leggatt stood, and a suggestion of pugnaciousness, but not more, I supposed, than his eminence and the circumstances warranted, and he spoke and behaved without bluster throughout.

'What do you want?' Leggatt repeated, but lacking quite the same tension as when I'd entered; and it crossed my mind as he spoke that with his passion for security they would be recording the conversation, and that I was speaking into an open microphone somewhere out of sight.

I said carefully, 'I came to make arrangements for returning the property of two of your journalists, Owen Watts and Jay Erskine.'

'Return it then,' Leggatt said brusquely.

'I would be so glad,' I said, 'if you would tell me why they needed to climb a ladder set against Bobby Allardeck's house at one in the morning.'

'What's it to you?'

'We found them, you understand, with telephone tapping equipment. Up a ladder, with tools, at the point where the telephone wires enter the Allardecks' house. What were they doing there?'

There was a pause, then Tunny flicked his fingers again.

'He's Allardeck's brother-in-law. Mrs Allardeck's brother.'

'Quite right,' I said. 'I was staying with them last night when your men came to break in.'

'They didn't break in,' Leggatt said. 'On the contrary, they were, I understand, quite savagely attacked. Allardeck should be arrested for assault.'

'We thought they were burglars. What would you think if you found people climbing a ladder set against your house at dead of night? It was only after we'd chased them off that we found they weren't after the silver.'

'Found? How found?'

'They left their jackets behind, full of credit cards and other things with their names on.'

'Which you propose to return.'

'Naturally. But I'd like a proper explanation of why they were there at all. Wire-tapping is illegal, and we disturbed them in the act of removing a tap which had been in place for at least two weeks, according to the telephone engineer who came this morning to complete the dismantling.'

They said nothing, just waited with calculating eyes.

I went on. 'Your paper mounted an unprovoked and damaging attack on Bobby Allardeck, using information gleaned by illegal means. Tell me why.'

They said nothing.

I said, 'You were sent, Mr Leggatt, a special delivery letter containing proof that all of Bobby Allardeck's creditors had been paid and he was not going bankrupt. Why don't you now try to undo a fraction of the misery you've caused him and my sister? Why don't you print conspicuously in Intimate Details an apology for misrepresenting Bobby's position? Why don't you outline the paragraph in red and get your two busy nocturnal journalists to scoot up to Newmarket with the edition hot off the presses like before, and while the town is asleep deliver a copy personally to every recipient who was on their earlier round? And why don't you send a red-inked copy to each of Bobby's owners, as before? That would be most pleasing, don't you think?'

They didn't looked pleased in the slightest.

'It's unfortunate,' I said mildly, 'that it's one's duty as a citizen to report illegal acts to the relevant authorities.'

Without any show of emotion Sam Leggatt turned his head towards the silent Mr Evans. After a pause Mr Evans briefly nodded.

'Do it,' Sam Leggatt said to Tunny.

Tunny was thunderstruck. 'No.'

'Print the apology and get the papers delivered.'

'But . . .'

'Don't you know a barrel when you see one?' He looked back at me. 'And in return?'

'Watts's credit cards and Erskine's Press Club pass.'

'And you'll still have . . .?'

'Their jackets, a chequebook, photos, letters, notebooks, a diary and a neat little bugging system.'

He nodded. 'And for those?'

'Well,' I said slowly, 'how about if you asked your lawyers what you would be forced to pay to Bobby if the wire-tapping came to court? If you cared to compensate him at that level now we would press no charges and save you the bad publicity and the costs and the penalties of a trial.'

'I have no authority for that.'

'But you could get it.'

He merely stared, without assent or denial.

'Also,' I said, 'the answer to why the attack was made. Who suggested it? Did you direct your journalists to break the law? Did they do it at their own instigation? Were they paid to do it, and if so by whom?'

'Those questions can't be answered.'

'Do you yourself know the answers?'

He said flatly, 'Your bargaining position is strong enough only for the apology and the delivery of the apology, and you shall have those, and I will consult on the question of compensation. Beyond that, nothing.'

I knew a stone wall when I saw one. The never-reveal-your-sources syndrome at its most flexible. Leggatt was telling me directly that answering my questions would cause the *Flag* more trouble than my reporting them for wire-tapping, which being so I would indeed get nothing else.

'We'll settle for the compensation,' I said. 'We would have to report the wire-tapping quite soon. Within a few days.' I paused. 'When a sufficient apology appears in the paper on Friday morning, and I've checked on the Newmarket deliveries, I'll see that the credit cards and the Press Club pass reach you here at your front desk.'

'Acceptable,' Leggatt said, smothering a protest from Tunny. 'I agree to that.'

I nodded to them and turned and went out through the door, and when I'd gone three steps felt a hand on my arm and found Leggatt had followed me.

'Off the record,' he said, 'what would you do if you discovered who had suggested the Allardeck attacks?'

I looked into sandy brown eyes, at one with the hair. At the businesslike outward presentation of the man who daily printed sneers, innuendo, distrust and spite, and spoke without showing a trace of them.

'Off the record,' I said, 'bash his face in.'

CHAPTER ELEVEN

I didn't suppose an apology printed in the *Flag* would melt Bobby's bank manager's cash register heart, and I was afraid that the *Flag*'s compensation, if they paid it, wouldn't be enough, or soon enough, to make much difference.

I thought with a sigh of the manager in my own bank, who had seen me uncomplainingly through bad patches in the past and had stuck out his neck later to lend me capital for one or two business excursions, never pressing prematurely for repayment. Now that I looked like being solvent for the foreseeable future he behaved the same as ever, friendly, helpful, a generous source of advice.

Getting the apology printed was more a gesture than an end to Bobby's troubles, but at least it should reassure the owners and put rock back under the quicksands for the tradespeople in Newmarket. If the stable could be saved, it would be saved alive, not comatose.

I'd got from Sam Leggatt a tacit admission that the *Flag* had been at fault, and the certainty that he knew the answers to my questions. I needed those answers immediately and had no hope of unlocking his tongue.

With a sense of failure and frustration I booked into a nearby hotel for the night, feeling more tired than I liked to admit and afraid of falling asleep on the seventy dark miles home. I ordered something to eat from room service and made a great many telephone calls between yawns.

First, to Holly.

'Well done, today,' she said.

'What?'

'Your win, of course.'

'Oh, yes.' It seemed a lifetime ago. 'Thanks.'

'Where are you?' she said. 'I tried the cottage.'

'In London.' I told her the hotel and my room number. 'How are things?'

'Awful.'

I told her about the *Flag* promising to print the apology, which cheered her a little but not much.

'Bobby's out. He's gone walking on the Heath. It's all dreadful. I wish he'd come back.'

The anxiety was raw in her voice and I spent some time trying to reassure her, saying Bobby would certainly return soon, he would know how she worried; and privately wondering if he wasn't sunk so deep in his own despair that he'd have no room for imagining Holly's.

'Listen,' I said after a while. 'Do something for me, will you?'

'Yes. What?'

'Look up in the form books for Maynard's horse Metavane. Do you remember, it won the 2000 Guineas about eight years ago?'

'Vaguely.'

'I want to know who owned it before Maynard.'

'Is it important?' She sounded uninterested and dispirited.

'Yes. See if you can find out, and ring me back.'

'All right.'

'And don't worry.'

'I can't help it.'

No one could help it, I thought, disconnecting. Her unhappiness settled heavily on me as if generated in my own mind.

I telephoned Rose Quince at the home number she had given me on my way out, and she answered breathlessly at the eighth ring saying she had just that minute come through the door.

'So they didn't throw you to the presses?' she said.

'No. But I fear I got bounced off the flak jacket.'

'Not surprising.'

'All the same, read Intimate Details on Friday. And by the way, do you know a man called Tunny? He edits Intimate Details.'

'Tunny,' she said. 'Tug Tunny. A memory like a floppy disc, instant recall at the flick of a switch. He's been in the gossip business all his life. He probably

pulled the wings off butterflies as a child and he's ful-
filled if he can goad any poor slob to a messy divorce.'

'He didn't look like that,' I said dubiously.

'Don't be put off by the parsonage exterior. Read
his column. That's *him*.'

'Yes. Thanks. And what about Owen Watts and Jay
Erskine?'

'The people who left their belongings in your sister's
garden?'

'That's right.'

'Owen Watts I've never heard of before today,' Rose
said. 'Jay Erskine . . . if it's the same Jay Erskine, he
used to work on the *Towncrier* as a crime reporter.'

There were reservations in her voice, and I said
persuasively, 'Tell me about him.'

'Hm.' She paused, then seemed to make up her
mind. 'He went to jail some time ago,' she said. 'He
was among criminals so much because of his job, he
grew to like them, like policemen sometimes do. He
got tried for conspiracy to obstruct the course of justice.
Anyway, if it's the same Jay Erskine, he was as hard as
nails but a terrific writer. If he wrote those pieces about
your brother-in-law, he's sold out for the money.'

'To eat,' I said.

'Don't get compassionate,' Rose said critically. 'Jay
Erskine wouldn't.'

'No,' I said. 'Thanks. Have you been inside the *Flag*
building?'

'Not since they did it up. I hear it's gruesome. When

Pollgate took over he let loose some decorator who'd been weaned on orange kitchen plastic. What's it like?'

'Gruesome,' I said, 'is an understatement. What's Pollgate like himself?'

'Nestor Pollgate, owner of the *Flag* as of a year ago,' she said, 'is reported to be a fairly young upwardly mobile shit of the first water. I've never met him myself. They say a charging rhinoceros is safer.'

'Does he have editorial control?' I asked. 'Does Sam Leggatt print to Pollgate's orders?'

'In the good old days proprietors never interfered,' she said nostalgically. 'Now, some do, some still don't. Bill Vaughnley gives general advice. The old Lord edited the *Towncrier* himself in the early years, which was different. Pollgate bought the *Flag* over several smarting dead bodies and you'll see old-guard *Flag* journalists weeping into their beer in Fleet Street bars over the whipped-up rancour they have to dip their pens in. The editor before Sam Leggatt threw in the sponge and retired. Pollgate has certainly dragged the *Flag* to new heights of depravity, but whether he stands over Leggatt with a whip, I don't know.'

'He wasn't around tonight, I don't think,' I said.

'He spends his time putting his weight about in the City, so I'm told. Incidentally, compared with Pollgate, your man Maynard is a babe in arms with his small takeovers and his saintly front. They say Pollgate doesn't give a damn what people think of him, and his financial bullying starts where Maynard's leaves off.'

'A right darling.'

'Sam Leggatt I understand,' she said. 'Pollgate I don't. If I were you I wouldn't twist the *Flag*'s tail any further.'

'Perhaps not.'

'Look what they did to your brother-in-law,' she said, 'and be warned.'

'Yes,' I said soberly. 'Thank you.'

'Any time.'

She said goodbye cheerfully and I sat drinking a glass of wine and thinking of Sam Leggatt and the fearsome manipulator behind him: wondering if the campaign against Maynard had originated from the very top, or from Leggatt or from Tunny, or from Watts and Erskine, or from outside the *Flag* altogether, or from one of Maynard's comet-trail of victims.

The telephone rang and I picked up the receiver, hearing Holly's voice saying without preamble, 'Maynard got Metavane when he was an unraced two-year-old, and I couldn't find the former owners in the form book. But Bobby has come back now, and he says he thinks they were called Perryside. He's sure his grandfather used to train for them, but they seem to have dropped right out of racing.'

'Um,' I said. 'Have you got any of those old *Racing Who's Who*s? They had pages of owners in them, with addresses. I've got them, but they're in the cottage, which isn't much good tonight.'

'I don't think we've got any from ten years ago,' she

said doubtfully, and I heard her asking Bobby. 'No, he says not.'

'Then I'll ring up Grandfather and ask him. I know he's kept them all, back to the beginning.'

'Bobby wants to know what's so important about Metavane after all these years.'

'Ask him if Maynard still owns any part of Metavane.'

The murmuring went on and the answer came back. 'He thinks Maynard still owns one share. He syndicated the rest for millions.'

I said, 'I don't know if Metavane's important. I'll know tomorrow. Keep the chin up, won't you?'

'Bobby says to tell you the dragon has started up the drive.'

I put the receiver down smiling. If Bobby could make jokes he had come back whole from the Heath.

Grandfather grumbled that he was ready for bed but consented to go downstairs in his pyjamas. 'Perryside,' he said, reading, 'Major Clement Perryside, The Firs, St Albans, Hertfordshire, telephone number attached.' Disgust filled the old voice. 'Did you know the fella had his horses with Allardeck?'

'Sorry, yes.'

'To hell with him, then. Anything else? No? Then goodnight.'

I telephoned to the Perryside number he'd given me and a voice at the other end said, Yes, it was The Firs, but the Perrysides hadn't lived there for about seven years. The voice had bought the house from Major and Mrs Perryside, and if I would wait they might find their new address and telephone number.

I waited. They found them. I thanked them; said goodnight.

At the new number another voice said, No, Major and Mrs Perryside don't live here any more. The voice had bought the bungalow from them several months back. They thought the Perrysides had gone into sheltered housing in Hitchin. Which sheltered housing? They couldn't say, but it was definitely in Hitchin. Or just outside. They thought.

Thank you, I said, sighing, and disconnected.

Major and Mrs Perryside, growing older and perhaps poorer, knowing Maynard had made millions from their horse: could they still hold a grievance obsessional enough to set them tilting at him at this late stage? But even if they hadn't, I thought it would be profitable to talk to them.

If I could find them; in Hitchin, or outside.

I telephoned to my answering machine in the cottage and collected my messages: four from various trainers, the one from Holly, and a final unidentified man asking me to ring him back, number supplied.

I got through to Wykeham Harlowe first because he, like my grandfather, went early to bed, and he, too, said he was in his pyjamas.

We talked for a while about that day's runners and those for the next day and the rest of the week, normal more or less nightly discussions. And as usual nowadays he said he wouldn't be coming to Towcester tomorrow, it was too far. Ascot, he said, on Friday and Saturday. He would go to Ascot, perhaps only on one day, but he'd be there.

'Great,' I said.

'You know how it is, Paul,' he said. 'Old bones, old bones.'

'Yes,' I said. 'I know. This is Kit.'

'Kit? Of course you're Kit. Who else would you be?'

'No one,' I said. 'I'll ring you tomorrow night.'

'Good, good. Take care of those novices. Goodnight, then, Paul.'

'Goodnight,' I said.

I talked after that with the three other trainers, all on the subject of the horses I'd be riding for them that week and next, and finally, after ten o'clock and yawning convulsively, I got through to the last, unidentified, number.

'This is Kit Fielding,' I said.

'Ah.' There was a pause, then a faint but discernible click. 'I'm offering you,' said a civilized voice, 'a golden opportunity.'

He paused. I said nothing. He went on, very smoothly, 'Three thousand before, ten thousand after.'

'No,' I said.

'You haven't heard the details.'

I'd heard quite enough. I disconnected without

206

saying another word and sat for a while staring at walls I didn't see.

I'd been propositioned before, but not quite like that. Never for such a large sum. The before-and-after merchants were always wanting jockeys to lose races to order, but I hadn't been approached by any of them seriously for years. Not since they'd tired of being told no.

Tonight's was an unknown voice, or one I hadn't heard often enough to recognize. High in register. Education to match. Prickles wriggled up my spine. The voice, the approach, the amount, the timing, all of them raised horrid little suggestions of entrapment.

I sat looking at the telephone number I'd been given.

A London number. The exchange 722. I got through to the operator and asked whereabouts in London one would find exchange 722, general information printed in London telephone directories. Hold on, she said, and told me almost immediately; 722 was Chalk Farm stroke Hampstead.

I thanked her. Chalk Farm stroke Hampstead meant absolutely nothing, except that it was not an area known for devotion to horse racing. Very much the reverse, I would have thought. Life in Hampstead tended to be intellectually inward-looking, not raucously open-air.

Why Hampstead . . .

I fell asleep in the chair.

*

After a night spent at least half in bed I drank some coffee in the morning and went out shopping, standing in draughty doorways in Tottenham Court Road, waiting for the electronic wizards to unbolt their steel-mesh shutters.

I found a place that would re-record Rose's professional three-quarter-inch tape of Maynard on to a domestic size to fit my own player, no copyright questions asked. The knowingly obliging youth who performed the service seemed disgusted and astounded that the contents weren't pornographic, but I cheered him up a little by buying a lightweight video-recording camera, a battery pack to run it off and a number of new tapes. He showed me in detail how to work everything and encouraged me to practise in the shop. He could point me to a helpful little bachelor club, he said, if I needed therapy.

I declined the offer, piled everything in the car, and set off north to Hitchin, which was not exactly on the direct route to Towcester but at least not in a diametrically opposite direction.

Finding the Perrysides when I got there was easy: they were in the telephone book. Major C. Perryside, 14 Conway Retreat, Ingle Barton. Helpful locals pointed me to the village of Ingle Barton, three miles outside the town, and others there explained how to find number 14 in the retirement homes.

The houses themselves were several long terraces of small one-storey units, each with its own brightly painted front door and strip of minute flower bed. Paths alone led to the houses: one had to park one's car on a tarmac area and walk along neatly paved ways between tiny segments of grass. Furniture removal men, I thought, would curse the lay-out roundly, but it certainly led to an air of unusual peace, even on a cold damp morning in November.

I walked along to number 14, carrying the video camera in its bag. Pressed the bell push. Waited.

Everywhere was quiet, and no one answered the door. After two or three more unsuccessful attempts at knocking and ringing I went to the door of the right-hand neighbour and tried there.

An old lady answered, round, bright-eyed, interested.

'They walked round to the shop,' she said.

'Do you know how long they'll be?'

'They take their time.'

'How would I know them?' I asked.

'The Major has white hair and walks with a stick. Lucy will be wearing a fishing hat, I should think. And if you're thinking of carrying their groceries home for them, young man, you'll be welcomed. But don't try to sell them encyclopaedias or life insurance. You'll be wasting your time.'

'I'm not selling,' I assured her.

'Then the shop is past the car park and down the lane to the left.' She gave me a sharp little nod and retreated behind her lavender door, and I went where she'd directed.

I found the easily recognizable Perrysides on the point of emerging from the tiny village stores, each of them carrying a basket and moving extremely slowly. I walked up to them without haste and asked if I could perhaps help.

'Decent of you,' said the Major gruffly, holding out his basket.

'What are you selling?' Lucy Perryside said suspiciously, relinquishing hers. 'Whatever it is, we're not buying.'

The baskets weren't heavy: the contents looked meagre.

'I'm not selling,' I said, turning to walk with them at the snail's pace apparently dictated by the Major's shaky legs. 'Would the name Fielding mean anything to you?'

They shook their heads.

Lucy under the battered tweed fishing hat had a thin imperious-looking face, heavily wrinkled with age but firm as to mouth. She spoke with clear upper-class diction and held her back ramrod straight as if in defiance of the onslaughts of time. Lucy Perryside, in various guises and various centuries, had pitched pride against bloody adversity and come through unbent.

'My name is Kit Fielding,' I said. 'My grandfather trains horses in Newmarket.'

The Major stopped altogether. 'Fielding. Yes. I remember. We don't like to talk about racing. Better keep off the subject, there's a good chap.'

I nodded slightly and we moved on as before, along the cold little lane with the bare trees fuzzy with the foreboding of drizzle; after a while Lucy said, 'That's why he came, Clement, to talk about racing.'

'Did you?' asked the Major apprehensively.

'I'm afraid so, yes.'

This time, however, he went on walking, with, it seemed to me, resignation; and I had an intense sense of the disappointments and downward adjustments he had made, swallowing his pain and behaving with dignity, civil in the face of disasters.

'Are you a journalist?' Lucy asked.

'No . . . a jockey.'

She gave me a sweeping glance from head to foot. 'You're too big for a jockey.'

'Steeplechasing,' I said.

'Oh.' She nodded. 'We didn't have jumpers.'

'I'm making a film,' I said. 'It's about hard luck stories in racing. And I wondered if you would help with one segment. For a fee, of course.'

They glanced at each other, searching each other's reactions, and in their private language apparently decided not to turn down the offer without listening.

'What would we have to do?' Lucy asked prosaically.

'Just talk. Talk to my camera.' I indicated the bag I

was carrying along with the baskets. 'It wouldn't be difficult.'

'Subject?' the Major asked, and before I could tell him he sighed and said, 'Metavane?'

'Yes,' I said.

They faced up to it as to a firing squad, and Lucy said eventually, 'For a fee. Very well.'

I mentioned an amount. They made no audible comment, but it was clear from their nods of acceptance that it was enough, that it was a relief, that they badly needed the money.

We made our slow progress across the car park and down the path and through their bright blue front door, and at their gestured invitation I brought out the camera and fed in a tape.

They grouped themselves naturally side by side on the sofa whose chintz cover had been patched here and there with different fabrics. They sat in a room unexpectedly spacious, facing large sliding windows which let out on to a tiny secluded paved area where in summer they could sit in the sun. There was a bedroom, Lucy said, and a kitchen and a bathroom, and they were comfortable, as I could see.

I could see that their furniture, although sparse, was antique, and that apart from that it looked as if everything saleable had been sold.

I adjusted the camera in the way I'd been taught and balanced it on a pile of books on a table, kneeling behind it to see through the viewfinder.

'OK,' I said, 'I'll ask you questions. Would you just look into the camera lens while you talk?'

They nodded. She took his hand: to give courage, I thought, rather than to receive.

I started the camera silently recording and said, 'Major, would you tell me how you came to buy Metavane?'

The Major swallowed and blinked, looking distinguished but unhappy.

'Major,' I repeated persuasively, 'please do tell me how you bought Metavane.'

He cleared his throat. 'I er . . . we . . . always had a horse, now and then. One at a time. Couldn't afford more, do you see? But loved them.' He paused. 'We asked our trainer . . . he was called Allardeck . . . to buy us a yearling at the sales. Not too expensive, don't you know. Not more than ten thousand. That was always the limit. But at that price we'd had a lot of fun, a lot of good times. A few thousand for a horse every four or five years, and the training fees. Comfortably off, do you see.'

'Go on, Major,' I said warmly as he stopped. 'You're doing absolutely fine.'

He swallowed. 'Allardeck bought us a colt that we liked very much. Not brilliant to look at, rather small, but good blood lines. Our sort of horse. We were delighted. He was broken in during the winter and during the spring he began to grow fast. Allardeck said we shouldn't race him then until the autumn, and of course we took his advice.' He paused. 'During the summer he developed splendidly and Allardeck told us he was very speedy and that we might have a really good one on our hands if all went well.'

The ancient memory of those heady days lit a faint glow in the eyes, and I saw the Major as he must have been then, full of boyish enthusiasm, inoffensively proud.

'And then, Major, what happened next?'

The light faded and disappeared. He shrugged. He said, 'Had a bit of bad luck, don't you know.'

He seemed at a loss to know how much to say, but Lucy, having contracted for gain, proved to have fewer inhibitions.

'Clement was a member of Lloyd's,' she said. 'He was in one of those syndicates which crashed . . . many racing people were, do you remember? He was called upon, of course, to make good his share of the losses.'

'I see,' I said, and indeed I did. Underwriting insurance was fine as long as one never actually had to pay out.

'A hundred and ninety-three thousand pounds,' the Major said heavily, as if the shock was still starkly fresh, 'over and above my Lloyd's deposit, which was another twenty-five. Lloyd's took that, of course, straight away. And it was a bad time to sell shares. The market was down. We cast about, do you see, to know what to do.' He paused gloomily, then went on, 'Our house was already mortgaged. Financial advisers, you understand, had always told us it was best to mortgage one's house and use the money for investments. But the investments had gone badly down ... some of them never recovered.'

The flesh on his old face drooped at the memory of failure. Lucy looked at him anxiously, protectively stroking his hand with one finger.

'It does no good to dwell on it,' she said uneasily. 'I'll tell you what happened. Allardeck got to hear of our problems and said his son Maynard could help us, he understood finance. We'd met Maynard once or twice and he'd been charming. So he came to our house and said if we liked, as we were such old owners of his father, he would lend us whatever we needed. The bank had agreed to advance us fifty thousand on the security of our shares, but that still left a hundred and forty. Am I boring you?'

'No, you are not,' I said with emphasis. 'Please go on.'

She sighed. 'Metavane was going to run in about six weeks and I suppose we were clutching at straws, we hoped he would win. We needed it so badly. We didn't want to have to sell him unraced for whatever we could get. If he won he would be worth very much more. So we were overwhelmed by Maynard's offer. It solved all our problems. We accepted. We were overjoyed. We banked his cheque and Clement paid off his losses at Lloyd's.'

215

Sardonic bitterness tugged at the corners of her mouth, but her neck was still stretched high.

'Was Maynard charging you interest?' I asked.

'Very low,' the Major said. 'Five per cent. Damned good of him, we thought.' The downward curve of his mouth matched his wife's. 'We knew it would be a struggle, but we were sure we would get back on our feet somehow. Economize, do you see. Sell things. Pay him back gradually. Sell Metavane, when he'd won.'

'Yes,' I said. 'What happened next?'

'Nothing much for about five weeks,' Lucy said. 'Then Maynard came to our house again in a terrible state and told us he had two very bad pieces of news for us. He said he would have to call in some of the money he had just lent us as he was in difficulties himself, and almost worse, his father had asked him to tell us that Metavane had lamed himself out at exercise so badly that the vet said he wouldn't be fit to run before the end of the season. It was late September by then. We'd counted on him running in October. We were absolutely, completely shattered, because of course we couldn't afford any longer to pay training fees for six months until racing started again in March, and worse than that, a lame unraced two-year-old at the end of the season isn't worth much. We wouldn't be able to sell him for even what we'd paid for him.'

She paused, staring wretchedly back to the heartbreak.

'Go on,' I said.

She sighed. 'Maynard offered to take Metavane off our hands.'

'Is that how he put it?'

'Yes. Exactly. Take him off our hands is what he said. He said moreover he would knock ten thousand off our debt, just as if the colt was still worth that much. But, he said, he desperately needed some cash, and couldn't we possibly raise a hundred thousand for him at once.' She looked at me bleakly. 'We simply couldn't. We went through it all with him, explaining. He could see that we couldn't pay him without borrowing from a moneylender at a huge interest and he said in no way would he let us do that. He was understanding and charming and looked so worried that in the end we found ourselves comforting him in his troubles, and assuring him we'd do everything humanly possible to repay him as soon as we could.'

'And then?'

'Then he said we'd better make it all legal, so we signed papers transferring ownership of Metavane to him. He changed the amount we owed him from a hundred and forty to a hundred and thirty thousand, and we signed a banker's order to pay him regularly month by month. We were all unhappy, but it seemed the best that could be done.'

'You let him have Metavane without contingencies?' I asked. 'You didn't ask for extra relief on your debt if the horse turned out well?'

Lucy shook her head wearily. 'We didn't think about

contingencies. Who thinks about contingencies for a lame horse?'

'Maynard said he would have to put our interest payments up to ten per cent,' the Major said. 'He kept apologizing, said he felt embarrassed.'

'Perhaps he was,' I said.

Lucy nodded. 'Embarrassed at his own wickedness. He went away leaving us utterly miserable, but it was nothing to what we felt two weeks later. Metavane ran in a two-year-old race at Newmarket and won by three lengths. We couldn't believe it. We saw the result in the paper. We telephoned Allardeck at once. And I suppose you'll have guessed what he said?'

I half nodded.

'He said he couldn't think why we thought Metavane was lame. He wasn't. He never had been. He had been working brilliantly of late on the Heath.'

CHAPTER TWELVE

'You hadn't thought, I suppose,' I said gently, 'to ask to see the vet's report? Or even to check with Allardeck?'

Lucy shook her head. 'We took Maynard's word.'

The Major nodded heavily. 'Trusted him. Allardeck's son, do you see.'

Lucy said, 'We protested vigorously, of course, that Maynard had told us a deliberate lie, and Maynard said he hadn't. He just denied he'd ever told us Metavane wouldn't run before spring. Took our breath away. Clement complained to the Jockey Club, and got nowhere. Maynard charmed them too. Told them we had misunderstood. The Stewards were very cool to Clement. And do you know what I think? I think Maynard told them we were trying to screw yet more money out of him, when he'd been so generous as to help us out of a dreadful hole.'

They were both beginning to look distressed and I had a few twinges of conscience of my own. But I said, 'Please tell me the state of your debt now, and how

219

much Maynard shared with you out of his winnings and the syndication of Metavane as a stallion.'

They both stared.

The Major said as if surprised, 'Nothing.'

'How do you mean, nothing?'

'He didn't give us a farthing.'

'He syndicated the horse for several millions,' I said.

The Major nodded. 'We read about it.'

'I wrote to him,' Lucy said, her cheeks slightly pink. 'I asked him to at least release us from what we owed him.'

'And?'

'He didn't answer.'

'Lucy wrote twice,' the Major said uncomfortably. 'The second time, she sent it special delivery, to be handed to him personally, so we know he must have received it.'

'He didn't reply,' Lucy said.

'We borrowed the money and that's that,' the Major said with resignation. 'Repayments and interest take most of our income, and I don't think we will ever finish.'

Lucy stroked his hand openly. 'We are both eighty-two, you see,' she said.

'And no children?' I asked.

'No children,' Lucy said regretfully. 'It wasn't to be.'

I packed away the camera, thanking them and giving them the cash I'd collected for paying Bobby's lads, proceeds of cashing one of Bobby's cheques with my valet at Newbury. My valet, a walking bank, had found the service routine and had agreed to bring cash for the other cheques to Towcester.

The Major and Lucy accepted the money with some embarrassment but more relief, and I wondered if they had feared I might not actually pay them once I'd got what I wanted. They'd learned in a hard school.

I looked at my watch and asked if I could make a quick credit card call on their telephone. They nodded in unison, and I got through to the manager where I banked.

'John,' I said.

'Kit.'

'Look, I'm in a hurry, on my way to ride at Towcester, but I've been thinking ... It's true, isn't it, that money can be paid into my account without my knowing?'

'Yes, by direct transfer from another bank, like your riding fees. But you'd see it on your next statement.'

'Well,' I said, 'except for my riding fees, could you see to it that nothing gets paid in? If anything else arrives, can you refuse to put it into my account?'

'Yes, I can,' he said doubtfully, 'but why?'

'Someone offered me a bribe last night,' I said. 'It felt too much like a set-up. I don't want to find I've been sneakily paid by a back door for something I don't intend to do. I don't want to find myself trying to tell the Stewards I didn't take the money.'

He said after a short pause, 'Is this one of your intuitions?'

'I just thought I'd take precautions.'

'Yes,' he said. 'All right. If anything comes, I'll check with you before crediting your account.'

'Thanks,' I said. 'Until further notice.'

'And perhaps you would drop me a line putting your instructions in writing? Then you would be wholly safe, if it came to the Stewards.'

'I do not know,' I said, 'what I would do without you.'

I said goodbye to the Perrysides and drove away, reflecting that it was their own total lack of sensible precautions which had crystallized in me the thought that I should prudently take my own.

They should have insured in the first place against a catastrophic loss at Lloyd's and they should have brought in an independent vet to examine Metavane. It was easy to see these things after the event. The trick for survival was to imagine them before.

Towcester was a deep-country course, all rolling green hills sixty miles to the north-west of London. I drove there with my mind on anything except the horses ahead.

Mostly I thought about precautions.

With me in the car, besides my overnight bag, I had the tapes of Maynard, the tape of the Perrysides, the video camera and a small hold-all of Holly's containing the jackets and other belongings of Jay Erskine and Owen Watts. Without all those things I would not be able to get any sort of compensation or future for Bobby and Holly, and it occurred to me that I should make sure that no one stole them.

Sam Leggatt or anyone else at the *Flag* would see that repossessing the journalists' belongings would be a lot cheaper and less painful than coughing up cash and printing and distributing humble apologies.

Owen Watts and Jay Erskine were bound to be revengeful after the damage they had suffered, and they could be literally anywhere, plotting heaven knew what.

I was driving to a time and place printed in more than half the daily newspapers: my name plain to see on the racing pages, declared overnight for the one-thirty, two o'clock, three o'clock and three-thirty races.

If I were Jay Erskine, I thought, I would be jemmying open Kit Fielding's Mercedes at one-thirty, two o'clock, three o'clock or three-thirty.

If I were Owen Watts, perhaps at those times, I would be breaking into Kit Fielding's cottage in Lambourn.

They might.

They might not.

I didn't think a little active breaking and entering would disturb their consciences in the least, especially as the current penalties for a conviction for wire-tapping ran to a two thousand pound fine or up to two years in prison, or both.

I didn't know that I would recognize them from the mêlée in the dark. They could however make it their business to know me. To watch for my arrival in the jockeys' car park. To note my car.

It took forty-five minutes to drive from the Perrysides' village to Towcester racecourse and for half the journey I thought I was being unnecessarily fanciful.

Then abruptly I drove into the centre of the town of Bletchley and booked myself into an old and prosperous looking hotel, the Golden Lion. They took an impression of my credit card and I was shown to a pleasant room, where I hung Watt's and Erskine's jackets in the closet, draped my night things around the bathroom and stowed everything else in a drawer. The receptionist nodded pleasantly and impersonally when I left the key at the desk on my way out, and no one else took any notice; and with a wince at my watch but feeling decidedly safer I broke the speed limit to Towcester.

The princess's novices were the first and last of my booked rides, with another for Wykeham and one for the Lambourn trainer in between.

The princess was waiting with her usual lambent patina in the parade ring when I went out there, and so was Danielle, dressed on that damp day in a blazing red shiny coat over the black trousers. I suppose my pleasure showed. Certainly both of them smiled down their noses in the way women do when they know they're admired, and Danielle, instead of shaking my hand, gave me a brief peck of a kiss on the cheek, a half touch of skin to skin, unpremeditated, the sensation lingering surprisingly in my nerve endings.

She laughed. 'How're you doing?' she said.

'Fine. And you?'

'Great.'

The princess said mildly, 'What do we expect from Kinley, Kit?'

I had a blank second of non-comprehension before remembering that Kinley was her horse. The one I was about to ride: three years old, still entire, a dappled grey going to the starting gate as second favourite for the first race of his life. High time, I thought, that I concentrated on my job.

'Dusty says he's travelled well; he's excited but not sweating,' I said.

'And that's good?' Danielle asked.

'That's good,' said the princess, nodding.

'He's mature for three, he jumps super at home and I think he's fast,' I said.

'And it all depends, I suppose, on whether he enjoys it today.'

'Yes,' I said. 'I'll do my best.'

'Enjoys it?' Danielle asked, surprised.

'Most horses enjoy it,' I said. 'If they don't, they won't race.'

'Do you remember Snowline?' the princess said. I

nodded, and she said to Danielle, 'Snowline was a mare I had a long time ago. She was beautiful to look at and had won two or three times on the Flat, and I bought her to be a hurdler, partly, I must confess, because of her name, but she didn't like jumping. I kept her in training for two years because I had a soft spot for her, but it was a waste of money and hope.' She smiled. 'Wykeham tried other jockeys, do you remember, Kit? For the second of those she wouldn't even start. I learned a great lesson. If a horse doesn't like racing, cut your losses.'

'What became of Snowline?' Danielle said.

'I sold her as a brood mare. Two of her foals have been winners on the Flat.'

Danielle looked from her aunt to me and back again. 'You both totally love it, don't you?'

'Totally,' said the princess.

'Totally,' I agreed.

I got up on Kinley and walked him slowly up past the stands to let him take in the sounds and smells, and then down towards the start, giving him a long close look at a flight of hurdles, letting him stand chest-high, almost touching, looking out over the top. He pricked his ears and extended his nostrils, and I felt the instinct stir in him most satisfactorily, the in-bred compulsion that ran in the blood like a song, the surging will to race and win.

You, Kinley, I thought, know all I've been able to teach you about jumping, and if you mess it up today you'll be wasting all those mornings I've spent with you on the schooling grounds this autumn.

Kinley tossed his head. I smoothed a hand down his neck and took him on to the start, mingling there with two or three other complete novices and about ten who had run at least once before but never won. The youngest a horse was allowed to go jump racing in Britain was in the August of its three-year-old year, and Kinley's was a two-mile event for three-year-olds who hadn't yet won.

Some jockeys avoided doing schooling sessions, but I'd never minded, on the basis that if I'd taught the horse myself I'd know what it could and wouldn't do. Some trainers sent green horses to crash around racecourses with only the haziest idea of how to meet a jump right, but Wykeham and I were in accord: it was no good expecting virtuoso jumping in public without arpeggios at home.

Wykeham was in the habit of referring to Kinley as Kettering, a horse he'd trained in the distant past. It was amazing, I sometimes thought, that the right horses turned up at the meetings: Dusty's doing, no doubt.

Kinley circled and lined up with only an appropriate amount of nervousness and when the tapes went up, set off with a fierce plunge of speed. Everything was new to him, everything unknown; nothing on the home gallops ever prepared a horse for the first rocketing reality. I settled him gradually with hands and mind, careful not to do it too much, not to teach him that what he was really feeling was wrong but just to control it, to keep it simmering, to wait.

He met the first hurdle perfectly and jumped it cleanly and I clearly felt his reaction of recognition, his increase in confidence. He let me shorten his stride a little approaching the second hurdle so as to meet it right and avoid slowing to jump, and at the third flight he landed so far out on the other side that my spirits rose like a bird. Kinley was going to be good. One could tell sometimes right from the beginning, like watching a great actor in his first decent role.

I let him see every obstacle clearly, mostly by keeping him to the outside. Technically the inside was the shortest way, but also the more difficult. Time for squeezing through openings when he could reliably run straight.

Just keep it going, Kinley old son, I told him; you're doing all right. Just take a pull here, that's right, to get set for the next jump, and now go for it, go for it ... dear bloody hell, Kinley, you'll leave me behind, jumping like that, just wait while I get up here over your shoulders, I don't see why we can't kick for home, first time out, why not, it's been done, get on there, Kinley, you keep jumping like that and we'll damned near win.

I gave him a breather on the last uphill section and he was most aggrieved at my lack of urging, but once round the last bend, with one jump left before the run-in, I shook him up and told him aloud to get on with it, squeezing him with the calves of my legs, sending him rhythmic messages through my hands, telling him OK, my son, now fly, now run, now stretch out your bloody neck, this is what it's all about, this is your future, take it, embrace it, it's all yours.

He was bursting with pride when I pulled him up, learning at once that he'd done right, that the many pats I gave him were approval, that the applause greeting his arrival in the winners' enclosure was the curtain call for a smash hit. Heady stuff for a novice; and I reckoned that because of that day he would run his guts out to win all his life.

'He enjoyed it,' the princess said, glowing with pleasure.

'He sure did.'

'Those jumps . . .'

I unbuckled my saddle and drew it off on to my arm.

'He's very good,' I said. 'You have seriously got a good horse.'

She looked at me with speculation, and I nodded. 'You never know. Too soon to be sure.'

'What on earth are you talking about?' Danielle demanded.

'The Triumph Hurdle,' said her aunt.

I went to weigh in, change and weigh out and go through the whole rigmarole again with Wykeham's second runner, which didn't belong to the princess but to a couple in their seventies who cared just as much.

They owned only the one horse, an ageing 'chaser who'd been retired once and had pined until he'd been sent back into training, and I was truly pleased for them when, because of his experience, he stood up throughout the three miles as others fell, and against all the odds thundered along insouciantly into first place.

Wykeham might not go to the meetings, I thought, gratefully pulling up, he might have his mental grooves stuck in the past, but he sure as hell could still train winners.

I watched the next race after that from the jockeys' stand, and won the one after for the Lambourn trainer. One of those days, I thought contentedly. A treble. It happened once or twice a season, not much more.

It occurred to me as I was unbuckling my saddle in the winners' enclosure that Eric Olderjohn, the owner of the horse, who was present and quietly incandescent with delight, was something to do with the Civil Service on a high level, a fact I knew only because he occasionally lamented that government business would keep him away from seeing his pride and joy run.

I asked him on an impulse if I could talk to him for a few minutes after I'd weighed in and changed for the next race, and rather in the Vaughnley mould he said 'Anything' expansively, and was waiting there as promised when I went out.

We talked for a bit about his win, which was uppermost in his mind, and then he asked what I wanted. I wanted, I said, the answers to a couple of questions, and I wondered if he could – or would – get them for me.

'Fire away,' he said. 'I'm listening.'

I explained about the newspaper attacks on Bobby and Maynard, and to my surprise he nodded.

'I've heard about this, yes. What are your questions?'

'Well, first, whether Maynard was in fact being considered for a knighthood, and second, if he was, who would have known?'

He half laughed. 'You don't want much, do you?' He shook his head. 'Patronage is not my department.' He looked up at the sky and down at the colours I wore, which were by then the princess's. 'What good would it do you to find out?'

'I don't know,' I said frankly. 'But someone ought to make reparation to Bobby and my sister.'

'Hm. Why don't they ask these questions themselves?'

I said blankly, 'But they wouldn't.'

'They wouldn't, but you would.' His eyes were half assessing, half amused.

'Those newspaper articles were maliciously unfair,' I said positively. 'Bobby and my sister Holly are gentle well-intentioned people trying to make a success of training and doing no harm to anyone.'

'And the newspaper attack on them makes you angry?'

'Yes, it does. Wouldn't it you?'

231

He considered it. 'An attack on my daughter would, yes.' He nodded briefly. 'I don't promise, but I'll ask.'

'Thank you very much,' I said.

He smiled, turned to go and said, 'Win for me again next time out.'

I said I hoped to, and wondered why I'd described Bobby as gentle when the marks of his fists lay scattered on my body among the dark red attentions of the hurdlers. Bobby was brother to the wind, the seed of the tornado dormant in the calm.

I went back into the changing room for my helmet and stick and then out to the parade ring again for the sixth and last race of the day, the two-mile novice 'chase.

'Totally awesome,' Danielle said, standing there.

'What is?' I asked.

'We went down in the medic's car to one of the fences. We stood right by there watching you jump. That speed . . . so fast . . . you don't realize, from the stands.'

'In the three-mile 'chase,' the princess said, nodding.

'The medic said you were all going over there at better than thirty miles an hour. He says you're all crazy. He's right.'

The princess asked me if I thought I'd be making it four for the day, but I thought it unlikely: this one, Dhaulagiri, hadn't as much talent as Kinley.

'There's a woman riding in this race,' Danielle observed, watching the other jockeys standing in groups with the owners. She looked at me without archness. 'What do you think if you're beaten in a race by a woman?'

'That she had a faster horse,' I said.

'Ouch.'

The princess smiled but made no comment. She knew I didn't like racing against the very few women who rode professionally over jumps, not for fear of a male ego-battering, but because I couldn't rid myself of protectiveness. A male opponent could take his bumps, but I'd never learned to ride ruthlessly against a female; and moreover I didn't like the idea of what falls and horses' hooves could do to their faces and bodies. The women jockeys despised my concern for them, and took advantage of it if they could.

Dhaulagiri was looking well, I thought, watching him walk round. Better than when I'd schooled him the previous week. Tauter. A new lean line of muscle on the haunch. Something in the carriage of the head.

'What is it, Kit?' the princess asked.

I looked from the horse to her enquiring face. 'He's improved since last week,' I said.

'Wykeham said he seemed to like jumping fences better than hurdles.'

'Yes, he did.'

Her eyes smiled. 'Do you think, then . . .?'

'It would be nice, wouldn't it?'

'Exquisite,' she said.

I nodded and went away on Dhaulagiri to the start,

and in some odd way it seemed a jaunt to the horse as much as to me. Three winners raised my spirits euphorically. Dhaulagiri could jump. So why not, why bloody not make it four. Dhaulagiri took the mood from his jockey, as all horses do. I reckon Dhaulagiri on that afternoon would have light-heartedly jumped off a cliff if I'd asked him.

It wasn't the most advisable tactic for a horse running for the first time over the bigger fences and I dared say Wykeham would have deplored it, but Dhaulagiri and I went round the whole two miles in friendly, fully stretched recklessness, and at the winning post I thought for nearly the thousandth time in my life that there was nothing in existence comparable to the shared intense joy of victory. Better perhaps, but comparable, no. I was laughing aloud when we pulled up.

The exhilaration lasted all the way back to the changing room and in and out of the shower, and only marginally began to abate when my valet handed me a zipped webbing belt stuffed full of Bobby's money. Jockeys' valets washed one's breeches and took one's saddles and other belongings from racecourse to racecourse, turning up with everything clean every day. Besides that they were the grapevine, the machine oil, the comforters and the bank. My valet said he was lending me the money-belt he used himself on holidays, as he didn't like the idea of me walking around with all those thousands in my pockets.

Bobby, I thought, sighing. I would drive to Bletchley and collect my stuff from the Golden Lion, and then go on to Newmarket to give the money to Bobby so he could pay his lads at the normal time the next day and stack the rest away in his safe. I would sleep there and go direct to Ascot in the morning.

I strapped the belt against my skin and buttoned my shirt over it, the valet nodding approval. It didn't show, he said.

I thanked him for his thoughtfulness, finished dressing, and went out for a briefer than usual talk with the princess, whose eyes were still sparkling behind the sheltering lashes.

Vague thoughts I'd had of asking Danielle to help celebrate my four winners over dinner disintegrated when she said she was again due at her bureau at six-thirty, and they would be leaving for London at any moment.

'Do you work at weekends?' I asked.

'No.'

'Could ... er, could I ask you out on Saturday evening?'

She glanced at her aunt, and so did I, but as usual one could tell nothing from the princess's face that she didn't want one to see. I felt no withdrawal, though, coming from her mind, and nor, it seemed, did her niece.

'Yes,' Danielle said, 'you could. I'll be coming to Ascot. After the races, we might make plans.'

Extraordinary, I thought. She understood. She had of course come close to seeing her ride from Devon to London evaporate at the third hurdle two days ago. Two days. That too was extraordinary. I seemed to have known her for longer.

'Tomorrow at Ascot,' the princess said to me, shaking my hand in goodbye. 'How long can we go on winning?'

'Until Christmas.'

She smiled. 'Christmas Fielding.'

'Yes.'

Danielle said, 'What do you mean, Christmas Fielding?'

'It's my name,' I said.

'What? I mean, I know it says C. Fielding on the number boards, but I took it for granted that Kit was for Christopher.'

I shook my head. 'We were born on Christmas morning. Christmas and Holly. No accounting for parents.'

There was warmth in her eyes as well as in the princess's. I left them saying their thanks to their hosts for the day before starting home, and with swelling contentment walked out to my own car.

At the sight of it most of the contentment vanished into anger. All four tyres were flat, the window on the driver's side was broken, and the lid of the boot hovered halfway open.

I said aloud and precisely about four obscene words

and then shrugged and turned to go back into the racecourse to telephone. The AA could deal with it. I could hire another car. The things I'd feared losing were safe in the Golden Lion and if that was what the vandals had been looking for, they were out of luck.

Most people had already left, but there were still a few cars in the park, still a person or two moving about. I was thinking chiefly of inconvenience and paying little attention to anything else, and very suddenly there was a voice at my left ear saying, 'Stand still, Fielding', and another man crowding against my right elbow with the same message.

I did stand still, too taken by surprise to think of doing anything else.

From each side the message reached me clearly.

Reached through my jacket, through my shirt and into my skin, somewhere above the money-belt.

'That's right,' said the one who'd spoken before. 'We've come to repossess some property. You don't want to get cut, do you?'

CHAPTER THIRTEEN

I certainly didn't.

'See that grey Ford over there right by the road,' said the man on my left. 'We're going to get into it, nice and easy. Then you'll tell us where to go for some jackets and the things in the pockets. We'll be sitting one each side of you on the back seat, and we're going to tie your hands, and if you make any sudden moves we'll slice your tendons so you won't stand again, never mind ride horses. You got that?'

Dry mouthed, I nodded.

'You've got to learn there's people you can't push around. We're here to teach you. So now walk.'

They were not Owen Watts and Jay Erskine. Different build, different voices, older and much heavier. They underlined their intentions with jabs against my lower ribs, and I did walk. Walked stiff-legged towards the grey Ford.

I would give them what they wanted: that was simple. Owen Watts's credit cards and Jay Erskine's Press Club pass weren't worth being crippled for. It was what would happen after the Golden Lion that seized up the imagination and quivered in the gut. They weren't going to release me with a handshake and a smile. They had as good as said so.

There was a third man, a driver, sitting in the Ford. At our approach he got out of the car and opened both rear doors. The car itself was pointing in the direction of the way out to the main road.

There seemed to be no one within shouting distance. No one near enough to help. I decided sharply and suddenly that all the same I wouldn't get into the car. I would run. Take my chances in the open air. Better under the sky than in some little dark corner; than on the back seat of a car with my hands tied. I would have given them the jackets but their priority was damage, and their intention of it was reaching me like shock waves.

It came to the point of now or never, and I was already tensing my muscles for it to be now, when a large quiet black car rolled along the road towards the racecourse exit and stopped barely six feet away from where I stood closely flanked. The nearside rear window slid down and a familiar voice said, 'Are you in trouble, Kit?'

I never was more pleased to see the princess in all my life.

'Say no,' the man on the left directed into my ear, screwing his knife round a notch. 'Get rid of them.'

'Kit?'

'Yes,' I said.

The princess's face didn't change. The rear door of her Rolls swung widely open and she said economically, 'Get in.'

I leapt. I jumped. I dived into her car head first, landing on my hands as lightly as possible across her ankles and Danielle's, flicking from there to the floor.

The car was moving forward quite fast even before the princess said, 'Drive on, Thomas' to her chauffeur, and I saw the angry faces of my three would-be captors staring in through the windows, heard their fists beating on the glossy bodywork, their hands trying to open the already centrally locked doors.

'They've got knives,' Danielle said in horror. 'I mean . . . *knives*.'

Thomas accelerated further, setting the heavy men running alongside and then leaving them behind, and I fumbled my way up on to one of the rear-facing folding seats and said I was sorry.

'Sorry!' Danielle exclaimed.

'For involving you in such a mess,' I said to the princess. I rubbed my hand across my face. 'I'm very sorry.'

Thomas said without noticeable alarm, 'Madam, those three men are intending to follow us in a grey Ford car.'

I looked out through the tinted rear window and saw that he was right. The last of them was scrambling in, fingers urgently pointing.

'Then we'd better find a policeman,' the princess said calmly; but as on every other racing day the police had left the racecourse as soon as the crowds had gone. There was no one at the racecourse gate directing traffic, since there was no longer any need. Thomas slowed and turned in the direction of London and put his foot smoothly on the accelerator.

'If I might suggest, madam?' he said.

'Yes. Go on.'

'You would all be safer if we kept going. I don't know where the police station is in Stony Stratford, which is the first town we come to. I would have to stop to ask directions.'

'If we go to a police station,' Danielle said anxiously, 'they'll keep us there for ages, taking statements, and I'll be terribly late.'

'Kit?' the princess asked.

'Keep going,' I said. 'If that's all right.'

'Keep going then, Thomas,' said the princess, and Thomas, nodding, complied. 'And now, Kit,' she said, 'tell us why you needed to be rescued in such a melo-dramatic fashion.'

'They had knives on him,' Danielle said.

'So I observed. But why?'

'They wanted something I've got.' I took a deep breath, trying to damp down the incredible relief of not being a prisoner in the car behind, trying to stop myself trembling. 'It started with some newspaper art-icles about my brother-in-law, Bobby Allardeck.'

She nodded. 'I heard about those from Lord Vaughnley yesterday, after you'd gone.'

'I've got blood on my leg,' Danielle said abruptly. 'How did I get . . .' She was looking down at her ankles, and then lifted her head suddenly and said to me, 'When you flew in like an acrobat, were you bleeding? Are you still bleeding?'

'I suppose so.'

'What do you mean, you suppose so? Can't you feel it?'

'No.' I looked inside my jacket, right and left.

'Well?' Danielle demanded.

'A bit,' I said.

Maybe the heavies hadn't expected me to jump with their knives already in. Certainly they'd reacted too slowly to stop me, ripping purposefully, but too late. The sting had been momentary, the aftermath ignorable. A little blood, however, went a long way.

The princess said resignedly, 'Don't we carry a first-aid box, Thomas?'

Thomas said 'Yes, madam' and produced a black box from a built-in compartment. He held it over his shoulder, and I took it, opened it, and found it contained useful-sized padded absorbent sterile dressings and all manner of ointments and sticky tapes. I took out one of the thick dressings and found two pairs of eyes watching.

'Excuse me,' I said awkwardly.

'You're embarrassed!' Danielle said.

242

'Mm.'

I was embarrassed by the whole situation. The princess turned her head away and studied the passing fields while I groped around under my shirt for somewhere to stick the dressing. The cuts, wherever they were, proved to be too far round for me to see them.

'For heaven's sake,' Danielle said, still watching, 'let me do it.'

She removed herself from the rear seat facing me to the folding seat by my side, took the dressing out of my hand and told me to hold my shirt and jacket up so that she could see the action. When I did she lifted her head slowly and looked at me directly.

'I simply don't believe you can't feel that.'

I smiled into her eyes. Whatever I felt was a pinprick to what I'd been facing. 'Stick the dressing on,' I said.

'All right.'

She stuck it on, and we changed places so she could do the other one, on my left. 'What a mess,' she said, wiping her hands and returning to the rear seat while I tucked my shirt untidily into my trousers. 'That first cut is long and horribly deep and needs stitches.'

The princess stopped staring out of the window and looked at me assessingly.

'I'll be all right for racing tomorrow,' I said.

Her mouth twitched. 'I would expect you to say that, if you had two broken legs.'

'I probably would.'

'Madam,' Thomas said, 'we're approaching the motorway and the grey Ford is still on our tail.'

The princess made an indecisive gesture with her hands. 'I suppose we'd better go on,' she said. 'What do you think?'

'On,' Danielle said positively, and Thomas and I nodded.

'Very well. On to London. And now, Kit, tell us what was happening.'

I told them about Bobby and me finding the journalists dismantling their wire-tap, and about removing their jackets before letting them go.

The princess blinked.

I said I had offered to return the jackets if the *Flag* would print an apology to Bobby and also pay some compensation. I explained about finding my car broken into, and about the suddenness with which my assailants had appeared.

'They wanted those jackets,' I said. 'And although I'd thought about robbery, I hadn't expected violence.' I couldn't think why not, after the violence of Bobby's assault on Owen Watts. I paused. 'I can't thank you enough.'

'Thank Thomas,' the princess said. 'Thomas said you were in trouble. I wouldn't have known.'

'Thank you, Thomas.'

'You could see it a mile off,' he said.

'You were pretty quick getting away.'

'I went to a lecture once about how not to get your employer kidnapped.'

'Thomas!' said the princess. 'Did you really?'

He said seriously, 'I wouldn't want to lose you, madam.'

The princess was moved and for once without an easy surface answer. Thomas, who had driven her devotedly for years, was a large quiet middle-aged Londoner with whom I talked briefly most days in racecourse car parks, where he sat and read books in the Rolls. I'd asked him once long ago if he didn't get bored going to the races every day when he wasn't much interested in horses and didn't gamble, and he'd said no, he liked the long journeys, he liked his solitude and most of all he liked the princess. He and I both, in many ways opposites, would I dare say have died for the lady.

I thought, all the same, that she wouldn't much care for the alarms of the continuing present. I looked back to the grey car still steadfastly following and began to consider what to do to vanish. I was thinking about perhaps diving down into thick undergrowth once we'd left the motorway, when the car behind suddenly swerved dangerously from the centre lane, cut across the slow lane to a wild blowing of horns and disappeared down a side road.

Thomas made a sort of growl in his throat and said with relief, 'They've gone into the service station.'

'You mean we've lost them?' Danielle said, twisting to look back.

'They peeled off.' To telephone, I supposed, a no-success story.

The princess said 'Good' as if that ended the matter entirely, and, greatly released, began to talk of her horses, of the day's triumphs, of more pleasing excitements, tracking with intent and expertise away from the alien violent terror of maiming steel back to the safe familiar danger of breaking one's neck.

By the time we reached central London she had returned the atmosphere to a semblance of full normality, behaving as if my presence in her car were commonplace, the tempestuous entrance overlooked. She would have gone with good manners to the scaffold, I thought, and was grateful for the calm she had laid upon us.

Within the last mile home, with dusk turning to full night, the princess asked Thomas if he would drive her niece to Chiswick as usual and return for her when she'd finished work.

'Certainly, madam.'

'Perhaps,' I said, 'I could fetch Danielle instead? Save Thomas the trip.'

'At two in the morning?' Danielle said.

'Why not?'

'OK.'

The princess made no comment, showed no feeling. 'It seems you have the night off, Thomas' was all she said; and to me, 'If you are wanting to go to the police, Thomas will drive you.'

I shook my head. 'I'm not going to the police.'

'But,' she said doubtfully, 'those horrid men . . .'

'If I go to the police, you will be in the newspapers.'

She said 'Oh' blankly. Cavorting about saving her jockey from a bunch of knife-wielding heavies was not the sort of publicity she yearned for. 'Do what you think best,' she said faintly.

'Yes.'

Thomas braked to a halt outside her house in Eaton Square and opened the car door for us to disembark. On the pavement I thanked the princess for the journey. Politeness conquered all. With the faintest gleam of amusement she said she would no doubt see me at Ascot, and as on ordinary days held out her hand for a formal shake, accepting the sketch of a bow.

'I don't believe it,' Danielle said.

'If you get the form of things right,' the princess said to her sweetly, 'every peril can be tamed.'

I bought a shirt and an anorak and booked into a hotel for the night, stopping in the lobby to rent a car from an agency booth there.

'I want a good one,' I said. 'A Mercedes, if you have one.'

They would try, they assured me.

Upstairs I changed from the slashed bloodstained

shirt and jacket into the new clothes, and began another orgy of telephoning.

The Golden Lion via directory enquiries said there was no problem, they would hold my room for another day, they had my credit card number, too bad I'd been unexpectedly detained, my belongings would be perfectly safe.

The AA said not to worry, they would rescue my car from Towcester racecourse within the hour. If I phoned in the morning, they would tell me where they'd taken it for repairs.

My answering system in the cottage had been hard-worked with please-ring-back messages from the police, my neighbour, my bank manager, Rose Quince, three trainers and Sam Leggatt.

My neighbour, an elderly widow, sounded uncommonly agitated, so I called her back first.

'Kit, dear, I hope I did right,' she said. 'I saw a strange man moving about in your cottage and I told the police.'

'You did right,' I agreed.

'It was lunchtime and I knew you'd be at Towcester, I always follow your doings. Four winners! It was on the radio just now. Well done.'

'Thanks . . . What happened at the cottage?'

'Nothing, really. I went over when the police came to let them in with my key. They couldn't have been more than five minutes getting there, but there wasn't anyone in the cottage. I felt so foolish, but then one of the policemen said a window was broken, and when they looked around a bit more they said someone had been in there searching. I couldn't see anything missing. Your racing trophies weren't touched. Just the window broken in the cloakroom.'

I sighed. 'Thank you,' I said. 'You are a dear.'

'I got Pedro from down the road to mend the window. I didn't like to leave it. I mean, anyone could get in.'

'I'll take you for a drink in the pub when I get back.'

She chuckled. 'Thank you, dear. That'll be nice.'

The police themselves had nothing to add. I should return, they said, to check my losses.

I got through to my bank manager at his home and listened to him chewing while he spoke. 'Sorry. Piece of toast,' he said. 'A man came into the bank at lunch-time to pay three thousand pounds into your account.'

'What man?'

'I didn't see him, unfortunately. I was out. It was a banker's draft, not a personal cheque.'

'Damn,' I said feelingly.

'Don't worry, it won't appear on your account. I've put a stop on anything being paid into it, as we agreed. The banker's draft is locked in the safe in my office. What do you want me to do with it?'

'Tear it up in front of witnesses,' I said.

'I can't do that,' he protested. 'Someone paid three thousand pounds for it.'

'Where was it issued?'

'At a bank in the City.'

'Can you ask them if they remember who bought it?'

'Yes, I'll try tomorrow. And be a good chap, let me have the no-paying-in instruction in writing pronto.'

'Yes,' I said.

'And well done with the winners. It was on the radio.'

I thanked him and disconnected, and after some thought left the hotel, walked down the street to an Underground station and from a public phone rang Sam Leggatt at the *Flag*.

There was no delay this time. His voice came immediately on the line, brisk and uncompromising.

'Our lawyers say that what you said here yesterday was tantamount to blackmail.'

'What your reporters did at my brother-in-law's house was tantamount to a jail sentence.'

'Our lawyers say if your brother-in-law thinks he has a case for settlement out of court, his lawyers should contact our lawyers.'

'Yeah,' I said. 'And how long would that take?'

'Our lawyers are of the opinion that no compensation should be paid. The information used in the column was essentially true.'

'Are you printing the apology?'

'Not yet. We haven't gone to press yet.'

'Will you print it?'

He paused too long.

'Did you know,' I said, 'that today someone searched

my cottage, someone smashed their way into my car, two men attacked me with knives, and someone tried to bribe me with three thousand pounds, paid directly into my bank account?'

More silence.

'I'll be telling everyone I can think of about the wire-tapping,' I said. 'Starting now.'

'Where are you?' he said.

'At the other end of the telephone line.'

'Wait,' he said. 'Ring me back, will you?'

'How long?'

'Fifteen minutes.'

'All right.'

I put the receiver down and stood looking at it, drumming my fingers and wondering if the *Flag* really did have equipment which could trace where I'd called from, or whether I was being fanciful.

I couldn't afford, I thought, any more punch-ups. I left the Underground station, walked along the street for ten minutes, went into a pub, rang the *Flag*. My call was again expected: the switchboard put me straight through.

When Sam Leggatt said 'Yes' there were voices raised loudly in the backgound.

'Fielding,' I said.

'You're early.' The backgound voices abruptly stopped.

'Your decision,' I said.

'We want to talk to you.'

'You're talking.'

'No. Here, in my office.'

I didn't answer immediately, and he said sharply, 'Are you still there?'

'Yes,' I said. 'What time do you go to press?'

'First edition, six-thirty, to catch the West Country trains. We can hold until seven. That's the limit.'

I looked at my watch. Fourteen minutes after six. Too late, to my mind, for talking.

'Look,' I said. 'Why don't you just print and distribute the apology? It's surely no big deal. It'll cost you nothing but the petrol to Newmarket. I'll come to your office when you assure me that you're doing that.'

'You'd trust my word?'

'Do you trust mine?'

He said grudgingly, 'Yes, I suppose I do expect you to return what you said.'

'I'll do it. I'll act in good faith. But so must you. You seriously did damage Bobby Allardeck, and you must at least try to put it right.'

'Our lawyers say an apology would be an acknowledgment of liability. They say we can't do it.'

'That's it, then,' I said. 'Goodbye.'

'No, Fielding, wait.'

'Your lawyers are fools,' I said, and put down the receiver.

I went out into the street and rubbed a hand over my head, over my hair, feeling depressed and a loser.

Four winners, I thought. It happened so seldom. I

should be knee-deep in champagne, not banging myself against a brick wall that kicked back so viciously.

The cuts on my ribs hurt. I could no longer ignore them.

I walked dispiritedly along to yet another telephone and rang up a long-time surgical ally.

'Oh, hello,' he said cheerfully. 'What is it this time? A little clandestine bone-setting?'

'Sewing,' I said.

'Ah. And when are you racing?'

'Tomorrow.'

'Toddle round, then.'

'Thanks.'

I went in a taxi and got stitched.

'That's not a horseshoe slash,' he observed, dabbing anaesthetic into my right side. 'That's a knife.'

'Yeah.'

'Did you know the bone is showing?'

'I can't see it.'

'Don't tear it open again tomorrow.'

'Then fix it up tight.'

He worked for a while before patting my shoulder. 'It's got absorbable stitches, also clips and gripping tape, but whether it would stand another four winners is anyone's guess.'

I turned my head. I'd said nothing about the winners.

'I heard it on the news,' he said.

He worked less lengthily on the other cut and

said lightly, 'I didn't think getting knifed was your sort of thing.'

'Nor did I.'

'Want to tell me why it happened?'

He was asking, I saw, for reassurance. He would come to my aid on the quiet, but it was important to him that I should be honest.

'Do you mean,' I said, 'have I got myself into trouble with gamblers and race-fixers and such?'

'I suppose so.'

'Then no, I promise you.' I told him briefly of Bobby's problems and felt his reservations fade.

'And the bruises?' he said.

'I fell under some hurdlers the day before yesterday.'

He nodded prosaically. I paid his fee in cash and he showed me to his door.

'Good luck,' he said. 'Come back when you need.'

I thanked him, caught a taxi and rode back to the hotel thinking of the *Flag* thundering off the presses at that moment without carrying the apology. Thinking of Leggatt and the people behind him; lawyers, Nestor Pollgate, Tug Tunny, Owen Watts and Jay Erskine. Thinking of the forces and the furies I had somehow unleashed. You've got to learn there's people you can't push around, one of the knifemen had said.

Well, I was learning.

The rented car booth in the lobby told me I was in luck, they'd got me a Mercedes; here were the keys, it was in the underground car park; the porter would show me when I wanted to go out. I thanked them. We try harder, they said.

Up in my room I ordered some food from room service and telephoned Wykeham to tell him how his winners had won, catching at least an echo of the elation of the afternoon.

'Did they get home all right?' I asked.

'Yes, they all ate up. Dhaulagiri looks as if he had a hard race but Dusty said he won easy.'

'Dhaulagiri ran great,' I said. 'They all did. Kinley's as good as any you've got.'

We talked of Kinley's future and of the runners at Ascot the next day and Saturday. For Wykeham the months of October, November and December were the peak: his horses came annually into their best form then, the present flourish of successes expected and planned for.

Between 30 September and New Year's Day he ran every horse in his charge as often as he could. 'Seize the moment,' he would say. After Christmas, with meetings disrupted by frost and snow, he let his stable more or less hibernate, resting, regrouping, aiming for a second intense flowering in March. My life followed his rhythms to a great extent, as natural to me as to his horses.

'Get some rest, now,' he said jovially. 'You've got six rides tomorrow, another five on Saturday. Get some good sleep.'

'Yes,' I said. 'Goodnight, Wykeham.'

DICK FRANCIS

'Goodnight, Paul.'

My food came and I ate bits of it and drank some wine while I got through to the other trainers who'd left messages, and after that I rang Rose Quince.

'Four winners,' she said. 'Laying it on a bit thick, aren't you?'

'These things happen.'

'Oh, sure. Just hold on to your moment of glory, buddy boy, because I've some negative news for you.'

'How negative?'

'A firm and positive thumbs down from the producer of *How's Trade*. There's no way on earth he's going to say who sicked him on to Maynard Allardeck.'

'But someone did?'

'Oh, sure. He just won't say who. I'd guess he got paid to do it as well as paid not to, if you see what I mean.'

'Whoever paid him to do it must be feeling betrayed.'

'Too bad,' she said. 'See you.'

'Listen,' I said hastily, 'what did Jay Erskine go to jail for?'

'I told you. Conspiracy to obstruct the course of justice.'

'But what did he actually do?'

'As far as I remember, he put some frighteners on to a chief prosecution witness who then skipped the country and never gave evidence, so the villain got off. Why?'

'I just wondered. How long did he get?'

'Five years, but he was out in a lot less.'

'Thanks.'

'You're welcome. And by the way, one of the favours you owed me is cancelled. I took your advice. The venom worked a treat and I'm freed, I'm no longer under the jurisdiction of the chauvinist. So thanks, and goodnight.'

'Goodnight.'

If the *Flag* wanted frighteners, Jay Erskine could get them.

I sighed and rubbed my eyes and thought about Holly, who had been hovering in my mind for ages, telling me to ring her up. She would want the money I still wore round my waist and I was going to have to persuade her and Bobby to come to London or Ascot in the morning to fetch it.

I was going to have to tell her that I hadn't after all managed to get the apology printed. That hers and Bobby's lawyers could grind on for ever and get nothing. That reporting the wire-tapping to all and sundry might inconvenience the *Flag*, but would do nothing to change their bank manager's mind. I put the call through to Holly reluctantly.

'Of course we'll come to fetch the money,' she said. 'Will you please stop talking about it and listen.'

'OK.'

'Sam Leggatt telephoned. The editor of the *Flag*.'

'Did he? When?'

'About an hour ago. An hour and a half. About seven o'clock. He said you were in London, somewhere in the Knightsbridge area, and did I know where you would be staying?'

'What did you say?' I asked, alarmed.

'I told him where you stayed last night. I told him to try there. He said that wasn't in Knightsbridge and I said of course not, but hadn't he heard of taxis. Anyway he wanted to get a message to you urgently, he said. He wanted me to write it down. He said to tell you the apology was being printed at that moment and will be delivered.'

'What! Why on earth didn't you say so?'

'But you told me last night it was going to happen. I mean, I thought you knew.'

'Christ Almighty,' I said.

'Also,' Holly said, 'he wants you to go to the *Flag* tonight. He said if you could get there before ten there would be someone there you wanted to meet.'

CHAPTER FOURTEEN

When I pressed the buzzer and walked unannounced through his unlatching door he was sitting alone in his office, shirt-sleeved behind his shiny black desk, reading the *Flag*.

He stood up slowly, his fingers spread on the paper as if to give himself leverage, a short solid man with authority carried easily, as of right.

I was not who he'd expected. A voice behind me was saying, 'Here it is, Sam', and a man came walking close, waving a folder.

'Yes, Dan, just leave it with me, will you?' Leggatt said, stretching out a hand and taking it. 'I'll get back to you.'

'Oh? OK.' The man Dan went away, looking at me curiously, closing the door with a click.

'I got your message,' I said.

He looked down at his copy of the *Flag*, turned a page, reversed the paper and pushed it towards me across the desk.

I read the Intimate Details that would be titillating

a few million Friday breakfasts and saw that at least he'd played fair. The paragraph was in bold black type in a black-outlined box.

It said:

The Daily Flag *acknowledges that the Newmarket racing stable of Robertson (Bobby) Allardeck (32) is a sound business and is not in debt to local traders. The* Daily Flag *apologizes to Mr Allardeck for any inconvenience he may have suffered in consequence of reports to the contrary printed in this column earlier.*

'Well,' he said, when I'd read.

'Thank you.'

'Bobby Allardeck should thank God for his brother-in-law.'

I looked at him in surprise, and I thought of Bobby's schizophrenic untrustable regard for me, and of my sister, for whom I truly acted. That paragraph should at least settle the nerves of the town and the owners and put the stable back into functionable order: given, of course, that its uneasy underlying finances could be equally sorted out.

'What changed your mind?' I asked.

He shrugged. 'You did. The lawyers said you would back down. I said you wouldn't. They think they can intimidate anybody with their threats of long expensive lawsuits.' He smiled twistedly. 'I said you'd be real poisonous trouble if we didn't print, and you would have been, wouldn't you?'

'Yes.'

He nodded. 'I persuaded them we didn't want Jay Erskine and Owen Watts in court, where you would put them.'

'Particularly as Jay Erskine has a criminal record already.'

He was momentarily still. 'Yes,' he said.

It had been that one fact, I thought, that had swayed them.

'Did Jay Erskine write the attacks on Bobby?' I asked.

After a slight hesitation he nodded. 'He wrote everything except the apology. I wrote that myself.'

He pressed a button on an intercom on his desk and said, 'Fielding's here' neutrally to the general air.

'Where are the credit cards, now we've printed?' he asked.

'You'll get them tomorrow, after the newspapers have been delivered, like I said.'

'You never let up, do you? Owen Watts has set off to Newmarket already and the others are in the post.' He looked at me broodingly. 'How did you find out about the bank?'

'I thought you might try to discredit me. I put a stop on all ingoing payments.'

He compressed his mouth. 'They can't see what they're dealing with,' he said.

The buzzer on his door sounded and he pushed the release instantly. I turned and saw a man I didn't know walking in with interest and no caution. Fairly tall, with a receding hairline over a pale forehead, he wore an ordinary dark suit with a brightly striped tie and had a habit of rubbing his fingers together, like a schoolmaster brushing off chalk.

'David Morse, head of our legal department,' said Sam Leggatt briefly.

No one offered to shake hands. David Morse looked me over as an exhibit, up and down, gaze wandering over the unzipped anorak and the blue shirt and tie beneath.

'The jockey,' he said coolly. 'The one making the fuss.'

I gave no reply, as none seemed useful, and through the open door behind him came another man who brought power with him like an aura and walked softly on the outsides of his feet. This one, as tall as the lawyer, had oiled dark hair, olive skin, a rounded chin, a small mouth and eyes like bright dark beads: also heavy shoulders and a flat stomach in smooth navy suiting. He was younger than either Sam Leggatt or Morse and was indefinably their boss.

'I'm Nestor Pollgate,' he announced, giving me a repeat of the Morse inspection and the same absence of greeting. 'I am tired of your antics. You will return my journalists' possessions immediately.'

His voice, like his body, was virile, reverberatingly bass in unaccented basic English.

'Did you ask me here just for that?' I said.

Don't twist their tail, Rose Quince had said. Ah well.

Pollgate's mouth contracted and he moved round to Leggatt's side of the desk, and the lawyer also, so that they were ranged there in a row like a triumvirate of judges with myself before them, as it were, on the carpet.

I had stood before the racing Disciplinary Stewards once or twice in that configuration, and I'd learned to let neither fright nor defiance show. Every bad experience, it seemed, could bring unexpected dividends. I stood without fidgeting and waited.

'Your contention that we mounted a deliberate campaign to ruin your brother-in-law is rubbish,' Pollgate said flatly. 'If you utter that opinion in public we will sue you.'

'You mounted a campaign to ruin Maynard Allardeck's chance of a knighthood,' I said. 'You aimed to destroy his credibility and you didn't give a damn who else you hurt in the process. Your paper was ruthlessly callous. It often is. I will utter that opinion as often as I care to.'

Pollgate perceptibly stiffened. The lawyer's mouth opened a little and Leggatt looked on the verge of inner amusement.

'Tell me why you wanted to wreck Maynard Allardeck,' I said.

'None of your business.' Pollgate answered with the finality of a bank-vault door, and I acknowledged that if I ever found out it wouldn't be by straightforward questions put to anyone in that room.

'You judged,' I said instead, 'that a sideways swipe at Maynard would be most effective, and you decided to get at him through his son. You gave not a thought to the ruin you were bringing on the son. You used him. You should compensate him for that use.'

'No,' Pollgate said.

'We admit nothing,' the lawyer said. A classically lawyer-like phrase. We may be guilty but we'll never say so. He went on, 'If you persist in trying to extort money by menaces, the *Daily Flag* will have you arrested and charged.'

I listened not so much to the words as to the voice, knowing I'd heard it somewhere recently, sorting out the distinctive high pitch and the precision of consonants and the lack of belief in any intelligence I might have.

'Do you live in Hampstead?' I said thoughtfully.

'What's that got to do with anything?' Pollgate said, coldly impatient.

'Three thousand before, ten after.'

'You're talking gibberish,' Pollgate said.

I shook my head. David Morse was looking as if he'd bitten a wasp.

'You were clumsy,' I said to him. 'You don't know the first thing about bribing a jockey.'

'What is the first thing?' Sam Leggatt asked.

I almost smiled. 'The name of the horse.'

'You admit you take bribes, then,' Morse said defensively.

'No I don't, but I've been propositioned now and then, and you didn't sound right. Also you were recording your offer on tape. I heard you start the machine. True would-be corrupters wouldn't do that.'

'I did advise caution,' Sam Leggatt said mildly.

'You've no proof of any of this,' Pollgate said with finality.

'My bank manager's holding a three thousand pound draft issued in the City. He intends on my behalf to ask questions about its origins.'

'He'll get nowhere,' Pollgate said positively.

'Then perhaps he'll do what I asked him first, which is to tear it up.'

There was a short stark silence. If they asked for the draft back they would admit they'd delivered it, and if they didn't, their failed ploy would have cost them the money.

'Or it could be transferred to Bobby Allardeck, as a first small instalment of compensation.'

'I've heard enough,' Pollgate said brusquely. 'Return the property of our journalists immediately. There will be no compensation, do you understand? None. You will come to wish, I promise you, that you had never tried to extort it.'

Under the civilized suiting he hunched his shoulders like a boxer, rotating them as a physical warning of an imminent onslaught, a flexing of literal muscles before an explosion of mental aggression. I saw in his face all the brutality of his newspaper and also the arrogance of absolute power. No one, I thought, could have defied him for too long, and he didn't intend that I should be an exception.

'If you make trouble for us in the courts,' he said grittily, 'I'll smash you. I mean it. I'll see to it that you yourself are accused of some crime that you'll hate, and I'll get you convicted and sent to prison, and you'll go down, I promise you, dishonoured and reviled, with maximum publicity and disgrace.'

The final words were savagely biting, the intention vibratingly real.

Both Leggatt and Morse looked impassive and I wondered what any of them could read on my own face. Show no fright . . . ye gods.

He surely wouldn't do it, I thought wildly. The threat must be only to deter. Surely a man in his position wouldn't risk his own status to frame and jail an adversary who wanted so little, who represented no life-or-death danger to his paper or to himself, who wielded no corporate power.

All the same, it looked horrible. Jockeys were eternally vulnerable to accusations of dishonesty and it took little to disillusion a cynical public. The assumption of guilt would be strong. He could try harder and more subtly to frame me for taking bribes, and certainly for things worse. What his paper had already set their hand to, they could do again and more thoroughly. A crime I would hate.

I could find no immediate words to reply to him, and while I stood there in the lengthening silence the door alarm buzzed fiercely, making Morse jump.

Sam Leggatt flicked a switch. 'Who is it?' he said.

'Erskine.'

Leggatt looked at Pollgate, who nodded. Leggatt pressed the button that unlatched the door, and the man I'd shaken off the ladder came quietly in.

He was of about my height, reddish haired going bald, with a drooping moustache and chillingly unsmiling eyes. He nodded to the triumvirate as if he'd been talking to them earlier and turned to face me directly, chin tucked in, stomach thrust out, a man with a ruined life behind him and a present mind full of malice.

'You'll give me my stuff,' he said. Not a question, not a statement: more a threat.

'Eventually,' I said.

There was a certain quality of stillness, of stiffening, on the far side of Leggatt's desk. I looked at Pollgate's thunderous expression and realized that I had almost without intending it told him with that one word that his threat, his promise, hadn't immediately worked.

'He's yours, Jay,' he said thickly.

I didn't have time to wonder what he meant. Jay Erskine caught hold of my right wrist and twisted my arm behind my back with a strength and speed that spoke of practice. I had done much the same to him in Bobby's garden, pressing his face into the mud, and into my ear with the satisfaction of an account paid he said, 'You tell me where my gear is or I'll break your shoulder so bad you'll ride no more races this side of Doomsday.'

His vigour hurt. I checked the three watching faces. No surprise, not even from the lawyer. Was this, I wondered fleetingly, a normal course of events in the editor's office of the *Daily Flag*?

'Tell me,' Erskine said, shoving.

I took a sharp half-pace backwards, cannoning into him. I went down in a crouch, head nearly to the floor, then straightened my legs with the fiercest possible jerk, pitching Jay Erskine bodily forwards over my shoulders, where he let go of my wrist and sailed sprawlingly into the air. He landed with a crash on a potted palm against the far wall while I completed the rolling somersault and ended upright on my feet. The manoeuvre took a scant second in the execution: the stunned silence afterwards lasted at least twice as long.

Jay Erskine furiously tore a leaf from his mouth and struggled pugnaciously to right himself, almost pawing the carpet like a bull for a second charge.

'That's enough,' I said. 'That's bloody enough.'

I looked directly at Nestor Pollgate. 'Compensation,' I said. 'Another of your banker's drafts. One hundred thousand pounds. Tomorrow. Bobby Allardeck will be coming to Ascot races. You can give it to him there. It could cost you about that much to manufacture a crime I didn't commit and have me convicted. Why not save yourself the trouble.'

Jay Erskine was upright and looking utterly malignant.

I said to him, 'Pray the compensation's paid ... Do you want another dose of the slammer?'

I walked to the door and looked briefly back. Pollgate, Leggatt and Morse had wiped-slate faces: Jay Erskine's was glitteringly cold.

I wondered fearfully for a second if the door's unlatching mechanism also locked and would keep me in; but it seemed not. The handle turned easily, came smoothly towards me, opening the path of escape.

Out of the office, along the passage to the lifts my feet felt alarmingly detached from my legs. If I believed Pollgate's threats I was walking into the bleakest of futures: if I believed Erskine's malevolence it would be violent and soon. Why in God's name, I thought despairingly, hadn't I given in, given them the jackets, let Bobby go bust.

There were running footsteps behind me across the mock-marble hallway outside the lifts, and I turned fast, expecting Erskine and danger, but finding, as once before, Sam Leggatt.

His eyes widened at the speed with which I'd faced him.

'You expected another attack,' he said.

'Mm.'

'I'll come down with you.' He pressed the button for descent and stared at me for a while without speaking while we waited.

'One hundred thousand,' he said finally, 'is too much. I thought you meant less.'

'Yesterday, I did.'

'And today?'

'Today I met Pollgate. He would sneer at a small demand. He doesn't think in peanuts.'

Sam Leggatt went back to staring, blinking his sandy lashes, not showing his unspoken thoughts.

'That threat,' I said slowly, 'about sending me to prison. Has he used that before?'

'What do you mean?'

'On someone else.'

'What makes you think so?'

'You and your lawyer,' I said, 'showed no surprise.'

The lift purred to a halt inside the shaft and the doors opened. Leggatt and I stepped inside.

'Also,' I said, as the doors closed, 'the words he used sounded almost rehearsed. "You'll go down, I promise you, dishonoured and reviled, with maximum publicity and disgrace." Like a play, don't you think?'

He said curiously, 'You remember the exact words?'

'One wouldn't easily forget them.' I paused. 'Did he mean it?'

'Probably.'

'What happened before?'

'He wasn't put to the test.'

'Do you mean, the threat worked?' I asked.

'Twice.'

'Jesus,' I said.

I absent-mindedly rubbed my right shoulder, digging in under the anorak with the left thumb and fingers to massage. 'Does he always get his way by threats?'

Leggatt said evenly, 'The threats vary to suit the circumstances. Does that hurt?'

'What?'

'Your shoulder.'

'Oh. Yes, I suppose so. Not much. No worse than a fall.'

'How did you do that? Fling him off you, like that?'

I half grinned. 'I haven't done it since I was about fifteen, same as the other guy. I wasn't sure it would work with a grown man, but it did, a treat.'

We reached the ground floor and stepped out of the lift.

'Where are you staying?' he asked casually.

'With a friend,' I said.

He came with me halfway across the ornate entrance hall, stopping beside the small fountain.

'Why did Nestor Pollgate want to crunch Maynard Allardeck?' I said.

'I don't know.'

'Then it wasn't your idea or Erskine's? It came from the top?'

'From the top.'

'And beyond,' I said.

'What do you mean?'

I frowned. 'I don't know. Do you?'

'As far as I know, Nestor Pollgate started it.'

I said ruefully, 'Then I didn't exactly smash his face in.'

'Not far off.'

There was no shade of disloyalty in his voice, but I had the impression that he was in some way apologizing: the chief's sworn lieutenant offering comfort to the outcast. The chief's man, I thought. Remember it.

'What do you plan to do next?' he said.

'Ride at Ascot.'

He looked steadily into my eyes and I looked right back. I might have liked him, I thought, if he'd steered any other ship.

'Goodbye,' I said.

He seemed to hesitate a fraction but in the end said merely, 'Goodbye' and turned back to the lifts: and I went out into Fleet Street and breathed great gulps of free air under the stars.

I walked the two miles back to the hotel and sat in my room for a while there contemplating the walls, and then I went down to find the rented Mercedes in the underground park and drove it out to Chiswick.

'You're incredibly early,' Danielle said, faintly alarmed at my arrival. 'I did say two a.m., not half after eleven.'

'I thought I might just sit here and watch you, as no one seemed to mind me being here last time.'

'You'll be bored crazy.'

'No.'

'OK.'

She pointed to a desk and chair close to hers. 'No one's using that tonight. You'll be all right there. Did you get that cut fixed?'

'Yes, it's fine.'

I sat in the chair and listened to the mysteries of newsgathering, American style, for the folks back home. The big six-thirty evening slot, eastern US time, was being aired at that moment, it appeared. The day's major hassle had just ended. From now until two, Danielle said, she would be working on anything new and urgent which might make the eleven o'clock news back home, but would otherwise be on the screens at breakfast.

'Does much news happen here at this time of night?' I asked.

'Right now we've got an out-of-control fire in an oil terminal in Scotland and at midnight Devil-Boy goes on stage at a royal charity gala to unveil a new smash.'

'Who?' I said.

273

'Never mind. A billion teenagers can't be wrong.'

'And then what?' I said.

'After we get the pictures? Transmit them back here from a mobile van, edit them, and transmit the finished article to the studios in New York. Sometimes at midday here we do live interviews, mostly for the seven-to-nine morning show back home, but nothing live at nights.'

'You do edit the tapes here?'

'Sure. Usually. Want to see?'

'Yes, very much.'

'After I've made these calls.' She gestured to the telephone and I nodded, and subsequently listened to her talking to someone at the fire.

'The talent is on his way back by helicopter from the race riot and should be with you in ten minutes. Get him to call me when he can. How close to the blaze are you? OK, when Cervano gets to you try to go closer, from that distance a volcano would look like a sparkler. OK, tell him to call me when he's reached you. Yeah, OK, get him to call me.'

She put down the receiver, grimacing. 'They're a good mile off. They might as well be in Brooklyn.'

'Who's the talent?' I said.

'Ed Cervano. Oh . . . the talent is any person behind a microphone talking to the camera. News reporter, anchor, anyone.'

She looked along the headings on the board on the

wall behind her chair. 'Slug. That's the story we're working on. Oil fire. Devil-Boy. Embassy. So on.'

'Yes,' I said.

'Locations, obvious. Time, obvious. Crew. That's the camera crew which is allocated to that story, and also the talent. Format, that's how fully we're covering a story. Package means the works, camera crew, talent, interviews, the lot. Voice-over is just a cameraman, with the commentary tagged on later. So on.'

'And it's you who decides who goes where for what?'

She half nodded. 'The bureau chief, and the other coordinators, who work in the daytime, and me, yes.'

'Some job,' I said.

She smiled with her eyes. 'If we do well, the company's ratings go up. If we do badly, we get fired.'

'The news is the news, surely,' I said.

'Oh yes? Which would you prefer, an oil fire from a mile off or to think you feel the flames?'

'Mm.'

Her telephone rang. 'News,' she said, and listened. 'Look,' she said, sounding exasperated, 'if he's late, it's news. If he's sick, it's news. If he doesn't make it on to the stage at a royal gala, it's news. You just stay there, whatever happens is news, OK? Get some shots of royalty leaving, if all else fails.' She put down the receiver. 'Devil-Boy hasn't arrived at the theatre and it takes him a good hour to dress.'

'The joys of the non-event.'

'I don't want to be scooped by one of the other broadcasting companies, now do I?'

'Where do you get the news from in the first place?'

'Oh . . . the press agencies, newspapers, police broadcasts, publicity releases, things like that.'

'I guess I never wondered before how the news arrived on the box.'

'Ten seconds' worth can take all day to gather.'

Her telephone rang again, with the helicoptering Ed Cervano now down to earth at the other end. Danielle asked him in gentle tones to go get himself a first degree burn, and from her smile it seemed he was willing to go up in flames entirely for her sake.

'A sweet-talking guy,' she said, putting down the receiver. 'And he writes like a poet.' Her eyes were shining over the talent's talents, her mouth curving from his honey.

'Writes?' I said.

'Writes what he says on the news. All our news reporters write their own stuff.'

Another message came through from the royal gala: Devil-Boy, horns and all, was reported on his way to the theatre in a bell-ringing ambulance.

'Is he sick?' Danielle asked. 'If it's a stunt, make sure you catch it.' She disconnected, shrugging resignedly. 'The hip-wriggling imp of Satan will get double the oil fire exposure. Real hell stands no chance against the fake. Do you want to see the editing rooms?'

'Yes,' I said, and followed her across the large office and down a passage, admiring the neatness of her walk and wanting to put my hands deep into her cloud of dark hair, wanting to kiss her, wanting quite fiercely to take her to bed.

She said, 'I'll show you the studio first, it's more interesting,' and veered down a secondary passage towards a door warningly marked 'If red light shows, do not enter'. No red light shone. We went in. The room was moderate in size, furnished barely with a couple of armchairs, a coffee table, a television camera, a television set, a teleprompter and a silent coffee machine with paper cups. The only surprise was the window, through which one could see a stretch of the Thames and Hammersmith Bridge, all decked with lights and busily living.

'We do live interviews in here in front of the window,' Danielle said. 'Mostly politicians but also actors, authors, sportsmen, anyone in the news. Red buses go across the bridge in the background. It's impressive.'

'I'm sure,' I said.

She gave me a swift look. 'Am I boring you?'

'Absolutely not.'

She wore pink lipstick and had eyebrows like wings. Dark smiling eyes, creamy skin, long neck to hidden breasts like apples on a slender stem ... For Christ's sake, Kit, I thought, drag your mind off it and ask some sensible questions.

'How does your stuff get from here to America?' I said.

'From in here.' She walked over to a closed door in one of the walls, and opened it. Beyond it was another room, much smaller, dimly lit, which was warm and hummed faintly with walls of machines.

'This is the transmitter room,' she said. 'Everything goes from in here by satellite, but don't ask me how, we have a man with a haunted expression twiddling the knobs and we leave it to him.'

She closed the transmitter room door and we went through the studio, into the passage and back to the editing rooms, of which there were three.

'OK,' she said, switching a light on and revealing a small area walled on one side by three television screens, several video recorders and racks of tape cassettes, 'this is what we still use, though I'm told there's a load of new technology round the corner. Our guys here like these machines, so I guess we'll have them around for a while yet.'

'How do they work?' I asked.

'You run the unedited tape through on the left-hand screen and pick out the best bits, then you record just those on to the second tape, showing on the second screen. You can switch it all around until it looks good and you get a good feeling. We transmit it like that, but New York often cuts it shorter. Depends how much else they've got to fit in.'

'Can you work these machines yourself?' I asked.

'I'm slow. If you really want to know now, you can watch Joe later when we get the oil fire and Devil-Boy tapes – he's one of the best.'

'Great,' I said.

'I'm surprised you're so interested.'

'Well, I've some tapes I want to edit myself. It would be nice to learn how.'

'Is that why you came here so early?' She sounded as if I might say yes without at all offending her.

I said, 'Partly. Mostly to see you . . . and what you do.'

She was close enough to hug and I had no insight at all into what she was thinking. A brick wall between minds. Disconcerting.

She looked with friendliness but nothing else into my face, and the only thing I was sure of was that she didn't feel as I did about a little uninhibited love-making on the spot.

She asked if I would like to see the library and I said yes please: and the library turned out to be not books but rows and rows of recorded tapes, past years of news stories forgotten but waiting like bombs in the dark, records of things said, undeniable.

'Mostly used for obituaries,' Danielle said. 'Reactivated scandals. Things like that.'

We returned to her news desk, where over the next hour I sat and listened to the progress of events (Devil-Boy had arrived at the stage door, fit, well and fully made-up in a blaze of technicolor lights to the gratified hysterics of a streetful of fans) and met Danielle's working companions, the bureau chief, Joe the editor, the gaunt transmitter expert, two spare cameramen and a bored and unallocated female talent. About sixty people altogether worked for the bureau, Danielle said, but of course never all at one time. The day shift, from ten to six-thirty, was much bigger: in the daytime there were two to do her job.

At one o'clock Ed Cervano telephoned to say they'd gotten a whole load of spectacular shots of the oil fire but the blaze was now under control and the story was as dead as tomorrow's ashes.

'Bring back the tapes anyway,' Danielle said. 'We don't have any oil fire stock shots in the library.'

She put down the receiver resignedly. 'So it goes.'

The crew from the royal gala returned noisily bearing Devil-Boy's capers themselves, and at the same time a delivery man brought a stock of morning news-papers to put on Danielle's desk for her to look through for possible stories. The *Daily Flag*, as it happened, lay on top, and I opened it at Intimate Details to re-read Leggatt's words.

'What are you looking at?' Danielle asked.

I pointed. She read the apology and blinked.

'I didn't think you stood a chance,' she said frankly. 'Did they agree to the compensation also?'

'Not so far.'

'They'll have to,' she said. 'They've practically admitted liability.'

I shook my head. 'British courts don't award huge damages for libel. It's doubtful whether Bobby would actually win if he sued, and even if he won, unless the *Flag* was ordered to pay his costs, which also isn't certain, he simply couldn't afford the lawyers' fees.'

She gazed at me. 'Back home you don't pay the lawyers unless you win. Then the lawyers take their slice of the damages. Forty per cent, sometimes.'

'It's not like that here.'

Here, I thought numbly, one bargained with threats. On the one side: I'll get your wrist slapped by the Press Council, I'll get questions asked in Parliament, I'll see your ex-convict journalist back in the dock. And on the other, I'll slice your tendons, I'll lose you your jockey's licence for taking bribes, I'll put you in prison. Reviled, dishonoured, and with publicity, disgraced.

Catch me first, I thought.

CHAPTER FIFTEEN

I watched Joe the editor, dark-skinned and with rapid fingers, sort his way through a mass of noisy peacock footage, clicking his tongue as a sort of commentary to himself, punctuating the lifted sections he was stringing together to make the most flamboyant impact. Kaleidoscope arrival of Devil-Boy, earlier entrance of royals, wriggling release of new incomprehensible song.

'Thirty seconds,' he said, running through the finished sequence. 'Maybe they'll use it all, maybe they won't.'

'It looks good to me.'

'Thirty seconds is a long news item.' He took the spooled tape from the machine, put it into an already labelled box and handed it to the gaunt transmitter man, who was waiting to take it away. 'Danielle says you want to learn to edit, so what do you want to know?'

'Er . . . what these machines will do, for a start.'

'Quite a lot.' He fluttered his dark fingers over the banks of controls, barely touching them. 'They'll take any size tape, any make, and record on any other. You can bring the sound up, cut it out, transpose it, superimpose any sounds you like. You can put the sound from one tape on to the pictures of another, you can cut two tapes together so that it looks as if the people are talking to each other when they were recorded hours and miles apart, you can tell lies and goddam lies and put a false face on truth.'

'Anything else?'

'That about covers it.'

He showed me how to achieve some of his effects, but his speed confounded me.

'Have you got an actual tape you want to edit?' he asked finally.

'Yes, but I want to add to it first, if I can.'

He looked at me assessingly, a poised black man of perhaps my own age with a touch of humour in the eyes but a rarely smiling mouth. I felt untidy in my anorak beside his neat suit and cream shirt; also battered and sweaty and dim. It had been, I thought ruefully, too long a day.

'Danielle says you're OK,' he said surprisingly. 'I don't see why you can't ask the chief to rent you the use of this room some night we're not busy. You tell me what you want, and I'll edit your tapes for you, if you like.'

*

283

'Joe's a nice guy,' Danielle said, stretching lazily beside me in the rented Mercedes on her way home. 'Sure, if he said he'd edit your tape, he means it. He gets bored. He waited three hours tonight for the Devil-Boy slot. He loves editing. Has a passion for it. He wants to work in movies. He'll enjoy doing your tape.'

The bureau chief, solicited, had proved equally generous. 'If Joe's using the machines, go ahead.' He'd looked over to where Danielle was eyes down marking paragraphs in the morning papers. 'I had New York on the line this evening congratulating me on the upswing of our output recently. That's her doing. She says you're OK, you're OK.'

For her too it had been a long day.

'Towcester,' she said, yawning, 'seems light years back.'

'Mm,' I said. 'What did Princess Casilia say after you went in, when you got back to Eaton Square?'

Danielle looked at me with amusement. 'In the hall she told me that good manners were a sign of strength, and in the drawing room she asked if I thought you would really be fit for Ascot.'

'What did you say?' I asked, faintly alarmed.

'I said yes, you would.'

I relaxed. 'That's all right, then.'

'I did not say,' Danielle said mildly, 'that you were insane, but only that you didn't appear to notice when you'd been injured. Aunt Casilia said she thought this to be fairly typical of steeplechase jockeys.'

'I do notice,' I said.

'But?'

'Well . . . if I don't race, I don't earn. Almost worse, if I miss a race on a horse and it wins, the happy owner may put up that winning jockey the next time, so I can lose not just the one fee but maybe the rides on that horse for ever.'

She looked almost disappointed. 'So it's purely economic, this refusal to look filleted ribs in the face?'

'At least half.'

'And the rest?'

'What you feel for your job. What Joe feels for his. Much the same.'

She nodded, and after a pause said, 'Aunt Casilia wouldn't do that, though. Keep another jockey on, after you were fit again.'

'No, she never has. But your aunt is special.'

'She said,' Danielle said reflectively, 'that I wasn't to think of you as a jockey.'

'But I am.'

'That's what she said this morning on the way to Towcester.'

'Did she explain what she meant?'

'No. I asked her. She said something vague about essences.' She yawned. 'Anyway, this evening she told Uncle Roland all about those horrid men with knives, as she put it, and although he was scandalized and said she shouldn't get involved in such sordid brawls, she seemed quite serene and unaffected. She may look like porcelain, but she's quite tough. The more I get to know her, the more, to be honest, I adore her.'

The road from Chiswick to Eaton Square, clogged by day with stop-go traffic, was at two-fifteen in the morning regrettably empty. Red lights turned green at our approach and even sticking rigidly to the speed limit didn't much seem to lengthen the journey. We slid to a halt outside the princess's house far too soon.

Neither of us made a move to spring at once out of the car: we sat rather for a moment letting the day die in peace.

I said, 'I'll see you then, on Saturday.'

'Yes,' she sighed for no clear reason. 'I guess so.'

'You don't have to,' I said.

'Oh no,' she half laughed. 'I suppose I meant . . . Saturday's some way off.'

I took her hand. She let it lie in mine, passive, waiting.

'We might have,' I said, 'a lot of Saturdays.'

'Yes, we might.'

I leaned over and kissed her mouth, tasting her pink lipstick, feeling her breath on my cheek, sensing the tremble somewhere in her body. She neither drew back nor clutched forward, but kissed as I'd kissed, as an announcement, as a promise perhaps; as an invitation.

I sat away from her and smiled into her eyes, and then got out of the car and went round to open her door.

We stood briefly together on the pavement.

'Where are you sleeping?' she said. 'It's so late.'

'In a hotel.'

'Near here?'

'Less than a mile.'

'Good . . . you won't have far to drive.'

'No distance.'

'Goodnight, then,' she said.

'Goodnight.'

We kissed again, as before. Then, laughing, she turned away, walked across the pavement and let herself through the princess's porticoed front door with a latchkey: and I drove away thinking that if the princess had disapproved of her jockey making approaches to her niece, she would by now have let both of us know.

I slept like the dead for five hours, then rolled stiffly out of bed, blinked blearily at the heavy cold rain making a mess of the day, and pointed the Mercedes towards Bletchley.

The Golden Lion was warm and alive with the smells of breakfast, and I ate there while the desk processed my bill. Then I telephoned the AA for news of my car (ready Monday) and to Holly to check that the marked *Flag* copies had been delivered as promised (which they had: the feed-merchant had telephoned) and after that I packed all my gear into the car and headed straight back towards the hotel I'd slept in.

No problem, they said helpfully at reception, I could retain my present room for as long as I wanted, and yes, certainly, I could leave items in the strongroom for safe-keeping.

Upstairs I put Jay Erskine's Press Club pass and Owen Watts's credit cards into an envelope and wrote 'URGENT DELIVER TO MR LEGGATT IMMEDIATELY' in large letters on the outside. Then I put the video recordings and all of the journalists' other possessions, except their jackets, into one of the hotel's laundry bags, rolling it into a neat bundle which downstairs was fastened with sticky-tape and labelled before vanishing into the vault.

After that I drove to Fleet Street, parked where I shouldn't, ran through the rain to leave the envelope for Sam Leggatt at the *Flag* front desk, fielded the car from under the nose of a traffic warden, and went lightheartedly to Ascot.

It was a rotten afternoon there in many ways. Sleet fell almost ceaselessly, needle-sharp, ice-cold and slanting, soaking every jockey to the skin before the start and proving a blinding hazard thereafter. Goggles were useless, caked with flying mud; gloves slipped wetly on the reins; racing boots clung clammily to waterlogged feet. A day for gritting one's teeth and getting round safely, for meeting fences exactly right and not slithering along on one's nose on landing. Raw November at its worst.

The crowd was sparse, deterred before it started out by the visible downpour and the drenching forecast, and the few people standing in the open were huddled inside dripping coats looking like mushrooms with their umbrellas.

Holly and Bobby both came but wouldn't stay, arriving after I'd won the first race more by luck than inspiration, and leaving before the second. They took the money out of the money-belt, which I returned to the valet with thanks.

Holly hugged me. 'Three people telephoned, after I'd talked to you, to say they were pleased about the apology,' she said. 'They're offering credit again. It's made all the difference.'

'Take care how you go with running up bills,' I said.

'Of course we will. The bank manager haunts us.'

I said to Bobby, 'I borrowed some of that money. I'll repay it next week.'

'It's all yours, really.' He spoke calmly in friendship, but the life-force was again at a low ebb. No vigour. Too much apathy. Not what was needed.

Holly looked frozen and was shivering. 'Keep the baby warm,' I said. 'Go into the trainers' bar.'

'We're going home.' She kissed me with cold lips. 'We would stay to watch you, but I feel sick. I feel sick most of the time. It's the pits.'

Bobby put his arm round her protectively and took her away under a large umbrella, both of them leaning head down against the icy wind, and I felt depressed for them, and thought also of the risks that lay ahead, before they could be safe.

The princess had invited to her box the friends of hers that I cared for least, a quartet of aristocrats from her old country, and as always when they were there I saw little of her. With two of them she came in red oilskins down to the parade ring before the first of her two runners, smiling cheerfully through the freezing rain and asking what I thought of her chances, and with the other two she repeated the enquiry an hour and a half later.

In each case I said, 'Reasonable.' The first runner finished reasonably fourth, the second runner, second. Neither time did she come down to the unsaddling enclosure, for which one couldn't blame her, and nor did I go up to her box, partly because it was a perfunctory routine when those friends were there, but mostly on account of crashing to the ground on the far side of the course in the last race. By the time I got in and changed, she would be gone.

Oh well, I thought dimly, scraping myself up; six rides, one winner, one second, one fourth, two also-rans, one fall. You can't win four every day, old son. And nothing broken. Even the stitches had survived without leaking. I waited in the blowing sleet for the car to pick me up, and took off my helmet to let the water run through my hair, embracing in a way the wild day, feeling at home. Winter and horses, the old song in the blood.

There was no fruit cake left in the changing room.

'Rotten buggers,' I said.

'But you never eat cake,' my valet said, heaving off my sodden boots.

'Every so often,' I said, 'like on freezing wet Fridays after a fall in the last race.'

'There's some tea still. It's hot.'

I drank the tea, feeling the warmth slide down, heating from inside. There was always tea and fruit cake in the changing rooms; instant energy, instant comfort. Everyone ate cake now and then.

An official put his head through the door: someone to see you, he said.

I pulled on a shirt and shoes and went out to the door from the weighing room to the outside world. No one all day had appeared with a banker's draft from Pollgate, and I suppose I went out with an incredulous flicker of hope. Hope soon extinguished. It was only Dusty, huddled in the weighing room doorway, blue of face, eyes watering with cold.

'Is the horse all right?' I asked. 'I heard you caught him.'

'Yes. Useless bugger. What about you?'

'No damage. I got passed by the doctor. I'll be riding tomorrow.'

'Right, I'll tell the guv'nor. We'll be off, then. So long.'

'So long.'

He scurried away into the leaden early dusk, a small dedicated man who liked to check for himself after I'd fallen that I was in good enough shape to do his charges justice next time out. He had been known to advise Wykeham to stand me down. Wykeham had been known to take the advice. Passing Dusty was sometimes harder than passing the medics.

I showered and dressed and left the racecourse via the cheaper enclosures, walking from there into the darkening town, where I'd left the rented Mercedes in a public parking place in the morning. Maybe it was unlikely that a repeat ambush would be set in the nearly deserted jockeys' car park long after the last race, but I was taking no chances. I climbed unmolested into the Mercedes and drove in safety to London.

There in my comfortable bolthole I again made additions to my astronomical phone bill, arranging first for my obliging neighbour to go into my cottage in the morning and pack one of my suits and some shirts and other things into a suitcase.

'Of course I will, Kit dear, but I thought you'd be back here for sure tonight, after riding at Ascot.'

'Staying with friends,' I said. 'I'll get someone to pick up the suitcase from your place tomorrow morning to take it to Ascot. Would that be all right?'

'Of course, dear.'

I persuaded another jockey who lived in Lambourn to collect the case and bring it with him, and he said sure he would, if he remembered.

I telephoned Wykeham when I judged he'd be indoors after his evening tour of the horses and told him his winner had been steadfast, the princess's two as good as could be hoped for, and one of the also-rans disappointing.

'And Dusty says you made a clear balls-up of the hurdle down by Swinley Bottom in the last.'

'Yeah,' I said. 'If Dusty can see clearly half a mile through driving sleet in poor light he's got better eyesight than I thought.'

'Er . . .' Wykeham said. 'What happened?'

'The one in front fell. Mine went down over him. He wouldn't have won, if that's any consolation. He was beginning to tire already, and he was hating the weather.'

Wykeham grunted assent. 'He's a sun-lover, true-bred. Kit, tomorrow there's Inchcape for the princess in the big race and he's in grand form, jumping out of his skin, improved a mile since you saw him last week.'

'Inchcape,' I said resignedly, 'is dead.'

'What? Did I say Inchcape? No, not Inchcape. What's the princess's horse?'

'Icefall.'

'Icicle's full brother,' he said, not quite making it a question.

'Yes.'

'Of course.' He cleared his throat. 'Icefall. Naturally. He should win, Kit, seriously.'

'Will you be there?' I asked. 'I half expected you today.'

'In that weather?' He sounded surprised. 'No, no, Dusty and you and the princess, you'll do fine.'

293

'But you've had a whole bunch of winners this week and you haven't seen one of them.'

'I see them here in the yard. I see them on video tapes. You tell Inchcape he's the greatest, and he'll jump Ben Nevis.'

'All right,' I said. Icefall, Inchcape, what did it matter?

'Good. Great. Goodnight, Kit.'

'Goodnight, Wykeham,' I said.

I got through to my answering machine and collected the messages, one of which was from Eric Olderjohn, the civil servant owner of the horse I'd won on for the Lambourn trainer at Towcester.

I called him back without delay at the London number he'd given, and caught him, it seemed, on the point of going out.

'Oh, Kit, yes. Look, I suppose you're in Lambourn?'

'No, actually. In London.'

'Really? That's fine. I've something you might be interested to see, but I can't let it out of my hands.' He paused for thought. 'Would you be free this evening after nine?'

'Yes,' I said.

'Right. Come round to my house, I'll be back by then.' He gave me directions to a street south of Sloane Square, not more than a mile from where I was staying. 'Coffee and brandy, right? Got to run. Bye.'

He disconnected abruptly and I put down my own receiver more slowly saying 'Wow' to myself silently. I hadn't expected much action from Eric Olderjohn, civil servant, and certainly none with such speed.

I sat for a while thinking of the tape of Maynard, and of the list of companies at the end, of those who had suffered from Maynard's philanthropy. Short of finding somewhere to replay the tape, I would have to rely on memory, and the only name I could remember for certain was Purfleet Electronics; chiefly because I'd spent a summer sailing holiday with a schoolfriend there long ago.

Purfleet Electronics, directory enquiries told me, was not listed.

I sucked my teeth a bit and reflected that the only way to find things was to look in the right place. I would go to Purfleet, as to Hitchin, in the morning.

I filled in the evening with eating and more phone calls, and by nine had walked down Sloane Street and found Eric Olderjohn's house. It was narrow, two storeys, one of a long terrace built for low-income early Victorians, now inhabited by the affluent as pieds-à-terre: or so Eric Olderjohn affably told me, opening his dark green front door and waving me in.

From the street one stepped straight into the sitting room, which stretched from side to side of the house; all of four metres. The remarkably small space glowed with pinks and light greens, textured trellised wall-paper, swagged satin curtains, round tables with skirts, china birds, silver photograph frames, fat buttoned arm-chairs, Chinese creamy rugs on the floor. There were softly glowing lamps, and the trellised wallpaper covered the ceiling also, enclosing the crowded contents in an impression of a summer grotto.

My host watched my smile of appreciation as if the reaction were only what he would have expected.

'It's great,' I said.

'My daughter did it.'

'The one you would defend from the *Flag*?'

'My only daughter. Yes. Sit down. Has it stopped raining? You'd like a brandy, I dare say?' He moved the one necessary step to a silver tray of bottles on one of the round tables and poured cognac into two modest balloon glasses. 'I've set some coffee ready. I'll just fetch it. Sit down, do.' He vanished through a rear door camouflaged by trellis and I looked at the photographs in the frames, seeing a well-groomed young woman who might be his daughter, seeing the horse that he owned, with myself on its back.

He returned with another small tray, setting it alongside the first.

'My daughter,' he said, nodding, as he saw I'd been looking. 'She lives here part of the time, part with her mother.' He shrugged. 'One of those things.'

'I'm sorry.'

'Yes. Well, it happens. Coffee?' He poured into two small cups and handed me one. 'Sugar? No, I suppose not. Sit down. Here's the brandy.'

He was neat in movement as in dress, and I found myself thinking 'dapper'; but there was purposefulness there under the surface, the developed faculty of getting things done. I sat in one of the armchairs with coffee and brandy beside me, and he sat also, and sipped, and looked at me over his cup.

'You were in luck,' he said finally. 'I put out a few feelers this morning and was told a certain person might be lunching at his club.' He paused. 'I was sufficiently interested in your problem to arrange for a friend of mine to meet and sound out that person, whom he knows well, and their conversation was, one might say, fruitful. As a result I myself went to a certain person's office this afternoon, and the upshot of that meeting was some information which I'll presently show you.'

His care over the choice of words was typical, I supposed, of the stratosphere of the civil service: the wheeler-dealers in subtlety, obliqueness and not saying quite what one meant. I never discovered the exact identity of the certain person, on the basis no doubt that it wasn't something I needed to know, and in view of what he'd allowed me a sight of, I could scarcely complain.

'I have some letters,' Eric Olderjohn said. 'More precisely, photocopies of letters. You can read them, but I am directly commanded not to let you take them away. I have to return them on Monday. Is all that ... er ... quite clear?'

'Yes,' I said.

'Good.'

Without haste he finished his coffee and put down

the cup. Then, raising the skirt of the table which bore the trays, he bent and brought out a brown leather attaché case, which he rested on his knees. He snapped open the locks, raised the lid and paused again.

'They're interesting,' he said, frowning.

I waited.

As if coming to a decision which until that moment he had left open, he drew a single sheet of paper out of the case and passed it across.

The letter had been addressed to the Prime Minister and had been sent in September from a company which made fine china for export. The chairman, who had written the letter, explained that he and the other directors were unanimous in suggesting some signal honour for Mr Maynard Allardeck, in recognition of his great and patriotic services to industry.

Mr Allardeck had come generously to the aid of the historic company, and thanks entirely to his efforts the jobs of two hundred and fifty people had been saved. The skills of many of these people were priceless and included the ability to paint and gild porcelain to the world's highest standards. The company was now exporting more than before and was looking forward to the brightest of futures.

The board would like to propose a knighthood for Mr Allardeck.

I finished reading and looked over at Eric Olderjohn.

'Is this sort of letter normal?' I asked.

'Entirely.' He nodded. 'Most awards are the result

of recommendations to the Prime Minister's office. Anyone can suggest anyone for anything. If the cause seems just, an award is given. The patronage people draw up a list of awards they deem suitable, and the list is passed to the Prime Minister for approval.'

I said, 'So all these people in the honours lists who get medals ... firefighters, music teachers, postmen, people like that, it's because their mates have written in to suggest it?'

'Er, yes. More often their employers, but sometimes their mates.'

He produced a second letter from his briefcase and handed it over. This one also was from an exporting company and stressed Maynard's invaluable contributions to worthwhile industry, chief among them the saving of very many jobs in an area of great local unemployment.

It was impossible to overestimate Mr Allardeck's services to his country in industry, and the firm unreservedly recommended that he should be offered a knighthood.

'Naturally,' I said, 'the patronage people checked that all this was true?'

'Naturally,' Eric Olderjohn said.

'And of course it was?'

'I am assured so. The certain person with whom I talked this afternoon told me that occasionally, if they receive six or seven similar letters all proposing someone unknown to the general public, they may begin to suspect that the person is busily proposing himself by persuading his friends to write in. The writers of the two letters I've shown you were specifically asked, as their recommendations were so similar, if Maynard himself had suggested they write. Each of them emphatically denied any such thing.'

'Mm,' I said. 'Well they would, wouldn't they, if they stood to gain from Maynard for his knighthood.'

'That's a thoroughly scurrilous remark.'

'So it is,' I said cheerfully. 'And your certain person, did he put Maynard down for his Sir?'

He nodded. 'Provisionally. To be considered. Then they received a third letter, emphasizing substantial philanthropy that they already knew about, and the question mark was erased. Maynard Allardeck was definitely in line for his K. The letter inviting him to accept the honour was drafted, and would have been sent out in about ten days from now, at the normal time for the New Year's list.'

'Would have been?' I said.

'Would have been.' He smiled twistedly. 'It is not now considered appropriate, as a result of the stories in the *Daily Flag* and the opinion page in the *Towncrier*.'

'Rose Quince,' I said.

He looked uncomprehending.

'She wrote the piece in the *Towncrier*,' I said.

'Oh . . . yes.'

'Would your, er, certain person,' I asked, 'really take notice of those bits in the newspapers?'

'Oh, definitely. Particularly as in each case the paragraphs were delivered by hand to his office, outlined in red.'

'They weren't!'

Eric Olderjohn raised an eyebrow. 'That means something to you?' he asked.

I explained about the tradespeople and the owners all receiving similarly marked copies.

'There you are, then. A thorough job of demolition. Nothing left to chance.'

'You mentioned a third letter,' I said. 'The clincher.'

He peered carefully into his case and produced it. 'This one may surprise you,' he said.

The third letter was not from a commercial firm but from a charitable organization with a list of patrons that stretched half the way down the left side of the page. The recipients of the charity appeared to be the needy dependants of dead or disabled public servants. Widows, children, the old and the sick.

'How do you define a public servant?' I asked.

'The Civil Service, from the top down.'

Maynard Allardeck, the letter reported, had worked tirelessly over several years to improve the individual lives of those left in dire straits through no fault of their own. He unstintingly poured out his own fortune in aid, besides giving his time and extending a high level of compassionate ongoing care to families in need. The charitable organization said it would itself feel honoured if the reward of a knighthood should be given to one of its most stalwart pillars: to the man they had unanimously chosen to be their next chairman, the appointment to be effective from 1 December of that year.

The letter had been signed by no fewer than four of the charity's officers: the retiring chairman, the head of the board of management, and two of the senior patrons. It was the fourth of these signatures which had me lifting my head in astonishment.

'Well?' Eric Olderjohn asked, watching.

'That's odd,' I said blankly.

'Yes, curious, I agree.'

He held out his hand for the letters, took them from me, snapped them safely back into his case. I sat with thoughts tumbling over themselves and unquestioned assumptions melting like wax.

Was it true, I had wanted to know, if Maynard Allardeck was being considered for a knighthood, and if so, who knew?

The people who had proposed him; they knew.

The letter from the charity, dated 1 October, had been signed by Lord Vaughnley.

CHAPTER SIXTEEN

'Why,' I said, 'did your certain person allow you to show these letters to me?'

'Ah.' Eric Olderjohn joined his fingers together in a steeple and studied them for a while. 'Why do you think?'

'I would suppose,' I said, 'he might think it possible I would stir up a few ponds, get a few muddy answers, without him having to do it himself.'

Eric Olderjohn switched his attention from his hands to my face. 'Something like that,' he said. 'He would like to know for sure Maynard Allardeck isn't just the victim of a hate campaign, for instance. He wants to do him justice. To put him back on the list, perhaps, for a knighthood next time around, in the summer.'

'He wants proof?' I asked.

'Can you supply it?'

'Yes, I think so.'

'What are you planning to do,' he asked with dry humour, 'when you have to give up race-riding?'

'Jump off a cliff, I dare say.'

I stood up, and he also. I thanked him sincerely for the trouble he'd taken. He said he would expect me to win again on his horse next time out. Do my best, I said, and took a last appreciative glance round his bower of a sitting room before making my way back to the hotel.

Lord Vaughnley, I thought.

On 1 October he had recommended Maynard for a knighthood. By the end of that month or the beginning of November there had been a tap on Bobby's telephone.

The tap had been installed by Jay Erskine, who had listened for two weeks and then written the articles in the *Flag*.

Jay Erskine had once worked for Lord Vaughnley, as crime reporter on the *Towncrier*.

But if Lord Vaughnley had got Jay Erskine to attack Maynard Allardeck, why was Nestor Pollgate so aggressive?

Because he didn't want to have to pay compensation, or to admit his paper had done wrong.

Well . . . perhaps.

I went round in circles and came back always to the central and unexpected question: Was it really Lord Vaughnley who had prompted the attacks, and if so, why?

From my hotel room I telephoned Rose Quince's home, catching her again soon after she had come in.

'Bill?' she said. 'Civil Service charity? Oh, sure, he's

a patron of dozens of things. All sorts. Keeps him in touch, he says.'

'Mm,' I said. 'When you wrote that piece about Maynard Allardeck, did he suggest it?'

'Who? Bill? Yes, sure he did. He put the clippings from the *Flag* on my desk and said it looked my sort of thing. I may know him from way back, but he's still the ultimate boss. When he wants something written, it gets written. Martin, our big white chief, always agrees to that.'

'And, er, how did you get on to the *How's Trade* interview? I mean, did you see the programme when it was broadcast?'

'Do me a favour. Of course not.' She paused. 'Bill suggested I try the television company, to ask for a private re-run.'

'Which you did.'

'Yes, of course. Look,' she demanded, 'what's all this about? Bill often suggests subjects to me. There's nothing strange in it.'

'No,' I said. 'Sleep well, Rose.'

'And goodnight to you, too.'

I slept soundly and long, and early in the morning took the video camera and drove to Purfleet along the flat lands just north of the Thames estuary. The rains of the day before had drawn away, leaving the sky washed and pale, and there were seagulls wheeling high over the low-tide mud.

I asked in about twenty places, post office and shops,

before I found anyone who had heard of Purfleet Electronics, but was finally pointed towards someone who had worked there. 'You want George Tarker... he owned it,' he said.

Following a few further instructions from helpful locals, I eventually pulled up beside a shabby old wooden boatshed optimistically emblazoned with a signboard saying 'George Tarker Repairs All'.

Out of the car and walking across the pot-holed entrance yard to the door one could see that the sign had once had a bottom half, which had split off and was lying propped against the wall, and which read 'Boats and Marine Equipment'.

With a sinking feeling of having come entirely to the wrong place I pushed open the rickety door and stepped straight into the untidiest office in the world, a place where every surface and every shelf was covered with unidentifiable lumps of ships' hardware in advanced age, and where every patch of wall was occupied by ancient calendars, posters, bills and instructions, all attached not by drawing pins but by nails.

In a sagging old chair, oblivious to the mess, sat an elderly grey-bearded man with his feet up on a desk, reading a newspaper and drinking from a cup.

'Mr Tarker?' I said.

'That's me.' He lowered the paper, looking at me critically from over the soles of his shoes. 'What do you want repaired?' He looked towards the bag I was carrying which contained the camera. 'A bit off a boat?'

'I'm afraid I've come to the wrong place,' I said. 'I was looking for Mr George Tarker who used to own Purfleet Electronics.'

He put his cup down carefully on the desk, and his feet on the floor. He was old, I saw, from an inner weariness as much as from age: it lay in the sag of his shoulders and the droop of his eyes and shouted from the disarray of everything around him.

'That George Tarker was my son,' he said.

Was.

'I'm sorry,' I said.

'Do you want anything repaired, or don't you?'

'No,' I said. 'I want to talk about Maynard Allardeck.'

The cheeks fell inwards into shadowed hollows and the eyes seemed to recede darkly into the sockets. He had scattered grey hair, uncombed, and below the short beard, in the thin neck inside the unbuttoned and tieless shirt, the tendons tightened and began to quiver.

'I don't want to distress you,' I said: but I had. 'I'm making a film about the damage Maynard Allardeck has done to many people's lives. I hoped you ... I hoped your son ... might help me.' I gestured vaguely with one hand. 'I know it wouldn't sway you one way or another, but I'm offering a fee.'

He was silent, staring at my face but seeing, I thought, another scene altogether, looking back into memory and finding it almost past bearing. The strain in his face deepened to the point when I did actively regret having come.

'Will it destroy him, your film?' he said huskily.

'In some ways, yes.'

'He deserves hellfire and damnation.'

I took the video camera out of its bag and showed it to him, explaining about talking straight at the lens.

'Will you tell me what happened to your son?' I asked.

'Yes, I will.'

I balanced the camera on a heap of junk and started it running; and with few direct questions from me he repeated in essence the familiar story. Maynard had come smiling to the rescue in a temporary cash crisis caused by a rapid expansion of the business. He had lent at low rates, but at the last and worst moment demanded to be repaid; had taken over the firm and ousted George Tarker, and after a while had stripped the assets, sold the freehold and put the workforce on the dole.

'Charming,' George Tarker said. 'That's what he was. Like a con man, right to the end. Reasonable. Friendly. Then he was gone, and everything with him. My son's business, gone. He started it when he was only eighteen and worked and worked . . . and after twenty-three years it was growing too fast.'

The gaunt face stared starkly into the lens, and water stood in the corner of each eye.

'My son George . . . my only child . . . he blamed himself for everything . . . for all his workers losing their jobs. He began to drink. He knew such a lot about electricity.' The tears spilled over the lower eyelids and rolled down the lined cheeks to be lost in the beard. 'My son wired himself up . . . and hit the switch . . .'

The voice stopped as if with the jolt that had stopped his son's heart. I found it unbearable. I wished with an intensity of pity that I hadn't come. I turned off the camera and stood there in silence, not knowing how to apologize for such an intrusion.

He brushed the tears away with the back of his hand. 'Two years ago, just over,' he said. 'He was a good man, you know, my son George. That Allardeck . . . just destroyed him.'

I offered him the same amount that I'd given the Perrysides, setting it down in front of him on the desk. He stared at the flat bunch of banknotes for a while, and then pushed it towards me.

'I didn't tell you for money,' he said. 'You take it back. I told you for George.'

I hesitated.

'Go on,' he said. 'I don't want it. Doesn't feel right. Any time you have a boat, you pay me then for repairs.'

'All right,' I said.

He nodded and watched while I picked up the notes.

'You make your film good,' he said. 'Make it for George.'

'Yes,' I said; and he was still sitting there, staring with pain into the past, when I left.

I went to Ascot with the same precautions as before, leaving the Mercedes down in the town and walking into the racecourse from the opposite direction to the jockeys' official car park. No one that I could see took any notice of my arrival, beyond the gatemen with their usual good mornings.

I had rides in the first five of the six races; two for the princess, two others for Wykeham, one for the Lambourn trainer. Dusty reported Wykeham to have a crippling migraine headache which would keep him at home watching on television. Icefall, Dusty said, should zoom in, and all the lads had staked their wages. Dusty's manner to me was as usual a mixture of deference and truculence, a double attitude I had long ago sorted into components: I might do the actual winning for the stable, but the fitness of the horses was the gift of the lads in the yard, and I wasn't to forget it. Dusty and I had worked together for ten years in a truce founded on mutual need, active friendship being neither sought nor necessary. He said the guv'nor wanted me to give the princess and the other owners his regrets about his headache. I'd tell them, I said.

I rode one of Wykeham's horses in the first race with negligible results, and came third in the second race, for the Lambourn trainer. The third race was

Icefall for the princess, and she and Danielle were both waiting in the parade ring, rosily lunched and sparkling-eyed, when I went out there to greet them.

'Wykeham sends his regrets,' I said.

'The poor man.' The princess believed in the migraines as little as I did, but was willing to pretend. 'Will we give him a win to console him?'

'I'm afraid he expects it.'

We watched Icefall walk round, grey and well muscled under his coroneted rug, more compact than his full brother Icicle.

'I schooled him last week,' I said. 'Wykeham says he's come on a ton since then. So there's hope.'

'Hope!' Danielle said. 'He's hot favourite.'

'Odds on,' nodded the princess. 'It never makes one feel better.'

She and I exchanged glances of acknowledgement of the extra pressure that came with too much expectation, and when I went off to mount she said only, 'Get round safely, that's all.'

Icefall at six was at the top of his hurdling form with a string of successes behind him, and his race on that day was a much publicized, much sponsored two-mile event which had cut up, as big-prize races tended occasionally to do, into no more than six runners: Icefall at the top of the handicap, the other five at the bottom, the centre block having decided to duck out for less taxing contests.

Icefall was an easy horse to ride, as willing as his

brother and naturally courageous, and the only foreseeable problem was the amount of weight he carried
in relation to the others: twenty pounds and more.
Wykeham never liked his horses to be front runners
and had tried to dissuade me sometimes from running
Icefall in that way; but the horse positively preferred
it and let me know it at every start, and even with the
weights so much against us, when the tapes went up
we were there where he wanted to be, setting the pace.

I'd learned in my teens from an American flat-race
jockey how to start a clock in my head, to judge the
speed of each section of the race against the clock, and
to judge how fast I could go in each section in order to
finish at or near the horse's own best time for the
distance.

Icefall's best time for two miles at Ascot at almost
the same weights on the same sort of wet ground was
three minutes forty-eight seconds, and I set out to take
him to the finish line in precisely that period, and at a
more or less even speed the whole way.

It seemed to the crowd on the stands, I was told
afterwards, that I'd set off too fast, that some of the
lightweights would definitely catch me; but I'd looked
up their times also in the form book, and none of them
had ever completed two miles as fast as I aimed to.

All Icefall had to do was jump with perfection, and
that he did, informing me of his joy in mid-air at every
hurdle. The lightweights never came near us, and we
finished ahead, without slackening, by eight lengths, a

margin that would do Icefall's handicap no good at all next time out.

Maybe, I thought, pulling up and patting the grey neck hugely, it would have been better for the future not to have won by so far, but the present was what mattered, and with those weights one couldn't take risks.

The princess was flushed and laughing and delighted, and as usual intensified my own pleasure in winning. Victories for glum and grumbling owners were never so sweet.

'My friends say it's sacrilege,' she said, 'for a top-weight to set off so fast and try to make all the running after rain like yesterday's. They were pitying me up in the box, telling me you were mad.'

I smiled at her, unbuckling my saddle. 'When he jumps like today, he can run this course even on wet gound in three minutes forty-eight seconds. That's what we did, more or less.'

Her eyes widened. 'You planned it! You didn't tell me. I didn't expect you to go off so fast, even though he likes it in front.'

'If he'd made a hash of any of the hurdles, I'd have looked a right idiot.' I patted the grey neck over and over. 'He understands racing,' I said. 'He's a great horse to ride. Very generous. He enjoys it.'

'You talk as if horses were people,' Danielle said, standing behind her aunt, listening.

'Yes, they are,' I said. 'Not human, but individuals, all different.'

I took the saddle in and sat on the scales, and changed into other colours and weighed out again for the next race. Then put the princess's colours back on, on top of the others, and went out bareheaded for the sponsors' presentations.

Lord Vaughnley was among the crowd round the sponsors' table of prizes, and he came straight over to me when I went out.

'My dear chap, what a race! I thought you'd gone off your rocker, I'm sorry to say. Now, you are coming to our box, aren't you? Like we agreed?'

He was a puzzle. His grey eyes smiled blandly in the big face, full of friendliness, empty of guile.

'Yes,' I said. 'Thank you. After the fifth race, when I'll have finished for the day, if that's all right?'

Lady Vaughnley appeared at his elbow, reinforcing the invitation. 'Delighted to have you. Do come.'

The princess, overhearing, said, 'Come along to me after,' taking my compliance for granted, not expecting an answer. 'Did you know,' she said with humour, 'the time Icefall took?'

'No, not yet.'

'Three minutes forty-nine seconds.'

'We were one second late.'

'Yes, indeed. Next time, go faster.'

Lady Vaughnley looked at her in astonishment.

'How can you say that?' she protested, and then understood it was merely a joke. 'Oh. For a moment . . .'

The princess patted her arm consolingly, and I watched Danielle, on the far side of the green-baized pot-laden table, talking to the sponsors as to the winning habit born. She turned her head and looked straight at me, and I felt the tingle of that visual connection run right down my spine. She's beautiful, I thought. I want her in bed.

It seemed that she had broken off in the middle of whatever she was saying. The sponsor spoke to her enquiringly. She looked at him blankly, and then with another glance at me seemed to sort out her thoughts and answer whatever he'd asked.

I looked down at the trophies, afraid that my feelings were naked. I had two races and a lot of box-talk to get through before we could be in any real way together, and the memory of her kisses was no help.

The presentations were made, the princess and the others melted away, and I peeled off the princess's colours and went out and rode another winner for Wykeham, scrambling home that time by a neck, all elbows, no elegance, practically throwing the horse ahead of himself, hard on him, squeezing him, making him stretch beyond where he thought he could go.

'Bloody hell,' said his owner, in the winners' unsaddling area. 'Bloody hell, I'd not like you on my back.' He seemed pleased enough all the same, a Sussex farmer, big and forthright, surrounded by chattering friends. 'You're a bloody demon, lad, that's what you are. Hard as bloody nails. He'll know he's had a race, I'll tell you.'

'Yes, well, Mr Davis, he can take it, he's tough, he'd not thank you to be soft. Like his owner, wouldn't you say, Mr Davis?'

He gave a great guffaw and clapped me largely on the shoulder, and I went and weighed in, and changed into the princess's colours again for the fifth race.

The princess's runner, Allegheny, was the second of her only two mares (Bernina being the other), as the princess, perhaps because of her own femininity, had a definite preference for male horses. Not as temperamental as Bernina, Allegheny was a friendly old pudding, running moderately well always but without fire. I'd tried to get Wykeham to persuade the princess to sell her but he wouldn't: Princess Casilia, he said, knew her own mind.

Allegheny's seconds, thirds, fourths, fifths, sixths, also-rans never seemed to disappoint her. It wasn't essential to her, he said, for all her children to be stars.

Allegheny and I set off amicably but as usual my attempts to jolly her into *joie de vivre* got little response. We turned into the straight for the first time lying fourth, going easily, approaching a plain fence, meeting it right, launching into the air, landing, accelerating away . . .

In one of her hind legs a suspensory ligament tore apart at the fetlock, and Allegheny went lame in three strides, all rhythm gone; like driving a car on a suddenly flat tyre. I pulled her up and jumped off her back, and walked her a few paces to make sure she hadn't broken a bone.

Just the tendon, I thought in relief. Bad enough, but not a death sentence. Losing a horse to the bolt of a humane killer upset everyone for days. Wykeham had wept sometimes for dead horses, and I also, and the princess. One couldn't help it, sometimes.

The vet sped round in his car, looked her over and pronounced her fit to walk, so I led her back up the course, her head nodding every time she put the injured foot to the ground. The princess and Danielle came down anxiously to the unsaddling area and Dusty assured them the guv'nor would get a vet to Allegheny as soon as possible.

'What do you think?' the princess asked me in depression, as Dusty and the mare's lad led her, nodding, away.

'I don't know.'

'Yes, you do. Tell me.'

The princess's eyes were deep blue. I said, 'She'll be a year off the racecourse, at least.'

She sighed. 'Yes, I suppose so.'

'You could patch her up,' I said, 'and sell her as a brood mare. She's got good blood lines. She could breed in the spring.'

'Oh!' She seemed pleased. 'I'm fond of her, you know.'

317

'Yes, I know.'

'I do begin to see,' Danielle said, 'what racing is all about.'

My neighbour and the Lambourn fellow jockey having come up trumps in the matter of a suitcase of clothes, I went up to Lord Vaughnley's box in a change for the better. I appeared to have chosen, though, the doldrums of time between events when everyone had gone down to look at the horses or to bet, and not yet returned to watch the race.

There was only one person in there, standing nervously beside the table now laid for tea, shifting from foot to foot: and I was surprised to see it was Hugh Vaughnley, Lord Vaughnley's son.

'Hello,' I said. 'No one's here ... I'll come back.'

'Don't go.'

His voice was urgent. I looked at him curiously, thinking of the family row which had so clearly been in operation on the previous Saturday, seeing only trouble still in the usually cheerful face. Much thinner than his father, more like his mother in build, he had neat features well placed, two disarming dimples, and youth still in the indecision of his mouth. Around nineteen, I thought. Maybe twenty. Not more.

'I ... er ...' he said. 'Do stay. I want someone here, to be honest, when they come back.'

'Do you?'

'Er...' he said. 'They don't know I'm here. I mean ... Dad might be furious, and he can't be, can he, in front of strangers? That's why I came here, to the races. I mean, I know you're not a stranger, but you know what I mean.'

'Your mother will surely be glad to see you.'

He swallowed. 'I hate quarrelling with them. I can't bear it. To be honest, Dad threw me out almost a month ago. He's making me live with Saul Bradley, and I can't bear it much longer, I want to go home.'

'He threw you out?' I must have sounded as surprised as I felt. 'You always seemed such a solid family. Does he think you should stand on your own two feet? Something like that?'

'Nothing like that. I just wish it was. I did something ... I didn't know he'd be so desperately angry ... not really ...'

I didn't want to hear what it was, with so much else on my mind.

'Drugs?' I said, without sympathy.

'What?'

'Did you take drugs?'

I saw from his face that it hadn't been that. He was simply bewildered by the suggestion.

'I mean,' he said plaintively, 'he thought so much of him. He said so. I mean, I thought he approved of him.'

'Who?' I said.

He looked over my shoulder however and didn't answer, a fresh wave of anxiety blotting out all else.

I turned. Lord and Lady Vaughnley had come through the door from the passage and were advancing towards us. I saw their expressions with clarity when they caught sight of their son. Lady Vaughnley's face lifted into a spontaneous uncomplicated smile.

Lord Vaughnley looked from his son to myself, and his reaction wasn't forgiveness, apathy, irritation or even anger.

It was alarm. It was horror.

CHAPTER SEVENTEEN

He recovered fast to some extent. Lady Vaughnley put her arms around Hugh and hugged him, and her husband looked on, stony-faced and displeased. Others of their guests came in good spirits back to the box, and Hugh was proved right to the extent that his father was not ready to fight with him in public.

Lord Vaughnley, in fact, addressed himself solely to me, fussing about cups of tea and making sure I talked no more to his son, seemingly unaware that his instant reaction and his current manner were telling me a good deal more than he probably meant.

'There we are,' he said heartily, getting a waitress to pass me a cup. 'Milk? Sugar? No? Princess Casilia's mare is all right, isn't she? So sad when a horse breaks down in a race. Sandwich?'

I said the mare wouldn't race again, and no thanks to the sandwich.

'Hugh been bothering you with his troubles, has he?' he said.

'Not really.'

'What did he say?'

I glanced at the grey eyes from where the blandness had flown and watchfulness taken over.

'He said he had quarrelled with you and wanted to make it up.'

'Hmph.' An unforgiving noise from a compressed mouth. 'As long as he didn't bother you?'

'No.'

'Good. Good. Then you'll be wanting to talk to Princess Casilia, eh? Let me take your cup. Good of you to come up. Yes. Off you go, then. Can't keep her waiting.'

Short of rudeness I couldn't have stayed, and rudeness at that point, I thought, would accomplish no good that I could think of. I went obediently along to the princess's well-populated box and drank more tea and averted my stomach from another sandwich, and tried not to look too much at Danielle.

'You're abstracted,' the princess said. 'You are not here.'

'I was thinking of Lord Vaughnley... I just came from his box.'

'Such a nice man.'

'Mm.'

'And for Danielle, this evening, what are your plans?'

I shut out the thoughts of what I would like. If I could read the princess's mind, she could also on occasion read mine.

'I expect we'll talk, and eat, and I'll bring her home.'

She patted my arm. She set me to talk to her guests, most of whom I knew, and I worked my way round to Danielle scattering politeness like confetti.

'Hi,' she said. 'Am I going back with Aunt Casilia, or what?'

'Coming with me from here, if you will.'

'OK.'

We went out on to the balcony with everyone else to watch the sixth race, and afterwards said goodbye correctly to the princess and left.

'Where are we going?' Danielle asked.

'For a walk, for a drink, for dinner. First of all we're walking to Ascot town, where I left the car, so as not to be carved up again in the car park.'

'You're too much,' she said.

I collected my suitcase from the changing room and we walked down through the cheaper enclosures to the furthest gate, and from there again safely to the rented Mercedes.

'I guess I never gave a thought to it happening again,' she said.

'And next time there would be no princess to the rescue.'

'Do you seriously think they'd be lying in wait?'

'I still have what they wanted.' And I'd twisted their tail fiercely, besides. 'I just go where they don't know I'm going, and hope.'

'Yes, but,' she said faintly, 'for how long?'

'Um,' I said, 'I suppose Joe doesn't work on Sundays?'

'No. Not till Monday night, like me. Not weekends. What's that got to do with how long?'

'Tuesday or Wednesday,' I said.

'You're not making much sense.'

'It's because I don't know for sure.' We got into the car and I started the engine. 'I feel like a juggler. Half a dozen clubs in the air and all likely to fall in a heap.'

'With you underneath?'

'Not,' I said, 'if I can help it.'

I drove not very fast to Henley, and stopped near a telephone box to try to reach Rose Quince, who was out. She had an answering machine which invited me to give a number for her to call back. I would try later, I said.

Henley-on-Thames was bright with lights and late Saturday afternoon shopping. Danielle and I left the car in a parking place and walked slowly along in the bustle.

'Where are we going?' she asked.

'To buy you a present.'

'What present?'

'Anything you'd like.'

She stopped walking. 'Are you crazy?'

'No.' We were outside a shop selling sport goods. 'Tennis racket?'

'I don't play tennis.'

I waved at the next shop along. 'Piano?'

'I can't play a piano.'

'Over there,' I pointed at a flower shop. 'Orchids?'

'In their place, but not to pin on me.'

'And over there, an antique chair?'

She laughed, her eyes crinkling. 'Tell me, too, what you like, and what you don't.'

'All right.'

We walked along the shopfronts, looking and telling. She liked blues and pinks but not yellow, she liked things with flowers and birds on, not geometric patterns, she liked baskets and nylon-tipped pens and aquamarines and seedless grapes and books about Leonardo da Vinci. She would choose for me, she said, something simple. If I were giving her a present, I would have to have one as well.

'OK,' I said. 'Twenty minutes. Meet me back at the car. Here's the key, in case you get there first.'

'And not expensive,' she said, 'or I'm not playing.'

'All right.'

When I returned with my parcel she was sitting in the car already, and smiling.

'You've been half an hour,' she said. 'You're disqualified.'

'Too bad.'

I climbed into the car beside her and we sat looking at each other's packages, mine to her in brown paper, hers to me flatter, in a carrier bag.

'Guess,' she said.

I tried to, and nothing came. I said with regret, 'I don't know.'

She eyed the brown-wrapped parcel in my hands. 'Three books? Three pounds of chocolates? A jack-in-a-box?'

'All wrong.'

We exchanged the presents and began to unwrap them. 'More fun than Christmas,' she said. 'Oh. How odd. I'd forgotten it was your name.' She paused very briefly for thought and said it the other way round. 'Christmas is more fun.'

It sounded all right in American. I opened the paper carrier she'd given me and found that our walk along the street had taught her a good deal about me, too. I drew out a soft brown leather zipped-around case which looked as if it would hold a pad of writing paper and a few envelopes: and it had KIT stamped in gold on the top.

'Go on, open it,' she said. 'I couldn't resist it. And you like neat small things, the way I do.'

I unzipped the case, opened it flat, and smiled with pure pleasure. It contained on one side a tool kit and on the other pens, a pocket calculator and a notepad; all in slots, all of top quality, solidly made.

'You do like it,' she said with satisfaction. 'I thought you would. It had your name on it, literally.'

She finished taking off the brown paper and showed me that I had pleased her also, and as much. I'd given her a baby antique chest of drawers which smelled faintly of polish, had little brass handles, and ran smoothly as silk. Neat, small, well-crafted, useful, good-looking, efficient: like the kit.

She looked long at the implications of the presents, and then at my face.

'That,' she said slowly, 'really is amazing, that we should both get it right.'

'Yes, it is.'

'And you broke the rules. That chest's not cheap.'

'So did you. Nor's the kit.'

'God bless credit cards.'

I kissed her, the same way as before, the gifts still on our laps. 'Thank you for mine.'

'Thank you for mine.'

'Well,' I said, reaching over to put my tool kit on the back seat. 'By the time we get there, the pub might be open.'

'What pub?'

'Where we're going.'

'Anyone who wants to know what you're not about to tell them,' she said, 'has a darned sticky time.'

I drove in contentment to the French Horn at Sonning, where the food was legendary and floodlights shone on willow trees drooping over the Thames. We went inside and sat on a sofa, and watched ducks roast on a spit over an open fire, and drank champagne. I stretched and breathed deeply, and felt the tensions of the long week relax: and I'd got to phone Rose Quince.

I went and phoned her. Answering machine again. I

said, 'Rose, Rose, I love you. Rose, I need you. If you come home before eleven, please, I beg you, ring me at the French Horn Hotel, the number is 0734 692204, tell them I'm in the restaurant having dinner.'

I telephoned Wykeham. 'Is the headache better?' I said.

'What?'

'Never mind. How's the mare?'

The mare was sore but eating, Mr Davis's horse was exhausted, Inchcape hardly looked as if he'd had a race.

'Icefall,' I said.

'What? I wish you wouldn't ride him from so far in front.'

'He liked it. And it worked.'

'I was watching on TV. Can you come and school on Tuesday? We have no runners that day, I'm not sending any to Southwell.'

'Yes, all right.'

'Well done, today,' he said with sincerity. 'Very well done.'

'Thanks.'

'Yes. Er. Goodnight then, Paul.'

'Goodnight, Wykeham,' I said.

I went back to Danielle and we spent the whole evening talking and later eating in the restaurant with silver and candlelight gleaming on the tables and a living vine growing over the ceiling; and at the last minute Rose Quince called me back.

'It's after eleven,' she said, 'but I just took a chance.'

'You're a dear.'

'I sure am. So what is so urgent, buddy boy?'

'Um,' I said. 'Does the name Saul Bradfield or Saul Bradley . . . something like that . . . mean anything to you?'

'Saul Bradley? Of course it does. What's so urgent about him?'

'Who is he?'

'He used to be the sports editor of the *Towncrier*. He retired last year . . . everyone's universal father-figure, an old friend of Bill's.'

'Do you know where he lives?'

'Good heavens. Wait while I think. Why do you want him?'

'In the general area of demolishing our business friend of the tapes.'

'Oh. Well, let's see. He moved. He said he was taking his wife to live by the sea. I'd've thought it would drive him mad but no accounting for taste. Worthing, or somewhere. No. Selsey.' Her voice strengthened. 'I remember, Selsey, in Sussex.'

'Terrific,' I said. 'And Lord Vaughnley. Where does he live?'

'Mostly in Regent's Park, in one of the Nash terraces. They've a place in Kent too, near Sevenoaks.'

'Could you tell me exactly?' I said. 'I mean . . . I'd like to write to thank him for my Towncrier trophy, and for all his other help.'

'Sure,' she said easily, and told me both his addresses

right down to the postal codes, tacking on the telephone numbers for good measure. 'You might need those. They're not in the directory.'

'I'm back in your debt,' I said, writing it all down.

'Deep, deep, buddy boy.'

I replaced the receiver feeling perfidious but unrepentant, and went to fetch Danielle to drive her home. It was midnight, more or less, when I pulled up in Eaton Square: and it wasn't where I would have preferred to have taken her, but where it was best.

'Thank you,' she said, 'for a great day.'

'What about tomorrow?'

'OK.'

'I don't know what time,' I said. 'I've something to do first.'

'Call me.'

'Yes.'

We sat in the car looking at each other, as if we hadn't been doing that already for hours. I've known her since Tuesday, I thought. In five days she'd grown roots in my life. I kissed her with much more hunger than before, which didn't seem to worry her, and I thought not long, not long . . . but not yet. When it was right, not before.

We said goodnight again on the pavement, and I watched her go into the house, carrying her present and waving as she closed the door. Princess Casilia, I thought, you are severely inhibiting, but I said I'd bring your niece home, and I have; and I don't even know what Danielle wanted, I can't read her mind and she didn't tell me in words, and tomorrow . . . tomorrow maybe I'd ask.

Early in the morning I drove to Selsey on the South Coast and looked up Saul Bradley in the local telephone book, and there he was, address and all, 15 Sea View Lane.

His house was on two floors and looked more suburban than seaside with mock-Tudor beams in its cream plastered gables. The mock-Tudor door, when I rang the bell, was opened by a grey-haired bespectacled motherly looking person in a flowered overall, and I could smell bacon frying.

'Hugh?' she said in reply to my question. 'Yes, he's still here, but he's still in bed. You know what boys are.'

'I'll wait,' I said.

She looked doubtful.

'I do very much want to see him,' I said.

'You'd better come in,' she said. 'I'll ask my husband. I think he's shaving, but he'll be down soon.'

She led me across the entrance hall into a smallish kitchen, all yellow and white tiles, with sunlight flooding in.

'A friend of Hugh's?' she said.

'Yes . . . I was talking to him yesterday.'

She shook her head worriedly. 'It's all most upsetting.

He shouldn't have gone to the races. He was more miserable than ever when he came back.'

'I'll do my best,' I said, 'to make things better.'

She attended to the breakfast she was frying, pushing the bacon round with a spatula. 'Did you say Fielding, your name was?' She turned from the cooker, the spatula in the air, motion arrested. 'Kit Fielding? The jockey?'

'Yes.'

She didn't know what to make of it, which wasn't surprising. She said uncertainly, 'I'm brewing some tea,' and I said I'd wait until after I'd seen her husband and Hugh.

Her husband came enquiringly into the kitchen, hearing my voice, and he knew me immediately by sight. A sports editor would, I supposed. Bunty Ireland's ex-boss was comfortably large with a bald head and shrewd eyes and a voice grown fruity, as from beer.

My presence nonplussed him, as it had his wife.

'You want to help Hugh? I suppose it's all right. Bill Vaughnley was speaking highly of you a few days ago. I'll go and get Hugh up. He's not good in the mornings. Want some breakfast?'

I hesitated.

'Like that, is it?' He chuckled. 'Starving and daren't put on an ounce.'

He went away into the house and presently returned,

followed shortly by Hugh, tousle-haired, in jeans and a T-shirt, his eyes puffed from sleep.

'Hello,' he said, bewildered. 'How did you find me?'

'You told me where you were staying.'

'Did I? I suppose I did. Er . . . sorry and all that, but what do you want?'

I wanted, I said, to take him out for a drive, to talk things over and see what could be done to help him: and with no more persuasion, he came.

He didn't seem to realize that his father had made sure he didn't speak to me further on the previous day. It had been done too skilfully for him to notice, especially in the anxiety he'd been suffering.

'Your father made you come back here,' I said, as we drove along Sea View Lane. 'Wouldn't let you go home?'

'It's so unfair.' There was self-pity in his voice, and also acceptance. The exile had been earned, I thought, and Hugh knew it.

'Tell me, then,' I said.

'Well, you know him. He's your father-in-law. I mean, no, he's your sister's father-in-law.'

I breathed deeply. 'Maynard Allardeck.'

'Yes. He caused it all. I'd kill him, if I could.'

I glanced at the good-looking immature face, at the dimples. Even the word kill came oddly from that mouth.

'I mean,' he said in an aggrieved voice, 'he's a member of the Jockey Club. Respected. I thought it was all right. I mean, he and Dad are patrons of the same charity. How was I to know? How was I?'

'You weren't,' I said. 'What happened?'

'He introduced me to his bookmaker.'

Whatever I'd imagined he might say, it wasn't that. I rolled the car to a halt in a parking place which at that time on a Sunday November morning was deserted. There was a distant glimpse of shingle banks and scrubby grass and sea glittering in the early sun, and nearby there was little but an acre of tarmac edged by a low brick wall, and a summer ice cream stall firmly shut.

'I've got a video camera,' I said. 'If you'd care to speak into that, I'll show the tape to your father, get him to hear your side of things, see if I can persuade him to let you go home.'

'Would you?' he said, hopefully.

'Yes, I would.'

I stretched behind my seat for the bag with the camera. 'Let's sit on the wall,' I said. 'It might be a bit chilly, but we'd get a better picture than inside the car.'

He made no objection, but came and sat on the wall, where I steadied the camera on one knee bent up, framed his face in the viewfinder and asked him to speak straight at the lens.

'Say that again,' I prompted, 'about the bookmaker.'

'I was at the races with my parents one day and having a bet, and a bookmaker was saying I wasn't old enough and making a fuss, and Maynard Allardeck was

there and he said not to worry, he would introduce me
to his own bookmaker instead.'

'How do you mean, he was there?'

Hugh's brow furrowed. 'He was just standing there. I
mean, I didn't know who he was, but he explained he
was a friend of my father.'

'And how old were you, and when did this happen?'

'That's what's so silly. I was twenty. I mean, you can
bet on your eighteenth birthday. Do I look seventeen?'

'No,' I said truthfully. 'You look twenty.'

'I was twenty-one, actually, in August. It was right
back in April when I met Maynard Allardeck.'

'So you started betting with Maynard Allardeck's
bookmaker . . . regularly?'

'Well, yes,' Hugh said unhappily. 'He made it so easy,
always so friendly, and he never seemed to worry when
I didn't pay his accounts.'

'There isn't a bookmaker born who doesn't insist on
his money.'

'This one didn't,' Hugh said defensively. 'I used to
apologize. He'd say never mind, one day, I know you'll
pay when you can, and he used to joke . . . and let me
bet again . . .'

'He let you bet until you were very deeply in debt?'

'Yes. Encouraged me. I mean, I suppose I should
have known . . . but he was so friendly, you see. All the
summer . . . Flat racing, every day . . . on the telephone.'

'Until all this happened,' I said, 'did you bet much?'

'I've always liked betting. Studying the form. Picking

the good things, following hunches. Never any good, I suppose, but probably any money I ever had went on horses. I'd get someone to put it on for me, on the Tote, when I was ten, and so on. Always. I mean, I won often too, of course. Terrific wins, quite often.'

'Mm.'

'Everyone who goes racing bets,' he said. 'What else do they go for? I mean, there's nothing wrong with a gamble, everyone does it. It's fun.'

'Mm,' I said again. 'But you were betting every day, several bets a day, even though you didn't go.'

'I suppose so, yes.'

'And then one day,' I said, 'it stopped being fun?'

'The Hove Stakes at Brighton,' he said. 'In September.'

'What about it?'

'Three runners. Slateroof couldn't be beaten. Maynard Allardeck told me. Help yourself, he said. Recoup your losses.'

'When did he tell you?'

'Few days before. At the races. Ascot. I went with my parents, and he happened to be there too.'

'And did you go to Brighton?'

'No.' He shook his head. 'Rang up the bookmaker. He said he couldn't give me a good price, Slateroof was a certainty, everyone knew it. Five to one on, he said. If I bet twenty, I could win four.'

'So you bet twenty pounds?'

'No.' Hugh looked surprised. 'Twenty thousand.'

'Twenty . . . thousand.' I kept my voice steady, unemotional. 'Was that, er, a big bet, for you, by that time?'

'Biggish. I mean, you can't win much in fivers, can you?'

You couldn't lose much either, I thought. I said, 'What was normal?'

'Anything between one thousand and twenty. I mean, I got there gradually, I suppose. I got used to it. Maynard Allardeck said one had to think big. I never thought of how much they really were. They were just numbers.' He paused, looking unhappy. 'I know it sounds stupid to say it now, but none of it seemed real. I mean, I never had to pay anything out. It was all done on paper. When I won, I felt great. When I lost I didn't really worry. I don't suppose you'll understand. Dad didn't. He couldn't understand how I could have been so stupid. But it just seemed like a game . . . and everyone smiled . . .'

'So Slateroof got beaten?'

'He didn't even start. He got left flat-footed in the stalls.'

'Oh yes,' I said. 'I remember reading about it. There was an enquiry and the jockey got fined.'

'Yes, but the bets stood, of course.'

'So what happened next?' I said.

'I got this frightful account from the bookmaker. He'd totted up everything, he said, and it seemed to be getting out of hand, and he'd like to be paid. I mean, there were pages of it.'

'Records of all the bets you'd made with him?'

'Yes, that's right. Winners and losers. Many more losers. I mean, there were some losers I couldn't remember backing; though he swore I had, he said he would produce his office records to prove it, if I liked, but he said I was ungenerous to make such a suggestion when he'd been so accommodating and patient.' Hugh swallowed. 'I don't know if he cheated me, I just don't. I mean, I did bet on two horses in the same race quite often, I know that, but I didn't realize I'd done it so much.'

'And you'd kept no record, yourself, of how much you'd bet, and what on?'

'I didn't think of it. I mean, I could remember. I mean, I thought I could.'

'Mm. Well, what next?'

'Maynard Allardeck telephoned me at home and said he'd heard from our mutual bookmaker that I was in difficulties, and could he help, as he felt sort of responsible, having introduced me, so to speak. He said we could meet somewhere and perhaps he could suggest some solutions. So I met him for lunch in a restaurant in London, and talked it all over. He said I should confess to my father and get him to pay my debts but I said I couldn't, he would be so angry, he'd no idea I'd gambled so much, he was always lecturing me about taking care of money. And I didn't want to disappoint him, if you can understand that? I didn't want him to be upset. I mean, I expect it sounds silly, but it wasn't really out of fear, it was, well, sort of love, really, only it's difficult to explain.'

'Yes,' I said, 'go on.'

'Maynard Allardeck said not to worry, he could see why I couldn't tell my father, it reflected well on me, he said, and he would lend me the money himself, and I could pay him back slowly, and he would just charge me a little over, if I thought that was fair. And I did think it was fair, of course. I was so extremely relieved. I thanked him a lot, over and over.'

'So Maynard Allardeck paid your bookmaker?'

'Yes.' Hugh nodded. 'I got a final account from him marked "Paid with thanks", and a note saying it would be best if I laid off betting for a while, but if I needed him in the future, he would accommodate me again. I mean, I thought it very fair and kind, wouldn't you?'

'Mm,' I said dryly. 'And then after a while Maynard Allardeck told you he was short of money himself and would have to call in the debt?'

'Yes,' Hugh said in surprise. 'How did you know? He was so apologetic and embarrassed I almost felt sorry for him, though he was putting me in a terrible hole. Terrible. And then he suggested a way round it, which was so easy ... so simple ... like the sun

coming out. I couldn't think why I hadn't thought of it
myself.'

'Hugh,' I asked slowly, 'what did you have, that he
wanted?'

'My shares in the *Towncrier*,' he said.

CHAPTER EIGHTEEN

He took my breath away. Oh my Christ, I thought. Bloody bingo.

Talk about the sun coming out. So simple, so easy. Why hadn't I thought of it myself.

'Your shares in the *Towncrier* . . .'

'Yes,' Hugh said. 'They were left to me by my grandfather. I mean, I didn't know I had them, until I was twenty-one.'

'In August.'

'Yes. That's right. Anyway, it seemed to solve everything. I mean it did solve everything, didn't it? Maynard Allardeck looked up the proper market value and everything, and gave me two or three forms to sign, which I did, and then he said that was fine, we were all square, I had no more debts. I mean, it was so easy. And it wasn't all of my shares. Not even half.'

'How much were the shares worth, that you gave Allardeck?'

He said as if such figures were commonplace, 'Two hundred and fifty-four thousand pounds.'

After a pause I said, 'Didn't it upset you . . . so much money?'

'Of course not. It was only on paper. And Maynard Allardeck laughed and said if I ever felt like gambling again, well, I had the collateral, and we could always come to the same arrangement again, if it was necessary. I begged him not to tell my father, and he said no, he wouldn't.'

'But your father found out?'

'Yes, it was something to do with voting shares, or preference shares or debentures. I'm really not sure, I didn't know what they were talking about, but they were busy fending off a takeover. They're always fending off takeovers, but this one had them all dead worried, and somewhere in the *Towncrier* they discovered that half of my shares had gone, and Dad made me tell him what I'd done . . . and he was so angry . . . I'd never seen him angry . . . never like that . . .'

His voice faded away, his eyes stark with remembrance.

'He sent me here to Saul Bradley and he said if I ever bet on anything ever again I could never go home . . . I want him . . . I do . . . to forgive me. I want to go home.'

He stopped. The intensity of his feelings stared into the lens. I let the camera run for a few silent seconds, and then turned it off.

'I'll show him the film,' I said.

'Do you think . . .?'

'In time he'll forgive you? Yes, I'd say so.'

'I could go back to just the odd bet in cash on the Tote.' His eyes were speculative, his air much too hopeful. The infection too deep in his system.

'Hugh,' I said, 'would you mind if I gave you some advice?'

'No. Fire away.'

'Take some practical lessons about money. Go away without any, find out it's not just numbers on a page, learn it's the difference between eating and hunger. Bet your dinner, and if you lose, see if it's worth it.'

He said earnestly, 'Yes, I do see what you mean. But I might win.' And I wondered doubtfully whether one could ever reform an irresponsible gambler, be he rich, poor, or the heir to the *Towncrier*.

I drove back to London, added the Hugh Vaughnley tape to the others in the hotel's care, and went upstairs for another session of staring blindly at the walls. Then I telephoned Holly, and got Bobby instead.

'How's things?' I said.

'Not much different. Holly's lying down, do you want to talk to her?'

'You'll do fine.'

'I've had some more cheques from the owners. Almost everyone's paid.'

'That's great.'

'They're a drop in the ocean.' His voice sounded tired. 'Will your valet cash them again?'

'Sure to.'

'Even then,' he said, 'we're right at the end.'

'I suppose,' I said, 'you haven't heard any more from the *Flag*? No letter? No money?'

'Not a thing.'

I sighed internally and said, 'Bobby, I want to talk to your father.'

'It won't do any good. You know what he was like the other day. He's stubborn and mean, and he hates us.'

'He hates me,' I said, 'and Holly. Not you.'

'One wouldn't guess it,' he said bitterly.

'I've no rides on Tuesday,' I said. 'Persuade him to come to your house on Tuesday afternoon. I'm schooling at Wykeham's place in the morning.'

'It's impossible. He wouldn't come here.'

'He might,' I said, 'if you tell him he was right all along, every Fielding is your enemy, and you want his help in getting rid of me, out of your life.'

'Kit!' He was outraged. 'I can't do that. It's the last thing I want.'

'And if you can bring yourself to it, tell him you're getting tired of Holly, as well.'

'No. How can I? I love her so much . . . I couldn't make it sound true.'

'Bobby, nothing less will bring him. Can you think

of anything else? I've been thinking for hours. If you can get him there some other way, we'll do it your way.'

After a pause he said, 'He would come out of hate. Isn't that awful? He's my father . . .'

'Yes. I'm sorry.'

'What do you want to talk to him about?'

'A proposition. Help for you in return for something he'd want. But don't tell him that. Don't tell him I'm coming. Just get him there, if you can.'

He said doubtfully, 'He'll never help us. Never.'

'Well, we'll see. At least give it a try.'

'Yes, all right, but for heaven's sake, Kit . . .'

'What?'

'It's dreadful to say it, but where you're concerned . . . I think he's dangerous.'

'I'll be careful.'

'It goes back so far . . . When I was little he taught me to hit things . . . with my fists, with a stick, anything, and he told me to think I was hitting Kit Fielding.'

I took a breath. 'Like in the garden?'

'God, Kit . . . I've been so sorry.'

'I told you. I mean it. It's all right.'

'I've been thinking about you, and remembering so much. Things I'd forgotten, like him telling me the Fieldings would eat me if I was naughty . . . I must have been three or four. I was scared stiff.'

'When you were four, I was two.'

'It was your father and your grandfather who would eat me. Then when you were growing up he told me

345

to hit Kit Fielding, he taught me how, he said one day it would be you and I, we would have to fight. I'd forgotten all that . . . but I remember it now.'

'My grandfather,' I sighed, 'gave me a punchbag and taught me how to hit it. That's Bobby Allardeck, he said. Bash him.'

'Do you mean it?'

'Ask Holly. She knows.'

'Bloody, weren't they.'

'It's finished now,' I said.

We disconnected and I got through to Danielle and said how about lunch and tea and dinner.

'Are you planning to eat all those?' she said.

'All or any.'

'All, then.'

'I'll come straight round.'

She opened the Eaton Square front door as I braked to a halt and came across the pavement with a spring in her step, an evocation of summer in a flower-patterned jacket over cream trousers, the chintz band holding back the fluffy hair.

She climbed into the car beside me and kissed me as if from old habit.

'Aunt Casilia sends her regards and hopes we'll have a nice day.'

'And back by midnight?'

'I would think so, wouldn't you?'

'Does she notice?'

'She sure does. I go past their rooms to get to mine

– she and Uncle Roland sleep separately – and the floors creak. She called me in last night to ask if I'd enjoyed myself. She was sitting in bed, reading, looking a knock-out as usual. I told her what we'd done and showed her the chest of drawers ... we had quite a long talk.'

I studied her face. She looked seriously back.

'What did she say?' I asked.

'It matters to you, doesn't it, what she thinks?'

'Yes.'

'I guess she'd be glad.'

'Tell me, then.'

'Not yet.' She smiled swiftly, almost secretly. 'What about this lunch?'

We went to a restaurant up a tower and ate looking out over half of London. 'Consommé and strawberries ... you'll be good for my figure,' she said.

'Have some sugar and cream.'

'Not if you don't.'

'You're thin enough,' I said.

'Don't you get tired of it?'

'Of not eating much? I sure do.'

'But you never let up?'

'A pound overweight in the saddle,' I said wryly, 'can mean a length's difference at the winning post.'

'End of discussion.'

Over coffee I asked if there was anywhere she'd like to go, though I apologized that most of London seemed to shut on Sundays, especially in November.

'I'd like to see where you live,' she said. 'I'd like to see Lambourn.'

'Right,' I said, and drove her there, seventy miles westwards down the M4 motorway, heading back towards Devon, keeping this time law-abidingly within the speed limit, curling off into the large village, small town, where the church stood at the main crossroads and a thousand thoroughbreds lived in boxes.

'It's quiet,' she said.

'It's Sunday.'

'Where's your cottage?'

'We'll drive past there,' I said. 'But we're not going in.'

She was puzzled, and, it seemed, disappointed, looking across at me lengthily. 'Why not?'

I explained about the break in, and the police saying the place had been searched. 'The intruders found nothing they wanted, and they stole nothing. But I'd bet they left something behind.'

'What do you mean?'

'Creepy-crawlies.'

'Bugs?'

'Mm,' I said. 'That's it over there.'

We went past slowly. There was no sign of life. No sign of heavy men lying in the bushes with sharp knives, which they wouldn't be by then, not after three days. Too boring, too cold. Listening somewhere, though, those two, or others.

The cottage was brick-built, rather plain, and would perhaps have looked better in June, with the roses.

'It's all right inside,' I said.

'Yuh.' She sounded downcast. 'OK. That's that.'

I drove around and up a hill and took her to the new house instead.

'Whose is this?' she said. 'This is great.'

'This is mine.' I got out of the car, fishing for keys. 'It's empty. Come and look.'

The bright day was fading but there was enough direct sunlight to shine horizontally through the windows and light the big empty rooms, and although the air inside was cold, the central heating, when I switched it on, went into smooth operation with barely a hiccup. There were a few light sockets with bulbs in, but no shades. No curtains. No carpets. Wood-block floor everywhere, swept but not polished. Signs of builders all over the place.

'They're just starting to paint,' I said, opening the double doors from the hall to the sitting room. 'I'll move in alongside, if they don't hurry up.'

There were trestles in the sitting room set up for reaching the ceiling, and an army of tubs of paint, and dustsheets all over the flooring to avoid spatters.

'It's huge,' she said. 'Incredible.'

'It's got a great kitchen. An office. Lots of things.' I explained about the bankrupt builder. 'He designed it for himself.'

We went around and through everywhere and ended

in the big room which led directly off the sitting room, the room where I would sleep. It seemed that the decorators had started with that: it was clean, bare and finished, the bathroom painted and tiled, the wood-blocks faintly gleaming with the first layer of polish, the western sun splashing in patches on the white walls.

Danielle stood by the window looking out at the muddy expanse which by summer would be a terrace, with geraniums in pots. The right person . . . in the right place . . . at the right time.

'Will you lie in my bedroom?' I said.

She turned, silhouetted against the sun, her hair like a halo, her face in shadow, hard to read. It seemed that she was listening still to what I'd said, as if to be sure that she had heard right and not misunderstood.

'On the bare floor?' Her voice was steady, uncommitted, friendly and light.

'We could, er, fetch some dustsheets, perhaps.'

She considered it.

'OK,' she said.

We brought a few dustsheets from the sitting room and arranged them in a rough rectangle, with pillows.

'I've seen better marriage beds,' she said.

We took all our clothes off, not hurrying, dropping them in heaps. No real surprises. She was as I had thought, flat and rounded, her skin glowing now in the sun. She stretched out her fingers, touching lightly the stitches, the fading bruises, the known places.

She said, 'When you looked at me at the races yesterday, over those cups, were you thinking of this?'

'Something like this. Was it so obvious?'

'Blinding.'

'I was afraid so.'

We didn't talk a great deal after that. We stood together for a while, and lay down, and on the hard cotton surface learned the ultimate things about each other, pleasing and pleased, with advances and retreats, with murmurs and intensities and breathless primeval energy.

The sunlight faded slowly, the sky lit still with afterglow, gleams reflecting in her eyes and on her teeth, darknesses deepening in hollows and in her hair.

At the end of a long calm afterwards she said prosaically, 'I suppose the water's not hot?'

'Bound to be,' I said lazily. 'It's combined with the heating. Everything's working, lights, plumbing, the lot.'

We got up and went into the bathroom, switching on taps but not lights. It was darker in there and we moved like shadows, more substance than shape.

I turned on the shower, running it warm. Danielle stepped into it with me, and we made love again there in the spray, with tenderness, with passion and in friendship, her arms round my neck, her stomach flat on mine, united as I'd never been before in my life.

I turned off the tap, in the end.

'There aren't any towels,' I said.

'Always the dustsheets.'

We took our bed apart and dried ourselves, and got dressed, and kissed again with temperance, feeling clean. In almost full darkness we dumped the dust sheets in the sitting room, switched off the heating, and went out of the house, locking it behind us.

Danielle looked back before getting into the car. 'I wonder what the house thinks,' she said.

'It thinks holy wow.'

'As a matter of fact, so do I.'

We drove back to London along the old roads, not the motorway, winding through the empty Sunday evening streets of a string of towns, stopping at traffic lights, stretching the journey. I parked the car in central London and we walked for a while, stopping to read menus, and eating eventually in a busy French bistro with red checked tablecloths and an androgynous guitarist; sitting in a corner, holding hands, reading the bill of fare chalked on a blackboard.

'Aunt Casilia,' Danielle said, sometime later over coffee, her eyes shining with amusement, 'said last night, among other things, that while decorum was essential, abstinence was not.'

I laughed in surprise, and kissed her, and in a while and in decorum drove her back to Eaton Square.

I raced at Windsor the next day, parking the car at the railway station and taking a taxi from there right to the jockeys' entrance gate near the weighing room on the racecourse.

The princess had no runners and wasn't expected; I rode two horses each for Wykeham and the Lambourn trainer and got all of them round into the first or second place, which pleased the owners and put grins on the stable lads. Bunty Ireland, beaming, told me I was on the winning streak of all time, and I calculated the odds that I'd come crashing down again by Thursday, and hoped that I wouldn't, and that he was right.

My valet said, sure, he would return me to the station in his van – a not too abnormal service. He was reading aloud from the *Flag* with disfavour. 'Reality is sweaty armpits, sordid sex, junkies dead in public lavatories, it says here.' He threw the paper on to the bench. 'Reality is the gas bill, remembering the wife's birthday, a beer with your mates, that's more like it. Get in the van, Kit, it's right outside the weighing room. I've just about finished here.'

Reality, I thought, going out, was speed over fences, a game of manners, love in a shower: to each his own.

I travelled without incident back to the hotel and telephoned on time to Wykeham.

'Where are you?' he said. 'People keep asking for you.'

'Who?' I said.

'They don't say. Four fellows, at least. All day. Where are you?'

'Staying with friends.'

'Oh.' He didn't ask further. He himself didn't care. We talked about his winner and his second, and discussed the horses I would be schooling in the morning.

'One of those fellows who rang wanted you for some lunch party or other in London,' he said, as if suddenly remembering. 'They invited me, too. The sponsors of Inchcape's race, last Saturday. The princess is going, and they wanted us as well. They said it was a great opportunity as they could see from tomorrow's race programmes that we hadn't any runners.'

'Are you going?'

'No, no. I said I couldn't. But it might be better if you came here early, and do the schooling in good time.'

I agreed, and said goodnight.

'Goodnight, Kit,' he said.

I got through to my answering machine, and there among the messages were the sponsors of Icefall's race, inviting me to lunch the next day. They would be delighted if I could join them and the princess in celebrating our victory in their race, please could I ring back at the given number.

I rang the number and got an answering machine referring me on, reaching finally the head of the sponsors himself.

'Great, great, you can come?' he said. 'Twelve-thirty at the Guineas restaurant in Curzon Street. See you there. That's splendid.'

Sponsors got advertising from racing and in return

pumped in generous cash. There was an unspoken understanding among racing people that sponsors were to be appreciated, and that jockeys should turn up if possible where invited. Part of the job. And I wanted to go, besides, to talk to the princess.

I answered my other messages, none of which were important, and then got through to Holly.

'Bobby spoke to his father,' she said. 'The beast said he would come only if you were there. Bobby didn't like it.'

'Did Bobby say I would be there anyway?'

'No, he waited to know what you wanted him to say. He has to ring back to his father.'

I didn't like it any more than Bobby. 'Why does Maynard want me?' I said. 'I didn't think he would come at all if he knew I'd be there.'

'He said he would help Bobby get rid of you once and for all, but that you had to be there.'

Bang, I thought, goes any advantage of surprise. 'All right,' I said. 'Tell Bobby to tell him I'll be coming. At about four o'clock, I should think. I'm going to a sponsors' lunch in London.'

'Kit . . . whatever you're planning, don't do it.'

'Must.'

'I've a feeling . . .'

'Stifle it. How's the baby?'

'Never have one,' she said. 'It's the pits.'

*

I collected all four recorded video tapes from the hotel's vaults and took them with six others, unused, to Chiswick: and kissed Danielle with circumspection at her desk.

'Hi,' she said, smiling deeply in her eyes.

'Hi, yourself.'

'How did it go, today?'

'Two wins, two seconds.'

'And no crunches.'

'No crunches.'

She seemed to relax. 'I'm glad you're OK.'

Joe appeared from the passage to the editing rooms saying he was biting his fingernails with inactivity and had I by any chance brought my tapes. I picked the four recorded tapes off Danielle's desk and he pounced on them, bearing them away.

I followed him with the spare tapes into an editing room and sat beside him while he played the interviews through, one by one, his dark face showing shock.

'Can you stick them together?' I asked, when he'd finished.

'I sure can,' he said sombrely. 'What you need is some voice-over linkage. You got anything else? Shots of scenery, anything like that?'

I shook my head. 'I didn't think of it.'

'It's no good putting a voice-over on a black screen,' he explained. 'You've got to have pictures, to hold interest. We're bound to have something here in the library that we can use.'

Danielle appeared at the doorway, looking enquiring.

'How's it going?' she said.

'I guess you know what's on these tapes,' Joe said.

'No. Kit hasn't told me.'

'Good,' Joe said. 'When I've finished, we'll try it out on you. Get a reaction.'

'OK,' she said. 'It's a quiet night for news, thank goodness.'

She went away and Joe got me to speak into a microphone, explaining who the Perrysides were, giving George Tarker a location, introducing Hugh Vaughnley. I wanted them in that order, I said.

'Right,' he said. 'Now you go away and talk to Danielle and leave it to me, and if you don't like the result, no problem, we can always change it.'

'I brought these unused tapes,' I said, giving them to him. 'Once we've settled on the final version, could we make copies?'

He took one of the new tapes, peeled off the cellophane wrapping and put it into a machine. 'A breeze,' he said.

He spent two or three hours on it, coming out whistling a couple of times to see if the station chief was still happy (which he appeared to be), telling me Spielberg couldn't do better, drinking coffee from a machine, going cheerfully back.

Danielle worked sporadically on a story about a police hunt for a rapist who lurked in bus shelters and had just been arrested, which she said would probably not make it on to network news back home, but kept everyone working, at least. No Devil-Boys, no oil fires that night.

Aunt Casilia, Danielle said, was looking forward to tomorrow's lunch party and hoped I would be there.

'Will you be going?' I asked.

'Nope. Aunt Casilia would have gotten me invited, but I've a college friend passing through London. We're having lunch. Long time date, I can't break it.'

'Pity.'

'You're going? Shall I tell her?'

I nodded. 'I'm schooling some of her horses in the morning, and I'll be coming along after.'

Joe came out finally, stretching his backbone and flexing his fingers.

'Come on, then,' he said. 'Come and see.'

We all went, the station chief as well, sitting in chairs collected from adjoining rooms. Joe started his machine, and there, immediately, was the uncut version of the television interview of Maynard and his tormentor, followed by the list of firms Maynard had acquired. At the end of that the tape returned to repeat the interviewer's outline of Metavane's story, and then came my voice, superimposed on views of horses exercising on Newmarket Health, explaining who Major and Mrs Perryside were, and where they now lived.

The Perrysides appeared in entirety, poignant and

brave; and at the end the tape returned to the television interviewer again repeating the takeover list. This time it stopped after the mention of Purfleet Electronics, and then, over a view of mudflats in the Thames estuary, my voice introduced George Tarker. The whole of that interview was there also, and when he said in tears about his son wiring himself up, Danielle's own eyes filled . . .

Joe left the shot of George Tarker's ravaged face running as long as I'd taped it, and then there was my voice again, this time over a printing press in full production, explaining that the next person to appear would be the son of Lord Vaughnley, who owned the *Daily* and *Sunday Towncrier* newspapers.

All of Hugh's tape was there, ending with his impassioned plea to come home. On the screen after that came a long shot taken from the cut televised version of *How's Trade*, of Maynard smiling and looking noble. The soundtrack of that had been erased, so that one saw him in silence. Then the screen went silently into solid black for about ten seconds before reverting to snow and background crackle.

Even though I'd recorded three of the main segments myself, the total effect was overpowering. Run together they were a punch to the brain, emotional, damning the wicked.

The station chief said, 'Christ', and Danielle blew her nose.

'It runs for one hour, thirteen minutes,' Joe said to me, 'if you're interested.'

'I can't thank you enough.'

'I hope the bastard burns,' he said.

In the morning I went to Wykeham's place south of London and on the Downs there spent two profitable hours teaching his absolute novices how to jump and refreshing the memories of others. We gave the one who had fallen at Ascot a pop to help him get his confidence back after being brought down, and talked about the runners for the rest of that week.

'Thank you for coming,' he said. 'Good of you.'

'A pleasure.'

'Goodbye, P . . . er . . . Kit.'

'Goodbye, Wykeham,' I said.

I went back to London, showered, dressed in grey suit, white shirt, quiet tie, presenting a civilized face to the sponsors.

I put one of the six copies Joe had made of the Allardeck production into a large envelope, sticking it shut, and then zipped a second of them into the big inside pocket of my blue anorak. The other four I took downstairs and lodged in the hotel vault, and carrying both the envelope and the anorak went by taxi to Eric Olderjohn's terrace house behind Sloane Square.

The taxi waited while I rang the bell beside the green door, and not much to my surprise there was no one at home. I wrote on the envelope: 'Mr Olderjohn, Please give this to a Certain Person, for his eyes only. Regards, Kit Fielding' and pushed it through the letter box.

'Right,' I said to the taxi driver. 'The Guineas restaurant, Curzon Street.'

The Guineas, where I'd been several times before, was principally a collection of private dining rooms of various sizes, chiefly used for private parties such as the one I was bound for. Opulent and discreet, it went in for dark green flocked wallpaper, gilded cherubs and waiters in gloves. Every time I had been there, there had been noisettes of lamb.

I left my anorak in the cloakroom downstairs and put the ticket in my pocket, walked up the broad stairs to the next floor, turned right, went down a passage and ended, as directed, at the sponsors' party in the One Thousand Room.

The sponsors greeted me effusively. 'Come in, come in. Have some champagne.' They gave me a glass.

The princess was there, dressed in a cream silk suit with gold and citrines, dark hair piled high, smiling.

'I'm so pleased you've come,' she said, shaking my hand.

'I wouldn't have missed it.'

'How are my horses? How is Icefall? How is my

361

poor Allegheny? Did you know that Lord Vaughnley is here?'

'Is he?'

I looked around. There were about thirty people present, more perhaps than I'd expected. From across the room Lady Vaughnley saw me, and waved.

'The *Towncrier* joined forces with the Icefall people,' the princess said. 'It's a double party, now.'

The Icefall sponsors came to bear her away. 'Do come . . . may I present . . .'

Lord Vaughnley approached, looking blander than bland.

'Now, everybody,' said one of the sponsors loudly, 'we're all going into another room to see films of our two races, both won by our most honoured guest, Princess Casilia.'

There was a little light applause, and everyone began to move to the door. Lord Vaughnley stood at my elbow. The princess looked back. 'You're coming, Kit?'

'In a minute,' Lord Vaughnley said. 'Just want to ask him something.'

The princess smiled and nodded and went on. Lord Vaughnley shepherded everyone out, and when the room was empty, closed the door and stood with his back to it.

'I wanted to reach you,' I said; but I don't think he heard. He was looking towards a second door, set in a side wall.

The door opened, and two people came through it.

Nestor Pollgate.

Jay Erskine.

Pollgate looked satisfied and Jay Erskine was smirking.

CHAPTER NINETEEN

'Neatly done,' Pollgate said to Lord Vaughnley.

'It worked out well,' he replied, his big head nodding.

He still stood four-square in front of the door. Erskine stood similarly, with folded arms, in front of the other.

There were chairs and tables round the green walls, tables with white cloths bearing bowls of nuts and cigarette-filled ashtrays. Champagne goblets all over the place, some still with bubble contents. There would be waiters, I thought, coming to clear the rubble.

'We won't be disturbed,' Pollgate told Lord Vaughnley. 'The "do not enter" signs are on both doors, and Mario says we have the room for an hour.'

'The lunch will be before that,' Lord Vaughnley said. 'The films take half an hour, no more.'

'He's not going to the lunch,' Pollgate said, meaning me.

'Er, no, perhaps not. But I should be there.'

I thought numbly: catch me first.

It had taken five days . . . and the princess.

'You are going to give us,' Pollgate said to me directly, 'the wire-tap and my journalists' belongings. And that will be the end of it.'

The power of the man was such that the words themselves were a threat. What would happen if I didn't comply wasn't mentioned. My compliance was assumed; no discussion.

He walked over to Jay Erskine, producing a flat box from a pocket and taking Jay Erskine's place guarding the door.

Jay Erskine's smirk grew to a twisted smile of antici-pation. I disliked intensely the cold eyes, the drooping moustache, his callous pen and his violent nature; and most of all I disliked the message in his sneer.

Pollgate opened the box and held it out to Jay Erskine, who took from it something that looked like the hand-held remote control of a television set. He settled it into his hand and walked in my direction. He came without the wariness one might have expected after I'd thrown him across a room, and he put the remote control thing smoothly between the open fronts of my jacket, on to my shirt.

I felt something like a thud, and the next thing I knew I was lying flat on my back on the floor, wholly disorientated, not sure where I was or what had happened.

Jay Erskine and Lord Vaughnley bent down, took my arms, helped me up, and dropped me on to a chair.

The chair had arms. I held on to them. I felt dazed, and couldn't work out why.

Jay Erskine smiled nastily and put the black object again against my shirt.

The thud had a burn to it that time. And so fast. No time to draw breath.

I would have shot out of the chair if they hadn't held me in it. My wits scattered instantly to the four winds. My muscles didn't work. I wasn't sure who I was or where I was, and nor did I care. Time passed. Time was relative. It was minutes, anyway. Not very quick.

The haze in my brain slowly resolved itself to the point where I knew I was sitting in a chair, and knew the people round me were Nestor Pollgate, Lord Vaughnley and Jay Erskine.

'Right,' Pollgate said. 'Can you hear me?'

I said, after a pause, 'Yes.' It didn't sound like my voice. More a croak.

'You're going to give us the wire-tap,' he said. 'And the other things.'

Some sort of electricity, I thought dimly. Those thuds were electric shocks. Like touching a cold metal doorknob after walking on nylon carpet, but magnified monstrously.

'You understand?' he said.

I didn't answer. I understood, but I didn't know whether I was going to give him the things or not.

'Where are they?' he said.

To hell with it, I thought.

'Where are they?'

Silence.

I didn't even see Jay Erskine put his hand against me the third time. I felt a great burning jolt and went shooting into space, floating for several millennia in a disorientated limbo, ordinary consciousness suspended, living as in dream-state, docile and drifting. I could see them in a way, but I didn't know who they were. I didn't know anything. I existed. I had no form.

Whatever would be done, wherever they might take me, whatever God-awful crime they might plant me in, I couldn't resist.

Thought came back again slowly. There were burns somewhere, stinging. I heard Lord Vaughnley's voice saying something, and Pollgate answering, 'Five thousand volts.'

'He's awake,' Erskine said.

Lord Vaughnley leaned over me, his face close and worried. 'Are you sure he's all right?'

'Yes,' Pollgate said. 'There'll be no permanent harm.'

Thank you, I thought wryly, for that. I felt dizzy and sick. Just as well that with lunch in view I had missed breakfast.

Pollgate was looking at his watch and shaking his head. 'He was dazed for twelve minutes that time. A three-second shock is too much. The two-second is better, but it's taking too long. Twenty minutes already.' He glared down at me. 'I can't waste any more time. You'll give me those things, now, at once.'

It was he who held the electric device now, not Erskine.

I thought I could speak. Tried it. Something came out: the same sort of croak. I said 'It will take . . . days.'

It wasn't heroics. I thought vaguely that if they believed it would take days they would give up trying, right there and then. Logic, at that point, was at a low ebb.

Pollgate stepped within touching distance of me and showed me five thousand volts at close range.

'Stun gun,' he said.

It had two short flat metal prongs protruding five centimetres apart from one end of a flat plastic case. He squeezed some switch or other, and between the prongs leapt an electric spark the length of a thumb, bright blue, thick and crackling.

The spark fizzed for a long three seconds of painful promise and disappeared as fast as it had come.

I looked from the stun gun up to Pollgate's face, staring straight at the shiny-bead eyes.

'Weeks,' I said.

It certainly nonplussed him. 'Give us the wire-tap,' he said; and he seemed to be looking, as I was, at a long, tiring battle of wills, much of which I would half sleep through, I supposed.

Lord Vaughnley said to Pollgate uncomfortably, 'You can't go on with this.'

A certain amount of coherence returned to my brain.

The battle of wills, I thought gratefully, shouldn't be necessary.

'He's going to give us those things,' Pollgate said obstinately. 'I'm not letting some clod like this get the better of me.' Pride, loss of face, all the deadly intangibles.

Lord Vaughnley looked down at me anxiously.

'I'll give you,' I said to him, 'something better.'

'What?'

My voice was steadier. Less hoarse, less slow. I moved in the chair, arms and legs coming back into coordination. It seemed to alarm Jay Erskine but I was still a long way from playing judo.

'What will you give us?' Lord Vaughnley said.

I concentrated on making my throat and tongue work properly. 'It's in Newmarket,' I said. 'We'll have to go there for it. Now, this afternoon.'

Pollgate said with impatience. 'That's ridiculous.'

'I'll give you,' I said to Lord Vaughnley, 'Maynard Allardeck.'

A short burst of stun couldn't have had more effect.

'How do you mean?' he said; not with puzzlement, but with hope.

'On a plate,' I said. 'In your power. Where you want him, don't you?'

They both wanted him. I could see it in Pollgate's face just as clearly as in Lord Vaughnley's. I suppose that I had guessed in a way that it would be both.

Jay Erskine said aggressively, 'Are our things in Newmarket, then?'

I said with an effort, 'That's where you left them.'

'All right, then.'

He seemed to think that the purpose of their expedition had been achieved, and I didn't tell him differently.

Nestor Pollgate said, 'Jay, fetch the car to the side entrance, will you?' and the obnoxious Erskine went away.

Pollgate and Lord Vaughnley agreed that Mario, whoever he was, should tell Icefall's sponsors not to expect their guests back for lunch, saying I'd had a bilious attack and Lord Vaughnley was helping me. 'But Mario can't tell them until after we've gone,' Lord Vaughnley said, 'or you'll have my wife and I daresay the princess out here in a flash to mother him.'

I sat and listened lethargically, capable of movement but not wanting to move, no longer sick, all right in my head, peaceful, extraordinarily, and totally without energy.

After a while Jay Erskine came back, the exasperating smirk still in place.

'Can you walk?' Pollgate asked me.

I said, 'Yes' and stood up, and we went out of the side door, along a short passage and down some gilded deeply carpeted backstairs, where no doubt many a Guineas visitor made a discreet entrance and exit, avoiding public eyes in the front hall.

I went down the stairs shakily, holding on to the rail.

'Are you all right?' Lord Vaughnley said solicitously, putting his hand supportively under my elbow.

I glanced at him. How he could think I would be all right was beyond me. Perhaps he was remembering that I was used to damage, to falls, to concussion: but bruises and fractures were different from that day's little junket.

'I'm all right,' I said though, because it was true where it counted, and we went safely down to the bottom.

I stopped there. The exit door stood open ahead, a passage stretching away indoors to the right.

'Come along,' Pollgate said, gesturing to the door. 'If we're going, let's go.'

'My anorak,' I said, 'is in the cloakroom.' I produced the ticket from my pocket. 'Anorak,' I said.

'I'll get it,' Lord Vaughnley said, taking the ticket. 'And I'll see Mario. Wait for me in the car.'

It was a large car. Jay Erskine was driving. Nestor Pollgate sat watchfully beside me on the back seat, and Lord Vaughnley, when he returned, sat in the front.

'Your anorak,' he said, holding it out, and I thanked him and put it by my feet, on the floor.

'The films of the races have just ended, Mario says,' he reported to Pollgate. 'He's going straight in to make our apologies. It's all settled. Off we go.'

It took ages to get out of London, partly because of thick traffic, mostly because Jay Erskine was a rotten driver, all impatience and heavy on the brakes. An hour and a half to Newmarket, at that rate: and I would have to be better by then.

No one spoke much. Jay Erskine locked all the doors centrally and Nestor Pollgate put the stun gun in its case in his right-hand jacket pocket, hidden but available; and I sat beside him in ambiguity, half prisoner, half ringmaster, going willingly but under threat, waiting for energy to return, physical, mental and psychic.

Stun guns, I thought. I'd heard of them, never seen one before. Used originally by American police to subdue dangerous violent criminals without shooting them. Instantaneous. Effective. You don't say.

I remembered from long-ago physics lessons that if you squeezed piezoelectric crystals you got sparks, as in the flickering lighters used for gas cookers. Maybe stun guns were like that, multiplied. Maybe not. Maybe I would ask someone. Maybe not. Five thousand volts . . .

I looked with speculation at the back of Lord Vaughnley's head, wondering what he was thinking. He was eager, that was for sure. They had agreed to the journey like thirsty men in a drought. They were going without knowing for sure why, without demanding to be told. Anything that could do Maynard Allardeck harm must be worth doing, in their eyes: that had to be why, at the beginning, Lord Vaughnley had been happy enough to introduce me to Rose Quince, to let me loose on the files. The destruction of Maynard's credibility could only be helped along, he might have thought, by pin pricks from myself.

I dozed, woke with a start, found Pollgate's face turned my way, his eyes watching. He was looking, if anything, puzzled.

In my rag-doll state I could think of nothing useful to say, so I didn't, and presently he turned his head away and looked out of the window, and I still felt very conscious of his force, his ruthlessness, and of the ruin he could make of my life if I got the next few hours wrong.

I thought of how they had set their trap in the Guineas.

Icefall's sponsors, on my answering machine, inviting me to lunch. The sponsors hadn't said where, but they'd said tomorrow, Tuesday: today. The message would have been overheard and despatched to Pollgate, and sent from him to Lord Vaughnley, who would have said, Nothing simpler, my dear fellow, I'll join forces with those sponsors, which they can hardly refuse, and Kit Fielding will definitely come, he'd do anything to please the princess . . .

Pollgate had known the Guineas. Known Mario. Known he could get an isolated room for an hour. The sort of place he would know, for sure.

Maybe Lord Vaughnley had suggested the Guineas to Icefall's sponsors. Maybe he hadn't had to. There were often racing celebration parties at the Guineas.

The sponsors would very likely have chosen it themselves, knowing they could show the films there.

Unprofitable thoughts. However it had been planned, it had worked.

I thought also about the alliance between Lord Vaughnley and Nestor Pollgate, owners of snapping rival newspapers, always at each other's throats in print, and acting in private accord.

Allies, not friends. They didn't move comfortably around each other, as friends did.

On 1 October Lord Vaughnley had signed the charity letter recommending Maynard for a knighthood: signed it casually perhaps, not knowing him well.

Then later in October his son Hugh had confessed to his dealings with Maynard, and Lord Vaughnley, outraged, had sought to unzip Maynard's accolade by getting Pollgate and his *Flag* to do the demolition; because it was the *Flag*'s sort of thing . . . and Jay Erskine, who had worked for Lord Vaughnley once, was in place there in the *Flag*, and was known not to be averse to an illegal sortie, now and then.

I didn't know why Lord Vaughnley should have gone to Pollgate, should have expected him to help. Somewhere between them there was a reason. I didn't suppose I would get an answer, if I asked.

Lord Vaughnley, I thought, could have been expected to tell the charity he wanted to recant his approval of Maynard Allardeck's knighthood: but they might have said too bad, your son was a fool, but

Allardeck definitely helped him. Lord Vaughnley might as a newspaperman have seen a few destructive paragraphs as more certain, and more revengefully satisfying, besides.

Before that, though, I guessed it had been he who had gone to the producers of *How's Trade*, who said dig up what you can about Allardeck, discredit him, I'll pay you: and had been defeated by the producer himself, who according to Rose Quince was known for taking more money in return for helping his victims off the hook.

The *How's Trade* programme on Maynard had gone out loaded in Maynard's favour, which hadn't been the plan at all. And it was after that, I thought, that Lord Vaughnley had gone to Pollgate.

I shut my eyes and drifted. The car hummed. They had the heater on. I thought about horses; more honest than men. Tomorrow I was due to ride at Haydock. Thank God the racecourse doctor hadn't been at the Guineas.

Takeovers, I thought inconsequentially. Always fending off takeovers.

Pollgate would bury me if I didn't get it right.

Towards the end of the journey both mental and physical power came seeping slowly back, like a tide rising, and it was an extraordinary feeling: I hadn't known how much power I did have until I'd both lost it and felt its return. Like not realizing how ill one had been, until one was well.

I stretched thankfully with the renewed strength in my muscles and breathed deeply from the surge in my mind, and Pollgate, for whom the consciousness of power must have been normal, sensed in some way the vital recharging in me and sat up more tensely himself.

Erskine drove into Bobby's stableyard at five minutes past three, and in the middle of what should have been a quiet snooze in the life of the horses, it seemed that there were people and movement all over the place. Erskine stopped the car with his accustomed jerk, and, Pollgate having told him to unlock the doors, we climbed out.

Holly was looking distractedly in our direction, and there were besides three or four cars, a horse trailer with the ramp down and grooms wandering about with head-collars.

There was also, to my disbelief, Jermyn Graves.

Holly came running across to me and said, 'Do something, he's a madman, and Bobby's indoors with Maynard, he came early and they've been shouting at each other and I don't want to go in, and thank God you're here, it's a farce.'

Jermyn Graves, seeing me, followed Holly. His gaze swept over Pollgate, Jay Erskine and Lord Vaughnley and he said belligerently, 'Who the hell are these people? Now see here, Fielding, I've had enough of your smart-arse behaviour, I've come for my horses.'

I put my arm around Holly. 'Did his cheque go through?' I asked her.

'Yes, it bloody well did,' Graves said furiously.

Holly nodded. 'The feed-merchant told us. The cheque was cleared yesterday. He has his money.'

'Just what is all this?' Pollgate said heavily.

'You keep out of it,' Graves said rudely. 'It's you, Fielding, I want. You give me my bloody horses or I'll fetch the police to you.'

'Calm down, Mr Graves,' I said. 'You shall have your horses.'

'They're not in their boxes.' He glared with all his old fury; and it occurred to me that his total disregard of Pollgate was sublime. Perhaps one had to know one should be afraid of someone before one was.

'Mr Graves,' I said conversationally to the two proprietors and one journalist, 'is removing his horses because of what he read in Intimate Details. You see here in action the power of the Press.'

'Shut your trap and give me my horses,' Graves said.

'Yes, all right. Your grooms are going in the wrong direction.'

'Jasper,' Graves yelled. 'Come here.'

The luckless nephew approached, eyeing me warily.

'Come on,' I jerked my head. 'Round the back.'

Jay Erskine would have prevented my going, but Pollgate intervened. I took Jasper round to the other yard and pointed out the boxes that contained Graves's horses. 'Awfully sorry,' Jasper said.

'You're welcome,' I said, and I thought that but for him and his uncle we wouldn't have rigged the bell, and but for the bell we wouldn't have caught Jay Erskine up the ladder, and I felt quite grateful to the Graveses, on the whole.

I went back with Jasper walking behind me leading the first of the horses, and found them all standing there in much the same places, Jermyn Graves blustering on about not having faith when the trainer couldn't meet his bills.

'Bobby's better off without you, Mr Graves,' I said. 'Load your horses up and hop it.'

Apoplexy hovered. He opened and shut his mouth a couple of times and finally walked over to his trailer to let out his spleen on the luckless Jasper.

'Thank God for that,' Holly said. 'I can't stand him. I'm so glad you're here. Did you have a good time at your lunch?'

'Stunning,' I said.

They all heard and looked at me sharply.

Lord Vaughnley said, mystified, 'How can you laugh . . .?'

'What the hell,' I said. 'I'm here. I'm alive.'

Holly looked from one to the other of us, sensing something strongly, not knowing what. 'Something happened?' she said, searching my face.

I nodded a fraction. 'I'm OK.'

She said to Lord Vaughnley, 'He risks his life most days of the week. You can't frighten him much.'

They looked at her speechlessly, to my amusement.

I said to her, 'Do you know who you're talking to?'

and she shook her head slightly, half remembering but not sure.

'This is Lord Vaughnley who owns the *Towncrier*. This is Nestor Pollgate who owns the *Flag*. This is Jay Erskine who wrote the paragraphs in Intimate Details and put the tap on your telephone.' I paused, and to them I said, 'My sister, Bobby's wife.'

She moved closer beside me, her eyes shocked.

'Why are they here? Did you bring them?'

'We sort of brought each other,' I said. 'Where are Maynard and Bobby?'

'In the drawing room, I think.'

Jasper was crunching across the yard with the second horse, Jermyn shouting at him unabated. The other groom who had come with them was scurrying in and out of the trailer, attempting invisibility.

Nestor Pollgate said brusquely, 'We're not standing here watching all this.'

'I'm not leaving Holly alone to put up with that man,' I said. 'He's a menace. It's because of you that he's here, so we'll wait.'

Pollgate stirred restlessly, but there was nowhere particular for him to go. We waited in varying intensities of impatience while Jasper and the groom raised the ramp and clipped it shut, and while Jermyn Graves walked back several steps in our direction and shook his fist at me with the index finger sticking out, jabbing, and said no one messed with him and got away with it, and he'd see I'd be sorry. I'd pay for what I'd done.

'Kit,' Holly said, distressed.

I put my arm round her shoulders and didn't answer Graves, and after a while he turned abruptly on his heel, went over to his car, climbed in, slammed the door, and overburdened his engine, starting with a jerk that must have rocked his horses off their feet in the trailer.

'He's a pig,' Holly said. 'What will he do?'

'He's more threat than action.'

'I,' Pollgate said, 'am not.'

I looked at him, meeting his eyes.

'I do know that,' I said.

The time, I thought, had inescapably come.

Power when I needed it. Give me power, I thought.

I let go of Holly and leaned into the car we had come in, picking up my anorak off the floor.

I said to Holly, 'Will you take these three visitors into the sitting room? I'll get Bobby . . . and his father.'

She said with wide apprehensive eyes, 'Kit, do be careful.'

'I promise.'

She gave me a look of lingering doubt, but set off with me towards the house. We went in by long habit through the kitchen: I don't think it occurred to either of us to use the formal front door.

Pollgate, Lord Vaughnley and Jay Erskine followed, and in the hall Holly peeled them off into the sitting room, where in the evenings she and Bobby watched television sometimes. The larger drawing room lay ahead, and there were voices in there, or one voice, Maynard's, continuously talking.

I screwed up every inner resource to walk through that door, and it was a great and appalling mistake. Bobby told me afterwards that he saw me in the same way as in the stable and in the garden, the hooded, the enemy, the old foe of antiquity, of immense and dark threat.

Maynard was saying monotonously as if he had already said it over and over, ' . . . And if you want to get rid of him you'll do it, and you'll do it today . . .'

Maynard was holding a gun, a hand gun, small and black.

He stopped talking the moment I went in there. His eyes widened. He saw, I supposed, what Bobby saw: Fielding, satanic.

He gave Bobby the pistol, pressing it into his hand. 'Do it,' he said fiercely. 'Do it now.'

His son's eyes were glazed, as in the garden.

He wouldn't do it. He couldn't . . .

'Bobby,' I said explosively, beseechingly: and he raised the gun and pointed it straight at my chest.

CHAPTER TWENTY

I turned my back on him.

I didn't want to see him do it; tear our lives apart, mine and his, and Holly's and the baby's. If he was going to do it, I wasn't going to watch.

Time passed, stretched out, uncountable. Danielle, I thought.

I heard his voice, close behind my shoulder.

'Kit . . .'

I stood rigidly still. You can't frighten him much, Holly had said. Bobby with a gun frightened me into immobility and despair.

He came round in front of me, as white as I felt. He looked into my face. He was holding the gun flat, not aiming, and put it into my hand.

'Forgive me,' he said.

I couldn't speak. He turned away blindly and made for the door. Holly appeared there, questioning, and he enfolded her and hugged her as if he had survived an earthquake, which he had.

I heard a faint noise behind me and turned, and

found Maynard advancing, his face sweating, his teeth showing, the charming image long gone. I turned holding the gun, and he saw it in my hand and went back a pace, and then another and another, looking fearful, looking sick.

'You incited,' I said bitterly, 'your own son to murder. Brainwashed him.'

'It would have been an accident,' he said.

'An Allardeck killing a Fielding would not have been believed as an accident.'

'I would have sworn it,' he said.

I loathed him. I said, 'Go into the sitting room,' and I stood back to let him pass, keeping the gun pointing his way all the while.

He hadn't had the courage to shoot me himself. Making Bobby do it . . . that crime was worse.

It hadn't been a good idea to draw him there with the express purpose of getting rid of me once and for all. He'd too nearly succeeded. My own stupid fault.

We went down the hall and into the sitting room. Pollgate and Erskine and Lord Vaughnley were all there, standing in the centre, with Bobby and Holly, still entwined, to one side. I went in there feeling I was walking into a cageful of tigers, and Holly said later that with the gun in my hand I looked so dangerous she hardly recognized me as her brother.

'Sit down,' I said. 'You,' I pointed to Maynard, 'over there in that chair at the end.' It was a deep chair, enveloping, no good for springing out of suddenly. 'You next, beside him,' I said to Erskine. 'Then Lord Vaughnley, on the sofa.'

Pollgate looked at the spare place beside Lord Vaughnley and took it in silence.

'Take out the stunner,' I said to him. 'Put it on the floor. Kick it this way.'

I could feel the refusal in him, see it in his eyes. Then he shrugged, and took out the flat black box, and did as I'd said.

'Right,' I said, 'you're all going to watch a video.' I glanced down at the pistol. 'I'm not a good shot. I don't know what I'd hit. So stay sitting down.' I held out the anorak in Bobby's direction. 'The tape's zipped into one of the pockets.'

'Put it on now?' he said, finding it and bringing it out. His hands were shaking, his voice unsteady. Damn Maynard, I thought.

'Yes, now,' I said. 'Holly, close the curtains and put on a lamp, it'll be dark before we're finished.'

No one spoke while she shut out the chilly day, while Bobby switched on the video machine and the television, and fed the tape into the slot. Pollgate looked moodily at the anorak which Bobby had laid on a chair and Lord Vaughnley glanced at the gun, and at my face, and away again.

'Ready,' Bobby said.

'Start it off,' I said, 'and you and Holly sit down and watch.'

I shut the door and leaned against it as Lord

Vaughnley had done in the Guineas, and Maynard's face came up bright and clear and smiling on the television screen.

He started to struggle up from his deep chair.

'Sit down,' I said flatly.

He must have guessed that what was coming was the tape he thought he'd suppressed. He looked at the gun in my hand and judged the distance he would have to cover to reach me, and he subsided into the cushions as if suddenly weak.

The interview progressed and went from smooth politeness into direct attack, and Lord Vaughnley's mouth slowly opened.

'You've not seen this before?' I said to him.

He said, 'No, no' with his gaze uninterruptedly on the screen, and I supposed that Rose wouldn't have seen any need to go running to the proprietor with her purloined tape, the two days she had had it in the *Towncrier* building.

I looked at all their faces as they watched. Maynard sick, Erskine blank, Lord Vaughnley riveted, Pollgate awakening to acute interest, Bobby and Holly horrified. Bobby, I thought ruefully, was in for some frightful shocks: it couldn't be much fun to find one's father had done so much cruel damage.

The interview finished, to be replaced by the Perrysides telling how they'd lost Metavane, with George Tarker and his son's suicide after, and Hugh Vaughnley, begging to go home; and finally Maynard again, smugly smiling.

The impact of it all on me was still great, and in the others produced something like suspended animation. Their expressions at the end of the hour and thirteen minutes were identical, of total absorption and stretched eyes, and I thought Joe would have been satisfied with the effect of his cutting, and of his hammer blow of final silence.

The trial was over: the accused, condemned. The sentence alone remained to be delivered.

The screen ran from black into snow, and no one moved.

I peeled myself off the door and walked across and switched off the set.

'Right,' I said, 'now listen.'

The eyes of all of them were looking my way with unadulterated concentration, Maynard's dark with humiliation, his body slack and deep in the chair.

'You,' I said to Lord Vaughnley, 'and you,' I said to Nestor Pollgate. 'You or your newspapers will each pay to Bobby the sum of fifty thousand pounds in compensation. You'll write promissory notes, here and now, in this room, in front of witnesses, to pay the money within three days, and those notes will be legal and binding.'

Lord Vaughnley and Nestor Pollgate simply stared.

'And in return,' I said, 'you shall have the wire-tap and the other evidence of Jay Erskine's criminal activity. You shall have complete silence from me about your various assaults on me and my property. You shall have back the draft for three thousand pounds now lodged in my bank manager's safe. And you shall have the tape you've just watched.'

Maynard said, 'No' in anguished protest, and no one took any notice.

'You,' I said to Maynard, 'will write a promissory note promising to pay to Bobby within three days the sum of two hundred and fifty thousand pounds, which will wipe out the overdrafts and the loans and mortgages on this house and stables, which you and your father made Bobby pay for, and which should rightfully be his by inheritance.'

Maynard's mouth opened, but no sound came out.

'You will also,' I said, 'give to Major and Mrs Perryside the one share you still own in Metavane.'

He began to shake his head weakly.

'And in return,' I said, 'you will have my assurance that many copies of this tape will not turn up simultaneously in droves of sensitive places, such as with the Senior Steward of the Jockey Club, or among the patrons of the civil service charity of which you are the new chairman, or in a dozen places in the City.' I paused. 'When Bobby has the money safe in the bank, you will be safe from me also. But that safety will always be conditional on your doing no harm either to Bobby and Holly or to me in future. The tapes will always exist.'

Maynard found his voice, hoarse and shaken.

'That's extortion,' he said aridly. 'It's blackmail.'

'It's justice,' I said.

There was silence. Maynard shrank as if deflated into the chair, and neither Pollgate nor Lord Vaughnley said anything at all.

'Bobby,' I said, 'take the tape out of the machine and out of this room and put it somewhere safe, and bring back some writing paper for the notes.'

Bobby stood up slowly, looking numb.

'You said we could have the tape,' Pollgate said, demurring.

'So you can, when Bobby's been paid. If the money's all safely in the bank by Friday, you shall have it then, along with Erskine's escape from going to jail.'

Bobby took the tape away, and I contemplated Pollgate's and Lord Vaughnley's expressionless faces and thought they were being a good deal too quiet. Maynard, staring at me blackly from his chair, was simple by comparison, his reactions expected. Erskine looked his usual chilling self, but without the smirk, which was an improvement.

Bobby came back with some large sheets of the headed writing paper he used for the bills for the owners, and gave a sheet each to Nestor Pollgate and Lord Vaughnley, and with stiff legs and an arm outstretched as far as it would go, gave the third to his father with his head turned away, not wanting to look at his face.

I surveyed the three of them sitting there stonily holding the blank sheets, and into my head floated various disjointed words and phrases.

'Wait,' I said. 'Don't write yet.'

The words were 'invalid', and 'obtained by menaces', and 'invalid by reason of having been extorted at gunpoint'.

I wondered if the thought had come on its own or been generated somewhere else in that room, and I looked at their faces carefully, one by one, searching their eyes.

Not Maynard. Not Erskine. Not Lord Vaughnley.

Nestor Pollgate's eyelids flickered.

'Bobby,' I said, 'pick that black box up off the floor and drop it out of the window, into the garden.'

He looked bewildered, but did as I asked, the November air blowing in a great gust through the curtains into the room.

'Now the gun,' I said, and gave it to him.

He took it gingerly and threw it out, and shut the window again.

'Right,' I said, putting my hands with deliberation into my pockets, 'you've all heard the propositions. If you accept them, please write the notes.'

For a long moment no one moved. Then Lord Vaughnley stretched out an arm to the coffee table in front of him and picked up a magazine. He put the sheet of writing paper on the magazine for support. With a slightly pursed mouth but in continued quiet he lifted a pen from a pocket inside his jacket, pressed the top of it with a click, and wrote a short sentence, signing his name and adding the date.

He held it out towards Bobby, who stepped forward hesitantly and took it.

'Read it aloud,' I said.

Bobby's voice said shakily, 'I promise to pay Robertson Allardeck fifty thousand pounds within three days of this date.' He looked up at me. 'It is signed William Vaughnley, and the date is today's.'

I looked at Lord Vaughnley.

'Thank you,' I said neutrally.

He gave the supporting magazine to Nestor Pollgate, and offered his own pen. Nestor Pollgate took both with a completely unmoved face and wrote in his turn.

Bobby took the paper from him, glanced at me, and read aloud, 'I promise to pay Robertson Allardeck fifty thousand pounds within three days of this date. It's signed Nestor Pollgate. It's dated today.'

'Thank you,' I said to Pollgate.

Bobby looked slightly dazedly at the two documents he held. They would clear the debt for the unsold yearlings, I thought. When he sold them, anything he got would be profit.

Lord Vaughnley and Jay Erskine, as if in some ritual, passed the magazine and the pen along to Maynard.

With fury he wrote, the pen jabbing hard on the paper. I took the completed page from him myself and read it aloud, 'I promise to pay my son Robertson two hundred and fifty thousand pounds within three days. Maynard Allardeck. Today's date.'

I looked up at him. 'Thank you,' I said.

'Don't thank me. Your thanks are an insult.'

I was careful, in fact, to show no triumph, though in his case I did feel it: and I had to admit to myself ruefully that in that triumph there was a definite element of the old feud. A Fielding had got the better of an Allardeck, and I dared say my ancestors were gloating.

I gave Maynard's note to Bobby. It would clear all his debts and put him on a sure footing to earn a fair living as a trainer, and he held the paper unbelievingly, as if it would evaporate before his eyes.

'Well, gentlemen,' I said cheerfully, 'bankers' drafts by Friday, and you shall have the notes back, properly receipted.'

Maynard stood up, his greying fair hair still smooth, his face grimly composed, his expensive suit falling into uncreased shape; the outer shell intact, the man inside in shreds.

He looked at nobody, avoiding eyes. He walked to the door, opened it, went out, didn't look back. A silence lengthened behind his exit like the silence at the end of the tape; the enormity of Maynard struck one dumb.

Nestor Pollgate rose to his feet, tall, frowning, still with his power intact. He looked at me judiciously, gave me a brief single nod of the head, and said to Holly, 'Which way do I go out?'

'I'll show you,' she said, sounding subdued, and led the way into the hall.

Erskine followed, his face pinched, the drooping reddish moustache in some way announcing his continuing inflexible hatred of those he had damaged.

Bobby went after him, carrying his three notes carefully as if they were brittle, and Lord Vaughnley, last of all, stood up to go. He shook his head, shrugged his shoulders, spread his hands in a sort of embarrassment.

'What can I say?' he said. 'What am I to say when I see you on racecourses?'

'Good morning, Kit,' I said.

The grey eyes almost smiled before awkwardness returned. 'Yes, but,' he said, 'after what we did to you in the Guineas . . .'

I shrugged. 'Fortunes of war,' I said. 'I don't resent it, if that's what you mean. I took the war to the *Flag*. Seek the battle, don't complain of the wounds.'

He said curiously, 'Is that how you view race-riding? How you view life?'

'I hadn't thought of it, but yes, perhaps.'

'I'm sorry all the same,' he said. 'I had no idea what it would be like. Jay Erskine got the stun gun . . . he said two short shocks and you'd be putty. I don't think Nestor realized himself how bad it would be . . .'

'Yeah,' I said dryly, 'but he agreed to it.'

'That was because,' Lord Vaughnley explained with

a touch of earnestness, wanting me to understand, perhaps to absolve, 'because you ignored all his threats.'

'About prison?' I said.

He nodded. 'Sam Leggatt warned him you were intelligent . . . he said an attempt to frame you could blow up in their faces, that you would get the *Flag* and Nestor himself into deep serious gritty trouble . . . David Morse, their lawyer, was of the same opinion, so he agreed not to try. Sam Leggatt told me. But you have to understand Nestor. He doesn't like to be crossed. He said he wasn't going to be beaten by some . . . er . . . jockey.'

Expletives deleted, I thought, amused.

'You were elusive,' he said. 'Nestor was getting impatient . . .'

'And he had a tap on my telephone?'

'Er, yes.'

'Mm,' I said. 'Is it Maynard Allardeck who is trying to take over the *Towncrier*?'

He blinked, and said 'Er – ' and recovered. 'You guessed?'

'It seemed likely, Maynard got half of Hugh's shares by a trick. I thought it just might be him who was after the whole thing.'

Lord Vaughnley nodded. 'A company . . . Allardeck is behind it. When Hugh confessed, I got people digging up Allardeck's contacts. Just digging for dirt. I'd no idea until then that he owned the company . . . his name hadn't surfaced. All I knew was that it was the same company that nearly acquired the *Flag* a year ago. Very aggressive. It cost Nestor a fortune to cap their bid, far more than he would have had to pay otherwise.'

Holy wow, I thought.

'So when you found out that Maynard was the ultimate enemy,' I said, 'and knew also that he'd recently been proposed for a knighthood, you thought at least you could put paid to that, and casually asked Pollgate to do it in the *Flag*?'

'Not all that casually. Nestor said he'd be pleased to, if it was Allardeck who had cost him so much.'

'Didn't you even consider what hell you were manufacturing for Bobby?'

'Erskine found he couldn't get at Allardeck's phone system . . . they decided on his son.'

'Callous,' I said.

'Er . . . yes.'

'And appallingly spiteful to deliver all those copies to Bobby's suppliers.'

He said without much apology, 'Nestor thought the story would make more of a splash that way. Which it did.'

We began to walk from the sitting room into the hall. He'd told me what I hadn't asked: where the alliance began. In common enmity to Maynard, who had cost them both dear.

'Will you use the tape,' I asked, 'to stop Maynard now in his tracks?'

He glanced at me. 'That would be blackmail,' he said mildly.

'Absolutely.'

'Fifty thousand pounds,' he said. 'That tape's cheap at the price.'

We went into the kitchen and paused again.

'The *Towncrier* is the third newspaper,' he said, 'that has had trouble with Allardeck's company. One paper after another . . . he won't give up till he's got one.'

'He's obsessive,' I said. 'And besides, he's wanted all his life to have power over others . . . to be kowtowed to. To be a lord.'

Lord Vaughnley's mouth opened. I told him about my grandfather, and Maynard at nine. 'He hasn't changed,' I said. 'He still wants those things. Sir first, Lord after. And don't worry, he won't get them. I sent a copy of the tape to where you sent your charity letter.'

He was dumbstruck. He said weakly, 'How did you know about that letter?'

'I saw it,' I said. 'I was shown it. I wanted to know who knew Maynard might be up for a knighthood, and there it was, with your name.'

He shook his head: at life in general, it seemed.

We went on through the kitchen and out into the cold air. All the lights were on round the yard and some of the box doors were open, the lads working there in the routine of evening stables.

'Why did you try to stop me talking to Hugh?' I asked.

'I was wrong, I see that now. But at the time . . . by then you were pressing Nestor for large compensation. He wanted us simply to get back the wire-tap and shut you up.' He spread his hands. 'No one imagined, you see, that you would do all that you've done. I mean, when it was just a matter of disgracing Allardeck in the public eye, no one could have foreseen . . . no one even thought of your existence, let alone considered you a factor. No one knew you would defend your brother-in-law, or be . . . as you are.'

We walked across the yard to the car where Pollgate and Erskine were waiting, shadowy figures behind glass.

'If I were you,' I said, 'I'd find out if Maynard owns the bookmakers that Hugh bet with. If he does, you can threaten him with fraud, and get Hugh's shares back, I should think.'

We stopped a few feet from the car.

'You're generous,' he said.

We stood there, face to face, not knowing whether or not to shake hands.

'Hugh had no chance against Maynard,' I said.

'No.' He paused. 'I'll let him come home.'

He looked at me lengthily, the mind behind the grey eyes perhaps totting up, as I was, where we stood.

Even if he hadn't intended it, he had set in motion the attacks on Bobby; yet because of them Bobby would be much better off. From the dirt, gold.

If he offered his hand, I thought, I would take it.

Tentatively, unsure, that's what he did. I shook it briefly; an acknowledgement, a truce.

'See you at the races,' I said.

When they had gone I went and found the pistol and the stun gun outside the sitting-room window, and with them in my pockets returned to the kitchen, where Holly and Bobby were looking more dazed than happy.

'Tea?' I said hopefully.

They didn't seem to hear. I put the kettle on and got out some cups.

'Kit . . .' Holly said. 'Bobby told me . . .'

'Yeah . . . well . . . have you a lemon?' I said.

She dumbly fetched me one from the refrigerator, and sliced it.

Bobby said, 'I nearly killed you.'

His distress, I saw, was still blotting out any full realization – or celebration – of the change in his fortunes. He still looked pale, still gaunt round the eyes.

'But you didn't,' I said.

'No . . . when you turned your back on me, I thought, I can't shoot him in the back . . . not in the back . . . and I woke up. Like waking from a nightmare. I couldn't . . . how could I . . . I stood there with that gun, sweating at how near I'd come . . .'

'You frightened me silly,' I said. 'Let's forget it.'

'How can we?'

'Easily.' I punched his arm lightly. 'Concentrate, my old chum, on being a daddy.'

The kettle boiled and Holly made the tea; and we heard a car driving into the yard.

'They've come back,' Holly said in dismay.

We went out to see, all of us fearful.

The car was large and bewilderingly familiar. Two of its doors opened and from one came Thomas, the princess's chauffeur, in his best uniform, and from the other, scrambling and running, Danielle.

'Kit...' She ran headlong into my arms, her face screwed up with worry. 'Are you... are you really OK?'

'Yes, I am. You can see.'

She put her head on my shoulder and I held her close, and felt her trembling, and kissed her hair.

Thomas opened a third door of the car and helped out the princess, holding the sable coat for her to put on over the silk suit against the cold.

'I am glad, Kit,' she said calmly, snuggling into the fur, 'to see you are alive and well.' She looked from me to Bobby and Holly. 'You are Bobby, you are Holly, is that right?' She held out her hand to them, which they blankly shook.

'We are here,' she said, 'because my niece Danielle insisted that we come.' She was explaining, half apologizing for her presence. 'When I went home after the Icefall luncheon,' she said to me, 'Danielle was waiting on the pavement. She said you were in very great danger, and that you were at your sister's house in Newmarket. She didn't know how she knew, but she was certain. She said that we must come at once.'

Bobby and Holly looked astounded.

'As I know that with you, Kit, telepathy definitely exists,' the princess said, 'and as you had disappeared from the lunch and were reported to be ill, and as Danielle was distraught... we came. And I see she was right in part at least. You are here, at your sister's house.'

'She was right about the rest,' Holly said soberly. 'He was in that danger... a split second from dying.' She looked at my face. 'Did you think of her then?'

I swallowed. 'Yes, I did.'

'Holy wow,' Holly said.

'Kit says that too,' Danielle said, lifting her head from my neck and beginning to recover. 'It's awesome.'

'We always did,' Holly said. She looked at Danielle with growing interest and understanding, and slowly smiled with pleasure.

'She's like us, isn't she?' she said.

'I don't know,' I said. 'I've never known what she was thinking.'

'You might, after this'; and to Danielle, with friendship, she said, 'Think of something. See if he can tell what it is.'

'OK.'

There was a silence. The only thought in my head

was that telepathy was unpredictable and only sometimes worked to order.

I looked at the princess, and at Bobby and Holly,
and saw in their faces the same hope, the same expectation, the same realization that this moment might
matter in all our futures.

I smiled into Danielle's eyes. I knew, for a certainty.

'Dustsheets,' I said.

BANKER

*My sincere thanks for the
generous help of*
JEREMY H. THOMPSON MD FRCPI
*Professor of Pharmacology
University of California
Los Angeles
and of*
MICHAEL MELLUISH
and JOHN COOPER

Contents

The First Year

MAY

Gordon Michaels stood in the fountain with all his clothes on.

'My God,' Alec said. 'What is he doing?'

'Who?'

'Your boss,' Alec said. 'Standing in the fountain.'

I crossed to the window and stared downwards: down two floors to the ornamental fountain in the forecourt of the Paul Ekaterin merchant bank. Down to where three entwining plumes of water rose gracefully into the air and fell in a glittering circular curtain. To where, in the bowl, calf-deep, stood Gordon in his navy pin-striped suit ... in his white shirt and sober silk tie ... in his charcoal socks and black shoes ... in his gold cufflinks and onyx ring ... in his polished City persona ... soaking wet.

It was his immobility, I thought, which principally alarmed. Impossible to interpret this profoundly uncharacteristic behaviour as in any way an expression of lightheartedness, of celebration or of joy.

I whisked straight out of the deep-carpeted office,

through the fire doors, down the flights of gritty stone staircase and across the marbled expanse of entrance hall. The uniformed man at the security desk was staring towards the wide glass front doors with his fillings showing and two arriving visitors were looking stunned. I went past them at a rush into the open air and slowed only in the last few strides before the fountain.

'Gordon!' I said.

His eyes were open. Beads of water ran down his forehead from his dripping black hair and caught here and there on his lashes. The main fall of water slid in a crystal sheet just behind his shoulders with scatterings of drops spraying forwards onto him like rain. Gordon's eyes looked at me unblinkingly with earnest vagueness as if he were not at all sure who I was.

'Get into the fountain,' he said.

'Er . . . why, exactly?'

'They don't like water.'

'Who don't?'

'All those people. Those people with white faces. They don't like water. They won't follow you into the fountain. You'll be all right if you're wet.'

His voice sounded rational enough for me to wonder wildly whether this was not after all a joke: but Gordon's jokes were normally small, civilized, glinting commentaries on the stupidities of mankind, not whooping, gusty, practical affairs smacking of the surreal.

4

'Come out of there, Gordon,' I said uneasily.

'No, no. They're waiting for me. Send for the police. Ring them up. Tell them to come and take them all away.'

'But *who*, Gordon?'

'All those people, of course. Those people with white faces.' His head slowly turned from side to side, his eyes focused as if at a throng closely surrounding the whole fountain. Instinctively I too looked from side to side, but all I could see were the more distant stone and glass walls of Ekaterin's, with, now, a growing chorus of heads appearing disbelievingly at the windows.

I clung still to a hope of normality. 'They work here,' I said. 'Those people work here.'

'No, no. They came with me. In the car. Only two or three of them, I thought. But all the others, they were here, you know. They want me to go with them, but they can't reach me here, they don't like the water.'

He had spoken fairly loudly throughout so that I should hear him above the noise of the fountain, and the last of these remarks reached the chairman of the bank who came striding briskly across from the building.

'Now, Gordon, my dear chap,' the chairman said authoritatively, coming to a purposeful halt at my side, 'what's all this about, for God's sake?'

'He's having hallucinations,' I said.

The chairman's gaze flicked to my face, and back to Gordon, and Gordon seriously advised him to get into

5

the fountain, because the people with white faces couldn't reach him there, on account of disliking water.

'Do something, Tim,' the chairman said, so I stepped into the fountain and took Gordon's arm.

'Come on,' I said. 'If we're wet they won't touch us. We don't have to stay in the water. Being wet is enough.'

'Is it?' Gordon said. 'Did they tell you?'

'Yes, they did. They won't touch anyone who's wet.'

'Oh. All right. If you're sure.'

'Yes, I'm sure.'

He nodded understandingly and with only slight pressure from my arm took two sensible-seeming paces through the water and stepped over the knee-high coping onto the paving slabs of the forecourt. I held onto him firmly and hoped to heaven that the people with white faces would keep their distance; and although Gordon looked around apprehensively, it appeared that they were not so far trying to abduct him.

The chairman's expression of concern was deep and genuine, as he and Gordon were firm and long-time friends. Except in appearance they were much alike; essentially clever, intuitive, and with creative imaginations. Each in normal circumstances had a manner of speaking which expressed even the toughest commands in gentle politeness and both had a visible appetite for their occupation. They were both in their fifties, both at the top of their powers, both comfortably rich.

Gordon dripped onto the paving stones.

'I think,' the chairman said, casting a glance at the inhabited windows, 'that we should go indoors. Into the boardroom, perhaps. Come along, Gordon.'

He took Gordon Michaels by his other sodden sleeve, and between us one of the steadiest banking brains in London walked obediently in its disturbing fog.

'The people with white faces,' I said as we steered a calm course across the marble entrance hall between clearly human open-mouthed watchers, 'are they coming with us?'

'Of course,' Gordon said.

It was obvious also that some of them came up in the lift with us. Gordon watched them dubiously all the time. The others, as we gathered from his reluctance to step out into the top-floor hallway, were waiting for our arrival.

'It's all right,' I said to Gordon encouragingly. 'Don't forget, we're still wet.'

'Henry isn't,' he said, anxiously eyeing the chairman.

'We're all together,' I said. 'It will be all right.'

Gordon looked doubtful, but finally allowed himself to be drawn from the lift between his supporters. The white faces apparently parted before us, to let us through.

The chairman's personal assistant came hurrying along the corridor but the chairman waved him conclusively to a stop and said not to let anyone disturb us in the boardroom until he rang the bell; and Gordon and I in our wet shoes sloshed across the deep-piled green carpet to the long glossy mahogany boardroom table. Gordon consented to sit in one of the comfortable leather armchairs which surrounded it with me and the chairman alongside, and this time it was the chairman who asked if the people with white faces were still there.

'Of course,' Gordon said, looking around. 'They're sitting in all the chairs round the table. And standing behind them. Dozens of them. Surely you can see them?'

'What are they wearing?' the chairman asked.

Gordon looked at him in puzzlement, but answered simply enough. 'White suits of course. With black buttons. Down the front, three big black buttons.'

'All of them?' the chairman asked. 'All the same?'

'Oh yes, of course.'

'Clowns,' I exclaimed.

'What?'

'White-faced clowns.'

'Oh no,' Gordon said. 'They're not clowns. They're not funny.'

'White-faced clowns are sad.'

Gordon looked troubled and wary, and kept a good eye on his visitations.

'What's best to do?' wondered the chairman; but he was talking principally to himself. To me directly, after a pause, he said, 'I think we should take him home.

He's clearly not violent, and I see no benefit in calling in a doctor here, whom we don't know. I'll ring Judith and warn her, poor girl. I'll drive him in my car as I'm perhaps the only one who knows exactly where he lives. And I'd appreciate it, Tim, if you'd come along, sit with Gordon on the back seat, keep him reassured.'

'Certainly,' I agreed. 'And incidentally his own car's here. He said that when he drove in he thought there were two or three of the white faces with him. The rest were waiting here.'

'Did he?' The chairman pondered. 'He can't have been hallucinating when he actually left home. Surely Judith would have noticed.'

'But he seemed all right in the office when he came in,' I said. 'Quiet, but all right. He sat at his desk for nearly an hour before he went out and stood in the fountain.'

'Didn't you talk with him?'

'He doesn't like people to talk when he's thinking.'

The chairman nodded. 'First thing, then,' he said, 'see if you can find a blanket. Ask Peter to find one. And ... er ... how wet are you, yourself?'

'Not soaked, except for my legs. No problem, honestly. It's not cold.'

He nodded, and I went on the errand. Peter, the assistant, produced a red blanket with Fire written across one corner for no good reason that I could think of, and with this wrapped snugly round his, by now, naked chest Gordon allowed himself to be conveyed discreetly to the chairman's car. The chairman himself slid behind the wheel and with the direct effectiveness which shaped his whole life drove his still half-damp passengers southwards through the fair May morning.

Henry Shipton, chairman of Paul Ekaterin Ltd, was physically a big-framed man whose natural bulk was kept short of obesity by raw carrots, mineral water and will power. Half visionary, half gambler, he habitually subjected every soaring idea to rigorous analytic test: a man whose powerful instinctive urges were everywhere harnessed and put to work.

I admired him. One had to. During his twenty-year stint (including ten as chairman) Paul Ekaterin Ltd had grown from a moderately successful banking house into one of the senior league, accepted world-wide with respect. I could measure almost exactly the spread of public recognition of the bank's name, since it was mine also: Timothy Ekaterin, great-grandson of Paul the founder. In my schooldays people always said 'Timothy *who? E-kat-*erin? How do you spell it?' Quite often now they simply nodded – and expected me to have the fortune to match, which I hadn't.

'They're very peaceful, you know,' Gordon said after a while.

'The white faces?' I asked.

He nodded. 'They don't say anything. They're just waiting.'

'Here in the car?'

He looked at me uncertainly. 'They come and go.'

At least they weren't pink elephants, I thought irreverently; but Gordon, like the chairman, was abstemious beyond doubt. He looked pathetic in his red blanket, the sharp mind confused with dreams, the well-groomed businessman a pre-fountain memory, the patina stripped away. This was the warrior who dealt confidently every day in millions, this huddled mass of delusions going home in wet trousers. The dignity of man was everywhere tissue-paper thin.

He lived, it transpired, in leafy splendour by Clapham Common, in a late Victorian family pile surrounded by head-high garden walls. There were high cream-painted wooden gates which were shut, and which I opened, and a short gravelled driveway between tidy lawns.

Judith Michaels erupted from her opening front door to meet the chairman's car as it rolled to a stop, and the first thing she said, aiming it variously between Henry Shipton and myself was, 'I'll throttle that bloody doctor.'

After that she said, 'How is he?' and after that, in compassion, 'Come along, love, it's all right, come along in, darling, we'll get you warm and tucked into bed in no time.'

She put sheltering arms round the red blanket as her child of a husband stumbled out of the car, and to me and to Henry Shipton she said again in fury, 'I'll kill him. He ought to be struck off.'

'They're very bad these days about house calls,' the chairman said doubtfully, 'but surely . . . he's coming?'

'No, he's not. Now you lambs both go into the kitchen – there's some coffee in the pot – and I'll be down in a sec. Come on Gordon, my dear love, up those stairs . . .' She helped him through the front door, across a Persian-rugged hall and towards a panelled wood staircase, with me and the chairman following and doing as we were told.

Judith Michaels, somewhere in the later thirties, was a brown-haired woman in whom the life-force flowed strongly and with whom I could easily have fallen in love. I'd met her several times before that morning (at the bank's various social gatherings) and had been freshly conscious each time of the warmth and glamour which were as normal to her as breathing. Whether I in return held the slightest attraction for her I didn't know and hadn't tried to find out, as entangling oneself emotionally with one's boss's wife was hardly best for one's prospects. All the same I felt the same old tug, and wouldn't have minded taking Gordon's place on the staircase.

With these thoughts, I hoped, decently hidden, I went with Henry Shipton into the friendly kitchen and drank the offered coffee.

'A great girl, Judith,' the chairman said with feeling, and I looked at him in rueful surprise and agreed.

She came to join us after a while, still more annoyed than worried. 'Gordon says there are people with white faces sitting all round the room and they won't go away. It's really too bad. It's infuriating. I'm so angry I could *spit*.'

The chairman and I looked bewildered.

'Didn't I tell you?' she said, observing us. 'Oh no, I suppose I didn't. Gordon hates anyone to know about his illness. It isn't very bad, you see. Not bad enough for him to have to stop working, or anything like that.'

'Er . . .' said the chairman. 'What illness?'

'Oh, I suppose I'll have to tell you, now this has happened. I could kill that doctor, I really could.' She took a deep breath and said, 'Gordon's got mild Parkinson's disease. His left hand shakes a bit now and then. I don't expect you've noticed. He tries not to let people see.'

We blankly shook our heads.

'Our normal doctor's just retired, and this new man, he's one of those frightfully bumptious people who think they know better than everyone else. So he's taken Gordon off the old pills, which were fine as far as I could see, and put him on some new ones. As of the day before yesterday. So when I rang him just now in an absolute *panic* thinking Gordon had suddenly gone raving mad or something and I'd be spending the rest of my life visiting mental hospitals he says lightheartedly not to worry, this new drug quite often causes hallucinations, and it's just a matter of getting the dosage right. I tell you, if he hadn't been at the other end of a telephone wire, I'd have *strangled* him.'

Both Henry Shipton and I, however, were feeling markedly relieved.

'You mean,' the chairman asked, 'that this will all just ... wear off?'

She nodded. 'That bloody doctor said to stop taking the pills and Gordon would be perfectly normal in thirty-six hours. I *ask* you! And after that he's got to start taking them again, but only half the amount, and to see what happens. And if we were *worried*, he said pityingly, as if we'd no right to be, Gordon could toddle along to the surgery in a couple of days and discuss it with him, though as Gordon would be perfectly all right by tomorrow night we might think there was no need.'

She herself was shaking slightly with what still looked like anger but was more probably a release of tension, because she suddenly sobbed, twice, and said, 'Oh God,' and wiped crossly at her eyes.

'I was so frightened, when you told me,' she said, half apologetically. 'And when I rang the surgery I got that damned obstructive receptionist and had to argue for ten minutes before she let me even *talk* to the doctor.'

After a brief sympathetic pause the chairman, going as usual to the heart of things, said, 'Did the doctor say how long it would take to get the dosage right?'

She looked at him with a defeated grimace. 'He said that as Gordon had reacted so strongly to an average dose it might take as much as six weeks to get him thoroughly stabilized. He said each patient was dif-

14

ferent, but that if we would persevere it would be much the best drug for Gordon in the long run.'

Henry Shipton drove me pensively back to the City.

'I think,' he said, 'that we'll say – in the office – that Gordon felt flu coming on and took some pills which proved hallucinatory. We might say simply that he imagined that he was on holiday, and felt the need for a dip in a pool. Is that agreeable?'

'Sure,' I said mildly.

'Hallucinatory drugs are, after all, exceedingly common these days.'

'Yes.'

'No need, then, Tim, to mention white-faced clowns.'

'No,' I agreed.

'Nor Parkinson's disease, if Gordon doesn't wish it.'

'I'll say nothing,' I assured him.

The chairman grunted and lapsed into silence; and perhaps we both thought the same thoughts along the well-worn lines of drug-induced side-effects being more disturbing than the disease.

It wasn't until we were a mile from the bank that Henry Shipton spoke again, and then he said, 'You've been in Gordon's confidence for two years now, haven't you?'

'Nearly three,' I murmured, nodding.

'Can you hold the fort until he returns?'

It would be dishonest to say that the possibility of this offer hadn't been in my mind since approximately

15

ten-fifteen, so I accepted it with less excitement than relief.

There was no rigid hierarchy in Ekaterin's. Few explicit ranks: to be 'in so and so's confidence', as house jargon put it, meant one would normally be on course for more responsibility, but unlike the other various thirty-two-year-olds who crowded the building with their hopes and expectations I lived under the severe disadvantage of my name. The whole board of directors, consistently afraid of accusations of nepotism, made me double-earn every step.

'Thank you,' I said neutrally.

He smiled a shade. 'Consult,' he said, 'whenever you need help.'

I nodded. His words weren't meant as disparagement. Everyone consulted, in Ekaterin's, all the time. Communication between people and between departments was an absolute priority in Henry Shipton's book, and it was he who had swept away a host of small-room offices to form opened-up expanses. He himself sat always at one (fairly opulent) desk in a room that contained eight similar, his own flanked on one side by the vice-chairman's and on the other by that of the head of Corporate Finance. Further senior directors from other departments occupied a row of like desks opposite, all of them within easy talking earshot of each other.

As with all merchant banks, the business carried on by Ekaterin's was different and separate from that conducted by the High Street chains of clearing banks. At Ekaterin's one never actually saw any money. There were no tellers, no clerks, no counters, no paying-ins, no withdrawals and hardly any chequebooks.

There were three main departments, each with its separate function and each on its own floor of the building. Corporate Finance acted for major clients on mergers, takeovers and the raising of capital. Banking, which was where I worked with Gordon, lent money to enterprise and industry. And Investment Management, the oldest and largest department, aimed at producing the best possible returns for the vast investment funds of charities, companies, pensions, trusts and trade unions.

There were several small sections like Administration, which did everyone's paperwork; like Property, which bought, sold, developed and leased; like Research, which dug around; like Overseas Investments, growing fast; and like Foreign Exchange, where about ten frenetic young wizards bought and sold world currencies by the minute, risking millions on decimal point margins and burning themselves out by forty.

The lives of all the three hundred and fifty people who worked for Ekaterin's were devoted to making money work. To the manufacture, in the main, of business, trade, industry, pensions and jobs. It wasn't a bad thing to be convinced of the worth of what one did, and certainly there was a tough basic harmony in the place which persisted unruffled by the surface tensions and jealousies and territorial defences of everyday office life.

Events had already moved on by the time the chairman and I returned to the hive. The chairman was pounced upon immediately in the entrance hall by a worriedly waiting figure from Corporate Finance, and upstairs in Banking Alec was giggling into his blotter.

Alec, my own age, suffered, professionally speaking, from an uncontrollable bent for frivolity. It brightened up the office no end, but as court jesters seldom made it to the throne his career path was already observably sideways and erratic. The rest of us were probably hopelessly stuffy. Thank God, I often thought, for Alec.

He had a well-shaped face of scattered freckles on cream-pale skin; a high forehead, a mat of tight tow-coloured curls. Stiff blond eyelashes blinked over alert blue eyes behind gold-framed spectacles, and his mouth twitched easily as he saw the funny side. He was liked on sight by almost everybody, and it was only gradually that one came to wonder whether the examiner who had awarded him a First in Law at Oxford had been suffering from critical blindness.

'What's up?' I said, instinctively smiling to match the giggles.

'We've been leaked.' He lifted his head but tapped the paper which lay on his desk. 'My *dear*,' he said with mischievous pleasure, 'this came an hour ago and it seems we're leaking all over the place like a punctured bladder. Like a baby. Like the *Welsh*.'

Leeking like the Welsh . . . ah well.

He lifted up the paper, and all, or at least a great deal, was explained. There had recently appeared a slim bi-monthly publication called *What's Going On Where It Shouldn't*, which had fast caught the attention of most of the country and was reportedly read avidly by the police. Descendant of the flood of investigative journalism spawned by the tidal wave of Watergate, *What's Going On . . .* was said to be positively bombarded by informers telling *precisely* what was going on, and all the investigating the paper had to do was into the truth of the information: which task it had been known to perform less than thoroughly.

'What does it say?' I asked; as who wouldn't?

'Cutting out the larky innuendo,' he said, 'it says that someone at Ekaterin's has been selling inside information.'

'*Selling* . . .'

'Quite so.'

'About a takeover?'

'How did you guess?'

I thought of the man from Corporate Finance hopping from leg to leg with impatience while he waited for the chairman to return and knew that nothing but extreme urgency would have brought him down to the doorstep.

'Let's see,' I said, and took the paper from Alec.

The piece headed merely 'Tut tut' was only four paragraphs long, and the first three of those were taken up with explaining with seductive authority that in merchant banks it was possible for the managers of investment funds to learn at an early stage about a takeover being organized by their colleagues. It was strictly illegal, however, for an investment manager to act on this private knowledge, even though by doing so he might make a fortune for his clients.

The shares of a company about to be taken over were likely to rise in value. If one could buy them at a low price before even a rumour of takeover started, the gain could be huge.

Such unprofessional behaviour by a merchant bank would be instantly recognized simply *because* of the profits made, and no investment manager would invite personal disaster in that way.

However, [asked the article] What's Going On in the merchant bank of Paul Ekaterin Ltd? Three times in the past year takeovers managed by this prestigious firm have been 'scooped' by vigorous buying beforehand of the shares concerned. The buying itself cannot be traced to Ekaterin's investment managers, but we are informed that the information did come from within Ekaterin's, and that someone there has been selling the golden news, either for straight cash or a slice of the action.

'It's a guess,' I said flatly, giving Alec back the paper. 'There are absolutely no facts.'

'A bucket of cold water,' he complained, 'is a sunny day compared with you.'

'Do you *want* it to be true?' I asked curiously.

'Livens the place up a bit.'

And there, I thought, was the difference between Alec and me. For me the place was alive all the time, even though when I'd first gone there eight years earlier it had been unwillingly; a matter of being forced into it by my uncle. My mother had been bankrupt at that point, her flat stripped to the walls by the bailiffs of everything except a telephone (property of the Post Office) and a bed. My mother's bankruptcy, as both my uncle and I well knew, was without doubt her own fault, but it didn't stop him applying his blackmailing pressure.

'I'll clear her debts and arrange an allowance for her if you come and work in the bank.'

'But I don't want to.'

'I know that. And I know you're stupid enough to try to support her yourself. But if you do that she'll ruin you like she ruined your father. Just give the bank a chance, and if you hate it after three months I'll let you go.'

So I'd gone with mulish rebellion to tread the path of my great-grandfather, my grandfather and my uncle, and within three months you'd have had to prise me loose with a crowbar. I suppose it was in my blood. All the snooty teenage scorn I'd felt for 'money-grubbing', all the supercilious disapproval of my student days, all the negative attitudes bequeathed by my failure of a father, all had melted into comprehension, interest and finally delight. The art of money-management now held me as addicted as any junkie, and my working life was as fulfilling as any mortal could expect.

'Who do you think did it?' Alec said.

'If anyone did.'

'It must have happened,' he said positively. 'Three times in the last year... that's more than a coincidence.'

'And I'll bet that that coincidence is all the paper's working on. They're dangling a line. Baiting a hook. They don't even say which takeovers they mean, let alone give figures.'

True or not, though, the story itself was bad for the bank. Clients would back away fast if they couldn't trust, and *What's Going On* ... was right often enough to instil disquiet. Henry Shipton spent most of the afternoon in the boardroom conducting an emergency meeting of the directors, with ripples of unease spreading outwards from there through all departments. By going-home time that evening practically everyone in the building had read the bombshell, and although some took it as lightheartedly as Alec, it had the effect of almost totally deflecting speculation from Gordon Michaels.

I explained only twice about flu and pills: only two people asked. When the very reputation of the bank was being rocked, who cared about a dip in the ornamental fountain, even if the bather had had all his clothes on and was a director in Banking.

On the following day I found that filling Gordon's job was no lighthearted matter. Until then he had gradually given me power of decision over loans up to certain amounts, but anything larger was in his own domain entirely. Within my bracket, it meant that I could arrange any loan if I believed the client was sound and could repay principal and interest at an orderly rate: but if I judged wrong and the client went bust, the lenders lost both their money and their belief in my common sense. As the lenders were quite often the bank itself, I couldn't afford for it to happen too often.

With Gordon there, the ceiling of my possible disasters had at least been limited. For him, though, the ceiling hardly existed, except that with loans incurring millions it was normal for him to consult with others on the board.

These consultations, already easy and informal because of the open-plan layout, also tended to stretch over lunch, which the directors mostly ate together in their own private dining room. It was Gordon's habit to look with a pleased expression at his watch at five to one and take himself amiably off in the direction of a tomato juice and roast lamb; and he would return an hour later with his mind clarified and made up.

I'd been lent Gordon's job but not his seat on the

board, so I was without the benefit of the lunches; and
as he himself had been the most senior in our own
green pasture of office expanse, there was no one else
of his stature immediately at hand. Alec's advice tended
to swing between the brilliantly perceptive and the
maniacally reckless, but one was never quite sure which
was which at the time. All high-risk Cinderellas would
have gone to the ball under Alec's wand; the trick was
in choosing only those who would keep an eye on the
clock and deliver the crystal goods.

Gordon tended therefore to allocate only cast-iron
certainties to Alec's care and most of the Cinderella-
type to me, and he'd said once with a smile that in this
job one's nerve either toughened or broke, which I'd
thought faintly extravagant at the time. I understood,
though, what he meant when I faced without him a
task which lay untouched on his desk: a request for
financial backing for a series of animated cartoon films.

It was too easy to turn things down ... and perhaps
miss Peanuts or Mickey Mouse. A large slice of the
bank's profits came from the interest paid by borrowers.
If we didn't lend, we didn't earn. A toss-up. I picked
up the telephone and invited the hopeful cartoonist to
bring his proposals to the bank.

Most of Gordon's projects were halfway through,
his biggest at the moment being three point four million
for an extension to a cake factory. I had heard him
working on this one for a week, so I merely took on
where he had left off, telephoning people who some-

times had funds to lend and asking if they'd be interested in underwriting a chunk of Home-made Heaven. The bank itself, according to Gordon's list, was lending three hundred thousand only, which made me wonder whether he privately expected the populace to go back to eating bread.

There was also, tucked discreetly in a folder, a glossy prospectus invitation to participate in a multi-million project in Brazil, whereon Gordon had doodled in pencil an army of question marks and a couple of queries: *Do we or don't we? Remember Brasilia! Is coffee enough??* On the top of the front page, written in red, was a jump-to-it memo: *Preliminary answer by Friday.*

It was already Thursday. I picked up the prospectus and went along to the other and larger office at the end of the passage, where Gordon's almost-equal sat at one of the seven desks. Along there the carpet was still lush and the furniture still befitting the sums dealt with on its tops, but the view from the windows was different. No fountain, but the sunlit dome of St Paul's Cathedral rising like a Fabergé egg from the white stone lattice of the City.

'Problem?' asked Gordon's almost-equal. 'Can I help?'

'Do you know if Gordon meant to go any further with this?' I asked. 'Did he say?'

Gordon's colleague looked the prospectus over and shook his head. 'Who's along there with you today?'

'Only Alec. I asked him. He doesn't know.'

'Where's John?'

'On holiday. And Rupert is away because of his wife.'

The colleague nodded. Rupert's wife was imminently dying: cruel at twenty-six.

'I'd take it around,' he said. 'See if Gordon's put out feelers in Research, Overseas, anywhere. Form a view yourself. Then if you think it's worth pursuing you can take it to Val and Henry.' Val was head of Banking and Henry was Henry Shipton. I saw that to be Gordon was a big step up indeed, and was unsure whether to be glad or sorry that the elevation would be temporary.

I spent all afternoon drifting round with the prospectus and in the process learned less about Brazil than about the tizzy over the report in *What's Going On* ... Soul-searching appeared to be fashionable. Long faces enquired anxiously, 'Could one possibly ... without knowing ... have mentioned a takeover to an interested party?' And the short answer to that, it seemed to me, was No, one couldn't. Secrecy was everywhere second nature to bankers.

If the article in the paper were true there had to be three people involved: the seller, the buyer and the informant; and certainly neither the buyer nor the informant could have acted in ignorance or by chance. Greed and malice moved like worms in the dark. If one were infested by them, one knew.

Gordon seemed to have asked no one about Brazil,

and for me it was make-up-your-mind time. It would have been helpful to know what the other merchant banks thought, the sixteen British accepting houses like Schroder's, Hambro's, Morgan Grenfell, Kleinwort Benson, Hill Samuel, Warburg's, Robert Fleming, Singer and Friedlander . . . all permitted, like Paul Ekaterin's, to assume that the Bank of England would come to their aid in a crisis.

Gordon's opposite numbers in those banks would all be pursing mouths over the same prospectus, committing millions to a fruitful enterprise, pouring millions down the drain, deciding not to risk it either way.

Which?

One could hardly directly ask, and finding out via the grapevine took a little time.

I carried the prospectus finally to Val Fisher, head of Banking, who usually sat at one of the desks facing Henry Shipton, two floors up.

'Well, Tim, what's your own view?' he said. A short man, very smooth, very charming, with nerves like toughened ice.

'Gordon had reservations, obviously,' I said. 'I don't know enough, and no one else here seems to. I suppose we could either make a preliminary answer of cautious interest and then find out a bit more, or just trust to Gordon's instinct.'

He smiled faintly. 'Which?'

Ah, which?

'Trust to Gordon's instinct, I think,' I said.

'Right.'

He nodded and I went away and wrote a polite letter to the Brazil people expressing regret. And I wouldn't know for six or seven years, probably, whether that decision was right or wrong.

The gambles were all long term. You cast your bread on the waters and hoped it would float back in the future with butter and jam.

Mildew . . . too bad.

JUNE

Gordon telephoned three weeks later sounding thoroughly fit and well. I glanced across to where his desk stood mute and tidy, with all the paper action now transferred to my own.

'Judith and I wanted to thank you . . .' he was saying.

'Really no need,' I said. 'How are you?'

'Wasting time. It's ridiculous. Anyway, we've been offered a half-share in a box at Ascot next Thursday. We thought it might be fun . . . We've six places. Would you like to come? As our guest, of course. As a thank you.'

'I'd love it,' I said. 'But . . .'

'No buts,' he interrupted. 'If you'd like to, Henry will fix it. He's coming himself. He agreed you'd earned a day off, so all you have to do is decide.'

'Then I'd like to, very much.'

'Good. If you haven't a morning coat, don't worry. We're not in the Royal Enclosure.'

'If you're wearing one . . . I inherited my father's.'

'Ah. Good. Yes, then. One o'clock Thursday, for

lunch. I'll send the entrance tickets to you in the office. Both Judith and I are very pleased you can come. We're very grateful. Very.' He sounded suddenly half-embarrassed, and disconnected with a click.

I wondered how much he remembered about the white faces, but with Alec and Rupert and John all in earshot it had been impossible to ask. Maybe at the races he would tell me. Maybe not.

Going racing wasn't something I did very often nowadays, although as a child I'd spent countless afternoons waiting around the Tote queues while my mother in pleasurable agony backed her dozens of hunches and bankers and third strings and savers and lost money by the ton.

'I've won!' she would announce radiantly to all about her, waving an indisputably winning ticket: and the bunch of losses on the same race would be thrust into a pocket and later thrown away.

My father at the same time would be standing drinks in the bar, an amiable open-fisted lush with more good nature than sense. They would take me home at the end of the day giggling happily together in a hired chauffeur-driven Rolls, and until I was quite old I never questioned but that this contented affluence was built on rock.

I had been their only child and they'd given me a very good childhood to the extent that when I thought of holidays it was of yachts on warm seas or Christmas in the Alps. The villain of those days was my uncle who descended on us occasionally to utter Dire Warnings about the need for his brother (my father) to find a job.

My father, however, couldn't shape up to 'money-grubbing' and in any case had no real ability in any direction; and with no habit of working he had quietly scorned people who had. He never tired of his life of aimless ease, and if he earned no one's respect, few detested him either. A weak, friendly, unintelligent man. Not bad as a father. Not good at much else.

He dropped dead of a heart attack when I was nineteen and it was then that the point of the Dire Warnings became apparent. He and mother had lived on the capital inherited from grandfather, and there wasn't a great deal left. Enough just to see me through college; enough, with care, to bring mother a small income for life.

Not enough to finance her manner of betting, which she wouldn't or couldn't give up. A lot more of the Dire Warnings went unheeded, and finally, while I was trying to stem a hopeless tide by working (of all things) for a bookmaker, the bailiffs knocked on the door.

In twenty-five years, it seemed, my mother had gambled away the best part of half a million pounds; all gone on horses, fast and slow. It might well have sickened me altogether against racing, but in a curious way it hadn't. I remembered how much she and father had enjoyed themselves; and who was to say that it was a fortune ill spent?

'Good news?' Alec said, eyeing my no doubt ambivalent expression.

'Gordon's feeling better.'

'Hm,' he said judiciously, 'so he should be. Three weeks off for flu . . .' He grinned. 'Stretching it a bit.'

I made a non-committal grunt.

'Be glad, shall we, when he comes back?'

I glanced at his amused, quizzical face and saw that he knew as well as I did that when Gordon reappeared to repossess his kingdom, I wouldn't be glad at all. Doing Gordon's job, after the first breath-shortening initial plunge, had injected me with great feelings of vigour and good health; had found me running up stairs and singing in the bath and showing all the symptoms of a love affair; and like many a love affair it couldn't survive the return of the husband. I wondered how long I'd have to wait for such a chance again, and whether next time I'd feel as high.

'Don't think I haven't noticed,' Alec said, the eyes electric blue behind the gold-rimmed specs.

'Noticed what?' Rupert asked, raising his head above papers he'd been staring blindly at for ninety minutes.

Back from his pretty wife's death and burial poor Rupert still wore a glazed otherwhere look and tended too late to catch up with passing conversations. In the two days since his return he had written no letters, made no telephone calls, reached no decisions. Out of compassion one had had to give him time, and Alec and I continued to do his work surreptitiously without him realizing.

'Nothing,' I said.

Rupert nodded vaguely and looked down again, an automaton in his living grief. I'd never loved anyone, I thought, as painfully as that. I think I hoped that I never would.

John, freshly returned also, but from his holidays, glowed with a still-red sunburn and had difficulty in fitting the full lurid details of his sexual adventures into Rupert's brief absences to the washroom. Neither Alec nor I ever believed John's sagas, but at least Alec found them funny, which I didn't. There was an element lurking there of a hatred of women, as if every boasted possession (real or not) was a statement of spite. He didn't actually use the word possession. He said 'made' and 'screwed' and 'had it off with the little cow'. I didn't like him much and he thought me a prig: we were polite in the office and never went together to lunch. And it was he alone of all of us who actively looked forward to Gordon's return, he who couldn't disguise his dismay that it was I who was filling the empty shoes instead of himself.

'Of course, if I'd been here . . .' he said at least once a day; and Alec reported that John had been heard telling Gordon's almost-equal along the passage that now he, John, was back, Gordon's work should be transferred from me to him.

'Did you hear him?' I asked, surprised.

'Sure. And he was told in no uncertain terms that it was the Old Man himself who gave you the green light, and there was nothing John could do about it. Proper miffed was our Lothario. Says it's all because you are who you are, and all that.'

'Sod him.'

'Rather you than me.' He laughed gently into his blotter and picked up the telephone to find backers for a sewage and water purification plant in Norfolk.

'Did you know,' he said conversationally, busy dialling a number, 'that there are so few sewage farms in West Berlin that they pay the East Berliners to get rid of the extra?'

'No, I didn't.' I didn't especially want to know, either, but as usual Alec was full of useless information and possessed by the urge to pass it on.

'The East Berliners take the money and dump the stuff out in the open fields. Untreated, mind you.'

'Do shut up,' I said.

'I saw it,' he said. 'And smelled it. Absolutely disgusting.'

'It was probably fertilizer,' I said, 'and what were you doing in East Berlin?'

'Calling on Nefertiti.'

'She of the one eye?'

'My God, yes, isn't it a shock? Oh . . . hello . . .' He got through to his prospective money-source and for far too long and with a certain relish explained the need for extra facilities to reverse the swamp of effluent

34

which had been killing off the Broads. 'No risk involved, of course, with a water authority.' He listened. 'I'll put you in, then, shall I? Right.' He scribbled busily and in due course disconnected. 'Dead easy, this one. Ecology and all that. Good emotional stuff.'

I shuffled together a bunch of papers of my own that were very far from dead easy and went up to see Val Fisher, who happened to be almost alone in the big office. Henry Shipton, it seemed, was out on one of his frequent walkabouts through the other departments.

'It's a cartoonist,' I said. 'Can I consult?'

'Pull up a chair.' Val nodded and waved hospitably, and I sat beside him, spread out the papers, and explained about the wholly level-headed artist I had spent three hours with two weeks earlier.

'He's been turned down by his own local bank, and so far by three other firms like ourselves,' I said. 'He's got no realizable assets, no security. He rents a flat and is buying a car on HP. If we financed him, it would be out of faith.'

'Background?' he asked. 'Covenant?'

'Pretty solid. Son of a sales manager. Respected at art school as an original talent: I talked to the Principal. His bank manager gave him a clean bill but said that his head office wouldn't grant what he's asking. For the past two years he's worked for a studio making animated commercials. They say he's good at the job; understands it thoroughly. They know he wants to go it alone, they think he's capable and they don't want to lose him.'

'How old?'

'Twenty-four.'

Val gave me an 'Oh ho ho' look, knowing, as I did, that it was the cartoonist's age above all which had invited negative responses from the other banks.

'What's he asking?' Val said, but he too looked as if he were already deciding against.

'A studio, properly equipped. Funds to employ ten copying artists, with the expectation that it will be a year before any films are completed and can expect to make money. Funds for promotion. Funds for himself to live on. These sheets set out the probable figures.'

Val made a face over the pages, momentarily re-arranging the small neat features, slanting the tidy dark moustache, raising the arched eyebrows towards the black cap of hair.

'Why haven't you already turned him down?' he asked finally.

'Um,' I said. 'Look at his drawings.' Opened another file and spread out the riotously coloured progression of pages which established two characters and told a funny story. I watched Val's sophisticated world-weary face as he leafed through them: saw the awakening interest, heard the laugh.

'Exactly,' I said.

'Hmph.' He leaned back in his chair and gave me

an assessing stare. 'You're not saying you think we should take him on?'

'It's an unsecured risk, of course. But yes, I am. With a string or two, of course, like a cost accountant to keep tabs on things and a first option to finance future expansion.'

'Hm.' He pondered for several minutes, looking again at the drawings which still seemed funny to me even after a fortnight's close acquaintance. 'Well, I don't know. It's too like aiming at the moon with a bow and arrow.'

'They might watch those films one day on space shuttles,' I said mildly, and he gave me a fast amused glance while he squared up the drawings and returned them to their folder.

'Leave these all here, then, will you?' he said. 'I'll have a word with Henry over lunch.' And I guessed in a swift uncomfortable moment of insight that what they would discuss would be not primarily the cartoonist but the reliability or otherwise of my judgement. If they thought me a fool I'd be back behind John in the promotion queue in no time.

At four-thirty, however, when my inter-office telephone rang, it was Val at the other end.

'Come up and collect your papers,' he said. 'Henry says this decision is to be yours alone. So sink or swim, Tim, it's up to you.'

*

One's first exposure to the Royal Ascot meeting was, according to one's basic outlook, either a matter of surprised delight or of puritanical disapproval. Either the spirits lifted to the sight of emerald grass, massed flowers, bright dresses, fluffy hats and men elegant in grey formality, or one despised the expenditure, the frivolity, the shame of champagne and strawberries while some in the world starved.

I belonged, without doubt, to the hedonists, both by upbringing and inclination. The Royal meeting at Ascot was, as it happened, the one racing event from which my parents had perennially excluded me, children in any case being barred from the Royal Enclosure for three of the four days, and mother more interested on this occasion in socializing than betting. School, she had said firmly every year, must come first: though on other days it hadn't, necessarily. So it was with an extra sense of pleasure that I walked through the gates in my father's resurrected finery and made my way through the smiling throng to the appointed, high-up box.

'Welcome to the charade,' Gordon said cheerfully, handing me a bubbling glass, and 'Isn't this *fun*?' Judith exclaimed, humming with excitement in yellow silk.

'It's great,' I said, and meant it; and Gordon, looking sunburned and healthy, introduced me to the owner of the box.

'Dissdale, this is Tim Ekaterin. Works in the bank. Tim – Dissdale Smith.'

We shook hands. His was plump and warm, like his body, like his face. 'Delighted,' he said. 'Got a drink? Good. Met my wife? No? Bettina, darling, say hello to Tim.' He put an arm round the thin waist of a girl less than half his age whose clinging white black-dotted dress was cut low and bare at neck and armholes. There was also a wide black hat, beautiful skin and a sweet and practised smile.

'Hello, Tim,' she said. 'So glad you could come.' Her voice, I thought, was like the rest of her: manufactured, processed, not natural top drawer but a long way from the gutter.

The box itself was approximately five yards by three, most of the space being filled by a dining table laid with twelve places for lunch. The far end wall was of windows looking out over the green course, with a glass door opening to steps going down to the viewing balcony. The walls of the box were covered as if in a house with pale blue hessian, and a soft blue carpet, pink flowers and pictures lent an air of opulence far greater than the actual expense. Most of the walls of the boxes into which I'd peered on the way along to this one were of builders' universal margarine colour, and I wondered fleetingly whether it was Dissdale or Bettina who had the prettying mind.

Henry Shipton and his wife were standing in the doorway to the balcony, alternately facing out and in, like a couple of Januses. Henry across the room lifted his glass to me in a gesture of acknowledgement, and Lorna as ever looked as if faults were being found.

Lorna Shipton, tall, over-assured, and dressed that frilly day in repressive tailored grey, was a woman from whom disdain flowed outward like a tide, a woman who seemed not to know that words could wound and saw no reason not to air each ungenerous thought. I had met her about the same number of times as I'd met Judith Michaels and mostly upon the same occasions, and if I smothered love for the one, it was irritation I had to hide for the other. It was, I suppose, inevitable, that of the two it was Lorna Shipton I was placed next to at lunch.

More guests arrived behind me, Dissdale and Bettina greeting them with whoops and kisses and making the sort of indistinct introductions that one instantly forgets. Dissdale decided there would be less crush if everyone sat down and so took his place at the top of the table with Gordon, his back to the windows, at the foot. When each had arranged their guests around them there were two empty places, one next to Gordon, one up Dissdale's end.

Gordon had Lorna Shipton on his right, with me beside her: the space on his left, then Henry, then Judith. The girl on my right spent most of her time leaning forward to speak to her host Dissdale, so that although I grew to know quite well the blue chiffon back of her shoulder, I never actually learned her name.

Laughter, chatter, the study of race cards, the

refilling of glasses; Judith with yellow silk roses on her hat and Lorna telling me that my morning coat looked a size too small.

'It was my father's,' I said.

'Such a stupid man.'

I glanced at her face, but she was merely expressing her thoughts, not positively trying to offend.

'A beautiful day for racing,' I said.

'You should be working. Your Uncle Freddie won't like it, you know. I'm certain that when he bailed you out he made it a condition that you and your mother should both stay away from racecourses. And now look at you. It's really too bad. I'll have to tell him, of course.'

I wondered how Henry put up with it. Wondered, as one does, why he'd married her. He, however, his ear attuned across the table in a husbandly way, said to her pleasantly, 'Freddie knows that Tim is here, my dear. Gordon and I obtained dispensation, so to speak.' He gave me a glimmer of a smile. 'The wrath of God has been averted.'

'Oh.' Lorna Shipton looked disappointed and I noticed Judith trying not to laugh.

Uncle Freddie, ex-vice-chairman, now retired, still owned enough of the bank to make his unseen presence felt, and I knew he was in the habit of telephoning Henry two or three times a week to find out what was going on. Out of interest, one gathered, not from a desire to meddle; as certainly, once he had set his terms, he never meddled with mother and me.

Dissdale's last guest arrived at that point with an unseen flourish of trumpets, a man making an entrance as if well aware of newsworthiness. Dissdale leapt to his feet to greet him and pumped him warmly by the hand.

'Calder, this is great. Calder Jackson, everybody.'

There were yelps of delight from Dissdale's end and polite smiles round Gordon's. 'Calder Jackson,' Dissdale said down the table, 'you know, the miracle-worker. Brings dying horses back to life. You must have seen him on television.'

'Ah yes,' Gordon responded. 'Of course.'

Dissdale beamed and returned to his guest who was lapping up adulation with a show of modesty.

'Who did he say?' Lorna Shipton asked.

'Calder Jackson,' Gordon said.

'Who?'

Gordon shook his head, his ignorance showing. He raised his eyebrows in a question to me, but I fractionally shook my head also. We listened, however, and we learned.

Calder Jackson was a shortish man with a head of hair designed to be noticed. Designed literally, I guessed. He had a lot of dark curls going attractively grey, cut short towards the neck but free and fluffy on top of his head and over his forehead; and he had let his beard grow in a narrow fringe from in front of his ears round the line of his jaw, the hairs of this being also bushy and curly but grey to white. From in front his weathered face was thus circled with curls: from the side he looked as if he were wearing a helmet. Or a coal-scuttle, I thought unflatteringly. Once seen, in any case, never forgotten.

'It's just a gift,' he was saying deprecatingly in a voice that had an edge to it more compelling than loudness: an accent very slightly of the country but of no particular region; a confidence born of acclaim.

The girl sitting next to me was ecstatic. 'How *divine* to meet you. One has heard so *much* ... Do tell us, now do tell us your secret.'

Calder Jackson eyed her blandly, his gaze sliding for a second beyond her to me and then back again. Myself he quite openly discarded as being of no interest, but to the girl he obligingly said, 'There's no secret, my dear. None at all. Just good food, good care and a few age-old herbal remedies. And, of course ... well ... the laying on of hands.'

'But *how*,' asked the girl, 'how do you do that to horses?'

'I just ... touch them.' He smiled disarmingly. 'And then sometimes I feel them quiver, and I know the healing force is going from me into them.'

'Can you do it infallibly?' Henry asked politely, and I noted with interest that he'd let no implication of doubt sound in his voice: Henry, whose gullibility could be measured in micrograms, if at all.

Calder Jackson took his seriousness for granted and

slowly shook his head. 'If I have the horse in my care for long enough, it usually happens in the end. But not always. No, sadly, not always.'

'How fascinating,' Judith said, and earned another of those kind bland smiles. Charlatan or not, I thought, Calder Jackson had the mix just right: an arresting appearance, a modest demeanour, no promise of success. And for all I knew, he really could do what he said. Healers were an age-old phenomenon, so why not a healer of horses?

'Can you heal people too?' I asked in a mirror-image of Henry's tone. No doubts. Just enquiry.

The curly head turned my way with more civility than interest and he patiently answered the question he must have been asked a thousand times before. Answered in a sequence of words he had perhaps used almost as often. 'Whatever gift it is that I have is especially for horses. I have no feeling that I can heal humans, and I prefer not to try. I ask people not to ask me, because I don't like to disappoint them.'

I nodded my thanks, watched his head turn away and listened to him willingly answering the next question, from Bettina, as if it too had never before been asked. 'No, the healing very seldom happens instantaneously. I need to be near the horse for a while. Sometimes for only a few days. Sometimes for a few weeks. One can never tell.'

Dissdale basked in the success of having hooked his celebrity and told us all that two of Calder's ex-patients were running that very afternoon. 'Isn't that right, Calder?'

The curly head nodded. 'Cretonne, in the first race, she used to break blood vessels, and Molyneaux, in the fifth, he came to me with infected wounds. I feel they are my friends now. I feel I know them.'

'And shall we back them, Calder?' Dissdale asked roguishly. 'Are they going to win?'

The healer smiled forgivingly. 'If they're fast enough, Dissdale.'

Everyone laughed. Gordon refilled his own guests' glasses. Lorna Shipton said apropos of not much that she had occasionally considered becoming a Christian Scientist and Judith wondered what colour the Queen would be wearing. Dissdale's party talked animatedly among themselves, and the door from the corridor tentatively opened.

Any hopes I might have had that Gordon's sixth place was destined for a Bettina-equivalent for my especial benefit were immediately dashed. The lady who appeared and whom Judith greeted with a kiss on the cheek was nearer forty than twenty-five and more solid than lissom. She wore a brownish pink linen suit and a small white straw hat circled with a brownish pink ribbon. The suit, I diagnosed, was an old friend; the hat, new in honour of the occasion.

Judith in her turn introduced the newcomer: Penelope Warner – Pen – a good friend of hers and Gordon's. Pen Warner sat where invited, next to

Gordon, and made small-talk with Henry and Lorna. I half listened, and took in a few desultory details like no rings on the fingers, no polish on the nails, no grey in the short brown hair, no artifice in the voice. Worthy, I thought. Well intentioned; slightly boring. Probably runs the church.

A waitress appeared with an excellent lunch, during which Calder could from time to time be heard extolling the virtues of watercress for its iron content and garlic for the treatment of fever and diarrhoea.

'And of course in humans,' he was saying, 'garlic is literally a life saver in whooping cough. You make a poultice and bind it onto the bottom of the feet of the child every night, in a bandage and a sock, and in the morning you'll smell the garlic on the breath of the child, and the cough will abate. Garlic, in fact, cures almost anything. A truly marvellous life-giving plant.'

I saw Pen Warner lift her head to listen and I thought that I'd been wrong about the church. I had missed the worldliness of the eyes, the long sad knowledge of human frailty. A magistrate, perhaps? Yes, perhaps.

Judith leaned across the table and said teasingly, 'Tim, can't you forget you're a banker even at the races?'

'What?' I said.

'You look at everyone as if you're working out just how much you can lend them without risk.'

'I'd lend you my soul,' I said.

'For me to pay back with interest?'

46

'Pay in love and kisses.'

Harmless stuff, as frivolous as her hat. Henry, sitting next to her, said in the same vein, 'You're second in the queue, Tim. I've a first option, eh, Judith? Count on me, dear girl, for the last drop of blood.'

She patted his hand affectionately and glowed a little from the deep truth of our idle protestations; and Calder Jackson's voice came through with, 'Comfrey heals tissues with amazing speed and will cause chronic ulcers to disappear in a matter of days, and of course it mends fractures in half the time considered normal. Comfrey is miraculous.'

There was a good deal of speculation after that all round the table about a horse called Sandcastle that had won the 2,000 Guineas six weeks earlier and was hot favourite for the King Edward VII Stakes, the top Ascot race for three-year-old colts, due to be run that afternoon.

Dissdale had actually seen the Guineas at Newmarket and was enthusiastic. 'Daisy-cutter action. Positively eats up the ground.' He sprayed his opinions good naturedly to the furthest ear. 'Big rangy colt, full of courage.'

'Beaten in the Derby, though,' Henry said, judiciously responding.

'Well, yes,' Dissdale allowed. 'But fourth, you know. Not a total disgrace, would you say?'

'He was good as a two-year-old,' Henry said, nodding.

'Glory, yes,' said Dissdale fervently. 'And you can't fault his breeding. By Castle out of an Ampersand mare. You can't get much better than that.'

Several heads nodded respectfully in ignorance.

'He's my banker,' Dissdale said and then spread his arms wide and half laughed. 'OK, we've got a roomful of bankers. But Sandcastle is where I'm putting my money today. Doubling him with my bets in every other race. Trebles. Accumulators. The lot. You all listen to your Uncle Dissdale. Sandcastle is the soundest banker at Ascot.' His voice positively shook with evangelical belief. 'He simply can't be beaten.'

'Betting is out for you, Tim,' Lorna Shipton said severely in my ear.

'I'm not my mother,' I said mildly.

'Heredity,' Lorna said darkly. 'And your father drank.'

I smothered a bursting laugh and ate my straw-berries in good humour. Whatever I'd inherited from my parents it wasn't an addiction to their more expensive pleasures; rather a firm intention never again to lose my record collection to the bailiffs. Those stolid men had taken even the rocking horse on which at the age of six I'd ridden my fantasy Grand Nationals. They'd taken my books, my skis and my camera. Mother had fluttered around in tears saying those things were mine, not hers, and they should leave them, and the men had gone on marching out with all our stuff as if they were deaf. About her own disappearing treasures she had been distraught, her distress and grief hopelessly mixed with guilt.

I had been old enough at twenty-four to shrug off our actual losses and more or less replace them (except for the rocking horse) but the fury of that day had affected my whole life since; and I had been silent when it happened, white and dumb with rage.

Lorna Shipton removed her disapproval from me long enough to tell Henry not to have cream and sugar on his strawberries or she would have no sympathy if he put on weight, had a heart attack, or developed pimples. Henry looked resignedly at the forbidden delights which he wouldn't have eaten anyway. God preserve me, I thought, from marrying a Lorna Shipton.

By the coffee-brandy-cigar stage the tranquil seating pattern had broken up into people dashing out to back their hopes in the first race and I, not much of a gambler whatever Mrs Shipton might think, had wandered out onto the balcony to watch the Queen's procession of sleek horses, open carriages, gold, glitter and fluttering feathers trotting like a fairy tale up the green course.

'Isn't it *splendid*,' said Judith's voice at my shoulder, and I glanced at the characterful face and met the straight smiling eyes. Damn it to hell, I thought, I'd like to live with Gordon's wife.

'Gordon's gone to bet,' she said, 'so I thought I'd take the opportunity... He's appalled at what happened ... and we're really grateful to you, you know, for what you did that dreadful day.'

I shook my head. 'I did nothing, believe me.'

'Well, that's half the point. You *said* nothing. In the bank, I mean. Henry says there hasn't been a whisper.'

'But ... I wouldn't.'

'A lot of people *would*,' she said. 'Suppose you had been that Alec.'

I smiled involuntarily. 'Alec isn't unkind. He wouldn't have told.'

'Gordon says he's as discreet as a town-crier.'

'Do you want to go down and see the horses?' I asked.

'Yes. It's lovely up here, but too far from life.'

We went down to the paddock, saw the horses walk at close quarters round the ring and watched the jockeys mount ready to ride out onto the course. Judith smelled nice. Stop it, I told myself. Stop it.

'That horse over there,' I said, pointing, 'is the one Calder Jackson said he cured. Cretonne. The jockey in bright pink.'

'Are you going to back it?' she asked.

'If you like.'

She nodded the yellow silk roses and we queued up in good humour to make the wager. All around us in grey toppers and frothy dresses the Ascot crowd swirled, a feast to the eye in the sunshine, a ritual in make-believe, a suppression of gritty truth. My father's whole life had been a pursuit of the spirit I saw in these Royal Ascot faces; the pursuit and entrapment of happiness.

'What are you thinking,' Judith said, 'so solemnly?'

'That lotus-eaters do no harm. Let terrorists eat lotus.'

'As a steady diet,' she said, 'it would be sickening.'

'On a day like this one could fall in love.'

'Yes, one could.' She was reading her racecard over-intently. 'But should one?'

After a pause I said, 'No, I don't think so.'

'Nor do I.' She looked up with seriousness and understanding and with a smile in her mind. 'I've known you six years.'

'I haven't been faithful,' I said.

She laughed and the moment passed, but the declaration had quite plainly been made and in a way accepted. She showed no awkwardness in my continued presence but rather an increase of warmth, and in mutual contentment we agreed to stay in the paddock for the first short race rather than climb all the way up and find it was over by the time we'd reached the box.

The backs of the jockeys disappeared down the course as they cantered to the start, and I said, as a way of conversation, 'Who is Dissdale Smith?'

'Oh.' She looked amused. 'He's in the motor trade. He loves to make a splash, as no doubt you saw, but I don't think he's doing as well as he pretends. Anyway, he told Gordon he was looking for someone to share the expense of this box here and asked if Gordon would be interested in buying half the box for today. He's sold halves for the other days as well. I don't think he's supposed to, actually, so better say nothing to anyone else.'

'No.'

'Bettina's his third wife,' she said. 'She's a model.'

'Very pretty.'

'And not as dumb as she looks.'

I heard the dryness in her voice and acknowledged that I had myself sounded condescending.

'Mind you,' Judith said forgivingly, 'his second wife was the most gorgeous thing on earth, but without two thoughts to rub together. Even Dissdale got tired of the total vacancy behind the sensational violet eyes. It's all very well to get a buzz when all men light up on meeting your wife, but it rather kicks the stilts away when the same men diagnose total dimness within five minutes and start pitying you instead.'

'I can see that. What became of her?'

'Dissdale introduced her to a boy who'd inherited millions and had an IQ on a par with hers. The last I heard they were in a fog of bliss.'

From where we stood we couldn't see much of the race, only a head-on view of the horses as they came up to the winning post. In no way did I mind that, and when one of the leaders proved to carry bright pink Judith caught hold of my arm and shook it.

'That's Cretonne, isn't it?' She listened to the announcement of the winner's number. 'Do you realize,

Tim, that we've damned well won?' She was laughing with pleasure, her face full of sunshine and wonder.

'Bully for Calder Jackson.'

'You don't trust him,' she said. 'I could see it in all your faces, yours and Henry's and Gordon's. You all have the same way of peering into people's souls: you too, though you're so young. You were all being incredibly polite so that he shouldn't see your reservations.'

I smiled. 'That sounds disgusting.'

'I've been married to Gordon for nine years,' she said.

There was again a sudden moment of stillness in which we looked at each other in wordless question and answer. Then she shook her head slightly, and after a pause I nodded acquiescence; and I thought that with a woman so straightforwardly intelligent I could have been content for ever.

'Do we collect our winnings now or later?' she asked.

'Now, if we wait awhile.'

Waiting together for the jockeys to weigh-in and the all-clear to be given for the pay-out seemed as little hardship for her as for me. We talked about nothing much and the time passed in a flash; and eventually we made our way back to the box to find that everyone there too had backed Cretonne and was high with the same success. Calder Jackson beamed and looked modest, and Dissdale expansively opened more bottles of excellent Krug, champagne of Kings.

Escorting one's host's wife to the paddock was not merely acceptable but an expected civility, so that it was with a benign eye that Gordon greeted our return. I was both glad and sorry, looking at his unsuspecting friendliness, that he had nothing to worry about. The jewel in his house would stay there and be his alone. Unattached bachelors could lump it.

The whole party, by now markedly carefree, crowded the box's balcony for the big race. Dissdale said he had staked his all on his banker, Sandcastle; and although he said it with a laugh I saw the tremor in his hands which fidgeted with the raceglasses. He's in too deep, I thought. A bad way to bet.

Most of the others, fired by Dissdale's certainty, happily clutched tickets doubling Sandcastle every which-way. Even Lorna Shipton, with a pink glow on each bony cheekbone, confessed to Henry that just for once, as it was a special day, she had staked five pounds in forecasts.

'And you, Tim?' Henry teased. 'Your shirt?'

Lorna looked confused. I smiled. 'Buttons and all,' I said cheerfully.

'No, but . . .' Lorna said.

'Yes, but,' I said, 'I've dozens more shirts at home.'

Henry laughed and steered Lorna gently away, and I found myself standing next to Calder Jackson.

'Do you gamble?' I asked, for something to say.

'Only on certainties.' He smiled blandly in the way

that scarcely warmed his eyes. 'Though on certainties it's hardly a gamble.'

'And is Sandcastle a certainty?'

He shook his curly head. 'A probability. No racing bet's a certainty. The horse might feel ill. Might be kicked at the start.'

I glanced across at Dissdale who was faintly sweating, and hoped for his sake that the horse would feel well and come sweetly out of the stalls.

'Can you tell if a horse is sick just by looking at him?' I enquired. 'I mean, if you just watched him walk round the parade ring, could you tell?'

Calder answered in the way that revealed it was again an often-asked question. 'Of course sometimes you can see at once, but mostly a horse as ill as that wouldn't have been brought to the races. I prefer to look at a horse closely. To examine for instance the colour inside the eyelid and inside the nostril. In a sick horse, what should be a healthy pink may be pallid.' He stopped with apparent finality, as if that were the appointed end of that answer, but after a few seconds, during which the whole huge crowd watched Sandcastle stretch out in the sun in the canter to the post, he said almost with awe, 'That's a superb horse. Superb.' It sounded to me like his first spontaneous remark of the day and it vibrated with genuine enthusiasm.

'He looks great,' I agreed.

Calder Jackson smiled as if with indulgence at the shallowness of my judgement compared with the weight of his inside knowledge. 'He should have won the Derby,' he said. 'He got shut in on the rails, couldn't get out in time.'

My place at the great man's side was taken by Bettina, who threaded her arm through his and said, 'Dear Calder, come down to the front, you can see better than here at the back.' She gave me a photogenic little smile and pulled her captive after her down the steps.

In a buzz that rose to a roar the runners covered their mile and a half journey; longer than the 2,000 Guineas, the same length as the Derby. Sandcastle in scarlet and white was making no show at all to universal groans and lay only fifth as the field swept round the last bend, and Dissdale looked as if he might have a heart attack.

Alas for my shirt, I thought. Alas for Lorna's forecasts. Bang goes the banker that can't lose.

Dissdale, unable to watch, collapsed weakly onto one of the small chairs which dotted the balcony, and in the next-door boxes people were standing on top of theirs and jumping up and down and screaming.

'Sandcastle making his move . . .' the commentator's voice warbled over the loudspeakers, but the yells of the crowd drowned the rest.

The scarlet and white colours had moved to the outside. The daisy-cutter action was there for the world to see. The superb horse, the big rangy colt full of courage was eating up his ground.

Our box in the grandstand was almost a furlong down the course from the winning post, and when he reached us Sandcastle still had three horses ahead. He was flying, though, like a streak, and I found the sight of this fluid valour, this all-out striving, most immensely moving and exciting. I grabbed Dissdale by his despairing shoulder and hauled him forcefully to his feet.

'Look,' I shouted in his ear. 'Watch. Your banker's going to win. He's a marvel. He's a dream.'

He turned with a gaping mouth to stare in the direction of the winning post and he saw ... he saw Sandcastle among the tumult going like a javelin, free now of all the others, aiming straight for the prize.

'He's won,' Dissdale's mouth said slackly, though amid the noise I could hardly hear him. 'He's bloody won.'

I helped him up the steps into the box. His skin was grey and damp and he was stumbling.

'Sit down,' I said, pulling out the first chair I came to, but he shook his head weakly and made his shaky way to his own place at the head of the table. He almost fell into it, heavily, and stretched out a trembling hand to his champagne.

'My God,' he said, 'I'll never do that again. Never on God's earth.'

'Do what?'

He gave me a flickering glance over his glass and said, 'All on one throw.'

All. He'd said it before. 'All on the banker ...' He

57

surely couldn't, I thought, have meant literally *all*; but yet not much else could have produced such physical symptoms.

Everyone else piled back into the room with ballooning jollity. Everyone without exception had backed Sandcastle, thanks to Dissdale. Even Calder Jackson, when pressed by Bettina, admitted to 'a small something on the Tote. I don't usually, but just this once.' And if he'd lost, I thought, he wouldn't have confessed.

Dissdale, from near fainting, climbed rapidly to a pulse-throbbing high, the colour coming back to his plump cheeks in a hectic red. No one seemed to have noticed his near-collapse, certainly not his wife, who flirted prettily with the healer and got less than her due response. More wine easily made its way down every throat, and there was no doubt that for the now commingled party the whole day was a riotous success.

In a while Henry offered to take Judith to the paddock. Gordon to my relief invited Lorna, which left me with the mystery lady, Pen Warner, with whom I'd so far exchanged only the thrilling words 'How do you do.'

'Would you like to go down?' I asked.

'Yes, indeed. But you don't need to stay with me if it's too much bother.'

'Are you so insecure?'

There was a quick widening of the eyes and a visible mental shift. 'You're damned rude,' she said. 'And Judith said you were nice.'

58

I let her go past me out onto the landing and smiled as she went. 'I should like to stay with you,' I said, 'if it's not too much bother.'

She gave me a dry look, but as we more or less had to walk in single file along the narrow passageway owing to people going in the opposite direction she said little more until we had negotiated the lifts, the escalators and the pedestrian tunnel and had emerged into the daylight of the paddock.

It was her first time at Ascot, she said. Her first time, in fact, at the races.

'What do you think of it?'

'Very beautiful. Very brave. Quite mad.'

'Does sanity lie in ugliness and cowardice?' I asked.

'Life does, pretty often,' she said. 'Haven't you noticed?'

'And some aren't happy unless they're desperate.'

She quietly laughed. 'Tragedy inspires, so they say.'

'They can stick it,' I said. 'I'd rather lie in the sun.'

We stood on the raised tiers of steps to watch the horses walk round the ring, and she told me that she lived along the road from Judith in another house fronting the common. 'I've lived there all my life, long before Judith came. We met casually, as one does, in the local shops, and just walked home together one day several years ago. Been friends ever since.'

'Lucky,' I said.

'Yes.'

'Do you live alone?' I asked conversationally.

59

Her eyes slid my way with inner amusement. 'Yes, I do. Do you?'

I nodded.

'I prefer it,' she said.

Her skin was clear and still girlish, the thickened figure alone giving an impression of years passing. That and the look in the eyes, the 'I've seen the lot' sadness.

'Are you a magistrate?' I asked.

She looked startled. 'No, I'm not. What an odd thing to ask.'

I made an apologetic gesture. 'You just look as if you might be.'

She shook her head. 'Wouldn't have time, even if I had the urge.'

'But you do do good in the world.'

She was puzzled. 'What makes you say so?'

'I don't know. The way you look.' I smiled to take away any seriousness and said, 'Which horse do you like? Shall we choose one and bet?'

'What about Burnt Marshmallow?'

She liked the name, she said, so we queued briefly at a Tote window and invested some of the winnings from Cretonne and Sandcastle.

During our slow traverse of the paddock crowds on our way back towards the box we came upon Calder Jackson, who was surrounded by respectful listeners and didn't see us.

'Garlic is as good as penicillin,' he was saying. 'If you scatter grated garlic onto a septic wound it will kill

60

all the bacteria . . .' We slowed a little to hear. ' . . . and comfrey is miraculous,' Calder said. 'It knits bones and cures intractable skin ulcers in half the time you'd expect.'

'He said all that upstairs,' I said.

Pen Warner nodded, faintly smiling. 'Good sound herbal medicine,' she said. 'You can't fault him. Comfrey contains allantoin, a well-known cell proliferant.'

'Does it? I mean . . . do you know about it?'

'Mm.' We walked on, but she said nothing more until we were high up again in the passageway to the box. 'I don't know whether you'd think I do good in the world . . . but basically I dole out pills.'

'Er . . .?' I said.

She smiled. 'I'm a lady in a white coat. A pharmacist.'

I suppose I was in a way disappointed, and she sensed it.

'Well,' she sighed, 'we can't all be glamorous. I told you life was ugly and frightening, and from my point of view that's often what it is for my customers. I see fear every day . . . and I know its face.'

'Pen,' I said, 'forgive my frivolity. I'm duly chastened.'

We reached the box to find Judith alone there, Henry having loitered to place a bet.

'I told Tim I'm a pharmacist,' Pen said. 'He thinks it's boring.'

I got no further than the first words of protestation when Judith interrupted.

'She's not just "a" pharmacist,' she said. 'She owns her own place. Half the medics in London recommend her. You're talking to a walking gold-mine with a heart like a wet sponge.'

She put her arm round Pen's waist and the two of them together looked at me, their eyes shining with what perhaps looked like liking, but also with the mischievous feminine superiority of being five or six years older.

'Judith!' I said compulsively. 'I . . . I . . .' I stopped. 'Oh *damn* it,' I said. 'Have some Krug.'

Dissdale's friends returned giggling to disrupt the incautious minute and shortly Gordon, Henry and Lorna crowded in. The whole party pressed out onto the balcony to watch the race, and because it was a time out of reality Burnt Marshmallow romped home by three lengths.

The rest of the afternoon slid fast away. Henry at some point found himself alone out on the balcony beside me while inside the box the table was being spread with a tea that was beyond my stretched stomach entirely and a temptation from which the ever-hungry Henry had bodily removed himself.

'How's your cartoonist?' he said genially. 'Are we staking him, or are we not?'

'You're sure . . . I have to decide . . . all alone?'

'I said so. Yes.'

'Well . . . I got him to bring some more drawings to the bank. And his paints.'

'His *paints*?'

'Yes. I thought if I could see him at work, I'd know . . .' I shrugged. 'Anyway, I took him into the private interview room and asked him to paint the outline of a cartoon film while I watched; and he did it, there and then, in acrylics. Twenty-five outline sketches in bright colour, all within an hour. Same characters, different story, and terrifically funny. That was on Monday. I've been . . . well . . . dreaming about those cartoons. It sounds absurd. Maybe they're too much on my mind.'

'But you've decided?'

After a pause I said, 'Yes.'

'And?'

With a sense of burning bridges I said, 'To go ahead.'

'All right.' Henry seemed unalarmed. 'Keep me informed.'

'Yes, of course.'

He nodded and smoothly changed the subject. 'Lorna and I have won quite a bit today. How about you?'

'Enough to give Uncle Freddie fits about the effect on my unstable personality.'

Henry laughed aloud. 'Your Uncle Freddie,' he said, 'knows you better than you may think.'

*

At the end of that splendid afternoon the whole party descended together to ground level and made its way to the exit; to the gate which opened onto the main road, and across that to the car park and to the covered walk which led to the station.

Calder just ahead of me walked in front, the helmet of curls bent kindly over Bettina, the strong voice thanking her and Dissdale for 'a most enjoyable time'. Dissdale himself, not only fully recovered but incoherent with joy as most of his doubles, trebles and accumulators had come up, patted Calder plumply on the shoulder and invited him over to 'my place' for the weekend.

Henry and Gordon, undoubtedly the most sober of the party, were fiddling in their pockets for car keys and throwing their racecards into wastebins. Judith and Pen were talking to each other and Lorna was graciously unbending to Dissdale's friends. It seemed to be only I, with unoccupied eyes, who saw at all what was about to happen.

We were out on the pavement, still in a group, half-waiting for a chance to cross the road, soon to break up and scatter. All talking, laughing, busy; except me.

A boy stood there on the pavement, watchful and still. I noticed first the fixed, burning intent in the dark eyes, and quickly after that the jeans and faded shirt which contrasted sharply with our Ascot clothes, and then finally with incredulity the knife in his hand.

I had almost to guess at whom he was staring with

such deadly purpose, and had no time even to shout a warning. He moved across the pavement with stunning speed, the stab already on its upward travel.

I jumped almost without thinking; certainly without assessing consequences or chances. Most unbankerlike behaviour.

The steel was almost in Calder's stomach when I deflected it. I hit the boy's arm with my body in a sort of flying tackle and in a flashing view saw the weave of Calder's trousers, the polish on his shoes, the litter on the pavement. The boy fell beneath me and I thought in horror that somewhere between our bodies he still held that wicked blade.

He writhed under me, all muscle and fury, and tried to heave me off. He was lying on his back, his face just under mine, his eyes like slits and his teeth showing between drawn-back lips. I had an impression of dark eyebrows and white skin and I could hear the breath hissing between his teeth in a tempest of effort.

Both of his hands were under my chest and I could feel him trying to get space enough to up-end the knife. I pressed down onto him solidly with all my weight and in my mind I was saying, 'Don't do it, don't do it, you bloody fool'; and I was saying it *for his sake*, which seemed crazy to me at the time and even crazier in retrospect. He was trying to do me great harm and all I thought about was the trouble he'd be in if he succeeded.

We were both panting but I was taller and stronger

and I could have held him there for a good while longer but for the two policemen who had been out on the road directing traffic. They had seen the mêlée; seen as they supposed a man in morning dress attacking a pedestrian, seen us struggling on the ground. In any case the first I knew of their presence was the feel of vice-like hands fastening onto my arms and pulling me backwards.

I resisted with all my might. I didn't know they were policemen. I had eyes only for the boy: his eyes, his hands, his knife.

With peremptory strength they hauled me off, one of them anchoring my upper arms to my sides by encircling me from behind. I kicked furiously backwards and turned my head, and only then realized that the new assailants wore navy blue.

The boy comprehended the situation in a flash. He rolled over onto his feet, crouched for a split second like an athlete at the blocks and without lifting his head above waist-height slithered through the flow of the crowds still pouring out of the gates and disappeared out of sight inside the racecourse. Through there they would never find him. Through there he would escape to the cheaper rings and simply walk out of the lower gate.

I stopped struggling but the policemen didn't let go. They had no thought of chasing the boy. They were incongruously calling me 'sir' while treating me with contempt, which if I'd been calm enough for reflection I would have considered fairly normal.

'For God's sake,' I said finally to one of them, 'what do you think that knife's doing on the pavement?'

They looked down to where it lay; to where it had fallen when the boy ran. Eight inches of sharp steel kitchen knife with a black handle.

'He was trying to stab Calder Jackson,' I said. 'All I did was stop him. Why do you think he's gone?'

By this time Henry, Gordon, Laura, Judith and Pen were standing round in an anxious circle continually assuring the law that never in a million years would their friend attack anyone except out of direst need, and Calder was looking dazed and fingering a slit in the waistband of his trousers.

The farce slowly resolved itself into duller bureaucratic order. The policemen relinquished their hold and I brushed the dirt off the knees of my father's suit and straightened my tangled tie. Someone picked up my tumbled top hat and gave it to me. I grinned at Judith. It all seemed such a ridiculous mixture of death and bathos.

The aftermath took half of the evening and was boring in the extreme: police station, hard chairs, polystyrene cups of coffee.

No, I'd never seen the boy before.

Yes, I was sure the boy had been aiming at Calder specifically.

Yes, I was sure he was only a boy. About sixteen, probably.

Yes, I would know him again. Yes, I would help with an Identikit picture.

No. My fingerprints were positively not on the knife. The boy had held onto it until he ran.

Yes, of course they could take my prints, in case.

Calder, wholly mystified, repeated over and over that he had no idea who could want to kill him. He seemed scandalized, indeed, at the very idea. The police persisted: most people knew their murderers, they said, particularly when as seemed possible in this case the prospective killer had been purposefully waiting for his victim. According to Mr Ekaterin the boy had known Calder. That was quite possible, Calder said, because of his television appearances, but Calder had *not* known *him*.

Among some of the police there was a muted quality, among others a sort of defiant aggression, but it was only Calder who rather acidly pointed out that if they hadn't done such a good job of hauling me off, they would now have the boy in custody and wouldn't need to be looking for him.

'You could have asked first,' Calder said, but even I shook my head.

If I had indeed been the aggressor I could have killed the boy while the police were asking the onlookers just who was fighting whom. Act first, ask questions after was a policy full of danger, but getting it the wrong way round could be worse.

Eventually we both left the building, Calder on the way out trying his best with unrehearsed words. 'Er . . . Tim . . . Thanks are in order . . . If it hadn't been for you . . . I don't know what to say.'

'Say nothing,' I said. 'I did it without thinking. Glad you're OK.'

I had taken it for granted that everyone else would be long gone, but Dissdale and Bettina had waited for Calder, and Gordon, Judith and Pen for me, all of them standing in a group by some cars and talking to three or four strangers.

'We know you and Calder both came by train,' Gordon said, walking towards us, 'but we decided we'd drive you home.'

'You're extraordinarily kind,' I said.

'My dear Dissdale . . .' Calder said, seeming still at a loss for words. 'So grateful, really.'

They made a fuss of him; the endangered one, the lion delivered. The strangers round the cars turned out to be gentlemen of the press, to whom Calder Jackson was always news, alive or dead. To my horror they announced themselves, producing notebooks and a camera, and wrote down everything anyone said, except they got nothing from me because all I wanted to do was shut them up.

As well try to stop an avalanche with an outstretched palm. Dissdale and Bettina and Gordon and Judith and

Pen did a diabolical job, which was why for a short time afterwards I suffered from public notoriety as the man who had saved Calder Jackson's life.

No one seemed to speculate about his assailant setting out for a second try.

I looked at my photograph in the papers and wondered if the boy would see it, and know my name.

OCTOBER

Gordon was back at work with his faintly trembling left hand usually out of sight and unnoticeable.

During periods of activity, as on the day at Ascot, he seemed to forget to camouflage, but at other times he had taken to sitting forwards in a hunched way over his desk with his hand anchored down between his thighs. I thought it a pity. I thought the tremor so slight that none of the others would have remarked on it, either aloud or to themselves, but to Gordon it was clearly a burden.

Not that it seemed to have affected his work. He had come back in July with determination, thanked me briskly in the presence of the others for my stop-gapping and taken all major decisions off my desk and back to his.

John asked him, also in the hearing of Alec, Rupert and myself, to make it clear to us that it was he, John, who was the official next-in-line to Gordon, if the need should occur again. He pointed out that he was older and had worked much longer in the bank than I had. Tim, he said, shouldn't be jumping the queue.

Gordon eyed him blandly and said that if the need arose no doubt the chairman would take every factor into consideration. John made bitter and audible remarks under his breath about favouritism and unfair privilege, and Alec told him ironically to find a merchant bank where there *wasn't* a nephew or some such on the force.

'Be your age,' he said. 'Of *course* they want the next generation to join the family business. Why shouldn't they? It's natural.' But John was unplaced, and didn't see that his acid grudge against me was wasting a lot of his time. I seemed to be continually in his thoughts. He gave me truly vicious looks across the room and took every opportunity to sneer and denigrate. Messages never got passed on, and clients were given the impression that I was incompetent and only employed out of family charity. Occasionally on the telephone people refused to do business with me, saying they wanted John, and once a caller said straight out, 'Are you that playboy they're shoving ahead over better men's heads?'

John's gripe was basically understandable: in his place I'd have been cynical myself. Gordon did nothing to curb the escalating hate campaign and Alec found it funny. I thought long and hard about what to do and decided simply to work harder. I'd see it was very difficult for John to make his allegations stick.

His aggression showed in his body, which was roundedly muscular and looked the wrong shape for a city suit. Of moderate height, he wore his wiry brown hair very short so that it bristled above his collar, and his voice was loud, as if he thought volume equated authority: and so it might have done in schoolroom or on barrack square, instead of on a civilized patch of carpet.

He had come into banking via business school with high ambitions and good persuasive skills. I sometimes thought he would have made an excellent export salesman, but that wasn't the life he wanted. Alec said that John got his kicks from saying 'I am a merchant banker' to pretty girls and preening himself in their admiration.

Alec was a wicked fellow, really, and a shooter of perceptive arrows.

There came a day in October when three whirlwind things happened more or less simultaneously. The cartoonist telephoned; *What's Going On Where It Shouldn't* landed with a thud throughout the City; and Uncle Freddie descended on Ekaterin's for a tour of inspection.

To begin with the three events were unconnected, but by the end of the day, entwined.

I heard the cartoonist's rapid opening remarks with a sinking heart. 'I've engaged three extra animators and I need five more,' he said. 'Ten isn't nearly enough.

I've worked out the amount of increased loan needed to pay them all.'

'Wait,' I said.

He went right on. 'I also need more space, of course, but luckily that's no problem, as there's an empty warehouse next to this place. I've signed a lease for it and told them you'll be advancing the money, and of course more furniture, more materials . . .'

'*Stop*,' I said distractedly. 'You *can't*.'

'What? I can't what?' He sounded, of all things, bewildered.

'You can't just keep on borrowing. You've a limit. You can't go beyond it. Look for heaven's sake come over here quickly and we'll see what can be undone.'

'But you said,' his voice said plaintively, 'that you'd want to finance later expansion. That's what I'm doing. Expanding.'

I thought wildly that I'd be licking stamps for a living as soon as Henry heard. Dear *God* . . .

'*Listen*,' the cartoonist was saying, 'we all worked like hell and finished one whole film. Twelve minutes long, dubbed with music and sound effects, everything, titles, the lot. And we did some rough-cuts of three others, no music, no frills, but enough . . . and I've sold them.'

'You've what?'

'Sold them.' He laughed with excitement. 'It's solid, I promise you. That agent you sent me to, he's fixed the sale and the contract. All I have to do is sign. It's a major firm that's handling them, and I get a big perpetual royalty. Worldwide distribution, that's what they're talking about, and the BBC are taking them. But we've got to make twenty films in a year from now, not seven like I meant. Twenty! And if the public like them, that's just the start. Oh heck, I can't believe it. But to do twenty in the time I need a lot more money. Is it all right? I mean . . . I was so sure . . .'

'Yes,' I said weakly. 'It's all right. Bring the contract when you've signed it, and new figures, and we'll work things out.'

'Thanks,' he said. 'Thanks, Tim Ekaterin, God bless your darling bank.'

I put the receiver down feebly and ran a hand over my head and down the back of my neck.

'Trouble?' Gordon asked, watching.

'Well no, not exactly . . .' A laugh like the cartoonist's rose in my throat. 'I backed a winner. I think perhaps I backed a bloody geyser.' The laugh broke out aloud. 'Did you ever do that?'

'Ah yes.' Gordon nodded. 'Of course.'

I told him about the cartoonist and showed him the original set of drawings, which were still stowed in my desk; and when he looked through them, he laughed.

'Wasn't that application on my desk,' he said, wrinkling his forehead in an effort to remember, 'just before I was away?'

I thought back. 'Yes, it probably was.'

He nodded. 'I'd decided to turn it down.'

'Had you?'

'Mm. Isn't he too young, or something?'

'That sort of talent strikes at birth.'

He gave me a brief assessing look and handed the drawings back. 'Well,' he said. 'Good luck to him.'

The news that Uncle Freddie had been spotted in the building rippled through every department and stiffened a good many slouching backbones. Uncle Freddie was given to growling out devastatingly accurate judgements of people in their hearing, and it was not only I who'd found the bank more peaceful (if perhaps also more complacent) when he retired.

He was known as 'Mr Fred' as opposed to 'Mr Mark' (grandfather) and 'Mr Paul', the founder. No one ever called me 'Mr Tim'; sign of the changing times. If true to form Uncle Freddie would spend the morning in Investment Management, where he himself had worked all his office life, and after lunch in the boardroom would put at least his head into Corporate Finance, to be civil, and end with a march through Banking. On the way, by some telepathic process of his own, he would learn what moved in the bank's collective mind; sniff, as he had put it, the prevailing scent on the wind.

He had already arrived when the copies of *What's Going On . . .* hit the fan.

Alec as usual slipped out to the local paper shop at about the time they were delivered there and returned

76

with the six copies which the bank officially sanctioned. No one in the City could afford not to know about What Was Going On on their own doorstep.

Alec shunted around delivering one copy to each floor and keeping ours to himself to read first, a perk he said he deserved.

'Your uncle,' he reported on his return, 'is beating the shit out of poor Ted Lorrimer in Investments for failing to sell Winkler Consolidated when even a squint-eyed baboon could see it was overstretched in its Central American operation, and a neck sticking out asking for the comprehensive chop.'

Gordon chuckled mildly at the verbatim reporting, and Alec sat at his desk and opened the paper. Normal office life continued for perhaps five more minutes before Alec shot to his feet as if he'd been stung.

'Jes-us *Christ*,' he said.

'What is it?'

'Our leaker is at it again.'

'What?' Gordon said.

'You'd better read it.' He took the paper across to Gordon whose preliminary face of foreboding turned slowly to anger.

'It's disgraceful,' Gordon said. He made as if to pass the paper to me, but John, on his feet, as good as snatched it out of his hand.

'I should come first,' he said forcefully, and took the paper over to his own desk, sitting down methodically and spreading the paper open on the flat surface to read. Gordon watched him impassively and I said nothing to provoke. When John at his leisure had finished, showing little reaction but a tightened mouth, it was to Rupert he gave the paper, and Rupert, who read it with small gasps and widening eyes, who brought it eventually to me.

'It's bad,' Gordon said.

'So I gather.' I lolled back in my chair and lifted the offending column to eye level. Under a heading of 'Dinky Dirty Doings' it said:

It is perhaps not well known to readers that in many a merchant bank two thirds of the annual profits come from interest on loans. Investment and Trust management and Corporate Finance departments are the public faces and glamour machines of these very private banks. Their investments (of other people's money) in the stock market and their entrepreneurial role in mergers and takeovers earn the spotlight year by year in the City Pages.

Below stairs, so to speak, lies the tail that wags the dog, the secretive Banking department which quietly lends from its own deep coffers and rakes in vast profits in the shape of interest at rates they can set to suit themselves.

These rates are not necessarily high.

Who in Paul Ekaterin Ltd has been effectively lending to himself small fortunes from these coffers at FIVE per cent? Who in Paul Ekaterin Ltd has set up private companies which are NOT carrying on the business for which the money has ostensibly been lent? Who has not declared that these companies are his?

The man-in-the-street (poor slob) would be delighted to get unlimited cash from Paul Ekaterin Ltd at five per cent so that he could invest it in something else for more.

Don't Bankers have a fun time?

I looked up from the damaging page and across at Alec, and he was, predictably, grinning.

'I wonder who's had his hand in the cookie jar,' he said.

'And who caught it there,' I asked.

'Wow, yes.'

Gordon said bleakly, 'This is very serious.'

'If you believe it,' I said.

'But this paper . . .' he began.

'Yeah,' I interrupted. 'It had a dig at us before, remember? Way back in May. Remember the flap everyone got into?'

'I was at home . . . with flu.'

'Oh, yes. Well, the furore went on here for ages and no one came up with any answers. This column today is just as unspecific. So . . . supposing all it's designed to do is stir up trouble for the bank? Who's got it in for us? To what raving nut have we for instance refused a loan?'

Alec was regarding me with exaggerated wonder. 'Here we have Sherlock Holmes to the rescue,' he said admiringly. 'Now we can all go out to lunch.'

Gordon, however, said thoughtfully, 'It's perfectly possible, though, to set up a company and lend it money. All it would take would be paperwork. I could do it myself. So could anyone here, I suppose, up to his authorized ceiling, if he thought he could get away with it.'

John nodded. 'It's ridiculous of Tim and Alec to make a joke of this,' he said importantly. 'The very reputation of the bank is at stake.'

Gordon frowned, stood up, took the paper off my desk, and went along to see his almost-equal in the room facing St Paul's. Spreading consternation, I thought; bringing out cold sweats from palpitating banking hearts.

I ran a mental eye over everyone in the whole department who could possibly have had enough power along with the opportunity, from Val Fisher all the way down to myself; and there were twelve, perhaps, who could theoretically have done it.

But . . . not Rupert, with his sad mind still grieving, because he wouldn't have had the appetite or energy for fraud.

Not Alec, surely; because I liked him.

Not John: too self-regarding.

Not Val, not Gordon, unthinkable. Not myself.

That left the people along in the other pasture, and

I didn't know them well enough to judge. Maybe one of them did believe that a strong fiddle on the side was worth the ruin of discovery, but all of us were already generously paid, perhaps for the very reason that temptations would be more likely to be resisted if we weren't scratching around for the money for the gas.

Gordon didn't return. The morning limped down to lunchtime, when John bustled off announcing he was seeing a client, an Alec encouraged Rupert to go out with him for a pie and pint. I'd taken to working through lunch because of the quietness, and I was still there alone at two o'clock when Peter, Henry's assistant, came and asked me to go up to the top floor, because I was wanted.

Uncle Freddie, I thought. Uncle Freddie's read the rag and will be exploding like a warhead. In some way he'll make it out to be my fault. With a gusty sigh I left my desk and took the lift to face the old warrior with whom I had never in my life felt easy.

He was waiting in the top-floor hallway, talking to Henry. Both of them at six foot three over-topped me by three inches. Life would never have been as ominous, I thought, if Uncle Freddie had been small.

'Tim,' Henry said when he saw me, 'go along to the small conference room, will you?'

I nodded and made my way to the room next to the boardroom where four or five chairs surrounded a square polished table. A copy of *What's Going On . . .* lay there, already dog-eared from many thumbs.

'Now, Tim', said my uncle, coming into the room behind me, 'do you know what all this is about?'

I shook my head and said, 'No.'

My uncle growled in his throat and sat down, waving Henry and myself to seats. Henry might be chairman, might indeed in office terms have been Uncle Freddie's boss, but the white-haired old tyrant still personally owned the leasehold of the building itself and from long habit treated everyone in it as guests.

Henry absently fingered the newspaper. 'What do you think?' he said to me. '*Who* . . . do you think?'

'It might not be anyone.'

He half smiled. 'A stirrer?'

'Mm. Not a single concrete detail. Same as last time.'

'Last time,' Henry said, 'I asked the paper's editor where he got his information from. Never reveal sources, he said. Useless asking again.'

'Undisclosed sources,' Uncle Freddie said, 'never trust them.'

Henry said, 'Gordon says you can find out, Tim, how many concerns, if any, are borrowing from us at five per cent. There can't be many. A few from when interest rates were low. The few who got us in the past to agree to a long-term fixed rate.' The few, though he didn't say so, from before his time, before he put an end to such unprofitable straitjackets. 'If there are more recent ones among them, could you spot them?'

'I'll look,' I said.

We both knew it would take days rather than hours

and might produce no results. The fraud, if it existed, could have been going on for a decade. For half a century. Successful frauds tended to go on and on unnoticed, until someone tripped over them by accident. It might almost be easier to find out who had done the tripping, and why he'd told the paper instead of the bank.

'Anyway,' Henry said, 'that isn't primarily why we asked you up here.'

'No,' said my uncle, grunting. 'Time you were a director.'

I thought: I didn't hear that right.

'Er . . . what?' I said.

'A director. A director,' he said impatiently. 'Fellow who sits on the board. Never heard of them, I suppose.'

I looked at Henry, who was smiling and nodding.

'But,' I said, 'so soon . . .'

'Don't you want to, then?' demanded my uncle.

'Yes, I do.'

'Good. Don't let me down. I've had my eye on you since you were eight.'

I must have looked as surprised as I felt.

'You told me then,' he said, 'how much you had saved, and how much you would have if you went on saving a pound a month at four per cent compound interest for forty years, by which time you would be very old. I wrote down your figures and worked them out, and you were right.'

'It's only a formula,' I said.

'Oh sure. You could do it now in a drugged sleep. But at *eight*? You'd inherited the gift, all right. You were just robbed of the inclination.' He nodded heavily. 'Look at your father. My little brother. Got drunk nicely, never a mean thought, but hardly there when the brains were handed out. Look at the way he indulged your mother, letting her gamble like that. Look at the life he gave you. All pleasure, regardless of cost. I despaired of you at times. Thought you'd been ruined. But I knew the gift was there somewhere, might still be dormant, might grow if forced. So there you are, I was right.'

I was pretty well speechless.

'We all agree,' Henry said. 'The whole board was unanimous at our meeting this morning that it's time another Ekaterin took his proper place.'

I thought of John, and of the intensity of rage my promotion would bring forth.

'Would you,' I said slowly, 'have given me a directorship if my name had been Joe Bloggs?'

Henry levelly said, 'Probably not this very day. But soon, I promise you, yes. You're almost thirty-three, after all, and I was on the board here at thirty-four.'

'Thank you,' I said.

'Rest assured,' Henry said. 'You've earned it.' He stood up and formally shook hands. 'Your appointment officially starts as of the first of November, a week today. We will welcome you then to a short meeting in the boardroom, and afterwards to lunch.'

They must both have seen the depth of my pleasure, and they themselves looked satisfied. Hallelujah, I thought, I've made it. I've got there . . . I've barely started.

Gordon went down with me in the lift, also smiling.

'They've all been dithering about it on and off for months,' he said. 'Ever since you took over from me when I was ill, and did OK. Anyway I told them this morning about your news from the cartoonist. Some of them said it was just lucky. I told them you'd now been lucky too often for it to be a coincidence. So there you are.'

'I can't thank you . . .'

'It's your own doing.'

'John will have a fit.'

'You've coped all right so far with his envy.'

'I don't like it, though,' I said.

'Who would? Silly man, he's doing his career no good.'

Gordon straightaway told everyone in the office, and John went white and walked rigidly out of the room.

I went diffidently a week later to the induction and to the first lunch with the board, and then in a few days, as one does, I got used to the change of company and to the higher level of information. In the departments one heard about the decisions that had been made; in the dining room one heard the decisions being reached.

'Our daily board meeting,' Henry said. 'So much easier this way when everyone can simply say what they think without anyone taking notes.'

There were usually from ten to fifteen directors at lunch, although at a pinch the elongated oval table could accommodate the full complement of twenty-three. People would vanish at any moment to answer telephone calls, and to deal. Dealing, the buying and selling of stocks, took urgent precedence over food.

The food itself was no great feast, though perfectly presented. 'Always lamb on Wednesdays,' Gordon said at the buffet table as he took a couple from a row of trimmed lean cutlets. 'Some sort of chicken on Tuesdays, beef wellington most Thursdays. Henry never eats the crust.' Each day there was a clear soup before and fruit and cheese after. Alcohol if one chose, but most of them didn't. No one should deal in millions whose brain wanted to sleep, Henry said, drinking Malvern water steadily. Quite a change, all of it, from a rough-hewn sandwich at my desk.

They were all polite about my failure to discover 'paper' companies to whom the bank had been lending at five per cent, although Val and Henry, I knew, shared my own view that the report originated from malice and not from fact.

I had spent several days in the extra-wide office at the back of our floor, where the more mechanical parts of the banking operation were carried on. There in the huge expanse (grey carpet, this time) were row upon row of long desks whose tops were packed with telephones, adding machines and above all computers.

From there went out our own interest cheques to the depositors who had lent us money for us to lend to things like 'Home-made Heaven cakes' and 'Water Purification' plants in Norfolk. Into there came the interest paid *to* us by cakes and water and cartoonists and ten thousand such. Machines clattered, phone bells rang, people hurried about.

Many of the people working there were girls, and it had often puzzled me why there were so few women among the managers. Gordon said it was because few women wanted to commit their whole lives to making money and John (in the days when he was speaking to me) said with typical contempt that it was because they preferred to spend it. In any case, there were no female managers in banking, and none at all on the board.

Despite that, my best helper in the fraud search proved to be a curvy redhead called Patty who had taken the *What's Going On* ... article as a personal affront, as had many of her colleagues.

'No one could do that under our noses,' she protested.

'I'm afraid they could. You know they could. No one could blame any of you for not spotting it.'

'Well ... where do we start?'

'With all the borrowers paying a fixed rate of five per cent. Or perhaps four per cent, or five point seven five, or six or seven. Who knows if five is right?'

She looked at me frustratedly with wide amber eyes. 'But we haven't got them sorted like that.'

Sorted, she meant, on the computer. Each loan transaction would have its own agreement, which in itself could originally range from one single slip of paper to a contract of fifty pages, and each agreement should say at what rate the loan interest was to be levied, such as two above the current accepted base. There were thousands of such agreements typed onto and stored on computer discs. One could retrieve any one transaction by its identifying number, or alphabetically, or by the dates of commencement, or full term, or by the date when the next interest payment was due, but if you asked the computer who was paying at what per cent you'd get a blank screen and the microchip version of a raspberry.

'You can't sort them out by rates,' she said. 'The rates go up and down like see-saws.'

'But there must still be some loans being charged interest at a fixed rate.'

'Well, yes.'

'So when you punch in the new interest rate the computer adjusts the interest due on almost all the loans but doesn't touch those with a fixed rate.'

'I suppose that's right.'

'So somewhere in the computer there must be a code which tells it when not to adjust the rates.'

She smiled sweetly and told me to be patient, and

half a day later produced a cheerful-looking computer programmer to whom the problem was explained.

'Yeah, there's a code,' he said. 'I put it there myself. What you want, then, is a programme that will print out all the loans which have the code attached. That right?'

We nodded. He worked on paper for half an hour with a much-chewed pencil and then typed rapidly onto the computer, pressing buttons and being pleased with results.

'You leave this programme on here,' he said, 'then feed in the discs, and you'll get the results on that line-printer over there. And I've written it all out for you tidily in pencil, in case someone switches off your machine. Then just type it all in again, and you're back in business.'

We thanked him and he went away whistling, the aristocrat among ants.

The line-printer clattered away on and off for hours as we fed through the whole library of discs, and it finally produced a list of about a hundred of the ten-digit numbers used to identify an account.

'Now,' Patty said undaunted, 'do you want a complete print-out of all the original agreements for those loans?'

'I'm afraid so, yes.'

'Hang around.'

It took two days even with her help to check through all the resulting paper and by the end I couldn't spot any companies there that had no known physical existence, though short of actually tramping to all the addresses and making an on-the-spot enquiry, one couldn't be sure.

Henry, however, was against the expenditure of time. 'We'll just be more vigilant,' he said. 'Design some more safeguards, more tracking devices. Could you do that, Tim?'

'I could, with that programmer's help.'

'Right. Get on with it. Let us know.'

I wondered aloud to Patty whether someone in her own department, not one of the managers, could set up such a fraud, but once she'd got over her instinctive indignation she shook her head.

'Who would bother? It would be much simpler – in fact it's almost dead easy – to feed in a mythical firm who has lent *us* money, and to whom we are paying interest. Then the computer goes on sending out interest cheques for ever, and all the crook has to do is cash them.'

Henry, however, said we had already taken advice on that one, and the 'easy' route had been plugged by systematic checks by the auditors.

The paper-induced rumpus again gradually died down and became undiscussed if not forgotten. Life in our plot went on much as before with Rupert slowly recovering, Alec making jokes and Gordon stuffing his left hand anywhere out of sight. John continued to suffer from his obsession, not speaking to me, not looking at me if he could help it, and apparently telling clients outright that my promotion was a sham.

'Cosmetic of course,' Alec reported him of saying on the telephone. 'Makes the notepaper heading look impressive. Means nothing in real terms, you know. Get through to me, I'll see you right.'

'He said all that?' I asked.

'Word for word.' Alec grinned. 'Go and bop him on the nose.'

I shook my head, however, and wondered if I should get myself transferred along to the St Paul's-facing office. I didn't want to go, but it looked as if John wouldn't recover his balance unless I did. If I tried to get John himself transferred, would it make things that much worse?

I was gradually aware that Gordon, and behind him Henry, were not going to help, their thought being that I was a big boy now and should be able to resolve it myself. It was a freedom which brought responsibility, as all freedoms do, and I had to consider that for the bank's sake John needed to be a sensible member of the team.

I thought he should see a psychiatrist. I got Alec to say it to him lightly as a joke, out of my hearing ('what you need, old pal, is a friendly shrink'), but to John his own anger appeared rational, not a matter for treatment.

I tried saying to him straight, 'Look, John, I know how you feel. I know you think my promotion isn't fair. Well, maybe it is, maybe it isn't, but either way I can't help it. You'll be a lot better off if you just face things and forget it. You're good at your job, we all know it, but you're doing yourself no favours with all this bellyaching. So shut up, accept that life's bloody, and let's lend some money.'

It was a homily that fell on a closed mind, and in the end it was some redecorating which came to the rescue. For a week while painters re-whitened our walls the five of us in the fountain-facing office squeezed into the other one, desks jammed together in every corner, phone calls made with palms pressed to ears against the noise and even normally placid tempers itching to snap. Overcrowd the human race, I thought, and you always got a fight. In distance lay peace.

Anyway, I used the time to do some surreptitious persuasion and shuffling, so that when we returned to our own patch both John and Rupert stayed behind. The two oldest men from the St Paul's office came with Gordon, Alec and myself, and Gordon's almost-equal obligingly told John that it was great to be working again with a younger team of bright energetic brains.

NOVEMBER

Val Fisher said at lunch one day, 'I've received a fairly odd request.' (It was a Friday: grilled fish.)

'Something new?' Henry asked.

'Yes. Chap wants to borrow five million pounds to buy a racehorse.'

Everyone at the table laughed except Val himself.

'I thought I'd toss it at you,' he said. 'Kick it around some. See what you think.'

'What horse?' Henry said.

'Something called Sandcastle.'

Henry, Gordon and I all looked at Val with sharpened attention; almost perhaps with eagerness.

'Mean something to you three, does it?' he said, turning his head from one to the other of us.

Henry nodded. 'That day we all went to Ascot. Sandcastle ran there, and won. A stunning performance. Beautiful.'

Gordon said reminiscently, 'The man whose box we were in saved his whole business on that race. Do you remember Dissdale, Tim?'

'Certainly do.'

'I saw him a few weeks ago. On top of the world. God knows how much he won.'

'Or how much he staked,' I said.

'Yes, well,' Val said. 'Sandcastle. He won the 2,000 Guineas, as I understand, and the King Edward VII Stakes at Royal Ascot. Also the "Diamond" Stakes in July, and the Champion Stakes at Newmarket last month. This is, I believe, a record second only to winning the Derby or the Arc de Triomphe. He finished fourth, incidentally, in the Derby. He could race next year as a four-year-old, but if he flopped his value would be less than it is at the moment. Our prospective client wants to buy him now and put him to stud.'

The rest of the directors got on with their fillets of sole while listening interestedly. A stallion made a change, I suppose, from chemicals, electronics and oil.

'Who is our client?' Gordon asked. Gordon liked fish. He could eat it right handed with his fork, in no danger of shaking it off between plate and mouth.

'A man called Oliver Knowles,' Val said. 'He owns a stud farm. He got passed along to me by the horse's trainer, whom I know slightly because of our wives being distantly related. Oliver Knowles wants to buy, the present owner is willing to sell. All they need is the cash.' He smiled. 'Same old story.'

'What's your view?' Henry said.

Val shrugged his well-tailored shoulders. 'Too soon to have one of any consequence. But I thought, if it interested you at all, we could ask Tim to do a preliminary look-see. He has a background, after all, a lengthy acquaintance, shall we say, with racing.'

There was a murmur of dry amusement round the table.

'What do you think?' Henry asked me.

'I'll certainly do it if you like.'

Someone down the far end complained that it would be a waste of time and that merchant banks of our stature should not be associated with the Turf.

'Our own dear Queen,' someone said ironically, 'is associated with the Turf. And knows the Stud Book backwards, so they say.'

Henry smiled. 'I don't see why we shouldn't at least look into it.' He nodded in my direction. 'Go ahead, Tim. Let us know.'

I spent the next few working days alternately chewing pencils with the computer programmer and joining us to a syndicate with three other banks to lend twelve point four million pounds short term at high interest to an international construction company with a gap in its cash-flow. In between those I telephoned around for information and opinions about Oliver Knowles, in the normal investigative preliminaries to any loan for anything, not only for a hair-raising price for a stallion.

Establishing a covenant, it was called. Only if the

covenant was sound would any loan be further considered.

Oliver Knowles, I was told, was a sane, sober man of forty-one with a stud farm in Hertfordshire. There were three stallions standing there with ample provision for visiting mares, and he owned the one hundred and fifty acres outright, having inherited them on his father's death.

When talking to local bank managers one listened attentively for what they left out, but Oliver Knowles' bank manager left out not much. Without in the least discussing his client's affairs in detail he said that occasional fair-sized loans had so far been paid off as scheduled and that Mr Knowles' business sense could be commended. A rave notice from such a source.

'Oliver Knowles?' a racing acquaintance from the long past said. 'Don't know him myself. I'll ask around.' And an hour later called back with the news. 'He seems to be a good guy but his wife's just buggered off with a Canadian. He might be a secret wife-beater, who can tell? Otherwise the gen is that he's as honest as any horse-breeder, which you can take as you find it, and how's your mother?'

'She's fine, thanks. She remarried last year. Lives in Jersey.'

'Good. Lovely lady. Always buying us ice creams. I adored her.'

I put the receiver down with a smile and tried a

credit rating agency. No black marks, they said: the Knowles credit was good.

I told Gordon across the room that I seemed to be getting nothing but green lights, and at lunch that day repeated the news to Henry. He looked around the table, collecting a few nods, a few frowns and a great deal of indecision.

'We couldn't carry it all ourselves, of course,' Val said. 'And it isn't exactly something we could go to our regular sources with. They'd think us crackers.'

Henry nodded. 'We'd have to canvass friends for private money. I know a few people here or there who might come in. Two million, I think, is all we should consider ourselves. Two and a half at the outside.'

'I don't approve,' a dissenting director said. 'It's madness. Suppose the damn thing broke its leg?'

'Insurance,' Henry said mildly.

Into a small silence I said, 'If you felt like going into it further I could get some expert views on Sandcastle's breeding, and then arrange blood and fertility tests. And I know it's not usual with loans, but I do think someone like Val should go and personally meet Oliver Knowles and look at his place. It's too much of a risk to lend such a sum for a horse without going into it extremely carefully.'

'Just listen to who's talking,' said the dissenter, but without ill-will.

'Mm,' Henry said, considering. 'What do you think, Val?'

Val Fisher smoothed a hand over his always smooth face. 'Tim should go,' he said. 'He's done the ground-work, and all I know about horses is that they eat grass.'

The dissenting director almost rose to his feet with the urgency of his feelings.

'Look,' he said, 'all this is ridiculous. How can we possibly finance a *horse*?'

'Well, now,' Henry answered. 'The breeding of thoroughbreds is big business, tens of thousands of people round the world make their living from it. Look upon it as an industry like any other. We gamble here on shipbuilders, motors, textiles, you name it, and all of those can go bust. And none of them,' he finished with a near-grin, 'can procreate in their own image.'

The dissenter heavily shook his head. 'Madness. Utter madness.'

'Go and see Oliver Knowles, Tim,' Henry said.

Actually I thought it prudent to bone up on the finances of breeding in general before listening to Oliver Knowles himself, on the basis that I would then have a better idea of whether what he was proposing was sensible or not.

I didn't myself know anyone who knew much on the subject, but one of the beauties of merchant banking was the ramification of people who knew people who knew people who could find someone with the information that was wanted. I sent out the question mark smoke signal and from distant out-of-sight mountain tops the answer puff-puffed back.

Ursula Young, I was told, would put me right. 'She's a bloodstock agent. Very sharp, very talkative, knows her stuff. She used to work on a stud farm, so you've got it every which way. She says she'll tell you anything you want, only if you want to see her in person this week it will have to be at Doncaster races on Saturday, she's too busy to spend the time else.'

I went north to Doncaster by train and met the lady at the racecourse, where the last Flat meeting of the year was being held. She was waiting as arranged by the entrance to the Members' Club and wearing an identifying red velvet beret, and she swept me off to a secluded table in a bar where we wouldn't be interrupted.

She was fifty, tough, good-looking, dogmatic and inclined to treat me as a child. She also gave me a patient and invaluable lecture on the economics of owning a stallion.

'Stop me,' she said to begin with, 'if I say something you don't understand.'

I nodded.

'All right. Say you own a horse that's won the Derby and you want to capitalize on your gold-mine. You judge what you think you can get for the horse, then you divide that by forty and try to sell each of the forty shares at that price. Maybe you can, maybe you can't.

99

It depends on the horse. With Troy, now, they were queuing up. But if your winner isn't frightfully well bred or if it made little show *except* in the Derby you'll get a cool response and have to bring the price down. OK so far?'

'Um,' I said. 'Why only forty shares?'

She looked at me in amazement. 'You don't know a *thing* do you?'

'That's why I'm here.'

'Well, a stallion covers forty mares in a season, and the season, incidentally, lasts roughly from February to June. The mares come to *him*, of course. He doesn't travel, he stays put at home. Forty is just about average; physically I mean. Some can do more, but others get exhausted. So forty is the accepted number. Now, say you have a mare and you've worked out that if you mate her with a certain stallion you might get a top-class foal, you try to get one of those forty places. The places are called nominations. You apply for a nomination, either directly to the stud where the stallion is standing, or through an agent like me, or even by advertising in a breeders' newspaper. Follow?'

'Gasping.' I nodded.

She smiled briefly. 'People who invest in stallion shares sometimes have broodmares of their own they want to breed from.' She paused. 'Perhaps I should have explained more clearly that everyone who owns a share automatically has a nomination to the stallion every year.'

'Ah,' I said.

'Yes. So say you've got your share and consequently your nomination but you haven't a mare to send to the stallion, then you sell your nomination to someone who *has* a mare, in the ways I already described.'

'I'm with you.'

'After the first three years the nominations may vary in price and in fact are often auctioned, but of course for the first three years the price is fixed.'

'Why of course?'

She sighed and took a deep breath. 'For three years no one knows whether the progeny on the whole are going to be winners or not. The gestation period is eleven months, and the first crop of foals don't race until they're two. If you work it out, that means that the stallion has stood for three seasons, and therefore covered a hundred and twenty mares, before the crunch.'

'Right.'

'So to fix the stallion fee for the first three years you divide the price of the stallion by one hundred and twenty, and that's it. That's the fee charged for the stallion to cover a mare. That's the sum you receive if you sell your nomination.'

I blinked.

'That means,' I said, 'that if you sell your nomination for three years you have recovered the total amount of your original investment?'

'That's right.'

'And after that ... every time, every year you sell your nomination, it's clear profit?'

'Yes. But taxed, of course.'

'And how long does that go on?'

She shrugged. 'Ten to fifteen years. Depends on the stallion's potency.'

'But that's ...'

'Yes,' she said. 'One of the best investments on earth.'

The bar had filled up behind us with people crowding in, talking loudly, and breathing on their fingers against the chill of the raw day outside. Ursula Young accepted a warmer in the shape of whisky and ginger wine, while I had coffee.

'Don't you drink?' she asked with mild disapproval.

'Not often in the daytime.'

She nodded vaguely, her eyes scanning the company, her mind already on her normal job. 'Any more questions?' she asked.

'I'm bound to think of some the minute we part.'

She nodded. 'I'll be here until the end of racing. If you want me, you'll see me near the weighing room after each race.'

We were on the point of standing up to leave when a man whose head one could never forget came into the bar.

'Calder Jackson!' I exclaimed.

Ursula casually looked. 'So it is.'

'Do you know him?' I asked.

'Everyone does.' There was almost a conscious neutrality in her voice as if she didn't want to be caught with her thoughts showing. The same response, I reflected, that he had drawn from Henry and Gordon and me.

'You don't like him?' I suggested.

'I feel nothing either way.' She shrugged. 'He's part of the scene. From what people say, he's achieved some remarkable cures.' She glanced at me briefly. 'I suppose you've seen him on television, extolling the value of herbs?'

'I met him,' I said, 'at Ascot, back in June.'

'One tends to.' She got to her feet, and I with her, thanking her sincerely for her help.

'Think nothing of it,' she said. 'Any time.' She paused. 'I suppose it's no use asking what stallion prompted this chat?'

'Sorry, no. It's on behalf of a client.'

She smiled slightly. 'I'm here if he needs an agent.'

We made our way towards the door, a path, I saw, which would take us close to Calder. I wondered fleetingly whether he would know me, remember me after several months. I was after all not as memorable as himself, just a standard issue six foot with eyes, nose and mouth in roughly the right places, dark hair on top.

'Hello Ursula,' he said, his voice carrying easily through the general din. 'Bitter cold day.'

'Calder.' She nodded acknowledgement.

His gaze slid to my face, dismissed it, focused again on my companion. Then he did a classic double-take, his eyes widening with recognition.

'Tim,' he said incredulously. 'Tim . . .' he flicked his fingers to bring the difficult name to mind, '. . . Tim Ekaterin!'

I nodded.

He said to Ursula, 'Tim, here, saved my life.'

She was surprised until he explained, and then still surprised I hadn't told her. 'I read about it, of course,' she said, 'and congratulated you, Calder, on your escape.'

'Did you ever hear any more,' I asked him. 'From the police, or anyone?'

He shook his curly head. 'No, I didn't.'

'The boy didn't try again?'

'No.'

'Did you really have no idea where he came from?' I said. 'I know you told the police you didn't know, but . . . well . . . you just might have done.'

He shook his head very decisively, however, and said, 'If I could help to catch the little bastard I'd do it at once. But I don't know who he was. I hardly saw him properly, just enough to know I didn't know him from Satan.'

'How's the healing?' I said. 'The tingling touch.'

There was a brief flash in his eyes as if he had found the question flippant and in bad taste, but perhaps mindful that he owed me his present existence he answered civilly. 'Rewarding,' he said. 'Heartwarming.'

Standard responses, I thought. As before.

'Is your yard full, Calder?' Ursula asked.

'Always a vacancy if needed,' he replied hopefully. 'Have you a horse to send me?'

'One of my clients has a two-year-old which looks ill and half dead all the time, to the despair of the trainer, who can't get it fit. She – my client – was mentioning you.'

'I've had great success with that sort of general debility.'

Ursula wrinkled her forehead in indecision. 'She feels Ian Pargetter would think her disloyal if she sent you her colt. He's been treating him for weeks, I think, without success.'

Calder smiled reassuringly. 'Ian Pargetter and I are on good terms, I promise you. He's even persuaded owners himself sometimes to send me their horses. Very good of him. We talk each case over, you know, and act in agreement. After all, we both have the recovery of the patient as our prime objective.' Again the swift impression of a statement often needed.

'Is Ian Pargetter a vet?' I asked incuriously.

They both looked at me.

'Er . . . yes,' Calder said.

'One of a group practice in Newmarket,' Ursula

added. 'Very forward-looking. Tries new things. Dozens of trainers swear by him.'

'Just ask him, Ursula,' Calder said. 'Ian will tell you he doesn't mind owners sending me their horses. Even if he's a bit open-minded about the laying on of hands, at least he trusts me not to make the patient worse.' It was said as a self-deprecating joke, and we all smiled. Ursula Young and I in a moment or two walked on and out of the bar, and behind us we could hear Calder politely answering another of the everlasting questions.

'Yes,' he was saying, 'one of my favourite remedies for a prolonged cough in horses is liquorice root boiled in water with some figs. You strain the mixture and stir it into the horse's normal feed . . .'

The door closed behind us and shut him off.

'You'd think he'd get tired of explaining his methods,' I said. 'I wonder he never snaps.'

The lady said judiciously, 'Calder depends on television fame, good public relations and medical success, roughly in that order. He owns a yard with about thirty boxes on the outskirts of Newmarket – it used to be a regular training stables before he bought it – and the yard's almost always full. Short-term and long-term crocks, all sent to him either from true belief or as a last resort. I don't pretend to know anything about herbalism, and as for supernatural healing powers . . .' She shook her head. 'But there's no doubt that whatever his methods, horses do usually seem to leave his yard in a lot better health than when they went in.'

'Someone at Ascot said he'd brought dying horses back to life.'

'Hmph.'

'You don't believe it?'

She gave me a straight look, a canny businesswoman with a lifetime's devotion to thoroughbreds.

'Dying,' she said, 'is a relative term when it doesn't end in death.'

I made a nod into a slight bow of appreciation.

'But to be fair,' she said, 'I know for certain that he totally and permanently cured a ten-year-old broodmare of colitis X, which has a habit of being fatal.'

'They're not all horses in training, then, that he treats?'

'Oh no, he'll take anybody's pet from a pony to an event horse. Showjumpers, the lot. But the horse has to be worth it, to the owner, I mean. I don't think Calder's hospital is terribly cheap.'

'Exorbitant?'

'Not that I've heard. Fair, I suppose, if you consider the results.'

I seemed to have heard almost more about Calder Jackson than I had about stallion shares, but I did after all have a sort of vested interest. One tended to want a life one had saved to be of positive use in the world. Illogical, I dare say, but there it was. I was pleased that it was true that Calder cured horses, albeit in his own mysterious unorthodox ways; and if I wished that I could warm to him more as a person, that was unrealistic and sentimental.

Ursula Young went off about her business, and although I caught sight of both her and Calder during the afternoon, I didn't see them again to speak to. I went back to London on the train, spent two hours of Sunday morning on the telephone, and early Sunday afternoon drove off to Hertfordshire in search of Oliver Knowles.

He lived in a square hundred-year-old stark redbrick house which to my taste would have been friendlier if softened by trailing creeper. Blurred outlines, however, were not in Oliver Knowles' soul: a crisp bare tidiness was apparent in every corner of his spread.

His land was divided into a good number of paddocks of various sizes, each bordered by an immaculate fence of white rails; and the upkeep of those, I judged, as I pulled up on the weedless gravel before the front door, must alone cost a fortune. There was a scattering of mares and foals in the distance in the paddocks, mostly heads down to the grass, sniffing out the last tender shoots of the dying year. The day itself was cold with a muted sun dipping already towards distant hills, the sky quiet with the greyness of coming winter, the damp air smelling of mustiness, wood smoke and dead leaves.

There were no dead leaves as such to be seen. No

flower beds, no ornamental hedges, no nearby trees. A barren mind, I thought, behind a business whose aim was fertility and the creation of life.

Oliver Knowles himself opened his front door to my knock, proving to be a pleasant lean man with an efficient, cultured manner of authority and politeness. Accustomed to command, I diagnosed. Feels easy with it; second nature. Positive, straightforward, self-controlled. Charming also, in an understated way.

'Mr Ekaterin?' He shook hands, smiling. 'I must confess I expected someone . . . older.'

There were several answers to that, such as 'time will take care of it' and 'I'll be older tomorrow', but nothing seemed appropriate. Instead I said 'I report back' to reassure him, which it did, and he invited me into his house.

Predictably the interior was also painfully tidy, such papers and magazines as were to be seen being squared up with the surface they rested on. The furniture was antique, well polished, brass handles shining, and the carpets venerably from Persia. He led me into a sitting room which was also office, the walls thickly covered with framed photographs of horses, mares and foals, and the window giving on to a view of, across a further expanse of gravel, an archway leading into an extensive stable yard.

'Boxes for mares,' he said, following my eyes. 'Beyond them, the foaling boxes. Beyond those, the breeding pen, with the stallion boxes on the far side of that again. My stud groom's bungalow and the lads' hostel, those roofs you can see in the hollow, they're just beyond the stallions.' He paused. 'Would you care perhaps to look round?'

'Very much,' I said.

'Come along, then.' He led the way to a door at the back of the house, collecting an overcoat and a black retriever from a mud room on the way. 'Go on then, Squibs, old fellow,' he said, fondly watching his dog squeeze ecstatically through the opening outside door. 'Breath of fresh air won't hurt you.'

We walked across to the stable arch with Squibs circling and zig-zagging nose down to the gravel.

'It's our quietest time of year,' Oliver Knowles said. 'We have our own mares here, of course, and quite a few at livery.' He looked at my face to see if I understood and decided to explain anyway. 'They belong to people who own broodmares but have nowhere of their own to keep them. They pay us to board them.'

I nodded.

'Then we have the foals born to the mares this past spring, and of course the three stallions. Total of seventy-eight at the moment.'

'And next spring,' I said, 'the mares coming to your stallions will arrive?'

'That's right.' He nodded. 'They come here a month or five weeks before they're due to give birth to the foals they are already carrying, so as to be near the stallion within the month following. They have to

110

foal here, because the foals would be too delicate straight after birth to travel.'

'And ... how long do they stay here?'

'About three months altogether, by which time we hope the mare is safely in foal again.'

'There isn't much pause then,' I said. 'Between ... er ... pregnancies?'

He glanced at me with civil amusement. 'Mares come into use nine days after foaling, but normally we would think this a bit too soon for breeding. The oestrus – heat you would call it – lasts six days, then there's an interval of fifteen days, then the mare comes into use again for six days, and this time we breed her. Mind you,' he added, 'nature being what it is, this cycle doesn't work to the minute. In some mares the oestrus will last only two days, in some as much as eleven. We try to have the mare covered two or three times while she's in heat, for the best chance of getting her in foal. A great deal depends on the stud groom's judgement, and I've a great chap just now, he has a great feel for mares, a sixth sense, you might say.'

He led me briskly across the first big oblong yard where long dark equine heads peered inquisitively from over half-open stable doors, and through a passage on the far side which led to a second yard of almost the same size but whose doors were fully shut.

'None of these boxes is occupied at the moment,' he said, waving a hand around. 'We have to have the capacity, though, for when the mares come.'

Beyond the second yard lay a third, a good deal smaller and again with closed doors.

'Foaling boxes,' Oliver Knowles explained. 'All empty now, of course.'

The black dog trotted ahead of us, knowing the way. Beyond the foaling boxes lay a wide path between two small paddocks of about half an acre each, and at the end of the path, to the left, rose a fair-sized barn with a row of windows just below its roof.

'Breeding shed,' Oliver Knowles said economically, producing a heavy key ring from his trouser pocket and unlocking a door set into a large roll-aside entrance. He gestured to me to go in, and I found myself in a bare concrete-floored expanse surrounded by white walls topped with the high windows, through which the dying sun wanly shone.

'During the season of course the floor in here is covered with peat,' he said.

I nodded vaguely and thought of life being generated purposefully in that quiet place, and we returned prosaically to the outer world with Oliver Knowles locking the door again behind us.

Along another short path between two more small paddocks we came to another small stable yard, this time of only six boxes, with feed room, tack room, hay and peat storage alongside.

'Stallions,' Oliver Knowles said.

Three heads almost immediately appeared over the

half-doors, three sets of dark liquid eyes turning inquisitively our way.

'Rotaboy,' my host said, walking to the first head and producing a carrot unexpectedly. The black mobile lips whiffled over the outstretched palm and sucked the goodie in: strong teeth crunched a few times and Rotaboy nudged Oliver Knowles for a second helping. Oliver Knowles produced another carrot, held it out as before, and briefly patted the horse's neck.

'He'll be twenty next year,' he said. 'Getting old, eh, old fella?'

He walked along to the next box and repeated the carrot routine. 'This one is Diarist, rising sixteen.'

By the third box he said, 'This is Parakeet,' and delivered the treats and the pat. 'Parakeet turns twelve on January first.'

He stood a little away from the horse so that he could see all three heads at once and said, 'Rotaboy has been an outstanding stallion and still is, but one can't realistically expect more than another one or two seasons. Diarist is successful, with large numbers of winners among his progeny, but none of them absolutely top rank like those of Rotaboy. Parakeet hasn't proved as successful as I'd hoped. He turns out to breed better stayers than sprinters, and the world is mad nowadays for very fast two-year-olds. Parakeet's progeny tend to be better at three, four, five and six. Some of his first crops are now steeplechasing and jumping pretty well.'

'Isn't that good?' I asked, frowning, since he spoke with no great joy.

'I've had to reduce his fee,' he said. 'People won't send their top flat-racing mares to a stallion who breeds jumpers.'

'Oh.'

After a pause he said, 'You can see why I need new blood here. Rotaboy is old, Diarist is middle rank, Parakeet is unfashionable. I will soon have to replace Rotaboy, and I must be sure I replace him with something of at least equal quality. The *prestige* of a stud farm, quite apart from its income, depends on the drawing-power of its stallions.'

'Yes,' I said, 'I see.'

Rotaboy, Diarist and Parakeet lost interest in the conversation and hope in the matter of carrots, and one by one withdrew into the boxes. The black retriever trotted around smelling unimaginable scents and Oliver Knowles began to walk me back towards the house.

'On the bigger stud farms,' he said, 'you'll find stallions which are owned by syndicates.'

'Forty shares?' I suggested.

He gave me a brief smile. 'That's right. Stallions are owned by any number of people between one and forty. When I first acquired Rotaboy it was in partnership with five others. I bought two of them out – they needed the money – so now I own half. This means I have twenty nominations each year, and I have no trouble in selling all of them, which is most satisfactory.' He looked at me enquiringly to make sure I understood, which, thanks to Ursula Young, I did.

'I own Diarist outright. He was as expensive in the first place as Rotaboy, and as he's middle rank, so is the fee I can get for him. I don't always succeed in filling his forty places, and when that occurs I breed him to my own mares, and sell the resulting foals as yearlings.'

Fascinated, I nodded again.

'With Parakeet it's much the same. For the last three years I haven't been able to charge the fee I did to begin with, and if I fill his last places these days it's with mares from people who *prefer* steeplechasing, and this is increasingly destructive of his flat-racing image.'

We retraced our steps past the breeding shed and across the foaling yard.

'This place is expensive to run,' he said objectively. 'It makes a profit and I live comfortably, but I'm not getting any further. I have the capacity here for another stallion – enough accommodation, that is to say, for the extra forty mares. I have a good business sense and excellent health, and I feel underextended. If I am ever to achieve more I must have more capital ... and capital in the shape of a world-class stallion.'

'Which brings us,' I said, 'to Sandcastle.'

He nodded. 'If I acquired a horse like Sandcastle this stud would immediately be more widely known and more highly regarded.'

Understatement, I thought. The effect would be galvanic. 'A sort of overnight stardom?' I said.

'Well, yes,' he agreed with a satisfied smile. 'I'd say you might be right.'

The big yard nearest the house had come moderately to life, with two or three lads moving about carrying feed scoops, hay nets, buckets of water and sacks of muck. Squibs with madly wagging tail went in a straight line towards a stocky man who bent to fondle his black ears.

'That's Nigel, my stud groom,' Oliver Knowles said. 'Come and meet him.' And as we walked across he added, 'If I can expand this place I'll up-rate him to stud manager; give him more standing with the customers.'

We reached Nigel, who was of about my own age with crinkly light-brown hair and noticeably bushy eyebrows. Oliver Knowles introduced me merely as 'a friend' and Nigel treated me with casual courtesy but not as the possible source of future fortune. He had a Gloucestershire accent but not pronounced, and I would have placed him as a farmer's son, if I'd had to.

'Any problems?' Oliver Knowles asked him, and Nigel shook his head.

'Nothing except that Floating mare with the discharge.'

His manner to his employer was confident and without anxiety but at the same time diffident, and I had a strong impression that it was Nigel's personality which suited Oliver Knowles as much as any skill he might have with mares. Oliver Knowles was not a man, I judged, to surround himself with awkward, unpredictable characters: the behaviour of everyone around him had to be as tidy as his place.

I wondered idly about the wife who had 'just buggered off with a Canadian', and at that moment a horse trotted into the yard with a young woman aboard. A girl, I amended, as she kicked her feet from the stirrups and slid to the ground. A noticeably curved young girl in jeans and heavy sweater with her dark hair tied in a pony tail. She led her horse into one of the boxes and presently emerged carrying the saddle and bridle, which she dumped on the ground outside the box before closing the bottom half of the door and crossing the yard to join us.

'My daughter,' Oliver Knowles said.

'Ginnie,' added the girl, holding out a polite brown hand. 'Are you the reason we didn't go out to lunch?'

Her father gave an instinctive repressing movement and Nigel looked only fairly interested.

'I don't know,' I said. 'I wouldn't think so.'

'Oh, I would,' she said. 'Pa really doesn't like parties. He uses any old excuse to get out of them, don't you Pa?'

He gave her an indulgent smile while looking as if his thoughts were elsewhere.

'I didn't mind missing it,' Ginnie said to me, anxious not to embarrass. 'Twelve miles away and people all Pa's age . . . but they do have frightfully good canapés,

117

and also a lemon tree growing in their greenhouse. Did you know that a lemon tree has everything all at once – buds, flowers, little green knobbly fruit and big fat lemons, all going on all the time?'

'My daughter,' Oliver Knowles said unnecessarily, 'talks a lot.'

'No,' I said, 'I didn't know about lemon trees.'

She gave me an impish smile and I wondered if she was even younger than I'd first thought: and as if by telepathy she said, 'I'm fifteen.'

'Everyone has to go through it,' I said.

Her eyes widened. 'Did you hate it?'

I nodded. 'Spots, insecurity, a new body you're not yet comfortable in, self-consciousness . . . terrible.'

Oliver Knowles looked surprised. 'Ginnie isn't self-conscious, are you, Ginnie?'

She looked from him to me and back again and didn't answer. Oliver Knowles dismissed the subject as of no importance anyway and said he ought to walk along and see the mare with the discharge. Would I care to go with him?

I agreed without reservation and we all set off along one of the paths between the white-railed paddocks, Oliver Knowles and myself in front, Nigel and Ginnie following, Squibs sniffing at every fencing post and marking his territory. In between Oliver Knowles explaining that some mares preferred living out of doors permanently, others would go inside if it snowed, others went in at nights, others lived mostly in the boxes, I could hear Ginnie telling Nigel that school this term was a dreadful drag owing to the new head-mistress being a health fiend and making them all do jogging.

'How do you know what mares prefer?' I asked.

Oliver Knowles looked for the first time nonplussed. 'Er . . .' he said. 'I suppose . . . by the way they stand. If they feel cold and miserable they put their tails to the wind and look hunched. Some horses never do that, even in a blizzard. If they're obviously unhappy we bring them in. Otherwise they stay out. Same with the foals.' He paused. 'A lot of mares are miserable if you keep them inside. It's just . . . how they are.'

He seemed dissatisfied with the loose ends of his answer, but I found them reassuring. The one thing he had seemed to me to lack had been any emotional contact with the creatures he bred: even the carrots for the stallions had been slightly mechanical.

The mare with the discharge proved to be in one of the paddocks at the boundary of the farm, and while Oliver Knowles and Nigel peered at her rump end and made obscure remarks like 'With any luck she won't slip,' and 'It's clear enough, nothing yellow or bloody,' I spent my time looking past the last set of white rails to the hedge and fields beyond.

The contrast from the Knowles land was dramatic. Instead of extreme tidiness, a haphazard disorder. Instead of short green grass in well-tended rectangles, long unkempt brownish stalks straggling through an

119

army of drying thistles. Instead of rectangular brick-built stable yards, a ramshackle collection of wooden boxes, light grey from old creosote and with tarpaulins tied over patches of roof.

Ginnie followed my gaze. 'That's the Watcherleys' place,' she said. 'I used to go over there a lot but they're so grimy and gloomy these days, not a laugh in sight. And all the patients have gone, practically, and they don't even have the chimpanzees any more, they say they can't afford them.'

'What patients?' I said.

'Horse patients. It's the Watcherleys' hospital for sick horses. Haven't you heard of it?'

I shook my head.

'It's pretty well known,' Ginnie said. 'Or at least it was until that razzamatazz man Calder Jackson stole the show. Mind you, the Watcherleys were no great shakes, I suppose, with Bob off to the boozer at all hours and Maggie sweating her guts out carrying muck sacks, but at least they used to be fun. The place was *cosy*, you know, even if bits of the boxes were falling off their hinges and weeds were growing everywhere, and all the horses went home blooming, or most of them, even if Maggie had her knees through her jeans and wore the same jersey for weeks and weeks on end. But Calder Jackson, you see, is the *in* thing, with all those chat shows on television and the publicity and such, and the Watcherleys have sort of got elbowed out.'

Her father, listening to the last of these remarks, added his own view. 'They're disorganized,' he said. 'No business sense. People liked their gypsy style for a while, but, as Ginnie says, they've no answer to Calder Jackson.'

'How old are they?' I asked, frowning.

Oliver Knowles shrugged. 'Thirties. Going on forty. Hard to say.'

'I suppose they don't have a son of about sixteen, thin and intense, who hates Calder Jackson obsessively for ruining his parents' business?'

'What an extraordinary question,' said Oliver Knowles, and Ginnie shook her head. 'They've never had any children,' she said. 'Maggie can't. She told me. They just lavish all that love on animals. It's really grotty, what's happening to them.'

It would have been so neat, I thought, if Calder Jackson's would-be assassin had been a Watcherley son. Too neat, perhaps. But perhaps also there were others like the Watcherleys whose star had descended as Calder Jackson's rose. I said, 'Do you know of any other places, apart from this one and Calder Jackson's, where people send their sick horses?'

'I expect there *are* some,' Ginnie said. 'Bound to be.'

'Sure to be,' said Oliver Knowles, nodding. 'But of course we don't send away any horse which falls ill here. I have an excellent vet, great with mares, comes day or night in emergencies.'

We made the return journey, Oliver Knowles

pointing out to me various mares and foals of interest and distributing carrots to any head within armshot. Foals at foot, foals in utero; the fertility cycle swelling again to fruition through the quiet winter, life growing steadily in the dark.

Ginnie went off to see to the horse she'd been riding and Nigel to finish his inspections in the main yard, leaving Oliver Knowles, the dog and myself to go into the house. Squibs, poor fellow, got no further than his basket in the mud room, but Knowles and I returned to the sitting room office from which we'd started.

Thanks to my telephone calls of the morning I knew what the acquisition and management of Sandcastle would mean in the matter of taxation, and I'd also gone armed with sets of figures to cover the interest payable should the loan be approved. I found that I needed my knowledge not to instruct but to converse: Oliver Knowles was there before me.

'I've done this often, of course,' he said. 'I've had to arrange finance for buildings, for fencing, for buying the three stallions you saw, and for another two before them. I'm used to repaying fairly substantial bank loans. This new venture is of course huge by comparison, but if I didn't feel it was within my scope I assure you I shouldn't be contemplating it.' He gave me a brief charming smile. 'I'm not a nut case, you know. I really do know my business.'

'Yes,' I said. 'One can see.'

I told him that the maximum length of an Ekaterin

loan (if one was forthcoming at all) would be five years, to which he merely nodded.

'That basically means,' I insisted, 'that you'd have to receive getting on for eight million in that five years, even allowing for paying off some of the loan every year with consequently diminishing interest. It's a great deal of money . . . Are you sure you understand how much is involved?'

'Of course I understand,' he said. 'Even allowing for interest payments and the ridiculously high insurance premiums on a horse like Sandcastle, I'd be able to repay the loan in five years. That's the period I've used in planning.'

He spread out his sheets of neatly written calculations on his desk, pointing to each figure as he explained to me how he'd reached it. 'A stallion fee of forty thousand pounds will cover it. His racing record justifies that figure, and I've been most carefully into the breeding of Sandcastle himself, as you can imagine. There is absolutely nothing in the family to alarm. No trace of hereditary illness or undesirable tendencies. He comes from a healthy blue-blooded line of winners, and there's no reason why he shouldn't breed true.' He gave me a photocopied genealogical table. 'I wouldn't except you to advance a loan without getting an expert opinion on this. Please do take it with you.'

He gave me also some copies of his figures, and I packed them all into the briefcase I'd taken with me.

'Why don't you consider halving your risk to twenty-one shares?' I asked. 'Sell nineteen. You'd still outvote the other owners – there'd be no chance of them whisking Sandcastle off somewhere else – and you'd be less stretched.'

With a smile he shook his head. 'If I found for any reason that the repayments were causing me acute difficulty, I'd sell some shares as necessary. But I hope in five years time to own Sandcastle outright, and also as I told you to have attracted other stallions of that calibre, and to be numbered among the world's top-ranking stud farms.'

His pleasant manner took away any suggestion of megalomania, and I could see nothing of that nature in him.

Ginnie came into the office carrying two mugs with slightly anxious diffidence.

'I made some tea. Do you want some, Dad?'

'Yes, please,' I said immediately, before he could answer, and she looked almost painfully relieved. Oliver Knowles turned what had seemed like an incipient shake of the head into a nod, and Ginnie, handing over the mugs, said that if I wanted sugar she would go and fetch some. 'And a spoon, I guess.'

'My wife's away,' Oliver Knowles said abruptly.

'No sugar,' I said. 'This is great.'

'You won't forget, Dad, will you, about me going back to school?'

'Nigel will take you.'

'He's got visitors.'

'Oh . . . all right.' He looked at his watch. 'In half an hour, then.'

Ginnie looked even more relieved, particularly as I could clearly sense the irritation he was suppressing. 'The school run,' he said as the door closed behind his daughter, 'was one of the things my wife always did. Does . . .' He shrugged. 'She's away indefinitely. You might as well know.'

'I'm sorry,' I said.

'Can't be helped.' He looked at the tea mug in my hand. 'I was going to offer you something stronger.'

'This is fine.'

'Ginnie comes home on four Sundays a term. She's a boarder, of course.' He paused. 'She's not yet used to her mother not being here. It's bad for her, but there you are, life's like that.'

'She's a nice girl,' I said.

He gave me a glance in which I read both love for his daughter and a blindness to her needs. 'I don't suppose,' he said thoughtfully, 'that you go anywhere near High Wycombe on your way home?'

'Well,' I said obligingly, 'I could do.'

I consequently drove Ginnie back to her school, listening on the way to her views on the new head-mistress's compulsory jogging programme ('all our bosoms flopping up and down, bloody uncomfortable and absolutely *disgusting* to look at') and to her opinion of Nigel ('Dad thinks the sun shines out of his you-know-what and I dare say he is pretty good with the mares, they all seem to flourish, but what the lads get up to behind his back is nobody's business. They smoke in the feed sheds, I ask you! All that hay around ... Nigel never notices. He'd make a rotten school prefect.') and to her outlook on life in general ('I can't wait to get out of school uniform and out of dormitories and being bossed around, and I'm no good at lessons; the whole thing's a *mess*. Why has everything *changed*? I used to be happy, or at least I wasn't *unhappy*, which I mostly seem to be nowadays, and no, it isn't because of Mum going away, or not especially, as she was never a lovey-dovey sort of mother, always telling me to eat with my mouth shut and so on ... and you must be bored silly hearing all this.').

'No,' I said truthfully. 'I'm not bored.'

'I'm not even *beautiful*,' she said despairingly. 'I can suck in my cheeks until I faint but I'll never look pale and bony and interesting.'

I glanced at the still rounded child-woman face, at the peach-bloom skin and the worried eyes.

'Practically no one is beautiful at fifteen,' I said. 'It's too soon.'

'How do you mean – too soon?'

'Well,' I said, 'say at twelve you're a child and flat and undeveloped and so on, and at maybe seventeen or eighteen you're a full-grown adult, just think of the terrific changes your body goes through in that time. Appearance, desires, mental outlook, everything. So at fifteen, which isn't much more than halfway, it's still too soon to know exactly what the end product will be like. And if it's of any comfort to you, you do now look as if you may be beautiful in a year or two, or at least not unbearably ugly.'

She sat in uncharacteristic silence for quite a distance, and then she said, 'Why did you come today? I mean, who are you? If it's all right to ask?'

'It's all right. I'm a sort of financial adviser. I work in a bank.'

'Oh.' She sounded slightly disappointed but made no further comment, and soon after that gave me prosaic and accurate directions to the school.

'Thanks for the lift,' she said, politely shaking hands as we stood beside the car.

'A pleasure.'

'And thanks . . .' she hesitated. 'Thanks anyway.'

I nodded, and she half-walked, half-ran to join a group of other girls going into the buildings. Looking briefly back she gave me a sketchy wave, which I acknowledged. Nice child, I thought, pointing the car homewards. Mixed up, as who wasn't at that age? Middling brains, not quite pretty, her future a clean stretch of sand waiting for footprints.

DECEMBER

It made the headlines in the *Sporting Life* (OLIVER KNOWLES, KING OF THE SANDCASTLE) and turned up as the lead story under less fanciful banners on the racing pages of all the other dailies.

SANDCASTLE TO GO TO STUD, SANDCASTLE TO STAY IN BRITAIN, SANDCASTLE SHARES NOT FOR SALE, SANDCASTLE BOUGHT PRIVATELY FOR HUGE SUM. The story in every case was short and simple. One of the year's top stallions had been acquired by the owner of a heretofore moderately ranked stud farm. 'I am very happy,' Oliver Knowles was universally reported as saying. 'Sandcastle is a prize for British bloodstock.'

The buying price, all the papers said, was 'not unadjacent to five million pounds,' and a few of them added, 'the financing was private.'

'Well,' Henry said at lunch, tapping the *Sporting Life*, 'not many of our loans make so much splash.'

'It's a belly-flop,' muttered the obstinate dissenter, who on that day happened to be sitting at my elbow.

Henry didn't hear and was anyway in good spirits.

'If one of the foals runs in the Derby we'll take a party from the office. What do you say, Gordon? Fifty people on open-topped buses?'

Gordon agreed with the sort of smile which hoped he wouldn't actually be called upon to fulfil his promise.

'Forty mares,' Henry said musingly. 'Forty foals. Surely one of them might be Derby material.'

'Er,' I said, from new-found knowledge. 'Forty foals is stretching it. Thirty-five would be pretty good. Some mares won't "take", so to speak.'

Henry showed mild alarm. 'Does that mean that five or six fees will have to be returned? Doesn't that affect Knowles' programme of repayment?'

I shook my head. 'For a horse of Sandcastle's stature the fee is all up in front. Payable for services rendered, regardless of results. That's in Britain, of course, and Europe. In America they have the system of no foal, no fee, even for the top stallions. A live foal, that is. Alive, on its feet and suckling.'

Henry relaxed, leaning back in his chair and smiling. 'You've certainly learnt a lot, Tim, since this all started.'

'It's absorbing.'

He nodded. 'I know it isn't usual, but how do you feel about keeping an eye on the bank's money at close quarters? Would Knowles object to you dropping in from time to time?'

'I shouldn't think so. Not out of general interest.'

'Good. Do that, then. Bring us progress reports. I

must say I've never been as impressed with any horse as I was that day with Sandcastle.

Henry's direct admiration of the colt had led in the end to Ekaterin's advancing three of the five million to Oliver Knowles, with private individuals subscribing the other two. The fertility tests had been excellent, the owner had been paid, and Sandcastle already stood in the stallion yard in Hertfordshire alongside Rotaboy, Diarist and Parakeet.

December was marching along towards Christmas, with trees twinkling all over London and sleet falling bleakly in the afternoons. On an impulse I sent a card embossed with tasteful robins to Calder Jackson, wishing him well, and almost by return of post received (in the office) a missive (Stubbs reproduction) thanking me sincerely and asking if I would be interested some time in looking round his place. If so, he finished, would I telephone – number supplied.

I telephoned. He was affable and far more spontaneous than usual. 'Do come,' he said, and we made a date for the following Sunday.

I told Gordon I was going. We were working on an interbank loan of nine and a half million for five days to a competitor, a matter of little more than a few telephone calls and a promise. My hair had almost ceased to rise at the size and speed of such deals, and with only verbal agreement from Val and Henry I had recently on my own lent seven million for forty-eight hours. The trick was never to lend for a longer time than we ourselves were able to borrow the necessary funds; if we did, we ran the risk of having to pay a higher rate of interest than we were receiving on the loan, a process which physically hurt Val Fisher. There had been a time in the past when owing to a client repaying late he had had to borrow several million for eighteen days at twenty-five per cent, and he'd never got over it.

Most of our dealings weren't on such a heavy scale, and next on my agenda was a request for us to lend fifty-five thousand pounds to a man who had invented a waste-paper basket for use in cars and needed funds for development. I read the letter out to Gordon, who made a fast thumbs-down gesture.

'Pity,' I said. 'It's a sorely needed object.'

'He's asking too little.' He put his left hand hard between his knees and clamped it there. 'And there are far better inventions dying the death.'

I agreed with him and wrote a brief note of regret. Gordon looked up from his pages shortly after and asked me what I'd be doing at Christmas.

'Nothing much,' I said.

'Not going to your mother in Jersey?'

'They're cruising in the Caribbean.'

'Judith and I wondered . . .' he cleared his throat, '. . . if you'd care to stay with us. Come on Christmas Eve, stay three or four days? Just as you like, of course. I daresay you wouldn't find us too exciting . . . but the offer's there, anyway.'

Was it wise, I wondered, to spend three or four days with Judith when three or four *hours* at Ascot had tempted acutely? Was it wise, when the sight of her aroused so many natural urges, to sleep so long – and so near – under her roof?

Most unwise.

'I'd like to,' I said, 'very much'; and I thought you're a bloody stupid fool, Tim Ekaterin, and if you ache it'll be your own ridiculous fault.

'Good,' Gordon said, looking as if he meant it. 'Judith will be pleased. She was afraid you might have younger friends to go to.'

'Nothing fixed.'

He nodded contentedly and went back to his work, and I thought about Judith wanting me to stay, because if she hadn't wanted it I wouldn't have been asked.

If I had any sense I wouldn't go; but I knew I would.

Calder Jackson's place at Newmarket, seen that next Sunday morning, was a gem of public relations, where everything had been done to please those visiting the sick. The yard itself, a three-sided quadrangle, had been cosmetically planted with central grass and a graceful tree, and brightly painted tubs, bare now of flowers, stood at frequent intervals outside the boxes. There were park-bench type seats here and there, and ornamental gates and railings in black iron scroll-work, and a welcoming archway labelled 'Comfort Room This Way.'

Outside the main yard, and to one side, stood a small separate building painted glossy white. There was a large prominent red cross on the door, with, underneath it, the single word 'Surgery'.

The yard and the surgery were what the visitor first saw; beyond and screened by trees stood Calder Jackson's own house, more private from prying eyes than his business. I parked beside several other cars on a stretch of asphalt, and walked over to ring the bell. The front door was opened to me by a manservant in a white coat. Butler or nurse?

'This way, sir,' he said deferentially, when I announced my name. 'Mr Jackson is expecting you.'

Butler.

Interesting to see the dramatic haircut in its home setting, which was olde-worlde cottage on a grand scale. I had an impression of a huge room, oak rafters, stone flagged floor, rugs, dark oak furniture, great brick fireplace with burning logs ... and Calder advancing with a broad smile and outstretched arm.

'Tim!' he exclaimed, shaking hands vigorously. 'This is a pleasure, indeed it is.'

'Been looking forward to it,' I said.

'Come along to the fire. Come and warm yourself. How about a drink? And ... oh ... this is a friend of mine ...' He waved towards a second man already standing by the fireplace, '... Ian Pargetter.'

The friend and I nodded to each other and made the usual strangers-meeting signals, and the name tumbled over in my mind as something I'd heard somewhere before but couldn't quite recall.

Calder Jackson clinked bottles and glasses and upon consultation gave me a Scotch of noble proportions.

'And for you, Ian,' he said, 'a further tincture?'

Oh yes, I thought. The vet. Ian Pargetter, the vet who didn't mind consorting with unlicensed practitioners.

Ian Pargetter hesitated but shrugged and held out his glass as one succumbing to pleasurable temptation.

'A small one, then, Calder,' he said. 'I must be off.'

He was about forty, I judged; large and reliable-looking, with sandy greying hair, a heavy moustache and an air of being completely in charge of his life. Calder explained that it was I who had deflected the knife aimed at him at Ascot, and Ian Pargetter made predictable responses about luck, fast reactions and who could have wanted to kill Calder?

'That was altogether a memorable day,' Calder said, and I agreed with him.

'We all won a packet on Sandcastle,' Calder said. 'Pity he's going to stud so soon.'

I smiled. 'Maybe we'll win on his sons.'

There was no particular secret, as far as I knew, about where the finance for Sandcastle had come from, but it was up to Oliver Knowles to reveal it, not me. I thought Calder would have been interested, but bankers' ethics as usual kept me quiet.

'A superb horse,' Calder said, with all the enthusiasm he'd shown in Dissdale's box. 'One of the greats.'

Ian Pargetter nodded agreement, then finished his drink at a gulp and said he'd be going. 'Let me know how that pony fares, Calder.'

'Yes, of course.' Calder moved with his departing guest towards the door and slapped him on the shoulder. 'Thanks for dropping in, Ian. Appreciate it.'

There were sounds of Pargetter leaving by the front door, and Calder returned rubbing his hands together and saying that although it was cold outside, I might care to look round before his other guests arrived for lunch. Accordingly we walked across to the open-sided quadrangle, where Calder moved from box to box giving me a brief résumé of the illness and prospects of each patient.

'This pony only came yesterday ... it's a prize show pony supposedly, and look at it. Dull eyes, rough coat, altogether droopy. They say it's had diarrhoea on and off for weeks. I'm their last resort, they say.' He smiled philosophically. 'Can't think why they don't send me sick horses as a *first* resort. But there you are, they always try regular vets first. Can't blame them, I suppose.'

We moved along the line. 'This mare was coughing blood when she came three weeks ago. I was her owner's last resort.' He smiled again. 'She's doing fine now. The cough's almost gone. She's eating well, putting on condition.' The mare blinked at us lazily as we strolled away.

'This is a two-year-old filly,' Calder said, peering over a half-door. 'She'd had an infected ulcer on her withers for six weeks before she came here. Antibiotics had proved useless. Now the ulcer's dry and healing. Most satisfactory.'

We went on down the row.

'This is someone's favourite hunter, came all the way from Gloucestershire. I don't know what I can do for him, though of course I'll try. His trouble, truthfully, is just age.'

Further on: 'Here's a star three-day-eventer. Came to me with intermittent bleeding in the urine, intractable to antibiotics. He was clearly in great pain, and almost dangerous to deal with on account of it. But now he's fine. He'll be staying here for a while longer but I'm sure the trouble is cured.

'This is a three-year-old colt who won a race back in July but then started breaking blood vessels and went on doing it despite treatment. He's been here a fortnight. Last resort, of course!'

By the next box he said, 'Don't look at this one if you're squeamish. Poor wretched little filly, she's so weak she can't hold her head up and all her bones are sharp under the skin. Some sort of wasting sickness. Blood tests haven't shown what it is. I don't know if I can heal her. I've laid my hands on her twice so far, but there's been nothing. No . . . feeling. Sometimes it takes a long time. But I'm not giving up with her, and there's always hope.'

He turned his curly head and pointed to another box further ahead. 'There's a colt along there who's been here two months and is only just responding. His owners were in despair, and so was I, privately, but then just three days ago when I was in his box I could feel the force flowing down my arms and into him, and the next day he was mending.'

He spoke with a far more natural fluency on his home ground and less as if reciting from a script, but all the same I felt the same reservations about the healing touch as I had at Ascot. I was a doubter, I supposed. I would never in my life have put my trust in a seventh son of a seventh son, probably because the only direct knowledge I had of any human seeking out 'the touch' had been a close friend of mine at college who'd had hopeless cancer and had gone to a woman healer as a last resort, only to be told that he was dying because he wanted to. I could vividly remember his anger, and mine on his behalf; and standing in Calder's yard I wondered if that same woman would also think that *horses* got sick to death because they wanted to.

'Is there anything you can't treat?' I asked. 'Anything you turn away?'

'I'm afraid so, yes.' He smiled ruefully. 'There are some things like advanced laminitis, with which I feel hopeless, and as for coryne . . .' He shook his head, '. . . It's a killer.'

'You've lost me,' I said.

'So sorry. Well, laminitis is a condition of the feet where the bone eventually begins to crumble, and horses in the end can't bear the pain of standing up. They lie down, and horses can't live for more than a few days lying down.' He spoke with regret. 'And coryne,' he went on, 'is a frightful bacterial infection which is deadly to foals. It induces a sort of pneumonia with abscesses in the lungs. Terribly contagious. I know of one stud farm in America which lost seventy foals in one day.'

I listened in horror. 'Do we have it in England?' I asked.

'Sometimes, in pockets, but not widespread. It doesn't affect older horses. Foals of three months or over are safe.' He paused. 'Some very young foals do survive, of course, but they're likely to have scar tissue in the lungs which may impair their breathing for racing purposes.'

'Isn't there a vaccine?' I said.

He smiled indulgently. 'Very little research is done into equine diseases, chiefly because of the cost but also because horses are so large, and can't be kept in a laboratory for any controlled series of tests.'

I again had the impression that he had said all this many times before, but it was understandable and I was getting used to it. We proceeded on the hospital round (four-year-old with general debility, show-jumper with festering leg) and came at length to a box with an open door.

'We're giving this one sun treatment,' Calder said, indicating that I should look; and inside the box a thin youth was adjusting the angle of an ultra-violet lamp set on a head-high, wall-mounted bracket. It wasn't at the dappled grey that I looked, however, but at the lad, because in the first brief glimpse I thought he was the boy who had tried to attack Calder.

I opened my mouth . . . and shut it again.

He wasn't the boy. He was of the same height, same build, same litheness, same general colouring, but not with the same eyes or jawline or narrow nose.

Calder saw my reaction and smiled. 'For a split second, when I saw that boy move at Ascot, I thought it was Jason here. But it wasn't, of course.'

I shook my head. 'Alike but different.'

Calder nodded. 'And Jason wouldn't want to kill me, would you, Jason?' He spoke with a jocularity to which Jason didn't respond.

'No, sir,' he said stolidly.

'Jason is my right-hand man,' said Calder heartily. 'Indispensable.'

The right-hand man showed no satisfaction at the flattery and maintained an impassive countenance throughout. He touched the grey horse and told it to shift over a bit in the manner of one equal talking to another, and the horse obediently shifted.

'Mind your eyes with that lamp,' Calder said. 'Where are your glasses?'

Jason fished into the breast pocket of his shirt and produced some ultra-dark sun-shades. Calder nodded. 'Put them on,' he said, and Jason complied. Where before there had already been a lack of mobility of expression, there was now, with the obscured eyes, no way at all of guessing Jason's thoughts.

'I'll be finished with this one in ten minutes,' he said. 'Is there anything else after that, sir?'

Calder briefly pondered and shook his head. 'Just the evening rounds at four.'

'Your invalids get every care,' I said, complimenting them.

Jason's blacked-out eyes turned my way, but it was Calder who said, 'Hard work gets results.' And you've said that a thousand times, I thought.

We reached the last box in the yard, the first one which was empty.

'Emergency bed,' Calder said, jokingly, and I smiled and asked how much he charged for his patients.

He replied easily and without explanation or apology. 'Twice the training fees currently charged for horses in the top Newmarket stables. When their rates go up, so do mine.'

'*Twice* . . .?'

He nodded. 'I could charge more, you know. But if I charged less I'd be totally swamped by all those "last resort" people, and I simply haven't the room or the

time or the spiritual resources to take more cases than
I do.'

I wondered how one would ever get to the essence
of the man behind the temperate, considerate public
face, or indeed if the public face was not a façade at
all but the essence itself. I looked at the physical
strength of the shoulders below the helmet head and
listened to the plain words describing a mystical force,
considered the dominating voice and the mild manner,
and still found him a man to admire rather than like.

'The surgery,' he said, gesturing towards it as we
walked that way. 'My drug store!' He smiled at the
joke (how often, I wondered, had he said it?) and
produced a key to unlock the door. 'There's nothing
dangerous or illegal in here, of course, but one has to
protect against vandals. So sad, don't you think?'

The surgery, which had no windows, was basically a
large brick-built hut. The internal walls, like the outer,
were painted white, and the floor was tiled in red.
There were antiseptic-looking glass-fronted cabinets
along the two end walls and a wide bench with drawers
underneath along the wall facing the door. On the
bench, a delicate-looking set of scales, a pestle and
mortar and a pair of fine rubber gloves: behind the
glass of the cabinets, rows of bottles and boxes. Everything very businesslike and tidy; and along the wall
which contained the door stood three kitchen
appliances, refrigerator, cooker and sink.

Calder pointed vaguely towards the cabinets. 'In

there I keep the herbs in pill and powder form. Comfrey, myrrh, sarsaparilla, golden seal, fo-ti-tieng, things like that.'

'Er . . .' I said. 'What do they do?'

He ran through them obligingly. 'Comfrey knits bones, and heals wounds, myrrh is antiseptic and good for diarrhoea and rheumatism, sarsaparilla contains male hormones and increases physical strength, golden seal cures eczema, improves appetite and digestion, fo-ti-tieng is a revitalizing tonic second to none. Then there's liquorice for coughs and papaya enzymes for digesting proteins and passiflora to use as a general pacifier and tranquillizer.' He paused. 'There's ginseng also, of course, which is a marvellous rejuvenator and invigorator, but it's really too expensive in the quantities needed to do a horse significant good. It has to be taken continuously, for ever.' He sighed. 'Excellent for humans, though.'

The air in the windowless room was fresh and smelled very faintly fragrant, and as if to account for it Calder started showing me the contents of the drawers.

'I keep seeds in here,' he said. 'My patients eat them by the handful every day.' Three or four of the drawers contained large opaque plastic bags fastened by bull-dog clips. 'Sunflower seeds for vitamins, phosphorus and calcium, good for bones and teeth. Pumpkin seeds for vigour – they contain male hormones – and also for phosphorus and iron. Carrot seeds for calming nervous horses. Sesame seeds for general health.'

He walked along a yard or two and pulled open an extra-large deep drawer which contained larger bags; more like sacks. 'These are hops left after beer-making. They're packed full of all good things. A great tonic, and cheap enough to use in quantity. We have bagfuls of them over in the feed shed to grind up as chaff but I use these here as one ingredient of my special decoction, my concentrated tonic.'

'Do you make it . . . on the stove?' I asked.

He smiled. 'Like a chef.' He opened the refrigerator door. 'I store it in here. Want to see?'

I looked inside. Nearly the whole space was taken with gallon-sized plastic containers full of brownish liquid. 'We mix it in a bran mash, warmed of course, and the horses thrive.'

I knew nothing about the efficiency of his remedies, but I was definitely impressed.

'How do you get the horses to take pills?' I said.

'In an apple, usually. We scoop out half the core, put in the tablet or capsule, or indeed just powder, and replace the plug.'

So simple.

'And incidentally, I make most of my own pills and capsules. Some, like comfrey, are commercially available, but I prefer to buy the dried herbs in their pure form and make my own recipes.' He pulled open one of the lower drawers under the work-bench and lifted out a heavy wooden box. 'This,' he said, laying it on the work surface and opening the lid, 'contains the makings.'

I looked down at a whole array of brass dies, each a small square with a pill-sized cavity in its centre. The cavities varied from tiny to extra large, and from round to oblong.

'It's an antique,' he said with a touch of pride. 'Early Victorian. Dates from when pills were always made by hand – and it's still viable, of course. You put the required drug in powder form into whatever sized cavity you want, and compress it with the rod which exactly fits.' He lifted one of a series of short brass rods from its rack and fitted its end into one of the cavities, tamping it up and down; then picked the whole die out of the box and tipped it right over. 'Hey presto,' he said genially, catching the imaginary contents, 'a pill!'

'Neat,' I said, with positive pleasure.

He nodded. 'Capsules are quicker and more modern.' He pulled open another drawer and briefly showed me the empty tops and bottoms of a host of gelatin capsules, again of varying sizes, though mostly a little larger than those swallowed easily by humans. 'Veterinary size,' he explained.

He closed his gem of a pill-making box and returned it to its drawer, straightening up afterwards and casting a caring eye around the place to make sure everything was tidy. With a nod of private satisfaction he opened the door for us to return to the outside world, switching off the fluorescent lights and locking the door behind us.

A car was just rolling to a stop on the asphalt, and presently two recognized figures emerged from it: Dissdale Smith and his delectable Bettina.

'Hello, hello,' said Dissdale, striding across with ready hand. 'Calder said you were coming. Good to see you. Calder's been showing you all his treasures, eh? The conducted tour, eh, Calder?' I shook the hand. 'Calder's proud of his achievements here, aren't you, Calder?'

'With good reason,' I said civilly, and Calder gave me a swift glance and a genuine-looking smile.

Bettina drifted more slowly to join us, a delight in high-heeled boots and cuddling fur, a white silk scarf round her throat and smooth dark hair falling glossily to her shoulders. Her scent travelled sweetly across the quiet cold air and she laid a decorative hand on my arm in an intimate touch.

'Tim the saviour,' she said. 'Calder's hero.'

The over-packaged charm unaccountably brought the contrasting image of Ginnie sharply to my mind, and I briefly thought that the promise was more beckoning than the performance, that child more interesting than that woman.

Calder took us all soon into his maxi-cottage sitting room and distributed more drinks. Dissdale told me that Sandcastle had almost literally saved his business and metaphorically his life, and we all drank a toast to the wonder horse. Four further guests arrived – a married couple with their two twentyish daughters – and the occasion became an ordinarily enjoyable lunch party, undemanding, unmemorable, good food handed round by the manservant, cigars offered with the coffee.

Calder at some point said he was off to America in the New Year on a short lecture tour.

'Unfortunately,' he said, 'I'll be talking to health clubs, not horse people. American racehorse trainers aren't receptive to me. Or not yet. But then, it took a few years for Newmarket to decide I could make a contribution.'

Everyone smiled at the scepticism of America and Newmarket.

Calder said, 'January is often a quiet month here. We don't take any new admissions if I'm away, and of course my head lad just keeps the establishment routines going until I return. It works pretty well.' He smiled. 'If I'm lucky I'll get some skiing; and to be honest, I'm looking forward to the skiing much more than the talks.'

Everyone left soon after three, and I drove back to London through the short darkening afternoon wondering if the herbs of antiquity held secrets we'd almost wilfully lost.

'Caffeine,' Calder had been saying towards the end, 'is a get-up-and-go stimulant, tremendously useful. Found in coffee beans of course, and in tea and cocoa and in cola drinks. Good for asthma. Vigorous, marvellous tonic. A life-saver after shock. And now in America, I ask you, they're casting caffeine as a villain and are busy taking it out of everything it's naturally *in*. You might as well take the alcohol out of bread.'

'But Calder dear,' Bettina said, 'there's no alcohol in bread.'

He looked at her kindly as she sat on his right. 'Bread that is made with yeast definitely does contain alcohol before it's cooked. If you mix yeast with water and sugar you get alcohol and carbon dioxide, which is the gas which makes the dough rise. The air in a bakery smells of wine . . . simple chemistry, my dear girl, no magic in it. Bread is the staff of life and alcohol is good for you.'

There had been jokes and lifted glasses, and I could have listened to Calder for hours.

The Christmas party at Gordon Michael's home was in a way an echo, because Judith's apothecary friend Pen Warner was in attendance most of the time. I got to know her quite well and to like her very much, which Judith may or may not have intended. In any case, it was again the fairy-tale day at Ascot which had led on to friendly relations.

'Do you remember Burnt Marshmallow?' Pen said. 'I bought a painting with my winnings.'

'I spent mine on riotous living.'

'Oh yes?' She looked me up and down and shook her head. 'You haven't the air.'

'What do I have the air of?' I asked curiously, and she answered in amusement, 'Of intelligent laziness and boring virtue.'

'All wrong,' I said.

'Ho hum.'

She seemed to me to be slightly less physically solid than at Ascot, but it might have been only the change of clothes; there were still the sad eyes and the ingrained worthiness and the unexpected cast of humour. She had apparently spent twelve hours that day – it was Christmas Eve – doling out remedies to people whose illnesses showed no sense of timing, and proposed to go back at six in the morning. Meanwhile she appeared at the Michaels' house in a long festive caftan with mood to match, and during the evening the four of us ate quails with our fingers, and roasted chestnuts, and played a board game with childish gusto.

Judith wore rose pink and pearls and looked about twenty-five. Gordon in advance had instructed me 'Bring whatever you like as long as it's informal' and himself was resplendent in a plum velvet jacket and bow tie. My own newly bought cream wool shirt which in the shop had looked fairly theatrical seemed in the event to be right, so that on all levels the evening proved harmonious and fun, much more rounded and easy than I'd expected.

Judith's housekeeping throughout my stay proved a poem of invisibility. Food appeared from freezer and cupboard, remnants returned to dishwasher and dustbin. Jobs were distributed when essential but sitting and talking had priority; and nothing so smooth, I reflected, ever got done without hard work beforehand.

'Pen will be back soon after one tomorrow,' Judith said at midnight on that first evening. 'We'll have a drink then and open some presents, and have our Christmas feast at half past three. There will be breakfast in the morning, and Gordon and I will go to church.' She left an invitation lingering in the air, but I marginally shook my head. 'You can look after yourself, then, while we're gone.'

She kissed me goodnight, with affection and on the cheek. Gordon gave me a smile and a wave, and I went to bed across the hall from them and spent an hour before sleep deliberately not thinking at all about Judith in or out of her nightgown – or not much.

Breakfast was taken in dressing gowns. Judith's was red, quilted and unrevealing.

They changed and went to church. Pray for me, I said, and set out for a walk on the common.

There were brightly wrapped gifts waiting around the base of the silver-starred Christmas tree in the Michaels' drawing room, and a surreptitious inspection had revealed one from Pen addressed to me. I walked across the windy grass, shoulders hunched, hands in pockets, wondering what to do about one for her, and as quite often happens came by chance to a solution.

A small boy was out there with his father, flying a kite, and I stopped to watch.

149

'That's fun,' I said.

The boy took no notice but the father said, 'There's no satisfying the little bleeder. I give him this and he says he wants roller skates.'

The kite was a brilliant phosphorescent Chinese dragon with butterfly wings and a big frilly tail, soaring and circling like a joyful tethered spirit in the Christmas sky.

'Will you sell it to me?' I asked. 'Buy the roller skates instead?' I explained the problem, the need for an instant present.

Parent and child consulted and the deal was done. I wound up the string carefully and bore the trophy home, wondering what on earth the sober pharmacist would think of such a thing; but when she unwrapped it from gold paper (cadged from Judith for the purpose) she pronounced herself enchanted, and back we all went onto the common to watch her fly it.

The whole day was happy. I hadn't had so good a Christmas since I was a child. I told them so, and kissed Judith uninhibitedly under some mistletoe, which Gordon didn't seem to mind.

'You were born sunny,' Judith said, briefly stroking my cheek, and Gordon, nodding, said, 'A man without sorrows, unacquainted with grief.'

'Grief and sorrow come with time,' Pen said, but not as if she meant it imminently. 'They come to us all.'

*

On the morning after Christmas Day I drove Judith across London to Hampstead to put flowers on her mother's grave.

'I know you'll think me silly, but I always go. She died on Boxing Day when I was twelve. It's the only way I have of remembering her . . . of feeling I had a mother at all. I usually go by myself. Gordon thinks I'm sentimental and doesn't like coming.'

'Nothing wrong with sentiment,' I said.

Hampstead was where I lived in the upstairs half of a friend's house. I wasn't sure whether or not Judith knew it, and said nothing until she'd delivered the pink chrysanthemums to the square marble tablet let in flush with the grass and communed for a while with the memories floating there.

It was as we walked slowly back towards the iron gates that I neutrally said, 'My flat's only half a mile from here. This part of London is home ground.'

'Is it?'

'Mm.'

After a few steps she said, 'I knew you lived some-where here. If you remember, you wouldn't let us drive you all the way home from Ascot. You said Hampstead was too far.'

'So it was.'

'Not for Sir Galahad that starry night.'

We reached the gates and paused for her to look back. I was infinitely conscious of her nearness and of my own stifled desire; and she looked abruptly into my eyes and said, 'Gordon knows you live here, also.'

'And does he know how I feel?' I asked.

'I don't know. He hasn't said.'

I wanted very much to go that last half-mile: that short distance on wheels, that far journey in commitment. My body tingled . . . rippled . . . from hunger, and I found myself physically clenching my back teeth.

'What are you thinking?' she said.

'For God's sake . . . you know damn well what I'm thinking . . . and we're going back to Clapham right this minute.'

She sighed. 'Yes. I suppose we must.'

'What do you mean . . . you suppose?'

'Well, I . . .' she paused. 'I mean, yes we must. I'm sorry . . . it was just that . . . for a moment . . . I was tempted.'

'As at Ascot?' I said.

She nodded. 'As at Ascot.'

'Only here and now,' I said, 'we have the place and the time and the opportunity to do something about it.'

'Yes.'

'And what we're going to do . . . is . . . nothing.' It came out as half a question, half a statement: wholly an impossibility.

'Why do we *care*?' she said explosively. 'Why don't we just get into your bed and have a happy time? Why is the whole thing so tangled up with bloody concepts like honour?'

We walked down the road to where I'd parked the car and I drove southwards with careful observance at every red light; stop signals making round eyes at me all the way to Clapham.

'I'd have liked it,' Judith said as we pulled up outside her house.

'So would I.'

We went indoors in a sort of deprived companionship, and I realized only when I saw Gordon's smiling unsuspicious face that I couldn't have returned there if it had been in any other way.

It was at lunch that day, when Pen had again resurfaced from her stint among the pills that I told them about my visit to Calder. Pen, predictably, was acutely interested and said she'd dearly like to know what was in the decoction in the refrigerator.

'What's a decoction?' Judith asked.

'A preparation boiled with water. If you dissolve things in alcohol, that's a tincture.'

'One lives and bloody well learns!'

Pen laughed. 'How about carminative, anodyne and vermifuge . . . effects of drugs. They simply roll off the tongue with grandeur.'

'And what do they mean?' Gordon asked.

'Getting rid of gas, getting rid of pain, getting rid of worms.'

Gordon too was laughing. 'Have some anodyne

153

tincture of grape.' He poured wine into our glasses. 'Do you honestly believe, Tim, that Calder cures horses by touch?'

'I'm sure *he* believes it.' I reflected. 'I don't know if he will let anyone watch. And if he did, what would one see? I don't suppose with a horse it's a case of "take up your bed and walk."'

Judith said in surprise, 'You sound as if you'd like it to be true. You, that Gordon and Harry have trained to doubt!'

'Calder's impressive,' I admitted. 'So is his place. So are the fees he charges. He wouldn't be able to set his prices so high if he didn't get real results.'

'Do the herbs come extra?' Pen said.

'I didn't ask.'

'Would you expect them to?' Gordon said.

'Well . . .' Pen considered. 'Some of those that Tim mentioned are fairly exotic. Golden seal – that hydrastis – said in the past to cure practically anything you can mention, but mostly used nowadays in tiny amounts in eye-drops. Has to be imported from America. And fo-ti-tieng – which is *Hydrocotyle asiatica minor*, also called the source of the elixir of long life – that only grows as far as I know in the tropical jungles of the Far East. I mean, I would have thought that giving things like that to horses would be wildly expensive.'

If I'd been impressed with Calder I was probably more so with Pen. 'I didn't know pharmacists were so clued up on herbs,' I said.

'I was just interested so I learned their properties,' she explained. 'The age-old remedies are hardly even hinted at on the official pharmacy courses, though considering digitalis and penicillin one can't exactly see why. A lot of chemist's shops don't sell non-prescription herbal remedies, but I do, and honestly for a stack of people they seem to work.'

'And do you advocate garlic poultices for the feet of babies with whooping cough?' Gordon asked.

Pen didn't. There was more laughter. If one believed in Calder, Judith said firmly, one believed in him, garlic poultices and all.

The four of us spent a comfortable afternoon and evening together, and when Judith and Gordon went to bed I walked along with Pen to her house, where she'd been staying each night, filling my lungs with the fresh air off the common.

'You're going home tomorrow, aren't you?' she said, fishing out her key.

I nodded. 'In the morning.'

'It's been great fun.' She found the keys and fitted one in the lock. 'Would you like to come in?'

'No . . . I'll just walk for a bit.'

She opened the door and paused there. 'Thank you for the kite . . . it was brilliant. And goodbye for this time, though I guess if Judith can stand it I'll be seeing you again.'

'Stand what?' I asked.

She kissed me on the cheek. 'Goodnight,' she said.

'And believe it or not, the herb known as passion flower is good for insomnia.'

Her grin shone out like the Cheshire Cat's as she stepped inside her house and closed the door, and I stood hopelessly on her pathway wanting to call her back.

The Second Year

FEBRUARY

Ian Pargetter was murdered at about one in the morning on February the first.

I learned about his death from Calder when I telephoned that evening on impulse to thank him belatedly for the lunch party, invite him for a reciprocal dinner in London and hear whether or not he had enjoyed his American tour.

'Who?' he said vaguely when I announced myself. 'Who? Oh... Tim... Look, I can't talk now, I'm simply distracted, a friend of mine's been killed and I can't think of anything else.'

'I'm so sorry,' I said inadequately.

'Yes... Ian Pargetter... but I don't suppose you know...'

This time I remembered at once. The vet: big, reliable, sandy moustache.

'I met him,' I said, 'in your house.'

'Did you? Oh, yes. I'm so upset I can't concentrate. Look, Tim, ring some other time, will you?'

'Yes, of course.'

159

'It's not just that he's been a friend for years,' he said, 'but I don't know... I really don't know how my business will fare without him. He sent so many horses my way... such a good friend... I'm totally distraught... Look, ring me another time... Tim, so sorry.' He put his receiver down with the rattle of a shaking hand.

I thought at the time that he meant Ian Pargetter had been killed in some sort of accident, and it was only the next day when my eye was caught by a paragraph in a newspaper that I realized the difference.

Ian Pargetter, well-known, much respected New-market veterinary surgeon, was yesterday morning found dead in his home. Police suspect foul play. They state that Pargetter suffered head injuries and that certain supplies of drugs appear to be missing. Pargetter's body was discovered by Mrs Jane Halson, a daily cleaner. The vet is survived by his wife and three young daughters, all of whom were away from home at the time of the attack. Mrs Pargetter was reported last night to be very distressed and under sedation.

A lot of succinct bad news, I thought, for a lot of sad bereft people. He was the first person I'd known who'd been murdered, and in spite of our very brief meeting I found his death most disturbing: and if I felt so unsettled about a near-stranger, how, I wondered, did anyone ever recover from the murder of someone one knew well and loved. How did one deal with the anger? Come to terms with the urge to revenge?

I'd of course read reports of husbands and wives who pronounced themselves 'not bitter' over the slaughter of a spouse, and I'd never understood it. I felt furious on Ian Pargetter's behalf that anyone should have the arrogance to wipe him out.

Because of Ascot and Sandcastle my long-dormant interest in racecourses seemed thoroughly to have reawakened, and on three or four Saturday afternoons that winter I'd trekked to Kempton or Sandown or Newbury to watch the jumpers. Ursula Young had become a familiar face, and it was from this brisk well-informed lady bloodstock agent that I learnt most about Ian Pargetter and his death.

'Drink?' I suggested at Kempton, pulling up my coat collar against a bitter wind.

She looked at her watch (I'd never seen her do anything without checking the time) and agreed on a quick one. Whisky-mac for her, coffee for me, as at Doncaster.

'Now tell me,' she said, hugging her glass and yelling in my ear over the general din of a bar packed with other cold customers seeking inner warmth, 'when you asked all those questions about stallion shares, was it for Sandcastle?'

I smiled without actually answering, shielding my coffee inadequately from adjacent nudging elbows.

'Thought so,' she said. 'Look – there's a table. Grab it.'

We sat down in a corner with the racket going on over our heads and the closed-circuit television playing re-runs of the last race fortissimo. Ursula bent her head towards mine. 'A wow-sized coup for Oliver Knowles.'

'You approve?' I asked.

She nodded. 'He'll be among the greats in one throw. Smart move. Clever man.'

'Do you know him?'

'Yes. Meet him often at the sales. He had a snooty wife who left him for some Canadian millionaire or other, and maybe that's why he's aiming for the big-time; just to show her.' She smiled fiendishly. 'She was a real pain and I hope he makes it.'

She drank half her whisky and I said it was a shame about Ian Pargetter, and that I'd met him once at Calder's house.

She grimaced with a stronger echo of the anger I had myself felt. 'He'd been out all evening saving the life of a classic-class colt with colic. It's so beastly. He went home well after midnight, and they reckon whoever killed him was already in the house stealing whatever he could lay his hands on. Ian's wife and family were away visiting her mother, you see, and the police think the killer thought the house would be empty for the night.' She swallowed. 'He was hit on

the back of the head with a brass lamp off one of the
tables in the sitting room. Just casual. Unpremeditated.
Just . . . *stupid*.' She looked moved, as I guessed
everyone must have been who had known him. 'Such
a waste. He was a really nice man, a good vet, everyone
liked him. And all for practically nothing . . . The police
found a lot of silver and jewellery lying on a blanket
ready to be carried away, but they think the thief just
panicked and left it when Ian came home . . . all that
anyone can think of that's missing is his case of instruments and a few drugs that he'd had with him that evening
. . . nothing worth killing for . . . not even for an addict.
Nothing in it like that.' She fell silent and looked down
into her nearly empty glass, and I offered her a refill.

'No, thanks all the same, one's enough. I feel pretty
maudlin as it is. I liked Ian. He was a good sort. I'd
like to *throttle* the little beast who killed him.'

'I think Calder Jackson feels much as you do,' I said.

She glanced up, her good-looking fifty-ish face full
of genuine concern. 'Calder will miss Ian terribly. There
aren't that number of vets around who'd not only put
up with a faith-healer on their doorstep but actually
treat him as a colleague. Ian had no professional jealousy. Very rare. Very good man. Makes it all the worse.'

We went out again into the raw air and I lost five
pounds on the afternoon, which would have sent Lorna
Shipton swooning to Uncle Freddie, if she'd known.

*

Two weeks later with Oliver Knowles' warm approval I paid another visit to his farm in Hertfordshire, and although it was again a Sunday and still winter, the atmosphere of the place had fundamentally changed. Where there had been quiet sleepy near-hibernation there was now a wakeful bustle and eagerness, where a scattering of dams and foals across the paddocks, now a crowd of mares moving alone and slowly with big bellies.

The crop had come to the harvest. Life was ripening into the daylight, and into the darkness the new seed would be sown.

I had not been truly a country child (ten acres of wooded hill in Surrey) and to me the birth of animals still seemed a wonder and joy; to Oliver Knowles, he said, it meant constant worry and profit and loss. His grasp of essentials still rang out strong and clear, but there were lines on his forehead from the details.

'I suppose,' he said frankly, walking me into the first of the big yards, 'that the one thing I hadn't mentally prepared myself for was the value of the foals now being born here. I mean . . .' he gestured around at the atient heads looking over the rows of half-doors, '. . . these mares have been to the top stallions. They're carrying fabulous blood-lines. They're history.' His awe could be felt. 'I didn't realize, you know, what anxiety they would bring me. We've always done our best for the foals, of course we have, but if one died it wasn't a tragedy, but with this lot . . .' He smiled ruefully. 'It's not enough just owning Sandcastle. I have to make sure that our reputation for handling top broodmares is good and sound.'

We walked along beside one row of boxes with him telling me in detail the breeding of each mare we came to and of the foal she carried, and even to my ignorant ears it sounded as if every Derby and Oaks winner for the past half-century had had a hand in the coming generation.

'I had no trouble selling Sandcastle's nominations,' he said. 'Not even at forty thousand pounds a throw. I could even choose, to some extent, which mares to accept. It's been utterly amazing to be able to turn away mares that I considered wouldn't do him justice.'

'Is there a temptation,' I asked mildly, 'to sell more than forty places? To ... er ... accept an extra fee ... in untaxed cash ... on the quiet?'

He was more amused than offended. 'I wouldn't say it hasn't been done on every farm that ever existed. But I wouldn't do it with Sandcastle ... or at any rate not this year. He's still young. And untested, of course. Some stallions won't look at as many as forty mares ... though shy breeders do tend to run in families, and there's nothing in his pedigree to suggest he'll be any-thing but energetic and fertile. I wouldn't have embarked on all this if there had been any doubts.'

It seemed that he was trying to reassure himself as much as me; as if the size and responsibility of his undertaking had only just penetrated, and in penetrating, frightened.

I felt a faint tremor of dismay but stifled it with the reassurance that come hell or high water Sandcastle was worth his buying price and could be sold again even at this late date for not much less. The bank's money was safe on his hoof.

It was earlier in the day than my last visit – eleven in the morning – and more lads than before were to be seen mucking out the boxes and carrying feed and water.

'I've had to take on extra hands,' Oliver Knowles said matter-of-factly. 'Temporarily, for the season.'

'Has recruitment been difficult?' I asked.

'Not really. I do it every spring. I keep the good ones on for the whole year, if they'll stay, of course: these lads come and go as the whim takes them, the unmarried ones, that is. I keep the nucleus on and put them painting fences and such in the autumn and winter.'

We strolled into the second yard, where the burly figure of Nigel could be seen peering over a half-door into a box.

'You remember Nigel?' Oliver said. 'My stud manager?'

Nigel, I noted, had duly been promoted.

'And Ginnie,' I asked, as we walked over, 'is she home today?'

'Yes, she's somewhere about.' He looked around as

if expecting her to materialize at the sound of her name, but nothing happened.

'How's it going, Nigel?' he asked.

Nigel's hairy eyebrows withdrew from the box and aimed themselves in our direction. 'Floradora's eating again,' he said, indicating the inspected lady and sounding relieved. 'And Pattacake is still in labour. I'm just going back there.'

'We'll come,' Oliver said. 'If you'd like to?' he added, looking at me questioningly.

I nodded and walked on with them along the path into the third, smaller quadrangle, the foaling yard.

Here too, in this place that had been empty, there was purposeful life, and the box to which Nigel led us was larger than normal and thickly laid with straw.

'Foals usually drop at night,' Oliver said, and Nigel nodded. 'She started about midnight. She's just lazy, eh, girl?' He patted the brown rump. 'Very slow. Same thing every year.'

'She's not come for Sandcastle, then?' I said.

'No. She's one of mine,' Oliver said. 'The foal's by Diarist.'

We hovered for a few minutes but there was no change in Pattacake. Nigel, running delicately knowledgeable hands over the shape under her ribs, said she'd be another hour, perhaps, and that he would stay with her for a while. Oliver and I walked onwards, past the still closed breeding shed and down the path between the two small paddocks towards the stallion yard. Everything, as before, was meticulously tidy.

There was one four-legged figure in one of the paddocks, head down and placid. 'Parakeet,' Oliver said. 'Getting more air than grass, actually. It isn't warm enough yet for the new grass to grow.'

We came finally to the last yard, and there he was, the gilt-edged Sandcastle, looking over his door like any other horse.

One couldn't tell, I thought. True there was a poise to the well-shaped head, and an interested eye and alertly pricked ears, but nothing to announce that this was the marvellous creature I'd seen at Ascot. No one ever again, I reflected, would see that arrow-like raking gallop, that sublime throat-catching valour; and it seemed a shame that he should be denied his ability in the hope that he would pass it on.

A lad, broom in hand, was sweeping scatterings of peat off the concrete apron in front of the six stallion boxes, watched by Sandcastle, Rotaboy and Diarist with the same depth of interest as a bus queue would extend to a busker.

'Lenny,' Oliver said, 'you can take Sandcastle down to the small paddock opposite to the one with Parakeet.' He looked up at the sky as if to sniff the coming weather. 'Put him back in his box when you return for evening stables.'

'Yes, sir.'

Lenny was well into middle age, small, leathery and

of obviously long experience. He propped the broom against one of the empty boxes and disappeared into a doorway to reappear presently carrying a length of rope.

'Lenny is one of my trusted helpers,' Oliver Knowles said. 'Been with me several years. He's good with stallions and much stronger than he looks. Stallions can be quite difficult to handle, but Lenny gets on with them better than with mares. Don't know why.'

Lenny clipped the rope onto the headcollar which Sandcastle, along with every other equine resident, wore at all times. Upon the headcollar was stapled a metal plate bearing the horse's name, an absolute essential for identification. Shuffle all those mares together without their headcollars, I thought, and no one would ever sort them. I suggested the problem mildly to Oliver, who positively blenched. 'God forbid! Don't suggest such things. We're very careful. Have to be. Otherwise, as you say, we could breed the wrong mare to the wrong stallion and never know it.'

I wondered, but privately, how often that in fact had happened, or whether indeed it was possible for two mares or two foals to be permanently swapped. The opportunities for mistakes, if not for outright fraud, put computer manipulation in the shade.

Nigel arrived in the yard, and with his scarcely necessary help Lenny opened Sandcastle's door and led the colt out; and one could see in all their strength the sleek muscles, the tugging sinews, the spring-like joints. The body that was worth its weight in gold pranced and scrunched on the hard apron, wheeling round impatiently and tossing its uncomprehending head.

'Full of himself,' Oliver explained. 'We have to feed him well and keep him fairly fit, but of course he doesn't get the exercise he used to.'

We stepped to one side with undignified haste to avoid Sandcastle's restless hindquarters. 'Has he . . . er . . . started work yet?' I asked.

'Not yet,' Oliver said. 'Only one of his mares has foaled so far. She's almost through her foal-heat, so when she comes into use in fifteen or sixteen days' time, she'll be his first. After that there will be a pause – give him time to think! – then he'll be busy until into June.'

'How often . . .?' I murmured delicately.

Oliver fielded the question as if he, like Calder, had had to give the same answer countless times over.

'It depends on the stallion,' he said. 'Some can cover one mare in the morning and another in the afternoon and go on like that for days. Others haven't that much stamina or that much desire. Occasionally you get very shy and choosy stallions. Some of them won't go near some mares but will mate all right with others. Some will cover only one mare a fortnight, if that. Stallions aren't machines, you know, they're individuals like everyone else.'

With Nigel in attendance Lenny led Sandcastle out

of the yard, the long bay legs stalking in powerful strides beside the almost trotting little man.

'Sandcastle will be all right with mares,' Oliver said again firmly. 'Most stallions are.'

We stopped for Oliver to give two carrots and a pat each to Rotaboy and Diarist, so that we didn't ourselves see the calamity. We heard a distant clatter and a yell and the thud of fast hooves, and Oliver went white as he turned to run to the disaster.

I followed him, also sprinting.

Lenny lay against one of the white-painted posts of the small paddock's rails, dazedly trying to pull himself up. Sandcastle, loose and excited, had found his way into one of the paths between the larger paddocks and from his bolting speed must have taken the rails to be those of a racecourse.

Nigel stood by the open gate of the small paddock, his mouth wide as if arrested there by shock. He was still almost speechless when Oliver and I reached him, but had at least begun to unstick.

'For Christ's sake,' Oliver shouted. 'Get going. Get the Land Rover. He can get out onto the road that way through the Watcherleys'.' He ran off in the direction of his own house leaving a partially resurrected Nigel to stumble off towards the bungalow, half in sight beyond the stallion yard.

Lenny raised himself and began his excuses, but I didn't wait to listen. Unused to the problem and ignorant of how best to catch fleeing horses, I simply set off in Sandcastle's wake, following his path between the paddocks and seeing him disappear ahead of me behind a distant hedge.

I ran fast along the grassy path between the rails, past the groups of incurious mares in the paddocks, thinking that my brief January holiday skiing down the pistes at Gstaad might have its practical uses after all; there was currently a lot more muscle in my legs than was ever to be found by July.

Whereas on my last visit the hedge between Oliver Knowles' farm and the Watcherleys' run-down hospital for sick horses had been a thorny unbroken boundary, there were now two or three wide gaps, so that passing from one side to the other was easy. I pounded through the gap which lay straight ahead and noticed almost unconsciously that the Watcherleys' dilapidation had not only halted but partially reversed, with new fencing going up and repairs in hand on the roofs.

I ran towards the stable buildings across a thistly field in which there was no sign of Sandcastle, and through an as yet unmended gate which hung open on broken hinges on the far side. Beyond there between piles of rubble and rusting iron I reached the yard itself, to find Ginnie looking around her with unfocused anxiety and a man and a girl walking towards her enquiringly.

Ginnie saw me running, and her first instinctively cheerful greeting turned almost at once to alarm.

'What is it?' she said. 'Is one of the mares out?'

'Sandcastle.'

'Oh no . . .' It was a wail of despair. 'He can get on the road.' She turned away, already running, and I ran after her; out of the Watcherleys' yard, round their ramshackle house and down the short weedy gateless drive to the dangerous outside world where a car could kill a horse without even trying.

'We'll never catch him,' Ginnie said as we reached the road. 'It's no use running. We don't know which way he went.' She was in great distress: eyes flooding, tears on her cheeks. 'Where's Dad?'

'I should think he's out in his car, looking. And Nigel's in a Land Rover.'

'I heard a horse gallop through the Watcherleys',' she said. 'I was in one of the boxes with a foal. I never thought . . . I mean, I thought it might be a mare . . .'

A speeding car passed in front of us, followed closely by two others doing at least sixty miles an hour, one of them dicily passing a heavy articulated lorry which should have been home in its nest on a Sunday. The thought of Sandcastle loose in that battlefield was literally goose-pimpling and I began for the first time to believe in his imminent destruction. One of those charging monsters would be sure to hit him. He would waver across the road into their path, swerving, rudderless, hopelessly vulnerable . . . a five million-pound traffic accident in the making.

'Let's go this way,' I said, pointing to the left. A

motorcyclist roared from that direction, head down in a black visor, going too fast to stop.

Ginnie shook her head sharply. 'Dad and Nigel will be on the road. But there's a track over there . . .' She pointed slantwise across the road. 'He might just have found it. And there's a bit of a hill and even if he isn't up there at least we might see him from there . . . you can see the road in places . . . I often ride up there.' She was off again, running while she talked, and I fell in beside her. Her face was screwed up with the intensity of her feelings and I felt as much sympathy for her as dismay about the horse. Sandcastle was insured – I'd vetted the policy myself – but Oliver Knowles' prestige wasn't. The escape and death of the first great stallion in his care would hardly attract future business.

The track was muddy and rutted and slippery from recent rain. There were also a great many hoofprints, some looking new, some overtrodden and old. I pointed to them as we ran and asked Ginnie pantingly if she knew if any of those were Sandcastle's.

'Oh.' She stopped running suddenly. 'Yes. Of course. He hasn't got shoes on. The blacksmith came yesterday. Dad said . . .' She peered at the ground dubiously, '. . . he left Sandcastle without new shoes because he was going to make leather pads for under them . . . I wasn't really listening.' She pointed. 'I think that might be him. Those new marks . . . they could be, they really could.' She began running again up the track, impelled by hope now as well as horror, fit in her jeans and sweater and jodhpur boots after all that compulsory jogging.

I ran beside her thinking that mud anyway washed easily from shoes, socks and trouser legs. The ground began to rise sharply and to narrow between bare-branched scratchy bushes; and the jumble of hoof marks inexorably led on and on.

'Please be up here,' Ginnie was saying. 'Please, Sand-castle, please be up here.' Her urgency pumped in her legs and ran in misery down her cheeks. 'Oh please . . . *please* . . .'

The agony of adolescence, I thought. So real, so overpowering . . . so remembered.

The track curved through the bushes and opened suddenly into a wider place where grass grew in patches beside the rutted mud; and there stood Sandcastle, head high, nostrils twitching to the wind, a brown and black creature of power and beauty and majesty.

Ginnie stopped running in one stride and caught my arm fiercely.

'Don't move,' she said. 'I'll do it. You stay here. Keep still. Please keep still.'

I nodded obediently, respecting her experience. The colt looked ready to run again at the slightest untimely movement, his sides quivering, his legs stiff with tension, his tail sweeping up and down restlessly.

He's frightened, I thought suddenly. He's out here, lost, not knowing where to go. He's never been free before, but his instinct is still wild, still against being caught. Horses were never truly tamed, only accustomed to captivity.

Ginnie walked towards him making crooning noises and holding out her hand palm upwards, an offering hand with nothing to offer. 'Come on, boy,' she said. 'Come on boy, there's a good boy, it's all right, come on now.'

The horse watched her as if he'd never seen a human before, his alarm proclaimed in a general volatile trembling. The rope hung down from his headcollar, its free end curling on the ground; and I wondered whether Ginnie would be able to control the colt if she caught him, where Lenny with all his strength had let him go.

Ginnie came to within a foot of the horse's nose, offering her open left hand upwards and bringing her right hand up slowly under his chin, reaching for the headcollar itself, not the rope; her voice made soothing, murmuring sounds and my own tensed muscles began to relax.

At the last second Sandcastle would have none of it. He wheeled away with a squeal, knocking Ginnie to her knees; took two rocketing strides towards a dense patch of bushes, wheeled again, laid back his ears and accelerated in my direction. Past me lay the open track, downhill again to the slaughtering main road.

Ginnie, seen in peripheral vision, was struggling to her feet in desperation. Without thinking of anything much except perhaps what that horse meant to her family, I jumped not out of his way but at his flying head, my fingers curling for the headcollar and missing that and fastening round the rope.

He nearly tore my arms out of their sockets and all the skin off my palms. He yanked me off my feet, pulled me through the mud and trampled on my legs. I clung all the same with both hands to the rope and bumped against his shoulder and knee, and shortly more by weight than skill hauled him to the side of the track and into the bushes.

The bushes, indeed, acted as an anchor. He couldn't drag my heaviness through them, not if I kept hold of the rope; and I wound the rope clumsily round a stump of branch for leverage, and that was roughly that. Sandcastle stood the width of the bush away, crossly accepting the inevitable, tossing his head and quivering but no longer trying for full stampede.

Ginnie appeared round the curve in the track, running and if possible looking more than ever distraught. When she saw me she stumbled and half fell and came up to me uninhibitedly crying.

'Oh, I'm so glad, and you should never do that, you can be killed, you should never do it, and I'm so grateful, so glad . . . oh dear.' She leant against me weakly and like a child wiped her eyes and nose on my sleeve.

'Well,' I said pragmatically, 'what do we do with him now?'

What we decided, upon consideration, was that I and Sandcastle should stay where we were, and that

Ginnie should go and find Nigel or her father, neither she nor I being confident of leading our prize home without reinforcements.

While she was gone I made an inventory of damage, but so far as my clothes went there was nothing the cleaners couldn't see to, and as for the skin, it would grow again pretty soon. My legs though bruised were functioning, and there was nothing broken or frightful. I made a ball of my handkerchief in my right palm which was bleeding slightly and thought that one of these days a habit of launching oneself at things like fleeing stallions and boys with knives might prove to be unwise.

Oliver, Ginnie, Nigel and Lenny all appeared in the Land Rover, gears grinding and wheels spinning in the mud. Sandcastle, to their obvious relief, was upon inspection pronounced sound, and Oliver told me forcefully that *no one*, should *ever*, repeat *ever*, try to stop a bolting horse in that way.

'I'm sorry,' I said.

'You could have been killed.'

'So Ginnie said.'

'Didn't it occur to you?' He sounded almost angry; the aftermath of fright. 'Didn't you *think*?'

'No,' I said truthfully. 'I just did it.'

'Never do it again,' he said. 'And thanks.' He paused and swallowed and tried to make light of his own shattered state. 'Thanks for taking care of my investment.'

Lenny and Nigel had brought a different sort of

headcollar which involved a bit in the mouth and a fierce-looking curb chain, and with these in place the captive (if not chastened) fugitive was led away. There seemed to me to be a protest in the stalking hind-quarters, a statement of disgust at the injustices of life. I smiled at that fanciful thought: the pathetic fallacy, the ascribing to animals of emotions one felt only oneself.

Oliver drove Ginnie and me back in the Land Rover, travelling slowly behind the horse and telling how Nigel and Lenny had allowed him to go free.

'Sheer bloody carelessness,' he said forthrightly. 'Both of them should know better. They could see the horse was fresh and jumping out of his skin yet Lenny was apparently holding the rope with only one hand and stretching to swing the gate open with the other. He took his eyes off Sandcastle so he wasn't ready when Nigel made some sharp movement or other and the horse reared and ran backwards. I ask you! Lenny! Nigel! How can they be so bloody stupid after all these years?'

There seemed to be no answer to that so we just let him curse away, and he was still rumbling like distant thunder when the journey ended. Once home he hurried off to the stallion yard and Ginnie trenchantly said that if Nigel was as sloppy with discipline for animals as he was with the lads, it was no wonder any horse with any spirit would take advantage.

'Accidents happen,' I said mildly.

'Huh.' She was scornful. 'Dad's right. That accident

shouldn't have happened. It was an absolute miracle that Sandcastle came to no harm at all. Even if he hadn't got out on the road he could have tried to jump the paddock rails – horses often do – and broken his leg or something.' She sounded as angry as her father, and for the same reason: the flooding release after fear. I put my arm around her shoulders and gave her a quick hug, which seemed to disconcert her horribly. 'Oh dear, you must think me so silly . . . and crying like that . . . and everything.'

'I think you're a nice dear girl who's had a rotten morning,' I said. 'But all's well now, you know; it really is.'

I naturally believed what I said, but I was wrong.

APRIL

Calder Jackson finally came to dinner with me while he was staying in London to attend a world conference of herbalists. He would be glad, he said, to spend one of the evenings away from his colleagues, and I met him in a restaurant on the grounds that although my flat was civilized my cooking was not.

I sensed immediately a difference in him, though it was hard to define; rather as if he had become a figure still larger than life. Heads turned and voices whispered when we walked through the crowded place to our table, but because of television this would have happened anyway. Yet now, I thought, Calder really enjoyed it. There was still no overt arrogance, still a becoming modesty of manner, but something within him had intensified, crystallized, become a governing factor. He was now, I thought, even to himself, the Great Man.

I wondered what, if anything, had specifically altered him, and it turned out to be the one thing I would have least expected: Ian Pargetter's death.

Over a plateful of succulent smoked salmon Calder apologized for the abrupt way he'd brushed me off on the telephone on that disturbing night, and I said it was most understandable.

'Fact is,' Calder said, squeezing lemon juice, 'I was afraid my whole business would collapse. Ian's partners, you know, never approved of me. I was afraid they would influence everyone against me, once Ian had gone.'

'And it hasn't worked out that way?'

He shook his head, assembling a pink forkful. 'Remarkably not. Amazing.' He put the smoked salmon in his mouth and made appreciative noises, munching. I was aware, and I guessed he was, too, that the ears of the people at the tables on either side were almost visibly attuned to the distinctive voice, to the clear loud diction with its country edge. 'My yard's still full. People have faith, you know. I may not get quite so many racehorses, that's to be expected, but still a few.'

'And have you heard any more about Ian Pargetter's death? Did they ever find out who killed him?'

He looked regretful. 'I'm sure they haven't. I asked one of his partners the other day, and he said no one seemed to be asking questions any more. He was quite upset. And so am I. I suppose finding his murderer won't bring Ian back, but all the same one wants to *know*.'

'Tell me some of your recent successes,' I said, nodding, changing the subject and taking a slice of paper-thin brown bread and butter. 'I find your work tremendously interesting.' I also found it about the only thing else to talk about, as we seemed to have few other points of contact. Regret it as I might, there was still no drift towards an easy personal friendship.

Calder ate some more smoked salmon while he thought. 'I had a colt,' he said at last, 'a two-year-old in training. Ian had been treating him, and he'd seemed to be doing well. Then about three weeks after Ian died the colt started bleeding into his mouth and down his nose and went on and on doing it, and as Ian's partner couldn't find out the trouble the trainer persuaded the owner to send the horse to me.'

'And did you discover what was wrong?' I asked.

'Oh no.' He shook his head. 'It wasn't necessary. I laid my hands on him on three succeeding days, and the bleeding stopped immediately. I kept him at my place for two weeks altogether, and returned him on his way back to full good health.'

The adjacent tables were fascinated, as indeed I was myself.

'Did you give him herbs?' I asked.

'Certainly. Of course. And alfalfa in his hay. Excellent for many ills, alfalfa.'

I had only the haziest idea of what alfalfa looked like, beyond it being some sort of grass.

'The one thing you can't do with herbs,' he said confidently, 'is *harm*.'

I raised my eyebrows with my mouth full.

He gave the nearest thing to a grin. 'With ordinary medicines one has to be so careful because of their power and their side-effects, but if I'm not certain what's wrong with a horse I can give it all the herbal remedies I can think of all at once in the hope that one of them will hit the target, and it quite often does. It may be hopelessly unscientific, but if a trained vet can't tell exactly what's wrong with a horse, how can I?'

I smiled with undiluted pleasure. 'Have some wine,' I said.

He nodded the helmet of curls, and the movement I made towards the bottle in its ice-bucket was instantly forestalled by a watchful waiter who poured almost reverently into the healer's glass.

'How was the American trip,' I asked, 'way back in January?'

'Mm.' He sipped his wine. 'Interesting.' He frowned a little and went back to finishing the salmon, leaving me wondering whether that was his total answer. When he'd laid down his knife and fork, however, he sat back in his chair and told me that the most enjoyable part of his American journey had been, as he'd expected, his few days on the ski slopes; and we discussed skiing venues throughout the roast beef and burgundy which followed.

With the crêpes Suzette I asked after Dissdale and Bettina and heard that Dissdale had been to New York on a business trip and that Bettina had been acting a small part in a British movie, which Dissdale hadn't known whether to be pleased about or not. 'Too many gorgeous young studs around,' Calder said, smiling. 'Dissdale gets worried anyway, and he was away for ten days.'

I pondered briefly about Calder's own seemingly non-existent sex-life; but he'd never seen me with a girl either, and certainly there was no hint in him of the homosexual.

Over coffee, running out of subjects, I asked about his yard in general, and how was the right-hand man Jason in particular.

Calder shrugged. 'He's left. They come and go, you know. No loyalty these days.'

'And you don't fear ... well, that he'd take your knowledge with him?'

He looked amused. 'He didn't know much. I mean, I'd hand out a pill and tell Jason which horse to give it to. That sort of thing.'

We finished amiably enough with a glass of brandy for each and a cigar for him, and I tried not to wince over the bill.

'A very pleasant evening,' Calder said. 'You must come out to lunch again one day.'

'I'd like to.'

We sat for a final few minutes opposite each other in a pause of mutual appraisal: two people utterly different but bonded by one-tenth of a second on a pavement in Ascot. Saved and saver, inextricably interested each in the other; a continuing curiosity which would never quite lose touch. I smiled at him slowly and got a smile in return, but all surface, no depth, a mirror exactly of my own feelings.

In the office things were slowly changing. John had boasted too often of his sexual conquests and complained too often about my directorship, and Gordon's almost-equal had tired of such waste of time. I'd heard from Val Fisher in a perhaps edited version that at a small and special seniors meeting (held in my absence and without my knowledge) Gordon's almost-equal had said he would like to boot John vigorously over St Paul's. His opinion was respected. I heard from Alec one day merely that the mosquito which had stung me for so long had been squashed, and on going along the passage to investigate had found John's desk empty and his bull-like presence but a quiver in the past.

'He's gone to sell air-conditioning to Eskimos,' Alec said, and Gordon's almost-equal, smiling affably, corrected it more probably to a partnership with some brokers on the Stock Exchange.

Alec himself seemed restless, as if his own job no longer held him enthralled.

'It's all right for you,' he said once. 'You've the gift. You've the *sight*. I can't tell a gold-mine from a pomegranate at five paces, and it's taken me all these years to know it.'

'But you're a conjuror,' I said. 'You can rattle up outside money faster than anyone.'

'Gift of the old gab, you mean.' He looked uncharacteristically gloomy. 'Syrup with a chisel in it.' He waved his hand towards the desks of our new older colleagues, who had both gone out to lunch. 'I'll end up like them, still here, still smooth-talking, part of the furniture, coming up to *sixty*.' His voice held disbelief that such an age could be achieved. 'That isn't life, is it? That's not *all*?'

I said that I supposed it might be.

'Yes, but for you it's exciting,' he said. 'I mean, you love it. Your eyes *gleam*. You get your kicks right here in this room. But I'll never be made a director, let's face it, and I have this grotty feeling that time's slipping away, and soon it will be too late to start anything else.'

'Like what?'

'Like being an actor. Or a doctor. Or an acrobat.'

'It's been too late for that since you were six.'

'Yeah,' he said. 'Lousy, isn't it?' He put his heart and soul ten minutes later, however, into tracking down a source of a hundred thousand for several years and lending it to a businessman at a profitable rate, knitting together such loan packages all afternoon with diligence and success.

I hoped he would stay. He was the yeast of the office: my bubbles in the dough. As for myself, I had grown accustomed to being on the board and had slowly found I'd reached a new level of confidence. Gordon seemed to treat me unreservedly as an equal, though it was not until he had been doing it for some time that I looked back and realized.

Gordon's hitherto uniformly black hair had grown a streak or two of grey. His right hand now trembled also, and his handwriting had grown smaller through his efforts to control his fingers. I watched his valiant struggles to appear normal and respected his privacy by never making even a visual comment: it had become second nature to look anywhere but directly at his hands. In the brain department he remained energetic, but physically overall he was slowing down.

I had only seen Judith once since Christmas, and that had been in the office at a retirement party given for the head of Corporate Finance, a golden-handshake affair to which all managers' wives had been invited.

'How are you?' she said amid the throng, holding a glass of wine and an unidentifiable canapé and smelling of violets.

'Fine. And you?'

'Fine.'

She was wearing blue, with diamonds in her ears. I looked at her with absolute and unhappy love and saw the strain it put into her face.

'I'm sorry,' I said.

She shook her head and swallowed. 'I thought . . . it might be different . . . here in the bank.'

'No.'

She looked down at the canapé, which was squashy

and yellow. 'If I don't eat this damned thing soon it'll drop down my dress.'

I took it out of her fingers and deposited it in an ashtray. 'Invest in a salami cornet. They stay rock-hard for hours.'

'What's Tim telling you to invest in?' demanded Henry Shipton, turning to us a beaming face.

'Salami,' Judith said.

'Typical. He lent money to a seaweed processor last week. Judith, my darling, let me freshen your glass.'

He took the glass away to the bottles and left us again looking at each other with a hundred ears around.

'I was thinking,' I said, 'when it's warmer, could I take you and Gordon, and Pen if she'd like it, out somewhere one Sunday? Somewhere not ordinary. All day.'

She took longer than normal politeness allowed to answer, and I understood all the unspoken things, but finally, as Henry could be seen returning, she said, 'Yes. We'd all like it. I'd like it . . . very much.'

'Here you are,' Henry said. 'Tim, you go and fight for your own refill, and leave me to talk to this gorgeous girl.' He put his arm round her shoulders and swept her off, and although I was vividly aware all evening of her presence, we had no more moments alone.

From day to day when she wasn't around I didn't precisely suffer: her absence was more of a faint background ache. When I saw Gordon daily in the office I felt no constant envy, nor hated him, nor even thought much of where he slept. I liked him for the good clever man he was, and our office relationship continued unruffled and secure. Loving Judith was both pleasure and pain, delight and deprivation, wishes withdrawn, dreams denied. It might have been easier and more sensible to have met and fallen heavily for some young glamorous unattached stranger, but the one thing love never did have was logic.

'Easter,' I said to Gordon one day in the office. 'Are you and Judith going away?'

'We had plans – they fell through.'

'Did Judith mention that I'd like to take you both somewhere – and Pen Warner – as a thank you for Christmas?'

'Yes, I believe she did.'

'Easter Monday, then?'

He seemed pleased at the idea and reported the next day that Judith had asked Pen, and everyone was poised. 'Pen's bringing her kite,' he said. 'Unless it's a day trip to Manchester.'

'I'll think of something,' I said, laughing. 'Tell her it won't be raining.'

What I did eventually think of seemed to please them all splendidly and also to be acceptable to others concerned, and I consequently collected Gordon and Judith and Pen (but not the kite) from Clapham at eight-thirty on Easter Bank Holiday morning. Judith and Pen were in fizzing high spirits, though Gordon seemed already tired. I suggested abandoning what was bound to be a fairly taxing day for him, but he wouldn't hear of it.

'I want to go,' he said. 'Been looking forward to it all week. But I'll just sit in the back of the car and rest and sleep some of the way.' So Judith sat beside me while I drove and touched my hand now and then, not talking much but contenting me deeply by just being there. The journey to Newmarket lasted two and a half hours and I would as soon it had gone on for ever.

I was taking them to Calder's yard, to the utter fascination of Pen. 'But don't tell him I'm a pharmacist,' she said. 'He might clam up if he knew he had an informed audience.'

'We won't tell,' Judith assured her. 'It would absolutely spoil the fun.'

Poor Calder, I thought: but I wouldn't tell him either.

He greeted us expansively (making me feel guilty) and gave us coffee in the huge oak-beamed sitting room where the memory of Ian Pargetter hovered peripherally by the fireplace.

'Delighted to see you again,' Calder said, peering at Gordon, Judith and Pen as if trying to conjure a memory to fit their faces. He knew of course who they were by name, but Ascot was ten months since, and although it had been an especially memorable day for him he had met a great many new people between then and now. 'Ah *yes*,' he said with relief, his brow clearing. 'Yellow hat with roses.'

Judith laughed. 'Well done.'

'Can't forget anyone so pretty.'

She took it as it was meant, but indeed he hadn't forgotten: as one tended never to forget people whose vitality brought out the sun.

'I see Dissdale and Bettina quite often,' he said, making conversation, and Gordon agreed that he and Judith, also, sometimes saw Dissdale, though infrequently. As a topic it was hardly riveting, but served as an acceptable unwinding interval between the long car journey and the Grand Tour.

The patients in the boxes were all different but their ailments seemed the same; and I supposed surgeons could be excused their impersonal talk of 'the appendix in bed 14', when the occupants changed week by week but the operation didn't.

'This is a star three-day-eventer who came here five weeks ago with severe muscular weakness and no appetite. Wouldn't eat. Couldn't be ridden. He goes home tomorrow, strong and thriving. Looks well, eh?' Calder patted the glossy brown neck over the half-stable door. 'His owner thought he was dying, poor girl. She was weeping when she brought him here. It's really satisfying, you know, to be able to help.'

Gordon said civilly that it must be.

'This is a two-year-old not long in training. Came with an intractably infected wound on his fetlock. He's

been here a week, and he's healing. It was most grati-
fying that the trainer sent him without delay, since I'd
treated several of his horses in the past.'

'This mare,' Calder went on, moving us all along,
'came two or three days ago in great discomfort with
blood in her urine. She's responding well, I'm glad to
say.' He patted this one too, as he did them all.

'What was causing the bleeding?' Pen asked,
but with only an uninformed-member-of-the-public
intonation.

Calder shook his head. 'I don't know. His vet diagnosed a kidney infection complicated by crystalluria,
which means crystals in the urine, but he didn't know
the type of germ and every antibiotic he gave failed to
work. So the mare came here. Last resort.' He gave me
a wink. 'I'm thinking of simply re-naming this whole
place "Last Resort".'

'And you're treating her,' Gordon asked, 'with
herbs?'

'With everything I can think of,' Calder said. 'And
of course . . . with hands.'

'I suppose,' Judith said diffidently, 'that you'd never
let anyone watch . . .?'

'My dear lady, for you, anything,' Calder said. 'But
you'd see nothing. You might stand for half an hour,
and nothing would happen. It would be terribly boring.
And I might, perhaps, be *unable*, you know, if someone
was waiting and standing there.'

Judith smiled understandingly and the tour continued, ending as before in the surgery.

Pen stood looking about her with sociable blankness and then wandered over to the glass-fronted cabinets to peer myopically at the contents.

Calder, happily ignoring her in favour of Judith, was pulling out his antique tablet-maker and demonstrating it with pride.

'It's beautiful,' Judith said sincerely. 'Do you use it much?'

'All the time,' he said. 'Any herbalist worth the name makes his own pills and potions.'

'Tim said you had a universal magic potion in the fridge.'

Calder smiled and obligingly opened the refrigerator door, revealing the brown-filled plastic containers, as before.

'What's in it?' Judith asked.

'Trade secret,' he said smiling. 'Decoction of hops and other things.'

'Like beer?' Judith said.

'Yes, perhaps.'

'Horses do drink beer,' Gordon said. 'Or so I've heard.'

Pen bent down to pick up a small peach-coloured pill which was lying unobtrusively on the floor in the angle of one of the cupboards, and put it without comment on the bench.

'It's all so *absorbing*,' Judith said. 'So tremendously

kind of you to show us everything. I'll watch all your programmes with more fervour than ever.'

Calder responded to her warmly as all men did and asked us into the house again for a drink before we left. Gordon, however, was still showing signs of fatigue and now also hiding both hands in his pockets which meant he felt they were trembling badly, so the rest of us thanked Calder enthusiastically for his welcome and made admiring remarks about his hospital and climbed into the car, into the same places as before.

'Come back any time you like, Tim,' he said; and I said thank you and perhaps I would. We shook hands, and we smiled, caught in our odd relationship and unable to take it further. He waved, and I waved back as I drove away.

'Isn't he amazing?' Judith said. 'I must say, Tim, I do understand why you're impressed.'

Gordon grunted and said that theatrical surgeons weren't necessarily the best; but yes, Calder was impressive.

It was only Pen, after several miles, who expressed her reservations.

'I'm not saying he doesn't do a great deal of good for the horses. Of course he must do, to have amassed such a reputation. But I don't honestly think he does it all with herbs.'

'How do you mean?' Judith asked, twisting round so as to see her better.

Pen leaned forward. 'I found a pill on the floor. I don't suppose you noticed.'

'I did,' I said. 'You put it on the bench.'

'That's right. Well, that was no herb, it was plain straightforward warfarin.'

'It may be plain straightforward war-whatever to you,' Judith said. 'But not to me.'

Pen's voice was smiling. 'Warfarin is a drug used in humans, and I dare say in horses, after things like heart attacks. It's a coumarin – an anticoagulant. Makes the blood less likely to clot and block up the veins and arteries. Widely used all over the place.'

We digested the information in silence for a mile or two, and finally Gordon said, 'How did you know it was warfarin? I mean, how can you tell?'

'I handle it every day,' she said. 'I know the dosages, the sizes, the colours, the manufacturers' marks. You see all those things so often, you get to know them at a glance.'

'Do you mean,' I said interestedly, 'that if you saw fifty different pills laid out in a row you could identify the lot?'

'Probably. If they all came from major drug companies and weren't completely new, certainly, yes.'

'Like a wine-taster,' Judith said.

'Clever girl,' Gordon said, meaning Pen.

'It's just habit.' She thought. 'And something else in those cupboards wasn't strictly herbal, I suppose. He had one or two bags of potassium sulphate, bought from Goodison's Garden Centre, wherever that is.'

'Whatever for?' Judith asked. 'Isn't potassium sulphate a fertilizer?'

'Potassium's just as essential to animals as to plants,' Pen said. 'I wouldn't be surprised if it isn't one of the ingredients in that secret brew.'

'What else would you put in it, if you were making it?' I asked curiously.

'Oh heavens.' She pondered. 'Any sort of tonic. Perhaps liquorice root, which he once mentioned. Maybe caffeine. All sorts of vitamins. Just a pepping-up mish-mash.'

The hardest part of the day had been to find somewhere decent to have lunch, and the place I'd chosen via the various gourmet guides turned out, as so often happens, to have changed hands and chefs since the books were written. The resulting repast was slow to arrive and disappointing to eat, but the mood of my guests forgave all.

'You remember,' Gordon said thoughtfully over the coffee, 'that you told us on the way to Newmarket that Calder was worried about his business when that vet was killed?'

'Yes,' I said. 'He was, at the time.'

'Isn't it possible,' Gordon said, 'that the vet was letting Calder have regular official medicines, like warfarin, and Calder thought his supplies would dry up, when the vet died?'

197

'Gordon!' Judith said. 'How devious you are, darling.'

We all thought about it, however, and Pen nodded. 'He must have found another willing source, I should think.'

'But,' I protested, 'would vets really do that?'

'They're not particularly brilliantly paid,' Pen said. 'Not badly by my standards, but they're never *rich*.'

'But Ian Pargetter was very much liked,' I said.

'What's that got to do with it?' Pen said. 'Nothing to stop him passing on a few pills and advice to Calder in return for a fat untaxed fee.'

'To their mutual benefit,' Gordon murmured.

'The healer's feet of clay,' Judith said. 'What a shame.'

The supposition seemed slightly to deflate the remembered pleasure of the morning, but the afternoon's visit put the rest of the day up high.

We went this time to Oliver Knowles' stud farm and found the whole place flooded with foals and mares and activity.

'How *beautiful*,' Judith said, looking away over the stretches of white-railed paddocks with their colonies of mothers and babies. 'How speechlessly *great*.'

Oliver Knowles, introduced, was as welcoming as Calder and told Gordon several times that he would never, ever, be out of his debt of gratitude to Paul Ekaterin's, however soon he had paid off his loan.

The anxiety and misgivings to be seen in him on my

February visit had all disappeared: Oliver was again, and more so, the capable and decisive executive I had met first. The foals had done well, I gathered. Not one from the mares coming to Sandcastle had been lost, and none of those mares had had any infection, a triumph of care. He told me all this within the first ten minutes, and also that Sandcastle had proved thoroughly potent and fertile and was a dream of a stallion. 'He's tireless,' he said. 'Forty mares will be easy.'

'I'm so glad,' I said, and meant it from the bottom of my banking heart.

With his dog Squibs at his heels he showed us all again through the succession of yards, where since it was approximately four o'clock the evening ritual of mucking out and feeding was in full swing.

'A stud farm is not like a racing stable, of course,' Oliver was explaining to Gordon. 'One lad here can look after far more than three horses, because they don't have to be ridden. And here we have a more flexible system because the mares are sometimes in, sometimes out in the paddocks, and it would be impossible to assign particular mares to particular lads. So here a lad does a particular section of boxes, regardless of which animals are in them.'

Gordon nodded, genially interested.

'Why are some foals in the boxes and some out in the paddocks?' Judith asked, and Oliver without hesitation told her it was because the foals had to stay with their dams, and the mares with foals in the boxes were due to come into heat, or were already in heat, and would go from their boxes to visit the stallion. When their heat was over they would go out into the paddocks, with their foals.

'Oh,' Judith said, blinking slightly at this factory aspect. 'Yes, I see.'

In the foaling yard we came across Nigel and also Ginnie, who ran across to me when she saw me and gave me a great hug and a smacking kiss somewhere to the left of the mouth. Quite an advance in confidence, I thought, and hugged her back, lifting her off her feet and whirling her round in a circle. She was laughing when I put her down, and Oliver watched in some surprise.

'I've never known her so demonstrative,' he said.

Ginnie looked at him apprehensively and held onto my sleeve. 'You didn't mind, did you?' she asked me worriedly.

'I'm flattered,' I said, meaning it and also thinking that her father would kill off her spontaneity altogether if he wasn't careful.

Ginnie, reassured, tucked her arm into mine and said, 'Come and look at the newest foal. It was born only about twenty minutes ago. It's a colt. A darling.' She tugged me off, and I caught a fleeting glance of Judith's face which was showing a mixture of all sorts of unreadable thoughts.

'Oliver's daughter,' I said in explanation over my shoulder, and heard Oliver belatedly introducing Nigel.

They all came to look at the foal over the half-door; a glistening little creature half-lying, half-sitting on the thick straw, all long nose, huge eyes and folded legs, new life already making an effort to balance and stand up. The dam, on her feet, alternatively bent her head to the foal and looked up at us warily.

'It was an easy one,' Ginnie said. 'Nigel and I just watched.'

'Have you seen many foals born?' Pen asked her.

'Oh, hundreds. All my life. Most often at night.'

Pen looked at her as if she, as I did, felt the imagination stirred by such an unusual childhood: as if she, like myself, had never seen one single birth of any sort, let alone a whole procession by the age of fifteen.

'This mare has come to Sandcastle,' Oliver said.

'And will that foal win the Derby?' Gordon asked, smiling.

Oliver smiled in return. 'You never know. He has the breeding.' He breathed deeply, expanding his chest. 'I've never been able to say anything like that before this year. No foal born or conceived here has in the past won a classic, but now...' He gestured widely with his arm, '... one day, from these ...' He paused. 'It's a whole new world. It's ... tremendous.'

'As good as you hoped?' I asked.

'Better.'

He had a soul after all, I thought, under all that tidy martial efficiency. A vision of the peaks, which he was reaching in reality. And how soon, I wondered, before the glossy became commonplace, the classic winners a routine, the aristocrats the common herd. It would be what he'd aimed for; but in a way it would be blunting.

We left the foal and went on down the path past the breeding shed, where the main door was today wide open, showing the floor thickly covered with soft brown crumbly peat. Beyond succinctly explaining what went on there when it was inhabited, Oliver made no comment, and we all walked on without stopping to the heart of the place, to the stallions.

Lenny was there, walking one of the horses round the small yard and plodding with his head down as if he'd been doing it for some time. The horse was dripping with sweat, and from the position of the one open empty box I guessed he would be Rotaboy.

'He's just covered a mare,' Oliver said matter-of-factly. 'He's always like that afterwards.'

Judith and Gordon and Pen all looked as if the overt sex of the place was earthier than they'd expected, even without hearing, as I had at one moment, Oliver quietly discussing a vaginal disinfectant process with Nigel. They rallied valiantly, however, and gazed with proper awe at the head of Sandcastle which swam into view from the inside-box shadows.

He held himself almost imperiously, as if his new role had basically changed his character; and perhaps it had. I had myself seen during my renewed interest in racing how constant success endowed some horses with definite 'presence', and Sandcastle, even lost and frightened up on top of the hill, had perceptibly had it; but now, only two months later, there was a new quality one might almost call arrogance, a fresh certainty of his own supremacy.

'He's splendid,' Gordon exclaimed. 'What a treat to see him again after that great day at Ascot.'

Oliver gave Sandcastle the usual two carrots and a couple of pats, treating the King with familiarity. Neither Judith nor Pen, nor indeed Gordon or myself, tried even to touch the sensitive nose: afraid of getting our fingers bitten off at the wrist, no doubt. It was all right to admire, but distance had virtue.

Lenny put the calming-down Rotaboy back in his box and started mucking out Diarist next door.

'We have two lads looking after the stallions full time,' Oliver said. 'Lenny, here, and another much trusted man, Don. And Nigel feeds them.'

Pen caught the underlying thought behind his words and asked, 'Do you need much security?'

'Some,' he said, nodding. 'We have the yard wired for sound, so either Nigel or I, when we're in our houses, can hear if there are any irregular noises.'

'Like hooves taking a walk?' Judith suggested.

'Exactly.' He smiled at her. 'We also have smoke alarms and massive extinguishers.'

'And brick-built boxes and combination locks on these door bolts at night and lockable gates on all the ways out to the roads,' Ginnie said, chattily. 'Dad's really gone to town on security.'

'Glad to hear it,' Gordon said.

I smiled to myself at the classic example of bolting the stable door after the horse had done likewise, but indeed one could see that Oliver had learned a dire lesson and knew he'd been lucky to be given a second chance.

We began after a while to walk back towards the house, stopping again in the foaling yard to look at the new baby colt, who was now shakily on his feet and searching round for his supper.

Oliver drew me to one side and asked if I would like to see Sandcastle cover a mare, an event apparently scheduled for a short time hence.

'Yes, I would,' I said.

'I can't ask them all – there isn't room,' he said. 'I'll get Ginnie to show them the mares and foals in the paddocks and then take them indoors for tea.'

No one demurred at this suggested programme, especially as Oliver didn't mention where he and I were going: Judith, I was sure, would have preferred to join us. Ginnie took them and Squibs off, and I could hear her saying, 'Over there, next door, there's another yard. We could walk over that way if you like.'

Oliver, eyeing them amble along the path that Sandcastle had taken at a headlong gallop and I at a sprint, said, 'The Watcherleys look after any delicate foals or any mares with infections. It's all worked out most satisfactorily. I rent their place and they work for me, and their expertise with sick animals comes in very useful.'

'And you were mending their fences for them, I guess, when I came in February.'

'That's right.' He sighed ruefully. 'Another week and the gates would have been up in the hedge and across their driveway, and Sandcastle would never have got out.'

'No harm done,' I said.

'Thanks to you, no.'

We went slowly back towards the breeding shed. 'Have you seen a stallion at work before?' he asked.

'No, I haven't.'

After a pause he said, 'It may seem strong to you. Even violent. But it's normal to them. Remember that. And he'll probably bite her neck, but it's as much to keep himself in position as an expression of passion.'

'All right,' I said.

'This mare, the one we're breeding, is receptive, so there won't be any trouble. Some mares are shy, some are slow to arouse, some are irritable, just like humans.' He smiled faintly. 'This little lady is a born one-nighter.'

It was the first time I'd heard him make anything like a joke about his profession and I was almost startled. As if himself surprised at his own words he said more soberly, 'We put her to Sandcastle yesterday morning, and all went well.'

'The mares go more than once then, to the stallion?' I asked.

He nodded. 'It depends of course on the stud farm, but I'm very anxious as you can guess that all the mares here shall have the best possible chance of conceiving. I bring them all at least twice to the stallion during their heat, then we put them out in the paddocks and wait, and if they come into heat again it means they haven't conceived, so we repeat the breeding process.'

'And how long do you go on trying?'

'Until the end of July. That means the foal won't be born until well on in June, which is late in the year for racehorses. Puts them at a disadvantage as two-year-olds, racing against March and April foals which have had more growing time.' He smiled. 'With any luck Sandcastle won't have any late June foals. It's too early to be complacent, but none of the mares he covered three weeks or more ago has come back into use.'

We reached and entered the breeding shed where the mare already stood, held at the head in a loose twitch by one lad and being washed and attended to by another.

'She can't wait, sir,' that lad said, indicating her tail, which she was holding high, and Oliver replied rather repressively, 'Good.'

Nigel and Lenny came with Sandcastle, who looked eagerly aware of where he was and what for. Nigel closed the door to keep the ritual private; and the mating which followed was swift and sure and utterly primeval. A copulation of thrust and grandeur, of

206

vigour and pleasure, not without tenderness: remarkably touching.

'They're not all like that,' Oliver remarked prosaically, as Sandcastle slid out and backwards, and brought his forelegs to earth with a jolt. 'You've seen a good one.'

I thanked him for letting me be there, and in truth I felt I understood more about horses then than I'd ever imagined I would.

We walked back to the house with Oliver telling me that with the four stallions there were currently six, seven or eight matings a day in the breeding shed, Sundays included. The mind stuttered a bit at the thought of all that rampaging fertility, but that, after all, was what the bank's five million pounds was all about. Rarely, I thought, had anyone seen Ekaterin's money so fundamentally at work.

We set off homewards fortified by tea, scones and whisky, with Oliver and Gordon at the end competing over who thanked whom most warmly. Ginnie gave me another but more composed hug and begged me to come again, and Judith kissed her and offered female succour if ever needed.

'Nice child,' she said as we drove away. 'Growing up fast.'

'Fifteen,' I said.

'Sixteen. She had a birthday last week.'

'You got on well with her,' I said.

'Yes.' She looked round at Pen and Gordon, who were again sitting in the back. 'She told us about your little escapade here two months ago.'

'She didn't!'

'She sure did,' Pen said, smiling. 'Why ever didn't you say?'

'I know why,' Gordon said drily. 'He didn't want it to be known in the office that the loan he'd recommended had very nearly fallen under a lorry.'

'Is that right?' Judith asked.

'Very much so,' I admitted wryly. 'Some of the board were against the whole thing anyway, and I'd have never heard the end of the horse getting out.'

'What a coward,' Pen said, chuckling.

We pottered slowly back to Clapham through the stop-go end-of-Bank Holiday traffic, and Judith and Pen voted it the best day they'd had since Ascot. Gordon dozed, I drove with relaxation and so finally reached the tall gates by the common.

I went in with them for supper as already arranged, but all of them, not only Gordon, were tired from the long day, and I didn't stay late. Judith came out to the car to see me off and to shut the gates after I'd gone.

We didn't really talk. I held her in my arms, her head on my shoulder, my head on hers, close in the dark night, as far apart as planets.

208

We stood away and I took her hand, lingering, not wanting all contact lost.

'A great day,' she said, and I said, 'Mm', and kissed her very briefly.

Got into the car and drove away.

OCTOBER

Summer had come, summer had gone, sodden, cold and unloved. It had been overcast and windy during Royal Ascot week and Gordon and I, clamped to our telephones and pondering our options, had looked at the sullen sky and hardly minded that this year Dissdale hadn't needed to sell half-shares in his box.

Only with the autumn, far too late, had days of sunshine returned, and it was on a bright golden Saturday that I took the race train to Newbury to see the mixed meeting of two jump races and four flat.

Ursula Young was there, standing near the weighing room when I walked in from the station and earnestly reading her racecard.

'Hello,' she said when I greeted her. 'Haven't seen you for ages. How's the money-lending?'

'Profitable,' I said.

She laughed. 'Are you here for anything special?'

'No. Just fresh air and a flutter.'

'I'm supposed to meet a client.' She looked at her

watch. 'Time for a quick sandwich, though. Are you on?'

I was on, and bought her and myself a thin pallid slice of tasteless white meat between two thick pallid tasteless slices of soggy-crusted bread, the whole wrapped up in cardboard and cellophane and costing a fortune.

Ursula ate it in disgust. 'They used to serve proper luscious sandwiches, thick, juicy handmade affairs which came in a whole stack. I can't stand all this repulsive hygiene.' The rubbish from the sandwiches indeed littered most of the tables around us . . . 'Every so-called advance is a retreat from excellence,' she said, dogmatic as ever.

I totally agreed with her and we chewed in joyless accord.

'How's trade with you?' I said.

She shrugged. 'Fair. The cream of the yearlings are going for huge prices. They've all got high reserves on them because they've cost so much to produce – stallion fees and the cost of keeping the mare and foal to start with, let alone vet's fees and all the incidentals. My sort of clients on the whole settle for a second, third or fourth rank, and many a good horse, mind you, has come from the bargain counter.'

I smiled at the automatic sales pitch. 'Talking of vets,' I said, 'is the Pargetter murder still unsolved?'

She nodded regretfully. 'I was talking to his poor wife in Newmarket last week. We met in the street.

211

She's only half the girl she was, poor thing, no life in her. She said she asked the police recently if they were still even trying, and they assured her they were, but she doesn't believe it. It's been so long, nine months, and if they hadn't any leads to start with, how can they possibly have any now? She's very depressed, it's dreadful.'

I made sympathetic murmurs, and Ursula went on, 'The only good thing you could say is that he'd taken out decent life insurance and paid off the mortgage on their house, so at least she and the children aren't penniless as well. She was telling me how he'd been very careful in those ways, and she burst into tears, poor girl.'

Ursula looked as if the encounter had distressed her also.

'Have another whisky-mac,' I suggested. 'To cheer you up.'

She looked at her watch. 'All right. You get it, but I'll pay. My turn.'

Over the second drink, in a voice of philosophical irritation, she told me about the client she was presently due to meet, a small-time trainer of steeplechasers. 'He's such a fool to himself,' she said. 'He makes hasty decisions, acts on impulse, and then when things go wrong he feels victimized and cheated and gets angry. Yet he can be perfectly nice when he likes.'

I wasn't especially interested in the touchy trainer, but when I went outside again with Ursula he spotted her from a short distance away and practically pounced on her arm.

'There you are,' he said, as if she'd had no right to be anywhere but at his side. 'I've been looking all over.'

'It's only just time,' she said mildly.

He brushed that aside, a short wiry intense man of about forty with a pork-pie hat above a weatherbeaten face.

'I wanted you to see him before he's saddled,' he said. 'Do come on, Ursula. Come and look at his conformation.'

She opened her mouth to say something to me but he almost forcefully dragged her off, holding her sleeve and talking rapidly into her ear. She gave me an apologetic look of long-suffering and departed in the direction of the pre-parade ring, where the horses for the first race were being led round by their lads before going off to the saddling boxes.

I didn't follow but climbed onto the steps of the main parade ring, round which walked several of the runners already saddled. The last of the field to appear some time later was accompanied by the pork-pie hat, and also Ursula, and for something to do I looked the horse up in the racecard.

Zoomalong, five-year-old gelding, trained by F. Barnet.

F. Barnet continued his dissertation into Ursula's ear, aiming his words from approximately six inches away, which I would have found irritating but which she bore without flinching. According to the flickering numbers on the Tote board Zoomalong had a medium chance in the opinion of the public, so for interest I put a medium stake on him to finish in the first three.

I didn't see Ursula or F. Barnet during the race, but Zoomalong zoomed along quite nicely to finish third, and I walked down from the stands towards the unsaddling enclosure to watch the patting-on-the-back post-race routine.

F. Barnet was there, still talking to Ursula and pointing out parts of his now sweating and stamping charge. Ursula nodded non-committally, her own eyes knowledgeably raking the gelding from stem to stern, a neat competent good-looking fifty in a rust-coloured coat and brown velvet beret.

Eventually the horses were led away and the whole cycle of excitement began slowly to regenerate towards the second race.

Without in the least meaning to I again found myself standing near Ursula, and this time she introduced me to the pork-pie hat, who had temporarily stopped talking.

'This is Fred Barnet,' she said. 'And his wife Susan.' A rounded motherly person in blue. 'And their son, Ricky.' A boy taller than his father, dark-haired, pleasant-faced.

I shook hands with all three, and it was while I was still touching the son that Ursula in her clear voice said my name, 'Tim Ekaterin.'

The boy's hand jumped in mine as if my flesh had burned him. I was astonished, and then I looked at his whitening skin, at the suddenly frightened dark eyes, at the stiffening of the body, at the rising panic: and I wouldn't have known him if he hadn't reacted in that way.

'What's the matter, Ricky?' his mother said, puzzled.

He said 'Nothing' hoarsely and looked around for escape, but all too clearly he knew I knew exactly who he was now and could always find him however far he ran.

'What do you think, then, Ursula?' Fred Barnet demanded, returning to the business in hand. 'Will you buy him? Can I count on you?'

Ursula said she would have to consult her client.

'But he was third,' Fred Barnet insisted. 'A good third . . . In that company, a pretty good showing. And he'll win, I'm telling you. He'll win.'

'I'll tell my client all about him. I can't say fairer than that.'

'But you do like him, don't you? Look, Ursula, he's a good sort, easy to handle, just right for an amateur . . .' He went on for a while in this vein while his wife listened with a sort of aimless beam meaning nothing at all.

To the son, under cover of his father's hard sell, I quietly said, 'I want to talk to you, and if you run away from me now I'll be telephoning the police.'

He gave me a sick look and stood still.

215

'We'll walk down the course together to watch the next race,' I said. 'We won't be interrupted there. And you can tell me *why*. And then we'll see.'

It was easy enough for him to drop back unnoticed from his parents, who were still concentrating on Ursula, and he came with me through the gate and out across the track itself to the centre of the racecourse, stumbling slightly as if not in command of his feet. We walked down towards the last fence, and he told me why he'd tried to kill Calder Jackson.

'It doesn't seem real, not now, it doesn't really,' he said first. A young voice, slightly sloppy accent, full of strain.

'How old are you?' I asked.

'Seventeen.'

I hadn't been so far out, I thought, fifteen months ago.

'I never thought I'd see you again,' he said explosively, sounding faintly aggrieved at the twist of fate. 'I mean, the papers said you worked in a bank.'

'So I do. And I go racing.' I paused. 'You remembered my name.'

'Yeah. Could hardly forget it, could I? All over the papers.'

We went a few yards in silence. 'Go on,' I said.

He made a convulsive gesture of frustrated despair. 'All right. But if I tell you, you won't tell *them*, will you, not Mum and Dad?'

I glanced at him, but from his troubled face it was

clear that he meant exactly what he'd said: it wasn't my telling the police he minded most, but my telling his parents.

'Just get on with it,' I said.

He sighed. 'Well, we had this horse. Dad did. He'd bought it as a yearling and ran it as a two-year-old and at three, but it was a jumper really, and it turned out to be good.' He paused. 'Indian Silk, that's what it was called.'

I frowned. 'But Indian Silk ... didn't that win at Cheltenham this year, in March?'

He nodded. 'The Gold Cup. The very top. He's only seven now and he's bound to be brilliant for years.' The voice was bitter with a sort of resigned, stifled anger.

'But he doesn't any longer belong to your father?'

'No, he doesn't.' More bitterness, very sharp.

'Go on, then,' I said.

He swallowed and took his time, but eventually he said, 'Two years ago this month, when 'ndian Silk was five, like, he won the Hermitage 'Chase very easily here at Newbury, and everyone was tipping him for the Gold Cup *last* year, though Dad was saying he was still on the young side and to give him time. See, Dad was that proud of that horse. The best he'd ever trained, and it was his own, not someone else's. Don't know if you can understand that.'

'I do understand it,' I said.

He gave a split-second glance at my face. 'Well,

Indian Silk got sick,' he said. 'I mean, there was nothing you could put your finger on. He just lost his speed. He couldn't even gallop properly at home, couldn't beat the other horses in Dad's yard that he'd been running rings round all year. Dad couldn't run him in races. He could hardly train him. And the vet couldn't find out what was wrong with him. They took blood tests and all sorts, and they gave him antibiotics and purges, and they thought it might be worms or something, but it wasn't.'

We had reached the last fence, and stood there on the rough grass beside it while in twos and threes other enthusiasts straggled down from the grandstand towards us to watch the horses in action at close quarters.

'I was at school a lot of the time, see,' Ricky said. 'I was home every night of course but I was taking exams and had a lot of homework and I didn't really want to take much notice of Indian Silk getting so bad or anything. I mean, Dad does go on a bit, and I suppose I thought the horse just had the virus or something and would get better. But he just got slowly worse and one day Mum was crying.' He stopped suddenly, as if that part was the worst. 'I hadn't seen a grown-up cry before,' he said. 'Suppose you'll think it funny, but it upset me something awful.'

'I don't think it funny,' I said.

'Anyway,' he went on, seeming to gather confidence, 'it got so that Indian Silk was so weak he could barely walk down the road and he wasn't eating, and Dad was in real despair because there wasn't nothing anyone could do, and Mum couldn't bear the thought of him going to the knackers, and then some guy telephoned and offered to buy him.'

'To buy a sick horse?' I said, surprised.

'I don't think Dad was going to tell him just how bad he was. Well, I mean, at that point Indian Silk was worth just what the knackers would pay for his carcass, which wasn't much, and this man was offering nearly twice that. But the man said he knew Indian Silk couldn't race any more but he'd like to give him a good home in a nice field for as long as necessary, and it meant that Dad didn't have the expense of any more vets' bills and he and Mum didn't have to watch Indian Silk just getting worse and worse, and Mum wouldn't have to think of him going to the knackers for dog meat, so they let him go.'

The horses for the second race came out onto the course and galloped down past us, the jockeys' colours bright in the sun.

'And then what?' I said.

'Then nothing happened for weeks and we were getting over it, like, and then someone told Dad that Indian Silk was back in training and looking fine, and he couldn't believe it.'

'When was that?' I asked.

'It was last year, just before ... before Ascot.'

A small crowd gathered on the landing side of the

fence, and I drew him away down the course a bit further, to where the horses would set themselves right to take off.

'Go on,' I said.

'My exams were coming up,' he said. 'And I mean, they were important, they were going to affect my whole life, see?'

I nodded.

'Then Dad found that the man who'd bought Indian Silk hadn't put him in any field, he'd sent him straight down the road to Calder Jackson.'

'Ah,' I said.

'And there was this man saying Calder Jackson had the gift of healing, some sort of magic, and had simply touched Indian Silk and made him well. I ask you . . . And Dad was in a frightful state because someone had suggested he should send the horse there, to Calder Jackson, while he was so bad, of course, and Dad had said don't be so ridiculous, it was all a lot of rubbish. And then Mum was saying he should have listened to her, because she'd said why not try it, it couldn't do any harm, and he wouldn't do it, and they were having rows, and she was crying . . .' He gulped for air, the story now pouring out faster almost than he could speak. 'And I wasn't getting any work done with it all going on, they weren't ever talking about anything else, and I took the first exam and just sat there and couldn't do it, and I knew I'd failed and I was going to fail them all because I couldn't concentrate . . . and then there was Calder Jackson one evening talking on television, saying he'd got a friend of his to buy a dying horse, because the people who owned it would just have let it die because they didn't believe in healers, like a lot of people, and he hoped the horse would be great again some day, like before, thanks to him, and I knew he was talking about Indian Silk. And he said he was going to Ascot on that Thursday . . . and there was Dad screaming that Calder Jackson had stolen the horse away, it was all a filthy swindle, which of course it wasn't, but at the time I believed him . . . and it all got so that I hated Calder Jackson so much that I couldn't think straight. I mean, I thought *he* was the reason Mum was crying and I was failing my exams and Dad had lost the only really top horse he'd have in his whole life, and I just wanted to *kill* him.'

The bedrock words were out, and the flood suddenly stopped, leaving the echo of them on the October air.

'And did you fail your exams?' I asked, after a moment.

'Yeah. Most of them. But I took them again at Christmas and got good passes.' He shook his head, speaking more slowly, more quietly. 'I was glad, even that night, that you'd stopped me stabbing him. I mean . . . I'd have thrown my whole life away, I could see it afterwards, and all for nothing, because Dad wasn't going to get the horse back whatever I did, because it was a legal sale, like.'

I thought over what he'd told me while in the

distance the horses lined up and set off on their three-mile steeplechase.

'I was sort of mad,' he said. 'I can't really understand it now. I mean, I wouldn't go around trying to kill people. I really wouldn't. It seems like I was a different person.'

Adolescence, I thought, and not for the first time, could be hell.

'I took Mum's knife out of the kitchen,' he said. 'She never could think where it had gone.'

I wondered if the police still had it; with Ricky's fingerprints on file.

'I didn't know there would be so many people at Ascot,' he said. 'And so many gates into the course. Much more than Newmarket. I was getting frantic because I thought I wouldn't find him. I meant to do it earlier, see, when he arrived. I was out on the road, running up and down the pavement, mad, you know, really, looking for him and feeling the knife kind of burning in my sleeve, like I was burning in my mind . . . and I saw his head, all those curls, crossing the road, and I ran, but I was too late, he'd gone inside, through the gate.'

'And then,' I suggested. 'You simply waited for him to come out?'

He nodded. 'There were lots of people around. No one took any notice. I reckoned he'd come up that path from the station, and that was the way he would go back. It didn't seem long, the waiting. Went in a flash.'

The horses came over the next fence down the course like a multi-coloured wave and thundered towards the one where we were standing. The ground trembled from the thud of the hooves, the air rang with the curses of jockeys, the half-ton equine bodies brushed through the birch, the sweat and the effort and the speed filled eyes and ears and mind with pounding wonder and then were gone, flying away, leaving the silence. I had walked down several times before to watch from the fences, both there and on other tracks, and the fierce fast excitement had never grown stale.

'Who is it who owns Indian Silk now?' I asked.

'A Mr Chacksworth, comes from Birmingham,' Ricky answered. 'You see him at the races sometimes, slobbering all over Indian Silk. But it wasn't him that bought him from Dad. He bought him later, when he was all right again. Paid a proper price for him, so we heard. Made it all the worse.'

A sad and miserable tale, all of it.

'Who bought the horse from your father?' I said.

'I never met him ... his name was Smith. Some funny first name. Can't remember.'

Smith. Friend of Calder's.

'Could it,' I asked, surprised, 'have been *Dissdale* Smith?'

'Yeah. That sounds like it. How do you know?'

'He was there that day at Ascot,' I said. 'There on the pavement, right beside Calder Jackson.'

'Was he?' Ricky looked disconcerted. 'He was a dead liar, you know, all that talk about nice fields.'

'Who tells the truth,' I said, 'when buying or selling horses?'

The runners were round again on the far side of the track, racing hard now on the second circuit.

'What are you going to do?' Ricky said. 'About me, like? You won't tell Mum and Dad. You won't, will you?'

I looked directly at the boy-man, seeing the continuing anxiety but no longer the first panic-stricken fear. He seemed to sense now that I would very likely not drag him into court, but he wasn't sure of much else.

'Perhaps they should know,' I said.

'No!' His agitation rose quickly. 'They've had so much trouble and I would have made it so much worse if you hadn't stopped me, and afterwards I used to wake up sweating at what it would have done to them; and the only good thing was that I did learn that you can't put things right by killing people, you can only make things terrible for your family.'

After a long pause I said, 'All right. I won't tell them.' And heaven help me, I thought, if he ever attacked anyone again because he thought he could always get away with it.

The relief seemed to affect him almost as much as the anxiety. He blinked several times and turned his head away to where the race was again coming round into the straight with this time an all-out effort to the winning post. There was again the rise and fall of the field over the distant fences but now the one wave had split into separate components, the runners coming home not in a bunch but a procession.

I watched again the fierce surprising speed of horse and jockey jumping at close quarters and wished with some regret that I could have ridden like that; but like Alec I was wishing too late, even strong and healthy and thirty-three.

The horses galloped off towards the cheers on the grandstand and Ricky and I began a slow walk in their wake. He seemed quiet and composed in the aftermath of confession, the soul's evacuation giving him ease.

'What do you feel nowadays about Calder Jackson?' I asked.

He produced a lop-sided smile. 'Nothing much. That's what's so crazy. I mean, it wasn't his fault Dad was so stubborn.'

I digested this. 'You mean,' I said, 'that you think your father should have sent him the horse himself?'

'Yes, I reckon he should've, like Mum wanted. But he said it was rubbish and too expensive, and you don't know my dad but when he makes his mind up he just gets fighting angry if anyone tries to argue, and he shouts at her, and it isn't fair.'

'If your father had sent the horse to Calder Jackson, I suppose he would still own it,' I said thoughtfully.

'Yes, he would, and don't think he doesn't know it,

of course he does, but it's as much as anyone's life's worth to say it.'

We trudged back over the thick grass, and I asked him how Calder or Dissdale had known that Indian Silk was ill.

He shrugged. 'It was in the papers. He'd been favourite for the King George VI on Boxing Day, but of course he didn't run, and the press found out why.'

We came again to the gate into the grandstand enclosure and went through it, and I asked where he lived.

'Exning,' he said.

'Where's that?'

'Near Newmarket. Just outside.' He looked at me with slightly renewed apprehension. 'You meant it, didn't you, about not telling?'

'I meant it,' I said. 'Only . . .' I frowned a little, thinking of the hot-house effect of his living with his parents.

'Only what?' he asked.

I tried a different tack. 'What are you doing now? Are you still at school?'

'No, I left once I'd passed those exams. I really needed them, like. You can't get a halfway decent job without those bits of paper these days.'

'You're not working for your father, then?'

He must have heard the faint relief in my voice because for the first time he fully smiled. 'No, I reckon it wouldn't be good for his temper, and anyway I don't want to be a trainer, one long worry, if you ask me.'

'What do you do, then?' I asked.

'I'm learning electrical engineering in a firm near Cambridge. An apprentice, like.' He smiled again. 'But not with horses, not me.' He shook his head ruefully and delivered his young-Solomon judgement of life. 'Break your heart, horses do.'

NOVEMBER

To my great delight the cartoonist came up trumps, his twenty animated films being shown on television every weeknight for a month in the best time-slot for that sort of humour, seven in the evening, when older children were still up and the parents home from work. The nation sat up and giggled, and the cartoonist telephoned breathlessly to ask for a bigger loan.

'I do need a proper studio, not this converted warehouse. And more animators, and designers, and recordists, and equipment.'

'All right,' I said into the first gap. 'Draw up your requirements and come and see me.'

'Do you *realize*,' he said, as if he himself had difficulty, 'that they'll take as many films as I can make? No limit. They said just go on making them for years and years . . . they said *please* go on making them.'

'I'm very glad,' I said sincerely.

'You gave me faith in myself,' he said. 'You'll never believe it, but you did. I'd been turned down so often, and I was getting depressed, but when you lent me the money to start it was like being uncorked. The ideas just rushed out.'

'And are they still rushing?'

'Oh sure. I've got the next twenty films roughed out in drawings already and we're working on those, and now I'm starting on the batch after that.'

'It's terrific,' I said.

'It sure is, brother, life's amazing.' He put down his receiver and left me smiling into space.

'The cartoonist?' Gordon said.

I nodded. 'Going up like a rocket.'

'Congratulations.' There was warmth and genuine pleasure in his voice. Such a generous man, I thought: so impossible to do him harm.

'He looks like turning into a major industry,' I said.

'Disney, Hanna Barbera, eat your hearts out,' Alec said from across the room.

'Good business for the bank.' Gordon beamed. 'Henry will be pleased.'

Pleasing Henry, indeed, was the aim of us all.

'You must admit, Tim,' Alec said, 'that you're a fairish rocket yourself . . . so what's the secret?'

'Light the blue paper and retire immediately,' I said good humouredly, and he balled a page of jottings to throw at me, and missed.

At mid-morning he went out as customary for the six copies of *What's Going On Where It Shouldn't* and having distributed five was presently sitting back in his chair reading our own with relish.

Ekaterin's had been thankfully absent from the probing columns ever since the five per cent business, but it appeared that some of our colleagues along the road weren't so fortunate.

'Did you know,' Alec said conversationally, 'that some of our investment manager chums down on the corner have set up a nice little fiddle on the side, accepting pay-offs from brokers in return for steering business their way?'

'How do you know?' Gordon asked, looking up from a ledger.

Alec lifted the paper. 'The gospel according to this dicky bird.'

'Gospel meaning good news,' I said.

'Don't be so damned erudite.' He grinned at me with mischief and went back to reading aloud, '*Contrary to popular belief the general run of so-called managers in merchant banks are not in the princely bracket.*' He looked up briefly. 'You can say that again.' He went on, '*We hear that four of the investment managers in this establishment have been cosily supplementing their middle-incomes by steering fund money to three stockbrokers in particular. Names will be revealed in our next issue. Watch this space.*'

'It's happened before,' Gordon said philosophically, 'and will happen again. The temptation is always there.' He frowned. 'All the same, I'm surprised their senior managers and the directors haven't spotted it.'

'They'll have spotted it *now*,' Alec said.

'So they will.'

'It would be pretty easy,' I said musingly, 'to set up a computer programme to do the spotting for Ekaterin's, in case we should ever find the pestilence cropping up here.'

'Would it?' Gordon asked.

'Mm. Just a central programme to record every deal in the Investment Department with each stockbroker, with running totals, easy to see. Anything hugely unexpected could be investigated.'

'But that's a vast job, surely,' Gordon said.

I shook my head. 'I doubt it. I could get our tame programmer to have a go, if you like.'

'We'll put it to the others. See what they say.'

'There will be screeches from Investment Management,' Alec said. 'Cries of outraged virtue.'

'Guards them against innuendo like this, though,' Gordon said, pointing to *What's Going On* . . .

The board agreed, and in consequence I spent another two days with the programmer, building dykes against future leaks.

Gordon these days seemed no worse, his illness not having progressed in any visible way. There was no means of knowing how he felt, as he never said and hated to be asked, but on the few times I'd seen Judith since the day at Easter, she had said he was as well as could be hoped for.

The best of those times had been a Sunday in July when Pen had given a lunch party in her house in

Clapham; it was supposed to have been a lunch-in-the-garden party, but like so much that summer was frustrated by chilly winds. Inside was to me much better, as Pen had written place-cards for her long refectory table and put me next to Judith, with Gordon on her right hand.

The other guests remained a blur, most of them being doctors of some sort or another, or pharmacists like herself. Judith and I made polite noises to the faces on either side of us but spent most of the time talking to each other, carrying on two conversations at once, one with voice, one with eyes; both satisfactory.

When the main party had broken up and gone, Gordon and Judith and I stayed to supper, first helping Pen clear up from what she described as 'repaying so many dinners at one go.'

It had been a day when natural opportunities for touching people abounded, when kisses and hugs of greeting had been appropriate and could be warm, when all the world could watch and see nothing between Judith and me but an enduring and peaceful friendship: a day when I longed to have her for myself worse than ever.

Since then I'd seen her only twice, and both times were when she'd come to the bank to collect Gordon before they went on to other events. On each of these times I'd managed at least five minutes with her, stiffly circumspect, Gordon's colleague being polite until Gordon himself was ready to leave.

It wasn't usual for wives to come to the bank: husbands normally joined them at wherever they were going. Judith said, the second time, 'I won't do this often. I just wanted to see you, if you were around.'

'Always here,' I said.

She nodded. She was looking as fresh and poised as ever, wearing a neat blue coat with pearls showing. The brown hair was glossy, the eyes bright, the soft mouth half smiling, the glamour born in her and unconscious.

'I get ... well ... thirsty, sometimes,' she said.

'Permanent state with me,' I said lightly.

She swallowed. 'Just for a moment or two ...'

We were standing in the entrance hall, not touching, waiting for Gordon.

'Just to see you ...' She seemed uncertain that I understood, but I did.

'It's the same for me,' I assured her. 'I sometimes think of going to Clapham and waiting around just to see you walk down the street to the bakers. Just to see you, even for seconds.'

'Do you really?'

'I don't go, though. You might send Gordon to buy the bread.'

She laughed a small laugh, a fitting size for the bank; and he came, hurrying, struggling into his overcoat. I sprang to help him and he said to her, 'Sorry, darling, got held up on the telephone, you know how it is.'

'I've been perfectly happy,' she said, kissing him, 'talking to Tim.'

'Splendid. Splendid. Are we ready then?'

They went off to their evening smiling and waving and leaving me to hunger futilely for this and that.

In the office one day in November Gordon said, 'How about you coming over to lunch on Sunday? Judith was saying it's ages since she saw you properly.'

'I'd love to.'

'Pen's coming, Judith said.'

Pen, my friend; my chaperone.

'Great,' I said positively. 'Lovely.'

Gordon nodded contentedly and said it was a shame we couldn't all have a repeat of last Christmas, he and Judith had enjoyed it so much. They were going this year to his son and daughter-in-law in Edinburgh, a visit long promised; to his son by his first long-dead wife, and his grandchildren, twin boys of seven.

'You'll have fun,' I said regretfully.

'They're noisy little brutes.'

His telephone rang, and mine also, and money-lending proceeded. I would be dutiful, I thought, and spend Christmas with my mother in Jersey, as she wanted, and we would laugh and play backgammon, and I would sadden her as usual by bringing no girl-friend, no prospective producer of little brutes.

'*Why*, my love,' she'd said to me once a few years earlier in near despair, 'do you take out these perfectly presentable girls and never marry them?'

234

'There's always something I don't want to spend my life with.'

'But you do *sleep* with them?'

'Yes, darling, I do.'

'You're too choosy.'

'I expect so,' I said.

'You haven't had a single one that's lasted,' she complained. 'Everyone else's sons manage to have live-in girlfriends, sometimes going on for years even if they don't marry, so why can't you?'

I'd smiled at the encouragement to what would once have been called sin, and kissed her, and told her I preferred living alone, but that one day I'd find the perfect girl to love for ever; and it hadn't even fleetingly occurred to me that when I found her she would be married to someone else.

Sunday came and I went to Clapham: bitter-sweet hours, as ever.

Over lunch I told them tentatively that I'd seen the boy who had tried to kill Calder, and they reacted as strongly as I'd expected, Gordon saying, 'You've told the police, of course,' and Judith adding, 'He's dangerous, Tim.'

I shook my head. 'No. I don't think so. I hope not.' I smiled wryly and told them all about Ricky Barnet and Indian Silk, and the pressure which had led to the try at stabbing. 'I don't think he'll do anything like that again. He's grown so far away from it already that he feels a different person.'

'I hope you're right,' Gordon said.

'Fancy it being Dissdale who bought Indian Silk,' Pen said. 'Isn't it amazing?'

'Especially as he was saying he was short of cash and wanting to sell box-space at Ascot,' Judith added.

'Mm,' I said. 'But after Calder had cured the horse Dissdale sold it again pretty soon, and made a handsome profit, by what I gather.'

'Typical Dissdale behaviour,' Gordon said without criticism. 'Face the risk, stake all you can afford, take the loot if you're lucky, and get out fast.' He smiled. 'By Ascot I guess he'd blown the Indian Silk profit and was back to basics. It doesn't take someone like Dissdale any longer to lose thousands than it does to make them.'

'He must have colossal faith in Calder,' Pen said musingly.

'Not colossal, Pen,' Gordon said. 'Just twice what a knacker would pay for a carcass.'

'Would *you* buy a sick-to-death horse?' Judith asked. 'I mean, if Calder said buy it and I'll cure him, would you believe it?'

Gordon looked at her fondly. 'I'm not Dissdale, darling, and I don't think I'd buy it.'

'And that is precisely,' I pointed out, 'why Fred Barnet lost Indian Silk. He thought Calder's powers were all rubbish and he wouldn't lash out good money to put them to the test. But Dissdale *did*. Bought the horse and presumably also paid Calder . . . who boasted about his success on television and nearly got himself killed for it.'

'Ironic, the whole thing,' Pen said, and we went on discussing it desultorily over coffee.

I stayed until six, when Pen went off to her shop for a Sunday-evening stint and Gordon began to look tired, and I drove back to Hampstead in the usual post-Judith state: half-fulfilled, half-starved.

Towards the end of November, and at Oliver Knowles' invitation, I travelled to another Sunday lunch, this time at the stud farm in Hertfordshire.

It turned out, not surprisingly, to be one of Ginnie's days home from school, and it was she, whistling to Squibs, who set off with me through the yards.

'Did you know we had a hundred and fifty-two mares here all at the same time, back in May?' she said.

'That's a lot,' I said, impressed.

'They had a hundred and fourteen foals between them, and only one of the mares and three of the foals died. That's a terrifically good record, you know.'

'Your father's very skilled.'

'So is Nigel,' she said grudgingly. 'You have to give him his due.'

I smiled at the expression.

237

'He isn't here just now,' she said. 'He went off to Miami yesterday to lie in the sun.'

'Nigel?'

She nodded. 'He goes about this time every year. Sets him up for the winter, he says.'

'Always Miami?'

'Yes, he likes it.'

The whole atmosphere of the place was back to where I'd known it first, to the slow chill months of gestation. Ginnie, snuggling inside her padded jacket, gave carrots from her pocket to some of the mares in the first yard and walked me without stopping through the empty places, the second yard, the foaling yard, and past the breeding shed.

We came finally as always to the stallion yard where the curiosity of the residents brought their heads out the moment they heard our footsteps. Ginnie distributed carrots and pats with the aplomb of her father, and Sandcastle graciously allowed her to stroke his nose.

'He's quiet now,' she said. 'He's on a much lower diet at this time of year.'

I listened to the bulk of knowledge behind the calm words and I said, 'What are you going to do when you leave school?'

'This, of course.' She patted Sandcastle's neck. 'Help Dad. Be his assistant.'

'Nothing else?'

She shook her head. 'I love the foals. Seeing them

born and watching them grow. I don't want to do anything else, ever.'

We left the stallions and walked between the paddocks with their foals and dams, along the path to the Watcherleys', Squibs trotting on ahead and marking his fence posts. The neighbouring place, whose ramshackle state I'd only glimpsed on my pursuit of the loose five million, proved now to be almost as neat as the parent spread, with much fresh paint in evidence and weeds markedly absent.

'Dad can't bear mess,' Ginnie said when I remarked on the spit-and-polish. 'The Watcherleys are pretty lucky, really, with Dad paying them rent *and* doing up their place *and* employing them to look after the animals in this yard. Bob may still gripe a bit at not being on his own, but Maggie was telling me just last week that she would be everlastingly thankful that Calder Jackson stole their business.'

'He hardly stole it,' I said mildly.

'Well, you know what I mean. Did better at it, if you want to be pedantic.' She grinned. 'Anyway, Maggie's bought some new clothes at last, and I'm glad for her.'

We opened and went into a few of the boxes where she handed out the last of the carrots and fondled the inmates, both mares and growing foals, talking to them, and all of them responded amiably to her touch, nuzzling her gently. She looked at peace and where she belonged, all growing pains suspended.

239

The Third Year

APRIL

Alec had bought a bunch of yellow tulips when he went out for *What's Going On . . .*, and they stood on his desk in a beer mug, catching a shaft of spring sunshine and standing straight like guardsmen.

Gordon was making notes in a handwriting growing even smaller, and the two older colleagues were counting the weeks to their retirement. Office life: an ordinary day.

My telephone rang, and with eyes still bent on a letter from a tomato grower asking for more time to repay his original loan because of needing a new greenhouse (half an acre) right this minute, I slowly picked up the receiver.

'Oliver Knowles,' the voice said. 'Is that you, Tim?'

'Hello,' I replied warmly. 'Everything going well?'

'No.' The word was sickeningly abrupt, and both mentally and physically I sat up straighter.

'What's the matter?'

'Can you come down here?' he asked, not directly answering. 'I'm rather worried. I want to talk to you.'

'Well . . . I could come on Sunday,' I said.

'Could you come today? Or tomorrow?'

I reviewed my workload and a few appointments. 'Tomorrow afternoon, if you like,' I said. 'If it's bank business.'

'Yes, it is.' The anxiety in his voice was quite plain, and communicated itself with much ease to me.

'Can't you tell me what's the trouble?' I asked. 'Is Sandcastle all right?'

'I don't know,' he said. 'I'll tell you when you come.'

'But Oliver . . .'

'Listen,' he said. 'Sandcastle is in good health and he hasn't escaped again or anything like that. It's too difficult to explain on the telephone. I want your advice, that's all.'

He wouldn't say any more and left me with the dead receiver in my hand and some horrid suspenseful question marks in my mind.

'Sandcastle?' Gordon asked.

'Oliver says he's in good health.'

'That horse is insured against everything – those enormous premiums – so don't worry too much,' Gordon said. 'It's probably something minor.'

It hadn't sounded like anything minor, and when I reached the stud farm the next day I found that it certainly wasn't. Oliver came out to meet me as I braked to a standstill by his front door, and there were new deep lines on his face that hadn't been there before.

'Come in,' he said, clasping my hand. 'I'm seriously worried. I don't know what to do.'

He led the way through the house to the office-sitting room and gestured me to a chair. 'Sit down and read this,' he said, and gave me a letter.

There had been no time for 'nice day' or 'how is Ginnie?' introductory noises, just this stark command. I sat down, and I read, as directed.

The letter, dated April 21st, said:

Dear Oliver,

I'm not complaining, because of course one pays one's fee and takes one's chances, but I'm sorry to tell you that the Sandcastle foal out of my mare Spiral Binding has been born with a half of one ear missing. It's a filly, by the way, and I dare say it won't affect her speed, but her looks are ruined.

So sad.

I expect I'll see you one day at the sales.

Yours,

Jane.

'Is that very bad?' I asked, frowning.

In reply he wordlessly handed me another letter. This one said:

Dear Mr Knowles,

You asked me to let you know how my mare Girandette, whom you liked so much, fared on

245

foaling. She gave birth safely to a nice colt foal, but unfortunately he died at six days. We had a post mortem, and it was found that he had malformed heart-valves, like hole-in-the-heart babies.

This is a great blow to me, financially as well as all else, but that's life I suppose.

Yours sincerely,
George Page.

'And now this,' Oliver said, and handed me a third.

The heading was that of a highly regarded and well-known stud farm, the letter briefly impersonal.

Dear Sir,

Filly foal born March 31st to Poppingcorn.

Sire: Sandcastle.

Deformed foot, near fore.

Put down.

I gave him back the letters and with growing misgiving asked, 'How common are these malformations?'

Oliver said intensely, 'They happen. They happen occasionally. But those letters aren't all. I've had two telephone calls – one last night. Two other foals have died of holes in the heart. Two more! That's five with something wrong with them.' He stared at me, his eyes like dark pits. 'That's far too many.' He swallowed. 'And what about the others, the other thirty-five? Suppose . . . suppose there are more . . .'

'If you haven't heard, they're surely all right.'

He shook his head hopelessly. 'The mares are scattered all over the place, dropping Sandcastle's foals where they are due to be bred next. There's no automatic reason for those stud managers to tell me when a foal's born, or what it's like. I mean, some do it out of courtesy but they just don't usually bother, and nor do I. I tell the owner of the mare, not the manager of the stallion.'

'Yes, I see.'

'So there may be other foals with deformities . . . that I haven't heard about.'

There was a long fraught pause in which the enormity of the position sank coldly into my banking consciousness. Oliver developed sweat on his forehead and a tic beside his mouth, as if sharing his anxiety had doubled rather than halved it.

The telephone rang suddenly, making us both jump.

'You answer it,' he said. 'Please.'

I opened my mouth to protest that it would be only some routine call about anything else on earth, but then merely picked up the receiver.

'Is that Oliver Knowles?' a voice said.

'No . . . I'm his assistant.'

'Oh. Then will you give him a message?'

'Yes, I will.'

'Tell him that Patrick O'Marr rang him from Limballow, Ireland. Have you got that?'

'Yes,' I said. 'Go ahead.'

'It's about a foal we had born here three or four weeks ago. I thought I'd better let Mr Knowles know that we've had to put it down, though I'm sorry to give him bad news. Are you listening?'

'Yes,' I said, feeling hollow.

'The poor little fellow was born with a sort of curled-in hoof. The vet said it might straighten out in a week or two, but it didn't, so we had it X-rayed, and the lower pastern bone and the coffin bone were fused and tiny. The vet said there was no chance of them developing properly, and the little colt would never be able to walk, let alone race. A beautiful little fella too, in all other ways. Anyway, I'm telling Mr Knowles because of course he'll be looking out for Sandcastle's first crop to win for him, and I'm explaining why this one won't be there. Pink Roses, that's the mare's name. Tell him, will you? Pink Roses. She's come here to be bred to Dallaton. Nice mare. She's fine herself, tell Mr Knowles.'

'Yes,' I said. 'I'm very sorry.'

'One of those things.' The cultured Irish accent sounded not too despairing. 'The owner of Pink Roses is cut up about it, of course, but I believe he'd insured against a dead or deformed foal, so it's a case of wait another year and better luck next time.'

'I'll tell Mr Knowles,' I said. 'And thank you for letting us know.'

'Sorry and all,' he said. 'But there it is.'

I put the receiver down slowly and Oliver said dully, 'Another one? Not another one.'

I nodded and told him what Patrick O'Marr had said.

'That's six,' Oliver said starkly. 'And Pink Roses . . . that's the mare you saw Sandcastle cover, this time last year.'

'Was it?' I thought back to that majestic mating, that moment of such promise. Poor little colt, conceived in splendour and born with a club foot.

'What am I going to do?' Oliver said.

'Get out Sandcastle's insurance policy.'

He looked blank. 'No, I mean, about the mares. We have all the mares here who've come this year to Sandcastle. They've all foaled except one and nearly all of them have already been covered. I mean . . . there's another crop already growing, and suppose those . . . suppose all of those . . .' He stopped as if he simply couldn't make his tongue say the words. 'I was awake all night,' he said.

'The first thing,' I said again, 'is to look at that policy.'

He went unerringly to a neat row of files in a cupboard and pulled out the needed document, a many-paged affair, partly printed, partly typed. I spread it open and said to Oliver, 'How about some coffee? This is going to take ages.'

'Oh. All right.' He looked around him vaguely. 'There'll be some put ready for me for dinner. I'll go and plug it in.' He paused. 'Percolator,' he explained.

I knew all the symptoms of a mouth saying one thing while the mind was locked on to another. 'Yes,' I said. 'That would be fine.' He nodded with the same un-meshed mental gears, and I guessed that when he got to the kitchen he'd have trouble remembering what for.

The insurance policy had been written for the trade and not the customer, a matter of jargon-ridden sentences full of words that made plain sense only to people who used them for a living. I read it very care-fully for that reason; slowly and thoroughly from start to finish.

There were many definitions of the word 'accident', with stipulations about the number of veterinary sur-geons who should be consulted and should give their signed opinions before Sandcastle (hereinafter called the horse) could be humanely destroyed for any reason whatsoever. There were stipulations about fractures, naming those bones which should commonly be held to be repairable, and about common muscle, nerve and tendon troubles which would not be considered grounds for destruction, unless of such severity that the horse couldn't actually stand up.

Aside from these restrictions the horse was to be considered to be insured against death from any natural causes whatsoever, to be insured against accidental death occurring while the horse was free (such a contin-gency to be guarded against with diligence, gross negligence being a disqualifying condition), to be insured against death by fire should the stable be consumed, and against death caused maliciously by human hand. He was insured fully against malicious or accidental castration and against such accidental damage being caused by veterinarians acting in good faith to treat the horse. He was insured against infertility on a sliding scale, his full worth being in question only if he proved one hundred per cent infertile (which laboratory tests had shown was not the case).

He was insured against accidental or malicious poisoning and against impotence resulting from non-fatal illness, and against incapacitating or fatal injuries inflicted upon him by any other horse.

He was insured against death caused by the weather (storm, flood, lightning, etc.) and also, surprisingly, against death or incapacity caused by war, riot or civil commotion, causes usually specifically excluded from insurance.

He was insured against objects dropped from the sky and against being driven into by mechanical objects on the ground and against trees falling on him and against hidden wells opening under his feet.

He was insured against every foreseeable disaster except one. He was not insured against being put out of business because of congenital abnormalities among his progeny.

Oliver came back carrying a tray on which sat two kitchen mugs containing tea, not coffee. He put the tray on the desk and looked at my face, which seemed only very slightly to deepen his despair.

'I'm not insured, am I,' he said, 'against possessing a healthy potent stallion to whom no one will send their mares?'

'I don't know.'

'Yes . . . I see you do.' He was shaking slightly. 'When the policy was drawn up about six people, including myself and two vets, besides the insurers themselves, tried to think of every possible contingency, and to guard against it. We threw in everything we could think of.' He swallowed. 'No one . . . no one thought of a whole crop of deformed foals.'

'No,' I said.

'I mean, breeders usually insure their own mares, if they want to, and the foal, to protect the stallion fee, but many don't because of the premiums being high. And I . . . I'm paying this enormous premium . . . and the one thing . . . the one thing that happens is something we never . . . no one ever imagined . . . could happen.'

The policy, I thought, had been too specific. They should have been content with something like 'any factor resulting in the horse not being considered fit for stud purposes'; but perhaps the insurers themselves couldn't find underwriters for anything so open to interpretation and opinion. In any case, the damage was done. All-risk policies all too often were not what they said; and insurance companies never paid out if they could avoid it.

My own skin felt clammy. Three million pounds of the bank's money and two million subscribed by private people were tied up in the horse, and if Oliver couldn't repay, it was we who would lose.

I had recommended the loan. Henry had wanted the adventure and Val and Gordon had been willing, but it was my own report which had carried the day. I couldn't have foreseen the consequences any more than Oliver, but I felt most horribly and personally responsible for the mess.

'What shall I do?' he said again.

'About the mares?'

'And everything else.'

I stared into space. The disaster that for the bank would mean a loss of face and a sharp dip in the profits and to the private subscribers just a painful financial setback meant in effect total ruin for Oliver Knowles.

If Sandcastle couldn't generate income, Oliver would be bankrupt. His business was not a limited company, which meant that he would lose his farm, his horses, his house; everything he possessed. To him too, as to my mother, the bailiffs would come, carrying off his furniture and his treasures and Ginnie's books and toys . . .

I shook myself mentally and physically and said, 'The first thing to do is nothing. Keep quiet and don't tell anyone what you've told me. Wait to hear if any more of the foals are . . . wrong. I will consult with the other directors at Ekaterin's and see what can be done in the way of providing time. I mean . . . I'm not promising . . . but we might consider suspending repayments while we look into other possibilities.'

He looked bewildered. 'What possibilities?'

'Well . . . of having Sandcastle tested. If the original tests of his fertility weren't thorough enough, for instance, it might be possible to show that his sperm had always been defective in some way, and then the insurance policy would protect you. Or at least it's a very good chance.'

The insurers, I thought, might in that case sue the laboratory that had originally given the fertility all-clear, but that wasn't Oliver's problem, nor mine. What did matter was that all of a sudden he looked a fraction more cheerful, and drank his tea absentmindedly.

'And the mares?' he said.

I shook my head. 'In fairness to their owners you'll have to say that Sandcastle's off colour.'

'And repay their fees,' he said gloomily.

'Mm.'

'He'll have covered two today,' he said. 'I haven't mentioned any of this to Nigel. I mean, it's his job to organize the breeding sessions. He has a great eye for those mares, he knows when they are feeling receptive. I leave it to his judgement a good deal, and he told me this morning that two were ready for Sandcastle. I just nodded. I felt sick. I didn't tell him.'

'So how many does that leave, er, uncovered?'

He consulted a list, fumbling slightly. 'The one that hasn't foaled, and . . . four others.'

Thirty-five more mares, I thought numbly, could be carrying that seed.

'The mare that hasn't yet foaled,' Oliver said flatly, 'was bred to Sandcastle last year.'

I stared. 'You mean . . . one of his foals will be born *here*?'

'Yes.' He rubbed his hand over his face. 'Any day.'

There were footsteps outside the door and Ginnie came in, saying on a rising, enquiring inflection, 'Dad?'

She saw me immediately and her face lit up. 'Hello! How lovely. I didn't know you were coming.'

I stood up to give her a customarily enthusiastic greeting, but she sensed at once that the action didn't match the climate. 'What's the matter?' She looked into my eyes and then at her father. 'What's happened?'

'Nothing,' he said.

'Dad, you're lying.' She turned again to me. 'Tell me. I can see something bad has happened. I'm not a child any more. I'm seventeen.'

'I thought you'd be at school,' I said.

'I've left. At the end of last term. There wasn't any point in me going back for the summer when all I'm interested in is here.'

She looked far more assured, as if the schooldays had been a chrysalis and she were now the imago, flying free. The beauty she had longed for hadn't quite arrived, but her face was full of character and far from plain, and she would be very much liked, I thought, throughout her life.

'What is it?' she said. 'What's happened?'

Oliver made a small gesture of despair and capitulation. 'You'll have to know sometime.' He swallowed. 'Some of Sandcastle's foals . . . aren't perfect.'

'How do you mean, not perfect?'

He told her about all six and showed her the letters, and she went slowly, swaying, pale. 'Oh Dad, no. No. It can't be. Not Sandcastle. Not that beautiful boy.'

'Sit down,' I said, but she turned to me instead, burying her face against my chest and holding on to me tightly. I put my arms round her and kissed her hair and comforted her for an age as best I could.

I went to the office on the following morning, Friday, and with a slight gritting of teeth told Gordon the outcome of my visit to Oliver.

He said 'My God,' several times, and Alec came over from his desk to listen also, his blue eyes for once solemn behind the gold-rimmed spectacles, the blond eyelashes blinking slowly and the laughing mouth grimly shut.

'What will you do?' he said finally, when I stopped.

'I don't really know.'

Gordon stirred, his hands trembling unnoticed on his blotter in his overriding concern. 'The first thing, I suppose,' he said, 'is to tell Val and Henry. Though what any of us can do is a puzzle. As you said, Tim, we'll have to wait to assess quite how irretrievable the situation is, but I can't imagine anyone with a top-class broodmare having the confidence to send her to Sandcastle in future. Can you, really, Tim? Would *you*?'

I shook my head. 'No.'

'Well, there you are,' Gordon said. 'No one would.'

Henry and Val received the news with undisguised dismay and told the rest of the directors at lunch. The man who had been against the project from the beginning reacted with genuine anger and gave me a furious dressing-down over the grilled sole.

'No one could foresee this,' Henry protested, defending me.

'Anyone could foresee,' said the dissenting director caustically, 'that such a scatterbrained scheme would blow up in our faces. Tim has been given too much power too soon, and it's his judgement that's at fault here, his alone. If he'd had the common nous to recognize the dangers, you would have listened to him and turned the proposal down. It's certainly because of his stupidity and immaturity that the bank is facing this loss, and I shall put my views on record at the next board meeting.'

There were a few uncomfortable murmurs round the table, and Henry with unruffled geniality said, 'We are all to blame, if blame there is, and it is unfair to call Tim stupid for not foreseeing something that escaped the imaginations of all the various experts who drew up the insurance policy.'

The dissenter however repeated his 'I told you so' remarks endlessly through the cheese and coffee, and I sat there depressedly enduring his digs because I wouldn't give him the satisfaction of seeing me leave before he did.

'What will you do next?' Henry asked me, when at long last everyone rather silently stood up to drift back to their desks. 'What do you propose?'

I was grateful that by implication he was leaving me in the position I'd reached and not taking the decisions out of my hands. 'I'm going down to the farm tomorrow,' I said, 'to go through the financial situation. Add up the figures. They're bound to be frightful.'

He nodded with regret. 'Such a marvellous horse. And no one, Tim, whatever anyone says, could have dreamt he'd have such a flaw.'

I sighed. 'Oliver has asked me to stay tomorrow night and Sunday night. I don't really want to, but they do need support.'

'They?'

'Ginnie, his daughter, is with him. She's only just seventeen. It's very hard on them both. Shattering, in fact.'

Henry patted my arm and walked with me to the lift. 'Do what you can,' he said. 'Let us know the full state of affairs on Monday.'

*

Before I left home that Saturday morning I had a telephone call from Judith.

'Gordon's told me about Sandcastle. Tim, it's so terrible. Those poor, poor people.'

'Wretched,' I said.

'Tim, tell Ginnie how sorry I am. Sorry ... how hopeless words are, you say sorry if you bump someone in the supermarket. That dear child ... she wrote to me a couple of times from school, just asking for feminine information, like I'd told her to.'

'Did she?'

'Yes. She's such a nice girl. So sensible. But this ... this is too much. Gordon says they're in danger of losing *everything*.'

'I'm going down there today to see where he stands.'

'Gordon told me. Do please give them my love.'

'I will.' I paused fractionally. 'My love to you, too.'

'Tim ...'

'I just wanted to tell you. It's still the same.'

'We haven't seen you for weeks. I mean ... I haven't.'

'Is Gordon in the room with you?' I asked.

'Yes, that's right.'

I smiled twistedly. 'I do hear about you, you know,' I said. 'He mentions you quite often, and I ask after you ... it makes you feel closer.'

'Yes,' she said in a perfectly neutral voice. 'I know exactly what you mean. I feel the same about it exactly.'

'Judith ...' I took a breath and made my own voice

calm to match hers. 'Tell Gordon I'll telephone him at home, if he'd like, if there is anything that needs consultation before Monday.'

'I'll tell him. Hang on.' I heard her repeating the question and Gordon's distant rumble of an answer, and then she said, 'Yes, he says please do, we'll be at home this evening and most of tomorrow.'

'Perhaps you'll answer when the telephone rings.'

'Perhaps.'

After a brief silence I said, 'I'd better go.'

'Goodbye then, Tim,' she said. 'And do let us know. We'll both be thinking of you all day, I know we will.'

'I'll call,' I said. 'You can count on it.'

The afternoon was on the whole as miserable as I'd expected and in some respects worse. Oliver and Ginnie walked about like pale automatons making disconnected remarks and forgetting where they'd put things, and lunch, Ginnie version, had consisted of eggs boiled too hard and packets of potato crisps.

'We haven't told Nigel or the lads what's happening,' Oliver said. 'Fortunately there is a lull in Sandcastle's programme. He's been very busy because nearly all his mares foaled in mid-March, close together, except for four and the one who's still carrying.' He swallowed. 'And the other stallions, of course, their mares are all here too, and we have their foals to deliver and their matings to be seen to. I mean ... we have to go on. We have to.'

Towards four o'clock they both went out into the yards for evening stables, visibly squaring their shoulders to face the stable hands in a normal manner, and I began adding the columns of figures I'd drawn up from Oliver's records.

The tally when I'd finished was appalling and meant that Oliver could be an undischarged bankrupt for the rest of his life. I put the results away in my briefcase and tried to think of something more constructive; and Oliver's telephone rang.

'Oliver?' a voice said, sounding vaguely familiar.

'He's out,' I said. 'Can I take a message?'

'Get him to ring me. Ursula Young. I'll give you the number.'

'Ursula!' I said in surprise. 'This is Tim Ekaterin.'

'Really?' For her it was equally unexpected. 'What are *you* doing there?'

'Just staying the weekend. Can I help?'

She hesitated slightly but then said, 'Yes, I suppose you can. I'm afraid it's bad news for him, though. Disappointing, you might say.' She paused. 'I've a friend who has a small stud farm, just one stallion, but quite a good one, and she's been so excited this year because one of the mares booked to him was in foal to Sandcastle. She was thrilled, you see, to be having a foal of that calibre born on her place.'

'Yes,' I said.

261

'Well, she rang me this morning, and she was crying.' Ursula herself gulped: she might appear tough but other people's tears always moved her. 'She said the mare had dropped the Sandcastle foal during the night and she hadn't been there. She said the mare gave no sign yesterday evening, and the birth must have been quick and easy, and the mare was all right, but . . .'

'But what?' I said, scarcely breathing.

'She said the foal – a filly – was on her feet and suckling when she went to the mare's box this morning, and at first she was overjoyed, but then . . . but then . . .'

'Go on,' I said hopelessly.

'Then she saw. She says it's dreadful.'

'Ursula . . .'

'The foal has only one eye.'

Oh my God, I thought: dear *God*.

'She says there's nothing on the other side,' Ursula said. 'No proper socket.' She gulped again. 'Will you tell Oliver? I thought he'd better know. He'll be most disappointed. I'm so sorry.'

'I'll tell him.'

'These things happen, I suppose,' she said. 'But it's so upsetting when they happen to your friends.'

'You're very right.'

'Goodbye then, Tim. See you soon, I hope, at the races.'

I put down the receiver and wondered how I would ever tell them, and in fact I didn't tell Ginnie, only

Oliver, who sat with his head in his hands, despair in every line of his body.

'It's hopeless,' he said.

'Not yet,' I said encouragingly, though I wasn't as certain as I sounded. 'There are still the tests to be done on Sandcastle.'

He merely slumped lower. 'I'll get them done, but they won't help. The genes which are wrong will be minute. No one will see them, however powerful the microscope.'

'You can't tell. If they can see DNA, why not a horse's chromosomes?'

He raised his head slowly. 'Even then . . . it's such a long shot.' He sighed deeply. 'I think I'll ask the Equine Research Establishment at Newmarket to have him there, to see what they can find. I'll ring them on Monday.'

'I suppose,' I said tentatively. 'Well, I know it sounds silly, but I suppose it couldn't be anything as simple as something he'd *eaten*? Last year, of course.'

He shook his head. 'I thought of that. I've thought of bloody well everything, believe me. All the stallions had the same food, and none of the others' foals are affected . . . or at least we haven't heard of any. Nigel feeds the stallions himself out of the feed room in that yard, and we're always careful what we give them because of keeping them fit.'

'Carrots?' I said.

'I give carrots to every horse on the place. Everyone

263

here does. Carrots are good food. I buy them by the hundredweight and keep them in the first big yard where the main feed room is. I put handfuls in my pockets every day. You've seen me. Rotaboy, Diarist and Parakeet all had them. It can't possibly be anything to do with carrots.'

'Paint: something like that? Something new in the boxes, when you put in all the security? Something he could chew?'

He again shook his head. 'I've been over it and over it. We did all the boxes exactly the same as each other. There's nothing in Sandcastle's box that wasn't in the others. They're all exactly alike.' He moved restlessly. 'I've been down there to make sure there's nothing Sandcastle could reach to lick if he put his head right over the half-door as far as he could get. There's nothing, nothing at all.'

'Drinking pails?'

'No. They don't always have the same pails. I mean, when Lenny fills them he doesn't necessarily take them back to the particular boxes they come from. The pails don't have the stallions' names on, if that's what you mean.'

I didn't mean anything much: just grabbing at straws.

'Straw . . .' I said. 'How about an allergy? An allergy to something around him? Could an allergy have such an effect?'

'I've never heard of anything like that. I'll ask the Research people, though, on Monday.'

He got up to pour us both a drink. 'It's good to have you here,' he said. 'A sort of net over the bottomless pit.' He gave me the glass with a faint half-smile, and I had a definite impression that he would not in the end go to pieces.

I telephoned then to the Michaels' house and Gordon answered at the first ring as if he'd been passing near by. Nothing good to report, I said, except that Ginnie sent Judith her love. Gordon said Judith was in the garden picking parsley for supper, and he would tell her. 'Call tomorrow,' he said, 'if we can help.'

Our own supper, left ready in the refrigerator by Oliver's part-time housekeeper, filled the hollows left by lunch, and Ginnie went to bed straight afterwards, saying she would be up at two o'clock and out with Nigel in the foal yard.

'She goes most nights,' Oliver said. 'She and Nigel make a good team. He says she's a great help, particularly if three or four mares are foaling at the same time. I'm often out there myself, but with all the decisions and paperwork as well I get very tired if I do it too much. Fall asleep over meals, that sort of thing.'

We ourselves went to bed fairly early, and I awoke in the large high-ceilinged guest room while it was still blackly dark. It was one of those fast awakenings which mean that sleep won't come back easily, and I got out of bed and went to the window, which looked out over the yard.

I could see only roofs and security lights and a small

section of the first yard. There was no visible activity, and my watch showed four-thirty.

I wondered if Ginnie would mind if I joined her in the foaling yard; and got dressed and went.

They were all there, Nigel and Oliver as well as Ginnie, all in one open-doored box where a mare lay on her side on the straw. They all turned their heads as I approached but seemed unsurprised to see me and gave no particular greeting.

'This is Plus Factor,' Oliver said. 'In foal to Sandcastle.'

His voice was calm and so was Ginnie's manner, and I guessed that they still hadn't told Nigel about the deformities. There was hope, too, in their faces, as if they were sure that this one, after all, would be perfect.

'She's coming,' Nigel said quietly. 'Here we go.'

The mare gave a grunt and her swelling sides heaved. The rest of us stood silent, watching, taking no part. A glistening half-transparent membrane with a hoof showing within it appeared, followed by the long slim shape of the head, followed very rapidly by the whole foal, flopping out onto the straw, steaming, the membrane breaking open, the fresh air reaching the head, new life beginning with the first fluttering gasp of the lungs.

Amazing, I thought.

'Is he all right?' Oliver said, bending down, the anxiety raw, unstifled.

'Sure,' Nigel said. 'Fine little colt. Just his foreleg's doubled over . . .'

He knelt beside the foal who was already making the first feeble efforts to move his head, and he stretched out both hands gently to free the bent leg fully from the membrane, and to straighten it. He picked it up . . . and froze.

We could all see.

The leg wasn't bent. It ended in a stump at the knee. No cannon bone, no fetlock, no hoof.

Ginnie beside me gave a choking sob and turned abruptly towards the open door, towards the dark. She took one rocky pace and then another, and then was running: running nowhere, running away from the present, the future, the unimaginable. From the hopeless little creature on the straw.

I went after her, listening to her footsteps, hearing them on gravel and then losing them, guessing she had reached the grass. I went more slowly in her wake down the path to the breeding pen, not seeing her, but sure she was out somewhere in the paths round the paddocks. With eyes slowly acclimatizing I went that way and found her not far off, on her knees beside one of the posts, sobbing with the deep sound of a wholly adult desperation.

'Ginnie,' I said.

She stood up as if to turn to me was natural and clung to me fiercely, her body shaking from the sobs, her face pressed hard against my shoulder, my arms

267

tightly round her. We stood like that until the paroxysm passed; until, dragging a handkerchief from her jeans, she could speak.

'It's one thing knowing it in theory,' she said, her voice full of tears and her body still shaking spasmodically from aftersobs. 'I read those letters. I did know. But *seeing* it . . . that's different.'

'Yes,' I said.

'And it means . . .' She took gulps of air, trying hard for control. 'It means, doesn't it, that we'll lose our farm. Lose everything?'

'I don't know yet. Too soon to say that.'

'Poor Dad.' The tears were sliding slowly down her cheeks, but like harmless rain after a hurricane. 'I don't see how we can bear it.'

'Don't despair yet. If there's a way to save you, we'll find it.'

'Do you mean . . . your bank?'

'I mean everybody.'

She wiped her eyes and blew her nose, and finally moved away a pace, out of my arms, strong enough to leave shelter. We went slowly back to the foaling yard and found nobody there except horses. I undid the closed top half of Plus Factor's box and looked inside; looked at the mare standing there patiently without her foal and wondered if she felt any fretting sense of loss.

'Dad and Nigel have taken him, haven't they?' Ginnie said.

'Yes.'

She nodded, accepting that bit easily. Death to her was part of life, as to every child brought up close to animals. I closed Plus Factor's door and Ginnie and I went back to the house while the sky lightened in the east to the new day, Sunday.

The work of the place went on.

Oliver telephoned to various owners of the mares who had come to the other three stallions, reporting the birth of foals alive and well and one dead before foaling, very sorry. His voice sounded strong, civilized, controlled, the competent captain at the helm, and one could almost see the steel creeping back, hour by hour, into his battered spirit. I admired him for it; and I would fight to give him time, I thought, to come to some compromise to avert permanent ruin.

Ginnie, showered, breakfasted, tidy in sweater and shirt, went off to spend the morning at the Watcherleys' and came back smiling; the resilience of youth.

'Both of those mares are better from their infections,' she reported, 'and Maggie says she's heard Calder Jackson's not doing so well lately, his yard's half empty. Cheers Maggie up no end, she says.'

For the Watcherleys too, I thought briefly, the fall of Oliver's business could mean a return to rust and weeds, but I said, 'Not enough sick horses just now, perhaps.'

'Not enough sick horses with rich owners, Maggie says.'

In the afternoon Ginnie slept on the sofa looking very childlike and peaceful, and only with the awakening did the night's pain roll back.

'Oh dear . . .' The slow tears came. 'I was dreaming it was all right. That that foal was a dream, only a dream . . .'

'You and your father,' I said, 'are brave people.'

She sniffed a little, pressing against her nose with the back of her hand. 'Do you mean,' she said slowly, 'that whatever happens, we mustn't be defeated?'

'Mm.'

She looked at me, and after a while nodded. 'If we have to, we'll start again. We'll work. He did it all before, you know.'

'You both have the skills,' I said.

'I'm glad you came.' She brushed the drying tears from her cheeks. 'God knows what it would have been like without you.'

I went with her out into the yards for evening stables, where the muck-carrying and feeding went on as always. Ginnie fetched the usual pocketful of carrots from the feed room and gave them here and there to the mares, talking cheerfully to the lads while they bent to their chores. No one, watching and listening, could ever have imagined that she feared the sky was falling.

'Evening, Chris, how's her hoof today?'

'Hi, Danny. Did you bring this one in this morning?'

'Hello, Pete. She looks as if she'll foal any day now.'

'Evening, Shane. How's she doing?'

'Hi, Sammy, is she eating now OK?'

The lads answered her much as they spoke to Oliver himself, straightforwardly and with respect, and in most cases without stopping what they were doing. I looked back as we left the first big yard for the second, and for a moment took one of the lads to be Ricky Barnet.

'Who's that?' I said to Ginnie.

She followed my gaze to where the lad walked across to the yard tap, swinging an empty bucket with one hand and eating an apple with the other.

'Shane. Why?'

'He reminded me of someone I knew.'

She shrugged. 'He's all right. They all are, when Nigel's looking, which he doesn't do often enough.'

'He works all night,' I said mildly.

'I suppose so.'

The mares in the second yard had mostly given birth already and Ginnie that evening had special eyes for the foals. The lads hadn't yet reached those boxes and Ginnie didn't go into any of them, warning me that mares with young foals could be protective and snappy.

'You never know if they'll bite or kick you. Dad doesn't like me going in with them alone.' She smiled. 'He still thinks I'm a baby.'

We went on to the foaling yard, where a lad greeted as Dave was installing a heavy slow-walking mare into one of the boxes.

'Nigel says she'll foal tonight,' he told Ginnie.

'He's usually right.'

We went on past the breeding pen and came to the stallions, where Larry and Ron were washing down Diarist (who appeared to have been working) in the centre of the yard, using a lot of water, energy and oaths.

'Mind his feet,' Larry said. 'He's in one of his moods.'

Ginnie gave carrots to Parakeet and Rotaboy, and we came finally to Sandcastle. He looked as great, as charismatic as ever, but Ginnie gave him his tit-bit with her own lips compressed.

'He can't help it all, I suppose,' she said sighing. 'But I do wish he'd never won any races.'

'Or that we'd let him die that day on the main road?'

'Oh no!' She was shocked. 'We couldn't have done that, even if we'd known . . .'

Dear girl, I thought; many people would personally have mown him down with a truck.

We went back to the house via the paddocks, where she fondled any heads that came to the railings and parted with the last of the crunchy orange goodies. 'I can't believe that this will all end,' she said, looking over the horse-dotted acres. 'I just *can't* believe it.'

I tentatively suggested to both her and Oliver that they might prefer it if I went home that evening, but they both declared themselves against.

'Not yet,' Ginnie said anxiously and Oliver nodded forcefully. 'Please do stay, Tim, if you can.'

I nodded, and rang the Michaels, and this time got Judith.

'Do let me speak to her,' Ginnie said, taking the receiver out of my hand. 'I do so want to.'

And I, I thought wryly, I too want so much to talk to her, to hear her voice, to renew my own soul through her: I'm no one's universal pillar of strength, I need my comfort too.

I had my crumbs, after Ginnie. Ordinary words, all else implied; as always.

'Take care of yourself,' she said finally.

'You, too,' I said.

'Yes.' The word was a sigh, faint and receding, as if she'd said it with the receiver already away from her mouth. There was the click of disconnection, and Oliver was announcing briskly that it was time for whisky, time for supper; time for anything perhaps but thinking.

Ginnie decided that she felt too restless after supper to go to bed early, and would go for a walk instead.

'Do you want me to come?' I said.

'No. I'm all right. I just thought I'd go out. Look at the stars.' She kissed her father's forehead, pulling on a thick cardigan for warmth. 'I won't go off the farm. You'll probably find me in the foal yard, if you want me.'

He nodded to her fondly but absentmindedly, and with a small wave to me she went away. Oliver asked me gloomily, as if he'd been waiting for us to be alone, how soon I thought the bank would decide on his fate,

273

and we talked in snatches about his daunting prospects, an hour or two sliding by on possibilities.

Shortly before ten, when we had probably twice repeated all there was to say, there came a heavy hammering on the back door.

'Whoever's that?' Oliver frowned, rose to his feet and went to find out.

I didn't hear the opening words, but only the goose-pimpling urgency in the rising voice.

'She's where?' Oliver said loudly, plainly, in alarm. 'Where?'

I went quickly into the hallway. One of the lads stood in the open doorway, panting for breath, wide-eyed and looking very scared.

Oliver glanced at me over his shoulder, already on the move. 'He says Ginnie's lying on the ground unconscious.'

The lad turned and ran off, with Oliver following and myself close behind; and the lad's breathlessness, I soon found, was owing to Ginnie's being on the far side of the farm, away down beyond Nigel's bungalow and the lads' hostel, right down on the far drive, near the gate to the lower road.

We arrived there still running, the lad now doubling over in his fight for breath, and found Ginnie lying on her side on the hard asphalt surface with another of the lads on his knees beside her, dim figures in weak moonlight, blurred outlines of shadow.

Oliver and I too knelt there and Oliver was saying

to the lads, 'What happened, what happened? Did she fall?'

'We just found her,' the kneeling lad said. 'We were on our way back from the pub. She's coming round, though, sir, she's been saying things.'

Ginnie in fact moved slightly, and said, 'Dad.'

'Yes, Ginnie, I'm here.' He picked up her hand and patted it. 'We'll soon get you right.' There was relief in his voice, but short-lived.

'Dad,' Ginnie said, mumbling. 'Dad.'

'Yes, I'm here.'

'Dad . . .'

'She isn't hearing you,' I said worriedly.

He turned his head to me, his eyes liquid in the dark of his face. 'Get an ambulance. There's a telephone in Nigel's house. Tell him to get an ambulance here quickly. I don't think we'll move her . . . Get a blanket.'

I stood up to go on the errand but the breathless lad said, 'Nigel's out. I tried there. There's no one. It's all locked.'

'I'll go back to the house.'

I ran as fast on the way back and had to fight to control my own gulping breaths there to make my words intelligible. 'Tell them to take the lower road from the village . . . the smaller right fork . . . where the road divides. Nearly a mile from there . . . wide metal farm gate, on the left.'

'Understood,' a man said impersonally. 'They'll be on their way.'

I fetched the padded quilt off my bed and ran back across the farm and found everything much as I'd left it. 'They're coming,' I said. 'How is she?'

Oliver tucked the quilt round his daughter as best he could. 'She keeps saying things. Just sounds, not words.'

'Da—' Ginnie said.

Her eyelids trembled and slightly opened.

'Ginnie,' Oliver said urgently. 'This is Dad.'

Her lips moved in a mumbling unformed murmur. The eyes looked at nothing, unfocused, the gleam just reflected moonlight, not an awakening.

'Oh God,' Oliver said. 'What's happened to her? What can have happened?'

The two lads stood there, awkward and silent, not knowing the answer.

'Go and open the gate,' Oliver told them. 'Stand on the road. Signal to the ambulance when it comes.'

They went as if relieved; and the ambulance did come, lights flashing, with two brisk men in uniform who lifted Ginnie without much disturbing her onto a stretcher. Oliver asked them to wait while he fetched the Land Rover from Nigel's garage, and in a short time the ambulance set off to the hospital with Oliver and me following.

'Lucky you had the key,' I said, indicating it in the ignition. Just something to say: anything.

'We always keep it in that tin on the shelf.'

The tin said 'Blackcurrant Coughdrops. Take as Required'.

Oliver drove automatically, following the rear lights ahead. 'Why don't they go faster?' he said, though their speed was quite normal.

'Don't want to jolt her, perhaps.'

'Do you think it's a stroke?' he said.

'She's too young.'

'No. I had a cousin ... an aneurysm burst when he was sixteen.'

I glanced at his face: lined, grim, intent on the road.

The journey seemed endless, but ended at a huge bright hospital in a sprawling town. The men in uniform opened the rear doors of the ambulance while Oliver parked the Land Rover and we followed them into the brightly lit emergency reception area, seeing them wheel Ginnie into a curtained cubicle, watching them come out again with their stretcher, thanking them as they left.

A nurse told us to sit on some nearby chairs while she fetched a doctor. The place was empty, quiet, all readiness but no bustle. Ten o'clock on Sunday night.

A doctor came in a white coat, stethoscope dangling. An Indian, young, black-haired, rubbing his eyes with forefinger and thumb. He went behind the curtains with the nurse and for about a minute Oliver clasped and unclasped his fingers, unable to contain his anxiety.

The doctor's voice reached us clearly, the Indian accent making no difference.

'They shouldn't have brought her here,' he said. 'She's dead.'

Oliver was on his feet, bounding across the shining floor, pulling back the curtains with a frantic sweep of the arm.

'She's not dead. She was talking. Moving. She's not dead.'

In dread I followed him. She couldn't be dead, not like that, not so fast, not without the hospital fighting long to save her. She *couldn't* be.

The doctor straightened up from bending over her, withdrawing his hand from under Ginnie's head, looking at us across the small space.

'She's my daughter,' Oliver said. 'She's not dead.'

A sort of weary compassion drooped in the doctor's shoulders. 'I am sorry,' he said. 'Very sorry. She is gone.'

'No!' The word burst out of Oliver in an agony. 'You're wrong. Get someone else.'

The nurse made a shocked gesture but the young doctor said gently, 'There is no pulse. No heartbeat. No contraction of the pupils. She has been gone for perhaps ten minutes, perhaps twenty. I could get someone else, but there is nothing to be done.'

'But *why*?' Oliver said. 'She was talking.'

The dark doctor looked down to where Ginnie was lying on her back, eyes closed, brown hair falling about her head, face very pale. Her jerseys had both been unbuttoned for the stethoscope, the white bra showing, and the nurse had also undone the waistband of the skirt, pulling it loose. Ginnie looked very young, very defenceless, lying there so quiet and still, and I stood numbly, not believing it, unable, like Oliver, to accept such a monstrous change.

'Her skull is fractured,' the doctor said. 'If she was talking, she died on the way here, in the ambulance. With head injuries it can be like that. I am sorry.'

There was a sound of an ambulance's siren wailing outside, and sudden noise and rushing people by the doors where we had come in, voices raised in a jumble of instructions.

'Traffic accident,' someone shouted, and the doctor's eyes moved beyond us to the new need, to the future, not the past.

'I must go,' he said, and the nurse, nodding, handed me a flat white plastic bottle which she had been holding.

'You may as well take this,' she said. 'It was tucked into the waistband of her skirt, against the stomach.'

She made as if to cover Ginnie with a sheet, but Oliver stopped her.

'I'll do it,' he said. 'I want to be with her.'

The young doctor nodded, and he and I and the nurse stepped outside the cubicle, drawing the curtains behind us. The doctor looked in a brief pause of still-ness towards the three or four stretchers arriving at the entrance, taking a breath, seeming to summon up energy from deep reserves.

'I've been on duty for thirty hours,' he said to me. 'And now the pubs are out. Ten o'clock, Sundays. Drunk drivers, drunk pedestrians. Always the same.'

He walked away to his alive and bleeding patients and the nurse pinned a 'Do Not Enter' sign onto the curtains of Ginnie's cubicle, saying she would be taken care of later.

I sat drearily on a chair, waiting for Oliver. The white plastic bottle had a label stuck onto one side saying 'Shampoo'. I put it into my jacket pocket and wondered if it was just through overwork that the doctor hadn't asked how Ginnie's skull had been fractured, asked whether she'd fallen onto a rock or a kerb ... or been hit.

The rest of the night and all the next day were in their own way worse, a truly awful series of questions, answers, forms and officialdom, with the police slowly taking over from the hospital and Oliver trying to fight against a haze of grief.

It seemed to me wicked that no one would leave him alone. To them he was just one more in a long line of bereaved persons, and although they treated him with perfunctory sympathy, it was for their own paperwork and not for his benefit that they wanted signature, information and guesses.

Large numbers of policemen descended on the farm early in the morning, and it gradually appeared that that area of the country was being plagued by a stalker of young girls who jumped out of bushes, knocked them unconscious and sexually assaulted them.

'Not Ginnie . . .' Oliver protested in deepening horror.

The most senior of the policemen shook his head. 'It would appear not. She was still wearing her clothing. We can't discount, though, that it was the same man, and that he was disturbed by your grooms. When young girls are knocked unconscious at night, it's most often a sexual attack.'

'But she was on my own land,' he said, disbelieving.

The policeman shrugged. 'It's been known in suburban front gardens.'

He was a fair-haired man with a manner that was not exactly brutal but spoke of long years of acclimatization to dreadful experiences. Detective Chief Inspector Wyfold, he'd said, introducing himself. Forty-fiveish, I guessed, sensing the hardness within him at sight and judging him through that day more dogged than intuitive, looking for results from procedure, not hunches.

He was certain in his own mind that the attack on Ginnie had been sexual in intent and he scarcely considered anything else, particularly since she'd been carrying no money and had expressly said she wouldn't leave the farm.

'She could have talked to someone over the gate,' he said, having himself spent some time on the lower drive. 'Someone walking along the road. And there are all your grooms that we'll need detailed statements from, though from their preliminary answers it seems they weren't in the hostel but down at the village, in the pubs.'

He came and went and reappeared again with more questions at intervals through the day and I lost track altogether of the hours. I tried, in his presence and out, and in Oliver's the same, not to think much about Ginnie herself. I thought I would probably have wept if I had, of no use to anyone. I thrust her away into a defensive compartment knowing that later, alone, I would let her out.

Some time in the morning one of the lads came to the house and asked what they should do about one of the mares who was having difficulty foaling, and Lenny also arrived wanting to know when he should take Rotaboy to the breeding pen. Each of them stood awkwardly, not knowing where to put their hands, saying they were so shocked, so sorry, about Ginnie.

'Where's Nigel?' Oliver said.

They hadn't seen him, they said. He hadn't been out in the yards that morning.

'Didn't you try his house?' Oliver was annoyed rather than alarmed: another burden on a breaking back.

'He isn't there. The door's locked and he didn't answer.'

Oliver frowned, picked up the telephone and pressed the buttons: listened; no reply.

He said to me, 'There's a key to his bungalow over there on the board, third hook from the left. Would you go and look ... would you mind?'

'Sure.'

I walked down there with Lenny who told me repeatedly how broken up the lads were over what had happened, particularly Dave and Sammy, who'd found her. They'd all liked her, he said. All the lads who lived in the hostel were saying that perhaps if they'd come back sooner, she wouldn't have been attacked.

'You don't live in the hostel, then?' I said.

'No. Down in the village. Got a house. Only the ones who come just for the season, they're the ones in the hostel. It's shut up, see, all winter.'

We eventually reached Nigel's bungalow where I rang the doorbell and banged on the knocker without result. Shaking my head slightly I fitted the key in the lock, opened the door, went in.

Curtains were drawn across the windows, shutting out a good deal of daylight. I switched on a couple of lights and walked into the sitting room, where papers, clothes and dirty cups and plates were strewn haphazardly and the air smelled faintly of horse.

There was no sign of Nigel. I looked into the equally untidy kitchen and opened a door which proved to be that of a bathroom and another which revealed a room with bare-mattressed twin beds. The last door in the small inner hall led into Nigel's own bedroom . . . and there he was, face down, fully clothed, lying across the counterpane.

Lenny, still behind me, took two paces back.

I went over to the bed and felt Nigel's neck behind the ear. Felt the pulse going like a steam-hammer. Heard the rasp of air in the throat. His breath would have an anaesthetized a crocodile, and on the floor beside him lay an empty bottle of gin. I shook his shoulder unsympathetically with a complete lack of result.

'He's drunk,' I said to Lenny. 'Just drunk.'

Lenny looked all the same as if he was about to vomit. 'I thought . . . I thought.'

'I know,' I said; and I'd feared it also, instinctively, the one because of the other.

'What will we do, then, out in the yard?' Lenny asked.

'I'll find out.'

We went back into the sitting room where I used Nigel's telephone to call Oliver and report.

'He's flat out,' I said. 'I can't wake him. Lenny wants instructions.'

After a brief silence Oliver said dully, 'Tell him to take Rotaboy to the breeding shed in half an hour. I'll see to things in the yards. And Tim?'

'Yes?'

284

'Can I ask you ... would you mind ... helping me here in the office?'

'Coming straight back.'

The disjointed, terrible day wore on. I telephoned to Gordon in the bank explaining my absence and to Judith also, at Gordon's suggestion, to pass on the heartbreak, and I took countless incoming messages as the news spread. Outside on the farm nearly two hundred horses got fed and watered, and birth and procreation went inexorably on.

Oliver came back stumbling from fatigue at about two o'clock, and we ate some eggs, not tasting them, in the kitchen. He looked repeatedly at his watch and said finally, 'What's eight hours back from now? I can't even *think*.'

'Six in the morning,' I said.

'Oh.' He rubbed a hand over his face. 'I suppose I should have told Ginnie's mother last night.' His face twisted. 'My wife ... in Canada ...' He swallowed. 'Never mind, let her sleep. In two hours I'll tell her.'

I left him alone to that wretched task and took myself upstairs to wash and shave and lie for a while on the bed. It was in taking my jacket off for those purposes that I came across the plastic bottle in my pocket, and I took it out and stood it on the shelf in the bathroom while I shaved.

An odd sort of thing, I thought, for Ginnie to have tucked into her waistband. A plastic bottle of shampoo; about six inches high, four across, one deep, with a screw cap on one of the narrow ends. The white label saying 'Shampoo' had been handwritten and stuck on top of the bottle's original dark brown, white-printed label, of which quite a bit still showed round the edges.

'*Instructions*,' part of the underneath label said. '*Shake well. Be careful not to get the shampoo in the dog's eyes. Rub well into the coat and leave for ten or fifteen minutes before rinsing.*'

At the bottom, below the stuck-on label, were the words, in much smaller print, '*Manufactured by Eagle Inc., Michigan, U.S.A. List number 29931.*'

When I'd finished shaving I unscrewed the cap and tilted the bottle gently over the basin.

A thick greenish liquid appeared, smelling powerfully of soap.

Shampoo: what else?

The bottle was to all intents full. I screwed on the cap again and put it on the shelf, and thought about it while I lay on the bed with my hands behind my head.

Shampoo for dogs.

After a while I got up and went down to the kitchen, and in a high cupboard found a small collection of empty, washed, screw-top glass jars, the sort of thing my mother had always saved for herbs and picnics. I took one which would hold perhaps a cupful of liquid and returned upstairs, and over the washbasin I shook the bottle well, unscrewed the cap and carefully poured more than half of the shampoo into the jar.

I screwed the caps onto both the bottle and the

jar, copied what could be seen on the original label into the small engagement diary I carried with me everywhere, and stowed the now half full, round glass container from Oliver's kitchen inside my own sponge-bag; and when I went downstairs again I took the plastic bottle with me.

'Ginnie had it?' Oliver said dully, picking it up and squinting at it. 'Whatever for?'

'The nurse at the hospital said it was tucked into the waistband of her skirt.'

A smile flickered. 'She always did that when she was little. Plimsolls, books, bits of string, anything. To keep her hands free, she said. They all used to slip down into her little knickers, and there would be a whole shower of things sometimes when we undressed her.' His face went hopelessly bleak at this memory. 'I can't believe it, you know,' he said. 'I keep thinking she'll walk through the door.' He paused. 'My wife is flying over. She says she'll be here tomorrow morning.' His voice gave no indication as to whether that was good news or bad. 'Stay tonight, will you?'

'If you want.'

'Yes.'

Chief Inspector Wyfold turned up again at that point and we gave him the shampoo bottle, Oliver explaining about Ginnie's habit of carrying things in her clothes.

'Why didn't you give this to me earlier?' he asked me.

'I forgot I had it. It seemed so paltry at the time, compared with Ginnie dying.'

The Chief Inspector picked up the bottle by its serrated cap and read what one could see of the label, and to Oliver he said, 'Do you have a dog?'

'Yes.'

'Would this be what you usually use, to wash him?'

'I really don't know. I don't wash him myself. One of the lads does.'

'The lads being the grooms?'

'That's right.'

'Which lad washed your dog?' Wyfold asked.

'Um . . . any. Whoever I ask.'

The Chief Inspector produced a thin white folded paper bag from one of his pockets and put the bottle inside it. 'Who to your knowledge has handled this, besides yourselves?' he asked.

'I suppose,' I said, 'the nurse at the hospital . . . and Ginnie.'

'And it spent from last night until now in your pocket?' He shrugged. 'Hopeless for prints, I should think, but we'll try.' He fastened the bag shut and wrote on a section of it with a ball pen. To Oliver, almost as an aside, he said, 'I came to ask you about your daughter's relationship with men.'

Oliver said wearily, 'She didn't have any. She's only just left school.'

Wyfold made small negative movements with head

and hands as if amazed at the naivety of fathers. 'No sexual relationship to your knowledge?'

Oliver was too exhausted for anger. 'No,' he said.

'And you sir?' He turned to me. 'What were your relations with Virginia Knowles?'

'Friendship.'

'Including sexual intercourse?'

'No.'

Wyfold looked at Oliver who said tiredly, 'Tim is a business friend of mine. A financial adviser, staying here for the weekend, that's all.'

The policeman frowned at me with disillusion as if he didn't believe it. I gave him no amplified answer because I simply couldn't be bothered, and what could I have said? That with much affection I'd watched a child grow into an attractive young woman and yet not wanted to sleep with her? His mind ran on carnal rails, all else discounted.

He went away in the end taking the shampoo with him, and Oliver with immense fortitude said he had better go out into the yards to catch the tail end of evening stables. 'Those mares,' he said. 'Those foals . . . they still need the best of care.'

'I wish I could help,' I said, feeling useless.

'You do.'

I went with him on his rounds, and when we reached the foaling yard, Nigel, resurrected, was there.

His stocky figure leaned against the doorpost of an open box as if without its support he would collapse, and the face he slowly turned towards us had aged ten years. The bushy eyebrows stood out starkly over charcoal shadowed eyes, puffiness in his skin swelling the eyelids and sagging in deep bags on his cheeks. He was also unshaven, unkempt and feeling ill.

'Sorry,' he said. 'Heard about Ginnie. Very sorry.' I wasn't sure whether he was sympathizing with Oliver or apologizing for the drunkenness. 'A big noise of a policeman came asking if I'd killed her. As if I would.' He put a shaky hand on his head, almost as if physically to support it on his shoulders. 'I feel rotten. My own fault. Deserve it. This mare's likely to foal tonight. That shit of a policeman wanted to know if I was sleeping with Ginnie. Thought I'd tell you . . . I wasn't.'

Wyfold, I reflected, would ask each of the lads individually the same question. A matter of time, perhaps, before he asked Oliver himself; though Oliver and I, he had had to concede, gave each other a rock-solid alibi.

We walked on towards the stallions and I asked Oliver if Nigel often got drunk, since Oliver hadn't shown much surprise.

'Very seldom,' Oliver said. 'He's once or twice turned out in that state but we've never lost a foal because of it. I don't like it, but he's so good with the mares.' He shrugged. 'I overlook it.'

He gave carrots to all four stallions but scarcely glanced at Sandcastle, as if he could no longer bear the sight.

'I'll try the Research people tomorrow,' he said. 'Forgot about it, today.'

From the stallions he went, unusually, in the direction of the lower gate, past Nigel's bungalow and the hostel, to stand for a while at the place where Ginnie had lain in the dark on the night before.

The asphalt driveway showed no mark. Oliver looked to where the closed gate sixty feet away led to the road and in a drained voice said, 'Do you think she could have talked to someone out there?'

'She might have, I suppose.'

'Yes.' He turned to go back. 'It's all so *senseless*. And unreal. Nothing feels real.'

Exhaustion of mind and body finally overtook him after dinner and he went grey-faced to bed, but I in the first quiet of the long day went out again for restoration: for a look at the stars, as Ginnie had said.

Thinking only of her I walked slowly along some of the paths between the paddocks, the way lit by a half-moon with small clouds drifting, and stopped eventually at the place where on the previous morning I'd held her tight in her racking distress. The birth of the deformed foal seemed so long ago, yet it was only yesterday: the morning of the last day of Ginnie's life.

I thought about that day, about the despair in its dawn and the resolution of its afternoon. I thought of her tears and her courage, and of the waste of so much goodness. The engulfing, stupefying sense of loss which had hovered all day swamped into my brain until my body felt inadequate, as if it wanted to burst, as if it couldn't hold in so much feeling.

When Ian Pargetter had been murdered I had been angry on his behalf and had supposed that the more one loved the dead person the greater one's fury against the killer. But now I understood that anger could simply be crowded out by something altogther more over-whelming. As for Oliver, he had displayed shock, daze, desolation and disbelief in endless quantities all day, but of anger, barely a flicker.

It was too soon to care who had killed her. The fact of her death was too much. Anger was irrelevant, and no vengeance could give her life.

I had loved her more than I'd known, but not as I loved Judith, not with desire and pain and longing. I'd loved Ginnie as a friend; as a brother. I'd loved her, I thought, right back from the day when I'd returned her to school and listened to her fears. I'd loved her up on the hill, trying to catch Sandcastle, and I'd loved her for her expertise and for her growing adult certainty that here, in these fields, was where her future lay.

I'd thought of her young life once as being a clear stretch of sand waiting for footprints, and now there would be none, now only a blank, chopping end to all she could have been and done, to all the bright love she had scattered around her.

'Oh . . . *Ginnie*,' I said aloud, calling to her hopelessly

in   tearing   body-shaking   grief.   'Ginnie ... little
Ginnie ... come back.'

But she was gone from there. My voice fled away
into darkness, and there was no answer.

MAY

On and off for the next two weeks I worked on Oliver's financial chaos at my desk in the bank, and at a special board meeting argued the case for giving him time before we foreclosed and made him sell all he had.

I asked for three months, which was considered scandalously out of the question, but got him two, Gordon chuckling over it quietly as we went down together afterwards in the lift.

'I suppose two months was what you wanted?' he said.

'Er . . . yes.'

'I know you,' he said. 'They were talking of twenty-one days maximum before the meeting, and some wanted to bring in liquidators at once.'

I telephoned Oliver and told him. 'For two months you don't have to pay any interest or capital repayments, but this is only temporary, and it is a special, fairly unusual concession. I'm afraid, though, that if we can't find a solution to Sandcastle's problem or come up with a cast-iron reason for the insurance company to pay out, the prognosis is not good.'

'I understand,' he said, his voice sounding calm. 'I haven't much hope, but thank you, all the same, for the respite – I will at least be able to finish the programmes for the other stallions, and keep all the foals here until they're old enough to travel safely.'

'Have you heard anything about Sandcastle?'

'He's been at the Research Establishment for a week, but so far they can't find anything wrong with him. They don't hold out much hope, I'd better tell you, of being able to prove anything one way or another about his sperm, even though they're sending specimens to another laboratory, they say.'

'They'll do their best.'

'Yes, I know. But . . . I walk around here as if this place no longer belongs to me. As if it isn't mine. I know, inside, that I'm losing it. Don't feel too badly, Tim. When it comes, I'll be prepared.'

I put the receiver down not knowing whether such resignation was good because he would face whatever came without disintegration, or bad because he might be surrendering too soon. A great host of other troubles still lay ahead, mostly in the shape of breeders demanding the return of their stallion fees, and he needed energy to say that in most cases he couldn't return them. The money had already been lodged with us, and the whole situation would have to be sorted out by lawyers.

The news of Sandcastle's disgrace was so far only a

doubtful murmur here and there, but when it broke open with a screech it was, I suppose predictably, in *What's Going On Where It Shouldn't.*

The bank's six copies were read to rags before lunch on the day Alec fetched them, eyes lifting from the page with anything from fury to a wry smile.

Three short paragraphs headed 'House on Sand' said:

Build not your house on sand. Stake not your banking house on a Sandcastle.

The five million pounds advanced by a certain prestigious merchant bank for the purchase of the stallion Sandcastle now look like being washed away by the tide. Sadly, the investment has produced faulty stock, or in plain language, several deformed foals.

Speculation now abounds as to what the bank can do to minimize its losses, since Sandcastle himself must be considered as half a ton of highly priced dog-meat.

'That's done it,' Gordon said, and I nodded; and the dailies, who always read *What's Going On* . . . as a prime news source, came up in the racing columns the next day with a more cautious approach, asking 'Sandcastle's Progeny Flawed?' and saying things like 'rumours have reached us' and 'we are reliably informed.'

Since our own home-grown leaker for once hadn't mentioned the bank by name, none of the dailies did either, and for them of course the bank itself was unimportant compared with the implications of the news.

Oliver, in the next weekday issues, was reported as having been asked how many, precisely, of Sandcastle's foals were deformed, and as having answered that he didn't know. He had heard of some, certainly, yes. He had no further comment.

A day later still the papers began printing reports telephoned into them by the stud farms where Sandcastle's scattered progeny had been foaled, and the tally of disasters mounted. Oliver was reported this time as having said the horse was at the Equine Research Establishment at Newmarket, and everything possible was being done.

'It's a mess,' Henry said gloomily at lunch, and even the dissenting director had run out of insults, beyond saying four times that we were the laughing-stock of the City and it was all my fault.

'Have they found out who killed Knowles' daughter?' Val Fisher asked.

'No.' I shook my head. 'He says the police no longer come to the house.'

Val looked regretful. 'Such a sadness for him, on top of the other.'

There were murmurs of sympathy and I didn't think I'd spoil it by telling them what the police thought of Oliver's lads.

'That man Wyfold,' Oliver had said on the telephone during one of our almost daily conversations, 'he more or less said I was asking for trouble, having a young girl on the place with all those lads. What's more, it seems many of them were halfway drunk that night, and with three pubs in the village they weren't even all together and have no idea of who was where at what time, so one of Wyfold's theories is that one of them jumped her and Dave and Sammy interrupted him. Alternatively Nigel did it. Alternatively some stranger walking down the road did it. Wyfold's manner is downright abrasive but I'm past caring. He despises my discipline. He says I shouldn't let my lads get drunk – as if anyone could stop them. They're free men. It's their business, not mine, what they do with their money and time on Sunday nights. I can only take action if they don't turn up on Monday morning. And as for Nigel being paralytic!' Words momentarily failed him. 'How can Nigel possibly expect the lads to stay more or less sober if he gets like that? And he says he can't remember anything that happened the night Ginnie died. Nothing at all. Total, alcoholic black-out. He's been very subdued since.'

The directors, I felt, would not be any more impressed than the Detective Chief Inspector with the general level of insobriety, and I wondered whether Nigel's slackness with the lads in general had always stemmed from a knowledge of his own occasional weakness.

The police had found no weapon, Oliver said on another day. Wyfold had told him that there was no way of knowing what had been used to cause the depressed fracture at the base of her brain. Her hair over the fracture bore no traces of anything unexpected. The forensic surgeon was of the opinion that there had been a single very heavy blow. She would have been knocked unconscious instantly. She wouldn't even have known. The period of apparent semi-consciousness had been illusory: parts of her brain would have functioned but she would not have been aware of anything at all.

'I suppose it's a mercy,' Oliver said. 'With some girls you hear of . . . How do their parents bear it?'

His wife, he said, had gone back to Canada. Ginnie's death seemed not to have brought mother and father together, but to have made the separation complete.

'The dog shampoo?' Oliver repeated, when I asked. 'Wyfold says that's just what it was, they checked it. He asked Nigel and all the lads if it was theirs, if they'd used it for washing Squibs, but none of them had. He seems to think Ginnie may have seen it lying in the road and picked it up, or that she got into conversation over the gate with a man who gave her the shampoo for Squibs as a come-on and then killed her afterwards.'

'No,' I said.

'Why not?'

'Because he'd have taken the shampoo away again with him.'

'Wyfold says not if he couldn't find it, because of its

299

being dark and her having hidden it to all intents and purposes under her skirt and two jumpers, and not if Dave and Sammy arrived at that point.'

'I suppose it's possible,' I said doubtfully.

'Wyfold says that particular shampoo isn't on sale at all in England, it's American, and there's absolutely no way at all of tracing how it got here. There weren't any fingerprints of any use; all a blur except a few of yours and mine.'

Another day he said, 'Wyfold told me the hardest murders to solve were single blows on the head. He said the case would remain open, but they are busy again with another girl who was killed walking home from a dance, and this time she definitely is one of that dreadful series, poor child ... I was lucky, Tim, you know, that Dave and Sammy came back when they did.'

There came a fine May day in the office when Alec, deciding we needed some fresh air, opened one of the windows which looked down to the fountain. The fresh air duly entered but like a lion, not a lamb, and blew papers off all the desks.

'That's a hurricane,' I said. 'For God's sake shut it.'

Alec closed off the gale and turned round with a grin. 'Sorry and all that,' he said.

We all left our chairs and bent down like gleaners to retrieve our scattered work, and during my search for page 3 of a long assessment of a proposed sports complex I came across a severe and unwelcome shock in the shape of a small pale blue sheet off a memo pad.

There were words pencilled on it and crossed out with a wavy line, with other words underneath.

Build your castle not on Sand was crossed out, and so was *Sandcastle gone with the tide*, and underneath was written *Build not your house on Sand. Build not your banking house on a Sandcastle.*

'What's that?' Alec said quickly, seeing it in my hand and stretching out his own. 'Let's see.'

I shook my head and kept it in my own hand while I finished picking up the sportsdrome, and when order was restored throughout the office I said, 'Come along to the interview room.'

'Right now?'

'Right now.'

We went into the only room on our floor where any real privacy was possible and I said without shilly-shallying, 'This is your handwriting. Did you write the article in *What's Going On . . .*?'

He gave me a theatrical sigh and a tentative smile and a large shrug of the shoulders.

'That's just doodling,' he said. 'It means nothing.'

'It means, for a start,' I said, 'that you shouldn't have left it round the office.'

'Didn't know I had.'

'Did you write the article?'

301

The blue eyes unrepentantly gleamed at me from behind the gold rims. 'It's a fair cop, I suppose.'

'But *Alec* . . .' I protested.

'Yeah.'

'And the others,' I said, 'those other leaks, was that you?'

He sighed again, his mouth twisting.

'Was it?' I repeated, wanting above all things to hear him deny it.

'Look,' he said, 'what harm did it do? Yes, all right, the stories did come from me. I wrote them myself, actually, like that one.' He pointed to the memo paper in my hand. 'And don't give me any lectures on disloyalty because none of them did us any harm. Did us good, if anything.'

'Alec . . .'

'Yes,' he said, 'but just think, Tim, what did those pieces really do? They stirred everyone up, sure, and it was a laugh a minute to see all their faces, but what else? I've been thinking about it, I assure you. It wasn't why I did it in the first place, that was just wanting to stir things, I'll admit, but *because* of what I wrote we've now got much better security checks than we had before.'

I listened to him open-mouthed.

'All that work you did with the computer, making us safer against frauds, that was because of what I wrote. And the Corporate Finance boys, they now go around with their mouths zipped up like suitcases so as not to spill the beans to the investment managers. I did *good*, do you see, not harm.'

I stood and looked at him, at the tight tow-coloured curls, the cream-coloured freckled skin, the eyes that had laughed with me for eight years. I don't want to lose you, I thought: I wish you hadn't done it.

'And what about this piece about Sandcastle? What good has that done?' I said.

He half grinned. 'Too soon to say.'

I looked at the damaging scrap in my hands and almost automatically shook my head.

'You're going to say,' Alec said, 'that I'll have to leave.'

I looked up. His face was wholly calm.

'I knew I'd have to leave if any of you ever found out.'

'But don't you *care*?' I said frustratedly.

He smiled. 'I don't know. I'll miss *you*, and that's a fact. But as for the job ... well, I told you, it's not my whole life, like it is yours. I loved it, I grant you, when I came here. All I wanted was to be a merchant banker, it sounded great. But to be honest it was the glamour I suppose I wanted, and glamour never lasts once you've got used to something. I'm not a dedicated money-man at heart ... and there's honesty for you, I never thought I'd admit that, even to myself.'

'But you do it well.'

'Up to a point. We discussed all that.'

'I'm sorry,' I said helplessly.

303

'Yeah, well, so am I in a way, and in a way I'm not. I've been dithering for ages, and now that it isn't my choice I'm as much relieved as anything.'

'But . . . what will you do?'

He gave a full cherubic smile. 'I don't suppose you'll approve.'

'What, then?'

'*What's Going On . . .*,' he said, 'have offered me a whole-time job.' He looked at my shattered expression. 'I've written quite a bit for them, actually. About other things, of course, not us. But in most editions there's something of mine, a paragraph or two or a whole column. They've asked me several times to go, so now I will.'

I thought back to all those days when Alec had bounded out for the six copies and spent his next hour chuckling. Alec, the gatherer of news, who knew all the gossip.

'They get masses of information in,' Alec said, 'but they need someone to evaluate it all properly, and there aren't so many merchant bankers looking for that sort of job.'

'No,' I said drily. 'I can imagine. For a start, won't your salary be much less?'

'A bit,' he admitted, cheerfully. 'But my iconoclastic spirit will survive.'

I moved restlessly, wishing things had been different.

'I'll resign from here,' he said. 'Make it easier.'

Rather gloomily I nodded. 'And will you say why?'

He looked at me thoughtfully. 'If you really want me to, yes,' he said finally. 'Otherwise not. You can tell them yourself, though, after I've gone, if you want to.'

'You're a damned fool,' I said explosively, feeling the loss of him acutely. 'The office will be bloody dull without you.'

He grinned, my long-time colleague, and pointed to the piece of memo paper. 'I'll send you pin-pricks now and then. You won't forget me. Not a chance.'

Gordon, three days later, said to me in surprise, 'Alec's leaving, did you know?'

'I knew he was thinking of it.'

'But why? He's good at his job, and he always seemed happy here.'

I explained that Alec had been unsettled for some time and felt he needed to change direction.

'Amazing,' Gordon said. 'I tried to dissuade him, but he's adamant. He's going in four weeks.'

Alec, indeed, addressed his normal work with the bounce and zealousness of one about to be liberated, and for the rest of his stay in the office was better company than ever. Chains visibly dropped from his spirits, and I caught him several times scribbling speculatively on his memo pad with an anything but angelic grin.

Oliver had sent me at my request a list of all the breeders who had sent their mares to Sandcastle the previous year, and I spent two or three evenings on the telephone asking after those foals we didn't know about. Oliver himself, when I'd asked him, said he frankly couldn't face the task, and I didn't in the least blame him: my enquiries brought forth an ear-burning amount of blasphemy.

The final count came to:

Five foals born outwardly perfect but dead within two weeks because of internal abnormalities.
One foal born with one eye. (Put down.)
Five foals born with deformed legs, deformation varying from a malformed hoof to the absent half-leg of Plus Factor's colt. (All put down.)
Three foals born with part of one or both ears missing. (All still living.)
One foal born with no tail. (Still living.)
Two foals born with malformed mouths, the equivalent of human hare lip. (Both put down.)
One foal born with a grossly deformed head. (Foaled with heart-beat but couldn't breathe; died at once.)

Apart from this horrifying tally, four mares who had been sent home as in foal had subsequently 'slipped' and were barren; one mare had failed to conceive at all; three mares had not yet foaled (breeders' comments incendiary); and fourteen mares had produced live healthy foals with no defects of any sort.

I showed the list to Gordon and Henry, who went

shockedly silent for a while as if in mourning for the superb racer they had so admired.

'There may be more to come,' I said, not liking it. 'Oliver says thirty mares covered by Sandcastle this year are definitely in foal. Some of those will be all right . . . and some may not.'

'Isn't there a test you can do to see if a baby is abnormal?' Henry said. 'Can't they do that with the mares, and abort the deformed foals now, before they grow?'

I shook my head. 'I asked Oliver that. He says amniocentesis – that's what that process is called – isn't possible with mares. Something to do with not being able to reach the target with a sterile needle because of all the intestines in the way.'

Henry listened with the distaste of the non-medical to these clinical realities. 'What it means, I suppose,' he said, 'is that the owners of all of those thirty-one mares will have the foals aborted and demand their money back.'

'I'd think so, yes.'

He shook his head regretfully. 'So sad, isn't it? Such a shame. Quite apart from the financial loss, a tragedy in racing terms.'

Oliver said on the telephone one morning, 'Tim, I need to talk to you. Something's happened.'

'What?' I said, with misgivings.

307

'Someone has offered to buy Sandcastle.'

I sat in a mild state of shock, looking at Alec across the room sucking his pencil while he wrote his future.

'Are you there?' Oliver said.

'Yes. What for and for how much?'

'Well, he says to put back into training. I suppose it's possible. Sandcastle's only five. I suppose he could be got fit to race by August or September, and he might still win next year at six.'

'Good heavens.'

'He's offering twenty-five thousand pounds.'

'Um,' I said. 'Is that good or bad?'

'Realistically, it's as much as he's worth.'

'I'll consult with my seniors here,' I said. 'It's too soon, this minute, to say yes or no.'

'I did tell him that my bankers would have to agree, but he wants an answer fairly soon, because the longer the delay the less time there is for training and racing this season.'

'Yes,' I said, understanding. 'Where is he? Sandcastle, I mean.'

'Still in Newmarket. But it's pointless him staying there any longer. They haven't found any answers. They say they just don't know what's wrong with him, and I think they want me to take him away.'

'Well,' I pondered briefly. 'You may as well fetch him, I should think.'

'I'll arrange it,' he said.

'Before we go any further,' I said. 'Are you sure it's a bona fide offer and not just some crank?'

'I had a letter from him and I've talked to him on the telephone, and to me he sounds genuine,' Oliver answered. 'Would you like to meet him?'

'Perhaps, yes.'

We fixed a provisional date for the following Saturday morning, and almost as an afterthought I asked the potential buyer's name.

'Smith,' Oliver said. 'A Mr Dissdale Smith.'

I went to Hertfordshire on that Saturday with a whole host of question marks raising their eyebrows in my mind, but it was Dissdale, as it so happened, who had the deeper astonishment.

He drove up while I was still outside Oliver's house, still clasping hands in greeting and talking of Ginnie. Dissdale had come without Bettina, and the first thing he said, emerging from his car, was, 'Hello, Tim, what a surprise, didn't know you knew Oliver Knowles.'

He walked across, announced himself, shook hands with Oliver, and patted me chubbily on the shoulder. 'How's things, then? How are you doing, Tim?'

'Fine,' I said mildly.

Oliver looked from one of us to the other. 'You know each other already?'

Dissdale said, 'How do you mean, already?'

'Tim's my banker,' Oliver said in puzzlement. 'It

was his bank, Ekaterin's, which put up the money for Sandcastle.'

Dissdale stared at me in stunned amazement and looked bereft of speech.

'Didn't you know?' Oliver said. 'Didn't I mention it?'

Dissdale blankly shook his head and finally found his voice. 'You just said your banker was coming . . . I never for a moment thought . . .'

'It doesn't make much odds,' Oliver said. 'If you know each other it may simply save some time. Let's go indoors. There's some coffee ready.' He led the way through his immaculate house to the sitting room office, where a tray stood on the desk with coffee hot in a pot.

Oliver himself had had four weeks by then in that house without Ginnie, but to me, on my first visit back, she seemed still most sharply alive. It was I, this time, who kept expecting her to walk into the room; to give me a hug, to say hello with her eyes crinkling with welcome. I felt her presence vividly, to an extent that to start with I listened to Dissdale with only surface attention.

'It might be better to geld him,' he was saying. 'There are some good prizes, particularly overseas, for geldings.'

Oliver's instinctive response of horror subsided droopingly to defeat.

'It's too soon,' I said, 'to talk of that.'

'Tim, face facts,' Dissdale said expansively. 'At this moment in time that horse is a walking bomb. I'm making an offer for him because I'm a bit of a gambler, you know that, and I've a soft spot for him, whatever his faults, because of him winning so much for me that day the year before last, when we were all in my box at Ascot. You remember that, don't you?'

'I do indeed.'

'He saved my life, Sandcastle did.'

'It was partly because of that day,' I said, nodding, 'that Ekaterin's lent the money for him. When the request came in from Oliver, it was because Henry Shipton – our chairman, if you remember – and Gordon and I had all seen the horse in action that we seriously considered the proposition.'

Dissdale nodded his comprehension. 'A great surprise, though,' he said. 'I'm sorry it's you and Gordon. Sorry it's your bank, I mean, that's been hit so hard. I read about the deformed foals in the papers, of course, and that's what gave me the idea of buying Sandcastle in the first place, but it didn't say which bank . . .'

I wondered fleetingly if Alec could claim that omission as a virtue along with everything else.

Oliver offered Dissdale more coffee which he accepted with cream and sugar, drinking almost absent-mindedly while he worked through the possible alterations he would need in approach now he'd found he was dealing with semi-friends. Having had time myself over several days to do it, I could guess at the speed he was needing for reassessment.

'Dissdale,' I said neutrally, deciding to disrupt him, 'did the idea of buying Sandcastle come from your profitable caper with Indian Silk?'

His rounded features fell again into shock. 'How . . . er . . . did you know about that?'

I said vaguely, 'Heard it on the racecourse, I suppose. But didn't you buy Indian Silk for a pittance because he seemed to be dying, and then send him to Calder?'

'Well . . .'

'And didn't Calder cure him? And then you sold him again, but well this time, no doubt needing the money as don't we all, since when Indian Silk's won the Cheltenham Gold Cup? Isn't that right?'

Dissdale raised a plump hand palm upwards in a gesture of mock defeat. 'Don't know where you heard it, but yes, there's no secret, that's what happened.'

'Mm.' I smiled at him benignly. 'Calder said on television, didn't he, that buying Indian Silk was his idea originally, so I wondered . . . I'm wondering if this is his idea too. I mean, did he by any chance suggest a repeat of the gamble that came off so happily last time?'

Dissdale looked at me doubtfully.

'There's nothing wrong in it,' I said. 'Is it Calder's idea?'

'Well, yes,' he said, deciding to confide. 'But it's my money, of course.'

'And, um, if you do buy Sandcastle, will you send him too along to Calder, like Indian Silk?'

Dissdale seemed not to know whether to answer or not, but appearing to be reasssured by my friendly interest said finally, 'Calder said he could give him a quick pepping-up to get him fit quickly for racing, yes.'

Oliver, having listened restlessly up to this point, said, 'Calder Jackson can't do anything for Sandcastle that I can't.'

Both Dissdale and I looked at Oliver in the same way, hearing the orthodox view ringing out with conviction and knowing that it was very likely untrue.

'I've been thinking these past few days,' I said to Dissdale, 'first about Indian Silk. Didn't you tell Fred Barnet, when you offered him a rock-bottom price, that all you were doing was providing a dying horse with a nice quiet end in some gentle field?'

'Well, Tim,' he said knowingly. 'You know how it is. You buy for the best price you can. Fred Barnet, I know he goes round grousing that I cheated him, but I didn't, he could have sent his horse to Calder the same as I did.'

I nodded. 'So now, be honest, Dissdale, are you planning again to buy for the best price you can? I mean, does twenty-five thousand pounds for Sandcastle represent the same sort of bargain?'

'Tim,' Dissdale said, half affronted, half in sorrow, 'what a naughty suspicious mind. That's not friendly, not at all.'

I smiled. 'I don't think I'd be wise, though, do you, to recommend to my board of directors that we should accept your offer without thinking it over very carefully?'

For the first time there was a shade of dismay in the chubby face. 'Tim, it's a fair offer, anyone will tell you.'

'I think my board may invite other bids,' I said. 'If Sandcastle is to be sold, we must recoup the most we can.'

The dismay faded: man-of-the-world returned. 'That's fair,' he said. 'As long as you'll come back to me, if anyone tops me.'

'Sure,' I said. 'An auction, by telephone. When we're ready, I'll let you know.'

With a touch of anxiety he said, 'Don't wait too long. Time's money, you know.'

'I'll put your offer to the board tomorrow.'

He made a show of bluff contentment, but the anxiety was still there underneath. Oliver took the empty coffee cup which Dissdale still held and asked if he would like to see the horse he wanted to buy.

'But isn't he in Newmarket?' Dissdale said, again looking disconcerted.

'No, he's here. Came back yesterday.'

'Oh. Then yes, of course, yes, I'd like to see him.'

He's out of his depth, I thought abruptly: for some reason Dissdale is very very unsettled.

We went on the old familiar walk through the yards, with Oliver explaining the layout to the new visitor. To me there was now a visible thinning out of numbers, and Oliver, with hardly a quiver in his voice, said that he was sending the mares home with their foals in an orderly progression as usual, with in consequence lower feed bills, fewer lads to pay wages to, smaller expenses all round: he would play fair with the bank, he said, matter-of-factly, making sure to charge what he could and also to conserve what he could towards his debt. Dissdale gave him a glance of amused incredulity as if such a sense of honour belonged to a bygone age, and we came in the end to the stallion yard, where the four heads appeared in curiosity.

The stay in Newmarket hadn't done Sandcastle much good, I thought. He looked tired and dull, barely arching his neck to lift his nose over the half-door, and it was he, of the four, who turned away first and retreated into the gloom of his box.

'Is that Sandcastle?' Dissdale said, sounding disappointed. 'I expected something more, somehow.'

'He's had a taxing three weeks,' Oliver said. 'All he needs is some good food and fresh air.'

'And Calder's touch,' Dissdale said with conviction. 'That magic touch most of all.'

When Dissdale had driven away Oliver asked me what I thought, and I said, 'If Dissdale's offering twenty-five thousand he's certainly reckoning to make much more than that. He's right, he is a gambler, and I'll bet he has some scheme in mind. What we need to do is guess what the scheme is, and decide what we'll do on that basis, such as doubling or trebling the ante.'

Oliver was perplexed. 'How can we possibly guess?'

'Hm,' I said. 'Did you know about Indian Silk?'

'Not before today.'

'Well, suppose Dissdale acts to a pattern, which people so often do. He told Fred Barnet he was putting Indian Silk out to grass, which was diametrically untrue; he intended to send him to Calder and with luck put him back in training. He told *you* he was planning to put Sandcastle back into training, so suppose that's just what he *doesn't* plan to do. And he suggested gelding, didn't he?'

Oliver nodded.

'Then I'd expect gelding to be furthest from his mind,' I said. 'He just wants us to believe that's his intention.' I reflected 'Do you know what I might do if I wanted to have a real gamble with Sandcastle?'

'What?'

'It sounds pretty crazy,' I said. 'But with Calder's reputation it might just work.'

'What are you talking about?' Oliver said in some bewilderment. 'What gamble?'

'Suppose,' I said, 'that you could buy for a pittance a stallion whose perfect foals would be likely to win races.'

'But no one would risk . . .'

'Suppose,' I interrupted. 'There was nearly a fifty per cent chance, going on this year's figures, that you'd get a perfect foal. Suppose Dissdale offered Sandcastle as a sire at say a thousand pounds, the fee only payable if the foal was born perfect and lived a month.'

Oliver simply stared.

'Say Sandcastle's perfect progeny do win, as indeed they should. There are fourteen of them so far this year, don't forget. Say that in the passage of time his good foals proved to be worth the fifty per cent risk. Say Sandcastle stands in Calder's yard, with Calder's skill on the line. Isn't there a chance that over the years Dissdale's twenty-five thousand-pound investment would provide a nice steady return for them both?'

'It's impossible,' he said weakly.

'No, not impossible. A gamble.' I paused. 'You wouldn't get people sending the top mares, of course, but you might get enough dreamers among the breeders who'd chance it.'

'Tim . . .'

'Just think of it,' I said. 'A perfect foal by Sandcastle for peanuts. And if you got a malformed foal, well, some years your mare might slip or be barren anyway.'

He looked at his feet for a while, and then into the iddle distance, and then he said, 'Come with me. I've something to show you. Something you'd better know.'

He set off towards the Watcherleys', and would say nothing more on the way. I walked beside him down the familiar paths and thought about Ginnie because I couldn't help it, and we arrived in the next-door yard that was now of a neatness to be compared with all the others.

'Over here,' Oliver said, going across to one of the boxes. 'Look at that.'

I looked where directed: at a mare with a colt foal suckling, not unexpected in that place.

'He was born three days ago,' Oliver said. 'I do so wish Ginnie had seen him.'

'Why that one, especially?'

'The mare is one of my own,' he said. 'And that foal is Sandcastle's.'

It was my turn to stare. I looked from Oliver to the foal and back again. 'There's nothing wrong with him,' I said.

'No.'

'But . . .'

Oliver smiled twistedly. 'I was going to breed her to Diarist. She was along here at the Watcherleys' because the foal she had then was always ailing, but she herself was all right. I was along here looking at her one day when she'd been in season a while, and on impulse I led her along to the breeding pen and told Nigel to fetch Sandcastle, and we mated them there and then. That foal's the result.' He shook his head regretfully. 'He'll be sold, of course, with everything else. I wish I could have kept him, but there it is.'

'He should be worth quite a bit,' I said.

'I don't think so,' Oliver said. 'And that's the flaw in your gamble. It's not just the racing potential that raises prices at auction, it's the chance of breeding. And no one could be sure, breeding from Sandcastle's stock, that the genetic trouble wouldn't crop up for evermore. It's not on, I'm afraid. No serious breeder would send him mares, however great the bargain.'

We stood for a while in silence.

'It was a good idea,' I said, 'while it lasted.'

'My dear Tim . . . we're clutching at straws.'

'Yes.' I looked at his calm strong face; the captain whose ship was sinking. 'I'd try anything, you know, to save you,' I said.

'And to save the bank's money?'

'That too.'

He smiled faintly. 'I wish you could, but time's running out.'

The date for bringing in the receivers had been set, the insurance company had finally ducked, the lawyers were closing in and the respite I'd gained for him was trickling away with no tender plant of hope growing in the ruins.

We walked back towards the house, Oliver patting the mares as usual as they came to the fences.

'I suppose this may all be here next year,' he said, 'looking much the same. Someone will buy it . . . it's just I who'll be gone.'

He lifted his head, looking away over his white-painted rails to the long line of the roofs of his yards. The enormity of the loss of his life's work settled like a weight on his shoulders and there was a haggard set to his jaw.

'I try not to mind,' he said levelly. 'But I don't quite know how to bear it.'

When I reached home that evening my telephone was ringing. I went across the sitting room expecting it to stop the moment I reached it, but the summons continued, and on the other end was Judith.

'I just came in,' I said.

'We knew you were out. We've tried once or twice.'

'I went to see Oliver.'

'The poor, poor man.' Judith had been very distressed over Ginnie and still felt that Oliver needed more sympathy because of his daughter than because of his bankruptcy, which I wasn't sure was any longer the case. 'Anyway,' she said, 'Pen asked me to call you as she's tied up in her shop all day and you were out when she tried ... She says she's had the reply from America about the shampoo and are you still interested?'

'Yes, certainly.'

'Then ... if you're not doing anything else ... Gordon and I wondered if you'd care to come here for the day tomorrow, and Pen will bring the letter to show you.'

'I'll be there,' I said fervently, and she laughed.

'Good, then. See you.'

I was at Clapham with alacrity before noon, and Pen, over coffee, produced the letter from the drug company.

'I sent them a sample of what you gave me in that little glass jar,' she said. 'And, as you asked, I had some of the rest of it analysed here, but honestly, Tim, don't hope too much from it for finding out who killed Ginnie, it's just shampoo, as it says.'

I took the official-looking letter which was of two pages clipped together, with impressive headings.

Dear Madam,

We have received the enquiry from your pharmacy and also the sample you sent us, and we now reply with this report, which is a copy of that which we recently sent to the Hertfordshire police force on the same subject.

The shampoo in question is our 'Bannitch' which is formulated especially for dogs suffering from various skin troubles, including eczema. It is distributed to shops selling goods to dog owners and offering cosmetic canine services, but would not normally be used except on the advice of a veterinarian.

We enclose the list of active ingredients and excipients, as requested.

'What are excipients?' I asked, looking up.

'The things you put in with the active drug for

various reasons,' she said. 'Like for instance chalk for bulk in pills.'

I turned the top page over and read the list on the second.

BANNITCH

EXCIPIENTS

Bentonite
Ethylene glycol monostearate
Citric acid
Sodium phosphate
Glyceryl monoricinoleate
Perfume

ACTIVE INGREDIENTS

Captan
Amphoteric
Selenium

'Terrific,' I said blankly. 'What do they all mean?'

Pen, sitting beside me on the sofa, explained. 'From the top ... Bentonite is a thickening agent so that everything stays together and doesn't separate out. Ethylene glycol monostearate is a sort of wax, probably there to add bulk. Citric acid is to make the whole mixture acid, not alkaline, and the next one, sodium phosphate, is to keep the acidity level more or less constant. Glyceryl monoricinoleate is a soap, to make lather, and perfume is there so that the dog smells nice to the owner when she's washing him.'

'How do you know so much?' Gordon asked, marvelling.

'I looked some of them up,' said Pen frankly, with a smile. She turned back to me and pointed to the short lower column of active ingredients. 'Captan and amphoteric are both drugs for killing fungi on the skin, and selenium is also anti-fungal and is used in shampoos to cure dandruff.' She stopped and looked at me doubtfully. 'I did tell you not to hope too much. There's nothing there of any consequence.'

'And nothing in the sample that isn't on the manufacturer's list?'

She shook her head. 'The analysis from the British lab came yesterday, and the shampoo in Ginnie's bottle contained exactly what it should.'

'What did you expect, Tim?' Gordon asked.

'It wasn't so much expect, as hope,' I said regretfully. 'Hardly hope, really. Just a faint outside chance.'

'Of what?'

'Well . . . the police thought – think – that the purpose of killing Ginnie was sexual assault, because of those other poor girls in the neighbourhood.'

They all nodded.

'But it doesn't *feel* right, does it? Not when you know she wasn't walking home from anywhere, like the others, and not when she wasn't actually, well, interfered with. And then she had the shampoo . . . and the farm was in such trouble, and it seemed to me possible, just slightly possible, that she had somehow discovered

323

that something in that bottle was significant . . .' I paused, and then said slowly to Pen, 'I suppose what I was looking for was something that could have been put into Sandcastle's food or water that affected his reproductive organs. I don't know if that's possible. I don't know anything about drugs . . . I just *wondered*.'

They sat in silence with round eyes, and then Gordon, stirring, said with an inflection of hope, 'Is that possible, Pen? Could it be something like that?'

'Could it *possibly*?' Judith said.

'My loves,' Pen said. 'I don't know.' She looked also as if whatever she said would disappoint us. 'I've never heard of anything like that, I simply haven't.'

'That's why I took the shampoo and gave it to you,' I said. 'I know it's a wild and horrible idea, but I told Oliver I'd try everything, however unlikely.'

'What you're suggesting,' Judith said plainly, 'is that someone might *deliberately* have given something to Sandcastle to make him produce deformed foals, and that Ginnie found out . . . and was killed for it.'

There was silence.

'I'll go and get a book or two,' Pen said. 'We'll look up the ingredients, just in case. But honestly, don't *hope*.'

She went home leaving the three of us feeling subdued. For me this had been the last possibility, although since I'd heard from Oliver that the police check had revealed only the expected shampoo in the bottle, it had become more and more remote.

Pen came back in half an hour with a thick tome, a piece of paper, and worried creases across her forehead. 'I've been reading,' she said. 'Sorry to be so long. I've been checking up on sperm deformities, and it seems the most likely cause is radiation.'

I said instantly, 'Let's ring Oliver.'

They nodded and I got through to him with Pen's suggestion.

'Tim!' he said. 'I'll see if I can get anyone in Newmarket . . . even though it's Sunday . . . I'll ring you back.'

'Though how a stallion could get anywhere near a radioactive source,' Pen said while we were waiting, 'would be a first-class mystery in itself.' She looked down at the paper she carried. 'This is the analysis report from the British lab, bill attached, I'm afraid. Same ingredients, though written in the opposite order, practically, with selenium put at the top, which means that that's the predominant drug, I should think.'

Oliver telephoned again in a remarkably short time. 'I got the chief researcher at home. He says they did think of radiation but discounted it because it would be more likely to result in total sterility, and there's also the improbability of a horse being near any radioactive isotopes.' He sighed. 'Sandcastle has never even been X-rayed.'

'See if you can check,' I said. 'If he ever was irradiated in any way it would come into the category of accidental or even malicious damage, and we'd be back into the insurance policy.'

'All right,' he said. 'I'll try.'

I put down the receiver to find Pen turning the pages of her large pharmacological book with concentration.

'What's that?' Judith asked, pointing.

'Toxicity of minerals,' Pen answered absentmindedly. 'Ethylene glycol . . .' She turned pages, searching. 'Here we are.' She read down the column, shaking her head. 'Not that, anyway.' She again consulted the index, read the columns, shook her head. 'Selenium . . . selenium . . .' She turned the pages, read the columns, pursed her lips. 'It says that selenium is poisonous if taken internally, though it can be beneficial on the skin.' She read some more. 'It says that if animals eat plants which grow in soil which has much selenium in it, they can die.'

'What is selenium?' Judith asked.

'It's an element,' Pen said. 'Like potassium and sodium.' She read on, 'It says here that it is mostly found in rocks of the Cretaceous Age – such useful information – and that it's among the most poisonous of elements but also an essential nutrient in trace quantities for both animals and plants.' She looked up. 'It says it's useful for flower-growers because it kills insects, and that it accumulates mostly in plants which flourish where there's a low annual rainfall.'

'Is that all?' Gordon asked, sounding disappointed.

'No, there's pages of it. I'm just translating the gist into understandable English.'

She read on for a while, and then it seemed to me that she totally stopped breathing. She raised her head and looked at me, her eyes wide and dark.

'What is it?' I said.

'Read it.' She gave me the heavy book, pointing to the open page.

I read:

Selenium is absorbed easily from the intestines and affects every part of the body, more lodging in the liver, spleen, and kidneys than in brain and muscle. Selenium is teratogenic.

'What does teratogenic mean?' I asked.

'It means,' Pen said, 'that it produces deformed offspring.'

'*What*?' I exclaimed. 'You don't mean . . .'

Pen was shaking her head. 'It couldn't affect Sandcastle. It's impossible. It would simply poison his system. Teratogens have nothing to do with males.'

'Then what . . .?'

'They act on the developing embryo,' she said. Her face crumpled almost as if the knowledge was too much and would make her cry. 'You could get deformed foals if you fed selenium *to the mares*.'

*

327

I went on the following morning to see Detective Chief Inspector Wyfold, both Gordon and Harry concurring that the errand warranted time off from the bank. The forceful policeman shook my hand, gestured me to a chair and said briskly that he could give me fifteen minutes at the outside, as did I know that yet another young girl had been murdered and sexually assaulted the evening before, which was now a total of six, and that his superiors, the press and the whole flaming country were baying for an arrest? 'And we are no nearer now,' he added with anger, 'than we were five months ago, when it started.'

He listened all the same to what I said about selenium, but in conclusion shook his head.

'We looked it up ourselves. Did you know it's the main ingredient in an anti-dandruff shampoo sold off open shelves all over America in the drug stores? It used to be on sale here too, or something like it, but it's been discontinued. There's no mystery about it. It's not rare, nor illegal. Just ordinary.'

'But the deformities . . .'

'Look,' he said restively, 'I'll bear it in mind. But it's a big jump to decide from one bottle of ordinary dog shampoo that *that*'s what's the matter with those foals. I mean, is there any way of proving it?'

With regret I said, 'No, there isn't.' No animal, Pen's book had implied, would retain selenium in its system for longer than a day or two if it was eaten only once or twice and in non-fatal amounts.

'And how, anyway,' Wyfold said, 'would you get a whole lot of horses to drink anything as nasty as shampoo?' He shook his head. 'I know you're very anxious to catch Virginia Knowles' killer, and don't think we don't appreciate your coming here, but we've been into the shampoo question thoroughly, I assure you.'

His telephone buzzed and he picked up the receiver, his eyes still turned in my direction, but his mind already elsewhere. 'What?' he said. 'Yes, all right. Straightaway.' He put down the receiver. 'I'll have to go.'

'Listen,' I said, 'isn't it possible that one of the lads was giving selenium to the mares this year also, and that Ginnie somehow found out . . .'

He interrupted. 'We tried to fit that killing onto one of those lads, don't think we didn't, but there was no evidence, absolutely none at all.' He stood up and came round from behind his desk, already leaving me in mind as well as body. 'If you think of anything else Mr Ekaterin, by all means let us know. But for now – I'm sorry, but there's a bestial man out there we've got to catch – and I'm still of the opinion he tried for Virginia Knowles too, and was interrupted.'

He gave me a dismissing but not impatient nod, holding open the door and waiting for me to leave his office ahead of him. I obliged him by going, knowing that realistically he couldn't be expected to listen to any further unsubstantiated theories from me while another victim lay more horribly and recently dead.

Before I went back to him, I thought, I had better dig further and come up with connected, believable facts, and also a basis, at least, for proof.

Henry and Gordon heard with gloom in the bank before lunch that at present we were 'insufficient data' in a Wyfold pigeonhole.

'But you still believe, do you, Tim . . .?' Henry said enquiringly.

'We have to,' I answered. 'And yes, I do.'

'Hm.' He pondered. 'If you need more time off from the office, you'd better take it. If there's the slightest chance that there's nothing wrong with Sandcastle after all, we must do our absolute best not only to prove it to our own satisfaction but also to the world in general. Confidence would have to be restored to breeders, otherwise they wouldn't send their mares. It's a tall order altogether.'

'Yes,' I said. 'Well . . . I'll do all I can'; and after lunch and some thought I telephoned Oliver, whose hopes no one had so far raised.

'Sit down,' I said.

'What's the matter?' He sounded immediately anxious. 'What's happened?'

'Do you know what teratogenic means?' I said.

'Yes, of course. With mares one always has to be careful.'

330

'Mm . . . Well, there was a teratogenic drug in the bottle of dog shampoo that Ginnie had.'

'*What*?' His voice rose an octave on the word, vibrating with instinctive unthinking anger.

'Yes,' I said. 'Now calm down. The police say it proves nothing either way, but Gordon and Henry, our chairman, agree that it's the only hope we have left.'

'But Tim . . .' The realization hit him. 'That would mean . . . that would mean . . .'

'Yes,' I said. 'It would mean that Sandcastle was always breeding good and true and could return to gold-mine status.'

I could hear Oliver's heavily disturbed breathing and could only guess at his pulse rate.

'No,' he said. 'No. If shampoo had got into a batch of feed, all the mares who ate it would have been affected, not just those covered by Sandcastle.'

'If the shampoo got into the feed accidentally, yes. If it was given deliberately, no.'

'I can't . . . I can't . . .'

'I did tell you to sit down,' I said reasonably.

'Yes, so you did.' There was a pause. 'I'm sitting,' he said.

'It's at least possible,' I said, 'that the Equine Research people could find nothing wrong with Sandcastle because there actually *isn't* anything wrong with him.'

'Yes,' he agreed faintly.

'It is possible to give teratogenic substances to mares?'

'Yes.'

'But horses wouldn't drink shampoo.'

'No, thoroughbreds especially are very choosy.'

'So how would you give them shampoo, and when?'

After a pause he said, still breathlessly, 'I don't know how. They'd spit it out. But when it's easier, and that could probably be no more than three or four days after conception, is when the body tube is forming in the embryo ... that's when a small amount of teratogenic substance could do a lot of damage.'

'Do you mean,' I said, 'that giving a mare selenium just *once* would ensure a deformed foal?'

'Giving a mare what?'

'Sorry. Selenium. A drug for treating dandruff.'

'Good ... heavens.' He rallied towards his normal self. 'I suppose it would depend on the strength of the dose, and its timing. Perhaps three or four doses ... No one could really *know* because no one would have tried ... I mean, there wouldn't have been any research.'

'No,' I agreed. 'But supposing that in this instance someone got the dosage and the timing right, and also found a way of making the shampoo palatable, then *who was it*?'

There was a long quietness during which even his breathing abated.

'I don't know,' he said finally. 'Theoretically it could

have been me, Ginnie, Nigel, the Watcherleys or any of the lads who were here last year. No one else was on the place often enough.'

'Really no one? How about the vet or the blacksmith or just a visiting friend?'

'But there were *eighteen* deformed foals,' he said. 'I would think it would have to have been someone who could come and go here all the time.'

'And someone who knew which mares to pick,' I said. 'Would that knowledge be easy to come by?'

'Easy!' he said explosively. 'It is positively thrust at everyone on the place. There are lists in all the feed rooms and in the breeding pen itself saying which mares are to be bred to which stallion. Nigel has one, there's one in my office, one at the Watcherleys' – all over. Everyone is supposed to double-check the lists all the time, so that mistakes aren't made.'

'And all the horses,' I said slowly, 'wear headcollars with their names on.'

'Yes, that's right. An essential precaution.'

All made easy, I thought, for someone intending mischief towards particular mares and not to any others.

'Your own Sandcastle foal,' I said, 'he's perfect . . . and it may be because on the lists your mare was down for Diarist.'

'Tim!'

'Look after him,' I said. 'And look after Sandcastle.'

'I will,' he said fervently.

'And Oliver . . . is the lad called Shane still with you?'

'No, he's gone. So have Dave and Sammy, who found Ginnie.'

'Then could you send me at the bank a list of the names and addresses of all the people who were working for you last year, and also this year? And I mean *everyone*, even your housekeeper and anyone working for Nigel or cleaning the lads' hostel, things like that.'

'Even my part-time secretary girl?'

'Even her.'

'She only comes three mornings a week.'

'That might be enough.'

'All right,' he said. 'I'll do it straight away.'

'I went to see Chief Inspector Wyfold this morning,' I said. 'But he thinks it's just a coincidence that Ginnie had shampoo with a foal-deforming drug in it. We'll have to come up with a whole lot more, to convince him. So anything you can think of . . .'

'I'll think of nothing else.'

'If Dissdale Smith should telephone you, pressing for an answer,' I said, 'just say the bank are deliberating and keeping you waiting. Don't tell him anything about this new possibility. It might be best to keep it to ourselves until we can prove whether or not it's true.'

'Dear God,' he said fearfully, 'I hope it is.'

*

In the evening I talked to Pen, asking her if she knew of any way of getting the selenium out of the shampoo.

'The trouble seems to be,' I said, 'that you simply couldn't get the stuff into a horse as it is.'

'I'll work on it,' she said. 'But of course the manufacturer's chemists will have gone to a good deal of trouble to make sure the selenium stays suspended throughout the mixture and doesn't all fall to the bottom.'

'It did say "Shake Well" on the bottle.'

'Mm, but that might be for the soap content, not for the selenium.'

I thought. 'Well, could you get the soap out, then? It must be the soap the horses wouldn't like.'

'I'll try my hardest,' she promised. 'I'll ask a few friends.' She paused. 'There isn't much of the shampoo left. Only what I kept after sending the samples off to America and the British lab.'

'How much?' I said anxiously.

'Half an egg-cupful. Maybe less.'

'Is that enough?'

'If we work in test tubes . . . perhaps.'

'And Pen . . . Could you or your friends make a guess, as well, as to how much shampoo you'd need to provide enough selenium to give a teratogenic dose to a mare?'

'You sure do come up with some difficult questions, dearest Tim, but we'll certainly try.'

Three days later she sent a message with Gordon, saying that by that evening she might have some answers, if I would care to go down to her house after work.

I cared and went, and with a smiling face she opened her front door to let me in.

'Like a drink?' she said.

'Well, yes, but . . .'

'First things first.' She poured whisky carefully for me and Cinzano for herself. 'Hungry?'

'Pen . . .'

'It's only rolls with ham and lettuce in. I never cook much, as you know.' She disappeared to her seldom-used kitchen and returned with the offerings, which turned out to be nicely squelchy and much what I would have made for myself.

'All right,' she said finally, pushing away the empty plates. 'Now I'll tell you what we've managed.'

'At last.'

She grinned. 'Yes. Well then, we started from the premise that if someone had to use shampoo as the source of selenium then that someone didn't have direct or easy access to poisonous chemicals, which being so he also wouldn't have sophisticated machinery available for separating one ingredient from another – a centrifuge, for instance. OK so far?'

I nodded.

'So what we needed, as we saw it, was a *simple* method that involved only everyday equipment. Something anyone could do anywhere. So the first thing we did was to let the shampoo drip through a paper filter, and we think you could use almost anything for that purpose, like a paper towel, a folded tissue or thin blotting paper. We actually got the best and fastest results from a coffee filter, which is after all specially designed to retain very fine solids while letting liquids through easily.'

'Yes,' I said. 'Highly logical.'

Pen smiled. 'So there we were with some filter-papers in which, we hoped, the microscopic particles of selenium were trapped. The filters were stained bright green by the shampoo. I brought one here to show you . . . I'll get it.' She whisked off to the kitchen taking the empty supper plates with her, and returned carrying a small tray with two glasses on it.

One glass contained cut pieces of green-stained coffee filter lying in what looked like oil, and the second glass contained only an upright test tube, closed at the top with a cork and showing a dark half-inch of solution at the bottom.

'One of my friends in the lab knows a lot about horses,' Pen said, 'and he reckoned that all racehorses are used to the taste of linseed oil, which is given them in their feed quite often as a laxative. So we got some linseed oil and cut up the filter and soaked it.' She pointed to the glass. 'The selenium particles floated out of the paper into the oil.'

'Neat,' I said.

'Yes. So then we poured the result into the test tube and just waited twenty-four hours or so, and the selenium particles slowly gravitated through the oil to the bottom.' She looked at my face to make sure I understood. 'We transferred the selenium from the wax-soap base in which it would remain suspended into an oil base, in which it *wouldn't* remain suspended.'

'I do understand,' I assured her.

'So here in the test tube,' she said with a conjuror's flourish, 'we have concentrated selenium with the surplus oil poured off.' She picked the tube out of the glass, keeping it upright, and showed me the brownish shadowy liquid lying there, darkest at the bottom, almost clear amber at the top. 'We had such a small sample to start with that this is all we managed to collect. But that dark stuff is definitely selenium sulphide. We checked it on a sort of scanner called a gas chromatograph.' She grinned. 'No point in not using the sophisticated apparatus when it's there right beside you – and we were in a research lab of a teaching hospital, incidentally.'

'You're marvellous.'

'Quite brilliant,' she agreed with comic modesty. 'We also calculated that that particular shampoo was almost ten per cent selenium, which is a very much higher proportion than you'd find in shampoos for humans. We all agree that this much, in the test tube, is enough to cause deformity in a foal – or in any other species, for that matter. We found many more references in other books – lambs born with deformed feet, for instance, where the sheep had browsed off plants growing on selenium-rich soil. We all agree that it's the *time* when the mare ingests the selenium that's most crucial, and we think that to be sure of getting the desired result you'd have to give selenium every day for three or four days, starting two or three days after conception.'

I slowly nodded. 'That's the same sort of time-scale that Oliver said.'

'And if you gave too much,' she said, 'too large a dose, you'd be more likely to get abortions than really gross deformities. The embryo would only go on growing at all, that is, if the damage done to it by the selenium was relatively minor.'

'There were a lot of *different* deformities,' I said.

'Oh sure. It could have affected any developing cell, regardless.'

I picked up the test tube and peered closely at its murky contents. 'I suppose all you'd have to do would be stir this into a cupful of oats.'

'That's right.'

'Or . . . could you enclose it in a capsule?'

'Yes, if you had the makings. We could have done it quite easily in the lab. You'd need to get rid of as much oil as possible, of course, in that case, and just scrape concentrated selenium into the capsules.'

'Mm. Calder could do it, I suppose?'

'Calder Jackson? Why yes, I guess he could if you

wanted him to. He had everything there that you'd need.' She lifted her head, remembering something. 'He's on the television tomorrow night, incidentally.'

'Is he?'

'Yes. They were advertising it tonight just after the news, before you came. He's going to be a guest on that chat show ... Micky Bonwith's show ... Do you ever see it?'

'Sometimes,' I said, thoughtfully. 'It's transmitted live, isn't it?'

'Yes, that's right.' She looked at me with slight puzzlement. 'What's going on in that computer brain?'

'A slight calculation of risk,' I said slowly, 'and of grasping unrepeatable opportunities. And tell me, dearest Pen, if I found myself again in Calder's surgery, what should I look for, to bring out?'

She stared at me literally with her mouth open. Then, recovering, she said, 'You can't mean ... *Calder*?'

'Well,' I said soberly. 'What I'd really like to do is to make sure one way or another. Because it does seem to me, sad though it is to admit it, that if you tie in Dissdale's offer for Sandcastle with someone deliberately poisoning the mares, and then add Calder's expertise with herbs – in which selenium-soaked plants might be included – you do at least get a *question mark*. You do want to know for sure, don't you think, whether or not Calder and Dissdale set out deliberately to debase Sandcastle's worth so that they could buy him for peanuts ... So that Calder could perform a well-publicized "miracle cure" of some sort on Sandcastle, who would thereafter always sire perfect foals, and gradually climb back into favour. Whose fees might never return to forty thousand pounds, but would over the years add up to a fortune.'

'But they couldn't,' Pen said, aghast. 'I mean ... Calder and Dissdale ... we *know* them.'

'And you in your trade, as I in mine, must have met presentable, confidence-inspiring crooks.'

She fell silent, staring at me in a troubled way, until finally I said, 'There's one other thing. Again nothing I could swear to – but the first time I went to Calder's place he had a lad there who reminded me sharply of the boy with the knife at Ascot.'

'Ricky Barnet,' Pen said, nodding.

'Yes. I can't remember Calder's lad's name, and I wouldn't identify him at all now after all this time, but at Oliver's I saw another lad, called Shane, who *also* reminded me of Ricky Barnet. I've no idea whether Shane and Calder's lad are one and the same person, though maybe not, because I don't think Calder's lad was called Shane, or I *would* have remembered, if you see what I mean.'

'Got you,' she said.

'But *if* – and it's a big if – if Shane did once work for Calder, he might *still* be working for him ... feeding selenium to mares.'

Pen took her time with gravity in the experienced

341

eyes, and at last said, '*Someone* would have had to be there on the spot to do the feeding, and it certainly couldn't have been Calder or Dissdale. But couldn't it have been that manager, Nigel? It would have been easy for him. Suppose Dissdale and Calder paid him...? Suppose they promised to employ him, or even give him a share in Sandcastle, once they'd got hold of the horse.'

I shook my head. 'I did wonder. I did think of Nigel. There's one good reason why it probably isn't him, though, and that's because he and only he besides Oliver knew that one of the mares down for Diarist was covered by Sandcastle.' I explained about Oliver's impulse mating. 'The foal is perfect, but might very likely not have been if it was Nigel who was doing the feeding.'

'Not conclusive,' Pen said, slowly.

'No.'

She stirred. 'Did you tell the police all this?'

'I meant to,' I said, 'but when I was there with Wyfold on Monday it seemed impossible. It was all so insubstantial. Such a lot of guesses. Maybe wrong conclusions. Dissdale's offer could be genuine. And a lad I'd seen for half a minute eighteen months ago... it's difficult to remember a strange face for half an hour, let alone all that time. I have only an impression of blankness and of sunglasses... and I don't have the same impression of Oliver's lad Shane. Wyfold isn't the sort of man to be vague to. I thought I'd better come up with something more definite before I went back to him.'

She bit her thumb. 'Can't you take another good look at this Shane?'

I shook my head. 'Oliver's gradually letting lads go, as he does every year at this time, and Shane is one who has already left. Oliver doesn't know where he went and has no other address for him, which he doesn't think very unusual. It seems that lads can drift from stable to stable for ever with their papers always showing only the address of their last or current employer. But I think we *might* find Shane, if we're lucky.'

'How?'

'By photographing Ricky Barnet, side view, and asking around on racetracks.'

She smiled. 'It might work. It just might.'

'Worth a try.'

My mind drifted back to something else worth a try, and it seemed that hers followed.

'You don't really mean to break into Calder's surgery, do you?' she said.

'Pick the lock,' I said. 'Yes.'

'But . . .'

'Time's running out, and Oliver's future and the bank's money with it, and yes, sure, I'll do what I can.'

She curiously looked into my face. 'You have no real conception of danger, do you?'

'How do you mean?'

'I mean . . . I saw you, that day at Ascot, simply hurl yourself at that boy, at that knife. You could have been badly stabbed, very easily. And Ginnie told us that you frightened her to tears jumping at Sandcastle the way you did, to catch him. She said it was suicidal . . . and yet you yourself seemed to think nothing of it. And at Ascot, that evening, I remembered you being *bored* with the police questions, not stirred up high by a brush with death . . .'

Her words petered away. I considered them and found in myself a reason and an answer.

'Nothing that has happened so far in my life,' I said seriously, 'has made me fear I might die. I think . . . I know it sounds silly . . . I am unconvinced of my own mortality.'

JUNE

On the following day, Friday, June 1st, I took up a long-offered invitation and went to lunch with the board of a security firm to whom we had lent money for launching a new burglar alarm on the market. Not greatly to their surprise I was there to ask a favour, and after a repast of five times the calories of Ekaterin's they gave me with some amusement three keys which would unlock almost anything but the crown jewels, and also a concentrated course on how to use them.

'Those pickers are strictly for opening doors in emergencies,' the locksmiths said, smiling. 'If you end up in jail, we don't know you.'

'If I end up in jail, send me another set in a fruit cake.'

I thanked them and left, and practised discreetly on the office doors in the bank, with remarkable results. Going home I let myself in through my own front door with them, and locked and unlocked every cupboard and drawer which had a keyhole. Then I put on a dark roll-neck jersey over my shirt and tie and with scant trepidation drove to Newmarket.

I left my car at the side of the road some distance from Calder's house and finished the journey on foot, walking quietly into his yard in the last of the lingering summer dusk, checking against my watch that it was almost ten o'clock, the hour when Micky Bonwith led his guests to peacock chairs and dug publicly into their psyches.

Calder would give a great performance, I thought; and the regrets I felt about my suspicions of him redoubled as I looked at the outline of his house against the sky and remembered his uncomplicated hospitality.

The reserve which had always at bottom lain between us I now acknowledged as my own instinctive and stifled doubt. Wanting to see worth, I had seen it; and the process of now trying to prove myself wrong gave me more sadness than satisfaction.

His yard was dark and peaceful, all lads long gone. Within the hall of the house a single light burned, a dim point of yellow glimpsed through the bushes fluttering in a gentle breeze. Behind the closed doors of the boxes the patients would be snoozing, those patients with festering sores and bleeding guts and all manner of woes awaiting the touch.

Sandcastle, if I was right, had been destined to stand there, while Calder performed his 'miracle' without having to explain how he'd done it. He never had explained: he'd always broadcast publicly that he didn't know *how* his power worked, he just knew it did. Thousands, perhaps millions, believed in his power. Perhaps even breeders, those dreamers of dreams, would have believed, in the end.

I came to the surgery, a greyish block in the advancing night, and fitted one of the lock-pickers into the keyhole. The internal tumblers turned without protest, much oiled and used, and I pushed the door open and went in.

There were no windows to worry about. I closed the door behind me and switched on the light, and immediately began the search for which I'd come: to find selenium in home-made capsules, or in a filtering device, or in bottles of shampoo.

Pen had had doubts that anyone would have risked giving selenium a second year if the first year's work had proved so effective, but I'd reminded her that Sandcastle had already covered many new mares that year before the deformed foals had been reported.

'Whoever did it couldn't have known at that point that he'd been successful. So to make sure, I'd guess he'd go on, and maybe with an increased dose ... and if no selenium was being given this year, *why did Ginnie have it?*'

Pen had reluctantly given in. 'I suppose I'm just trying to find reasons for you not to go to Calder's.'

'If I find anything, Chief Inspector Wyfold can go there later with a search warrant. Don't worry so.'

'No,' she'd said, and gone straight on looking anxious.

The locked cabinets at both ends of Calder's surgery proved a doddle for the picks, but the contents were a puzzle, as so few of the jars and boxes were properly labelled. Some indeed had come from commercial suppliers, but these seemed mostly to be the herbs Calder had talked of: hydrastis, comfrey, fo-ti-tieng, myrrh, sarsaparilla, liquorice, passiflora, papaya, garlic; a good quantity of each.

Nothing was obligingly labelled selenium.

I had taken with me a thickish polythene bag which had a zip across one end and had formerly enclosed a silk tie and handkerchief, a present from my mother at Christmas. Into that I systematically put two or three capsules from each bottle, and two or three pills of each ort, and small sachets of herbs; and Pen, I thought, was going to have a fine old time sorting them all out.

With the bag almost half full of samples I carefully locked the cabinets again and turned to the refrigerator, which was of an ordinary domestic make with only a magnetic door fastening.

Inside there were no bottles of shampoo. No coffee filters. No linseed oil. There were simply the large plastic containers of Calder's cure-all tonic.

I thought I might as well take some to satisfy Pen's curiosity, and rooted around for a small container, finding some empty medicine bottles in a cupboard below the work-bench. Over the sink I poured some of the tonic into a medicine bottle, screwed on the cap, and returned the plastic container carefully to its place in the fridge. I stood the medicine bottle on the work-bench ready to take away, and turned finally to the drawers where Calder kept things like hops and also his antique pill-making equipment.

Everything was clean and tidy, as before. If he had made capsules containing selenium there, I could see no trace.

With mounting disappointment I went briefly through every drawer. Bags of seeds: sesame, pumpkin, sunflower. Bags of dried herbs, raspberry leaves, alfalfa. Boxes of the empty halves of gelatine capsules, waiting for contents. Empty unused pill bottles. All as before: nothing I hadn't already seen.

The largest bottom drawer still contained the plastic sacks of hops. I pulled open the neck of one of them and found only the expected strong-smelling crop; closed the neck again, moving the bag slightly to settle it back into its place, and saw that under the bags of hops lay a brown leather briefcase, ordinary size, six inches deep.

With a feeling of wasting time I hauled it out onto the working surface on top of the drawers, and tried to open it.

Both catches were locked. I fished for the keys in my trouser pocket and with the smallest of the picks delicately twisted until the mechanisms clicked.

Opened the lid. Found no bottles of dog shampoo,

but other things that turned me slowly to a state of stone.

The contents looked at first sight as if the case belonged to a doctor: stethoscope, pen torch, metal instruments, all in fitted compartments. A cardboard box without its lid held four or five small tubes of antibiotic ointment. A large bottle contained only a few small white pills, the bottle labelled with a long name I could scarcely read, let alone remember, with 'diuretic' in brackets underneath. A pad of prescription forms, blank, ready for use.

It was the name and address rubber-stamped onto the prescription forms and the initials heavily embossed in gold into the leather beneath the case's handle which stunned me totally.

I.A.P. on the case.

Ian A. Pargetter on the prescriptions.

Ian Pargetter, veterinary surgeon, address in Newmarket.

His case had vanished the night he died.

This case . . .

With fingers beginning to shake I took one of the tubes of antibiotics and some of the diuretic pills and three of the prescription forms and added them to my other spoils, and then with a heart at least beating at about twice normal speed checked that everything was in its place before closing the case.

I felt as much as heard the surgery door open, the current of air reaching me at the same instant as the night sounds. I turned thinking that one of Calder's lads had come on some late hospital rounds and wondering how I could ever explain my presence; and I saw that no explanation at all would do.

It was Calder himself crossing the threshold. Calder with the light on his curly halo, Calder who should have been a hundred miles away talking to the nation on the tube.

His first expression of surprise turned immediately to grim assessment, his gaze travelling from the medicine bottle of tonic mixture on the work-bench to the veterinary case lying open. Shock, disbelief and fury rose in an instantly violent reaction, and he acted with such speed that even if I'd guessed what he would do I could hardly have dodged.

His right arm swung in an arc, coming down against the wall beside the door and pulling from the bracket which held it a slim scarlet fire extinguisher. The swing seemed to me continuous. The red bulbous end of the fire extinguisher in a split second filled my vision and connected with a crash against my forehead, and consciousness ceased within a blink.

The world came back with the same sort of on–off switch: one second I was unaware, the next, awake. No grey area of daze, no shooting stars, simply on–off, off–on.

I was lying on my back on some smelly straw in an

electrically lit horse box with a brown horse peering at me suspiciously from six feet above.

I couldn't remember for a minute how I'd got there; it seemed such an improbable position to be in. Then I had a recollection of a red ball crashing above my eyes, and then, in a snap, total recall of the evening.

Calder.

I was in a box in Calder's yard. I was there because, presumably, Calder had put me there.

Pending? I wondered.

Pending what?

With no reassuring thoughts I made the moves to stand up, but found that though consciousness was total, recovery was not. A whirling dizziness set the walls tilting, the grey concrete blocks seeming to want to lean in and fall on me. Cursing slightly I tried again more slowly and made it to one elbow with eyes balancing precariously in their sockets.

The top half of the stable door abruptly opened with the sound of an unlatching bolt. Calder's head appeared in the doorway, his face showing shock and dismay as he saw me awake.

'I thought,' he said, 'that you'd be unconscious . . . that you wouldn't know. I hit you so hard . . . you're supposed to be out.' His voice saying these bizarre words sounded nothing but normal.

'Calder . . .' I said.

He was looking at me no longer with anger but

almost with apology. 'I'm sorry, Tim,' he said. 'I'm sorry you came.'

The walls seemed to be slowing down.

'Ian Pargetter . . .' I said. 'Did *you* . . . kill him? Not you?'

Calder produced an apple and fed it almost absent-mindedly to the horse. 'I'm sorry, Tim. He was so stubborn. He refused . . .' He patted the horse's neck. 'He wouldn't do what I wanted. Said it was over, he'd had enough. Said he'd stop me, you know.' He looked for a moment at the horse and then down to me. 'Why did you come? I've liked you. I wish you hadn't.'

I tried again to stand up and the whirling returned as before. Calder took a step backwards, but only one, stopping when he saw my inability to arise and charge.

'Ginnie,' I said. 'Not Ginnie . . . Say it wasn't you who hit Ginnie . . .'

He simply looked at me, and didn't say it. In the end he said merely, and with clear regret, 'I wish I'd hit you harder . . . but it seemed . . . enough.' He moved another step backwards so that I could see only the helmet of curls under the light and dark shadows where his eyes were; and then while I was still struggling to my knees he closed the half-door and bolted it, and from outside switched off the light.

Night-blindness made it even harder to stand up but at least I couldn't *see* the walls whirl, only feel they were spinning. I found myself leaning against one of them and ended more or less upright, spine supported, brain at last settling into equilibrium.

The grey oblong of window gradually detached itself from the blackness, and when my equine companion moved his head I saw the liquid reflection of an eye.

Window . . . way out.

I slithered round the walls to the window and found it barred on the inside, not so much to keep horses in, I supposed, but to prevent them breaking the glass. Five strong bars, in any case, were set in concrete top and bottom, as secure as any prison cell, and I shook them impotently with two hands in proving them immovable.

Through the dusty window panes I had a sideways view across the yard towards the surgery, and while I stood there and held onto the bars and watched, Calder went busily in and out of the open lighted doorway, carrying things from the surgery to his car. I saw what I was sure was Ian Pargetter's case go into the boot, and remembered with discomfiture that I'd left the bunch of picks in one of its locks. I saw him carry also an armful of the jars which contained unlabelled capsules and several boxes of unguessable contents, stowing them in the boot carefully and closing them in.

Calder was busy obliterating his tracks.

I yelled at him, calling his name, but he didn't even hear or turn his head. The only result was startled movement in the horse behind me, a stamping of hooves and a restless swinging round the box.

'All right,' I said soothingly. 'Steady down. All right. Don't be frightened.'

The big animal's alarm abated, and through the window I watched Calder switch off the surgery light, lock the door, get into his car and drive away.

He drove away out of his driveway, towards the main road, not towards his house. The lights of his car passed briefly over the trees as he turned out through the gates, and then were gone: and I seemed suddenly very alone, imprisoned in that dingy place for heaven knew how long.

Vision slowly expanded so that from the dim light of the sky I could see again the outlines within the box: walls, manger . . . horse. The big dark creature didn't like me being there and wouldn't settle, but I could think of no way to relieve him of my presence.

The ceiling was solid, not as in some stables open through the rafters to the roof. In many it would have been possible for an agile man to climb the partition from one box to the next, but not here; and in any case there was no promise of being better off next door. One would be in a different box but probably just as simply and securely bolted in.

There was nothing in my trouser pockets but a handkerchief. Penknife, money and house keys were all in my jacket in the boot of my own unlocked car out on the road. The dark jersey which had seemed good for speed, quiet and concealment had left me without even a coin for a screwdriver.

I thought concentratedly of what a man could do with his fingers that a horse couldn't do with superior strength, but found nothing in the darkness of the door to unwind or unhinge; nothing anywhere to pick loose. It looked most annoyingly as if that was where I was going to stay until Calder came back.

And then ... what?

If he'd intended to kill me, why hadn't he already made sure of it? Another swipe or two with the fire extinguisher would have done ... and I would have known nothing about it.

I thought of Ginnie, positive now that that was how it had been for her, that in one instant she had been thinking, and in the next ... not.

Thought of Ian Pargetter, dead from one blow of his own brass lamp. Thought of Calder's shock and grief at the event, probably none the less real despite his having killed the man he mourned. Calder shattered over the loss of a business friend ... the friend he had himself struck down.

He must have killed him, I thought, on a moment's ungovernable impulse, for not ... what had he said? ... for not wanting to go on, for wanting to stop Calder doing ... what Calder planned.

Calder had struck at me with the same sort of speed: without pause for consideration, without time to think of consequences. And he had lashed at me as a friend too, without hesitation, while saying shortly after that he liked me.

Calder, swinging the fire extinguisher, had ruthlessly aimed at killing the man who had saved his life.

Saved Calder's life ... Oh God, I thought, why ever did I do it?

The man in whom I had wanted to see only goodness had after that day killed Ian Pargetter, killed Ginnie; and if I hadn't saved him they would both have lived.

The despair of that thought filled me utterly, swelling with enormity, making me feel, as the simpler grief for Ginnie had done, that one's body couldn't hold so much emotion. Remorse and guilt could rise like dragons' teeth from good intentions, and there were in truth unexpected paths to hell.

I thought back to that distant moment that had affected so many lives: to that instinctive reflex, faster than thought, which had launched me at Ricky's knife. If I could have called it back I would have been looking away, not seeing, letting Calder die ... letting Ricky take his chances, letting him blast his young life to fragments, destroy his caring parents.

One couldn't help what came after.

A fireman or a lifeboatman or a surgeon might fight to the utmost stretch of skill to save a baby and find he had let loose a Hitler, a Nero, Jack the Ripper. It couldn't always be Beethoven or Pasteur whose life one extended. All one asked was an ordinary, moderately sinful, normally well-intentioned, fairly harmless human. And if he cured horses ... all the better.

Before that day at Ascot Calder couldn't even have

thought of owning Sandcastle, because Sandcastle at that moment was in mid-career with his stud value uncertain. But Calder had seen, as we all had, the majesty of that horse, and I had myself listened to the admiration in his voice.

At some time after that he must have thought of selenium, and from there the wickedness had grown to encompass us all: the wickedness which would have been extinguished before birth if I'd been looking another way.

I knew logically that I couldn't have not done what I did; but in heart and spirit that didn't matter. It didn't stop the engulfing misery or allow me any ease.

Grief and sorrow came to us all, Pen had said: and she was right.

The horse became more restive and began to paw the ground.

I looked at my watch, the digital figures bright in the darkness: twenty minutes or thereabouts since Calder had left. Twenty minutes that already seemed like twenty hours.

The horse swung round suddenly in the gloom with unwelcome vigour, bumping against me with his rump.

'Calm down now, boy,' I said soothingly. 'We're stuck with each other. Go to sleep.'

The horse's reply was the equivalent of unprintable: the crash of a steel-clad hoof against a wall.

Perhaps he didn't like me talking, I thought, or indeed even moving about. His head swung round towards the window, his bulk stamping restlessly from one side of the box to the other, and I saw that he, unlike Oliver's horses, wore no headcollar: nothing with which to hold him, while I calmed him, patting his neck.

His head reared up suddenly, tossing violently, and with a foreleg he lashed forward at the wall.

Not funny, I thought. Horrific to have been in the firing-line of that slashing hoof. For heaven's sake, I said to him mentally, I'll do you no harm. Just stay quiet. Go to sleep.

I was standing at that time with my back to the door, so that to the horse I must have been totally in shadow; but he would know I was there. He could smell my presence, hear my breathing. If he could see me as well, would it be better?

I took a tentative step towards the dim oblong of window, and had a clear, sharp, and swiftly terrifying view of one of his eyes.

No peace. No sleep. No prospect of anything like that. The horse's eye was stretched wide with white showing all round the usual darkness, staring not at me but as if blind, glaring wildly at nothing at all.

The black nostrils looked huge. The lips as I watched were drawing back from the teeth. The ears had gone flat to the head and there was froth forming in the mouth. It was the face, I thought incredulously, not of unrest or alarm . . . but of madness.

The horse backed suddenly away, crashing his hindquarters into the rear wall and rocking again forwards, but this time advancing with both forelegs off the ground, the gleams from thrashing hooves curving in silvery streaks in the gloom, the feet hitting the wall below the window with sickening intent.

I pressed in undoubted panic into the corner made by wall and door, but it gave no real protection. The box was roughly ten feet square by eight feet high, a space even at the best of times half filled by horse. For that horse at that moment it was a straitjacket confinement out of which he seemed intent on physically smashing his way.

The manger, I thought. Get in the manger.

The manger was built at about waist height diagonally across one of the box's rear corners; a smallish metal trough set into a sturdy wooden support. As a shelter it was pathetic, but at least I would be off the ground . . .

The horse turned and stood on his forelegs and let fly backwards with an almighty double kick that thudded into the concrete wall six inches from my head, and it was then, at that moment, that I began to fear that the crazed animal might not just hurt but kill me.

He wasn't purposely trying to attack; most of his kicks were in other directions. He wasn't trying to bite, though his now open mouth looked savage. He was uncontrollably wild, but not with me ... though that, in so small a space, made little difference.

He seemed in the next very few seconds to go utterly berserk. With speeds I could only guess at in the scurrying shadows he whirled and kicked and hurled his bulk against the walls, and I, still attempting to jump through the tempest into the manger, was finally knocked over by one of his flailing feet.

I didn't realize at that point that he'd actually broken one of my arms because the whole thing felt numb. I made it to the manger, tried to scramble up, got my foot in ... sat on the edge ... tried to raise my other, now dangling foot ... and couldn't do it fast enough. Another direct hit crunched on my ankle and I knew, that time, that there was damage.

The air about my head seemed to hiss with hooves and the horse was beginning a high bubbling whinny. Surely someone, I thought desperately, someone would hear the crashing and banging and come ...

I could see him in flashes against the window, a rearing, bucking, kicking, rocketing nightmare. He came wheeling round, half-seen, walking on his hind legs, head hard against the ceiling, the forelegs thrashing as if trying to climb invisible walls ... and he knocked me off my precarious perch with a swiping punch in the chest that had half a ton of weight behind it and no particular aim.

I fell twisting onto the straw and tried to curl my head away from those lethal feet, to save instinctively one's face and gut . . . and leave backbone and kidney to their fate. Another crushing thud landed on the back of my shoulder and jarred like a hammer through every bone, and I could feel a scream forming somewhere inside me, a wrenching cry for mercy, for escape, for an end to battering, for release from terror.

His mania if anything grew worse, and it was he who was finally screaming, not me. The noise filled my ears, bounced off the walls, stunning, mind-blowing, the roaring of furies.

He somehow got one hoof inside my rolled body and tumbled me fast over, and I could see him arching above me, the tendons like strings, the torment in him too, the rage of the gods bursting from his stretched throat, his forelegs so high that he was hitting the ceiling.

This is death, I thought. This is dreadful, pulverizing extinction. Only for this second would I see and feel . . . and one of his feet would land on my head and I'd go . . . I'd go . . .

Before I'd even finished the thought his forelegs came crashing down with a hoof so close it brushed my hair; and then again, as if driven beyond endurance, he reared dementedly on his hind legs, the head going up like a reverse thunderbolt towards the sky, the skull meeting the ceiling with the force of a ram. The whole building shook with the impact, and the horse, his voice cut off, fell in a huge collapsing mass across my legs, spasms shuddering through his body, muscles jerking in stiff kicks, the air still ringing with the echoes of extremity.

He was dying in stages, unconscious, reluctant, the brain finished, the nerve messages still passing to convulsing muscles, turmoil churning without direction in stomach and gut, the head already inert on the straw.

An age passed before it was done. Then the heavy body fell flaccid, all systems spent, and lay in perpetual astonishing silence, pinning me beneath.

The relief of finding him dead and myself alive lasted quite a long time, but then, as always happens with the human race, simple gratitude for existence progressed to discontent that things weren't better.

He had fallen with his spine towards me, his bulk lying across my legs from my knees down; and getting out from under him was proving an impossibility.

The left ankle, which felt broken, protested screechingly at any attempted movement. I couldn't lift my arm for the same reason. There was acute soreness in my chest, making breathing itself painful and coughing frightful; and the only good thing I could think of was that I was lying on my back and not face down in the straw.

A very long time passed very slowly. The crushing weight of the horse slowly numbed my legs altogether and transferred the chief area of agony to the whole of my left arm, which I might have thought totally mangled if I hadn't been able to see it dimly lying there looking the same as usual, covered in blue sweater, white cuff slightly showing, hand with clean nails, gold watch on wrist.

Physical discomfort for a while shut out much in the way of thought, but eventually I began to add up memories and ask questions, and the biggest, most immediate question was what would Calder do when he came back and found me alive?

He wouldn't expect it. No one could really expect anyone to survive being locked in with a mad horse, and the fact that I had was a trick of fate.

I remembered him giving the horse an apple while I'd struggled within the spinning walls to stand up. Giving his apple so routinely, and patting the horse's neck.

I remembered Calder saying on my first visit that he gave his remedies to horses in hollowed-out apples. But this time it had been no remedy, this time something opposite, this time a drug to make crazy, to turn a normal steel-shod horse into a killing machine.

What had he said when he'd first found me conscious? Those bizarre words ... 'I thought you'd be out. I thought you wouldn't know ...' And something else ... 'I wish I'd hit you harder, but it seemed enough.'

He had said also that he was sorry, that he wished I hadn't come ... He hadn't meant, I thought, that I should be aware of it when the horse killed me. At the very least, he hadn't meant me to see and hear and suffer that death. But also, when he found me awake, it hadn't prevented him from *then* giving the apple, although he knew that I *would* see, *would* hear, would . . . suffer.

The horse hadn't completed the task. When Calder returned, he would make good the deficit. It was certain.

I tried, on that thought, again to slide my legs out, though how much it would have helped if I had succeeded was debatable. It was as excruciating as before, since the numbness proved temporary. I concluded somewhat sadly that dragging a broken ankle from beneath a dead horse was no jolly entertainment, and in fact, given the state of the rest of me, couldn't be done.

I had never broken any bones before, not even skiing. I'd never been injured beyond the transient bumps of childhood. Never been to hospital, never troubled a surgeon, never slept from anaesthetic. For thirty-four years I'd been thoroughly healthy and, apart from chicken-pox and such, never ill. I even had good teeth.

I was unprepared in any way for the onslaught of so much pain all at once, and also not quite sure how to deal with it. All I knew was that when I tried to pull out my ankle the protests throughout my body brought actual tears into my eyes and no amount of theoretical resolution could give me the power to continue. I wondered if what I felt was cowardice. I didn't much care if it was. I lay with everything stiffening and getting cold and worse, and I'd have given a good deal to be as oblivious as the horse.

The oblong of window at length began to lighten towards the new day: Saturday, June 2nd, Calder would come back and finish the job, and no reasonable pathologist would swear the last blow had been delivered hours after the first. Calder would say in bewilderment, 'But I had no idea Tim was coming to see me ... I was in London for the television ... I have no idea how he came to shut himself into one of the boxes ... because it's just possible to do that, you know, if you're not careful ... I've no idea why the horse should have kicked him, because he's a placid old boy, as you can see ... the whole thing's a terrible accident, and I'm shattered ... most distressed ...', and anyone would look at the horse from whose bloodstream the crazing drug would have departed and conclude that I'd been pretty unintelligent and also unlucky, and too bad.

Ian Pargetter's veterinary case had gone to a securer hiding place or to destruction, and there would be only a slight chance left of proving Calder a murderer. Whichever way one considered it, the outlook was discouraging.

I couldn't be bothered to roll my wrist over to see the time. The sun rose and shone slantingly through the bars with the pale brilliance of dawn. It had to be five o'clock, or after.

Time drifted. The sun moved away. The horse and I lay in intimate silence, dead and half dead; waiting.

A car drove up fast outside and doors slammed.

It will be now, I thought. Now. Very soon.

There were voices in the distance, calling to each other. Female and male. *Strangers.*

Not Calder's distinctive, loud, edgy, public voice. Not his at all.

Hope thumped back with a tremendous surge and I called out myself, saying, 'Here ... Come here,' but it was at best a croak, inaudible beyond the door.

Suppose they were looking for Calder, and when they didn't find him, drove away ... I took all possible breath into my lungs and yelled, 'Help ... Come here.'

Nothing happened. My voice ricocheted off the walls and mocked me, and I dragged in another grinding lungful and shouted again ... and again ... and again.

The top half of the door swung outward and let in a dazzle of light, and a voice yelled incredulously, 'He's *here*. He's in here ...'

The bolt on the lower half-door clattered and the daylight grew to an oblong, and against the light three figures appeared, coming forward, concerned, speaking with anxiety and joy and bringing life.

Judith and Gordon and Pen.

Judith was gulping and so I think was I.

'Thank God,' Gordon said. 'Thank God.'

'You didn't go home,' Pen said. 'We were worried.'

'Are you all right?' Judith said.

'Not really ... but everything's relative. I've never been happier, so who cares.'

'If we put our arms under your shoulders,' Gordon said, surveying the problem, 'we should be able to pull you out.'

'Don't do that,' I said.

'Why not?'

'One shoulder feels broken. Get a knacker.'

'My dear Tim,' he said, puzzled.

'They'll come with a lorry . . . and a winch. Their job is dead horses.'

'Yes, I see.'

'And an ambulance,' Pen said. 'I should think.'

I smiled at them with much love, my fairly incompetent saviours. They asked how I'd got where I was, and to their horror I briefly told them; and I in turn asked why they'd come, and they explained that they'd been worried because Calder's television programme had been cancelled.

'Micky Bonwith was taken ill,' Pen said. 'They just announced it during the evening. There would be no live Micky Bonwith show, just an old recording, very sorry, expect Calder Jackson at a later date.'

'Pen telephoned and told us where you were going, and why,' Judith said.

'And we were worried,' Gordon added.

'You didn't go home . . . didn't telephone,' Pen said.

'We've been awake all night,' Gordon said. 'The girls were growing more and more anxious . . . so we came.'

They'd come a hundred miles. You couldn't ask for better friends.

Gordon drove away to find a public telephone and Pen asked if I'd found what I'd come for.

'I don't know,' I said. 'Half the things had no labels.'

'Don't talk any more,' Judith said. 'Enough is enough.'

'I might as well.'

'Take your mind off it,' Pen nodded, understanding.

'What time is it?' I asked.

Judith looked at her watch. 'Ten to eight.'

'Calder will come back . . .' And the lads too, I thought. He'd come when the lads turned up for work. About that time. He'd need witnesses to the way he'd found me.

'Tim,' Pen said with decision, 'if he's coming . . . Did you take any samples? Did you get a chance?'

I nodded weakly.

'I suppose you can't remember what they were . . .'

'I hid them.'

'Wouldn't he have found them?' She was gentle and prepared to be disappointed; careful not to blame.

I smiled at her. 'He didn't find them. They're here.'

She looked blankly round the box and then at my face. 'Didn't he search you?' she said in surprise. 'Pockets . . . of course, he would.'

'I don't know . . . but he didn't find the pills.'

'Then where *are* they?'

'I learned from Ginnie about keeping your hands free,' I said. 'They're in a plastic bag . . . below my waistband . . . inside my pants.'

369

They stared incredulously, and then they laughed, and Judith with tears in her eyes said, 'Do you mean . . . all the time . . .?'

'All the time,' I agreed. 'And go easy getting them out.'

Some things would be best forgotten but are impossible to forget, and I reckon one could put the next half-hour into that category: at the end of it I lay on a table-like stretcher in the open air, and my dead-weight pal was half up the ramp of the knacker's van that Gordon with exceptional persuasiveness had conjured out at that hour of the morning.

The three lads who had at length arrived for work stood around looking helpless, and the two ambulance men, who were not paramedics, were farcically trying to get an answer on a radio with transmission troubles as to where they were supposed to take me.

Gordon was telling the knacker's men that I said it was essential to remove a blood sample from the horse and that the carcass was not to be disposed of until that was done. Judith and Pen both looked tired, and were yawning. I wearily watched some birds wheeling high in the fair blue sky and wished I were up there with them, as light as air; and into this riveting tableau drove Calder.

Impossible to know what he thought when he saw

370

all the activity, but as he came striding from his car his mouth formed an oval of apprehension and shock.

He seemed first to fasten his attention on Gordon, and then on the knacker's man who was saying loudly, 'If you want a blood sample you'll have to give us a written authorization, because of calling in a vet and paying him.'

Calder looked from him to the dead horse still halfway up the ramp, and from there towards the horse's normal box, where the door stood wide open.

From there he turned with bewilderment to Judith, and then with horror saw the bag Pen held tightly, the transparent plastic bag with the capsules, pills and other assorted treasures showing clearly inside.

Pen remarkably found her voice and in words that must have sounded like doom to Calder said, 'I didn't tell you before . . . I'm a pharmacist.'

'Where did you get that?' Calder said, staring at the bag as if his eyes would burn it. 'Where . . .'

'Tim had it.'

Her gaze went to me and Calder seemed finally to realize that my undoubted stillness was not that of death. He took two paces towards the stretcher and looked down at my face and saw me alive, awake, aware.

Neither of us spoke. His eyes seemed to retreat in the sockets and the shape of the upper jaw stood out starkly. He saw in me I dare say the ravages of the

371

night and I saw in him the realization become certainty
that my survival meant his ruin.

I thought: you certainly should have hit harder; and
maybe he thought it too. He looked at me with a
searing intensity that defied analysis and then turned
abruptly away and walked with jerky steps back to his
car.

Gordon took two or three hesitant steps towards
perhaps stopping him, but Calder without looking back
started his engine, put his foot on the accelerator and
with protesting tyres made a tight semicircular turn
and headed for the gate.

'We should get the police,' Gordon said, watching
him go.

Judith and Pen showed scant enthusiasm and I none
at all. I supposed we would have to bring in the police
in the end, but the longer the boring rituals could be
postponed, from my point of view, the better. Britain
was a small island, and Calder too well known to go far.

Pen looked down at the plastic storehouse in her
hands and then without actual comment opened her
handbag and put the whole thing inside. She glanced
briefly at me and smiled faintly, and I nodded with relief
that she and her friends would have the unravelling of
the capsules to themselves.

On that same Saturday, at about two-thirty in the afternoon, a family of picnickers came across a car which

had been parked out of sight of any road behind some clumps of gorse bushes. The engine of the car was running and the children of the family, peering through the windows, saw a man slumped on the back seat with a tube in his mouth.

They knew him because of his curly hair, and his beard.

The children were reported to be in a state of hysterical shock and the parents were angry, as if some authority, somewhere or other, should prevent suicides spoiling the countryside.

Tributes to Calder's miracle-working appeared on television that evening, and I thought it ironic that the master who had known so much about drugs should have chosen to gas his way out.

He had driven barely thirty miles from his yard. He had left no note. The people who had been working with him on the postponed Micky Bonwith show said they couldn't understand it, and Dissdale telephoned Oliver to say that in view of Calder's tragic death he would have to withdraw his offer for Sandcastle.

I, by the time I heard all this, was half covered in infinitely irritating plaster of Paris, there being more grating edges of bone inside me than I cared to hear about, and horseshoe-shaped crimson bruises besides.

I had been given rather grudgingly a room to myself, privacy in illness being considered a sinful luxury in the National Health Service, and on Monday evening

Pen came all the way from London again to report on the laboratory findings.

She frowned after she'd kissed me. 'You look exhausted,' she said.

'Tiring place, hospital.'

'I suppose it must be. I'd never thought . . .'

She put a bunch of roses in my drinking-water jug and said they were from Gordon and Judith's garden.

'They send their love,' she said chattily, 'and their garden's looking lovely.'

'Pen . . .'

'Yes. Well.' She pulled the visitor's chair closer to the bed upon which I half sat, half lay in my plaster and borrowed dressing gown on top of the blankets. 'You have really, as they say, hit the jackpot.'

'Do you mean it?' I exclaimed.

She grinned cheerfully. 'It's no wonder that Calder killed himself, not after seeing you alive and hearing you were going to get the dead horse tested, and knowing that after all you had taken all those things from his surgery. It was either that or years in jail and total disgrace.'

'A lot of people would prefer disgrace.'

'Not Calder, though.'

'No.'

She opened a slim black briefcase on her knees and produced several typewritten pages.

'We worked all yesterday and this morning,' she said. 'But first I'll tell you that Gordon got the dead horse's

374

blood test done immediately at the Equine Research Establishment, and they told him on the telephone this morning that the horse had been given ethyl isobutrazine, which was contrary to normal veterinary practice.'

'You don't say.'

Her eyes gleamed. 'The Research people told Gordon that any horse given ethyl isobutrazine would go utterly berserk and literally try to climb the walls.'

'That's just what he did,' I said soberly.

'It's a drug which is used all the time as a tranquillizer to stop dogs barking or getting car-sick, but it has an absolutely manic effect on horses. One of its brand names is Diquel, in case you're interested. All the veterinary books warn against giving it to horses.'

'But normally . . . in a horse . . . it would wear off?'

'Yes, in six hours or so, with no trace.'

Six hours, I thought bleakly. *Six hours* . . .

'In your bag of goodies,' Pen said, 'guess what we found? Three tablets of Diquel.'

'Really?'

She nodded. 'Really. And now pin back your ears, dearest Tim, because when we found what Calder had been doing, words simply failed us.'

They seemed indeed to fail her again, for she sat looking at the pages with a faraway expression.

'You remember,' she said at last, 'when we went to Calder's yard that time at Easter, we saw a horse that had been bleeding in its urine . . . crystalluria was what he called it . . . that antibiotics hadn't been able to cure?'

'Yes,' I said. 'Other times too, he cured horses with that.'

'Mm. And those patients had been previously treated by Ian Pargetter before he died, hadn't they?'

I thought back. 'Some of them, certainly.'

'Well . . . you know you told me before they carted you off in the ambulance on Saturday that some of the jars of capsules in the cupboards were labelled only with letters like a+w, b+w, and c+s?'

I nodded.

'Three capsules each with one transparent and one blue end, *did* contain c and s. Vitamin C, and sulphanilamide.' She looked at me for a possible reaction, but vitamin C and sulphanilamide sounded quite harmless, and I said so.

'Yes,' she said, 'separately they do nothing but good, but *together they can cause crystalluria.*'

I stared at her.

'Calder had made those capsules expressly to *cause the horse's illness* in the first place, so that he could "cure" it afterwards. And then the only miracle he'd have to work would be to stop giving the capsules.'

'My God,' I said.

She nodded. 'We could hardly believe it. It meant, you see, that Ian Pargetter almost certainly *knew*. Because it was he, you see, who could have given the horse's trainer or owner or lad or whatever a bottle of capsules labelled "antibiotic" to dole out every day. And those capsules were precisely what was making the horse ill.'

'*Pen!*'

'I'd better explain just a little, if you can bear it,' she said. 'If you give sulpha drugs to anyone – horse or person – who doesn't need them, you won't do much harm because urine is normally slightly alkaline or only slightly acid and you'll get rid of the sulpha safely. But vitamin C is ascorbic acid and makes the urine *more* acid, and the acid works with sulpha drugs to form crystals, and the crystals cause pain and bleeding . . . like powdered glass.'

There was a fairly long silence, and then I said, 'It's diabolical.'

She nodded. 'Once Calder had the horse in his yard he could speed up the cure by giving him bicarbonate of soda, which will make the urine alkaline again and also dissolve the crystals, and with plenty of water to drink the horse would be well in no time. Miraculously fast, in fact.' She paused and smiled, and went on, 'We tested a few more things which were perfectly harmless herbal remedies and then we came to three more home-made capsules, with pale green ends this time, and we reckon that they were your a+w.'

'Go on, then,' I said. 'What's a, and what's w?'

'A is antibiotic, and w is warfarin. And before you ask, warfarin is a drug used in humans for reducing the clotting ability of the blood.'

'That pink pill you found on the surgery floor,' I said. 'That's what you said.'

'Oh yes.' She looked surprised. 'So I did. I'd forgotten. Well . . . if you give certain antibiotics *with* warfarin you increase the effect of the warfarin to the extent that blood will hardly clot at all . . . and you get severe bleeding from the stomach, from the mouth, from anywhere where a small blood vessel breaks . . . when normally it would clot and mend at once.'

I let out a held breath. 'Every time I went, there was a bleeder.'

She nodded. 'Warfarin acts by drastically reducing the effect of vitamin K, which is needed for normal clotting, so all Calder had to do to reverse things was feed lots of vitamin K . . . which is found in large quantities in alfalfa.'

'And b+w?' I asked numbly.

'Barbiturate and warfarin. Different mechanism, but if you used them together and then stopped just the barbiturate, you could cause a sort of delayed bleeding about three weeks later.' She paused. 'We've all been looking up our pharmacology textbooks, and there are warnings there, plain to see if you're looking for them, about prescribing antibiotics or barbiturates or indeed phenylbutazone or anabolic steroids for people on warfarin without carefully adjusting the warfarin dosage. And you see,' she went on, 'putting two drugs together in one capsule was really brilliant, because no one would think they were giving a horse two drugs, but just one . . . and we reckon Ian Pargetter could have put Calder's capsules into any regular bottle, and the horse's owner would think that he was giving the horse what it said on the label.'

I blinked. 'It's incredible.'

'It's easy,' she said. 'And it gets easier as it goes on.'

'There's more?'

'Sure there's more.' She grinned. 'How about all those poor animals with extreme debility who were so weak they could hardly walk?'

I swallowed. 'How about them?'

'You said you found a large bottle in Ian Pargetter's case with only a few pills in it? A bottle labelled "diuretic", or in other words, pills designed to increase the passing of urine?'

I nodded.

'Well, we identified the ones you took, and if you simply gave those particular thiazide diuretic pills over a long period to a horse you would cause *exactly* the sort of general progressive debility shown by those horses.'

I was past speech.

'And to cure the debility,' she said, 'you just stop the diuretics and provide good food and water. And hey presto!' She smiled blissfully. 'Chemically, it's so elegant. The debility is caused by constant excessive excretion of potassium which the body needs for strength, and the cure is to restore potassium as fast as safely possible . . . with potassium salts, which you can buy anywhere.'

I gazed at her with awe.

She was enjoying her revelations. 'We come now to the horses with non-healing ulcers and sores.'

Always those, too, in the yard, I thought.

'Ulcers and sores are usually cleared up fairly quickly by applications of antibiotic cream. Well . . . by this time we were absolutely bristling with suspicions, so last of all we took that little tube of antibiotic cream you found in Ian Pargetter's case, and we tested it. And lo and behold, it didn't contain antibiotic cream at all.'

'What then?'

'Cortisone cream.'

She looked at my non-comprehension and smiled. 'Cortisone cream is fine for eczema and allergies, but *not* for general healing. In fact, if you scratched a horse and smeared some dirt into the wound to infect it and then religiously applied cortisone cream twice a day you would get a nice little ulcer which would never heal. Until, of course, you sent your horse to Calder, who would lay his hands upon your precious . . . and apply antibiotics at once, to let normal healing begin.'

'Dear God in heaven.'

'Never put cortisone cream on a cut,' she said. 'A lot of people do. It's stupid.'

'I never will,' I said fervently.

Pen grinned. 'They always fill toothpaste from the

blunt end. We looked very closely and found that the end of the tube had been unwound and then resealed. Very neat.'

She seemed to have stopped, so I asked, 'Is that the lot?'

'That's the lot.'

We sat for a while and pondered.

'It does answer an awful lot of questions,' I said finally.

'Such as?'

'Such as why Calder killed Ian Pargetter,' I said. 'Ian Pargetter wanted to stop something . . . which must have been this illness caper. Said he'd had enough. Said also that he would stop Calder too, which must have been his death warrant.'

Pen said, 'Is that what Calder actually told you?'

'Yes, that's what he said, but at the time I didn't understand what he meant.'

'I wonder,' Pen said, 'why Ian Pargetter wanted to stop altogether? They must have had a nice steady income going between the two of them. Calder must have recruited him years ago.'

'Selenium,' I said.

'What?'

'Selenium was different. Making horses ill in order to cure them wasn't risking much permanent damage, if any at all. But selenium would be for ever. The foals would be deformed. I'd guess when Calder suggested it the idea sickened Ian Pargetter. Revolted him, probably, because he was after all a vet.'

'And Calder wanted to go on with it all ... enough to kill.'

I nodded. 'Calder would have had his sights on a fortune as well as an income. And but for Ginnie somehow getting hold of that shampoo, he would very likely have achieved it.'

'I wonder how she did,' Pen said.

'Mm.' I shifted uncomfortably on the bed. 'I've remembered the name of the lad Calder had who looked like Ricky Barnet. It was Jason. I remembered it the other night ... in that yard ... funny the way the mind works.'

'What about him?' Pen said sympathetically.

'I remembered Calder saying he gave the pills to Jason for Jason to give to the horses. The herb pills, he meant. But with Ian Pargetter gone, Calder would have needed someone else to give those double-edged capsules to horses ... because he still had horses in his yard with those same troubles long after Ian Pargetter was dead.'

'So he did,' she said blankly. 'Except ...'

'Except what?'

'Only that when we got to the yard last Saturday, before I heard you calling, we looked into several other boxes, and there weren't many horses there. The place wasn't full, like it had been.'

'I should think,' I said slowly, 'that it was because

Jason had been busy working for three months or more at Oliver's farm, feeding selenium apples.'

A visual memory flashed in my brain. *Apples* . . . Shane, the stable lad, walking across the yard, swinging a bucket and eating an apple. Shane, Jason: one and the same.

'What is it?' Pen said.

'Photos of Ricky Barnet.'

'Oh yes.'

'They say I can leave here tomorrow,' I said, 'if I insist.'

She looked at me with mock despair. 'What exactly did you break?'

'They said this top lot was scapula, clavicle, humerus, sternum and ribs. Down there,' I pointed, 'they lost me. I didn't know there *were* so many bones in one ankle.'

'Did they pin it?'

'God knows.'

'How will you look after yourself?'

'In my usual clumsy fashion.'

'Don't be silly,' she said. 'Stay until it stops hurting.'

'That might be weeks . . . there's some problem with ligaments or tendons or something.'

'What problem?'

'I didn't really listen.'

'*Tim*.' She was exasperated.

'Well . . . it's so boring,' I said.

She gave an eyes-to-heaven laugh. 'I brought you a

present from my shop.' She dug into her handbag. 'Here you are, with my love.'

I took the small white box she offered, and looked at the label on its side.

Comfrey, it said.

She grinned. 'You might as well try it,' she said. 'Comfrey does contain allantoin, which helps to knit bones. And you never know ... Calder really was an absolute expert with all sorts of drugs.'

On Tuesday, June 5th, Oliver Knowles collected me from the hospital to drive me on some errands and then take me to his home, not primarily as an act of compassion but mostly to talk business. I had expected him to accept my temporary disabilities in a straight-forward and unemotional manner, and so he did, although he did say drily when he saw me that when I had invited myself over the telephone I had referred to a 'crack or two' and not to half an acre of plaster with clothes strung on in patches.

'Never mind,' I said. 'I can hop and I can sit and my right arm is fine.'

'Yes. So I see.'

The nurse who had wheeled me in a chair to his car said, however, 'He can't hop, it jars him,' and handed Oliver a slip of paper. 'There's a place along that road ...' She pointed, '... where you can hire wheel-chairs.' To me she said, 'Get a comfortable one. And

one which lets your leg lie straight out, like this one.
You'll ache less. All right?'

'All right,' I said.

'Hm. Well . . . take care.'

She helped me into the car with friendly competence
and went away with the hospital transport, and Oliver
and I did as she advised, storing the resulting
cushioned and chromium comfort into the boot of his
car.

'Right,' I said. 'Then the next thing to do is buy a
good instant camera and a stack of films.'

Oliver found a shop and bought the camera while I
sat in the front passenger seat as patiently as possible.

'Where next?' he said, coming back with parcels.

'Cambridge. An engineering works. Here's the
address.' I handed him the piece of paper on which
I'd written Ricky Barnet's personal directions. 'We're
meeting him when he comes out of work.'

'Who?' Oliver said. 'Who are we meeting?'

'You'll see.'

We parked across the road from the firm's gate and
waited, and at four-thirty on the dot the exodus
occurred.

Ricky Barnet came out and looked this way and that
in searching for us, and beside me I heard Oliver stir
and say, 'But that's Shane,' in surprise, and then relax
and add doubtfully, 'No it isn't.'

'No, it isn't.' I leaned out of the open window and
called to him, 'Ricky . . . over here.'

He crossed the road and stopped beside the car.

'Hop in,' I said.

'You been in an accident?' he said disbelievingly.

'Sort of.'

He climbed into the back of the car. He hadn't been too keen to have his photograph taken for the purpose I'd outlined, but he was in no great position to refuse; and I'd made my blackmailing pressure sound like honey, which I wasn't too bad at, in my way. He still wasn't pleased, however, which had its own virtues, as the last thing I wanted was forty prints of him grinning.

Oliver drove off and stopped where I asked at a suitably neutral background – a grey-painted factory wall – and he said he would take the photographs if I explained what I wanted.

'Ricky looks like Shane,' I said. 'So take pictures of Ricky in the way he *most* looks like Shane. Get him to turn his head slowly like he did when he came out of work, and tell him to hold it where it's best.'

'All right.'

Ricky got out of the car and stood in front of the wall, with Oliver focusing at head-and-shoulder distance. He took the first picture and we waited for it to develop.

Oliver looked at it, grunted, adjusted the light meter, and tried again.

'This one's all right,' he said, watching the colours emerge. 'Looks like Shane. Quite amazing.'

With a faint shade of sullenness Ricky held his pose

386

for as long as it took to shoot four boxes of film. Oliver passed each print to me as it came out of the camera, and I laid them in rows along the seat beside me while they developed.

'That's fine,' I said, when the films were finished. 'Thank you, Ricky.'

He came over to the car window and I asked him without any great emphasis, 'Do you remember, when Indian Silk got so ill with debility, which vet was treating him?'

'Yeah, sure, that fellow that was murdered. Him and his partners. The best, Dad said.'

I nodded non-committally. 'Do you want a ride to Newmarket?'

'Got my motorbike, thanks.'

We took him back to his engineering works where I finally cheered him up with payment for his time and trouble, and watched while he roared off with a flourish of self-conscious bravado.

'What's now?' Oliver said. 'Did you say Newmarket?'

I nodded. 'I've arranged to meet Ursula Young.'

He gave me a glance of bewilderment and drove without protest, pulling duly into the mid-town car park where Ursula had said to come.

We arrived there first, the photography not having taken as long as I'd expected, and Oliver finally gave voice to a long-restrained question.

'Just what,' he said, 'are the photographs *for*?'

'For finding Shane.'

'But why?'

'Don't explode.'

'No.'

'Because I think he gave the selenium to your mares.'

Oliver sat very still. 'You asked about him before,' he said. 'I did wonder . . . if you thought . . . he killed Ginnie.'

It was my own turn for quiet.

'I don't know if he did,' I said at last. 'I don't know.'

Ursula arrived in her car with a rush, checking her watch and apologizing all the same, although she was on time. She, like Oliver and Ricky, looked taken aback at my unorthodox attire, but rallied in her usual no-nonsense fashion and shuffled into the back seat of Oliver's car, leaning forward to bring her face on a level with ours.

I passed her thirty of the forty pictures of Ricky Barnet who, of course, she knew immediately.

'Yes, but,' I explained, 'Ricky looks like a lad who worked for Oliver, and it's *that* lad we want to find.'

'Well, all right. How important is it?'

Oliver answered her before I could. 'Ursula, if you find him, we might be able to prove there's nothing wrong with Sandcastle. And don't ask me how, just believe it.'

Her mouth had opened.

'And Ursula,' Oliver said, 'if you find him – Shane,

that lad – I'll put business your way for the rest of my life.'

I could see that to her, a middle-rank bloodstock agent, it was no mean promise.

'All right,' she said briskly. 'You're on. I'll start spreading the pictures about at once, tonight, and call you with results.'

'Ursula,' I said. 'If you find where he is now, make sure he isn't frightened off. We don't want to lose him.'

She looked at me shrewdly. 'This is roughly police work?'

I nodded. 'Also, if you find anyone who employed him in the past, ask if by any chance a horse he looked after fell ill. Or any horse in the yard, for that matter. And don't give him a name ... he isn't always called Shane.'

'Is he dangerous?' she said straightly.

'We don't want him challenged,' I said. 'Just found.'

'All right. I trust you both, so I'll do my best. And I suppose one day you'll explain what it's all about?'

'If he's done what we think,' I said, 'we'll make sure the whole world knows. You can count on it.'

She smiled briefly and patted my unplastered shoulder. 'You look grey,' she said, and to Oliver, 'Tim told me a horse kicked him and broke his arm. Is that right?'

'He told me that, too.'

'And what else?' she asked me astringently. 'How did you get in this state?'

'The horse didn't know its own strength.' I smiled at her. 'Clumsy brute.'

She knew I was dodging in some way, but she lived in a world where the danger of horse kicks was ever present and always to be avoided, and she made no more demur. Stowing the photographs in her capacious handbag she wriggled her way out of the car, and with assurances of action drove off in her own.

'What now?' Oliver said.

'A bottle of Scotch.'

He gave me an austere look which then swept over my general state and softened to understanding.

'Can you wait until we get home?' he said.

That evening, bit by bit, I told Oliver about Pen's analysis of the treasures from Calder's surgery and of Calder's patients' drug-induced illnesses. I told him that Calder had killed Ian Pargetter, and why, and I explained again how the idea of first discrediting, then buying and rebuilding Sandcastle had followed the pattern of Indian Silk.

'There may be others besides Indian Silk that we haven't heard of,' I said thoughtfully. 'Show jumpers, eventers, even prize ponies. You never know. Dissdale might have gone along more than twice with his offer to buy the no-hoper.'

'He withdrew his offer for Sandcastle the same night Calder died.'

'What exactly did he say?' I asked.

'He was very upset. Said he'd lost his closest friend, and that without Calder to work his miracles there was no point in buying Sandcastle.'

I frowned. 'Do you think it was genuine?'

'His distress? Yes, certainly.'

'And the belief in miracles?'

'He did *sound* as if he believed.'

I wondered if it was in the least possible that Dissdale was an innocent and duped accomplice and hadn't known that his bargains had been first made ill. His pride in knowing the Great Man had been obvious at Ascot, and perhaps he had been flattered and foolish but not wicked after all.

Oliver asked in the end how I'd found out about the drug-induced illnesses and Ian Pargetter's murder, and I told him that too, as flatly as possible.

He sat staring at me, his gaze on the plaster.

'You're very lucky to be in a wheelchair, and not a coffin,' he said. 'Damn lucky.'

'Yes.'

He poured more of the brandy we had progressed to after dinner. Anaesthesia was coming along nicely.

'I'm almost beginning to believe,' he said, 'that somehow or other I'll still be here next year, even if I do have to sell Sandcastle and whatever else is necessary.'

I drank from my replenished glass. 'Tomorrow we'll make a plan contingent upon Sandcastle's being reinstated in the eyes of the world. Look out the figures, see what the final damage is likely to be, draw up a time-scale for recovery. I can't promise because it isn't my final say-so, but if the bank gets all its money in the end, it'll most likely be flexible about when.'

'Good of you,' Oliver said, hiding emotion behind his clipped martial manner.

'Frankly,' I said, 'you're more use to us salvaged than bust.'

He smiled wryly. 'A banker to the last drop of blood.'

Because of stairs being difficult I slept on the sofa where Ginnie had dozed on her last afternoon, and I dreamed of her walking up a path towards me looking happy. Not a significant dream, but an awakening of fresh regret. I spent a good deal of the following day thinking of her instead of concentrating on profit and loss.

In the evening Ursula telephoned with triumph in her strong voice and also a continual undercurrent of amazement.

'You won't believe it,' she said, 'but I've already found three racing stables in Newmarket where he worked last summer and autumn, and in *every case* one of the horses in the yard fell sick!'

I hadn't any trouble at all with belief and asked what sort of sickness.

'They all had crystalluria. That's crystals . . .'

'I know what it is,' I said.

'And . . . it's absolutely incredible but all three were in stables which had in the past sent horses to Calder Jackson, and these were sent as well, and he cured them straight away. Two of the trainers said they would swear by Calder, he had cured horses for them for years.'

'Was the lad called Shane?' I asked.

'No. Bret. Bret Williams. The same in all three places.'

She dictated the addresses of the stables, the names of the trainers, and the dates (approximate) when Shane – Jason – Bret had been in their yards.

'These lads just come and go,' she said. 'He didn't work for any of them for as long as a month. Just didn't turn up one morning. It happens all the time.'

'You're marvellous,' I said.

'I have a feeling,' she said with less excitement, 'that what I'm telling you is what you expected to hear.'

'Hoped.'

'The implications are unbelievable.'

'Believe them.'

'But *Calder*,' she protested. 'He couldn't . . .'

'Shane worked for Calder,' I said. 'All the time. Permanently. Wherever he went, it was to manufacture patients for Calder.'

She was silent so long that in the end I said, 'Ursula?'

'I'm here,' she said. 'Do you want me to go on with the photos?'

'Yes, if you would. To find him.'

393

'Hanging's too good for him,' she said grimly. 'I'll do what I can.'

She disconnected, and I told Oliver what she'd said.

'Bret Williams? He was Shane Williams here.'

'How did you come to employ him?' I asked.

Oliver frowned, looking back. 'Good lads aren't that easy to find, you know. You can advertise until you're blue in the face and only get third- or fourth-rate applicants. But Nigel said Shane impressed him at the interview and that we should give him a month's trial, and of course after that we kept him on, and took him back gladly this year when he telephoned asking, because he was quick and competent and knew the job backwards, and was polite and a good time-keeper . . .'

'A paragon,' I said drily.

'As lads go, yes.'

I nodded. He would have to have been good; to have taken pride in his deception, with the devotion of all traitors. I considered those fancy names and thought that he must have seen himself as a sort of macho hero, the great foreign agent playing out his fantasies in the day to day tasks, feeling superior to his employers while he tricked them with contempt.

He could have filled the hollowed cores of apples with capsules, and taken a bite or two round the outside to convince, and fed what looked like remainders to his victims. No one would ever have suspected, because suspicion was impossible.

I slept again on the sofa and the following morning

Oliver telephoned to Detective Chief Inspector Wyfold and asked him to come to the farm. Wyfold needed persuading; reluctantly agreed; and nearly walked out in a U-turn when he saw me waiting in Oliver's office.

'No. Look,' he protested, 'Mr Ekaterin's already approached me with his ideas and I simply haven't time . . .'

Oliver interrupted. 'We have a great deal more now. Please do listen. We quite understand that you are busy with all those other poor girls, but at the very least we can take Ginnie off that list for you.'

Wyfold finally consented to sit down and accept some coffee and listen to what we had to say: and as we told him in turns and in detail what had been happening his air of impatience dissipated and his natural sharpness took over.

We gave him copies of Pen's analyses, the names of 'Bret's' recent employers and the last ten photographs of Ricky. He glanced at them briefly and said, 'We interviewed this groom, but . . .'

'No, you didn't,' Oliver said. 'The photo is of a boy who looks like him if you don't know either of them well.'

Wyfold pursed his lips, but nodded. 'Fair enough.'

'We do think he may have killed Ginnie, even if you couldn't prove it,' Oliver said.

Wyfold began putting together the papers we'd given him. 'We will certainly redirect our enquiries,' he said, and giving me a dour look added, 'If you had left it to the police to search Calder's surgery, sir, Calder Jackson would not have had the opportunity of disposing of Ian Pargetter's case and any other material evidence. These things are always mishandled by amateurs.' He looked pointedly at my plaster jacket. 'Better have left it to the professionals.'

I gave him an amused look but Oliver was gasping. 'Left to you,' he said, 'there would have been no search at all ... or certainly not in time to save my business.'

Wyfold's expression said plainly that saving people's businesses wasn't his prime concern, but beyond mentioning that picking locks and stealing medicinal substances constituted a breach of the law he kept any further disapproval to himself.

He was on his feet ready to go when Ursula rang again, and he could almost hear every word she said because of her enthusiasm.

'I'm in Gloucestershire,' she shouted. 'I thought I'd work from the other end, if you see what I mean. I remembered Calder had miraculously cured Binty Rockingham's utterly brilliant three-day-eventer who was so weak he could hardly totter, so I came here to her house to ask her, and guess what?'

'What?' I asked obligingly.

'That lad worked for her!' The triumph exploded. 'A good lad, she says, would you believe it? He called himself Clint. She can't remember his last name, it was more than two years ago and he was only here a few weeks.'

'Ask her if it was Williams,' I said.

There was some murmuring at the other end and then Ursula's voice back again, 'She thinks so, yes.'

'You're a dear, Ursula,' I said.

She gave an embarrassed laugh. 'Do you want me to go on down the road to Rube Golby's place? He had a show pony Calder cured a fair time ago of a weeping wound that wouldn't heal.'

'Just one more, then, Ursula. It's pretty conclusive already, I'd say.'

'Best to be sure,' she said cheerfully. 'And I'm enjoying myself, actually, now I'm over the shock.'

I wrote down the details she gave me and when she'd gone off the line I handed the new information to Wyfold.

'Clint,' he said with disillusion. 'Elvis next, I shouldn't wonder.'

I shook my head. 'A man of action, our Shane.'

Perhaps through needing to solve at least one murder while reviled for not catching his rapist, Wyfold put his best muscle into the search. It took him two weeks only to find Shane, who was arrested on leaving a pub in the racing village of Malton, Yorkshire, where he had been heard boasting several times about secret exploits of undisclosed daring.

Wyfold told Oliver, who telephoned me in the office,

to which I'd returned via a newly installed wheelchair ramp up the front steps.

'He called himself Dean,' Oliver said. 'Dean Williams. It seems the police are transferring him from Yorkshire back here to Hertfordshire, and Wyfold wants you to come to his police headquarters to identify Shane as the man called Jason at Calder's yard.'

I said I would.

I didn't say that with honesty I couldn't.

'Tomorrow,' Oliver added. 'They're in a hurry because of holding him without a good enough change, or something.'

'I'll be there.'

I went in a chauffeur-driven hired car, a luxury I seemed to have spent half my salary on since leaving Oliver's house.

I was living nearer the office than usual with a friend whose flat was in a block with a lift, not up stairs like my own. The pains in my immobile joints refused obstinately to depart, but owing to a further gift from Pen (via Gordon) were forgettable most of the time. A new pattern of 'normal' life had evolved, and all I dearly wanted was a bath.

I arrived at Wyfold's police station at the same time as Oliver, and together we were shown into an office, Oliver pushing me as if born to it. Two months minimum, they'd warned me to expect of life on wheels. Even if my shoulder would be mended before then, it wouldn't stand my weight on crutches. Patience, I'd been told. Be patient. My ankle had been in bits and they'd restored it like a jigsaw puzzle and I couldn't expect miracles, they'd said.

Wyfold arrived, shook hands briskly (an advance) and said that this was not a normal identity parade, as of course Oliver knew Shane very well, and I obviously knew him also, because of Ricky Barnet.

'Just call him Jason,' Wyfold told me. 'If you are sure he's the same man you saw at Calder Jackson's.'

We left the office and went along a fiercely lit institutional corridor to a large interview room which contained a table, three chairs, a uniformed policeman standing . . . and Shane, sitting down.

He looked cocky, not cowed.

When he saw Oliver he tilted his head almost jauntily, showing not shame but pride, not apology but a sneer. On me he looked with only a flickering glance, neither knowing me from our two very brief meetings nor reckoning on trouble from my direction.

Wyfold raised his eyebrows at me to indicate the need for action.

'Hello, Jason,' I said.

His head snapped round immediately and this time he gave me a full stare.

'I met you at Calder Jackson's yard,' I said.

'You never did.'

Although I hadn't expected it, I remembered him clearly. 'You were giving sunlamp treatment to a horse and Calder Jackson told you to put on your sunglasses.'

He made no more effort to deny it. 'What of it, then?' he said.

'Conclusive evidence of your link with the place, I should think,' I said.

Oliver, seeming as much outraged by Shane's lack of contrition as by his sins, turned with force to Wyfold and in half-controlled bitterness said, 'Now prove he killed my daughter.'

'*What!*'

Shane had risen in panic to his feet, knocking his chair over behind him and losing in an instant the smart-alec assurance. 'I never did,' he said.

We all watched him with interest, and his gaze travelled fast from one face to another, seeing only assessment and disbelief and nowhere admiration.

'I didn't kill her,' he said, his voice hoarse and rising. 'I didn't. Straight up, I didn't. It was him. He did it.'

'Who?' I said.

'Calder. Mr Jackson. He did it. It was him, not me.' He looked across at us all again with desperation. 'Look, I'm telling you the truth, straight up I am. I never killed her, it was him.'

Wyfold began telling him in a flat voice that he had a right to remain silent and that anything he said might be written down and used in evidence, but Shane wasn't clever and fright had too firm a hold. His fantasy world had vanished in the face of unimaginable reality, and I found myself believing every word he said.

'We didn't know she was there, see. She heard us talking, but we didn't know. And when I carried the stuff back to the hostel he saw her moving so he hit her. I didn't see him do it, I didn't, but when I went back there he was with Ginnie on the ground and I said she was the boss's daughter, which he didn't even know, see, but he said all the worse if she was the boss's daughter because she would have gone straight off and told everybody.'

The words, explanations, excuses came tumbling out in self-righteous urgency and Wyfold thankfully showed no signs of regulating the flow into the careful officialese of a formal statement. The uniformed policeman, now sitting behind Shane, was writing at speed in a notebook, recording, I imagined, the gist.

'I don't believe you,' Wyfold said impatiently. 'What did he hit her with?'

Shane redoubled his efforts to convince, and from then on I admired Wyfold's slyly effective interrogatory technique.

'With a fire extinguisher,' Shane said. 'He kept it in his car, see, and he had it in his hand. He was real fussy about fire always. Would never let anyone smoke anywhere near the stables. That Nigel . . .' The sneer came back temporarily, '. . . the lads all smoked in the feed room, I ask you, behind his back. He'd no idea what went on.'

'Fire extinguisher . . .' Wyfold spoke doubtfully, shaking his head.

'Yeah, it was. It was. One of them red things about this long.' Shane anxiously held up his hands about fifteen inches apart. 'With the nozzle, sort of, at the top. He was holding it by that, sort of swinging it. Ginnie was lying flat on the ground, face down, like, and I said, "What have you gone and done?" and he said she'd been listening.'

Wyfold sniffed.

'It was like that, straight up,' Shane said urgently.

'Listening to what?'

'We were talking about the stuff, see.'

'The shampoo . . .'

'Yeah.' He seemed only briefly to feel the slightest alarm at the mention of it. 'I told him, see, that the stuff had really worked because there'd been a foal born that morning with half a leg, that Nigel had tried to hush it up but by afternoon he was half cut and told one of the lads so we all knew. So I told Mr Jackson and he said great, because it was time we'd heard, and there hadn't been a murmur in the papers and he was getting worried he hadn't got the dose right, or something. So anyway when I told him about the foal with half a leg he laughed, see, he was so pleased, and he said this was probably the last lot I'd have to do, just do the six bottles he'd brought and then scarper.'

Oliver looked very pale, with sweat along his hairline and whitely clenched fists. His mouth was rigidly closed with the effort of self-control, and he listened throughout without once interrupting or cursing.

'I took the six bottles off to the hostel but when I got there I'd only got five, so I went back to look for the one I'd dropped, but I forgot it, see, when I saw him standing there over Ginnie and him saying she'd heard us talking, and then he said for me to come with him down to the village in his car and he'd drop me at a pub where the other lads were, so as I couldn't have been back home killing the boss's daughter, see? I remembered about the bottle I'd dropped when we were on our way to the village but I didn't think he'd be best pleased and anyway I reckoned I'd find it all right when I went back, but I never did. I didn't think it would matter much, because no one would know what it was for, it was just dog shampoo, and anyway I reckoned I'd skip using the new bottles after all because of the fuss there would be over Ginnie. But if it hadn't been for that bottle I wouldn't have gone out again at all, see, and I wouldn't know it was him that killed her, and it wasn't me, it *wasn't*.'

He came to what appeared in his own mind to be a halt, but as far as Wyfold, Oliver and myself were concerned he had stopped short of enough.

'Are you saying,' Wyfold said, 'that you walked back from the village with the other grooms, knowing what you would find?'

'Well, yeah. Only Dave and Sammy, see, they'd got back first, and when I got back there was an ambulance there and such, and I just kept in the background.'

'What did you do with the other five bottles of

shampoo?' Wyfold asked. 'We searched all the rooms in the hostel. We didn't find any shampoo.'

The first overwhelming promptings of fear were beginning to die down in Shane, but he answered with only minimal hesitation, 'I took them down the road a ways and threw them in a ditch. That was after they'd all gone off to the hospital.' He nodded in the general direction of Oliver and myself. 'Panicked me a bit, it did, when Dave said she was talking, like. But I was glad I'd got rid of the stuff afterwards, when she was dead after all, with everyone snooping around.'

'You could show me which ditch?' Wyfold said.

'Yeah, I could.'

'Good.'

'You mean,' Shane said, with relief, 'you believe what I told you . . .'

'No, I don't mean that,' Wyfold said repressively. 'I'll need to know what you ordinarily did with the shampoo.'

'What?'

'How you prepared it and gave it to the mares.'

'Oh.' An echo of the cocky cleverness came back: a swagger to the shoulders, a curl to the lip. 'It was dead easy, see. Mr Jackson showed me how. I just had to put a coffee filter in a wash basin and pour the shampoo through it, so's the shampoo all ran down the drain and there was that stuff left on the paper, then I just turned the coffee filter inside out and soaked it in a little jar with some linseed oil from the feed shed, and then I'd stir a quarter of it into the feed if it was for a mare I was looking after anyway, or let the stuff fall to the bottom and scrape up a teaspoonful and put it in an apple for the others. Mr Jackson showed me how. Dead easy, the whole thing.'

'How many mares did you give it to?'

'Don't rightly know. Dozens, counting last year. Some I missed. Mr Jackson said better to miss some than be found out. He liked me to do the oil best. Said too many apples would be noticed.' A certain amount of anxiety returned. 'Look, now I've told you all this, you know I didn't kill her, don't you?'

Wyfold said impasssively, 'How often did Mr Jackson bring you bottles of shampoo?'

'He didn't. I mean, I had a case of it under my bed. Brought it with me when I moved in, see, same as last year. But this year I ran out, like, so I rang him up from the village one night for some more. So he said he'd meet me at the back gate at nine on Sunday when all the lads would be down in the pub.'

'That was a risk he wouldn't take,' Wyfold said sceptically.

'Well, he did.'

Wyfold shook his head.

Shane's panic resurfaced completely. 'He was there,' he almost shouted. 'He was. He *was*.'

Wyfold still looked studiedly unconvinced and told Shane that it would be best if he now made a formal statement, which the sergeant would write down for him to sign when he, Shane, was satisfied that it represented what he had already told us; and Shane in slight bewilderment agreed.

Wyfold nodded to the sergeant, opened the door of the room, and gestured to Oliver and me to leave. Oliver in undiluted grimness silently pushed me out. Wyfold, with a satisfied air, said in his plain uncushioning way, 'There you are then, Mr Knowles, that's how your daughter died, and you're luckier than some. That little sod's telling the truth. Proud of himself, like a lot of crooks. Wants the world to know.' He shook hands perfunctorily with Oliver and nodded briefly to me, and walked away to his unsolved horrors where the papers called for his blood and other fathers choked on their tears.

Oliver pushed me back to the outside world but not directly to where my temporary chauffeur had said he would wait. I found myself making an unscheduled turn into a small public garden, where Oliver abruptly left me beside the first seat we came to and walked jerkily away.

I watched his back, ramrod stiff, disappearing behind bushes and trees. In grief, as in all else, he would be tidy.

A boy came along the path on roller skates and wheeled round to a stop in front of me.

'You want pushing?' he said.

'No. But thanks all the same.'

He looked at me judiciously. 'Can you make that chair go straight, using just one arm?'

'No. I go round in a circle and end where I started.'

'Thought so.' He considered me gravely. 'Just like the earth,' he said.

He pushed off with one foot and sailed away straight on the other and presently, walking firmly, Oliver came back.

He sat on the bench beside me, his eyelids slightly reddened, his manner calm.

'Sorry,' he said, after a while.

'She died happy,' I said. 'It's better than nothing.'

'How do you mean?'

'She heard what they were doing. She picked up the shampoo Shane dropped. She was coming to tell you that everything was all right, there was nothing wrong with Sandcastle and you wouldn't lose the farm. At the moment she died she must have been full of joy.'

Oliver raised his face to the pale summer sky.

'Do you think so?'

'Yes, I do.'

'Then I'll believe it,' he said.

OCTOBER

Gordon was coming up to sixty, the age at which everyone retired from Ekaterin's, like it or not. The bustle of young brains, the founder Paul had said, was what kept money moving, and his concept still ruled in the house.

Gordon had his regrets but they were balanced, it seemed to me, by a sense of relief. He had battled for three years now against his palsy and had finished the allotted work span honourably in the face of the enemy within. He began saying he was looking forward to his leisure, and that he and Judith would go on a celebratory journey as soon as possible. Before that, however, he was to be away for a day of medical tests in hospital.

'Such a bore,' he said, 'but they want to make these checks and set me up before we travel.'

'Very sensible,' I said. 'Where will you go?'

He smiled with enthusiasm. 'I've always wanted to see Australia. Never been there, you know.'

'Nor have I.'

He nodded and we continued with our normal work in the accord we had felt together for so many years. I would miss him badly for his own sake, I thought, and even more because through him I would no longer have constant news and contact with Judith. The days seemed to gallop towards his birthday and my spirits grew heavy as his lightened.

Oliver's problems were no longer the day-to-day communiqués at lunch. The dissenting director had conceded that even blue-chip certainties weren't always proof against well-planned malice and no longer grumbled about my part in things, particularly since the day that Henry in his mild-steel voice made observations about defending the bank's money beyond the call of duty.

'And beyond the call of common sense,' Val murmured in my ear. 'Thank goodness.'

Oliver's plight had been extensively aired by Alec in *What's Going On Where It Shouldn't*, thanks to comprehensive leaks from one of Ekaterin's directors; to wit, me.

Some of the regular newspapers had danced round the subject, since with Shane still awaiting trial the business of poisoning mares was supposed to be sub judice. Alec's paper with its usual disrespect for secrecy had managed to let everyone in the bloodstock industry know that Sandcastle himself was a rock-solid investment, and that any foals already born perfect would not be carrying any damaging genes.

As for the mares covered this year, [the paper continued] there is a lottery as to whether they will produce deformed foals or not. Breeders are advised to let their mares go to term, because there is a roughly fifty per cent chance that the foal will be perfect. Breeders of mares who produce deformed or imperfect foals will, we understand, have their stallion fees refunded and expenses reimbursed.

The bloodstock industry is drawing up its own special guidelines to deal with this exceptional case.

Meanwhile, fear not. Sandcastle is potent, fertile and fully reinstated. Apply without delay for a place in next year's programme.

Alec himself telephoned me in the office two days after the column appeared.

'How do you like it?' he said.

'Absolutely great.'

'The editor says the newsagents in Newmarket have been ringing up like mad for extra copies.'

'Hm,' I said. 'I think perhaps I'll get a list of all breeders and bloodstock agents and personally – I mean anonymously – send each of them a copy of your column, if your editor would agree.'

'Do it without asking him,' Alec said. 'He would probably prefer it. We won't sue you for infringement of copyright, I'll promise you.'

'Thanks a lot,' I said. 'You've been really great.'

'Wait till you get an eyeful of the next issue. I'm

working on it now. *Do-it-yourself Miracles*, that's the heading. How does it grab you?'

'Fine.'

'The dead can't sue,' he said cheerfully. 'I just hope I spell the drugs right.'

'I sent you the list,' I protested.

'The typesetters,' he said, 'can scramble eggs, let alone sulphanilamide.'

'See you someday,' I said, smiling.

'Yeah. Pie and beer. We'll fix it.'

His miracle-working column in the next issue demolished Calder's reputation entirely and made further progress towards restoring Sandcastle's and after a third bang on the Sandcastle-is-tops gong in the issue after that, Oliver thankfully reported that confidence both in his stallion and his stud farm was creeping back. Two-thirds of the nominations were filled already, and enquiries were arriving for the rest.

'One of the breeders whose mare is in foal now is threatening to sue me for negligence, but the blood-stock associations are trying to dissuade him. He can't do anything, anyway, until after Shane's trial and after the foal is born, and I just hope to God it's one that's perfect.'

From the bank's point of view his affairs were no longer in turmoil. The board had agreed to extend the period of the loan for three extra years, and Val, Gordon and I had worked out the rates at which Oliver could repay without crippling himself. All finally rested on Sandcastle, but if his progeny should prove to have inherited his speed, Oliver should in the end reach the prosperity and prestige for which he had aimed.

'But let's not,' Henry said, smiling one day over roast lamb, 'let's not make a habit of going to the races.'

Gordon came to the office one Monday saying he had met Dissdale the day before at lunch in a restaurant which they both liked.

'He was most embarrassed to see me,' Gordon said. 'But I had quite a talk with him. He really didn't know, you know, that Calder was a fake. He says he can hardly believe, even now, that the cures weren't cures, or that Calder actually killed two people. Very subdued, he was, for Dissdale.'

'I suppose,' I said diffidently, 'you didn't ask him if he and Calder had ever bought, cured and sold sick animals before Indian Silk.'

'Yes, I did, actually, because of your thoughts. But he said they hadn't. Indian Silk was the first, and Dissdale rather despondently said he supposed Calder and Ian Pargetter couldn't bear to see all their time and trouble go to waste, so when Ian Pargetter couldn't persuade Fred Barnet to try Calder, Calder sent Dissdale to buy the horse outright.'

'And it worked a treat.'

Gordon nodded. 'Another thing Dissdale said was that Calder was as stunned as he was himself to find it was Ekaterin's who had lent the money for Sandcastle. There had been no mention of it in the papers. Dissdale

asked me to tell you that when he told Calder who it was who had actually put up the money, Calder said "My God" several times and walked up and down all evening and drank far more than usual. Dissdale didn't know why, and Calder wouldn't tell him, but Dissdale says he thinks now it was because Calder was feeling remorse at hammering Ekaterin's after an Ekaterin had saved his life.'

'Dissdale,' I said drily, 'is still trying to find excuses for his hero.'

'And for his own admiration of him,' Gordon agreed. 'But perhaps it's true. Dissdale said Calder had liked you very much.'

Liked me, and apologized, and tried to kill me: that too.

Movement had slowly returned to my shoulder and arm once the body-restricting plaster had come off, and via electrical treatment, exercise and massage normal strength had returned.

In the ankle department things weren't quite so good: I still after more than four months wore a brace, though now of removable aluminium, and strapping, not plaster. No one would promise I'd be able to ski on the final outcome and meanwhile all but the shortest journeys required sticks. I had tired of hopping up and down my Hampstead stairs on my return there to the extent of renting a flat of my own with a lift to take me aloft and a garage in the basement, and I reckoned life had basically become reasonable again on the day

I drove out of there in my car: automatic gear change, no work for the left foot, perfect.

A day or two before he was due to go into hospital for his check-up Gordon mentioned in passing that Judith was coming to collect him from the bank after work to go with him to the hospital, where he would be spending the night so as to be rested for the whole day of tests on Friday.

She would collect him again on Friday evening and they would go home together, and he would have the weekend to rest in before he returned to the office on Monday.

'I'll be glad when it's over,' he said frankly. 'I hate all the needles and the pulling and pushing about.'

'When Judith has settled you in, would she like me to give her some dinner before she goes home?' I said.

He looked across with interest, the idea taking root. 'I should think she would love it. I'll ask her.'

He returned the next day saying Judith was pleased, and we arranged between us that when she left him in the hospital she would come to join me in a convenient restaurant that we all knew well; and on the following day, Thursday, the plan was duly carried out.

She came with a glowing face, eyes sparkling, white teeth gleaming; wearing a blue full-skirted dress and shoes with high heels.

'Gordon is fine, apart from grumbling about

414

tomorrow,' she reported, 'and they gave him almost no supper, to his disgust. He says to think of him during our fillet steaks.'

I doubt if we did. I don't remember what we ate. The feast was there before me on the other side of the small table, Judith looking beautiful and telling me nonsensical things like what happens to a blasé refrigerator when you pull its plug out.

'What, then?'

'It loses its cool.'

I laughed at the stupidity of it and brimmed over with the intoxication of having her there to myself, and I wished she was my own wife so fiercely that my muscles ached.

'You'll be going to Australia . . .' I said.

'Australia?' She hesitated. 'We leave in three weeks.'

'It's so soon.'

'Gordon's sixty the week after next,' she said. 'You know he is. There's the party.'

Henry, Val and I had clubbed together to give Gordon a small sending-off in the office after his last day's work, an affair to which most of the banking managers and their wives had been invited.

'I hate him going,' I said.

'To Australia?'

'From the bank.'

We drank wine and coffee and told each other much without saying a word. Not until we were nearly leaving did she say tentatively, 'We'll be away for months, you know.'

My feelings must have shown. 'Months ... How many?'

'We don't know. We're going to all the places Gordon or I have wanted to see that couldn't be fitted into an ordinary holiday. We're going to potter. Bits of Europe, bits of the Middle East. India, Singapore, Bali, then Australia, New Zealand, Tahiti, Fiji, Hawaii, America.' She fell silent, her eyes not laughing now but full of sadness.

I swallowed. 'Gordon will find it exhausting.'

'He says not. He passionately wants to go, and I know he's always yearned to have the time to see things ... and we're going slowly, with lots of rests.'

The restaurant had emptied around us and the waiters hovered with polite faces willing us to go. Judith put on her blue coat and we went outside onto the cold pavement.

'How do you plan to go home now?' I asked.

'Underground.'

'I'll drive you,' I said.

She gave me a small smile and nodded, and we walked slowly across the road to where I'd left the car. She sat in beside me and I did all the automatic things like switching on the lights and letting off the hand-brake, and I drove all the way to Clapham without consciously seeing the road.

Gordon's house behind the big gates lay quiet and

dark. Judith looked up at its bulk and then at me, and I leaned across in the car and put my arms round her and kissed her. She came close to me, kissing me back with a feeling and a need that seemed as intense as my own, and for a while we stayed in that way, floating in passion, dreaming in deep unaccustomed touch.

As if of one mind we each at the same time drew back and slowly relaxed against the seat. She put her hand on mine and threaded her fingers through, holding tight.

I looked ahead through the windscreen, seeing trees against the stars; seeing nothing.

A long time passed.

'We can't,' I said eventually.

'No.'

'Especially not,' I said, 'in his own house.'

'No.'

After another long minute she let go of my hand and opened the door beside her, and I too opened mine.

'Don't get out,' she said, 'because of your ankle.'

I stood up, however, on the driveway and she walked round the car towards me. We hugged each other but without kissing, a long hungry minute of body against body; commitment and farewell.

'I'll see you,' she said, 'at the party'; and we both knew how it would be, with Lorna Shipton talking about watching Henry's weight and Henry flirting

417

roguishly with Judith whenever he could, and everyone talking loudly and clapping Gordon on the back.

She walked over to the front door and unlocked it, and looked back, briefly, once, and then went in, putting the walls between us in final, mutual, painful decision.

DECEMBER

I felt alone and also lonely, which I'd never been before, and I telephoned Pen one Sunday in December and suggested taking her out to lunch. She said to come early as she had to open her shop at four, and I arrived at eleven-thirty to find coffee percolating richly and Pen trying to unravel the string of the Christmas kite.

'I found it when I was looking for some books,' she said. 'It's so pretty. When we've had coffee, let's go out and fly it.'

We took it onto the common, and let the string out gradually until the dragon was high on the wind, circling and darting and fluttering its frilly tail. It took us slowly after it across the grass, Pen delightedly intent and I simply pleased to be back there in that place.

She glanced at me over her shoulder. 'Are we going too far for your ankle? Or too fast?'

'No and no,' I said.

'Still taking the comfrey?'

'Religiously.'

The bones and other tissues round my shoulder had

mended fast, I'd been told, and although the ankle still lagged I was prepared to give comfrey the benefit of the doubt. Anything which would restore decent mobility attracted my enthusiasm: life with brace and walking stick, still boringly necessary, made even buying groceries a pest.

We had reached a spot on a level with Gordon and Judith's house when a gust of wind took the kite suddenly higher, setting it weaving and diving in bright-coloured arcs and stretching its land-line to tautness. Before anything could be done the string snapped and the dazzling butterfly wings soared away free, rising in a spiral, disappearing to a shape, to a black dot, to nothing.

'What a pity,' Pen said, turning to me with disappointment and then pausing, seeing where my own gaze had travelled downwards to the tall cream gates, firmly shut.

'Let her go,' Pen said soberly, 'like the kite.'

'She'll come back.'

'Take out some other girl,' she urged.

I smiled lop-sidedly. 'I'm out of practice.'

'But you can't spend your whole life . . .' She stopped momentarily, and then said, 'Parkinson's disease isn't fatal. Gordon could live to be eighty or more.'

'I wouldn't want him dead,' I protested. 'How could you think it?'

'Then what?'

'Just to go on, I suppose, as we are.'

She took my arm and turned me away from the gates to return to her house.

'Give it time,' she said. 'You've got months. You both have.'

I glanced at her. 'Both?'

'Gordon and I don't go around with our eyes shut.'

'He's never said anything . . .'

She smiled. 'Gordon likes you better than you like him, if possible. Trusts you, too.' She paused. 'Let her go, Tim, for your own sake.'

We went silently back to her house and I thought of all that had happened since the day Gordon stood in the fountain, and of all I had learned and felt and loved and lost. Thought of Ginnie and Oliver and Calder, and of all the gateways I'd gone through to grief and pain and the knowledge of death. So much – too much – compressed into so small a span.

'You're a child of the light,' Pen said contentedly. 'Both you and Judith. You always take sunshine with you. I don't suppose you know it, but everything brightens when people like you walk in.' She glanced down at my slow foot. 'Sorry. When you limp in. So carry the sunlight to a new young girl who isn't married to Gordon and doesn't break your heart.' She paused. 'That's good pharmacological advice, so take it.'

'Yes, doctor,' I said; and knew I couldn't.

*

On Christmas Eve when I had packed to go to Jersey and was checking around the flat before leaving, the telephone rang.

'Hello,' I said.

There was a series of clicks and hums and I was about to put the receiver down when a breathless voice said, 'Tim . . .'

'Judith?' I said incredulously.

'Yes.'

'Where are you?'

'Listen, just listen. I don't know who else to ask, not at Christmas . . . Gordon's ill and I'm alone and I don't know, I don't know . . .'

'Where are you?'

'India . . . He's in hospital. They're very good, very kind, but he's so ill . . . unconscious . . . they say cerebral haemorrhage . . . I'm so afraid . . . I do so love him . . .' She was suddenly crying, and trying not to, the words coming out at intervals when control was possible. 'It's so much to ask . . . but I need . . . help.'

'Tell me where,' I said. 'I'll come at once.'

'Oh . . .'

She told me where. I was packed and ready to go, and I went.

Because of the date and the off-track destination there were delays and it took me forty hours to get there. Gordon died before I reached her, on the day after Christmas, like her mother.